A CROWN OF SWORDS

Book Seven of The Wheel of Time®

By Robert Jordan

The Wheel of Time®
The Eye of the World
The Great Hunt
The Dragon Reborn
The Shadow Rising
The Fires of Heaven
Lord of Chaos
A Crown of Swords
The Path of Daggers
Winter's Heart
Crossroads of Twilight
Knife of Dreams
The Gathering Storm
(by Robert Jordan and Brandon Sanderson)
Towers of Midnight
(by Robert Jordan and Brandon Sanderson)
A Memory of Light
(by Robert Jordan and Brandon Sanderson)

New Spring

The Wheel of Time Companion
(with Harriet McDougal, Alan Romanczuk
and Maria Simons)

The World of Robert Jordan's The Wheel of Time®
(with Teresa Patterson)

*

The Conan Chronicles 1
The Conan Chronicles 2

A CROWN OF SWORDS

Book Seven of The Wheel of Time®

ROBERT JORDAN

orbitbooks.net

ORBIT

First published in Great Britain in 1996 by Orbit
This paperback edition published in 2014 by Orbit
This paperback edition published in 2021 by Orbit

10

Copyright © 1996 by Robert Jordan

The moral right of the author has been asserted.

The phrases 'The Wheel of Time®' and 'The Dragon Reborn™',
and the snake-wheel symbol are trademarks of Robert Jordan.

Maps by Thomas Canty and Ellisa Mitchell
Interior illustrations by Matthew C. Nielsen and Ellisa Mitchell

*All characters and events in this publication, other than those
clearly in the public domain, are fictitious and any resemblance
to real persons, living or dead, is purely coincidental.*

All rights reserved.
No part of this publication may be reproduced, stored in a
retrieval system, or transmitted, in any form or by any means, without
the prior permission in writing of the publisher, nor be otherwise circulated
in any form of binding or cover other than that in which it is published
and without a similar condition including this condition being
imposed on the subsequent purchaser.

A CIP catalogue record for this book is available from the British Library.

ISBN 978-0-356-51706-3

Typeset in Garamond by M Rules
Printed and bound in Great Britain by Clays Ltd, Elcograf S.p.A.

Papers used by Orbit are from well-managed forests
and other responsible sources.

Orbit
An imprint of
Little, Brown Book Group
Carmelite House
50 Victoria Embankment
London EC4Y 0DZ

An Hachette UK Company
www.hachette.co.uk

www.orbitbooks.net

To Harriet,
who deserves the credit
once again.

Contents

	MAPS	x–xi, 269
	PROLOGUE Lightnings	1
1	High Chasaline	49
2	The Butcher's Yard	64
3	Hill of the Golden Dawn	88
4	Into Cairhien	104
5	A Broken Crown	117
6	Old Fear, and New Fear	130
7	Pitfalls and Tripwires	141
8	The Figurehead	161
9	A Pair of Silverpike	173
10	Unseen Eyes	194
11	An Oath	215
12	A Morning of Victory	235
13	The Bowl of the Winds	268
14	White Plumes	288
15	Insects	304
16	A Touch on the Cheek	313
17	The Triumph of Logic	327
18	As the Plow Breaks the Earth	345
19	Diamonds and Stars	360
20	Patterns Within Patterns	375
21	Swovan Night	387
22	Small Sacrifices	401
23	Next Door to a Weaver	417

24	The Kin	436
25	Mindtrap	445
26	The Irrevocable Words	454
27	To Be Alone	475
28	Bread and Cheese	485
29	The Festival of Birds	502
30	The First Cup	514
31	*Mashiara*	526
32	Sealed to the Flame	544
33	A Bath	561
34	*Ta'veren*	573
35	Into the Woods	587
36	Blades	604
37	A Note from the Palace	625
38	Six Stories	635
39	Promises to Keep	657
40	Spears	679
41	A Crown of Swords	695
	GLOSSARY	729

There can be no health in us, nor any good thing grow, for the land is one with the Dragon Reborn, and he one with the land. Soul of fire, heart of stone, in pride he conquers, forcing the proud to yield. He calls upon the mountains to kneel, and the seas to give way, and the very skies to bow. Pray that the heart of stone remembers tears, and the soul of fires, love.

> From a much-disputed translation of
> *The Prophecies of the Dragon*,
> by the poet Kyera Termendal, of Shiota,
> believed to have been published between FY 700 and FY 800.

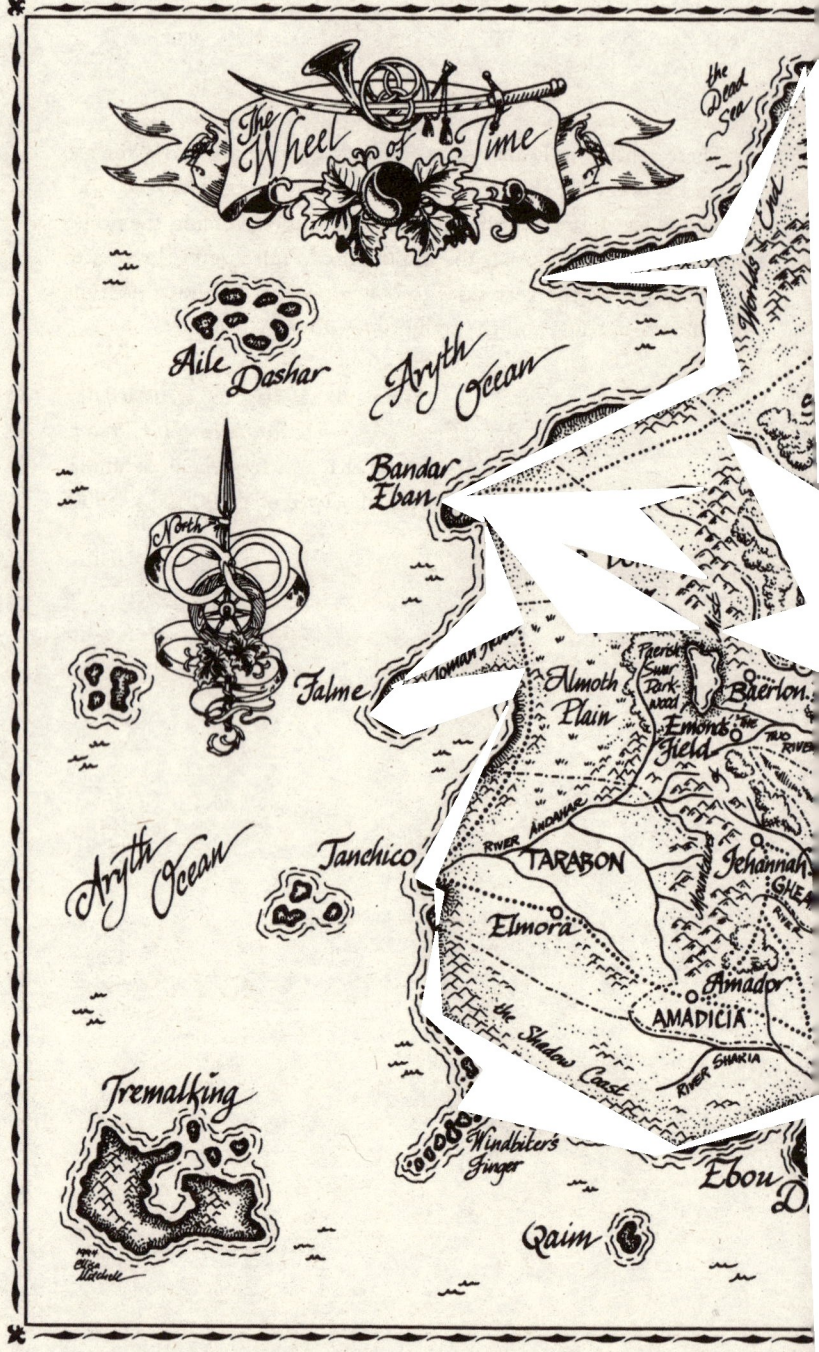

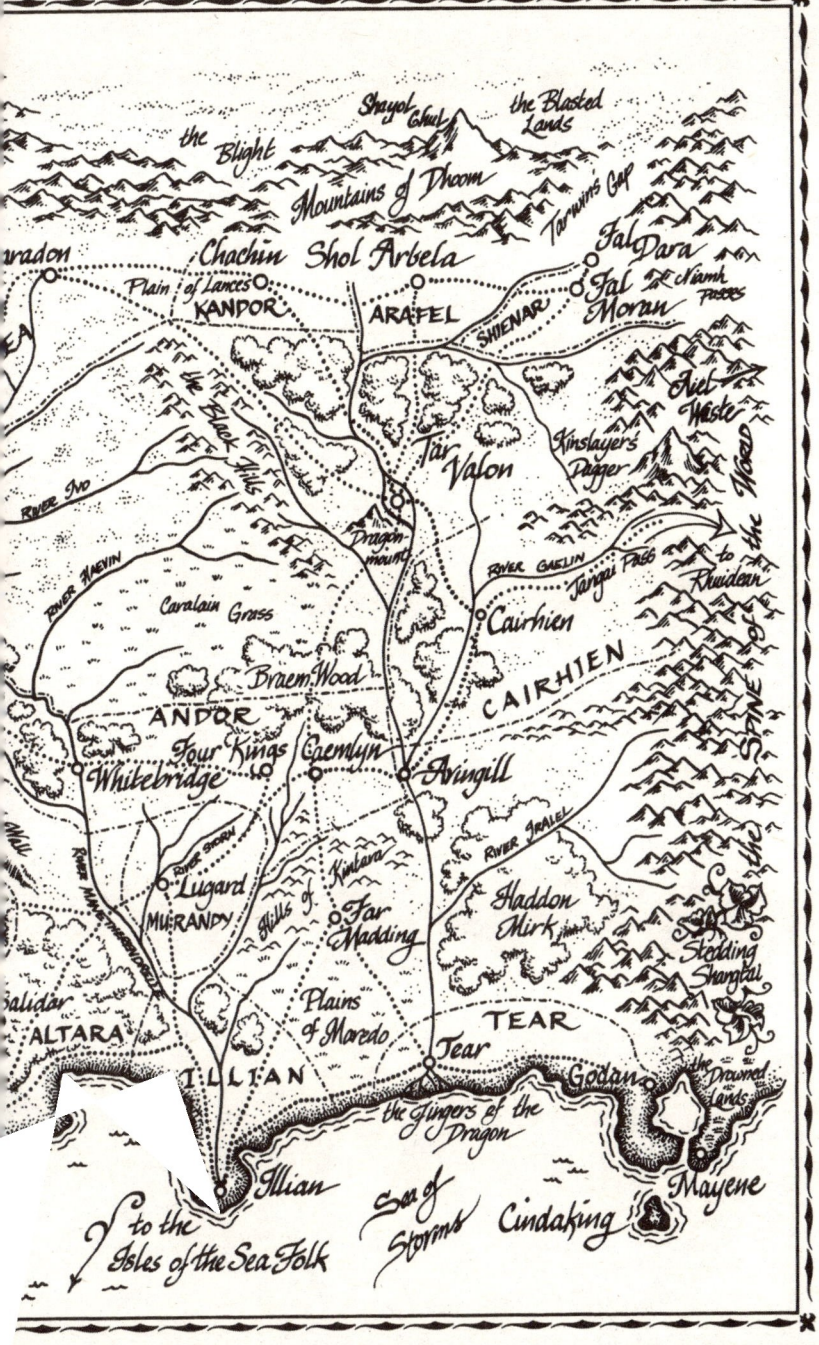

PROLOGUE

Lightnings

From the tall arched window, close onto eighty spans above the ground, not far below the top of the White Tower, Elaida could see for miles beyond Tar Valon, to the rolling plains and forests that bordered the broad River Erinin, running down from north and west before it divided around the white walls of the great island city. On the ground, long morning shadows must be dappling the city, but from this prominence all seemed clear and bright. Not even the fabled 'topless towers' of Cairhien had truly rivaled the White Tower. Certainly none of Tar Valon's lesser towers did, for all that men spoke far and wide of them and their vaulting sky-bridges.

This high, an almost constant breeze lessened the unnatural heat gripping the world. The Feast of Lights past, snow should have covered the ground deep, yet the weather belonged in the depths of a hard summer. Another sign that the Last Battle approached and the Dark One touched the world, if more were needed. Elaida did not let the heat touch her even when she descended, of course. The breeze was not why she had had her quarters moved up here, despite the inconvenience of so many stairs, to these simple rooms.

Plain russet floor tiles and white marble walls decorated by a few tapestries could not compare with the grandeur of the Amyrlin's study and the rooms that went with it far below. She still used those rooms occasionally – they held associations with the power of the

Amyrlin Seat in some minds — but she resided here, and worked here more often than not. For the view. Not of city or river or forests, though. Of what was beginning in the Tower grounds.

Great diggings and foundations spread across what had been the Warders' practice yard, tall wooden cranes and stacks of cut marble and granite. Masons and laborers swarmed over the workings like ants, and endless streams of wagons trailed through the gates onto the Tower grounds, bringing more stone. To one side stood a wooden 'working model,' as the masons called it, big enough for men to enter crouching on their heels and see every detail, where every stone should go. Most of the workmen could not read, after all — neither words nor mason's drawn plans. The 'working model' was as large as some manor houses.

When any king or queen had a palace, why should the Amyrlin Seat be relegated to apartments little better than those of many ordinary sisters? Her palace would match the White Tower for splendor, and have a great spire ten spans higher than the Tower itself. The blood had drained from the chief mason's face when he heard that. The Tower had been Ogier-built, with assistance from sisters using the Power. One look at Elaida's face, however, set Master Lerman bowing and stammering that of course all would be done as she wished. As if there had been any question.

Her mouth tightened with exasperation. She had wanted Ogier masons again, but the Ogier were confining themselves to their *stedding* for some reason. Her summons to the nearest, Stedding Jentoine, in the Black Hills, had been met with refusal. Polite, yet still refusal, without explanation, even to the Amyrlin Seat. Ogier were reclusive at best. Or they might be withdrawing from a world full of turmoil; Ogier stayed clear of human strife.

Firmly Elaida dismissed the Ogier from her mind. She prided herself on separating what could be from what could not. Ogier were a triviality. They had no part in the world beyond the cities they had built so long ago and seldom visited now except to make repairs.

The men below, crawling beetle-like over the building site, made her frown slightly. Construction went forward by inches. Ogier might be out of the question, yet perhaps the One Power could be used again. Few sisters possessed real strength in weaving

Earth, but not that much was required to reinforce stone, or bind stone to stone. Yes. In her mind, the palace stood finished, colonnaded walks and great domes shining with gilt and that one spire reaching to the heavens ... Her eyes rose to the cloudless sky, to where the spire would peak, and she let out a long sigh. Yes. The orders would be issued today.

The towering case clock in the room behind her chimed Third Rise, and in the city gongs and bells pealed the hour, the sound faint here, so high above. With a smile, Elaida left the window, smoothing her red-slashed dress of cream silk and adjusting the broad, striped stole of the Amyrlin Seat on her shoulders.

On the ornately gilded clock, small figures of gold and silver and enamel moved with the chimes. Horned and snouted Trollocs fled from a cloaked Aes Sedai on one level; on another a man representing a false Dragon tried to fend off silver lightning bolts that had obviously been hurled by a second sister. And above the clockface, itself above her head, a crowned king and queen knelt before an Amyrlin Seat in her enameled stole, with the Flame of Tar Valon, carved from a large moonstone, atop a golden arch over her head.

She did not laugh often, but she could not help a quietly pleased chuckle at the clock. Cemaile Sorenthaine, raised from the Gray, had commissioned it dreaming of a return to the days before the Trolloc Wars, when no ruler held a throne without the Tower's approval. Cemaile's grand plans came to naught, however, as did Cemaile, and for three centuries the clock sat in a dusty storage room, an embarrassment no one dared display. Until Elaida. The Wheel of Time turned. What was once, could be again. *Would* be again.

The case clock balanced the door to her sitting room, and her bedchamber and dressing room beyond. Fine tapestries, colorful work from Tear and Kandor and Arad Doman, with thread-of-gold and thread-of-silver glittering among the merely dyed, hung each exactly opposite its mate. She had always liked order. The carpet covering most of the tiles came from Tarabon, patterned in red and green and gold; silk carpets were the most precious. In each corner of the room a marble plinth carved in unpretentious verticals held a white vase of fragile Sea Folk porcelain with two dozen carefully arranged red roses. To make roses bloom now required the One Power, especially with the drought and heat; a worthwhile use, in her opinion. Gilded carving covered both the only chair – no one sat in her presence now – and the writing table, but in the stark style of Cairhien. A simple room, really, with a ceiling barely two spans high, yet it would do until her palace was ready. With the view, it would.

The tall chairback held the Flame of Tar Valon picked out in moonstones above her dark head as she sat. Nothing marred the polished surface of the table except for three boxes of Altaran lacquerwork, arranged just so. Opening the box covered with golden hawks among white clouds, she removed a slim strip of thin paper from atop the pile of reports and correspondence inside.

For what must have been the hundredth time, she read the message come from Cairhien by pigeon twelve days ago. Few in the Tower knew of its existence. None but she knew its contents, or would have a glimmer of what it meant if they did. The thought almost made her laugh again.

The ring has been placed in the bull's nose. I expect a pleasant journey to market.

No signature, yet she needed none. Only Galina Casban had known to send that glorious message. Galina, whom Elaida trusted to do what she would have trusted to no one else save herself. Not that she trusted anyone fully, but the head of the Red Ajah more than any other. She herself had been raised from the Red, after all, and in many ways still thought of herself as Red.

The ring has been placed in the bull's nose.

Rand al'Thor – the Dragon Reborn, the man who had seemed on the point of swallowing the world, the man who had swallowed entirely too much of it – Rand al'Thor was shielded and in Galina's control. And none who might support him knew. Even a chance of that, and the wording would have been different. By various earlier messages, it seemed he had rediscovered how to Travel, a Talent lost to Aes Sedai since the Breaking, yet that had not saved him. It had even played into Galina's hands. Apparently he had a habit of coming and going without warning. Who would suspect that this time he had not gone, but been taken? Something very like a giggle rose in her.

Inside another week, two at most, al'Thor would be in the Tower, closely supervised and guided safely until Tarmon Gai'don, his ravaging of the world stopped. It was madness to allow any man who could channel to run free, but most of all the man prophecy said must face the Dark One in the Last Battle, the Light send that it lay years off yet in spite of the weather. Years would be needed to arrange the world properly, beginning with undoing what al'Thor had done.

Of course, the damage he had wrought was nothing beside what he could have caused, free. Not to mention the possibility that he might have gotten himself killed before he was needed. Well, that troublesome young man would be wrapped in swaddling and kept safe as an infant in his mother's arms until time to take him to Shayol Ghul. After that, if he survived ...

Elaida's lips pursed. The Prophecies of the Dragon seemed to say he would not, which undeniably would be for the best.

'Mother?' Elaida almost gave a start as Alviarin spoke. Entering without so much as a knock! 'I have word from the Ajahs, Mother.' Slim and cool-faced, Alviarin wore the Keeper's narrow stole in white, matching her dress, to show she had been raised from the White, but in her mouth 'Mother' became less a title of respect and more an address to an equal.

Alviarin's presence was enough to dent Elaida's good mood. That the Keeper of Chronicles came from the White, not the Red, always served as a biting reminder of her weakness when she was first raised. Some of that had been dispelled, true, but not all. Not yet. She was tired of regretting that she had so few personal eyes-and-ears outside Andor. And that her predecessor and Alviarin's had escaped – been helped to escape; they must have had help! – escaped before the keys to the Amyrlin's great network could be wrested out of them.

She more than wanted the network that was hers by right. By strong tradition the Ajahs sent to the Keeper whatever dribbles from their own eyes-and-ears they were willing to share with the Amyrlin, but Elaida was convinced the woman kept back some of even that trickle. Yet she could not ask the Ajahs for information directly. Bad enough to be weak without going begging to the world. The Tower, anyway, which was as much of the world as really counted.

Elaida kept her own face every bit as cool as the other woman's, acknowledging her only with a nod while she pretended to examine papers from the lacquered box. Slowly she turned them over one by one, returned them to the box slowly. Without really seeing a word. Making Alviarin wait was bitter, because it was petty, and petty ways were all she had to strike at one who should have been her servant.

An Amyrlin could issue any decree she wished, her word law and absolute. Yet as a practical matter, without support from the Hall of the Tower, many of those decrees were wasted ink and paper. No sister would disobey an Amyrlin, not directly at least, yet many decrees required a hundred other things ordered to implement them. In the best of times that could come slowly, on occasion so slowly it never happened, and these were far from the best.

Alviarin stood there, calm as a frozen pond. Closing the Altaran box, Elaida kept out the strip of paper that announced her sure victory. Unconsciously she fingered it, a talisman. 'Has Teslyn or Joline finally deigned to send more than word of their safe arrival?'

That was meant to remind Alviarin that no one could consider herself immune. Nobody cared what happened in Ebou Dar, Elaida least of all; the capital of Altara could fall into the sea, and except for the merchants, not even the rest of Altara would notice. But Teslyn had sat in the Hall nearly fifteen years before Elaida had commanded her to resign her chair. If Elaida could send a Sitter – a *Red* Sitter – who had supported her rise off as ambassador to a flyspeck throne with no one sure why but a hundred rumors flowering, then she could come down on anyone. Joline was a different matter. She had held her chair for the Green only a matter of weeks, and everyone was sure the Greens had selected her to show they would not be cowed by the new Amyrlin, who had handed her a fearsome penance. That bit of insolence could not be allowed to pass, of course, and had not been. Everyone knew that, too.

It was meant to remind Alviarin that she was vulnerable, but the slim woman merely smiled her cool smile. So long as the Hall remained as it was, she *was* immune. She riffled through the papers in her hand, plucking one out. 'No word from Teslyn or Joline, Mother, no, though with the news you have received so far from the thrones ...' That smile deepened into something dangerously close to amusement. 'They all mean to try their wings, to see if you are as strong as ... as your predecessor.' Even Alviarin had enough sense not to speak the Sanche woman's name in her presence. It was true, though; every king and queen, even mere nobles, seemed to be testing the limits of her power. She must make examples.

Glancing at the paper, Alviarin went on. 'There is word from Ebou Dar, however. Through the Gray.' Had she emphasized that, to drive the splinter deeper? 'It appears Elayne Trakand and Nynaeve al'Meara are there. Posing as full sisters, with the blessings of the rebel ... *embassy* ... to Queen Tylin. There are two others, not identified, who may be doing the same. The lists of who is with the rebels are incomplete. Or they may just be companions. The Grays are uncertain.'

'Why under the Light would they be in Ebou Dar?' Elaida said dismissively. Certainly Teslyn would have sent news of *that*. 'The Gray must be passing along rumors, now. Tarna's message said they are with the rebels in Salidar.' Tarna Feir had reported Siuan Sanche there, too. And Logain Ablar, spreading those vicious lies no Red sister could lower herself to acknowledge, much less deny. The Sanche woman had a hand in that obscenity, or the sun would rise in the west tomorrow. Why could she not simply have crawled away and died, decently out of sight, like other stilled women?

It required effort not to draw a deep breath. Logain could be hanged quietly as soon as the rebels were dealt with; most of the world thought him dead long since. The filthy slander that the Red Ajah had set him up as a false Dragon would die with him. When the rebels were dealt with, the Sanche woman could be made to hand over the keys to the Amyrlin's eyes-and-ears. And name the traitors who had helped her escape. A foolish hope to wish that Alviarin would be named among them. 'I can hardly see the al'Meara girl running to Ebou Dar claiming to be Aes Sedai, much less Elayne, can you?'

'You did order Elayne found, Mother. As important as putting a leash on al'Thor, you said. When she was among three hundred rebels in Salidar, it was impossible to do anything, but she will not be so well protected in the Tarasin Palace.'

'I have no time for gossip and rumors.' Elaida bit off each word with contempt. Did Alviarin know more than she should, mentioning al'Thor, and leashing? 'I suggest you read Tarna's report again, then ask yourself whether even *rebels* would allow Accepted to pretend to the shawl.'

Alviarin waited with visible patience for her to finish, then examined her sheaf again and pulled out four more sheets. 'The Gray agent sent sketches,' she said blandly, proffering the pages. 'He is no artist, but Elayne and Nynaeve are recognizable.' After a moment, when Elaida did not take the drawings, she slipped them under the rest.

Elaida felt the color of anger and embarrassment rising in her cheeks. Alviarin had led her down this path deliberately by not bringing out those sketches at the first. She ignored that – anything else would only be more embarrassing still – but her voice became cold. 'I want them taken, and brought to me.'

The lack of curiosity on Alviarin's face made Elaida wonder again how much the woman knew that she was not supposed to. The al'Meara girl might well provide a handle on al'Thor, coming from the same village. All the sisters knew that, just as they knew that Elayne was Daughter-Heir of Andor, and that her mother was dead. Vague rumors linking Morgase to the Whitecloaks were so much nonsense, for she would never have gone to the Children of the Light for help. She was dead, leaving not even a corpse behind, and Elayne would be Queen. If she could be wrested away from the rebels before the Andoran Houses put Dyelin on the Lion Throne instead. It was not widely known what made Elayne more important than any other noble with a strong claim to a throne. Aside from the fact that she would be Aes Sedai one day, of course.

Elaida had the Foretelling sometimes, a Talent many thought lost before her, and long ago she had Foretold that the Royal House of Andor held the key to winning the Last Battle. Twenty-five years gone and more, as soon as it became clear that Morgase Trakand would gain the throne in the Succession, Elaida had fastened herself to the girl, as she was then. How Elayne was crucial, Elaida did not know, but Foretelling never lied. Sometimes she almost hated the Talent. She hated things she could not control.

'I want all four of them, Alviarin.' The other two were unimportant, certainly, but she would take no chances. 'Send my command to Teslyn immediately. Tell her – *and* Joline – that if they fail to send regular reports from now on, they will wish they had never been born. Include the information from the Macura woman.' Her mouth twisted around that last.

The name made Alviarin shift uneasily, too, and no wonder. Ronde Macura's nasty little infusion was something to make any sister uncomfortable. Forkroot was not lethal – at least you woke, if you drank enough to sleep – but a tea that deadened a woman's ability to channel seemed aimed too directly at Aes Sedai. A pity the information had not been received before Galina went; if forkroot worked on men as well as it seemed to on women, it would have made her task considerably easier.

Alviarin's ill ease lasted only a moment; a mere instant and she was all self-possession again, unyielding as a wall of ice. 'As you wish, Mother. I am sure they will leap to obey, as of course they should.'

A sudden flash of irritation swept Elaida like fire in dry pasture. The fate of the world in her hands, and petty stumbling blocks kept rising beneath her feet. Bad enough that she had rebels and recalcitrant rulers to handle, but too many Sitters still brooded and grumbled behind her back, fertile ground for the other woman to plow. Only six were firmly under her own thumb, and she suspected as many at least listened closely to Alviarin before they voted. Certainly nothing of importance passed through the Hall unless Alviarin agreed to it. Not open agreement, not with any acknowledgment that Alviarin bore a shred more influence or power than a Keeper should, but if Alviarin opposed . . . At least they had not gone so far as to reject anything Elaida sent them. They simply dragged their feet and too often let what she wanted starve on the floor. A pitifully small thing for which to be happy. Some Amyrlins had become little more than puppets once the Hall acquired a taste for rejecting what they put forward.

Her hands clenched, and a tiny crackle came from the strip of paper.

The ring has been placed in the bull's nose.

Alviarin looked as composed as a marble statue, but Elaida no longer cared. The shepherd was on his way to her. The rebels would be crushed and the Hall cowed, Alviarin forced to her knees and every fractious ruler brought to heel, from Tenobia of Saldaea, who had gone into hiding to avoid her emissary, to Mattin Stepaneos of Illian, who was trying to play all sides at once again, trying to agree with her *and* the Whitecloaks, and with al'Thor for all she knew. Elayne would be placed on the throne in Caemlyn, without her brother to get in the way and with a full knowledge of who had set her there. A little time back in the Tower would make the girl damp clay in Elaida's hands.

'I want *those men* rooted out, Alviarin.' There was no need to say who she meant; half the Tower could talk of nothing but *those men* in their *Black* Tower, and the other half whispered about them in corners.

'There are disturbing reports, Mother.' Alviarin looked through her papers once more, but Elaida thought it was only for something to do. She did not pluck out any more pages, and if nothing else disturbed the woman for long, this unholy midden outside Caemlyn must.

'*More* rumors? Do you believe the tales of thousands flocking to Caemlyn in answer to that obscene *amnesty?*' Not the least of what al'Thor had done, but hardly cause for worry. Just a pile of filth that must be safely cleared before Elayne was crowned in Caemlyn.

'Of course not, Mother, but—'

'Toveine is to lead; this task belongs properly to the Red.' Toveine Gazal had been fifteen years away from the Tower, until Elaida summoned her back. The other two Red Sitters who had resigned and gone into a 'voluntary' retreat at the same time were nervous-eyed women now, but unlike Lirene and Tsutama, Toveine had only hardened in her solitary exile. 'She is to have fifty sisters.' There could not be more than two or three men at this *Black* Tower actually able to channel, Elaida was certain. Fifty sisters could overwhelm them easily. Yet there might be others to deal with. Hangers-on, camp followers, fools full of futile hopes and insane ambitions. 'And she is to take a hundred – no, two hundred – of the Guard.'

'Are you certain that is wise? The rumors of thousands are certainly madness, but a Green agent in Caemlyn claims there are over four hundred in this Black Tower. A clever fellow. It seems he counted the supply carts that go out from the city. And you are aware of the rumors Mazrim Taim is with them.'

Elaida fought to keep her features smooth, and barely succeeded. She had forbidden mention of Taim's name, and it was bitter that she did not dare – did not dare! – impose the penalty on Alviarin. The woman looked her straight in the eyes; the absence of so much as a perfunctory 'Mother' this time was marked. And the *temerity* of asking whether her actions were *wise*! She was the Amyrlin Seat! Not first among equals; the Amyrlin Seat!

Opening the largest of the lacquered boxes revealed carved ivory miniatures laid out on gray velvet. Often just handling her collection soothed her, but more, like the knitting she enjoyed, it let whoever was attending her know their place, if she seemed to give more attention to the miniatures than to what they had to say. Fingering first an exquisite cat, sleek and flowing, then an elaborately robed woman with a peculiar little animal, some fantasy of the carver, almost like a man covered in hair, crouched on her shoulder, at length Elaida chose a curving fish, so delicately carved that it seemed nearly real despite the aged yellow of the ivory.

'Four hundred rabble, Alviarin.' She felt calmer already, for Alviarin's mouth had thinned. Just a fraction, but she savored any crack in the woman's façade. 'If there are that many. Only a fool could believe that more than one or two can channel. At most! In ten years, we have found only six men with the ability. Just twenty-four in the last twenty years. And you know how the land has been scoured. As for Taim ...' The name burned her mouth; the only false Dragon ever to escape being gentled once in the hands of Aes Sedai. Not a thing she wanted in the Chronicles under her reign, certainly not until she decided how it should be recorded. At present the Chronicles told nothing after his capture.

She stroked her thumb along the fish's scales. 'He is dead, Alviarin, else we would have heard from him long since. And not serving al'Thor. Can you think he went from claiming to be the Dragon Reborn to *serving* the Dragon Reborn? Can you think he could be in Caemlyn without Davram Bashere at least trying to kill him?' Her thumb moved faster on the ivory fish as she reminded herself that the Marshal-General of Saldaea was in Caemlyn taking orders from al'Thor. What *was* Tenobia playing at? Elaida held it all inside, though, presenting a face as calm as one of her carvings.

'Twenty-four is a dangerous number to speak aloud,' Alviarin said with an ominous quiet, 'as dangerous as two thousand. The Chronicles record only sixteen. The last thing needed now is for those years to rear up again. Or for sisters who know only what they were told to learn the truth. Even those you brought back hold their silence.'

Elaida put on a bemused look. So far as she knew, Alviarin had learned the truth of those years only on being raised Keeper, but her own knowledge was more personal. Not that Alviarin could be aware of that. Not for certain, anyway. 'Daughter, whatever comes out, I have no fear. Who is going to impose a penance on *me*, and on what charge?' That skirted truth nicely, but apparently it impressed the other woman not at all.

'The Chronicles record a number of Amyrlins who took on public penance for some usually obscure reason, but it has always seemed to me that is how an Amyrlin might have it written if she found herself with no choice except—'

Elaida's hand slapped down on the table. 'Enough, daughter! I *am* Tower law! What has been hidden will remain hidden, for the same reason it has for twenty years – the good of the White Tower.' Only then did she feel the bruise beginning on her palm; she lifted her hand to reveal the fish, broken in two. How old had it been? Five hundred years? A thousand? It was all she could do not to quiver with rage. Her voice certainly thickened with it. 'Toveine is to lead fifty sisters and two hundred of the Tower Guards to Caemlyn, to this Black Tower, where they will gentle any man they find able to channel and hang him, along with as many others as they can take alive.' Alviarin did not even blink at the violation of Tower law. Elaida had spoken the truth as she meant it to be; with this, with everything, she *was* Tower law. 'For that matter, hang up the dead as well. Let them be a warning to any man who thinks of touching the True Source. Have Toveine attend me. I will want to hear her plan.'

'It will be as you command, Mother.' The woman's reply was as cool and smooth as her face. 'Though if I may suggest, you might wish to reconsider sending so many sisters away from the Tower. Apparently the rebels found your offer wanting. They are no longer in Salidar. They are on the march. The reports come from Altara, but they must be into Murandy by now. And they have chosen themselves an Amyrlin.' She scanned the top sheet of her sheaf of papers as if searching for the name. 'Egwene al'Vere, it seems.'

That Alviarin had left this, the most important piece of news, until now, should have made Elaida explode in fury. Instead, she threw back her head and laughed. Only a firm hold on dignity kept her from drumming her heels on the floor. The surprise on Alviarin's face made her laugh harder, till she had to wipe her eyes with her fingers.

'You do not see it,' she said when she could speak between ripples of mirth. 'As well you are Keeper, Alviarin, not a Sitter. In the Hall, blind as you are, within a month the others would be holding you in a cabinet and taking you out when they needed your vote.'

'I see enough, Mother.' Alviarin's voice held no heat; if anything, it should have coated the walls with frost. 'I see three hundred rebel Aes Sedai, perhaps more, marching on Tar Valon with an army led by Gareth Bryne, acknowledged a great captain. Discounting the more ridiculous reports, that army may number over twenty thousand, and with Bryne to lead they will gain more at every village and town they pass. I do not say they have hope of taking the city, of course, but it is hardly a matter for laughter. High Captain Chubain should be ordered to increase recruiting for the Tower Guard.'

Elaida's gaze fell sourly on the broken fish, and she stood and stalked to the nearest window, her back to Alviarin. The palace under construction took away the bitter taste, that and the slip of paper she still clutched.

She smiled down on her palace-to-be. 'Three hundred rebels, yes, but you should read Tarna's account again. At least a hundred are on the point of breaking already.' She trusted Tarna to some extent, a Red with no room in her head for nonsense, and she said the rebels were ready to jump at shadows. Quietly desperate sheep looking for a shepherd, she said. A wilder, of course, yet still sensible. Tarna should be back soon, and able to give a fuller report. Not that it was needed. Elaida's plans were already working among the rebels. But that was her secret.

'Tarna has always been sure she could make people do what it was clear they would not.' Had there been an emphasis in that, a significance of tone? Elaida decided to ignore it. She had to ignore too much from Alviarin, but the day would come. Soon.

'As for their army, daughter, she says two or three thousand men at most. If they had more, they would have made sure she saw them, to overawe us.' In Elaida's opinion, eyes-and-ears always exaggerated, to make their information seem more valuable. Only sisters could be truly trusted. Red sisters, anyway. Some of them. 'But I would not care if they did have twenty thousand, or fifty, or a hundred. Can you even begin to guess why?' When she turned, Alviarin's face was all smooth composure, a mask over blind ignorance. 'You seem to be conversant with all the aspects of Tower law. What penalty do rebels face?'

'For the leaders,' Alviarin said slowly, 'stilling.' She frowned slightly, skirts swaying just barely as her feet shifted. Good. Even Accepted knew this, and she could not understand why Elaida asked. Very good. 'For many of the rest, too.'

'Perhaps.' The leaders might themselves escape that, most of them, if they submitted properly. The minimum penalty in law was to be birched in the Grand Hall before the assembled sisters, followed by at least a year and a day in public penance. Yet nothing said the penance must be served all at once; a month here, a month there, and they would still be atoning their crimes ten years from now, constant reminders of what came of resisting her. Some would be stilled, of course – Sheriam, a few of the more prominent so-called Sitters – but only sufficient to make the rest fear putting a foot wrong again, not enough to weaken the Tower. The White Tower had to be whole, and it had to be strong. Strong, and firmly in her grasp.

'Only one crime among those they have committed *demands* stilling.' Alviarin opened her mouth. There had been ancient rebellions, buried so deep that few among the sisters knew; the Chronicles stood mute, the lists of stilled and executed confined to records open only to Amyrlin, Keeper and Sitters, aside from the few librarians who kept them. Elaida allowed Alviarin no opportunity to speak. 'Any woman who falsely claims the title of Amyrlin Seat *must* be stilled. If they believed they had any chance of success, Sheriam would be their *Amyrlin*, or Lelaine, or Carlinya, or one of the others.' Tarna reported that Romanda Cassin had come out of her retirement; Romanda surely would have seized the stole with both hands if she saw the tenth part of a chance. 'Instead, they have plucked out an *Accepted*!'

Elaida shook her head in wry amusement. She could quote every word of the law setting out how a woman was chosen Amyrlin – she had made good use of it herself, after all – and never once did it require that the woman be a full sister. Obviously she *must* be, so those who framed the law never stated it, and the rebels had squirmed through that crack. 'They know their cause is hopeless, Alviarin. They plan to strut and bluster, try to dig out some protection against penalty for themselves, then yield the girl as a sacrifice.' Which was a pity. The al'Vere girl was another possible handle on al'Thor, and when she reached her full strength in the One Power, she would have been one of the strongest in a thousand years or more. A true pity.

'Gareth Bryne and an army hardly sound like strutting to me. It will take their army five or six months to reach Tar Valon. In that time, High Captain Chubain could increase the Guard—'

'Their *army*,' Elaida sneered. Alviarin was such a fool; for all her cool exterior, she was a rabbit. Next she would be spouting the Sanche woman's nonsense about the Forsaken being loose. Of course, she did not know the secret, but just the same ... 'Farmers carrying pikes, butchers with bows and tailors on horseback! And every step of the way, thinking of the Shining Walls, that held Artur Hawkwing at bay.' No, not a rabbit. A weasel. Yet soon or late, she would be weasel-fur trim on Elaida's cloak. The Light send it soon. 'Every step of the way, they will lose a man, if not ten. I would not be surprised if our rebels appear with nothing more than their Warders.' Too many people knew of the division in the Tower. Once the rebellion was broken, of course, it could be made to seem all a ploy, a part of gaining control of young al'Thor perhaps. An effort of years, that, and generations before memories faded. Every last rebel would pay for that on her knees.

Elaida clenched her fist as though she held all the rebels by the throat. Or Alviarin. 'I mean to break them, daughter. They will split open like a rotten melon.' Her secret assured that, however many farmers and tailors Lord Bryne hung on to, but let the other woman think as she would. Suddenly the Foretelling took hold of her, a certainty about things she could not see stronger than if they had been laid out before her. She would have been willing to step blindly over a cliff on that certainty. 'The White Tower will be whole again, except for remnants cast out and scorned, whole and stronger than ever. Rand al'Thor will face the Amyrlin Seat and know her anger. The Black Tower will be rent in blood and fire, and sisters will walk its grounds. This I Foretell.'

As usual, the Foretelling left her trembling, gasping for breath. She forced herself to stand still and straight, to breathe slowly; she never let anyone see weakness. But Alviarin ... Her eyes were wide as they could open, lips parted as if she had forgotten the words she meant to speak. A paper slid from the sheaf in her hands and almost fell before she could catch it. That recalled her to herself. In a flash she regained her serene mask, a perfect picture of Aes Sedai calm, but she definitely had been jolted to her heels. Oh, very good. Let her chew on the certain surety of Elaida's victory. Chew and break her teeth.

Elaida drew a deep breath and seated herself behind her writing table again, putting the broken ivory fish to one side where she did not have to look at it. It was time to exploit her victory. 'There is work to be done today, daughter. The first message is to go to the Lady Caraline Damodred ...'

Elaida spun out her plans, enlarging on what Alviarin knew, revealing some that she did not, because at the last an Amyrlin did have to work through her Keeper, however much she hated the woman. There was a pleasure in watching Alviarin's eyes, watching her wonder what else she still did not know. But while Elaida ordered, divided and assigned the world between the Aryth Ocean and the Spine of the World, in her mind frolicked the image of young al'Thor on his way to her like a caged bear, to be taught to dance for his dinner.

The Chronicles could hardly record the years of the Last Battle without mentioning the Dragon Reborn, but she knew that one name would be written larger than all others. Elaida do Avriny a'Roihan, youngest daughter of a minor House in the north of Murandy, would go down in history as the greatest and most powerful Amyrlin Seat of all time. The most powerful woman in the history of the world. The woman who saved humankind.

The Aiel standing in a deep fold in the low, brown-grass hills seemed like carved figures, ignoring sheets of dust sweeping ahead of a gusting wind. That snow should have been deep on the ground this time of year did not bother them; none had ever seen snow, and this oven heat, with the sun still well short of its peak, was less than where they came from. Their attention remained fixed on the southern rise, waiting for the signal that would announce the arrival of the destiny of the Shaido Aiel.

Outwardly, Sevanna looked like the others, though a ring of Maidens marked her out, resting easily on their heels, dark veils already hiding their faces to the eyes. She also waited, and more impatiently than she let on, but not to the exclusion of everything else. That was one reason why she commanded and the rest followed. The second was that she saw what could be if you refused to let outworn custom and stale tradition tie your hands.

A slight flicker of her green eyes to the left showed twelve men and one woman, each with round bull-hide buckler and three or four short spears, garbed in gray-and-brown *cadin'sor* that blended as well with the terrain here as in the Three-fold Land. Efalin, short graying hair hidden by the *shoufa* wrapped around her head, sometimes glanced Sevanna's way; if a Maiden of the Spear could be said to be uneasy, Efalin was. Some Shaido Maidens had gone south, joining the fools capering around Rand al'Thor, and Sevanna did not doubt others talked of it. Efalin must be wondering whether providing Sevanna with an escort of Maidens, as if she had been *Far*

Dareis Mai once herself, was enough to balance that. At least Efalin had no doubts where true power lay.

Like Efalin, the men led Shaido warrior societies, and they eyed one another between watching the rise. Especially blocky Maeric, who was *Seia Doon*, and scar-faced Bendhuin, of *Far Aldazar Din*. After today, no longer would anything hold back the Shaido from sending a man to Rhuidean, to be marked as the clan chief if he survived. Until that happened, Sevanna spoke as the clan chief since she was the widow of the last chief. Of the last two chiefs. And let those who muttered that she carried bad luck choke on it.

Gold and ivory bracelets clattered softly as she straightened the dark shawl over her arms and adjusted her necklaces. Most of those were gold and ivory too, but one was a mass of pearls and rubies that had belonged to a wetlander noblewoman – the woman now wore white and hauled and fetched alongside the other *gai'shain* back in the mountains called Kinslayer's Dagger – with a ruby the size of a small hen's egg nestled between her breasts. The wetlands held rich prizes. A large emerald on her finger caught sunlight in green fire; finger rings were one wetlander custom worth adopting, no matter the stares often aimed at hers. She would have more, if they matched this one for magnificence.

Most of the men thought Maeric or Bendhuin would be first to receive the Wise Ones' permission to try Rhuidean. Only Efalin in that group suspected that none would, and she only suspected; she also was astute enough to voice her suspicions circumspectly to Sevanna and not at all to anyone else. Their minds could not encompass the possibility of shedding the old, and in truth, if Sevanna was impatient to don the new, she was also aware that she must bring them to it slowly. Much had changed already in the old ways since the Shaido crossed the Dragonwall into the wetlands – still wet, compared to the Three-fold Land – yet more would change. Once Rand al'Thor was in her hands, once she had wed the *Car'a'carn*, the chief of chiefs of all the Aiel – this nonsense of the Dragon Reborn was wetlander foolishness – there would be a new way of naming clan chiefs, and sept chiefs as well. Perhaps even the heads of the warrior societies. Rand al'Thor would name them. Pointing where she told him, of course. And that would be only the beginning. The wetlander notion of handing down rank to your children, and their children, for instance.

The wind swept higher for a moment, blowing south. It would cover the sound of the wetlanders' horses and wagons.

She shifted her shawl again, then suppressed a grimace. At all costs she must not appear nervous. A glance to the right stilled worry as soon as begun. Over two hundred Shaido Wise Ones clustered there, and normally at least some would be watching her like vultures, but their eyes were all on the rise. More than one adjusted her shawl uneasily or smoothed bulky skirts. Sevanna's lip curled. Sweat beaded on some of those faces. Sweat! Where was their honor that they showed nerves before every gaze?

Everyone stiffened slightly as a young *Sovin Nai* appeared above them, lowering his veil as he scrambled down. He came straight to her, as was proper, but to her irritation he raised his voice enough for all to hear. 'One of their forward scouts escaped. He was wounded, but still on his horse.'

The society leaders began to move before he finished speaking. That would never do. They would lead in the actual fighting — Sevanna had never more than held a spear in her life — but she would not let them forget for a moment who she was. 'Throw every last spear against them,' she ordered loudly, 'before they can ready themselves.' They rounded on her as one.

'Every spear?' Bendhuin demanded incredulously. 'You mean except for the screens—'

Glowering, Maeric spoke right on top of him. 'If we keep no reserve, we can be—'

Sevanna cut them both off. 'Every spear! These are Aes Sedai we dance with. We must overwhelm them immediately!' Efalin and most of the others schooled their faces to stillness, but Bendhuin and Maeric frowned, ready to argue. Fools. They faced a few dozen Aes Sedai, a few hundred wetlander soldiers, yet with the more than forty thousand *algai'd'siswai* they had insisted on, they still wanted their screens of scouts and their spears in reserve as if they faced other Aiel or a wetlander army. 'I speak as the clan chief of the Shaido.' She should not have to say that, but a reminder could do no harm. 'They are a handful.' She weighted every word with contempt now. 'They can be run down if the spears move quickly. You were ready to avenge Desaine this sunrise. Do I smell fear now? Fear of a few wetlanders? Has honor gone from the Shaido?'

That turned their faces to stone, as intended. Even Efalin showed eyes like polished gray gems as she veiled; her fingers moved in Maiden handtalk, and as the society leaders sprinted up the rise, the Maidens around Sevanna followed. *That* was not what she had intended, but at least the spears were moving. Even from the bottom of the fold she could see what had seemed bare ground disgorging *cadin'sor*-clad figures, all hurrying south with the long strides that could run down horses. There was no time to waste. With a thought to have words with Efalin later, Sevanna turned to the Wise Ones.

Chosen from the strongest of the Shaido Wise Ones who could wield the One Power, they were six or seven for every Aes Sedai around Rand al'Thor, yet Sevanna saw doubt. They tried to hide it behind stony faces, but it was there, in shifting eyes, in tongues wetting lips. Many traditions fell today, traditions old and strong as law. Wise Ones did not take part in battles. Wise Ones kept far from Aes Sedai. They knew the ancient tales, that the Aiel had been sent to the Three-fold Land for failing the Aes Sedai, that they would be destroyed if ever they failed them again. They had heard the stories, what Rand al'Thor had claimed before all, that as part of their service to the Aes Sedai, the Aiel had sworn to do no violence.

Once Sevanna had been sure those stories were lies, but of late she believed the Wise Ones knew them for truth. None had told her so, of course. It did not matter. She herself had never made the two journeys to Rhuidean required to become a Wise One, but the others had accepted her, however reluctant some had been. Now they had no choice but to go on accepting. Useless traditions would be carved into new.

'Aes Sedai,' she said softly. They leaned toward her in a muted clatter of bracelets and necklaces, to catch her low words. 'They hold Rand al'Thor, the *Car'a'carn*. We must take him from them.' There were scattered frowns. Most believed she wanted the *Car'a'carn* taken alive in order to avenge the death of Couladin, her second husband. They understood that, but they would not have come here for it. 'Aes Sedai,' she hissed angrily. 'We kept our pledge, but they broke theirs. We violated nothing, but they have violated everything. You know how Desaine was murdered.' And of course they did. The eyes watching her were suddenly sharper. Killing a Wise One ranked with killing a pregnant woman, a child or a blacksmith. Some of those eyes were *very* sharp. Therava's, Rhiale's, others'. 'If we allow these women to walk away from that, then *we* are less than animals, *we* will have no honor. I hold my honor.'

On that she gathered her skirts with dignity and climbed the slope, head high, not looking back. She was certain the others would follow. Therava and Norlea and Dailin would see to that, and Rhiale and Tion and Meira and the rest who had accompanied her a few days past to see Rand al'Thor beaten and put back into his wooden chest by the Aes Sedai. Her reminder had been for those thirteen even more than the others, and they dared not fail her. The truth of how Desaine had died tied them to her.

Wise Ones with their skirts looped over their arms to free their legs could not keep up with the *algai'd'siswai* in *cadin'sor*, however hard they ran, though race they did. Five miles across those low rolling hills, not a long run, and they topped a crest to see the dance of spears already begun. After a fashion.

Thousands of *algai'd'siswai* made a huge pool of veiled gray-and-brown surging around a circle of wetlander wagons, which itself surrounded one of the small clumps of trees that dotted this region. Sevanna drew an angry breath. The Aes Sedai had even had time to bring all of their horses inside. The spears encircled the wagons, pressed in on them, showered arrows toward them, but those at the front seemed to push against an invisible wall. At first the arrows that arched highest passed over this wall, but then they too began striking something unseen and bouncing back. A low murmur rose among the Wise Ones.

'You see what the Aes Sedai do?' Sevanna demanded, as though she also could see the One Power being woven. She wanted to sneer; the Aes Sedai were fools, with their vaunted Three Oaths. When they finally decided they must use the Power as a weapon instead of just to make barriers, it would be too late. Provided the Wise

Ones did not stand too long staring. Somewhere in those wagons was Rand al'Thor, perhaps still doubled into a chest like a bolt of silk. Waiting for her to pick him up. If the Aes Sedai could hold him, then she could, with the Wise Ones. And a promise. 'Therava, take your half to the west now. Be ready to strike when I do. For Desaine, and the *toh* the Aes Sedai owe us. We will make them meet *toh* as no one ever has before.'

It was a foolish boast to speak of making someone meet an obligation they had not acknowledged, yet in the angry mutters from the other women, Sevanna heard other furious promises to make the Aes Sedai meet *toh*. Only those who had killed Desaine on Sevanna's orders stood silent. Therava's narrow lips tightened slightly, but finally she said, 'It will be as you say, Sevanna.'

At an easy lope, Sevanna led her half of the Wise Ones to the east side of the battle, if it could be called that yet. She had wanted to remain on a rise where she could have a good view – that was how a clan chief or battle leader directed the dance of spears – but in this one thing she found no support even from Therava and the others who shared the secret of Desaine's death. The Wise Ones made a sharp contrast with the *algai'd'siswai* as she lined them up in their white *algode* blouses and dark wool skirts and shawls, their glittering bracelets and necklaces and their waist-length hair held back by dark folded scarves. For all their decision that if they were to be in the dance of the spears, they would be in it, not on a rise apart, she did not believe they yet realized that the true battle today was theirs to fight. After today, nothing would be the same again, and tethering Rand al'Thor was the smallest part.

Among the *algai'd'siswai* staring toward the wagons only height quickly told men from Maidens. Veils and *shoufa* hid heads and faces, and *cadin'sor* was *cadin'sor* aside from the differences of cut that marked clan and sept and society. Those at the outer edge of the encirclement appeared confused, grumbling among themselves as they waited for something to happen. They had come prepared to dance with Aes Sedai lightning, and now they milled impatiently, too far back even to use the horn bows still in leather cases on their backs. They would not have to wait much longer if Sevanna had her way.

Hands on hips, she addressed the other Wise Ones. 'Those to the south of me will disrupt what the Aes Sedai are doing. Those to the north will attack. Forward the spears!' With the command, she turned to watch the destruction of the Aes Sedai who thought they had only steel to face.

Nothing happened. In front of her the mass of *algai'd'siswai* seethed uselessly, and the loudest sound was the occasional drumming of spears on bucklers. Sevanna gathered her anger, winding it like thread from the spinning. She had been so sure they were ready after Desaine's butchered corpse was displayed to them, but if they still found attacking Aes Sedai unthinkable, she would chivvy them to it if she had to shame them all till they demanded to put on *gai'shain* white.

Suddenly a ball of pure flame the size of a man's head arched toward the wagons, sizzling and hissing, then another, dozens. The knot in her middle loosened. More fireballs came from the west, from Therava and the rest. Smoke began to rise from burning wagons, first gray wisps, then thickening black pillars; the murmurs of the *algai'd'siswai* changed pitch, and if those directly in front of her moved little, there was a sudden sense of pressing forward. Shouts drifted from the wagons, men yelling in anger, bellowing in pain. Whatever barriers the Aes Sedai had made were down. It had begun, and there could be only one ending. Rand al'Thor would be hers; he would give her the Aiel, to take all of the wetlands, and before he died he would give her daughters and sons to lead the Aiel after her. She might enjoy that; he was quite pretty, really, strong and young.

She did not expect the Aes Sedai to go down easily, and they did not. Fireballs fell among the spears, turning *cadin'sor*-clad figures to torches, and lightnings struck from a clear sky, hurling men and earth into the air. The Wise Ones learned from what they saw, though, or perhaps they already knew and had hesitated before; most channeled so seldom, especially where anyone besides Wise Ones could see, that only another Wise One knew whether any given woman could. Whatever the reason, no sooner did lightning begin to fall among the Shaido spears than more struck toward the wagons.

Not all reached its target. Balls of fire streaking through the air, some large as horses now, silver lightning stabbing toward the ground like spears from the heavens, sometimes suddenly darted aside as if striking an invisible shield, or erupted violently in midair, or simply vanished altogether. Roars and crashes filled the air, warring with shouts and screams. Sevanna stared at the sky in delight. It was like the Illuminators' displays she had read about.

Suddenly the world turned white in her eyes; she seemed to be floating. When she could see again, she was flat on the ground a dozen paces from where she had stood, aching in every muscle, struggling for breath and covered with a scattering of dirt. Her hair wanted to lift away from her. Other Wise Ones were down as well, around a ragged hole a span across torn in the ground; thin tendrils of smoke rose from the dresses of some. Not everyone had fallen – the battle of fire and lightning continued in the sky – but too many. She had to throw them back into the dance.

Forcing herself to breathe, she scrambled to her feet, not bothering to brush off the dirt. 'Push spears!' she shouted. Seizing Estalaine's angular shoulders, she started to drag the woman to her feet, then realized from her staring blue eyes that she was dead and let her fall. She pulled a dazed Dorailla erect instead, then seized up a spear from a fallen Thunder Walker and waved it high. 'Forward the spears!' Some of the Wise Ones seemed to take her literally, plunging into the mass of *algai'd'siswai*. Others kept their heads better, helping those who could rise, and the storm of fire and lightning continued as she raged up and down the line of Wise Ones, waving her spear and shouting. 'Push spears! Forward the spears!'

She felt like laughing; she did laugh. With dirt all over her and the battle raging, she had never been so exhilarated before in her life. Almost she wished she had chosen to become a Maiden of the Spear. Almost. No *Far Dareis Mai* could ever be clan chief, any more than a man could be a Wise One; a Maiden's route to power was to give up the spear and become a Wise One. As wife of a clan chief she had been wielding power at an age when a Maiden was barely trusted to carry a spear or a Wise One's apprentice to fetch water. And now she had it all, Wise One and clan chief, though it would take some doing yet to have that last title in truth. Titles mattered little so long as she had the power, but why should she not have both?

A sudden scream made her turn, and she gaped at the sight of a shaggy gray wolf ripping Dosera's throat out. Without thought she plunged her spear into its side. Even as it twisted to snap at the spear haft, another waist-tall wolf bounded past her to hurl itself onto the back of one of the *algai'd'siswai*, then another wolf, and more, tearing into *cadin'sor*-clad figures wherever she looked.

Superstitious fear lanced through her as she pulled her spear free. The Aes Sedai had called wolves to fight for them. She could not take her gaze from the wolf she had killed. The Aes Sedai had ... No. No! It could change nothing. She would not let it.

Finally she managed to pull her eyes away, but before she could shout encouragement to the Wise Ones again, something else stilled her tongue and made her stare. A knot of wetlander horsemen in red helmets and breastplates, laying about them with swords, thrusting with long lances, in the middle of the *algai'd'-siswai*. Where had *they* come from?

She did not realize she had spoken aloud until Rhiale answered her. 'I tried to tell you, Sevanna, but you would not listen.' The flame-haired woman eyed her bloody spear distastefully; Wise Ones were not supposed to carry spears. She ostentatiously laid the weapon in the crook of her elbow, the way she had seen chiefs do, as Rhiale went on. 'Wetlanders have attacked from the south. Wetlanders and *siswai'aman*.' She imbued the word with all the scorn proper for those would name themselves Spears of the Dragon. 'Maidens as well. And ... And there are Wise Ones.'

'Fighting?' Sevanna said incredulously before realizing how it sounded. If she could toss out decayed custom, surely those sun-blinded fools to the south who still called themselves Aiel could as well. She had not expected it, though. No doubt Sorilea had brought them; that old woman reminded Sevanna of a landslide plunging down a mountain, carrying all before it. 'We must attack them at once. They will not have Rand al'Thor. Or ruin our vengeance for Desaine,' she added when Rhiale's eyes widened.

'They are Wise Ones,' the other woman said in a flat tone, and Sevanna understood bitterly. Joining the dance of spears was bad enough, but Wise One attacking Wise One was more than even Rhiale would countenance. She had agreed that Desaine must die – how else could the other Wise Ones, not to mention the *algai'd'siswai*, be brought to attack Aes Sedai, which they must do to put Rand al'Thor in their hands, and with him all the Aiel – yet that was done in secret, surrounded by like-minded women. This would be before everyone. Fools and cowards, all of them!

'Then fight those enemies you can bring yourself to fight, Rhiale.' She bit off every word with as much scorn as she could, but Rhiale merely nodded, adjusted her shawl with another glance at the spear on Sevanna's arm and returned to her place in the line.

Perhaps there was a way to make the other Wise Ones move first. Better to attack by surprise, but better anything than that they should snatch Rand al'Thor from her very hands. What she would not give for a woman who could channel and would do as she was told without balking. What she would not give to be on a rise, where she could see how the battle went.

Keeping her spear ready and a wary eye out for wolves – those she could see were either killing men and women in *cadin'sor* or were dead themselves – she returned to shouting encouragement. To the south more fire and lightning fell among the Shaido than before, but it made no difference that she could tell. That battle, with its explosions of flame and earth and people, continued unabated.

'Push spears!' she shouted, waving hers. 'Push spears!' Among the churning *algai'd'siswai* she could not make out any of the fools who had tied a bit of red cloth around their temples and named themselves *siswai'aman*. Perhaps they were too few to alter the course of events. The knots of wetlanders certainly seemed few and far between. Even as she watched, one was swarmed under, men and horses, by stabbing spears. 'Push spears! Push spears!' Exultation filled her voice. If the Aes Sedai called ten thousand wolves, if Sorilea had brought a thousand Wise Ones and a hundred thousand spears, the Shaido would still emerge victorious today. The Shaido, and herself. Sevanna of the Jumai Shaido would be a name remembered forever.

Suddenly a hollow boom sounded amid the roar of battle. It

seemed to come from the direction of the Aes Sedai wagons, but nothing told her whether they had caused it, or the Wise Ones. She disliked things she did not understand, yet she was not about to ask Rhiale or the others and flaunt her ignorance. And her lack of the ability all here had, save her. It counted for nothing among themselves, but another thing she did not like was for others to have power she did not.

A flicker of light among the *algai'd'siswai*, a sense of something turning, caught the corner of her eye, but when she turned to look, there was nothing. Again the same thing happened, a flash of light seen on the edge of vision, and again when she looked there was nothing to see. Too many things she did not understand.

Shouting encouragement, she eyed the line of Shaido Wise Ones. Some appeared bedraggled, head scarves gone and long hair hanging loose, skirts and blouses covered with dirt or even singed. At least a dozen lay stretched out in a row, groaning, and seven more were still, shawls laid over their faces. It was those on their feet that interested her. Rhiale, and Alarys with her rare black hair all awry. Someryn, who had taken to wearing her blouse unlaced to show even more generous cleavage than Sevanna herself, and Meira, with her long face yet more grim than usual. Stout Tion, and skinny Belinde, and Modarra, as tall as most men.

One of them should have told her if they did something new. The secret of Desaine bound them to her; even for a Wise One, revelation of that would lead to a lifetime of pain – and worse, shame – trying to meet *toh*, if the one revealed was not simply driven naked into the wilderness to live or die as she could, likely to be killed like a beast by any who found her. Even so, Sevanna was sure they took as much delight as the rest in concealing things from her, the things that Wise Ones learned during their apprenticeships, and in the journeys to Rhuidean. Something would have to be done about that, but later. She would not display weakness by asking what they did now.

Turning back to the battle, she found the balance changing, and in her favor it appeared. To the south fireballs and lightning bolts plummeted as heavily as ever, but not in front of her, and it seemed not to the west or north either. What struck toward the wagons still failed to reach the ground more often than not, yet there was a definite slackening of the Aes Sedai's efforts. They had been forced onto the defensive. She *was* winning!

Even as the thought flushed through her like pure heat, the Aes Sedai went silent. Only to the south did fire and lightning still fall among the *algai'd'siswai*. She opened her mouth to shout victory, and another realization silenced her. Fire and lightning stormed down toward the wagons, stormed down and crashed against some unseen obstruction. Smoke from burning wagons was beginning to outline the shape of a dome as it streamed up and finally billowed from a hole in the top of the invisible enclosure.

Sevanna whirled to confront the line of Wise Ones, her face such that several flinched back from her, and maybe from the spear in her hand. She knew she looked ready to use it; she was ready. 'Why have you let them do this?' she raged. 'Why? You were to obstruct whatever they did, not allow them to make more walls!'

Tion looked ready to empty her stomach, but she planted her fists on broad hips and faced Sevanna directly. 'It was not the Aes Sedai.'

'Not the Aes Sedai?' Sevanna spat. 'Then who? The other Wise Ones? I told you we must attack them!'

'It was not women,' Rhiale said, her voice faltering. 'It was not—' Face pale, she swallowed.

Sevanna turned slowly to stare at the dome, only then remembering to breathe again. Something had risen through the hole where the smoke gushed out. One of the wetlander banners. The smoke was not enough to obscure it completely. Crimson, with a disc half white and half black, the colors divided by a sinuous line, just like the piece of cloth the *siswai'aman* wore. Rand al'Thor's banner. Could he possibly be strong enough to have broken free, overwhelmed all the Aes Sedai and raised that? It had to be.

The storm still battered at the dome, but Sevanna heard murmurs behind her. The other women were thinking of retreat. Not her. She had always known that the easiest path to power lay through conquering men who already possessed it, and even as a child she was sure she had been born with the weapons to conquer them. Suladric, clan chief of the Shaido, fell to her at sixteen, and when he died, she chose those most likely to succeed. Muradin and Couladin each believed he alone had captured her interest, and when Muradin failed to return from Rhuidean, as so many men did, one smile convinced Couladin that he had overwhelmed her. But the power of a clan chief paled beside that of the *Car'a'carn*, and even that was nothing beside what she saw before her. She shivered as if she had just seen the most beautiful man imaginable in the sweat tent. When Rand al'Thor was hers, she would conquer the whole world.

'Press harder,' she commanded. 'Harder! We will humble these Aes Sedai for Desaine!' And she would have Rand al'Thor.

Abruptly there was a roar from the front of the battle, men shouting, screaming. She cursed that she could not see what was happening. Again she shouted for the Wise Ones to press harder, but if anything, it seemed the fall of flame and lightning against the dome lessened. And then there was something she could see.

Close to the wagons, *cadin'sor*-clad figures and earth erupted into the air with a thunderous crash, not in one place, but in a long line. Again the ground exploded, and again, again, each time a little farther from the encircled wagons. Not a line, but a solid ring of exploding ground and men and Maidens that she had no doubt ran all the way around the wagons. Again and again and again, ever expanding, and suddenly *algai'd'siswai* were pushing past her, buffeting through the line of Wise Ones, running.

Sevanna beat at them with her spear, flailing at heads and shoulders, not caring when the spearhead came away redder than before. 'Stand and fight! Stand, for the honor of the Shaido!' They rushed by unheeding. 'Have you no honor! Stand and fight!' She stabbed a fleeing Maiden in the back, but the rest just trampled over the fallen woman. Abruptly she realized that some of the Wise Ones were gone, and others picking up the injured. Rhiale turned to run, and Sevanna seized the taller woman's arm, threatening her with the spear. She did not care that Rhiale could channel. 'We must stand! We can still have him!'

The other woman's face was a mask of fear. 'If we stand, we die! Or else we end chained outside Rand al'Thor's tent! Stay and die if you wish, Sevanna. I am no Stone Dog!' Ripping her arm free, she sped eastward.

For a moment more, Sevanna stood there, letting the men and Maidens push her this way and that as they streamed by in panic. Then she tossed down the spear and felt her belt pouch, where a small cube of intricately carved stone lay. Well that she had hesitated over throwing that away. She had another cord for her bow yet. Gathering her skirts to bare her legs, she joined in the chaotic flight, but if all the rest fled in terror, she ran with plans whirling through her head. She *would* have Rand al'Thor on his knees before her, and the Aes Sedai as well.

Alviarin finally left Elaida's apartments, as cool and collected as ever on the surface. Inside, she felt wrung out like a damp cloth. She managed to keep her legs steady down the long curving flights of stairs, marble even in the very heights. Liveried servants bowed and curtsied as they scurried about their tasks, seeing only the Keeper in all her Aes Sedai serenity. As she went lower, sisters began to appear, many wearing their shawls, fringed in the colors of their Ajahs, as if to emphasize by formality that they *were* full sisters. They eyed her as she passed, uneasy often as not. The only one to ignore her was Danelle, a dreamy Brown sister. She had been part of bringing down Siuan Sanche and raising Elaida, but lost in her own thoughts, a solitary with no friends even in her own Ajah, she seemed unaware that she had been shoved aside. Others were all too aware. Berisha, a lean and hard-eyed Gray, and Kera, with the fair hair and blue eyes that appeared occasionally among Tairens and all the arrogance so common to Greens, went so far as to curtsy. Norine made as if to, then did not; big-eyed and nearly as dreamy as Danelle at times, and as friendless, she resented Alviarin; if the Keeper came from the White, in her eyes it should have been Norine Dovarna.

The courtesy was not required toward the Keeper, not from a sister, but no doubt they hoped she might intercede with Elaida should that become necessary. The others merely wondered what commands she carried, whether another sister was to be singled out today for some failure in the Amyrlin's eyes. Not even Reds went within five levels of the Amyrlin's new apartments unless summoned, and more than one sister actually hid when Elaida came below. The very air seemed heated, thick with a fear that had nothing to do with rebels or men channeling.

Several sisters tried to speak, but Alviarin brushed past, barely polite, hardly noticing worry bloom in their eyes when she refused to pause. Elaida filled her mind as much as theirs. A woman of many layers, Elaida. The first look at her showed a beautiful woman filled with dignified reserve, the second a woman of steel, stern as a bared blade. She overwhelmed where others persuaded, bludgeoned where others tried diplomacy or the Game of Houses. Anyone who knew her saw her intelligence, but only after a time did you realize that for all her brains, she saw what she wanted to see, would try to make true what she wanted to be true. Of the two indisputably frightening things about her, the lesser was that she so often succeeded. The greater was her Talent for Foretelling.

So easy to forget that, erratic and infrequent; it had been so long since the last Foretelling that the very unpredictability made it strike like a thunderbolt. No one could say when it would come, not even Elaida, and no one could say what it would reveal. Now Alviarin almost felt the woman's shadowy presence following and watching.

It might be necessary to kill her yet. If so, Elaida would not be the first she had killed in secret. Still, she hesitated to take that step without orders, or at least permission.

She entered her own apartments with a sense of relief, as though Elaida's shade could not cross the threshold. A foolish thought. If Elaida had a suspicion of the truth, a thousand leagues would not keep her from Alviarin's throat. Elaida would expect her to be hard at work, personally penning orders for the Amyrlin's signature and seal – but which of those orders were actually to be carried out had yet to be decided. Not by Elaida, of course. Nor by herself.

The rooms were smaller than those Elaida occupied, though the ceilings reached higher, and a balcony looked over the great square in front of the Tower from a hundred feet up. Sometimes she went out on the balcony to see Tar Valon spread out before her, the greatest city in the world, filled with countless thousands who were less than pieces on a stones board. The furnishings were Domani, pale striped wood inlaid with pearlshell and amber, bright carpets in patterns of flowers and scrolls, brighter tapestries of forest and flowers and grazing deer. They had belonged to the last occupant of these rooms, and if she retained them for any reason beyond not wanting to waste time choosing new, it was to remind herself of the price of failure. Leane Sharif had dabbled in schemes and failed, and now she was cut off from the One Power forever, a helpless refugee dependent on charity, doomed to a life of misery until she either ended it or simply put her face to the wall and died. Alviarin had heard of a few stilled women who managed to survive, but she would doubt those stories until she met one. Not that she had the slightest desire to do so.

Through the windows she could see the brightness of early afternoon, yet before she was halfway across her sitting room, the light suddenly faded into dim evening. The darkness did not surprise her. She turned and went to her knees immediately. 'Great Mistress, I live to serve.' A tall woman of dark shadow and silver light stood before her. Mesaana.

'Tell me what happened, child.' The voice was crystal chimes.

On her knees, Alviarin repeated every word that Elaida had said, though she wondered why it was necessary. In the beginning she had left out unimportant bits, and Mesaana knew every time, demanded *every* word, every gesture and facial expression. Plainly she eavesdropped on those meetings. Alviarin had tried to work out the logic of it and failed. Some things did work to logic, though.

She had met others of the Chosen, whom fools called the Forsaken. Lanfear had come within the Tower, and Graendal, imperious in their strength and knowledge, making it clear without words that Alviarin was far beneath them, a scullery maid to run errands and wriggle with pleasure if she received a kind word. Be'lal had snatched Alviarin away in the night while she slept – to where she still did not know; she had wakened back in her own bed, and that had terrified her even more than being in the presence of a man who could channel. To him she was not even a worm, not even a living thing, just a piece in a game, to move at his command. First had been Ishamael, years before the others, plucking her out of the hidden mass of the Black Ajah to place her at its head.

To each she had knelt, saying that she lived to serve and meaning it, obeying as they commanded, whatever the command. After all, they stood only a step below the Great Lord of the Dark himself, and if she wanted the rewards of her service, the immortality it seemed they already possessed, it was well to obey. To each she knelt, and only Mesaana had appeared with an inhuman face. This cloak of shadow and light must be woven with the One Power, but Alviarin could see no weave. She had felt the strength of Lanfear and Graendal, had known from the first instant how much stronger in the Power they were than she, but in Mesaana she sensed . . . nothing. As if the woman could not channel at all.

The logic was clear, and stunning. Mesaana hid herself because she might be recognized. She must reside in the Tower itself. On the face of it, that seemed impossible, yet nothing else fit. Given that, she must be one of the sisters; surely she was not among servants, bound to labor and sweat. But who? Too many women had been out of the Tower for years before Elaida's summons, too many had no close friends, or none at all. Mesaana must be one of those. Alviarin very much wanted to know. Even if she could make no use of it, knowledge was power.

'So our Elaida has had a Foretelling,' Mesaana chimed, and Alviarin realized with a start that she had reached the end of her recital. Her knees hurt, but she knew better than to rise without permission. A finger of shadow tapped silver lips thoughtfully. Had she seen any sister make that gesture? 'Strange that she should be so clear and so erratic at the same time. It was always a rare Talent, and most who had it spoke so only poets could understand. Usually until it was too late to matter, at least. Everything always became clear then.' Alviarin kept silent. None of the Chosen conversed; they commanded or demanded. 'Interesting predictions. The rebels breaking – like a rotten melon? – was that part of it?'

'I am not certain, Great Mistress,' she said slowly – had it been? – but Mesaana only shrugged.

'Either it is or it is not, and either way can be used.'

'She is dangerous, Great Mistress. Her Talent could reveal what should not be revealed.'

Crystalline laughter answered her. 'Such as? You? Your Black Ajah sisters? Or perhaps you think to safeguard me? You are a good girl sometimes, child.' That silvery voice was amused. Alviarin felt her face heat and hoped that Mesaana read the shame, not the anger. 'Do you suggest that our Elaida should be disposed of, child? Not yet, I think. She has her uses still. At least until young al'Thor reaches us, and very likely after. Write out her orders and see to them. Watching her play her little games is certainly amusing. You children almost match the *Ajah* at times. Will she succeed in having the King of Illian and the Queen of Saldaea kidnapped? You *Aes Sedai* used to do that, didn't you, but not for – what? – two thousand years? Who will she try to put on the throne of Cairhien? Will the offer of being king in Tear overcome the High Lord Darlin's dislike of Aes Sedai? Will our Elaida choke on her own frustration first? A pity she resists the idea of a larger army. I'd have thought her ambitions would leap at that.'

The interview was coming to a close – they never lasted longer than for Alviarin to report and be given her own orders – but she had a question yet to ask. 'The Black Tower, Great Mistress.' Alviarin wet her lips. She had learned much since Ishamael appeared to her, not least that the Chosen were neither omnipotent nor all-knowing. She had risen because Ishamael killed her predecessor in his wrath at discovering what Jarna Malari had begun, yet it had not ended for another two years, after the death of another Amyrlin. She often wondered whether Elaida had had any hand in the death of that one, Sierin Vayu; certainly the Black Ajah had not. Jarna had had Tamra Ospenya, the Amyrlin before Sierin, squeezed like a bunch of grapes – obtaining little juice, as it turned out – and made her appear to have died in her sleep, but Alviarin and the other twelve sisters of the Supreme Council had paid in pain before they could convince Ishamael they had no responsibility for it. The Chosen were not all-powerful, and they did not know everything, yet sometimes they knew what no one else did. Asking could be dangerous, though. 'Why' was the most dangerous; the Chosen never liked to be asked why. 'Is it safe to send fifty sisters to deal with them, Great Mistress?'

Eyes glowing like twin full moons regarded her in silence, and a chill slid up Alviarin's spine. Jarna's fate flashed into her mind. Publicly Gray, Jarna had never shown any interest in the *ter'angreal* no one knew a use for – until the day she became snared in one untried for centuries. How to activate it remained a mystery still. For ten days no one could reach her, only listen to her throat-wrenching shrieks. Most of the Tower thought Jarna a model of virtue; when what could be recovered was buried, every sister in Tar Valon and everyone who could reach the city in time attended the funeral.

'You have curiosity, child,' Mesaana said finally. 'That can be an asset, properly directed. Wrongly directed . . .' The threat hung in the air like a gleaming dagger.

'I will direct it as you command, Great Mistress,' Alviarin breathed hoarsely. Her mouth was dry as dust. 'Only as you command.' But she would still see that no Black sisters went with Toveine. Mesaana moved, looming over her so she had to crane her neck to look up at that face of light and shadow, and suddenly she wondered whether the Chosen knew her thoughts.

'If you would serve me, child, then you must serve and obey me. Not Semirhage or Demandred. Not Graendal or anyone else. Only me. And the Great Lord, of course, but me above all save him.'

'I live to serve you, Great Mistress.' That came out in a croak, but she managed to emphasize the added word.

For a long moment silvery eyes stared down at her unblinking. Then Mesaana said, 'Good. I will teach you, then. But remember that a pupil is not a teacher. I choose who learns what, and I decide when they can make use of it. Should I find you have passed on the smallest scrap or used even a hair of it without my direction, I will extinguish you.'

Alviarin worked moisture back into her mouth. There was no anger in those chimes, only certainty. 'I live to serve you, Great Mistress. I live to obey you, Great Mistress.' She had just learned something about the Chosen that she could hardly credit. Knowledge was power.

'You have a little strength, child. Not much, but enough.'

A weave appeared seemingly from nowhere.

'This,' Mesaana chimed, 'is called a gateway.'

Pedron Niall grunted as Morgase placed a white stone on the board with a smile of triumph. Lesser players might set two dozen more stones each yet, but he could see the inevitable course now, and so could she. In the beginning the golden-haired woman seated on the other side of the small table had played to lose, to make the game close enough to be interesting for him, but it had not taken her long to learn that that led to obliteration. Not to mention that he was clever enough to see through the subterfuge and would not tolerate it. Now she plied all her skill and managed to win nearly half their games. No one had beaten him so often in a good many years.

'The game is yours,' he told her, and the Queen of Andor nodded. Well, she would be Queen again; he would see to that. In green silk, with a high lace collar brushing her chin, she looked every inch a queen despite the sheen of perspiration on her smooth cheeks. She hardly appeared old enough to have a daughter Elayne's age, though, much less a son Gawyn's.

'You did not realize I saw the trap you were laying from your thirty-first stone, Lord Niall, and you took my feint from the forty-third stone to be my real attack.' Excitement sparkled in her blue eyes; Morgase liked to win. She liked playing to win.

It was all meant to lull him, of course, the playing at stones, the politeness. Morgase knew she was a prisoner in the Fortress of the Light in all but name, albeit a luxuriously pampered prisoner. And a secret one. He had allowed stories of her presence to spread, but issued no proclamations. Andor had too strong a history of opposing the Children of the Light. He would announce nothing until legions moved into Andor, with her their figurehead. Morgase certainly knew that, as well. Very probably she also knew he was aware of her attempts to soften him. The treaty she had signed gave the Children rights in Andor they had never possessed anywhere except here in Amadicia, and he expected that she already planned how to lighten his hand on her land, how to remove his hand altogether as soon as she could. She had only signed because he backed her into a corner, yet confined in that corner, she fought on as skillfully as she maneuvered on a stones board. For one so beautiful, she was a tough woman. No, she was tough, and that was that. She did let herself be caught up in the pure pleasure of the game, but he could not count that a fault when it gave him so many pleasant moments.

Had he been even twenty years younger, he might have played

more to her true game. Long years as a widower stretched behind him, and the Lord Captain Commander of the Children of the Light had little time for pleasantries with women, little time for anything except *being* Lord Captain Commander. Had he been twenty years younger – well, twenty-five – and she not trained by the Tar Valon witches. It was easy to forget that, in her presence. The White Tower was a sink of iniquity and the Shadow, and she was touched deeply by it. Rhadam Asunawa, the High Inquisitor, would have tried her for her months in the White Tower and hanged her without delay, had Niall allowed it. He sighed regretfully.

Morgase kept her victorious smile, but those big eyes studied his face with an intelligence she could not hide. He filled her goblet and his own with wine from the silver pitcher sitting in a bowl of cool water that had been ice a little while ago.

'My Lord Niall . . .' The hesitation was just right, the slim hand half-stretched across the table toward him, the added respect in how she addressed him. Once she had called him simply Niall, with more contempt than she would have handed a drunken groom. The hesitation would have been just right had he not had the measure of her. 'My Lord Niall, surely you can order Galad to Amador so I may see him. Just for a day.'

'I regret,' he replied smoothly, 'that Galad's duties keep him in the north. You should be proud; he is one of the best young officers among the Children.' Her stepson was a lever to use on her at need, one best used now by keeping him away. The young man *was* a good officer, perhaps the best to join the Children in Niall's time, and there was no need to put strains on his oath by letting him know his mother was here, and a 'guest' only by courtesy.

No more than a slight tightening of her mouth, quickly gone, betrayed her disappointment. This was not the first time she had made that request, nor would it be the last. Morgase Trakand did not surrender just because it was plain she was beaten. 'As you say, my Lord Niall,' she said, so meekly that he nearly choked on his wine. Submissiveness was a new tactic, one she must have worked up with difficulty. 'It is just a mother's—'

'My Lord Captain Commander?' a deep, resonant voice broke in from the doorway. 'I fear I have important news that cannot wait, my Lord.' Abdel Omerna stood tall in the white-and-gold tabard of a Lord Captain of the Children of the Light, bold face framed by wings of white at his temples, dark eyes deep and thoughtful. From head to toe he was fearless and commanding. And a fool, though that was not apparent at a glance.

Morgase drew in on herself at the sight of Omerna, so small a motion most men would not have noticed. She believed him spymaster for the Children, as everyone did, a man to be feared almost as much as Asunawa, perhaps more. Even Omerna himself did not know he was but a decoy to keep eyes away from the true master of spies, a man known only to Niall himself. Sebban Balwer, Niall's dry little stick of a secretary. Yet decoy or not, something useful did pass through Omerna's hands on occasion. On rare occasions, something dire. Niall had no doubts what the man had brought; nothing else except Rand al'Thor at the gates would have sent him barging in this way. The Light send it was all a rug merchant's madness.

'I fear our gaming is done for this morning,' Niall told Morgase, standing. He offered her a slight bow as she rose, and she acknowledged it by inclining her head.

'Until this evening, perhaps?' Her voice still held that almost docile tone. 'That is, if you will dine with me?'

Niall accepted, of course. He did not know where she was leading with this new tactic — not where an oaf might suppose, he was sure — but it would be amusing to find out. The woman was full of surprises. Such a pity she was tainted by the witches.

Omerna advanced as far as the great sunflare of gold, set in the floor, that had been worn by feet and knees over centuries. It was a plain room aside from that and the captured banners that lined the walls high beneath the ceiling, age-tattered and worn. Omerna watched her skirt around him without really acknowledging his presence, and when the door closed behind her, he said, 'I have not yet found Elayne or Gawyn, my Lord.'

'Is *that* your important news?' Niall demanded irritably. Balwer reported Morgase's daughter in Ebou Dar, still mired to her neck with the witches; orders concerning her had already been sent to Jaichim Carridin. Her other son still toiled with the witches as well, it seemed, in Tar Valon, where even Balwer possessed few eyes-and-ears.

Niall took a long swallow of cool wine. His bones felt old and brittle and cold of late, yet the Shadow-spawned heat made his skin sweat enough, and dried his mouth.

Omerna gave a start. 'Ah ... no, my Lord.' He fumbled in a pocket of his white undercoat and pulled out a tiny bone cylinder with three red stripes running its length. 'You wanted this brought as soon as the pigeon arrived in the—' He cut off as Niall snatched the tube.

This was what he had been waiting for, the reason a legion was not already on its way to Andor with Morgase riding at its head, if not leading. If it was not all Varadin's madness, the ravings of a man unbalanced by watching Tarabon collapse into anarchy, Andor would have to wait. Andor, and maybe more.

'I ... I have confirmation that the White Tower truly has broken,' Omerna went on. 'The ... the Black Ajah has seized Tar Valon.' No wonder he sounded nervous, speaking heresy. There was no Black Ajah; all of the witches were Darkfriends.

Niall ignored him and broke the wax sealing the tube with his thumbnail. He had used Balwer to start those rumors, and now they came back to him. Omerna believed every rumor his ears caught, and his ears caught them all.

'And there are reports that the witches are conferring with the false Dragon al'Thor, my Lord.'

Of course the witches were conferring with him! He was their creation, their puppet. Niall shut out the fool's blather and moved back to the gaming table while he drew a slim roll of paper from the tube. He never let anyone know more of these messages than that they existed, and few knew that much. His hands trembled as they unrolled the thin paper. His hands had not trembled since he was a boy facing his first battle, more than seventy years ago. Those hands seemed little more than bone and sinew now, but they still possessed enough strength for what he had to do.

The writing was not that of Varadin, but of Faisar, sent to Tarabon for a different purpose. Niall's stomach twisted into a knot as he read; it was in clear language, not Varadin's cipher. Varadin's reports had been the work of a man on the brink of madness if not over, yet Faisar confirmed the worst of it and more. Much more.

Al'Thor was a rabid beast, a destroyer who must be stopped, but now a second mad animal had appeared, one that might be even more dangerous than the Tar Valon witches with their tame false Dragon. But how under the Light could he fight both?

'It . . . it seems that Queen Tenobia has left Saldaea, my Lord. And the . . . the Dragonsworn are burning and killing across Altara and Murandy. I have heard the Horn of Valere has been found, in Kandor.'

Still half-distracted, Niall looked up to find Omerna at his side, licking his lips and wiping sweat from his forehead with the back of his hand. No doubt he hoped for a glance at what was in the message. Well, everyone would know soon enough.

'It seems one of your wilder fancies wasn't so wild after all,' Niall said, and that was when he felt the knife go in under his ribs.

Shock froze him long enough for Omerna to pull the dagger free and plunge it in again. Other Lord Captain Commanders had died this way before him, yet he had never thought it would be Omerna. He tried to grapple with his killer, but there was no force in his arms. He hung on to Omerna with the man supporting him, the pair of them eye to eye.

Omerna's face was red; he looked ready to weep. 'It had to be done. It had to be. You let the witches sit there in Salidar unhindered, and . . .' As if suddenly realizing that he had his arms around the man he was murdering, he pushed Niall away.

Strength had gone from Niall's legs now as well as his arms. He fell heavily against the gaming table, turning it over. Black and white stones scattered across the polished wooden floor around him; the silver pitcher bounced and splashed wine. The cold in his bones was leaching out into the rest of him.

He was not certain whether time had slowed for him or everything really did happen so quickly. Boots thudded across the floor, and he lifted his head wearily to see Omerna gaping and wide-eyed, backing away from Eamon Valda. Every bit as much the picture of a Lord Captain as Omerna in his white-and-gold tabard and white undercoat, Valda was not so tall, not so plainly commanding, but the dark man's face was hard, as ever, and he had a sword in his hands, the heron-mark blade he prized so highly.

'Treason!' Valda bellowed, and drove the sword through Omerna's chest.

Niall would have laughed if he could; breath came hard, and he could hear it bubbling in the blood in his throat. He had never liked Valda – in fact, he despised the man – but someone had to know. His eyes shifted, found the slip of paper from Tanchico lying not far from his hand; it might be missed there, but not if his corpse clutched it. And that message had to be read. His hand seemed to crawl across the floorboards so slowly, brushing the paper, pushing it as he fumbled to take hold. His vision was growing misty. He tried to force himself to see. He had to ... The fog was thicker. Part of him tried to shake that thought; there was no fog. The fog was thicker, and there was an enemy out there, unseen, hidden, as dangerous as al'Thor or more. The message. What? What message? It was time to mount and out sword, time for one last attack. By the Light, win or die, he was coming! He tried to snarl.

Valda wiped his blade on Omerna's tabard, then suddenly realized the old wolf still breathed, a rasping, bubbling sound. Grimacing, he bent to make an end – and a gaunt, long-fingered hand caught his arm.

'Would you be Lord Captain Commander now, my son?' Asunawa's emaciated face belonged on a martyr, yet his dark eyes burned with a fervor to unnerve even those who did not know who he was. 'You may well be, after I attest that you killed Pedron Niall's assassin. But not if I must say that you ripped open Niall's throat as well.'

Baring teeth in what could pass for a smile, Valda straightened. Asunawa had a love of truth, a strange love; he could tie it into knots, or hang it up and flay it while it screamed, but so far as Valda knew, he never actually lied. A look at Niall's glazed eyes, and the pool of blood spreading beneath him, satisfied Valda. The old man was dying.

'May, Asunawa?'

The High Inquisitor's gaze burned hotter as Asunawa stepped back, moving the snowy cloak away from Niall's blood. Even a Lord Captain was not supposed to be that familiar. 'I said may, my son. You have been oddly reluctant to agree that the witch Morgase must be given to the Hand of the Light. Unless you give that assurance—'

'Morgase is needed yet.' Breaking in gave Valda considerable pleasure. He did not like Questioners, the Hand of the Light as they called themselves. Who could like men who never met an enemy not disarmed and in chains? They held themselves apart from the Children, separate. Asunawa's cloak bore only the scarlet shepherd's crook of the Questioners, not the flaring golden sun of the Children that graced his own tabard. Worse, they seemed to think their work with racks and hot irons was the only true work of the Children. 'Morgase gives us Andor, so you cannot have her before we have it. And we cannot take Andor until the Prophet's mobs are crushed.' The Prophet had to be first, preaching the coming of the Dragon Reborn, his mobs burning villages too slow to proclaim for al'Thor. Niall's chest barely moved, now. 'Unless you want to trade Amadicia for Andor, instead of holding both? I mean to see al'Thor hung and the White Tower ground to dust, Asunawa, and I did not go along with your plan just to see you toss it all on the midden.'

Asunawa was not taken aback; he was no coward. Not here, with hundreds of Questioners in the Fortress and most of the Children wary of putting a foot wrong around them. He ignored the sword in Valda's hands, and that martyr's face took on a look of sadness. His sweat seemed to be tears of regret. 'In that case, since Lord Captain Canvele believes that the law must be obeyed, I fear—'

'*I* fear Canvele agrees with me, Asunawa.' Since dawn he did, since he realized that Valda had brought half a legion into the Fortress. Canvele was no fool. 'The question is not whether I will be Lord Captain Commander when the sun sets today, but who will guide the Hand of the Light in its digging for truth.'

No coward, Asunawa, and even less a fool than Canvele. He neither flinched nor demanded how Valda thought to bring this about. 'I see,' he said after a moment, and then, mildly, 'Do you mean to flout the law entirely, my son?'

Valda almost laughed. 'You can examine Morgase, but she is not to be put to the question. You can have her for that when I am done with her.' Which might take a little time; finding a replacement for the Lion Throne, one who understood her proper relationship to the Children as King Ailron did here, would not happen overnight.

Perhaps Asunawa understood and perhaps not. He opened his

mouth, and there was a gasp from the doorway. Niall's pinch-faced secretary stood there, purse-mouthed and knobby, narrow eyes trying to stare at everything except the bodies stretched out on the floor.

'A sad day, Master Balwer,' Asunawa intoned, his voice sorrowful iron. 'The traitor Omerna has slain our Lord Captain Commander Pedron Niall, the Light illumine his soul.' Not an advance on the truth; Niall's chest no longer moved, and killing him had been treason. 'Lord Captain Valda entered too late to save him, but he did slay Omerna in the full depth of his sin.' Balwer gave a start and began dry-washing his hands.

The birdlike fellow made Valda itch. 'Since you are here, Balwer, you may as well be useful.' He disliked useless people, and the scribbler was the very form of uselessness. 'Carry this message to each Lord Captain in the Fortress. Tell them the Lord Captain Commander has been murdered, and I call for a meeting of the Council of the Anointed.' His first act on being named Lord Captain Commander would be to boot the dried-up little man out of the Fortress, boot him so far he bounced twice, and choose a secretary who did not twitch. 'Whether Omerna was bought by the witches or the Prophet, I mean to see Pedron Niall avenged.'

'As you say, my Lord.' Balwer's voice was dry and narrow. 'It shall be as you say.' He apparently found himself able to look on Niall's body at last; as he bowed himself out jerkily, he hardly looked at anything else.

'So it seems you will be our next Lord Captain Commander after all,' Asunawa said once Balwer was gone.

'So it seems,' Valda answered dryly. A tiny slip of paper lay next to Niall's outstretched hand, the sort used in sending messages by pigeon. Valda bent and picked it up, then exhaled in disgust. The paper had been sitting in a puddle of wine; whatever had been written on it was lost, the ink a blur.

'And the Hand will have Morgase when your need for her is done.' That was not in the slightest a question.

'I will hand her to you myself.' Perhaps a little something might be arranged to sate Asunawa's appetite for a while. It might make sure Morgase remained amenable, too. Valda dropped the bit of rubbish on Niall's corpse. The old wolf had lost his cunning and his nerve with age, and now it would be up to Eamon Valda to bring the witches and their false Dragon to heel.

Flat on his belly on a rise, Gawyn surveyed disaster beneath the afternoon sun. Dumai's Wells lay miles to the south now, across rolling plain and low hills, but he could still see the smoke from burning wagons. What had happened there after he led what he could gather of the Younglings in breaking out, he did not know. Al'Thor had seemed well in charge, al'Thor and those black-coated men who appeared to be channeling, taking down Aes Sedai and Aiel alike. It had been the realization that sisters were fleeing that told him it was time to go.

He wished he could have killed al'Thor. For his mother, dead by the man's doing; Egwene denied it, but she had no proof. For his sister. If Min had spoken the truth – he should have made her leave the camp with him, whatever she wanted; there was too much he should have done differently today – if Min was right, and Elayne loved al'Thor, then that dreadful fate was reason enough to kill. Maybe the Aiel had done the work for him. He doubted it, though.

With a sour laugh he raised the tube of his looking glass. One of the golden bands bore an inscription. 'From Morgase, Queen of Andor, to her beloved son, Gawyn. May he be a living sword for his sister and Andor.' Bitter words, now.

There was not much to see beyond sere grass and small, scattered clumps of trees. The wind still gusted, raising waves of dust. Occasionally a flash of movement in a crease between squat ridges spoke of men on the move. Aiel, he was sure. They blended with the land too well to be green-coated Younglings. The Light send that more had escaped than those he had brought out.

He was a fool. He should have killed al'Thor; he had to kill him. But he could not. Not because the man was the Dragon Reborn, but because he had promised Egwene not to raise a hand against al'Thor. As a lowly Accepted, she had vanished from Cairhien, leaving Gawyn only a letter that he had read and reread until the paper was ready to tear along the folds, and he would be unsurprised to learn she had gone to aid al'Thor in some way. He could not break his word, least of all to the woman he loved. Never his word to her. Whatever the cost to himself. He hoped she would accept the compromise he had made with his honor; he had raised not a hand to harm, but none to help, either. The Light send she never asked that of him. It was said that love addled men's brains, and he was the proof.

Suddenly he pressed the looking glass to his eye as a woman galloped a tall black horse into the open. He could not make out her face, but no servant would be wearing a dress divided for riding. So at least one Aes Sedai had managed to escape. If sisters had made it out of the trap alive, maybe more of the Younglings had too. With luck, he could find them before they were killed in small groups by the Aiel. First there was the matter of this sister, though. In many ways he would rather have gone on without her, but leaving her alone, maybe to take an arrow she never saw coming, was not an option he could allow himself. As he started to rise and wave to her, though, the horse stumbled and fell, pitching her over its head.

He cursed, then again when the looking glass showed him an arrow standing up from the black's side. Hastily he scanned the hills, and bit down on another curse; maybe two dozen veiled Aiel stood on a crest staring toward downed horse and rider, less than a hundred paces from the Aes Sedai. Quickly he glanced back. The sister rose unsteadily to her feet. If she kept her wits and used the Power, there should be no way a few Aiel could harm her, especially if she took shelter against more arrows behind the fallen horse. Even so, he would feel better when he had gathered her in. Rolling away from the crest to lessen the chances of the Aiel seeing him, he slid down the reverse slope until he could stand.

He had brought five hundred and eighty-one Younglings south, almost every one who was far enough along in training to leave Tar Valon, but fewer than two hundred waited on their horses in the hollow. Before disaster struck at Dumai's Wells, he was certain there had been a plot afoot to see that he and the Younglings died without returning to the White Tower. Why, he did not know, nor whether the scheme came from Elaida or Galina, but it had succeeded well enough, if not exactly in the way its devisers had thought. Small wonder that he would have preferred to go on without Aes Sedai, had he any choice.

He stopped beside a tall gray gelding with a young rider. Young, as indeed all the Younglings were – many did not need to shave beyond every third day, and a few still only pretended even that – but Jisao wore the silver tower on his collar, marking him a veteran of the fighting when Siuan Sanche was deposed, and scars beneath his clothes from fighting since. He was one of those who could skip the razor most mornings; his dark eyes belonged to a man thirty years older, though. What did his own eyes look like, Gawyn wondered.

'Jisao, we have a sister to pull out of the—'

The hundred or so Aiel who came trotting over the low rise to the west recoiled in surprise at finding the Younglings below, but neither surprise nor the Younglings' superior numbers held them back. In a flash they veiled and plunged down the slope, darting in with spears stabbing at horses as often as riders, working in pairs. Yet if the Aiel knew how to fight men on horseback, the Younglings had recently had rough lessons in how to fight Aiel, and slow learners did not live long in their ranks. Some carried slender lances, ending in a foot and a half of steel with a crossguard to prevent the head penetrating too deeply, and all could use their swords as well as any but a blademaster. They fought in twos and threes, each man watching another's back, keeping their mounts moving so the Aiel could not hamstring the animals. Only the quickest Aiel managed to get inside those circles of flashing steel. The war-trained horses themselves were weapons, splitting skulls with their hooves, seizing men with their teeth and shaking them like dogs worrying rats, jaws tearing away half a man's face. The horses screamed as they fought, and men grunted with effort, shouted with the fever that overtook men in battle, the fever that said they were alive and would live to see another sunrise if they had to wade waist-deep in blood. They shouted as they killed, shouted as they died; there seemed little difference.

Gawyn had no time to watch or listen, though. The only Youngling afoot, he attracted attention. Three *cadin'sor*-clad figures dodged through the horsemen, rushing at him with spears ready. Perhaps they thought him easy meat, three on one. He disabused them. His sword left the scabbard smoothly, as smoothly as he flowed from The Falcon Stoops to The Creeper Embraces the Oak to The Moon Rises Over the Lakes. Three times he felt the shock in his wrists of blade meeting flesh, and that quickly three veiled Aielmen were down; two still moving weakly, but they were out of the fight as much as the other. The next to confront him was a different matter.

A lean fellow, overtopping Gawyn by a hand, he moved like a snake, spear flickering while his buckler darted and slanted to deflect sword strokes with a force Gawyn could feel to his shoulders. The Wood Grouse Dances became Folding the Air became The Courtier Taps His Fan, and the Aielman met each of them at the cost of a slash along his ribs, while Gawyn took a gash on his thigh that only a quick twist kept from being a stab clean through.

They circled one another, oblivious to whatever happened around them. Blood oozed hot down Gawyn's leg. The Aielman feinted, hoping to draw him off balance, feinted again; Gawyn shifted from stance to stance, sword now high, now low, hoping the man would extend one of those half-thrusts just a little too far.

In the end, it was chance that decided matters. The Aielman abruptly stumbled a step, and Gawyn ran him through the heart before he even saw the horse that had backed into the man.

Once he would have felt regret; he had grown up believing that if two men must fight, the duel should proceed honorably and cleanly. More than half a year of battles and skirmishes had taught him better. He put a foot on the Aielman's chest and wrenched his blade free. Ungallant, but fast, and in battle, slow was often dead.

Only, when his sword was free, there was no need for speed. Men were down, Younglings and Aielmen, some groaning, some still, and the rest of the Aiel streaming away to the east, harried by two dozen Younglings, including some who should know better. 'Hold!' he shouted. If the idiots allowed themselves to become separated, the Aiel would cut them to dogmeat. 'No pursuit! Hold, I said! Hold, burn you!' The Younglings pulled up reluctantly.

Jisao reined his gelding around. 'They just thought to cut a path through us on the way wherever they're going, my Lord.' His sword dripped red from half its length.

Gawyn caught the reins of his own bay stallion and swung into the saddle, not waiting to clean or sheath his blade. No time to see who was dead, who might live. 'Forget them. That sister is waiting for us. Hal, keep your half-troop to look after the wounded.

And watch those Aiel; just because they're dying doesn't mean they have quit. The rest, follow me.' Hal saluted with his sword, but Gawyn was already digging in his spurs.

The skirmish had not lasted long, yet too long however short. When Gawyn reached the crest, only the dead horse was to be seen, its saddlebags turned out. Scanning through his looking glass revealed not a sign of the sister, the Aiel or anything else living. All that moved was windblown dust and a dress on the ground near the horse, stirring in the gusts. The woman must have sprinted to be so completely out of sight so quickly.

'She can't have gone far, even running,' Jisao said. 'We can find her if we fan out.'

'We'll search after we see to the wounded,' Gawyn replied firmly. He was not about to split up his men with Aiel roaming loose. Only a few hours yet till sunset, and he wanted a tight camp on high ground before then. It might be as well if he did manage to find a sister or two; someone was going to have to explain this catastrophe to Elaida, and he would as soon it was an Aes Sedai facing her wrath, not him.

Turning his bay with a sigh, he rode back down to see what the butcher's bill had been this time. That had been his first real lesson as a soldier. You always had to pay the butcher. He had a feeling there would be bigger bills due soon. The world would forget Dumai's Wells in what was coming.

Chapter 1

High Chasaline

The Wheel of Time turns, and Ages come and pass, leaving memories that become legend. Legend fades to myth, and even myth is long forgotten when the Age that gave it birth comes again. In one Age, called the Third Age by some, an Age yet to come, an Age long past, a wind rose in the great forest called Braem Wood. The wind was not the beginning. There are neither beginnings nor endings to the turning of the Wheel of Time. But it was *a* beginning.

North and east the wind blew as the searing sun rose higher in a cloudless sky, north and east through parched trees with brown leaves and bare branches, through scattered villages where the air shimmered from the heat. The wind brought no relief, no hint of rain, much less snow. North and east it blew, past an ancient arch of finely worked stone that some said had been a gateway to a great city and others a monument to some long forgotten battle. Only weathered, illegible remnants of carving remained on the massive stones, mutely recalling the lost glories of storied Coremanda. A few wagons trundled by in sight of the arch, along the Tar Valon Road, and folk afoot shielded their eyes from dust raised by hooves and wagon wheels and driven by the wind. Most had no idea where they were going, only that the world seemed to turn somersaults, all order ending where it was not gone already. Fear drove some on, while others were drawn by something they could not quite see and did not understand, and most of them were afraid, too.

Onward the wind traveled, across the gray-green River Erinin, heeling ships that still carried trade north and south, for there had to be trade even in these days, though none could be sure where it was safe to trade. East of the river, the forests began to thin, giving way eventually to low rolling hills covered in brown, tinder-dry grass and dotted sparsely with small clumps of trees. Atop one of those hills stood a circle of wagons, many with the canvas scorched or else completely burned away from the iron hoops. On a makeshift flagstaff, trimmed from a young tree dead in the drought and lashed to a bare wagon hoop for more height, waved a crimson banner, a black-and-white disc in its heart. The Banner of Light, some called it, or al'Thor's Banner. Others had darker names, and shivered as they spoke them in whispers. The wind shook the banner hard and was gone quickly, as if glad to be away.

Perrin Aybara sat on the ground with his broad back against a wagon wheel, wishing the wind lingered. It had been cooler for a moment. And the wind from the south had cleared the scent of death from his nostrils, a scent that reminded him where he was supposed to be, the last place he wanted to be. Much better here, inside the wagon circle, his back to the north, where he could forget after a fashion. The surviving wagons had been hauled up to the hilltop yesterday, in the afternoon, once men could find strength to do more than thank the Light they still breathed. Now the sun climbed again, and the heat with it.

Irritably, he scratched at his short curly beard; the more he sweated, the more it itched. Sweat rolled down the face of every man he could see except the Aiel, and water lay nearly a mile away to the north now. But so did the horrors, and the smells. Most considered it a fair trade. He should have been doing his duty, yet the touch of guilt did not move him. Today was High Chasaline, and back home in the Two Rivers there would be feasting all day and dancing all night; the Day of Reflection, when you were supposed to remember all the good things in your life and anyone who voiced a complaint could find a bucket of water upended over his head to wash away bad luck. Not something anybody wanted when the weather was cold as it should be; a bucket of water would be a pleasure now. For a man lucky to be alive, he found it remarkably hard to pull up any good thoughts. He had learned things about himself yesterday. Or maybe it had been this morning, after it was all done.

He could sense a few of the wolves still, a handful of those that survived and were now on their way elsewhere, far from here, far from men. The wolves were still the talk of the camp, uneasy speculation over where they had appeared from and why. A few believed Rand had called them. Most thought the Aes Sedai had. The Aes Sedai did not say what they thought. No blame came from the wolves – what had happened, had happened – but he could not match their fatalism. They had come because he called them. Shoulders wide enough to make him seem shorter than he was slumped under the weight of responsibility. Now and then he heard other wolves, that had not come, speak with scorn to those that had: This was what came of mixing with the two-legs. Nothing else could be expected.

It was a strain to keep his thoughts to himself. He wanted to howl that the scornful ones were right. He wanted to be home, in the Two Rivers. Small chance of that, perhaps ever again. He wanted to be with his wife anywhere at all, and everything the way it was before. The chances of which seemed little better, maybe worse. Far more than the yearning for home, more even than the wolves, worry about Faile ate inside him like a ferret trying to burrow out of his middle. She had actually seemed glad to see him leave Cairhien. What was he to do about her? He could not think of words to describe how much he loved his wife, and needed her, but she was jealous where she had no cause, hurt where he had done nothing, angry where he could not see why. He must do something, but what? The answer eluded him. Careful thought was all he had, while Faile was flashing quicksilver.

'The Aiel should put some clothes on them,' Aram muttered primly, scowling at the ground. He squatted nearby, patiently holding the reins of a rangy gray gelding; he seldom went far from Perrin. The sword strapped to his back jarred with his green-striped Tinker coat, hanging undone for the heat. A rolled kerchief tied around his forehead kept sweat from his eyes. Once Perrin had thought him almost too good-looking for a man. A bleak darkness had settled in him, though, and now he wore a scowl as often as not. 'It isn't decent, Lord Perrin.'

Perrin put aside thoughts of Faile reluctantly. With time, he could puzzle it out. He had to. Somehow. 'It is their way, Aram.'

Aram grimaced as if he might spit. 'Well, it isn't a decent way. It keeps them under control, I suppose – nobody would run far or make trouble like that – but it isn't decent.'

There were Aiel all over the place, of course. Tall, aloof men in grays and browns and greens, their only bit of color the scarlet strip of cloth tied around their temples, with the black-and-white disc on their foreheads. *Siswai'aman*, they called themselves. Sometimes that word tickled the edge of his memory, like a word he should know. Ask one of the Aielmen, and he looked as if you had babbled nonsense. But then, they ignored the strips of cloth, too. No Maiden of the Spear wore the scarlet headband. Whether white-haired or looking barely old enough to leave her mother, every Maiden stalked about giving the *siswai'aman* challenging stares that seemed somehow self-satisfied, while the men looked back flat-eyed, with a smell almost of hunger, a matter of jealousy by the scent of all of them, though over what Perrin could not begin to imagine. Whatever it was, it was not new, and it did not seem likely to come to blows. A few of the Wise Ones were inside the wagons as well, in bulky skirts and white blouses, wearing their dark shawls in defiance of the heat, glittering bracelets and necklaces of gold and ivory making up for the plainness of the rest of their clothes. Some appeared amused by the Maidens and the *siswai'aman* and others exasperated. All of them – Wise Ones, Maidens and *siswai'aman* – ignored the Shaido the way Perrin would have a stool or a rug.

The Aiel had taken two hundred or so Shaido prisoners yesterday, men and Maidens – not many, considering the numbers involved – and they moved about freely. In a manner of speaking. Perrin would have been a lot more comfortable had they been guarded. And clothed. Instead, they fetched water and ran errands, naked as the day they were born. With other Aiel, they were meek as mice. Anyone else received a proudly defiant stare for noticing them. Perrin was not the only one who tried *not* to notice them, and Aram not the only one to mutter. A good many of the Two Rivers men in camp did one or both. A good many of the Cairhienin nearly had apoplexy whenever they saw one of the Shaido. The Mayeners just shook their heads as though it were all a joke. And ogled the women. They had as little shame as the Aiel, the Mayeners.

'Gaul explained it to me, Aram. You know what a *gai'shain* is, don't you? About *ji'e'toh* and serving a year and a day and all that?' The other man nodded, which was a good thing. Perrin did not know much himself. Gaul's explanations of Aiel ways often left him more confused. Gaul always thought it all self-evident. 'Well, *gai'shain* aren't allowed to wear anything one of the *algai'd'siswai* might wear – that means "spear fighters,"' he added at Aram's questioning frown. Suddenly he realized he was looking straight at one of the Shaido as she trotted in his general direction, a tall young woman, golden-haired and pretty despite a long thin scar down her cheek and other scars elsewhere. Very pretty and very naked. Clearing his throat roughly, he pulled his eyes away. He could feel his face heating. 'Anyway, that is why they are . . . the way they are. *Gai'shain* wear white robes, and they don't have any here. It's just their way.' *Burn Gaul and burn his explanations*, he thought. *They could cover them with something!*

'Perrin Goldeneyes,' said a woman's voice, 'Carahuin sends to know whether you wish water.' Aram's face went purple, and he jerked himself around in his squat, presenting his back to her.

'No, thank you.' Perrin did not need to look up to know it was the golden-haired Shaido woman. He kept peering off at nothing in another direction. Aiel had a peculiar sense of humor, and Maidens of the Spear – Carahuin was a Maiden – had the most peculiar. They had quickly seen how the wetlanders reacted to the Shaido – they would have needed to be blind not to – suddenly *gai'shain* were being sent to wetlanders left and right, and Aiel all but rolling on the ground at the blushes and stammers and even the shouting. He was sure that Carahuin and her friends were watching now. This was at least the tenth time one of the *gai'shain* women had been sent to ask him whether he wanted water or had a spare whetstone or some such bloody fool thing.

Abruptly a thought struck him. The Mayeners were seldom bothered this way. A handful of Cairhienin plainly enjoyed looking, if not so openly as the Mayeners, and some of the older Two Rivers men, who should have known better. The point was, none of them had had a second spurious message that he knew of. Those who reacted the most, on the other hand ... Cairhienin, who had shouted the loudest about indecency, and two or three of the younger Two Rivers men, who stammered and blushed so hard they looked ready to melt, had been pestered until they fled the wagons entirely ...

With an effort Perrin looked up at the *gai'shain*'s face. At her eyes. *Focus on her eyes*, he thought frantically. They were green, and large, and not at all meek. Her scent was pure fury. 'Thank Carahuin for me, and tell her you could oil my spare saddle, if she doesn't mind. And I don't have a clean shirt. If she wouldn't mind you doing some laundry?'

'She will not mind,' the woman said in a tight voice, then turned and trotted off.

Perrin whipped his eyes away, though the image did stay in his head. Light, Aram was right! But with luck, he might just have stopped any more visitations. He would have to point this out to Aram, and the Two Rivers men. Maybe the Cairhienin would listen too.

'What are we going to do about them, Lord Perrin?' Still looking away, Aram no longer spoke of *gai'shain*.

'That is Rand's to decide,' Perrin said slowly, satisfaction fading. It might be odd to think of people wandering about naked as a small problem, but this was definitely a bigger. And one he had been avoiding as hard as he had what lay to the north.

On the far side of the wagon circle, nearly two dozen women sat on the ground. All well-dressed for travel, many wore silk, most with light linen dustcloaks, but not a bead of sweat showed on any face. Three appeared young enough that he might have asked them for a dance before he married Faile.

If they weren't Aes Sedai, anyway, he thought wryly. Once he had danced with an Aes Sedai, and nearly swallowed his tongue when he realized who he swung about. And she had been a friend, if that word applied to Aes Sedai. *How new does an Aes Sedai have to be for me to put an age to her?* The others looked ageless, of course; maybe in their twenties, maybe their forties, changing from one glance to the next, always uncertain. That was what their faces said, though several showed gray in their hair. You just could not tell with Aes Sedai. About anything.

'At least those are no danger anymore,' Aram said, jerking his head toward three of the sisters a little apart from the rest.

One wept, face on her knees; the other two stared haggardly at nothing, one of them plucking aimlessly at her skirt. They had been much the same since yesterday; at least none was screaming any longer. If Perrin had the straight of it, which he was not sure he did, they had been stilled somehow when Rand broke free. They would never channel the One Power again. To Aes Sedai, it was probably better to be dead.

He would have expected the other Aes Sedai to comfort them, care for them somehow, but most ignored the three entirely, although a little too studied in looking anywhere and everywhere else. For that matter, the stilled Aes Sedai refused to acknowledge the rest, either. In the beginning, at least, a few of the other sisters had approached, each by herself, calm to the eye yet smelling sharply of aversion and reluctance, but they got nothing for their pains, not word or glance. None had gone near this morning.

Perrin shook his head. The Aes Sedai seemed to do a lot of ignoring of what they did not want to admit. For instance, the black-coated men standing over them. There was an Asha'man for each sister, even the three who had been stilled, and they never seemed to blink. For their part, the Aes Sedai looked past the Asha'man, or through them; they might as well not have existed.

It was quite a trick. He could not make himself disregard the Asha'man, and he was not under their guard. They ranged from fuzz-cheeked boys to gray-haired, balding gansers, and it was not their grim, high-collared black coats or the sword each wore at his hip that made them dangerous. Every Asha'man could channel, and somehow they were keeping the Aes Sedai from channeling. Men who could wield the One Power, a thing of nightmares. Rand could, of course, but he was Rand, and the Dragon Reborn besides. These fellows made Perrin's hackles rise.

The captive Aes Sedai's surviving Warders sat some distance off, under their own guard. Thirty or so of Lord Dobraine's armsmen in bell-shaped Cairhienin helmets and as many Mayener Winged Guards in red breastplates, each sharp-eyed as if guarding leopards. A good attitude, under the circumstances. More Warders than there were Aes Sedai; a number of the prisoners were Green Ajah, apparently. More guards than Warders, a good many more, and maybe few enough at that.

'The Light send we don't see any more grief from that lot,' Perrin muttered. Twice during the night the Warders had tried to break free. In truth, those outbreaks had been suppressed more by the Asha'man than by the Cairhienin or Mayeners, and they had not been gentle. None of the Warders had been killed, but at least a dozen nursed broken bones none of the sisters had yet been allowed to Heal.

'If the Lord Dragon cannot make the decision,' Aram said quietly, 'maybe it should be made by somebody else. To protect him.'

Perrin gave him a sidelong look. 'What decision? The sisters told them not to make another attempt, and they'll obey their Aes Sedai.' Broken bones or no, unarmed as they were, hands tied behind their backs, the Warders still looked like a wolfpack awaiting the lead wolf's command to attack. None would rest easy until his Aes Sedai was free, maybe until all of the sisters were free. Aes Sedai and Warders: a stack of well-aged oak, ready for a flame. But even Warders and Aes Sedai had proved no match for Asha'man.

'I did not mean the Warders.' Aram hesitated, then shuffled closer to Perrin and lowered his voice further, to a hoarse whisper. 'The Aes Sedai kidnapped the Lord Dragon. He can't trust them, not ever, but he won't do what he has to, either. If they died before he knew it—'

'What are you saying?' Perrin almost choked as he sat bolt upright. Not for the first time, he wondered whether there was any Tinker left in the other man. 'They're helpless, Aram! Helpless women!'

'They are Aes Sedai.' Dark eyes met Perrin's golden stare levelly. 'They cannot be trusted, and they cannot be turned loose. How long can Aes Sedai be held against their will? They've been doing what they do far longer than the Asha'man. They must know more. They're a danger to the Lord Dragon, and to you, Lord Perrin. I have seen them look at you.'

Across the wagon circle, the sisters were talking among themselves in whispers even Perrin could not hear, mouths held close to ears. Now and again one did look at him and Aram. At him, not Aram. He had caught a double handful of names. Nesune Bihara. Erian Boroleos and Katerine Alruddin. Coiren Saeldain, Sarene Nemdahl and Elza Penfell. Janine Pavlara, Beldeine Nyram, Marith Riven. Those last were the young sisters, but young or ageless, they watched him with faces so serene it seemed they had the upper hand despite the Asha'man. Defeating Aes Sedai was not easy; making them admit defeat lay on the far side of impossible.

He forced his hands to unknot and rest on his knees, giving an appearance of calm he was nowhere near feeling. They knew he was *ta'veren*, one of those few the Pattern would shape itself around for a time. Worse, they knew he was tied to Rand in some way nobody understood, least of all himself or Rand. Or Mat; Mat was in that tangle, too, another *ta'veren*, though neither of them as strongly as Rand. Given half a chance those women would have him – and Mat – inside the White Tower as fast as they would Rand, tethered like goats until the lion came. And they *had* kidnapped Rand, mistreated him. Aram was right about one thing; they could not be trusted. But what Aram suggested – he would not – could not! – countenance such a thing. The thought made him queasy.

'I'll hear no more of that,' he growled. The onetime Tinker opened his mouth, but Perrin cut him off. 'Not a word, Aram, do you hear me? Not one word!'

'As my Lord Perrin commands,' Aram murmured, inclining his head.

Perrin wished he could see the man's face. There was no anger in the smell of him, no resentment. That was the worst of it. There had been no anger scent even when Aram suggested murder.

A pair of Two Rivers men climbed up on the wheels of the next wagon, peering across the wagon bed and down the hill toward the north. Each wore a bristling quiver on his right hip and a stout, long-bladed knife, almost a short-sword, on his left. A good three hundred men from home had followed Perrin here. He cursed the first to call him Lord Perrin, cursed the day he had stopped trying to quash it. Even with the murmurs and noises usual in a camp this size, he had no trouble hearing the pair.

Tod al'Caar, a year younger than Perrin, let out a long breath, as if seeing what lay below for the first time. Perrin could almost sense the lanky man's lantern jaw working. Tod's mother had willingly let him go only for the honor of her son following Perrin Goldeneyes. 'A famous victory,' Tod said finally. 'That's what we won. Wasn't it, Jondyn?'

Grizzled Jondyn Barran, gnarled as an oak root, was one of the few older men among the three hundred. A better bowshot than anyone in the Two Rivers except Master al'Thor and a better hunter than anyone at all, he was one of the Two Rivers' less distinguished residents. Jondyn had not worked a day more than he had to since he was old enough to leave his father's farm. The forests and the hunt were all he cared about, that and drinking too much at feast-days. Now he spat loudly. 'If you say so, boy. Was those bloody Asha'man won it, anyway. And welcome to it, I say. Too bad they don't take it and go someplace else to celebrate.'

'They aren't so bad,' Tod protested. 'I wouldn't mind being one myself.' That sounded more boast and bluff than truth. Smelled it, too; without looking, Perrin was sure he was licking his lips. Likely Tod's mother had used tales of men who could channel to frighten him not so many years ago. 'I mean to say, Rand – that is, the Lord Dragon – it still sounds odd, doesn't it, Rand al'Thor being the Dragon Reborn and all?' Tod laughed, a short, uneasy sound. 'Well, he can channel, and it doesn't seem so – he doesn't – I mean . . . ' He swallowed loudly. 'Besides, what could we have done about all those Aes Sedai without them?' That came out in a whisper. He smelled afraid now. 'Jondyn, what are we going to do? I mean, Aes Sedai *prisoners?*'

The older man spat again, louder than before. He did not bother to lower his voice, either. Jondyn always said what he thought no matter who heard, another reason for his bad repute. 'Better for us if they'd all died yesterday, boy. We'll pay for that before it's done. Mark me, we'll pay large.'

Perrin shut out the rest, no easy task with his ears. First Aram, and now Jondyn and Tod, if not so directly. *Burn Jondyn!* No, the man might make Mat look industrious, but if he spoke it, others thought it. No Two Rivers man would willingly harm a woman, but who else wished the Aes Sedai prisoners dead? And who might try to achieve the wish?

He scanned the wagon circle uneasily. The thought that he might have to protect the Aes Sedai prisoners was not pleasant, but he did not shirk it. He had little fondness for any Aes Sedai, least of all for these, but he had grown up in the unspoken certainty that a man would put himself at risk to protect a woman as far as she allowed; whether he liked her or even knew her was beside the point. True, an Aes Sedai could tie any man she chose into a knot nine ways from next feastday, but cut off from the Power, they became like anyone else. That was the struggle whenever he looked at them. Two dozen Aes Sedai. Two dozen women who might not know *how* to defend themselves without the Power.

For a bit he studied the Asha'man guards, every one wearing a face like grim death. Except the three overseeing the stilled women. They tried to appear as somber as the rest, but under the attempt lay something else. Satisfaction, maybe. If only he was close enough to catch a scent of them. Any Aes Sedai was a threat to the Asha'man. Perhaps the reverse was true, too. Perhaps they would only still them. From the little he had picked up, stilling an Aes Sedai amounted to a killing that just took a few years for the corpse to lie down.

Whatever the case, he decided reluctantly, he had to leave the Asha'man to Rand. They spoke only to each other and the prisoners, and Perrin doubted they would listen to anyone but Rand. The question was, what would Rand say? And what could Perrin do if he said the wrong thing?

Putting that problem aside, he scratched his beard with one finger. The Cairhienin were too nervous about Aes Sedai to consider harming them, and the Mayeners too respectful, but he would keep an eye on them anyway. Who would have thought Jondyn would go as far as he had? Among the Cairhienin or Mayeners, he possessed some influence, though it would surely vanish if they once thought. He was really just a blacksmith, after all. That left the Aiel. Perrin sighed. He was not certain how much influence even Rand truly had with the Aiel.

It was difficult picking out individual scents with so many people around, but he had grown used to telling as much by smells as by what his eyes told him. The *siswai'aman* who came close enough smelled calm but alert, a smooth, strong scent. They hardly appeared to notice the Aes Sedai. The Maidens' aromas were spiky with suppressed fury and grew spikier when they looked at the prisoners. And the Wise Ones . . .

Every Wise One who had come here from Cairhien was able to channel, though none had the ageless face. He supposed they used the One Power too seldom. Still, smooth-cheeked like Edarra or as leathery-faced as white-haired Sorilea, they carried themselves with a self-possession easily matching the Aes Sedai's. Graceful women for the most part, most of them tall, as nearly all Aiel were, they seemed to ignore the sisters completely.

Sorilea's eyes passed across the prisoners without pausing, and she went right on talking softly to Edarra and another Wise One, a lean, yellow-haired woman he did not know by name. If only he could make out what they were saying. They walked by, not a line changing on those three unruffled faces, but their scents were another matter. When Sorilea's gaze swept over the Aes Sedai, the smell of her went cold and distant, grim and purposeful, and as she spoke to the other two, their scents changed to match hers.

'A fine bloody stew,' he growled.

'Trouble?' Aram asked, sitting up straighter on his heels, right hand poised to dart for the wolfhead-pommeled sword hilt jutting above his shoulder. He had become very good with that sword in a very short time, and he was never loath to use it.

'There's no trouble, Aram.' That was not quite a lie. Jolted out of his glum brooding, Perrin really looked at the others for the first time. At all of them together. He did not like what he saw, and the Aes Sedai were only part.

Cairhienin and Mayeners watched Aiel suspiciously, which was no more than the Aiel's return suspicion, especially toward the Cairhienin. No real surprise there. Aiel did have a certain reputation, after all, for being none too friendly to anyone born this side of the Spine of the World, Cairhienin least of all. Simple truth was, Aiel and Cairhienin hated each other about as hard as it was possible to hate. Neither side had really put their enmity aside – the best that could be said was that it was on a loose leash – yet up to now he had been convinced they would hold it in. For Rand's sake if no other reason. A mood hung in the camp, though, a tension that had wound everyone tight. Rand was free now, and temporary alliances were just that, after all; temporary. Aiel hefted their spears when they looked at the Cairhienin, and the Cairhienin grimly fingered their swords. So did the Mayeners; they had no quarrel with the Aiel, had never fought them except for the Aiel War when everybody had, but if it came to a fight, there was little doubt which side they would be on. The Two Rivers men, too, probably.

The dark mood had settled deepest into the Asha'man and the Wise Ones, though. The black-coated men paid no more heed to the Maidens and the *siswai'aman* than to Cairhienin or Mayeners or Two Rivers men, but they studied the Wise Ones with faces almost as dark as those they directed at the Aes Sedai. Very likely they made small distinction between one woman who could wield the Power and another. Any could be an enemy and dangerous; thirteen together were deadly dangerous, and there were better than ninety Wise Ones in the camp or nearby. Fewer than half the number of Asha'man, but still enough to do damage if they chose. Women who could channel, yet they seemed to follow Rand; they seemed to follow Rand, yet they were women who could channel.

The Wise Ones looked at the Asha'man only a trifle less coldly than they did the Aes Sedai. The Asha'man were men who could channel, but they followed Rand; they followed Rand, but ... Rand was a special case. According to Gaul, his channeling was not mentioned in the prophecies about their *Car'a'carn*, but the Aiel seemed to pretend that inconvenient fact did not exist. The Asha'man were not in those prophecies at all, though. It must be like discovering you had a pride of rabid lions fighting on your side. How long would they remain loyal? Maybe it would be better to put them down now.

His head fell back against the wagon wheel, eyes closed, and his chest heaved in silent, mirthless laughter. Think of the good things on High Chasaline. *Burn me,* he thought wryly, *I should have gone with Rand.* No, it was best to know, and better soon than late. But what in the Light was he to do? If the Aiel and the Cairhienin and Mayeners turned on one another, or worse, the Asha'man and the Wise Ones . . . A barrel full of snakes, and the only way to find out which were vipers was to stick your hand in. *Light, I wish I was home, with Faile, and a forge to work, and nobody calling me bloody lord.*

'Your horse, Lord Perrin. You didn't say whether you wanted Stepper or Stayer, so I saddled—' At Perrin's golden-eyed glare, Kenly Maerin shied back into the dun stallion he was leading.

Perrin made a soothing gesture. Not Kenly's fault. What could not be mended had to be endured. 'Easy, lad. You did right. Stepper will do just fine. You chose well.' He hated speaking to Kenly that way. Short and stocky, Kenly was barely old enough to marry or leave home – and certainly not old enough for the patchy beard he was trying to cultivate in imitation of Perrin – yet he had fought Trollocs at Emond's Field and done well yesterday. But he grinned broadly at praise from Lord Perrin bloody Goldeneyes.

Rising, Perrin took his axe from where he had propped it under the wagon, out of sight and for a little while out of mind, and thrust the haft through the loop on his belt. A heavy half-moon blade balanced by a thick curving spike; a thing made for no other purpose than killing. The axe-haft felt too familiar to his hands for comfort. Did he even remember what a good forge-hammer felt like? There were other things besides 'Lord Perrin' that it might be too late to change. A friend had once told him to keep the axe until he began to like using it. The thought made him shiver in spite of the heat.

He swung into Stepper's saddle, shadowed by Aram with the gray, and sat facing south, into the wagon circle. At least half again as tall as even the tallest of the Aiel, Loial was just stepping carefully over crossed wagon tongues. With the size of him, he did look as though he might break one of the heavy wooden shafts with a heedless step. As usual, the Ogier had a book in his hand, a thick finger marking his place, and the capacious pockets of his long coat bulged with more. He had spent the morning in a tiny clump of trees he called restful and shady, but whatever the shade among those trees, the heat was affecting him, too. He looked tired, and his coat was undone, his shirt unlaced, and his boots rolled down below his knees. Or maybe it was more than the heat. Just inside the wagons Loial paused, peering at the Aes Sedai and the Asha'man, and his tufted ears quivered uneasily. Eyes big as teacups rolled toward the Wise Ones, and his ears vibrated again. Ogier were sensitive to the mood of a place.

When he saw Perrin, Loial came striding across the camp. Sitting his saddle, Perrin was two or three hands shorter than Loial standing. 'Perrin,' Loial whispered, 'this is all wrong. It isn't right, and it is dangerous besides.' For an Ogier it was a whisper. He sounded like a bumblebee the size of a mastiff. Some of the Aes Sedai turned their heads.

'Could you speak a little louder?' Perrin said almost under his breath. 'I think somebody in Andor didn't hear. In the west of Andor.'

Loial looked startled, then grimaced, long eyebrows brushing his cheeks. 'I do know how to whisper, you know.' This time it was unlikely anyone could hear clearly more than three paces away or so. 'What are we going to do, Perrin? It is wrong holding Aes Sedai against their will, wrong and wrongheaded, too. I have said that before, and I will again. And that isn't even the worst. The feel here ... One spark, and this place will erupt like a wagonload of fireworks. Does Rand know about this?'

'I don't know,' Perrin said to both questions, and after a moment the Ogier nodded reluctantly.

'Someone has to know, Perrin. Someone has to do something.' Loial looked north, over the wagons behind Perrin, and Perrin knew there was no putting it off longer.

Unwillingly he turned Stepper. He would rather have worried over Aes Sedai and Asha'man and Wise Ones till his hair fell out, but what had to be done, had to be done. Think of the good on High Chasaline.

Chapter 2

The Butcher's Yard

At first Perrin did not look downslope toward where he would ride, where he should have gone with Rand this morning. Instead he sat his saddle at the edge of the wagons and sent his eyes anywhere else, though the view everywhere made him want to sick up. It was like being hit in the belly with a hammer.

Hammerstroke. Nineteen fresh graves atop a squat hill to the east; nineteen Two Rivers men who would never see home again. A blacksmith seldom had to see people die because of his decisions. At least the Two Rivers men had obeyed his orders. There would have been more graves, otherwise. Hammerstroke. Rectangles of newly turned earth blanketed the next slope over from that, as well, near to a hundred Mayeners, and more Cairhienin, who had come to Dumai's Wells to die. Never mind causes or reasons; they had followed Perrin Aybara. Hammerstroke. The ridge-face to the west seemed solid graves, maybe a thousand or more. A thousand Aiel, buried standing upright, to face each sunrise. A thousand. Some were Maidens. The men tied his stomach into knots; the women made him want to sit down and cry. He tried telling himself that they all had chosen to be here, that they had *had* to be here. Both things were true, but he had given the orders, and that made the responsibility for those graves his. Not Rand's, not the Aes Sedai's; his.

The living Aiel had only stopped singing over their dead a short while ago, haunting songs, sung in parts, that lingered in the mind.

Life is a dream – that knows no shade.
Life is a dream – of pain and woe.
A dream from which – we pray to wake.
A dream from which – we wake and go.

Who would sleep – when the new dawn waits?
Who would sleep – when the sweet winds blow?
A dream must end – when the new day comes.
This dream from which – we wake and go.

They appeared to find comfort in those songs. He wished he could, too, but as far as he could see, the Aiel truly did not seem to care whether they lived or died, and that was mad. Any sane man wanted to live. Any sane man would run as far as he could from a battle, run as hard as he could.

Stepper tossed his head, nostrils flaring at the smells from below, and Perrin patted the dun's neck. Aram was grinning as he looked at what Perrin tried to block out. Loial's face had so little expression it might have been carved from wood. His lips moved slightly, and Perrin thought he heard, 'Light, let me never see the like again.' Drawing a deep breath, he made his eyes follow theirs, to Dumai's Wells.

In some ways it was not as bad as the graves – he had known some of those people since he was a child – but it all crashed down on him at once anyway, like the scent in his nose made solid and smashing him between the eyes. The memories he wanted to forget came rushing back. Dumai's Wells had been a killing ground, a dying ground, but now it was worse. Less than a mile away, the charred remains of wagons stood around a small copse of trees nearly hiding the low stone copings of the wells. And surrounding that . . .

A seething sea of black, vultures and ravens and crows in tens of thousands, swirling up in waves and settling again, concealing the broken earth. For which Perrin was more than grateful. The Asha'man's methods had been brutal, destroying flesh and ground with equal impartiality. Too many Shaido had died to bury in less than days, even had anyone cared to bury them, so the vultures gorged, and the ravens, and the crows. The dead wolves were down there, too; he had wanted to bury them, but that was not the wolves' way. Three Aes Sedai corpses had been found, their channeling unable to save them from spears and arrows in the madness of battle, and half a dozen dead Warders, too. They were buried in the clearing near the wells.

The birds were not alone with the dead. Far from it. Black-feathered waves rose around Lord Dobraine Taborwin and over two hundred of his mounted Cairhienin armsmen, and Lord Lieutenant Havien Nurelle with all that remained of his Mayeners aside from the guards on the Warders. *Con* with two white diamonds on blue picked out the Cairhienin officers, all but Dobraine himself, and the Mayeners' red armor and red-streamered lances made a brave show amid the carnage, but Dobraine was not the only one who held a cloth to his nose. Here and there a man leaned from the saddle trying to empty a stomach already emptied earlier. Mazrim Taim, almost as tall as Rand, was afoot in his black coat with the blue-and-gold Dragons climbing the sleeves, and maybe a hundred more of the Asha'man. Some of them heaved up their bellies, too. There were Maidens by the score, more *siswai'aman* than Cairhienin and Mayeners and Asha'man combined, and several dozen Wise Ones to boot. All supposedly in case the Shaido returned, or perhaps in case some of the dead were only shamming, though Perrin thought anyone who pretended at being a corpse here would soon go insane. All centered around Rand.

Perrin should have been down there with the Two Rivers men. Rand had asked for them, spoken about trusting men from home, but Perrin had made no promises. *He'll have to settle for me, and late*, he thought. In a little bit, when he managed to steel himself to the butcher's yard below. Only, butchers' knives did not mow down people, and they were tidier than axes, tidier than vultures.

The black-coated Asha'man faded into the sea of birds, death swallowed by death, and ravens and crows surging up hid the others, but Rand stood out in the tattered white shirt he had been wearing when rescue came. Though perhaps he hardly needed deliverance by that time. The sight of Min, close beside Rand in pale red coat and snug breeches, made Perrin grimace. That was no place for her, or anyone, but she stayed closer to Rand since the rescue than even Taim did. Somehow Rand had managed to free both himself and her well before Perrin broke through, or even the Asha'man, and Perrin suspected she saw Rand's presence as the only real safety.

Sometimes as he strode across that charnel ground, Rand patted Min's arm or bent his head as if speaking to her, but not with his main attention. Dark clouds of birds billowed around them, the smaller darting away to feed elsewhere, the vultures giving ground reluctantly, some refusing to take wing, extending featherless necks and squawking defiantly as they waddled back. Now and then Rand stopped, bending over a corpse. Sometimes fire darted from his hands to strike down vultures that did not give way. Every time, Nandera, who led the Maidens, or Sulin, her second, argued with him. Sometimes Wise Ones did, too, from the way they tugged at the body's coat as if demonstrating something. And Rand would nod and move on. Not without backward glances, though. And only until another body caught his attention.

'What is he doing?' demanded a haughty voice at Perrin's knee. By scent he knew her before he looked down. Statuesque and elegant in a green silk riding dress and thin linen dust-cloak, Kiruna Nachiman was sister to King Paitar of Arafel and a powerful noble in her own right, and becoming Aes Sedai had done nothing to dampen her manner. Trapped in what he was watching, he had not heard her approach. 'Why is he down in that? He should not be.'

Not all the Aes Sedai in the camp were prisoners, though those who were not had been keeping out of sight since yesterday, talking among themselves, Perrin suspected, and trying to figure out what had happened at the last. Maybe trying to figure some way around it. Now they were out in force. Bera Harkin, another Green, stood at Kiruna's shoulder, a farmwife by looks despite her ageless face and fine woolen dress, but every scrap as proud as Kiruna in her own way. This farmwife would tell a king to scrape his boots before coming into her house and be sharp about it. She and Kiruna together led the sisters who had come to Dumai's Wells with Perrin, or perhaps passed leadership back and forth between them. It was not exactly clear, which was hardly unusual with Aes Sedai.

The other seven stood in a covey not far away. Or maybe in a pride, lionesses, not quail by their air of being in charge. Their Warders were arrayed behind them, and if the sisters were all outward serenity, the Warders made no bones of their feelings. They were disparate men, some in those color-shifting cloaks that seemed to make parts of them disappear, but whether short or tall, thick or thin, just standing there they looked like violence on a frayed leash.

Perrin knew two of those women well, Verin Mathwin and Alanna Mosvani. Short and stout and almost motherly at times in a distracted way, when she was not studying you like a bird studying a worm, Verin was Brown Ajah. Alanna, slim and darkly pretty though a little haggard around the eyes of late for some reason, was Green. Altogether, five of the nine were Green. Once, some time ago, Verin had told him not to trust Alanna too far, and he more than took her at her word. Nor did he trust any of the others, including Verin. Neither did Rand, for all they had fought on his side yesterday, and despite what had happened at the end. Which Perrin still was not sure he believed, even though he had seen it.

A good dozen Asha'man lounged by a wagon about twenty paces from the sisters. A cocky fellow named Charl Gedwyn had charge of them this morning, a hard-faced man who swaggered standing still. All wore a pin in the shape of a silver sword on their tall coat-collars, and four or five besides Gedwyn had a Dragon in gold-and-red enamel fastened on the other side. Perrin supposed that had to do with rank in some way. He had seen both on some of the other Asha'man. Not precisely guards, they managed to be wherever Kiruna and the others were. Just taking their ease. And keeping a sharp eye open. Not that the Aes Sedai took any notice, not that you could see. Even so, the sisters smelled wary, and puzzled, and infuriated. Part of that had to be because of the Asha'man.

'Well?' Kiruna's dark eyes flashed impatience. He doubted that many people kept her waiting.

'I don't know,' he lied, patting Stepper's neck again. 'Rand doesn't tell me everything.'

He understood a little – he thought he did – but he had no intention of telling anyone. That was Rand's to reveal, if he chose. Every body that Rand looked at belonged to a Maiden; Perrin was convinced of it. A Shaido Maiden without a doubt, but he was not sure how much difference that made to Rand. Last night he had walked away from the wagons to be by himself, and as the sound of men laughing because they were alive faded behind him, he found Rand. The Dragon Reborn, who made the world tremble, sitting on the ground, alone in the dark, his arms wrapped around himself, rocking back and forth.

To Perrin's eyes, the moon was nearly as good as the sun, but right then he wished for pitch blackness. Rand's face was drawn and twisted, the face of a man who wanted to scream, or maybe weep, and was fighting it down with every scrap of his fiber. Whatever trick the Aes Sedai knew to keep the heat from touching them, Rand and the Asha'man knew, too, but he was not using it now. The night's heat would have done for a more-than-warm summer day, and sweat slid down Rand's cheeks as much as Perrin's.

He did not look around, though Perrin's boots rustled loudly in the dead grass, yet he spoke hoarsely, still rocking. 'One hundred and fifty-one, Perrin. One hundred and fifty-one Maidens died today. For me. I promised them, you see. Don't argue with me! Shut up! Go away!' *Despite his sweat, Rand shivered.* 'Not you, Perrin; not you. I have to keep my promises, you see. Have to, no matter how it hurts. But I have to keep my promise to myself, too. No matter how it hurts.'

Perrin tried not to think about the fate of men who could channel. The lucky ones died before they went mad; the unlucky died after. Whether Rand was lucky or unlucky, everything rested on him. Everything. 'Rand, I don't know what to say, but—'

Rand seemed not to hear. Back and forth he rocked. Back and forth. 'Isan, of the Jarra Sept of the Chareen Aiel. She died for me today. Chuonde of the Spine Ridge Miagoma. She died for me today. Agirin of the Daryne . . .'

There had been nothing for it but to settle on his heels and listen to Rand recite all one hundred and fifty-one names in a voice like pain stretched to breaking, listen and hope Rand was holding on to sanity.

Whether or not Rand was still completely sane, though, if a Maiden who came to fight for him had been missed down there somehow, Perrin was sure that not only would she be buried decently with the others on the ridge, there would be one hundred and fifty-two names in that list. And that was none of Kiruna's business. Not that, or Perrin's doubts. Rand had to stay sane, or sane enough anyway, and that was that. Light, send it so!

And the Light burn me for thinking it so coldly, Perrin thought.

From the corner of his eye he saw her full mouth tighten momentarily. She liked not knowing everything about as well as being made to wait. She would have been beautiful, in a grand sort of manner, except that hers was a face used to getting what it wanted. Not petulant, just absolutely certain that whatever she wanted was right and proper and must be. 'With so many crows and ravens in one place, there are certainly hundreds, perhaps thousands, ready to report what they've seen to a Myrddraal.' She made no effort to mask her irritation; she sounded as though he had brought every bird there himself. 'In the borderlands, we kill them on sight. You have men, and they have bows.'

It was true, a raven or crow was all too likely to be a spy for the Shadow, but disgust welled up in him. Disgust and weariness. 'To what point?' With that many birds, the Two Rivers men and the Aiel could shoot every arrow they had and spies would still report. Most times there was no way to tell whether the bird you killed was the spy or the one that flew away. 'Hasn't there been enough killing? There will be more soon enough. Light, woman, even the *Asha'man* are sated!'

Eyebrows rose among the onlooking clutch of sisters. No one spoke to Aes Sedai that way, not a king or a queen. Bera gave him a look that said she was considering hauling him out of the saddle and boxing his ears. Still peering toward the shambles below, Kiruna smoothed her skirts, her face coldly determined. Loial's ears trembled. He had a deep but uneasy respect for Aes Sedai; close to twice as tall as most of the sisters, sometimes he behaved as though one might step on him without noticing if he got in her way.

Perrin gave Kiruna no chance to speak. Give an Aes Sedai a finger, and she took your whole arm, unless she decided to take more. 'You've been staying clear of me, but I have a few things to say to you. You disobeyed orders yesterday. If you want to call it changing the plan,' he pushed on when she opened her mouth, 'then call it that. If you think that makes it better.' She and the other eight had been told to stay with the Wise Ones, well back from the actual fighting, guarded by the Two Rivers men and the Mayeners. Instead they had plunged right into the thick of it, wading in where men were trying to cut one another into dogmeat with swords and spears. 'You took Havien Nurelle with you, and half the Mayeners died for it. You don't go your own way with no regard anymore. I won't see men die because you suddenly think you see a better way, and the Dark One take what everyone else thinks. Do you understand me?'

'Are you finished, farmboy?' Kiruna's voice was dangerously calm. The face she turned up to him might have been carved from some dark ice, and she reeked of affront. Standing on the ground, she somehow made it seem that she was looking down at him. Not an Aes Sedai trick, that; he had seen Faile do it. He suspected most women knew how. 'I will tell you something, though the meanest intelligence should be able to reason it out. By the Three Oaths, no sister may use the One Power as a weapon except against Shadowspawn or in defense of her life, or that of her Warders or another sister. We could have stood where you would have had us and watched until Tarmon Gai'don without ever being able to do anything effective. Not until we were in danger ourselves. I do not like having to explain my actions, farmboy. Do not make me do it again. Do *you* understand?'

Loial's ears wilted, and he stared straight ahead so hard that it was plain he wished he were anywhere but here, even with his mother, who wanted to marry him off. Aram's mouth hung open, and he always tried to pretend Aes Sedai did not impress him at all. Jondyn and Tod climbed down from their wagon wheel just a touch too casually; Jondyn managed to stroll away, but Tod ran, looking back over his shoulder.

Her explanation sounded reasonable; it was probably the truth. No, by another of the Three Oaths, it *was* the truth. There were loopholes, though. Like not speaking the whole truth, or talking around it. The sisters might well have put themselves in danger so they could use the Power as a weapon, but Perrin would eat his boots if they had not also been thinking they could reach Rand before anybody else. What would have happened then was anyone's guess, but he was certain their plans had not included anything like what actually happened.

'He's coming,' Loial said suddenly. 'Look! Rand is coming.' Dropping to a whisper, he added, 'Be careful, Perrin.' For an Ogier, it truly was a whisper. Aram and Kiruna probably heard quite clearly, and maybe Bera, but certainly no one besides. 'They did not swear anything to you!' His voice went back to its normal boom. 'Do you think he might talk to me about what went on inside the camp? For my book.' He was writing a book about the Dragon Reborn, or at least taking notes for one. 'I really didn't see much once the ... the fighting began.' He had been at Perrin's side in the thick of it, wielding an axe with a haft nearly as long as he was tall; it was hard to take note of much else when you were trying to stay alive. If you listened to Loial, you would think he was always somewhere else when things became dangerous. 'Do you think he might, Kiruna Sedai?'

Kiruna and Bera exchanged looks, then without a word glided across the ground to Verin and the others. Peering after them, Loial heaved a sigh, a wind through caverns.

'You really should have a care, Perrin,' he breathed. 'You're always so hasty with your tongue.' He sounded like a bumblebee the size of a cat instead of a mastiff. Perrin thought he might learn to whisper yet, if they spent enough time around Aes Sedai. He motioned the Ogier to be quiet, though, so he could listen. The sisters began talking right away, but not a sound reached Perrin's ears. Clearly they had erected a barrier with the One Power.

Clear to the Asha'man as well. They went from lounging to up on their toes in a heartbeat, every line of them focused on the sisters. Nothing said they had taken hold of *saidin*, the male half of the True Source, but Perrin would have wagered Stepper they had. By Gedwyn's angry sneer, he was ready to use it, too.

Whatever obstruction the Aes Sedai had raised, they must have dropped it. They folded their hands, turning to look down the slope in silence. Glances passed among the Asha'man, and finally Gedwyn waved them back to apparent indolence. He looked disappointed. Growling irritably, Perrin turned back to look beyond the wagons.

Rand was strolling up the slope with Min on his arm, patting her hand and talking with her. Once he threw back his head and laughed, and she ducked hers to do the same, brushing back dark ringlets that hung to her shoulders. You might have thought him a countryman out with his girl. Except that he had belted on his sword, and sometimes he ran his hand down the long hilt. And except for Taim right at his other shoulder. And the Wise Ones following almost as close behind. And the rings of Maidens and *siswai'aman*, Cairhienin and Mayeners that completed the procession.

What a relief that he would not have to ride down into that shambles after all; but he needed to warn Rand about all the tangled enmities he had seen this morning. What would he do if Rand did not listen? Rand had changed since leaving the Two Rivers, most of all since being kidnapped by Coiren and that lot. No. He *had* to be sane.

When Rand and Min entered the wagon-circle, most of the procession remained outside, though they hardly came alone, but with quite an assembly in its own right.

Taim shadowed Rand, of course, dark and slightly hook-nosed and what Perrin supposed most women would consider good-looking. A number of the Maidens had certainly given him second looks, and third; they were forward about that sort of thing. As Taim stepped inside, he glanced to Gedwyn, who shook his head just a hair. A grimace flashed across Taim's face, gone as soon as it appeared.

Nandera and Sulin were right at Rand's heels, equally of course, and Perrin wondered they did not bring twenty more Maidens. They hardly seemed to let Rand bathe without Maidens guarding the tub, that Perrin could see. He did not understand why Rand put up with it. Each had her *shoufa* draped around her shoulders, baring short hair cut with a tail at the back. Nandera was a sinewy woman, hair more gray than yellow, but her tough features managed to be handsome if not beautiful. Sulin – wiry, scarred, leathery and white-haired – made Nandera look pretty and almost soft. They glanced at the Asha'man, too, without exactly seeming to, then scanned both groups of Aes Sedai just as circumspectly.

Nandera's fingers flashed Maiden handtalk. Not for the first time, Perrin wished he could understand it, but a Maiden would give up the spear to marry a toad before teaching their handtalk to a man. A Maiden Perrin had not noticed, sitting on her heels against a wagon a few paces from Gedwyn, answered the same way, and so did another who until that moment had been playing at cat's cradle with a spear-sister near the prisoners.

Amys brought the Wise Ones in and took them aside to confer with Sorilea and a few of the others who had stayed inside the wagons. Despite a face too young for her waist-long white hair, Amys was an important woman, second among the Wise Ones to Sorilea. They used no One Power tricks to shield their talk, but seven or eight Maidens immediately encircled them and began singing softly to themselves. Some sat, some stood, some squatted on their heels, each by herself, and all happenstance. If you were a fool.

It seemed to Perrin that he sighed a great deal since he became mixed up with Aes Sedai and Wise Ones. Maidens, too. Women in general just seemed to give him fits of late.

Dobraine and Havien, leading their horses and minus their soldiers, brought up the rear. Havien had finally seen a battle; Perrin wondered whether he would be so eager to see the next. About the same age as Perrin, he did not look as young today as the day before yesterday. Dobraine, with the front of his long, mostly gray hair shaved in the style of Cairhienin soldiers, definitely was not young, and yesterday definitely had not been his first battle, yet the truth was, he looked older too, and worried. So did Havien. Their eyes sought out Perrin.

Another time, he would have waited to see what they wanted to talk about, but now he slipped from his saddle, tossed Stepper's reins to Aram, and went to Rand. Others were there ahead of him. Only Sulin and Nandera held their silence.

Kiruna and Bera had moved the moment Rand stepped inside the wagons, and as Perrin approached, Kiruna was saying grandly to Rand, 'You refused Healing yesterday, but anyone can see you are still in pain, even if Alanna was not ready to leap out of her—' She cut off as Bera touched her arm, but she picked up again almost without pause. 'Perhaps you are ready to be Healed now?' That had the sound of 'Perhaps you have come to your fool senses?'

'The matter of the Aes Sedai must be settled without any more delay, *Car'a'carn*,' Amys said formally, right atop Kiruna.

'They should be given into our care, Rand al'Thor,' Sorilea added at the same time that Taim spoke.

'The Aes Sedai problem does need to be settled, my Lord Dragon. My Asha'man know how to handle them. They could be held at the Black Tower easily.' Dark, slightly tilted eyes flickered toward Kiruna and Bera, and Perrin realized with a shock that Taim meant *all* the Aes Sedai, not just those who were prisoners now. For that matter, though Amys and Sorilea frowned at Taim, the looks they directed at the two Aes Sedai meant the same.

Kiruna smiled at Taim, at the Wise Ones, a thin smile to fit her lips. It was maybe a fraction harder when directed at the man in the black coat, but she seemed not to realize his intent yet. It was enough that he was who he was. What he was. 'Under the circumstances,' she said coolly, 'I am certain that Coiren Sedai and the others will give me their parole. You have no more need to worry—'

The others spoke all at once.

'These women have no honor,' Amys said contemptuously, and this time it was clear she included all of them. 'How could their parole mean anything? They—'

'They are *da'tsang*,' Sorilea said in a grim voice, as though pronouncing sentence, and Bera frowned at her. Perrin thought that was something in the Old Tongue – again, the word seemed almost something he should recognize – but he did not know why it should make the Aes Sedai scowl. Or why Sulin should suddenly nod agreement with the Wise One, who went on like a boulder rumbling downhill. 'They deserve no better than any other—'

'My Lord Dragon,' Taim said, as if belaboring the obvious, 'surely you want the Aes Sedai, all of them, in charge of those you trust, those you know can deal with them, and who better—?'

'Enough!' Rand shouted.

They fell silent as one, but their reactions were very different. Taim's features went blank, though he smelled of fury. Amys and Sorilea exchanged glances and adjusted their shawls in near unison;

their scents were identical, too, and matched their faces in pure determination. They wanted what they wanted and intended to have it, *Car'a'carn* or no. Looks passed between Kiruna and Bera, as well, speaking such volumes that Perrin wished he could read them the way his nose read scent. His eyes saw two serene Aes Sedai, in command of themselves and anything else they wished to be in command of; his nose smelled two women who were anxious, and more than a little afraid. Of Taim, he was sure. They still seemed to think they could deal with Rand, one way or another, and with the Wise Ones, but Taim and the *Asha'man* put the fear of the Light into them.

Min tugged at Rand's shirtsleeve – she had been studying everybody at once, and the scent of her was almost as worried as the sisters'. He patted her hand while glaring hard at everyone else. Including Perrin, when he opened his mouth. Everybody in the camp was watching, from the Two Rivers men to the Aes Sedai prisoners, though only a few Aiel stood close enough to hear anything. People might watch Rand, but they tended to stay clear of him, too, if they could.

'The Wise Ones will take charge of the prisoners,' Rand said at last, and Sorilea suddenly smelled so satisfied that Perrin knuckled his nose vigorously. Taim shook his head in exasperation, but Rand rounded on him before he could speak. He had tucked a thumb behind the buckle of his sword belt, a Dragon etched and gilded, and his knuckles were white from gripping it; his other hand worked on the dark boarhide of his sword hilt. 'The Asha'man are supposed to train – and recruit – not stand guard. Especially on Aes Sedai.' Perrin's hackles stirred as he realized what aroma wafted from Rand when he looked at Taim. Hatred, touched with fear. Light, he had to be sane.

Taim gave a short, reluctant nod. 'As you command, my Lord Dragon.' Min glanced uneasily at the black-coated man and moved closer to Rand.

Kiruna smelled of relief, but with one last glance at Bera, she drew herself up in stubborn certainty. 'These Aiel women are quite worthy – some might have done well, had they come to the Tower – but you cannot simply hand *Aes Sedai* over to them. It is unthinkable! Bera Sedai and I will—'

Rand raised a hand, and her words stopped in their tracks. Maybe it was his stare, like blue-gray stone. Or maybe it was what showed clearly through his torn sleeve, one of the red-and-gold Dragons that wound around his forearms. The Dragon glittered in the sunlight. 'Did you swear fealty to me?' Kiruna's eyes popped as though something had struck her in the pit of her stomach.

After a moment, she nodded, however unwillingly. She looked as disbelieving now as she had the day before, when she knelt down there by the wells at battle's end and swore beneath the Light and by her hope of salvation and rebirth to obey the Dragon Reborn and serve him until the Last Battle had come and gone. Perrin understood her shock. Even without the Three Oaths, had she denied it, he would have doubted his own memories. Nine Aes Sedai on their knees, faces aghast at the words coming out of their mouths, reeking of disbelief. Right now Bera's mouth was puckered up as though she had bitten a bad plum.

An Aielman joined the small group, a tall man about the same height as Rand, with a weathered face and touches of gray in his dark red hair, who nodded to Perrin and touched Amys' hand lightly. She might have pressed his hand for a moment in return. Rhuarc was her husband, but that was about as much affection as Aiel displayed in front of others. He was also clan chief of the Taardad Aiel – he and Gaul were the only two men who did not wear the *siswai'aman* headband – and since last night he and a thousand spears had been out scouting in force.

A blind man in another country could have sensed the temper around Rand, and Rhuarc was no fool. 'Is this the right moment, Rand al'Thor?' When Rand motioned him to speak, he went on. 'The Shaido dogs are still fleeing east as fast as they can run. I saw men with green coats on horses to the north, but they avoided us, and you said to let them go unless they gave trouble. I think they were hunting any Aes Sedai who escaped. There were several women with them.' Cold blue eyes glanced at the two Aes Sedai, anvil flat and anvil hard. Once, Rhuarc had walked lightly around Aes Sedai – any Aiel had – but that had ended yesterday, if not before.

'Good news. I'd give almost anything to have Galina, but still, good news.' Rand touched the hilt of his sword again, eased the blade in its dark scabbard. The action seemed unconscious. Galina, a Red, had been in charge of the sisters who held him prisoner, and if he was calm about her today, yesterday he had been in a fury that she had gotten away. Even now his calm was icy, the sort that could hide smoldering rage, and his scent made Perrin's skin crawl. 'They are going to pay. Every one of them.' There was nothing to say whether Rand meant the Shaido or the Aes Sedai who had escaped or both.

Bera moved her head uneasily, and he turned his attention back to her and Kiruna. 'You swore fealty, and I trust that.' He held up his hand, thumb and forefinger nearly touching to show how far. 'Aes Sedai always know better than anybody else, or so they think. So I trust you to do what I say, but you won't so much as take a bath without my permission. Or a Wise One's.'

This time it was Bera who looked as though she had been struck. Her light brown eyes swiveled to Amys and Sorilea with astonished indignation, and Kiruna quivered with the effort of not doing the same. The two Wise Ones merely shifted their shawls, but once again their aromas were identical. Contentment rolled off of them in waves, a very grim contentment. Perrin thought it a good thing the Aes Sedai did not have his nose, or they would have been ready to go to war right then and there. Or maybe run, and dignity be hanged. That was what he would have done.

Rhuarc stood there idly examining the point of one of his short spears. This was Wise Ones' business, and he always said he did not care what the Wise Ones did so long as they kept their fingers out of clan chiefs' business. But Taim . . . He made a show of not caring, folding his arms and looking around the camp with a bored expression, yet his scent was strange, complex. Perrin would have said the man was amused, definitely in a better humor than before.

'The oath we took,' Bera said at last, planting her hands on her ample hips, 'is sufficient to hold anyone but a Darkfriend.' The twist she gave to 'oath' was almost as bleak as the one she gave 'Darkfriend.' No, they did not like what they had sworn to. 'Do you dare to accuse us—?'

'If I thought that,' Rand snapped, 'you would be on your way to the Black Tower with Taim. You swore to obey. Well, obey!'

For a long moment Bera hesitated, then in an instant, was as regal from head to toe as any Aes Sedai could be. Which was saying something. An Aes Sedai could make a queen on her throne look a slattern. She curtsied slightly, stiffly inclining her head a fraction.

Kiruna, on the other hand, made a visible effort to take hold of herself, the calm she assumed hard and brittle as her voice. 'Must we then request *permission* of these *worthy* Aiel women to ask whether you are willing to be Healed yet? I know Galina treated you harshly. I know you are welts from shoulders to knees. Accept Healing. Please.' Even 'please' sounded part of an order.

Min stirred at Rand's side. 'You should be grateful for it, as I was, sheepherder. You don't like hurting. *Some*body has to do it, or else ...' She grinned mischievously, very nearly the Min Perrin remembered from before she was kidnapped. '... Or else you won't be able to sit a saddle.'

'Young men and fools,' Nandera said suddenly to no one in particular, 'sometimes bear pain they do not have to as a badge of their pride. And their foolishness.'

'The *Car'a'carn*,' Sulin added dryly, also to the air, 'is not a fool. I think.'

Rand smiled back at Min fondly, and gave Nandera and Sulin wry looks, but when he raised his eyes to Kiruna again, they were stone once more. 'Very well.' As she started forward, he added, 'But not from you.' Her face grew so stiff it appeared ready to crack. Taim's mouth quirked in a wry almost-smile, and he stepped toward Rand, but without taking his eyes from Kiruna, Rand flung out a hand behind him. 'From her. Come here, Alanna.'

Perrin gave a start. Rand had pointed straight to Alanna with never so much as a glance. That prickled something in the back of his head, but he could not make out what. It seemed to catch Taim, as well. The man's face became a bland mask, yet dark eyes flickered between Rand and Alanna, and the only name Perrin could put to the scent that writhed in his nose was 'puzzled.'

Alanna gave a start, too. For whatever reason, she had been on edge ever since joining Perrin on his way here, her serenity at best a thin veneer. Now she smoothed her skirts, shot a defiant stare at Kiruna and Bera of all people, and glided around in front of Rand. The other two sisters watched her, like teachers intending to make sure a pupil performed well and still not convinced she would. Which made no sense. One of them might be the leader, yet Alanna *was* Aes Sedai, the same as they. It all deepened Perrin's suspicion. Mixing with Aes Sedai was too much like wading the streams in the Waterwood near to the Mire. However peaceful the surface, currents beneath could snatch you off your feet. More undercurrents seemed to appear here every moment, and not all from the sisters.

Shockingly, Rand cupped Alanna's chin, turning her face up. There was a hiss of indrawn breath from Bera, and for once, Perrin agreed. Rand would not have been so forward with a girl at a dance back home, and Alanna was no girl at a dance. Just as surprising, her reaction was to blush and smell of uncertainty. Aes Sedai did not blush, in Perrin's experience, and they were *never* uncertain.

'Heal me,' Rand said, a command, not a request. The red in Alanna's face deepened, and anger touched her scent. Her hands trembled as she reached up to take his head between them.

Unconsciously Perrin rubbed the palm of his hand, the one a Shaido spear had laid open yesterday. Kiruna had Healed several gashes in him, and he had had healing before, too. It felt like being plunged headfirst into a freezing pond; it left you gasping and shaking and weak-kneed. Hungry, too, usually. The only sign Rand gave that anything had been done, though, was a slight shiver.

'How do you stand the pain?' Alanna whispered at him.

'It's done, then,' he said, removing her hands. And turned from her without a word of thanks. Seeming on the point of speaking, he paused, half-turning to look back toward Dumai's Wells.

'They have all been found, Rand al'Thor,' Amys said gently.

He nodded, then again, more briskly. 'It's time to be gone. Sorilea, will you name Wise Ones to take over the prisoners from the Asha'man? And also as companions for Kiruna and . . . my other liegewomen.' For an instant, he grinned. 'I wouldn't want them to err through ignorance.'

'It shall be done as you say, *Car'a'carn*.' Adjusting her shawl firmly, the leather-faced Wise One addressed the three sisters. 'Join your friends until I can find someone to hold your hands.' It was not unexpected that Bera would frown indignantly, or Kiruna become frost personified. Alanna gazed at the ground, resigned, almost sullen. Sorilea was having none of it. Clapping hands sharply, she made brisk shooing motions. 'Well? Move! Move!'

Reluctantly, the Aes Sedai let themselves be herded, making it seem they simply were going where they wished. Joining Sorilea, Amys whispered something that Perrin did not quite catch. The three Aes Sedai apparently did, though. They stopped dead, three *very* startled faces looking back at the Wise Ones. Sorilea just clapped her hands again, louder than before, and shooed even more briskly.

Scratching his beard, Perrin met Rhuarc's eyes. The clan chief smiled faintly and shrugged. Wise Ones' business. That was all very well for him; Aiel were fatalistic as wolves. Perrin glanced at Gedwyn. The fellow was watching Sorilea lecture the Aes Sedai. No, it was the sisters he watched, a fox staring at hens in a coop just out of his reach. *The Wise Ones have to be better than the Asha'man*, Perrin thought. *They have to be.*

If Rand noticed the byplay, he ignored it. 'Taim, you take the Asha'man back to the Black Tower as soon as the Wise Ones have charge of the prisoners. As soon as. Remember to keep an eye out for any man who learns too fast. And remember what I said about recruiting.'

'I can hardly forget, my Lord Dragon,' the black-coated man replied dryly. 'I will handle that trip personally. But if I may bring it up again ... You need a proper honor guard.'

'We have been over that,' Rand said curtly. 'I have better uses for the Asha'man. If I need an honor guard, those I *am* keeping will do. Perrin, will you—?'

'My Lord Dragon,' Taim broke in, 'you need more than a few Asha'man around you.'

Rand's head turned toward Taim. His face matched any Aes Sedai for giving nothing away, but his scent made Perrin's ears try to lie back. Razor-sharp rage abruptly vanished in curiosity and caution, the one thin and probing, the other foglike; then slashing, murderous fury consumed both. Rand shook his head just slightly, and his smell became stony determination. Nobody's scent changed that fast. Nobody's.

Taim had only his eyes to go by, of course, and all they could tell him was that Rand had shaken his head, if just barely. 'Think. You have chosen four Dedicated and four soldiers. You should have Asha'man.' Perrin did not understand that; he thought they were *all* Asha'man.

'You think I can't teach them as well as you?' Rand's voice was soft, the whisper of a blade sliding in its sheath.

'I think the Lord Dragon is too busy for teaching,' Taim replied smoothly, yet the anger smell rose again. 'Too important. Take men who need the least of it. I can choose the furthest along—'

'One,' Rand cut in. 'And I will choose.' Taim smiled, spreading his hands in acquiescence, but the scent of frustration nearly overwhelmed anger. Again Rand pointed without looking. 'Him.' This time, he seemed surprised to find he was pointing directly at a man in his middle years sitting atop an upturned cask on the other side of the wagon circle, paying no attention to the gathering around Rand. Instead, elbow on his knee and chin propped on his hand, he was frowning at the Aes Sedai prisoners. The sword and Dragon glittered on the high collar of his black coat. 'What is his name, Taim?'

'Dashiva,' Taim said slowly, studying Rand. He smelled even more surprised than Rand did, and irritated, too. 'Corlan Dashiva. From a farm in the Black Hills.'

'He will do,' Rand said, but he did not sound sure himself.

'Dashiva is gaining his strength rapidly, but his head is in the clouds often as not. Even when it isn't, he is not always entirely there. Maybe he's just a daydreamer, and maybe the taint on *saidin* is touching his brain already. Better for you to choose Torval or Rochaid or—'

Taim's opposition seemed to sweep away Rand's uncertainty. 'I said Dashiva will do. Tell him he's to come with me, then turn the prisoners over to the Wise Ones and go. I don't intend to stand here all day arguing. Perrin, ready everyone to move. Find me when they are.' Without another word he strode off, Min clinging to his arm, and Nandera and Sulin like shadows. Taim's dark eyes glittered;

then he was stalking away himself, shouting for Gedwyn and Rochaid, Torval and Kisman. Black-coated men came running.

Perrin grimaced. With everything he had to tell Rand, he had not opened his mouth once. At that, maybe it would come better away from the Aes Sedai and the Wise Ones. And Taim.

Really there was not much for him to do. He was supposed to be in charge since he had brought the rescue, but Rhuarc knew what needed doing better than he ever would, and a word to Dobraine and Havien was sufficient for the Cairhienin and Mayeners. They still wanted to say something, though they held back until they were alone and Perrin asked what it was.

Then Havien burst out, 'Lord Perrin, it's the Lord Dragon. All that searching through the corpses—'

'It seemed a little . . . excessive,' Dobraine interrupted smoothly. 'We worry for him, as you can understand. A great deal depends on him.' He might look a soldier, and he was, but he was a Cairhienin lord, too, and steeped in the Game of Houses, with all its careful talk, like any other Cairhienin.

Perrin was not steeped in the Game of Houses. 'He's still sane,' he said bluntly. Dobraine simply nodded, as if to say of course, shrugged to say he had never intended to question, but Havien went bright red. Watching them go to their men, Perrin shook his head. He hoped he was not lying.

Gathering the Two Rivers men, he told them to saddle their horses and ignored all the bowing, most of which looked spur-of-the-moment. Even Faile said that sometimes Two Rivers people carried bowing too far; she said they were still working out how to behave with a lord. He thought about shouting 'I am not a lord' at them, but he had done that before, and it never worked.

When all the others rushed for their animals, Dannil and Tell Lewin remained behind. Brothers, both were beanpoles and they looked much alike, except that Dannil affected mustaches like downturned horns in the Taraboner style, while Tell wore narrow lines of dark hair, in the fashion of Arad Doman, beneath a nose like a pickaxe. Refugees had brought a lot of new things into the Two Rivers.

'Those Asha'man coming with us?' Dannil asked. When Perrin

shook his head, he exhaled so hard in relief that his thick mustaches stirred.

'What about the Aes Sedai?' Ban said anxiously. 'They'll go free, now, won't they? I mean, Rand is free. The Lord Dragon, that is. They can't stay prisoners, not Aes Sedai.'

'You two just have everybody ready to ride,' Perrin said. 'Leave worrying about Aes Sedai to Rand.' The pair even winced alike. Two fingers rose to scratch worriedly at mustaches, and Perrin jerked his hand away from his chin. A man looked as if he had fleas when he did that.

The camp was abustle in no time. Everyone had been expecting to move soon, yet everyone had things left undone. The captive Aes Sedai's servants and wagon drivers hurriedly loaded the last items into the wagons and began hitching teams with a jingle of harness. Cairhienin and Mayeners seemed to be everywhere, checking saddles and bridles. Unclothed *gai'shain* went running every which way, though there did not seem to be much for the Aiel to ready.

Flashes of light outside the wagons announced the departure of Taim and the Asha'man. That made Perrin feel better. Of the nine who remained, another besides Dashiva was in his middle years, a stocky fellow with a farmer's face, and one, with a limp and a fringe of white hair, might easily have been a grandfather. The rest were younger, some little more than boys, yet they watched all the hubbub with the self-possession of men who had seen as much a dozen times. They did keep to themselves, though, and together except for Dashiva, who stood a few paces apart staring at nothing. Remembering Taim's caution about the fellow, Perrin hoped he was daydreaming.

He found Rand seated on a wooden crate with his elbows on his knees. Sulin and Nandera squatted easily to either side of Rand, both studiously avoiding looking at the sword at his hip. Holding their spears and bull-hide bucklers casually, here in the midst of people loyal to Rand, they kept a watch on anything that moved near him. Min sat on the ground at his feet with her legs tucked under, smiling up at him.

'I hope you know what you're doing, Rand,' Perrin said, shifting the axe haft so he could drop to his heels. No one was close enough to hear except for Rand and Min and the two Maidens. If Sulin or Nandera went running to the Wise Ones, so be it. Without more preamble he launched into what he had seen so far this morning. What he had smelled, too, though he did not say that. Rand was not among the few who knew about him and wolves; he made it all seem what he had seen and heard. The Asha'man and the Wise Ones. The Asha'man and the Aes Sedai. The Wise Ones and the Aes Sedai. The whole tangle of tinder that might burst into flame any moment. He did not spare the Two Rivers men. 'They're worried, Rand, and if they are sweating, you can be sure some Cairhienin is thinking about doing something. Or a Tairen. Maybe just helping the prisoners escape, maybe something worse. Light, I could see Dannil and Ban and fifty more besides helping them get away, if they knew how.'

'You think something else would be that much worse?' Rand said quietly, and Perrin's skin prickled.

He met Rand's gaze directly. 'A thousand times,' he said in just as quiet a voice. 'I won't be part of murder. If you will be, I'll stand in your way.' A silence stretched, unblinking blue-gray eyes meeting unblinking golden.

Frowning at each of them in turn, Min made an exasperated sound in her throat. 'You two woolheads! Rand, you know you'll never give an order like that, or let anyone else give it, either. Perrin, you know he won't. Now the pair of you stop acting like two strange roosters in a pen.'

Sulin chuckled, but Perrin wanted to ask Min how certain she was, although that was not a question he could voice here. Rand scrubbed his fingers through his hair, then shook his head, for all the world like a man disagreeing with somebody who was not there. The sort of voice that madmen heard.

'It's never easy, is it?' Rand said after a time, looking sad. 'The bitter truth is, I can't say which would be worse. I don't have any good choices. They saw to that themselves.' His face was despondent, but rage boiled in his scent. 'Alive or dead, they're a millstone on my back, and either way, they could break it.'

Perrin followed his gaze to the Aes Sedai prisoners. They were on their feet now, and all together, though even so they managed to put a little distance between the three who had been stilled and the rest. The Wise Ones around them were being curt with their orders, by the gestures they made and the tight faces on the sisters. Maybe the Wise Ones were better than Rand keeping them, too. If only he could be sure.

'Did you see anything, Min?' Rand said.

Perrin gave a start and directed a warning glance at Sulin and Nandera, but Min laughed softly. Leaning against Rand's knee, she really did look the Min he knew, for the first time since finding her at the wells. 'Perrin, they know about me. The Wise Ones, the Maidens, maybe all of them. And they don't care.' She had a talent she kept hidden, much as he did the wolves. Sometimes she saw images and auras around people, and sometimes she knew what they meant. 'You can't know what that's like, Perrin. I was twelve when it started, and I didn't know to make a secret of it. Everybody thought I was just making things up. Until I said a man on the next street was going to marry a woman I saw him with, only he was already married. When he ran off with her, his wife brought a mob to my aunts' house claiming I was responsible, that I'd used the One Power on her husband or given the two of them some kind of potion.' Min shook her head. 'She wasn't too clear. She just had to blame somebody. There was talk of me being a Darkfriend, too. There had been some Whitecloaks in town earlier, trying to stir people up. Anyway, Aunt Rana convinced me to say I had just overheard them talking, and Aunt Miren promised to spank me for spreading tales, and Aunt Jan said she'd dose me. They didn't, of course – they knew the truth – but if they hadn't been so matter-of-fact about it, about me just being a child, I could have been hurt, or even killed. Most people don't like somebody knowing things about their future; most people don't really want to know it themselves, not unless it's good anyway. Even my aunts didn't. But to the Aiel, I am sort of a Wise One by courtesy.'

'Some can do things others cannot,' Nandera said, as if that was enough explanation.

Min laughed again and reached out to touch the Maiden's knee. 'Thank you.' Settling her feet beneath her, she looked up at Rand. Now that she was laughing again, she seemed radiant. That held even after she became serious. Serious, and not very pleased. 'As for your question, nothing of any use. Taim has blood in his past and blood in his future, but you could guess that. He's a dangerous man. They seem to be gathering images like Aes Sedai.' A sidelong look through lowered eyelashes at Dashiva and the other Asha'man said who she meant. Most people had few images around them, but Min said Aes Sedai and Warders always did. 'The problem is, what I can see is all blurry. I think it's because they're holding the Power. That often seems true with Aes Sedai, and it's worse when they're actually channeling. Kiruna and that lot have all sorts of things around them, but they stay so close together that it all ... well ... jumbles together most of the time. It's even muddier with the prisoners.'

'Never mind the prisoners,' Rand told her. 'That's what they'll say.'

'But Rand, I keep feeling there is something important, if I could only pick it out. You need to know.'

'"If you don't know everything, you must go on with what you do know,"' Rand quoted wryly. 'It seems I never do know everything. Hardly enough, most of the time. But there's no choice but to go on, is there.' That was not at all a question.

Loial strode up, bubbling with energy despite his obvious weariness. 'Rand, they say they're ready to go, but you promised to talk to me while it's fresh.' Abruptly his ears twitched with embarrassment, and that booming voice became plaintive. 'I am sorry; I know it can't be enjoyable. But I must know. For the book. For the Ages.'

Laughing, Rand got to his feet and tugged at the Ogier's open coat. 'For the Ages? Do writers all talk like that? Don't worry, Loial. It will still be fresh when I tell you. I won't forget.' A grim, sour scent flashed from him despite the smile, and was gone. 'But back in Cairhien, after we all have a bath and sleep in a bed.' Rand motioned for Dashiva to come closer.

The man was not skinny, yet he moved in a hesitant, creeping way, hands folded at his waist, that made him seem so. 'My Lord Dragon?' he said, tilting his head.

'Can you make a gateway, Dashiva?'

'Of course.' Dashiva began dry-washing his hands, flicking at his lips with the tip of his tongue, and Perrin wondered whether the man was always this jittery, or just when speaking to the Dragon Reborn. 'That is to say, the M'hael teaches Traveling as soon as a student shows himself strong enough.'

'The M'Hael?' Rand said, blinking.

'The Lord Mazrim Taim's title, my Lord Dragon. It means "leader". In the Old Tongue.' The fellow's smile managed to be nervous and patronizing at the same time. 'I read a great deal on the farm. Every book the peddlers brought by.'

'The M'Hael,' Rand muttered disapprovingly. 'Well, be that as it may. Make me a gateway to near Cairhien, Dashiva. It's time to see what the world has been up to while I was away, and what I have to do about it.' He laughed then, in a rueful way, but the sound of it made Perrin's skin prickle.

Chapter 3

Hill of the Golden Dawn

On a wide low hilltop some miles north and east of the city of Cairhien, well away from any road or human habitation, a thin vertical slash of pure light appeared, taller than a man on a horse. The ground sloped away in every direction, undulating gently; nothing more than occasional brush obscured the view for more than a mile, all the way to the surrounding forest. Brown grass fell as the light seemed to rotate, widening into a square opening in midair. A number of the dead stems were slit lengthwise, sliced finer than any razor could have. By a hole in the air.

The instant the gateway was fully open, veiled Aiel poured out, men and Maidens, spreading in every direction to encircle the hill. Almost hidden in the torrent, four sharp-eyed Asha'man took up positions around the gateway itself, peering toward the encircling woodland. Nothing stirred except with the wind, dust, tall grass, and branches in the distance, yet each Asha'man studied the vista with the fervor of a starving hawk searching for a rabbit. A rabbit watching for a hawk might have been as intent, but never with that air of menace.

There was really no break in the flow. One moment it was a flood of Aiel, the next, mounted Cairhienin armsmen galloping out two by two, the crimson Banner of Light going up at their head as soon as it cleared the gateway. Without a pause Dobraine drew his men aside and began forming them up a little down the slope, helmeted and gauntleted in precise ranks, lances raised to the same angle. Seasoned campaigners, they were ready to wheel and charge in any direction at his gesture.

On the heels of the last Cairhienin, Perrin rode Stepper through, the dun passing in one stride from the hill below Dumai's Wells to the hill in Cairhien, and ducked in spite of himself. The upper edge of the thing stood well above his head, but he had seen the damage a gateway could do and had no wish to test whether they were safer standing still. Loial and Aram followed close behind – the Ogier, afoot with his long-hafted axe on his shoulder, bent his knees – and then the Two Rivers men, crouching on their saddles well beyond the gateway. Rad al'Dai carried the Red Wolfhead banner, Perrin's because everyone said it was, and Tell Lewin the Red Eagle.

Perrin tried not to look at those, especially the Red Eagle. The Two Rivers men wanted things both ways. He was a lord, so he had to have banners. He was a lord, but when he told them to get rid of those bloody banners, they never vanished for long. The Red Wolfhead named him something he was not and did not want to be, while the Red Eagle ... More than two thousand years after Manetheren died in the Trolloc Wars, close to a thousand after Andor swallowed part of what once had been Manetheren, that banner was still as good as an act of rebellion for an Andorman. Legends still walked in some men's minds. Of course it had been a few generations since Two Rivers folk had had any notion that they were Andormen, but Queens' minds did not change so easily.

He had met the new Queen of Andor what seemed a long time ago, in the Stone of Tear. She had not been Queen then – and was not yet, really, until she was crowned in Caemlyn – but Elayne seemed a pleasant young woman, and pretty, though he was not partial to fair-haired women. A bit taken with herself, of course, as Daughter-Heir. Taken with Rand, too, if snuggling in corners meant anything. Rand meant to give her not only the Lion Throne of Andor, but the Sun Throne of Cairhien. Surely she would be grateful enough to let the flying of a flag pass when it did not really mean anything. Watching the Two Rivers men deploy behind those banners, Perrin shook his head. It was a worry for another day, in any case.

There was nothing like armsmen's precision in the Two Rivers men, most boys like Tod, farmers' sons and shepherds, yet they knew what to do. Every fifth man took the reins of four more horses while the other riders hurriedly dismounted, longbows already strung and in hand. Those on the ground straggled together in rough lines, looking around with more interest than anything else, but they checked their quivers with practiced gestures and handled their bows with familiarity, the great Two Rivers bows, even when strung nearly as tall as the men who drew them. With those bows, not a man of them but could shoot farther than anyone outside the Two Rivers would believe. And hit what he aimed at.

Perrin hoped there would be none of that today. Sometimes he dreamed of a world where there never was. And Rand . . .

'Do you believe my enemies have been asleep while I was . . . away?' Rand had said suddenly as they stood waiting for Dashiva to open the gateway. He had on a coat rooted out of the wagons, well-cut green wool, but hardly what he usually wore now. Short of taking the coat off a Warder's back or a cadin'sor *from an Aielman, it was the only garment in the camp to fit him. Truth, you would have thought he insisted on silk and fine embroidery, the way he had had those wagons searched top to bottom, yesterday and this morning.*

The wagons stretched out in line, teams hitched, canvas covers and iron hoops taken down. Kiruna and the rest of the sworn sisters sat packed into the lead wagon, and not happy. They had ceased their protests as soon as they saw that protesting did no good, but Perrin could still hear coldly angry mutters. At least they rode. Their Warders surrounded the wagon afoot, silent and stony, while the Aes Sedai prisoners stood in a rigid, sullen cluster ringed by every Wise One who was not with Rand, which was to say all but Sorilea and Amys. The prisoners' Warders glowered in another clump a hundred paces off, cold death waiting despite their injuries and siswai'aman guards. Except for Kiruna's big black, its reins held by Rand, and a mouse-colored mare with fine ankles for Min, the Aes Sedai's and Warders' horses not assigned to Asha'man — or used to fill out wagon teams; that *had caused a commotion worse than making their owners walk!* — were all tied to long lead lines fastened to the wagons' tailgates.

'Do you believe it, Flinn? Grady?'

One of the Asha'man waiting to go through first, the stocky fellow with a farmer's face, looked at Rand uncertainly, then at the leathery old man with the limp. Each wore a silver-sword pin on his collar, but not the Dragon. 'Only a fool thinks his enemies stand still when he isn't looking, my Lord Dragon,' the old man said in a gruff voice. He sounded like a soldier.

'What about you, Dashiva?'

Dashiva gave a start, surprised to be addressed. 'I ... grew up on a farm.' He tugged his sword-belt straight, which it did not need. Supposedly they trained with the swords as much as with the Power, but Dashiva did not seem to know one end from the other. 'I don't know much about having enemies.' Despite his awkwardness, there was a kind of insolence to him. But then, the whole lot seemed weaned on arrogance.

'If you stay near me,' Rand said softly, 'you will.' His smile made Perrin shiver. He smiled while he gave orders to go through the gateway as though they would be attacked on the other side. There were enemies everywhere, he told them. Always remember that. There were enemies everywhere, and you never knew who.

The exodus continued unabated. Wagons rumbled from Dumai's Wells to Cairhien, the sisters in the first like statues of ice being lurched about. Their Warders trotted alongside, hands gripping sword hilts and eyes never resting on one spot; clearly they thought their Aes Sedai needed protection as much from those already on the hill as from anyone who might appear. The Wise Ones marched through herding their charges; a number used sticks to prod the

Aes Sedai along, though the sisters made a good job pretending there were neither Wise Ones nor prods. The Shaido *gai'shain* came, trotting in a column four wide under the gaze of a single Maiden; she pointed to a place out of the way before darting to join the other *Far Dareis Mai*, and the *gai'shain* knelt there in lines, naked as jaybirds and proud as eagles. The remaining Warders followed under their guard, radiating a massed fury that Perrin could smell over everything else, then Rhuarc with the rest of the *siswai'aman* and Maidens, and four more Asha'man, each leading a second horse for one of the first four, and Nurelle and his Winged Guards with their red-streamered lances.

The Mayeners were puffed up over being the rear guard, laughing and shouting boasts to the Cairhienin of what they would have done had the Shaido returned, though in fact they were not last. Last of all came Rand on Kiruna's gelding, and Min on her mare. Sorilea and Amys strode along to one side of the tall black horse, Nandera and half a dozen Maidens to the other, and Dashiva led a placid-looking bay mare at their heels. The gateway winked out, and Dashiva blinked at where it had been, smiling faintly, then scrambled clumsily into the mare's saddle. He seemed to be talking to himself, but it was probably because his sword tangled in his legs and he nearly fell. Surely he was not mad already.

An army covered the hill, all arrayed for an attack that plainly was not coming. A small army, only a few thousand, though it would have seemed fair-sized before the Aiel brought their numbers across the Dragonwall. Guiding his horse slowly toward Perrin, Rand scanned the countryside. The two Wise Ones followed closely, talking softly and watching him; Nandera and the Maidens followed, watching everything else. Had Rand been a wolf, Perrin would have said he was testing the air. He carried the Dragon Scepter across his high saddlebow, a two-foot length of spearhead decorated with a green-and-white tassel and carved with Dragons, and now and then he weighed it lightly in his hand as if to remind himself of it.

When Rand reined in, he studied Perrin as intently as he had the surrounding country. 'I trust you,' he said finally, nodding. Min stirred in her saddle, and he added, 'And you, Min, of course. And you, too, Loial.' The Ogier shifted uncertainly, with a hesitant glance for Perrin. Rand looked around the hillside, at the Aiel and the Asha'man and all the rest. 'So few I can trust,' he whispered tiredly. His scent was jumbled enough for two men, anger and fear, determination and despair. And woven through it all, weariness.

Be sane, Perrin wanted to tell him. *Hold on.* A wash of guilt held his tongue, though. Because it was the Dragon Reborn he wanted to say it to, not his friend since childhood. He wanted his friend to stay sane; the Dragon Reborn *had* to stay sane.

'My Lord Dragon,' one of the Asha'man called abruptly. He looked little more than a boy, with dark eyes as big as any girl's and neither sword nor Dragon on his collar, but pride in his bearing. Narishma, Perrin had heard him called. 'To the southwest.'

A figure had appeared, running out from the trees a mile or more away, a woman with skirts hiked to her thighs. To Perrin's eyes she was clearly Aiel. A Wise One, he thought, though there was no real way to tell at sight. He was just certain. The sight of her brought back all his edginess. Somebody out here, just where they happened to come out of the gateway, could not be good news. The Shaido had been troubling Cairhien again when he set off after Rand, but to the Aiel, a Wise One was a Wise One, whatever her clan. They visited like neighbors over for tea while their clans killed one another. Two Aiel trying to kill each other would step back to let a Wise One pass between. Maybe yesterday had changed that and maybe not. He exhaled wearily. At best she could not be good news.

Nearly everyone on the hill seemed to feel the same. Ripples of motion ran everywhere, spears hefted, arrows nocked. Cairhienin and Mayeners shifted in their saddles, and Aram drew his sword, eyes shining with anticipation. Loial leaned on his tall axe and fingered the edge regretfully. The head was shaped like that of a huge wood-axe, but engraved with leaves and scrolls and inlaid with gold. The inlay was a trifle scuffed from the axe's late use. If he had to use it again, he would, but with as much reluctance as Perrin used his and for many of the same reasons.

Rand simply sat his horse and watched, face unreadable. Min edged her mare close enough to stroke his shoulder like someone trying to soothe a mastiff with its hackles up.

The Wise Ones also gave no sign of disturbance, but neither did they stay still. Sorilea gestured, and a dozen of the women guarding the Aes Sedai broke off to join her and Amys, well away from Rand and out of even Perrin's hearing. Few had any gray in their hair, and Sorilea's was the only lined face, but then, there was hardly a gray hair to be seen on any of the Wise Ones here. The fact was, not many Aiel lived to have much gray hair. These women had position, though, or influence, however Wise Ones decided such things. Perrin had seen Sorilea and Amys confer with the same lot before, though confer was not quite the word. Sorilea spoke, with an occasional word from Amys, and the others listened. Edarra raised a protest, but Sorilea smothered it, apparently without breaking stride, then pointed out two of their number, Sotarin and Cosain. Immediately, they gathered their skirts over their arms and sped off toward the newcomer, legs flashing.

Perrin patted Stepper's neck. No more killing. Not yet.

The three Wise Ones met nearly half a mile from the hill and stopped. They spoke, just for a moment, and then all came on at a run, back to the hill. And straight to Sorilea. The newcomer, a youngish, long-nosed woman with a mass of incredibly red hair, spoke hurriedly. Sorilea's face grew stonier by the word. Finally the red-haired woman finished – or rather Sorilea cut her short with a few words – and the lot turned to face Rand. None made a move toward him, though. They waited, hands folded at their waists and shawls looped over their arms, inscrutable as any Aes Sedai.

'The *Car'a'carn*,' Rand muttered dryly under his breath. Swinging a leg over, he slid from his saddle then helped Min to the ground.

Perrin climbed down too, and led Stepper after them to the Wise Ones. Loial trailed along, and Aram followed on his horse, not dismounting until Perrin motioned him to. Aiel did not ride, not unless it was absolutely necessary anyway, and they considered it rude for anyone to face them from horseback. Rhuarc joined them, and Gaul, who wore a scowl for some reason. It went without saying that Nandera and Sulin and the Maidens came too.

The red-haired newcomer began as soon as Rand drew near. 'Bair and Megana set watches every way you might possibly come back to the treekillers' city, *Car'a'carn*, but in truth, no one thought this would be—'

'Feraighin,' Sorilea said, sharply enough to draw blood. The red-haired woman's teeth clicked as she snapped her mouth shut, and she stared fixedly at Rand with brilliant blue eyes, avoiding Sorilea's glare.

Finally Sorilea took a breath and turned her attention to Rand. 'There is trouble in the tents,' she said in a flat voice. 'Rumors began among the treekillers that you have gone to the White Tower with the Aes Sedai who came, gone to bend knee to the Amyrlin Seat. None who know the truth dared speak, or the result would have been worse.'

'And what is the result?' Rand asked quietly. He exuded tension, and Min began stroking his shoulder again.

'Many believe you have abandoned the Aiel,' Amys told him just as quietly. 'The bleakness has returned. Every day a thousand or more throw down their spears and vanish, unable to face our future, or our past. Some may be going to the Shaido.' For a moment disgust tinged her voice. 'There have been whispers that the true *Car'a'carn* would not give himself to the Aes Sedai. Indirian says if you have gone to the White Tower, it cannot be willingly. He is ready to take the Codarra north, to Tar Valon, and dance the spears with any Aes Sedai he finds. Or any wetlander; he says you must have been betrayed. Timolan mutters that if the tales are true, you have betrayed us, and he will take the Miagoma back to the Three-fold Land. After he sees you dead. Mandelain and Janwin hold their counsel, but they listen to Indirian and Timolan both.' Rhuarc grimaced, sucking air between his teeth; for an Aiel, that was as much as tearing his hair in despair.

'It's not good news,' Perrin protested, 'but you make it sound a death sentence. Once Rand shows himself, the rumors are done.'

Rand scrubbed a hand through his hair. 'If that was so, Sorilea wouldn't look like she had swallowed a lizard.' For that matter, Nandera and Sulin looked as though their lizards were still alive on the way down. 'What haven't you told me yet, Sorilea?'

The leather-faced woman gave him a thin, approving smile. 'You see beyond what is said. Good.' Her tone stayed flat as worked stone, though. 'You return with Aes Sedai. Some will believe that means you did bend knee. Whatever you say or do, they will believe you wear an Aes Sedai halter. And that is before it is known you were a prisoner. Secrets find crevices a flea could not slip through, and a secret known by so many has wings.'

Perrin eyed Dobraine and Nurelle, watching with their men, and swallowed queasily. How many of those who followed Rand did so because he had the weight of the Aiel massed behind him? Not all, certainly, but for every man who had chosen because Rand was the Dragon Reborn, five or even ten had come because the Light shone brightest on the strongest ranks. If the Aiel broke away, or splintered . . .

He did not want to think about that possibility. Defending the Two Rivers had stretched his abilities as far as they would go, maybe farther. *Ta'veren* or not, he had no illusions he was one of those men who ended up in the histories; that was for Rand. Village-sized problems were his limit. Yet he could not help himself. His mind churned. What to do if the worst came? Lists ran up in his head: who would remain loyal and who might try to slip away. The first list was sufficiently short and the second sufficiently long to dry his throat. Too many people still schemed for advantage as if they had never heard of the Prophecies of the Dragon or the Last Battle. He suspected some still would the day after Tarmon Gai'don began. The worst of it was, most would not be Darkfriends, just people looking out for their own interests first. Loial's ears hung limp; he saw it, too.

No sooner did Sorilea finish speaking to Rand than her eyes whipped to one side in a glare to bore holes in iron. 'You were told to remain in the wagon.' Bera and Kiruna came to an abrupt halt, and Alanna nearly stumbled into them. 'You were told not to touch the One Power without permission, but you listened to what was said here. You will learn that I mean what I say.'

Despite Sorilea's auguring stare, the three held their ground, Bera and Kiruna with icy dignity, Alanna with smoldering defiance. Loial's huge eyes rolled toward them, then toward the Wise One; if his ears had been limp before, now they wilted completely, and his long eyebrows dropped to his cheeks. Poring uneasily over his mental lists, Perrin wondered absently how far the Aes Sedai intended to push. Eavesdropping with the Power! They might find a reaction from the Wise Ones worse than Sorilea's bark. From Rand, too.

Not this time, however. Rand seemed unaware of them. He looked right through Sorilea. Or maybe listened to something nobody else could hear again. 'What of the wetlanders?' he said finally. 'Colavaere has been crowned queen, hasn't she?' It was not really a question.

Sorilea nodded, thumb tapping the hilt of her belt knife, but her attention never left the Aes Sedai. Who was chosen king or queen among the wetlanders was of small concern to Aiel, especially among the treekilling Cairhienin.

An icicle stabbed into Perrin's chest. That Colavaere of House Saighan wanted the Sun Throne was no secret; she had schemed for it from the day Galldrian Riatin was assassinated, before Rand had even declared himself the Dragon Reborn, and kept scheming after it became public knowledge that Rand meant the throne for Elayne. Few knew she was a cold-blooded murderer, however. And Faile was in the city. At least she was not alone. Bain and Chiad would be close to her. They were Maidens and her friends, maybe almost what the Aiel called near-sisters; they would not let her be harmed. The icicle would not go away, though. Colavaere hated Rand, and by extension anyone close to Rand. Such as, perhaps, the wife of a man who was Rand's friend. No. Bain and Chiad would keep her safe.

'This is a delicate situation.' Moving closer to Rand, remarkably, Kiruna ignored Sorilea. For such a scrawny woman, the Wise One had eyes like hammers. 'Whatever you do can have serious repercussions. I—'

'What has Colavaere said about me?' Rand asked Sorilea in a too-casual tone. 'Has she harmed Berelain?' Berelain, the First of Mayene, was who Rand had left in charge of Cairhien. Why did he not ask about Faile?

'Berelain sur Paendrag is well,' Sorilea murmured, without stopping her study of the Aes Sedai. Outwardly Kiruna stayed calm despite being interrupted and ignored, but the gaze she fixed on Rand could have frozen a forge-fire solid with the bellows pumping. For the rest, Sorilea gestured to Feraighin.

The red-haired woman gave a start and cleared her throat; plainly she had not expected to be allowed a word. She put dignity back on like a hastily donned garment. 'Colavaere Saighan says you have gone to Caemlyn, *Car'a'carn*, or maybe to Tear, but wherever you have gone, all must remember that you are the Dragon Reborn and must be obeyed.' Feraighin sniffed; the Dragon Reborn was no part of Aiel prophecies, only the *Car'a'carn*. 'She says you will return and confirm her on the throne. She speaks often to the chiefs, encouraging them to move the spears south. In obedience to you, she says. She does not see the Wise Ones, and hears only the wind when we speak.' This time her sniff was a fair approximation of Sorilea's. No one told the clan chiefs what to do, but angering the Wise Ones was a bad way to start convincing the chiefs of anything.

It made sense to Perrin, though, to the part of him that could think of anything beside Faile. Colavaere probably had never paid enough attention to the 'savages' to realize the Wise Ones did more than dispense herbs, but she would want every last Aiel out of Cairhien. The question was, given the circumstances, had any of the chiefs listened to her? But the question Rand asked was not the obvious.

'What else has happened in the city? Anything you've heard, Feraighin. Maybe something that might only seem important to a wetlander.'

She tossed her red mane contemptuously. 'Wetlanders are like sandflies, *Car'a'carn*: who can know what they find important? Strange things sometimes happen in the city, so I have heard, as they do among the tents. People sometimes see things that cannot be, only for a time, what cannot be, is. Men, women, children have died.' Perrin's skin prickled: he knew she meant what Rand called 'bubbles of evil,' rising from the Dark One's prison like froth in a fetid swamp, drifting along the Pattern till they burst. Perrin had been caught in one once; he never wanted to see another . . . 'If you mean what the wetlanders do,' she went on, 'who has time to watch sandflies? Unless they bite. That minds me of one thing. I do not understand it, but perhaps you do. These sandflies will bite sooner or later.'

'What sandflies? Wetlanders? What are you talking about?'

Feraighin was not as good as Sorilea at that level look, yet no Wise One that Perrin had seen appreciated others' impatience. Not even the chief of chiefs'. Thrusting her chin up, she gathered her shawl and answered. 'Three days ago the treekillers Caraline Damodred and Toram Riatin approached the city. They issued a proclamation that Colavaere Saighan is a usurper, but they sit in their camp south of the city and do nothing except send a few people into the city now and then. Away from their camp, a hundred of them will run from one *algai'd'siswai*, or even a *gai'shain*. The man called Darlin Sisnera and other Tairens arrived by ship below the city yesterday and joined them. They have been feasting and drinking ever since, as if celebrating something. Treekiller soldiers gather in the city at Colavaere Saighan's command, yet they watch our tents more than they do the other wetlanders' or the city itself. They watch, and do nothing. Perhaps you know the why of all this, *Car'a'carn*, but I do not, nor does Bair or Megana, or anyone else in the tents.'

Lady Caraline and Lord Toram led the Cairhienin who refused to accept that Rand and the Aiel had conquered Cairhien, just as High Lord Darlin led their counterparts in Tear. Neither revolt amounted to much; Caraline and Toram had been sitting in the foothills of the Spine of the World for months, making threats and claims, and Darlin the same down in Haddon Mirk. But not any longer, it seemed. Perrin found himself running a thumb lightly along the edge of his axe. The Aiel were in danger of slipping away, and Rand's enemies were coming together in one place. All it needed now was for the Forsaken to appear. And Sevanna with her Shaido. That would put the cream on the honeycake. Yet none of it was any more important than whether somebody saw a nightmare walking. Faile had to be safe; she just had to be.

'Better watching than fighting,' Rand murmured thoughtfully, listening to something unseen again.

Perrin agreed with Rand wholeheartedly – just about anything was better than fighting – but Aiel did not see it that way, not when it came to enemies. From Rhuarc to Sorilea, Feraighin to Nandera and Sulin, they stared as though Rand had said sand was better to drink than water.

Feraighin drew herself up practically on tiptoe. She was not particularly tall for an Aiel woman, not quite to Rand's shoulder, but she appeared to be trying to put herself nose-to-nose. 'There are few more than ten thousand in that wetlander camp,' she said reprovingly, 'and fewer in the city. They can be dealt with easily. Even Indirian remembers that you commanded no wetlander killed except in self-defense, but they will make trouble left to themselves. It does not help that there are Aes Sedai in the city. Who can know what they—'

'Aes Sedai?' The words came out cold, Rand's knuckles white on the Dragon Scepter. 'How many?' At the smell of him the skin between Perrin's shoulders crawled; suddenly he could *feel* the Aes Sedai prisoners watching, and Bera and Kiruna and the rest.

Sorilea lost all interest in Kiruna. Her hands planted themselves on her hips and her mouth narrowed. 'Why did you not tell me this?'

'You gave me no chance, Sorilea,' Feraighin protested a touch breathily, shoulders hunching. Blue eyes swung to Rand, and her voice firmed. 'There may be as many as ten or more, *Car'a'carn*. We avoid them, of course, especially since ...' Back to Sorilea and breathiness. 'You did not want to hear about the wetlanders, Sorilea. Only our own tents. You said so.' To Rand, her back straightening. 'Most of them stay beneath the roof of Arilyn Dhulaine, *Car'a'carn*, and seldom leave it.' To Sorilea, hunching. 'Sorilea, you know I would have told you everything. You cut me short.' As she realized how many were watching, and how many beginning to smile, among the Wise Ones anyway, Feraighin's eyes grew wild, and her cheeks reddened. Her head swung between Rand and Sorilea, and her mouth worked but no sound came out. Some of the Wise Ones began laughing behind their hands; Edarra did not bother with a hand. Rhuarc threw back his head and roared.

Perrin certainly did not feel like laughing. An Aiel could find something funny in having a sword stuck through him. Aes Sedai on top of everything else. Light! He cut straight through to what was important. 'Feraighin? My wife, Faile, is she well?'

She gave him a half-distracted stare, then visibly pulled together the tatters of her poise. 'I think Faile Aybara is well,

Sei'cair,' she said with cool composure. Or almost. She tried to sneak glances at Sorilea from the corner of her eye. Sorilea was not amused, or anything close to it; arms folded, she gave Feraighin a perusal that made the one she had given Kiruna seem mild.

Amys put a hand on Sorilea's arm. 'She is not at fault,' the younger woman murmured, too softly to reach any ears but the leathery Wise One's and Perrin's. Sorilea hesitated, then nodded; the flaying glare faded to her usual cantankerousness. Amys was the only one Perrin had seen able do that, the only one Sorilea did not trample down when she got in her way. Well, she did not trample Rhuarc, but with him it was more a boulder ignoring a thunderstorm; Amys could make it stop raining.

Perrin wanted more of Feraighin – she *thought* Faile was well? – but before he could open his mouth, Kiruna bulled in with her usual tact.

'Now, listen to me carefully,' she told Rand, gesturing emphatically under his nose. 'I called the situation delicate. It is not. The situation is complex beyond your imagining, so fragile a breath could shatter it. Bera and I will accompany you to the city. Yes, yes, Alanna; and you, as well.' She waved away the slender Aes Sedai impatiently. Perrin thought she was trying that looming trick. She did seem to be peering down her nose at Rand, though tall as she was, he stood head and shoulders taller. 'You must let yourself be guided by us. One wrong move, one wrong word, and you may deliver to Cairhien the same disaster you gave Tarabon and Arad Doman. Worse, you can do incalculable damage to matters about which you know almost nothing.'

Perrin winced. The whole speech could not have been better designed to inflame Rand. But Rand simply listened till she was done, then turned to Sorilea. 'Take the Aes Sedai to the tents. All of them, for now. Make sure everyone knows they're Aes Sedai. Let it be seen that they hop when you say toad. Since you hop when the *Car'a'carn* says it, that should convince everybody I'm not wearing an Aes Sedai leash.'

Kiruna's face grew bright red; she smelled of outrage and indignation so strongly that Perrin's nose itched. Bera tried to calm her, without much success, while shooting you-ignorant-young-lout looks at Rand, and Alanna bit her lip in an effort not to smile. Going by the odors drifting from Sorilea and the others, Alanna had no reason to be pleased.

Sorilea gave Rand a slash of smile. 'Perhaps, *Car'a'carn*,' she said dryly. Perrin doubted that she hopped for anyone. 'Perhaps it will.' She did not sound convinced.

With another shake of his head, Rand stalked off with Min, shadowed by the Maidens and issuing orders as to who was to go with him and who with the Wise Ones. Rhuarc began ordering the *siswai'aman*. Alanna followed Rand with her eyes. Perrin wished he knew what was going on there. Sorilea and the others watched Rand, too, and they smelled anything but gentle.

Feraighin was standing alone, he realized. Now was his chance. But when he tried to catch her up, Sorilea and Amys and the rest of the 'council' surrounded her, neatly shouldering him away. They moved some distance before they began showering her with questions, the sharp looks directed at Kiruna and the other two sisters leaving no doubt they would tolerate no further eavesdropping. Kiruna appeared to be considering it, glowering till it seemed a wonder her dark hair was not standing on end. Bera was speaking to her firmly, and without trying Perrin heard 'sensible' and 'patience,' 'cautious' and 'foolish.' Which applied to whom was not evident.

'There will be fighting when we reach the city.' Aram sounded eager.

'Of course not,' Loial said stoutly. His ears twitched, and he peered uncomfortably at his axe. 'There won't be, will there, Perrin?'

Perrin shook his head. He did not know. If only the other Wise Ones would leave Feraighin alone, just for a few moments. What did they have to talk about that was so important?

'Women,' Gaul muttered, 'are stranger than drunken wetlanders.'

'What?' Perrin said absently. What would happen should he simply push through the circle of Wise Ones? As if she had read his mind Edarra gave him a pointed frown. So did some of the others; sometimes it did seem women could read men's minds. Well . . .

'I said women are strange, Perrin Aybara. Chiad told me she would not lay a bridal wreath at my feet; she actually *told* me.' The Aielman sounded scandalized. 'She said she would take me for a lover, her and Bain, but no more.' Another time that would have shocked Perrin, though he had heard it before; Aiel were incredibly ... free ... about such things. 'As if I am not good enough for a husband.' Gaul snorted angrily. 'I do not like Bain, but I would marry her to make Chiad happy. If Chiad will not make a bridal wreath, she should stop trying to entice me. If I cannot catch her interest well enough for her to marry me, she should let me go.'

Perrin frowned at him. The green-eyed Aielman was taller than Rand, nearly a head taller than he. 'What are you talking about?'

'Chiad, of course. Have you not been listening? She avoids me, but every time I see her, she pauses long enough to make sure I have seen her. I do not know how you wetlanders do it, but with us, that is one of the ways a woman uses. When you least expect her, she is in your eyes, then gone. I did not even know she was with the Maidens until this morning.'

'You mean she's here?' Perrin whispered. That icicle was back, now a blade, hollowing him out. 'And Bain? Here, too?'

Gaul shrugged. 'One is seldom far from the other. But it is Chiad's interest I want, not Bain's.'

'Burn their bloody interest!' Perrin shouted. The Wise Ones turned to look at him. In fact, people all over the hillside did. Kiruna and Bera were staring, faces entirely too thoughtful. With an effort he managed to lower his voice. He could do nothing about the intensity, though. 'They were supposed to be protecting her! She's in the city, in the Royal Palace, with Colavaere — with Colavaere! — and they were supposed to be protecting her.'

Scratching his head, Gaul looked at Loial. 'Is this wetlander humor? Faile Aybara is out of short skirts.'

'I know she's not a child!' Perrin drew a deep breath. It was very hard keeping a level tone with his belly full of acid. 'Loial, will you explain to this ... to Gaul, that our women don't run around with spears, that Colavaere wouldn't offer to fight Faile, she'd just order somebody to cut her throat or throw her off a wall or ...' The images were too much. He was going to empty his stomach in a moment.

Loial patted him awkwardly on the shoulder. 'Perrin, I know you're worried. I know how I'd feel if I thought anything happened to Erith.' The tufts on his ears quivered. He was a fine one to talk;

he would run as hard as he could to avoid his mother and the young Ogier woman she had chosen for him. 'Ah. Well. Perrin, Faile is waiting for you, safe and sound. I know it. And you know she can care for herself. Why, she could care for herself and you and me, and Gaul, as well.' His booming laugh sounded forced, and it quickly faded to grave seriousness. 'Perrin . . . Perrin, you know you can't always be there to protect Faile, however much you want to. You are *ta'veren*; the Pattern spun you out for a purpose, and it will use you for that purpose.'

'Burn the Pattern,' Perrin growled. 'It can all burn, if it keeps her safe.' Loial's ears went rigid with shock, and even Gaul looked taken aback.

What does that make me? Perrin thought. He had been scornful of those who scribbled and scrabbled for their own ends, ignoring the Last Battle and the Dark One's shadow creeping over the world. How was he different from them?

Rand reined the black in beside him. 'Are you coming?'

'I'm coming,' Perrin said bleakly. He had no answer for his own questions, but he knew one thing. To him, Faile *was* the world.

CHAPTER 4

Into Cairhien

Perrin would have set a harder pace than Rand did, though he knew the horses could not have stood it long. Half the time they rode at a trot, the other half ran alongside their animals. Rand seemed unaware of anyone else, except that he always had a hand for Min if she stumbled. For the rest, he was lost in some other world, blinking in surprise when he noticed Perrin, or Loial. Truth to tell, nobody was any better. Dobraine's men and Havien's stared straight ahead, chewing their own worries over what they would find. The Two Rivers men had soaked in Perrin's dark mood. They liked Faile – truth be told, some worshiped her – and if she had been hurt in any way ... Even Aram's eagerness grew bleak once he realized that Faile might be in danger. Every man focused on the leagues before them, toward the city ahead. Except for the Asha'man, anyway; close behind Rand like a cluster of ravens, they studied the country the column crossed, still wary of an ambush. Dashiva slumped in his saddle like a sack, and muttered darkly to himself when he had to run; he glared as if he hoped there was an ambush.

Small chance of that. Sulin and a dozen *Far Dareis Mai* trotted ahead of the column in Perrin's sight, with as many more farther ahead, probing the way, and an equal number on the flanks. Some had thrust their short spears into the harnesses that held their bow cases on their backs, so the spearheads bobbed above their heads; the short horn bows were out, arrows nocked. They kept equally sharp watch for anything that might threaten the *Car'a'carn* and on Rand himself, as though they suspected he might vanish again. If any trap waited, any danger approached, they would find it.

Chiad was one of the Maidens with Sulin, a tall woman with dark reddish hair and gray eyes. Perrin stared at her back, willing her to drop behind the others and speak to him. Now and then she spared him a glance, but she avoided him as if he had three diseases, all catching. Bain was not with the column; most of the Maidens followed much the same route with Rhuarc and the *algai'd'siswai*, but moving more slowly because of the wagons and prisoners.

Faile's black mare trotted behind Stepper, her reins tied to his saddle. The Two Rivers men had brought Swallow from Caemlyn when they joined him before Dumai's Wells. Every time he looked at the mare prancing along behind him, his wife's face swelled in his thoughts, her bold nose and generous mouth, flashing dark eyes tilted above high cheekbones. She loved the animal, maybe almost as much as she did him. A woman as proud as she was beautiful, as fiery as she was proud. Davram Bashere's daughter would not hide, or even hold her tongue, not for the likes of Colavaere.

Four times they stopped to rest the mounts, and he ground his teeth at the delay. Taking good care of horses was second nature to him, he checked Stepper absently, gave the stallion a little water by rote. Swallow he was more careful with. If Swallow reached Cairhien safely ... A notion had planted itself in his mind. If he brought her mare to Cairhien, Faile would be all right. It was ludicrous, a boy's fancy, a *small* boy's *foolish* fancy, and it would not go away.

At each of those stops, Min tried to reassure him. With a bantering grin, she said he looked like death on a winter morning, just waiting for somebody to shovel his grave full. She told him if he approached his wife with a face like that, Faile would slam the door on him. But she had to admit that none of her viewings promised that Faile was unharmed.

'Light, Perrin,' she said at last in exasperated tones, snugging her gray riding gloves, 'if anyone tries to harm the woman, she'll make him wait out in the hall till she has time for him.' He very nearly growled at her. It was not that the two disliked each other, exactly.

Loial reminded Perrin that Hunters for the Horn could take care of themselves, that Faile had survived Trollocs unscathed. 'She is well, Perrin,' he boomed heartily, trotting beside Stepper with his long axe across his shoulders. 'I know she is.' But he said the same twenty times, and each time he sounded a little less hearty.

The Ogier's final attempt at heartening went further than Loial intended. 'I am sure Faile can look after herself, Perrin. She is not like Erith. I can hardly wait for Erith to make me her husband so I can tend her; I think I'd die if she changed her mind.' At the end of that, his mouth remained open, and his huge eyes popped; ears fluttering, he stumbled over his own boots and nearly fell. 'I never meant to say that,' he said hoarsely, striding along beside Perrin's horse once more. His ears still trembled. 'I am not sure I want to— I'm too young to get—' Swallowing hard, he gave Perrin an accusing look, and spared one for Rand up ahead, too. 'It is hardly safe to open your mouth with *two ta'veren* about. Anything at all might come out!' Nothing that might not have come off his tongue anyway, as he well knew, though it might have happened one time in a thousand, or a thousand times a thousand, without *ta'veren* there. Loial knew that also, and the fact of it seemed to frighten him as much as anything Perrin had ever seen. Some considerable time passed before the Ogier's ears stopped shaking.

Faile filled Perrin's mind, but he was not blind, not completely. What he at first saw without seeing, as they rode south and west, began to seep in at the edges. The weather had been hot when he headed north from Cairhien, less than two weeks ago, yet it seemed the Dark One's touch had gained a harder hold, grinding the land more desperately than before. Brittle grass crackled beneath the horses' hooves, shriveled brown creepers spiderwebbed rocks on the hillsides, and naked branches, not merely leafless but dead, cracked when the arid wind gusted. Evergreen pine and leatherleaf stood brown and yellow often as not.

Farms had begun appearing after a few miles, plain structures of dark stone laid out in squares, the first in isolated clearings in the forest, then coming more thickly as the woodland thinned to trees hardly deserving the name. A cart road straggled there, running over the shoulders and crests of hills, accommodating stone-walled fields more than the terrain. Most of those early farms looked deserted, here a ladderback chair lying on its side in front of a farmhouse, there a rag doll by the roadside. Slat-ribbed cattle and lethargic sheep dotted pastures where frequently ravens squabbled over carcasses; hardly a pasture but had a carcass or two. Streams ran in trickles down channels of dried mud. Cropland that should have been blanketed with snow looked ready to crumble to dust, where it was not dust already, blowing away.

A tall plume of dust marked the passage of the column, until the narrow dirt way joined the broad stone-paved road that led from Jangai Pass. Here there were people, though few, and those often lethargic, dull-eyed. With the sinking sun almost halfway down to the horizon now, the air was an oven. The occasional ox-cart or horse-drawn wagon hurried off the road, down narrow tracks or even into fields, out of the way. The drivers, and the handful of farm folk in the open, stood blank-faced as they watched the three banners pass.

Close to a thousand armed men was reason enough to stare. A thousand armed men, heading somewhere in a hurry, with a purpose. Reason enough to stare, and be thankful when they passed out of sight.

At last, when the sun had less than twice its own height yet to fall, the road topped a rise, and there two or three miles before them lay Cairhien. Rand drew rein, and the Maidens, all together now, dropped to their heels where they were. They kept those sharp eyes out, though.

Nothing could be seen moving on the nearly treeless hills around the city, a great mass of gray stone sinking toward the River Alguenya on the west, square-walled, square-towered and stark. Ships of all sizes lay anchored in the river, and some tied to the docks of the far bank, where the granaries were; a few vessels moved under sail or long sweeps. They gave an impression of peace and prosperity. With not a cloud in the sky, the light was sharp, and the huge banners flying from the city's towers stood plain enough to Perrin when the wind unfurled them. The scarlet Banner of Light and the white Dragon banner with its serpentine creature scaled scarlet and gold, the wavy-rayed Rising Sun of Cairhien, gold on blue. And a fourth, given equal prominence with the rest. A silver diamond on a field checked yellow and red.

Lowering a small looking glass from his eye, a scowling Dobraine stuffed it into a worked-leather tube tied to his saddle. 'I hoped the savages had it wrong somehow, but if House Saighan flies with the Rising Sun, Colavaere has the throne. She will have been distributing gifts in the city every day; coin, food, finery. It is traditional for the Coronation Festival. A ruler is never more popular than for the week after taking the throne.' He eyed Rand sideways; the strain of speaking straight out hollowed his face. 'The commoners could riot if they dislike what you do. The streets could run with blood.'

Havien's gray gelding danced his rider's impatience, and the man himself kept looking from Rand to the city and back. It was not his city; he had made it clear earlier that he cared little what ran in the streets, so long as his own ruler was safe.

For long moments Rand simply studied the city. Or seemed to, anyway; whatever he saw, his face was bleak. Min studied him, worriedly, maybe pityingly. 'I will try to see they don't,' he said at last. 'Flinn, remain here with the soldiers. Min—'

She broke in on him sharply. 'No! I am going where you go, Rand al'Thor. You need me, and you know it.' The last sounded more plea than demand, but when a woman planted her fists on her hips that way and fixed her eyes to you, she was not begging.

'I am going, too,' Loial added, leaning on his long-hafted axe. 'You always manage to do things when I'm somewhere else.' His voice took on a plaintive edge. 'It won't do, Rand. It will not do for the book. How can I write about things if I am not there?'

Still looking at Min, Rand half-raised a hand toward her, then let it fall. She met his gaze levelly.

'This is ... madness.' Holding his reins stiffly, Dashiva booted the plump mare closer to Rand's black. Reluctance twisted his features; perhaps even Asha'man worried at being too near Rand. 'All it needs is one man with a ... a bow, or a knife, and you don't see him in time. Send one of the Asha'man to do what needs doing, or more, if you think it's necessary. A gateway to the palace, and it can be done before anyone knows what has happened.'

'And sit here past dark,' Rand cut in, reining his gelding around to face Dashiva, 'until they know this place well enough to open one? That way brings bloodshed for sure. They've seen us from the walls, unless they're blind. Sooner or later they will send somebody to find out who we are, and how many.' The rest of the column remained hidden behind the rise, and the banners were down there, too, but men sitting their horses on a ridge with Maidens for company would indeed attract curiosity. 'I will do this my way.' His voice rose in anger, and he smelled of cold fury. 'Nobody dies unless it can't be avoided, Dashiva. I've had a bellyful of death. Do you understand me? Nobody!'

'As my Lord Dragon commands.' The fellow inclined his head, but he sounded sour, and he smelled ...

Perrin rubbed his nose. The smell ... skittered, dodging wildly through fear and hate and anger and a dozen more emotions almost too quickly to make out. He no longer doubted the man was mad, however good a face the fellow put on. Perrin no longer really cared, either. This close ...

Digging his heels into Stepper's flanks, he started for the city and Faile, not waiting for the rest, barely noticing Aram close behind. He did not have to see Aram to know he would be there. All he could think of was Faile. If he got Swallow safely into the city ... He made himself keep Stepper at no more than a quick walk. A galloping rider drew eyes, and questions, and delays.

At that pace, the others caught up with Aram and him fast enough, those who were coming. Min had gotten her way, it seemed, and so had Loial. The Maidens fanned out ahead, some giving Perrin sympathetic looks as they trotted by. Chiad studied the ground until she was beyond him.

'I still don't like this plan,' Havien muttered on one side of Rand. 'Forgive me, my Lord Dragon, but I do not.'

Dobraine, on Rand's other side, grunted. 'We have been over that, Mayener. If we did as you want, they would close the gates on us before we covered a mile.' Havien growled something under his breath and danced his horse a few paces. He had wanted every man to follow Rand into the city.

Perrin glanced over his shoulder, past the Asha'man. Damer Flinn, recognizable by his coat, and a few of the Two Rivers men were visible on the ridge, standing and holding their horses. Perrin sighed. He would not have minded having the Two Rivers men along. But Rand was probably right, and Dobraine had backed him up.

A few men could enter where a small army could not. If the gates were shut, the Aiel would have to besiege the city, if they still would, and then the killing began anew. Rand had stuffed the Dragon Scepter into one of the geldings' saddlebags so just the carved butt stuck out, and that plain coat looked like nothing the Dragon Reborn would wear. For the Asha'man, nobody in the city had any idea what a black coat meant. A few men were easier to kill than a small army, too, even if most of them could channel. Perrin had seen an Asha'man take a Shaido spear through his belly, and the man had died no harder than any other.

Dashiva grumbled under his breath; Perrin caught 'hero' and 'fool' in equally disparaging tones. Without Faile, he might have agreed. Once Rand peered toward the Aiel encampment sprawled over the hills two or three miles east of the city, and Perrin held his breath, but whatever thoughts Rand had, he kept on the road. Nothing mattered more than Faile. Nothing, whether or not Rand saw it so.

A good half-mile short of the gates, they rode into another camp, one that made Perrin frown. It was big enough for a city itself, a thick band of ramshackle brush huts and rickety tents made from scraps, on burned-over ground, clinging to the high gray walls as far as he could see. This had been called Foregate once, a warren of twisting streets and alleys, before the Shaido burned it. Some of the people stared in silence as the strange party passed, at an Ogier, and Aiel Maidens, but most scuttled about their business with wary, sullen faces and a care to notice nothing that was not right in front of them. The bright colors and often tattered cast-off finery worn by Foregaters mingled with the somber garb more usual for Cairhienin, the plain dark clothes of villagers and farmers. The Foregaters had been in the city when Perrin left, along with thousands of refugees from deeper inside the country. Many of those faces bore bruises and worse, cuts and slashes, often unbandaged. Colavaere must have put them out. They would not have left the shelter of the walls on their own; Foregaters and refugees alike feared the return of the Shaido the way a man who had been seared to the bone feared hot iron.

The road ran straight through the camp to the Jangai Gates, three tall square arches flanked by towers. Helmeted men lounged up on the battlements, peering down through the gaps in the stone teeth. Some stared off toward the men on the hilltop, and here and there an officer with a *con* held a looking glass to his eye. Rand's small party drew inquiring glances. Men ahorseback and Aiel Maidens; not common companions. Crossbows showed atop the serrated wall, but no one raised a weapon. The iron-bound gates stood open. Perrin held his breath. He wanted very much to gallop for the Sun Palace and Faile.

Just inside the gates sat a squat stone guardhouse, where strangers to the city were supposed to register before entering. A square-faced Cairhienin officer watched them pass with a disgruntled frown, eyeing the Maidens uneasily. He just stood there, watching.

'As I told you,' Dobraine said once they were by the guardhouse. 'Colavaere gave free access to the city for Coronation Festival. Not even someone under order of arrest can be denied or detained. It is tradition.' He sounded relieved, though. Min sighed audibly, and Loial let out a breath that could have been heard two streets over. Perrin's chest was still too tight for sighing. Swallow was inside Cairhien. Now, if he could only get her to the Royal Palace.

Up close, Cairhien carried out what it had promised from afar. The highest of the hills lay inside the walls, but terraced and faced with stone till they no longer seemed hills at all. Broad, crowded streets met at right angles. In this city, even the alleys made a grid. The streets rose and fell reluctantly with the hills, often simply cutting through. From shops to palaces, the buildings were all stark squares and severe rectangles, even the great buttressed towers, each wrapped in scaffolding on a hilltop, the once-fabled topless towers of Cairhien, still being rebuilt after burning in the Aiel War. The city seemed harder than stone, a bruising place, and shadows stretching across everything heightened the effect. Loial's tufted ears twitched almost without stopping; a worried frown creased his forehead, and his dangling eyebrows brushed his cheek.

There were few signs of Coronation Festival, or High Chasaline. Perrin had no notion what the Festival might entail, but in the Two Rivers, the Day of Reflection was a time of merriment and forgetting the bleakness of winter. Here, a near hush hung in the air, despite the number of people. Anywhere else, Perrin might have thought it the unnatural heat dragging people's spirits down, but except for Foregaters, Cairhienin were a sober, austere lot. On the surface, at least; what lay underneath, he would as soon not think about. The hawkers and cart-peddlers he remembered were gone from the streets, the musicians and tumblers and puppet shows. Those people would be in the ragtag camp outside the walls. A few closed, dark-painted sedan chairs threaded through the quiet throngs, some with House banners a little larger than *con* standing stiffly above. They moved as slowly as the ox-carts with goad-wielding drivers walking alongside, axles squealing in the stillness. Outlanders stood out, no matter how little color they wore, because few except outlanders rode. The almost inevitably shorter natives looked like pale-faced crows in their dark garb. Aiel stood out too, of course. Whether one alone or ten together, they walked in clearings through the crowds; eyes darted away and space just opened up around them wherever they went.

Aiel faces turned toward the party as it made its slow way through the crowds. Even if not all recognized Rand in his green coat, they knew who a tall wetlander escorted by Maidens must be. Those faces sent a chill down Perrin's spine: considering. They made him thankful Rand had left all of the Aes Sedai behind. Aside from the Aiel, the Dragon Reborn moved through a river of unconcern that parted for the Maidens and closed in again behind the Asha'man.

The Royal Palace of Cairhien, the Sun Palace, the Palace of the Rising Sun in Splendor – Cairhienin were great ones for names, each more extravagant than the last – stood atop the highest hill in the city, a dark mass of square stone with stepped towers looming over everything. The street, the Way of the Crown, became a long broad ramp rising toward the palace, and Perrin drew a deep breath as they started up. Faile was up there. She had to be, and safe. Whatever else, she had to be safe. He touched the knot holding Swallow's reins to a ring on his pommel, stroked the axe at his waist. The horses' shod hooves rang loudly on the paving stones. The Maidens made no sound at all.

The guards on the great, open bronze gates watched their slow approach and exchanged glances. They were colorful for Cairhienin soldiers, ten men with the Rising Sun in gold on their dark breastplates and scarves in House Saighan's colors tied below the heads of their halberds. Perrin could have written out their thoughts. Thirteen men on horseback, but in no hurry, and only two wearing armor, one in Mayener red. Any trouble would come from Caraline Damodred and Toram Riatin, and Mayeners had no place in that. And there was a woman, and an Ogier. Surely they intended no trouble. Still, three dozen or so Maidens trotting ahead of the horses hardly looked as though they were coming for tea. For an instant all hung balanced. Then a Maiden veiled herself. The guards jerked as if goosed, and one slanted his halberd and darted for the gates. Two steps he took, and stopped, rigid as a statue. Every guard stood stiff; nothing moved but their heads.

'Good,' Rand murmured. 'Now tie off the flows and leave them for later.'

Perrin shrugged uncomfortably. The Asha'man had spread out behind, taking up most of the width of the ramp; they must be using the Power. Very likely the eight of them could tear the whole palace apart. Maybe Rand could have by himself. But if those towers began spewing crossbow bolts, they would die with everyone else, caught in the open on this ramp that no longer seemed so wide.

Nobody sped up. Any eyes at the tall narrow windows of the palace, on the colonnaded walks high above must see nothing out of the ordinary. Sulin flashed Maiden handtalk, and the one who had veiled lowered the black cloth hurriedly, face flushing. A slow walk, up the stone ramp. Some of the guards' helmeted heads shook wildly, eyes rolling; one seemed to have fainted, slumping upright with his chin on his chest. Their mouths strained, open, but no sound came out. Perrin tried not to think about what had gagged them. A slow walk, through the open bronze gates, into the main courtyard.

There were no soldiers here. The stone balconies around the courtyard stood empty. Liveried servants rushed out with downcast eyes to take the horses' reins and hold stirrups. Stripes of red and yellow and silver ran down the sleeves of otherwise dark coats and dresses, and each had the Rising Sun small on the left breast. That was more color than Perrin had seen on a Cairhienin servant before. They could not see the guards outside, and likely would have done little different if they had. In Cairhien, servants played their own version of *Daes Dae'mar*, the Game of Houses, but they pretended to ignore the doings of those above them. Taking too much notice of what happened among your betters – or at least, being seen to take notice – might mean being caught up in it. In Cairhien, maybe in most lands, ordinary folk could be crushed unnoticed where the mighty walked.

A blocky woman led Stepper and Swallow away without ever really looking at him. Swallow was inside the Sun Palace, and it made no difference. He still did not know whether Faile was alive or dead. A fool boy's fool fancy.

Shifting his axe at his hip, he followed Rand up the broad gray stairs at the far end of the courtyard, and nodded when Aram reached over his shoulder again to ease his sword. Liveried men swung open the great doors at the head of the stairs, bronze like the outer gates and marked large with the Rising Sun of Cairhien.

Once, the entry hall would have stunned Perrin with its grandeur. Thick square columns of dark marble held a square-vaulted ceiling ten paces above floor tiles that alternated dark blue and deep gold. Gilded Rising Suns marched around the cornices, and friezes carved in the walls showed Cairhienin triumphs in battle. The hall was empty, save for a handful of young men clustered beneath one of the friezes who fell silent when Perrin and the rest entered.

Not all men, he realized. All wore swords, but four of the seven were women, in coats and snug breeches much like Min's, their hair cut short as the men's. Not that that was particularly short; men and women alike had it gathered in a kind of tail that reached their shoulders, tied with a dark ribbon. One of the women wore green a little paler than normal for Cairhienin, and another bright blue; all the rest were in dark colors, with a few bright stripes across their chests. They studied Rand's party – with an especial view for himself, Perrin realized; his yellow eyes took people aback, although he hardly noticed it any more unless somebody jumped, or made a commotion – studied in silence until the last of the Asha'man was in and the doors swung shut. The boom of the closing covered a moment of fierce whispering; then they came swaggering closer, the women strutting even more arrogantly than the men, which took some doing. Even the way they knelt was arrogant.

The green-clad woman glanced at the one in blue, who had her head down, and said, 'My Lord Dragon, I am Camaille Nolaisen. Selande Darengil leads our society . . .' She blinked at a fierce look from the woman in blue. Despite the glare, Selande smelled afraid to her bones, if Perrin was making out who was who properly. Clearing her throat, Camaille went on, 'We did not think— We did not expect you to return – so soon.'

'Yes,' Rand said softly. 'I doubt anyone thought I would return – so soon. None of you has any reason to be afraid of me. None at all.

If you believe anything, believe that.' Surprisingly, he looked right at Selande when he said that. Her head whipped up, and as she stared at him, the fear-smell faded. Not completely, but down to a tatter. How had Rand known it was there? 'Where is Colavaere?' Rand asked.

Camaille opened her mouth, but it was Selande who answered. 'In the Grand Hall of the Sun.' Her voice grew stronger as she spoke, the scent of her fear growing weaker. Oddly, a slight tinge of jealousy touched it once, just for an instant, when she glanced at Min. Sometimes his sense of smell was more confusing than enlightening. 'It is the third Sunset Convocation,' she went on. 'We are not important enough to attend. Besides, I think we of the societies make her uneasy.'

'The third,' Dobraine muttered. 'The ninth sunset after her coronation already. She wasted no time. At least they will all be together. No one of any rank or pretension will miss it, Cairhienin or Tairen.'

Drawing herself up on her knees, Selande managed to make it seem she was meeting Rand eye-to-eye. 'We are ready to dance the blades for you, my Lord Dragon.' Sulin shook her head, wincing, and another Maiden groaned audibly; several looked and smelled ready to do some violence then and there. The Aiel could not decide what to make of these young wetlanders. The problem in Aiel eyes were that they were trying to be Aiel, in a way, to follow *ji'e'toh*, their version of it, anyway. These seven were not the lot; hundreds of the idiots, at least, could be found all over the city, organized into societies in imitation of the Aiel. Half the Aiel Perrin had heard mention them wanted to help; the other half wanted to strangle them.

For himself, he did not care whether they mangled *ji'e'toh* to mincemeat. 'Where is my wife?' he demanded. 'Where is Faile?' The young fools exchanged guarded looks. Guarded!

'She is in the Grand Hall of the Sun,' Selande said slowly. 'She – she is one of Queen – of Colavaere's lady attendants.'

'Put your eyes back in your head, Perrin,' Min whispered. 'She must have a good reason. You know she must.'

Shrugging inside his coat, Perrin tried to gather himself. One of

Colavaere's *attendants*? Whatever her reason, it must be good. That much he was sure of. But what could it be?

Selande and the others were passing guarded looks about again. One of the men, a young fellow with a pointed nose, whispered fierce and low, 'We swore not to tell anyone! Not anyone! On water oath!'

Before Perrin could demand to be told, Rand spoke. 'Selande, lead the way to the Grand Hall. There will be no blades. I am here to see justice done, to all who deserve it.'

Something in his voice made Perrin's hackles rise. A hardness grim as a hammer's face. Faile *did* have a good reason. She had to.

Chapter 5

A Broken Crown

Wide and tall as the corridors were, they felt close, and dim despite tall gilded stand-lamps with mirrors on every branch, lit wherever daylight could not penetrate. Tapestries hung few and far between on the walls, scenes of hunt or battle with people and animals arranged more precisely than ever nature had. Scattered niches held bowls and vases and now and then a small statue, in gold or silver or alabaster, but even the statues seemed to emphasize that they were stone or metal, as if the sculptors had tried to banish curves.

The city's hush was magnified here. The sound of their boots on the floor tiles echoed, a hollow foreboding march, and Perrin did not think it was so to his ears alone. Loial's quivered at every other step, and he peered down crossing corridors as though wondering what might leap out. Min held herself stiffly and took ginger steps, grimacing ruefully when she glanced at Rand; she seemed to make an effort not to walk closer to him, and not particularly pleased with herself over it. The young Cairhienin started off swaggering like peacocks, but that arrogance faded as the drumming of their heels reverberated. Even the Maidens felt it; Sulin was the only one whose hand did not sometimes rise toward the veil hanging down her chest.

There were servants everywhere, of course, pale, narrow-faced men and women in dark coats and dresses with the Rising Sun on the left breast and sleeves striped in Colavaere's colors. Some gaped in recognition as Rand passed by; a handful dropped to their knees, heads bowed. Most went on about their tasks after a small pause for deep bow or curtsy. It was just as in the courtyard. Show proper respect to your betters, whoever they are; obey them and otherwise ignore what they do, and perhaps you will not be entangled in it. It was a way of thinking that set Perrin's teeth on edge. Nobody should have to live that way.

Two fellows in Colavaere's livery, standing before the gilt-covered doors to the Grand Hall of the Sun, frowned at sight of the Maidens, and maybe at the young Cairhienin. Older folk usually looked askance at the younglings' carrying on every bit as much as the Aiel did. More than one parent had tried to put an end to it, had ordered sons or daughters to give over, instructed armsmen and servants to chase off others' like-minded sons and daughters like common vagrants or street ruffians. Perrin would not have been surprised if these doormen slanted their gilded staffs to stop Selande and her friends from going through the open doorway, nobility or not, and perhaps even the Maidens. Few Cairhienin still dared call Aiel savages, not where they could be heard, but most thought it. The pair gathered themselves, drew deep breaths – and saw Rand over the Maidens' heads. Their eyes nearly popped out of their faces. Each man glanced sideways at the other, and then they were on their knees. One stared fixedly at the floor; the other squeezed his eyes shut, and Perrin heard him praying under his breath.

'So am I loved,' Rand said softly. He hardly sounded himself. Min touched his arm, her face pained. Rand patted her hand without looking at her, and for some reason that seemed to pain her even more.

The Grand Hall of the Sun was immense, with an angle-vaulted ceiling a full fifty paces high at its peak and great golden lamps hung on gilded chains thick enough to move the gates of a fortress. It was immense, and it was full, people crowding among massive square columns of blue-black veined marble that stood in two rows to either side of the center aisle. The folk at the rear noticed the newcomers first. In long coats and short, some in bright colors or embroidered, some travel-worn, they stared curiously. Intently. The few women in the back of the hall wore riding dresses and had faces as hard as the men, gazes as direct.

Hunters for the Horn, Perrin thought. Dobraine had said that every noble who could be there would, and most Hunters were nobly born, or claimed to be. Whether or not they recognized Rand, they sensed something, hands feeling for swords and daggers that were not there this evening. More Hunters than not sought adventure and a place in the histories along with the Horn of Valere. Even if they did not know the Dragon Reborn, they knew danger when they saw it.

The others in the Grand Hall were less attuned to danger, or rather, more to intrigues and plots than to open hazard. Perrin was a third of the way down the long center aisle, close on Rand's heels, before gasps ran through the chamber like a wind. Pale Cairhienin Lords with colorful slashes across the chests of their dark silk coats, some with the front of their heads shaved and powdered; Cairhienin ladies with stripes on their dark high-necked gowns and lace falls covering their hands, their hair in intricate towers that often added a good foot of height. Tairen High Lords and Lords of the Land with oiled beards trimmed to points, in velvet hats and coats of red and blue and every color, with puffy, satin-striped sleeves; Tairen ladies in even more colorful gowns, with wide lace ruffs and close caps studded with pearls and moonstones, firedrops and rubies. They knew Perrin, and they knew Dobraine and even Havien and Min, but most importantly, they knew Rand. A ripple of knowing that kept pace up the Hall with him. Eyes widening, jaws dropping, they went so stiff Perrin almost thought the Asha'man had bound them like the guards outside the palace. The chamber was a sea of sweet perfumes, and beneath that undercurrents of salty sweat, but through it oozed fear, a quivering sort of smell.

His attention was all on the far end of the Hall, though, on the deep blue marble dais where the Sun Throne stood, shining like its namesake with gilt, the wavy-rayed Rising Sun huge atop the high back. Colavaere rose slowly, peering down the aisle over Rand's head. Her nearly black dress bore not a single stripe of nobility, but the great mass of curls rising above her head had to have been dressed around the crown she wore, the Rising Sun in gold and yellow diamonds. Seven young women flanked the Sun Throne in dark-bodiced gowns with lace snugged under their chins and skirts striped vertically in Colavaere's yellow and red and silver. It seemed that Cairhienin fashion was different for the Queen, and the Queen's attendants.

A flicker of motion behind the throne picked out an eighth woman, hidden, but Perrin cared about neither Colavaere nor anyone else except the woman to her immediate right. Faile. Her slightly tilted eyes fastened on him, dark liquid moons, yet not a line altered of her coolly decorous expression. If anything, her face grew tighter. His nose strained for the scent of her, but the perfume was too strong, and the fear. She had a reason for being there on the dais, a good reason. She did.

Rand touched Sulin's sleeve. 'Wait here,' he said. Scowling, the scar on her leathery face standing out as white as her hair, she scanned his face, then nodded with obvious reluctance. Her free hand gestured anyway, and another gasp ran through the chamber as the Maidens veiled. It was almost laughable; the eight men in black coats, trying to watch everywhere at once, could probably kill them all before the first Maiden drove home a spear, but no one knew who or what they were. No one looked at them twice, a handful of men with their swords sheathed. Only at the Maidens. And Rand. Hadn't they noticed that not a one of those men sweated a drop more than Rand? Perrin felt as if he were bathing in his.

Stepping past the Maidens with Min still close beside him, Rand stopped as first Perrin, then Dobraine and Havien joined him. And Aram, of course, like Perrin's shadow. Rand studied them each in turn, nodding slowly. He studied Perrin longest, and took the longest time to nod. The gray-haired Cairhienin and the young Mayener wore faces like death. Perrin did not know how his own looked, but his jaw was locked tight. No one was going to harm Faile, no matter what she had done, no matter why. No matter what he had to do to stop it.

Their boots drummed loud in the silence as they crossed the huge golden mosaic of the Rising Sun in the blue-tiled floor and approached the throne. Hands gripping her skirts, Colavaere wet her lips, and her eyes darted between Rand and the doors behind him.

'Looking for Aes Sedai?' Rand's voice echoed. He smiled unpleasantly. 'I sent them to the Aiel camp. If the Aiel can't teach them manners, no one can.' A shocked murmur rose, and fell raggedly. Fear became stronger than the perfumes in Perrin's nose.

Colavaere gave a start. 'Why would I—?' Drawing a deep breath, she gathered dignity. A more than handsome woman in her middle years, without a touch of gray in her dark hair, she bore a regal presence that had nothing to do with the crown. She had been born to command; to reign, so she thought. And her eyes, weighing and measuring, betrayed a hard intelligence. 'My Lord Dragon,' she said, making a curtsy so deep it nearly mocked itself, 'I welcome you back. Cairhien welcomes you back.' The way she said it, she seemed to be repeating herself.

Slowly Rand climbed the steps of the dais. Min half-made to follow him, then folded her arms. Perrin did follow, to be nearer Faile, but only partway. It was her gaze that stopped him. A gaze that probed every bit as much as Colavaere's. At him as much as at Rand. Perrin wished he could smell her. Not to try discovering why or what, just for the smell of her. The wash of perfumes and fright was too great. Why did she not speak? Why did she not come to him? Or smile? Just a smile.

Colavaere stiffened a splinter's worth, but only that. Her head came no more than level with Rand's chest, though her towered hair rose almost as tall as he. His eyes slid from her face and along the women lined up on either side of the throne. He might have paused on Faile. Perrin could not be sure.

Rand rested his hand on one heavy arm of the Sun Throne. 'You know I mean this for Elayne Trakand.' His voice was emotionless.

'My Lord Dragon,' Colavaere replied smoothly, 'Cairhien had been too long without a ruler. A Cairhienin ruler. You yourself said you have no interest in the Sun Throne for yourself. Elayne Trakand would have had some claim,' a small, quick gesture dismissed such a claim, 'if she were alive. Rumor says she is dead, like her mother.' A dangerous thing to say. A good many rumors said Rand had killed both mother and daughter. The woman was no coward.

'Elayne is alive.' The words were still flat as a planed board, but Rand's eyes burned. Perrin could not pick out his smell any more than Faile's, but he did not need his nose to know rage bottled right in front of him. 'She will have the crowns of Andor, and of Cairhien.'

'My Lord Dragon, what is done cannot be undone. If anything has offended you—'

For all her dignity, all her courage, Colavaere made a visible effort not to flinch as Rand reached out and took hold of the Sun Crown. There was a loud crack of metal snapping, and the crown flexed, hardly disarraying her tower of curls as it pulled away, slowly straightening. A few of the brilliant yellow stones popped from their settings and fell. He held up the stretched arc of metal, and slowly it bent back on itself until the ends met, and . . . Maybe the Asha'man could see what happened, could understand, but to Perrin, one moment the crown was broken, the next it was whole again. No one among the nobles made a sound, not even a shuffling of boots; Perrin thought they might be afraid to. To his nose, stark terror was stronger than any other scent now. It did not quiver; it spasmed wildly.

'Whatever can be done,' Rand said softly, 'can be undone.'

Colavaere's face drained of blood. The few wisps of hair that had escaped her coiffure made her seem wild, at bay. Swallowing, she opened her mouth twice before any words came out. 'My Lord Dragon . . .' It was a breathy whisper, but as she went on, her voice became stronger. And edged with desperation. She seemed to forget anyone else was present. 'I have kept the laws you made, maintained your policies. Even those that go against the ancient laws of Cairhien, against all custom.' She probably meant the laws that had let a noble kill a farmer or craftsman and walk away. 'My Lord Dragon, the Sun Throne is yours to give. I . . . know that. I – I was wrong to take it without your leave. But I have the right to it, by birth and blood. If I must have it from your hand, then give it to me, by your hand. I have the right!' Rand only looked at her; he said nothing. He seemed to be listening, but not to her.

Perrin cleared his throat. Why was Rand dragging this out? It was done, or nearly. Let whatever else had to be done, be done. Then he could take Faile away, where they could talk. 'Did you have the right to murder Lord Maringil and High Lord Meilan?' Perrin demanded. There was no doubt in his mind she had had it done; they had been her biggest rivals for the throne. Or she, and they, thought they were, anyway. Why was Rand just standing there? He knew all of this. 'Where is Berelain?'

Before the name was off his tongue he wanted to call it back. Faile only glanced at him, her face still a cool mask of propriety, but that glance could have set water aflame. 'A jealous wife is like a hornets' nest in your mattress,' the saying went. No matter how you twitched, you got stung.

'You dare accuse me of so vile a crime?' Colavaere demanded. 'There is no proof. There can be no proof! Not when I am innocent.' Abruptly she seemed to become aware of where she was, of the nobles crowded shoulder-to-shoulder among the columns, watching and listening. Whatever else could be said of her, she did have courage. Standing straight, she did her best to stare Rand in the eye without tilting her head too far back. 'My Lord Dragon, eight days ago at sunrise I was crowned Queen of Cairhien according to the laws and usages of Cairhien. I will keep my oath of fealty to you, but I *am* Queen of Cairhien.' Rand only stared at her, silent. And troubled, Perrin would have said. 'My Lord Dragon, I am Queen, unless you would rip all our laws away.' Still silence from Rand, and an unblinking stare.

Why doesn't he end it? Perrin wondered.

'These charges against me are false. They are mad!' Only that silent stare for answer. Colavaere moved her head uneasily. 'Annoura, advise me. Come, Annoura! Advise me!'

Perrin thought she spoke to one of the women with Faile, but the woman who stepped from behind the throne did not wear the striped skirts of an attendant. A broad face with a wide mouth and a beak of a nose regarded Rand from beneath dozens of long thin dark braids. An ageless face. To Perrin's surprise, Havien made a sound in his throat and began grinning. His own hackles were standing straight.

'I cannot do this, Colavaere,' the Aes Sedai said in a Taraboner accent, shifting her gray-fringed shawl. 'I fear I have allowed you to misperceive my relationship to you.' Drawing a deep breath, she added, 'There ... there is no need for this, Master al'Thor.' Her voice became slightly unsteady for a moment. 'Or my Lord Dragon, if you prefer. I assure you, I harbor no ill intentions toward you. If I did, I would have struck before you knew I was here.'

'You might well have died if you had.' Rand's voice was icy steel; his face made it seem soft. 'I'm not who has you shielded, Aes Sedai. Who are you? Why are you here? Answer me! I don't have much patience with ... your kind. Unless you want to be hauled out to the Aiel camp? I wager the Wise Ones can make you speak freely.'

This Annoura was not slow-witted. Her eyes darted to Aram, then to the aisle where the Asha'man stood. And she knew. They had to be who he meant, in their black coats, grim faces dry when every other but hers and Rand's glistened. Young Jahar was watching her like a hawk watching a rabbit. Incongruously, Loial stood in the midst of them with his axe propped against his shoulder. One big hand managed to hold an ink bottle and an open book, pressed awkwardly against his chest, while the other scribbled as fast as he could dip a pen fatter than Perrin's thumb. He was taking notes. Here!

The nobles heard Rand as well as Annoura did. They had been watching the veiled Maidens uneasily; now they crowded back from the Asha'man, pressing together like fish in a barrel. Here and there someone sagged in a faint, held up by the throng.

Shivering, Annoura adjusted her shawl, and regained all the vaunted Aes Sedai composure. 'I am Annoura Larisen, my Lord Dragon. Of the Gray Ajah.' Nothing about her said that she was shielded, and in the presence of men who could channel. She seemed to answer as a favor. 'I am the advisor to Berelain, First of Mayene.' So that was why Havien was grinning like a madman; he had recognized the woman. Perrin did not feel like grinning at all. 'This has been kept secret, you understand,' she went on, 'because of the attitude of Tear both toward Mayene and toward Aes Sedai, but I think me the time for secrets, it is past, yes?' Annoura turned to Colavaere, and her mouth firmed. 'I let you think what you would think, but Aes Sedai do not become advisors simply because someone tells them they are. Most especially when they already advise someone else.'

'If Berelain confirms your story,' Rand said, 'I will parole you to her custody.' Looking at the crown, he seemed to realize for the first time that the spray of gold and gems was still in his hand. Very gently he set it on the silk-covered seat of the Sun Throne. 'I don't think every Aes Sedai is my enemy, not entirely, but I won't be schemed against, and I won't be manipulated, not anymore. It's your choice, Annoura, but if you make the wrong one, you will go to the Wise Ones. If you live long enough. I won't hobble the Asha'man, and a mistake could cost you.'

'The Asha'man,' Annoura said calmly. 'I quite understand.' But she touched her lips with her tongue.

'My Lord Dragon, Colavaere plotted to break her oath of fealty.' Perrin had wished so hard for Faile to speak that he jumped when she did, stepping out of the line of attendants. Choosing her words carefully, she confronted the would-be queen like a stooping eagle. Light, but she was beautiful! 'Colavaere swore to obey you in all things and uphold your laws, but she has made plans to rid Cairhien of the Aiel, to send them south and return all to as it was before you came. She also said that if you ever returned, you would not dare change anything she had done. The woman she told these things, Maire, was one of her attendants. Maire vanished soon after telling me. I have no proof, but I believe she is dead. I believe Colavaere regretted revealing too much of her mind, too soon.'

Dobraine strode up the steps to the dais, his helmet under his arm. His face might have been cold iron. 'Colavaere Saighan,' he announced in a formal voice that carried to every corner of the

Grand Hall, 'by my immortal soul, under the Light, I, Dobraine, High Seat of House Taborwin, do arraign and censure you of treason, the penalty for which is death.'

Rand's head went back, eyes closed. His mouth moved slightly, but Perrin knew that only he and Rand heard what was said. 'No. I cannot. I will not.' Perrin understood the delay now. Rand was searching for a way out. Perrin wished he could see one.

Colavaere certainly did not hear, but she wanted a way out, too. She looked around wildly, to the Sun Throne, to her other attendants, to the assembled nobility, as though they might step forward to defend her. Their feet could as well have been set in cement; a sea of carefully blank, sweaty faces confronted her, and eyes that avoided hers. Some of those eyes rolled toward the Asha'man, but not too openly. The already considerable space between nobles and Asha'man widened noticeably.

'Lies!' she hissed, hands knotted in her skirts. 'All lies! You sneaking little—!' She took a step toward Faile. Rand stretched his arm between them, though Colavaere appeared not to see it, and Faile looked as though she wished he had not. Anyone who attacked her was in for a surprise.

'Faile does not lie!' Perrin growled. Well, not about something like this.

Once again Colavaere recovered herself. Slight as her height was, she drew up every inch of it. Perrin almost admired her. Except for Meilan, and Maringil, and this Maire, and the Light alone knew how many others. 'I demand justice, my Lord Dragon.' Her voice was calm, stately. Royal. 'There is no proof of any of this ... this filth. A claim that someone who is no longer in Cairhien says I spoke words I never did? I demand the Lord Dragon's justice. By your own laws, there must be proof.'

'How do you know she is no longer in Cairhien?' Dobraine demanded. 'Where is she?'

'I assume she has gone.' She addressed her answer to Rand. 'Maire left my service, and I replaced her with Reale, there.' She gestured toward the third attendant on the left: 'I have no idea where she is. Bring her forward if she is in the city, and let her make these ridiculous charges to my face. I will fling her lies in her face.'

Faile looked murder at her. Perrin hoped she would not produce one of those knives she kept hidden about her; she had a habit of doing that when she became angry enough.

Annoura cleared her throat. She had been studying Rand much too closely for Perrin's comfort. She reminded him of Verin suddenly, that look of a bird examining a worm. 'May I speak, Master ... ah ... my Lord Dragon?' At his curt nod, she went on, adjusting her shawl. 'Of young Maire, I know nothing except that one morning she was here, and before nightfall, she was nowhere to be found and none knew where she had gone. But Lord Maringil and High Lord Meilan, they are a different matter. The First of Mayene, she brought with her two most excellent thief-catchers, men experienced in ferreting out crimes. They have brought before me two of the men who waylaid the High Lord Meilan in the streets, though both insist they only held his arms while others did the stabbing. Also they brought me the servant who put poison in the spiced wine Lord Maringil liked to drink at bedtime. She also protests her true innocence; her invalid mother would have died, and she herself, had Lord Maringil not. So she says, and in her case, I believe she speaks truly. Her solace at confession was not false, I think. Both the men and the woman agree in this: the orders for their actions came from the mouth of Lady Colavaere herself.'

Word by word the defiance leached out of Colavaere. She still stood, yet it seemed a wonder; she appeared as limp as a damp rag. 'They promised,' she mumbled to Rand. 'They promised you would never return.' Too late, she clamped both hands over her mouth. Her eyes bulged. Perrin wished he could not hear the sounds coming from her throat. No one should make sounds like that.

'Treason and murder.' Dobraine sounded satisfied. Those whimpered screams did not touch him. 'The penalty is the same, my Lord Dragon. Death. Except, by your new law, it is hanging for murder.' For some reason, Rand looked at Min. She returned his gaze with profound sadness. Not for Colavaere. For Rand. Perrin wondered whether a viewing was involved.

'I – I demand the headsman,' Colavaere managed in a strangled voice. Her face sagged. She had become old on the spot, and her eyes were mirrors of stark terror. But with nothing left, she fought on, for the scraps. 'It is – it is my right. I will not be . . . hanged like some commoner!'

Rand seemed to struggle with himself, shaking his head in that disturbing way. When he spoke at last, his words were winter cold and anvil hard. 'Colavaere Saighan, I strip you of your titles.' He drove the words like nails. 'I strip you of your lands and estates and possessions, of everything but the dress you stand in. Do you own – did you own a farm? A small farm?'

Each sentence staggered the woman. She swayed drunkenly on her feet, soundlessly mouthing the word 'farm' as if she had never heard it before. Annoura, Faile, everyone stared at Rand in amazement or curiosity or both. Perrin not least. A *farm*? If there had been silence in the Grand Hall before, now it seemed that no one even breathed.

'Dobraine, did she own a small farm?'

'She owns . . . owned . . . many farms, my Lord Dragon,' the Cairhienin replied slowly. Clearly he understood no more than Perrin did. 'Most are large. But the lands near the Dragonwall have always been divided into smallholdings, less than fifty hides. All of the tenants abandoned them during the Aiel War.'

Rand nodded. 'Time to change that. Too much land has lain fallow too long. I want to move people back there, to farm again. Dobraine, you will find out which farm of those Colavaere owned near the Dragonwall is the smallest. Colavaere, I exile you to that farm. Dobraine will see you're provided with what is needed to make a farm work, and with someone to teach you how to till the soil. And with guards to see that you never go farther from it than you can walk in a day, so long as you live. See to it, Dobraine. In a week I want her on her way.' A bewildered Dobraine hesitated before nodding. Perrin could catch murmurs from the assembly behind him now. This was unheard of. None understood why she was not to die. And the rest! Estates had been confiscated before, but never all, never nobility itself. Nobles had been exiled, even for life, but never to a *farm*.

Colavaere's response was immediate. Eyes rolling up in her head, she collapsed, crumpling backward toward the steps.

Perrin darted to catch her, but someone was ahead of him. Before he had taken a full step, her fall simply stopped. She slumped in midair, slanting over the steps to the dais, head dangling. Slowly, her unconscious form rose, swung around and settled gently in front of the Sun Throne. Rand. Perrin was sure the Asha'man would have let her fall.

Annoura *tsk*ed. She did not appear surprised, or perturbed, except that her thumbs rubbed her forefingers nervously. 'I suspect she would have preferred the headsman. I will see to her if you have your man, your ... Asha'man ...'

'She's not your concern,' Rand said roughly. 'She is alive, and ... She is alive.' He drew a long, ragged breath. Min was there before he let it out; she only stood near him, yet she looked as if she wanted to do something more. Slowly his face firmed. 'Annoura, you will take me to Berelain. Release her, Jahar; she'll be no trouble. Not with one of her and nine of us. I want to find out what has been going on while I was away, Annoura. And what Berelain means bringing you here behind my back. No, don't speak. I'll hear it from her. Perrin, I know you want some time with Faile. I—'

Rand's gaze swept slowly around the hall, over all the nobles waiting silently. Under his stare, none dared move a muscle. The scent of fear far outweighed any other, convulsing sharply. Except for the Hunters, everyone there had given him the same oath as had Colavaere. Perhaps just being in this gathering was treason, too? Perrin did not know.

'This audience is at an end,' Rand said. 'I will forget every face that departs now.'

Those at the front, the highest-ranking, the most powerful, began their progress toward the doors without too much haste, avoiding the Maidens and the Asha'man standing in the aisle, while the rest waited their turn. Every mind must have been turning over what Rand had said, though. What precisely did he mean by 'now'? Purposeful strides quickened, skirts were lifted. Hunters, nearest the doors, began slipping out, first one at a time, then in a flood, and seeing them, lesser nobles among the Cairhienin and Tairens darted ahead of the higher. In moments it was a milling mass at the doors, men and women pushing and elbowing to get out. Not one looked back at the woman stretched out before the throne she had held so briefly.

Chapter 6

Old Fear, and New Fear

Rand passed through the struggling mob without any difficulty, of course. Maybe it was the presence of the Maidens and the Asha'man, or maybe Rand or one of the black-coated fellows did something with the Power, but the crowd parted for him, with Min holding to his arm, and a very subdued Annoura attempting to speak to him, and Loial, who was still trying with some difficulty to write in his book *and* carry his axe. Staring at one another, Perrin and Faile missed their chance to join them before the crowd closed up again.

She said nothing for a time, and neither did he, not what he wanted to say, not with Aram there, staring at them like some worshipful hound. And Dobraine, frowning down at the unconscious woman put in his charge. No one else remained on the dais. Havien had gone with Rand, to find Berelain, and as soon as Rand went, the other attendants had darted away toward the doors without a second glance at Perrin or Faile. Or Colavaere. Without the first glance, for that matter. They just lifted their striped skirts and ran. Grunts and curses drifted from the pack, not all in men's voices. Even with Rand gone, those people wanted to be elsewhere, and now. Perhaps they thought Perrin stayed to watch and report, though had any glanced back, they would have seen his eyes were not on them.

Climbing the rest of the way, he took Faile's hand and breathed in the scent of her. This close, the lingering perfumes did not matter. Anything else could wait. She produced a red lace fan from somewhere, and before spreading it to cool herself, touched first her cheek, then his. There was a whole language of fans in her native Saldaea. She had taught him a little. He wished he knew what the cheek-touching meant; it must be something good. On the other hand, her scent carried a spiky shading he knew too well.

'He should have sent her to the block,' Dobraine muttered, and Perrin shrugged uncomfortably. From the man's tone, it was not clear whether he meant that that was what the law called for or that it would have been more merciful. Dobraine did not understand. Rand could have sprouted wings first.

Faile's fan slowed to barely moving, and she eyed Dobraine sideways over the crimson lace. 'Her death might be best for everyone. That is the prescribed penalty. What will you do, Lord Dobraine?' Sidelong or not, it still managed to be very direct, a very meaningful gaze.

Perrin frowned. Not a word for him, but questions for Dobraine? And there was that undertone of jealousy in her aroma, making him sigh.

The Cairhienin gave her a level look in return while thrusting his gauntlets behind his sword belt. 'What I was commanded to do. I keep my oaths, Lady Faile.'

The fan snapped open and shut, faster than thought. 'He actually sent Aes Sedai to the Aiel? As prisoners?' Disbelief tinged her voice.

'Some, Lady Faile.' Dobraine hesitated. 'Some swore fealty on their knees. This I saw with my own eyes. They went to the Aiel, too, but I do not think they can be called prisoners.'

'I saw it, too, my Lady,' Aram put in from his place on the steps, and a wide smile split his face when she glanced at him.

Red lace described a fluttering hitch. What she did with the fan seemed almost unconscious. 'You both saw.' The relief in her voice — and in her scent — was so strong that Perrin stared.

'What did you think, Faile? Why would Rand lie, especially when everyone would know in a day?'

Instead of answering immediately, she frowned down at Colavaere. 'Is she still under? Not that it matters, I suppose. She knows more than I would say here. Everything we worked so hard to keep hidden. She let that slip to Maire, too. She knows too much.'

Dobraine thumbed one of Colavaere's eyes open none too gently. 'As if hit with a mace. A pity she did not break her neck on the steps. But she will go to her exile and learn to live as a farmer.' A brief, jaggedy, vexed smell wafted from Faile.

Abruptly it hit Perrin what his wife had been proposing, so obliquely; what Dobraine had rejected just as indirectly. Every hair on his body tried to stand. From the start he had known that he had married a very dangerous woman. Just not how dangerous. Aram was peering at Colavaere, his lips pursed in dark thought; the man would do anything for Faile.

'I don't think Rand would like it if anything prevented her reaching that farm,' Perrin said firmly, eyeing Aram and Faile in turn. '*I* wouldn't like it, either.' He felt rather proud of himself. That was talking around the point as well as any of them.

Aram bowed his head briefly – he understood – but Faile tried to look innocent above her gently fluttering fan, with no notion what he was talking about. Suddenly he realized not all the fear scent came from the people still milling at the door. A thin, quivering thread of it wafted from her. Fear under control, yet it was there.

'What's the matter, Faile? Light, you'd think Coiren and that lot had won instead of . . .' Her face did not change, but the thread grew thicker. 'Is that why you didn't say anything at first?' he asked softly. 'Were you afraid we had come back as puppets, and them pulling the strings?'

She eyed the rapidly diminishing crowd across the Grand Hall. The nearest of them was a long way, and all making a good deal of noise, but she lowered her voice even so. 'Aes Sedai can do that sort of thing, I've heard. My husband, no one knows more than I that even Aes Sedai would find hard times trying to make you dance for a puppet, much harder than a man who's just the Dragon Reborn, but when you walked in here, I was more afraid than at any time since you left.' Amusement trickled through in the first of that, like tiny bubbles in his nose, and warm fondness, and love, the smell of her, clear and pure and strong, but all of those faded by the end, leaving that thin trembling thread.

'Light, Faile, it's true. Every word Rand said. You heard Dobraine, and Aram.' She smiled, and nodded, and worked her fan. That thread still quivered in his nostrils, though. *Blood and ashes, what does it take to convince her?* 'Would it help if he had Verin dance the *sa'sara*? She will, if he tells her to.' He meant it for a joke. All he knew of the *sa'sara* was that it was scandalous – and that Faile had once admitted knowing how to dance it, though recently she sidestepped and all but denied it. He meant it for a joke, but she closed her fan and tapped it on her wrist. He knew that one. *I am giving your suggestion serious thought.*

'I don't know what would be enough, Perrin.' She shivered slightly. 'Is there anything an Aes Sedai would not do, or put up with, if the White Tower told her to? I have studied my history, and I was taught to read between the lines. Mashera Donavelle bore seven children for a man she loathed, whatever the stories say, and Isebaille Tobanyi delivered the brothers she loved to their enemies and the throne of Arad Doman with them, and Jestian Redhill . . .' She shivered again, not so slightly.

'It's all right,' he murmured, wrapping her in his arms. He had studied several books of history himself, but he had never seen those names. The daughter of a lord received a different education from a blacksmith's apprentice. 'It really is true.' Dobraine averted his eyes, and so did Aram, though with a pleased grin.

She resisted at first, but not very hard. He could never be sure when she would avoid a public embrace and when welcome it, only that if she did not want one, she made it clear in no uncertain terms, with or without words. This time she snuggled her face into his chest and hugged him back, squeezing harder.

'If any Aes Sedai ever harms you,' she whispered, 'I will kill her.' He believed her. 'You belong to me, Perrin t'Bashere Aybara. To me.' He believed that, too. As her hug grew fiercer, so did the thorny scent of jealousy. He almost chuckled. It seemed the right to put a knife in him was reserved to her. He would have chuckled, except that filament of fear remained. That, and what she had said about Maire. He could not smell himself, but he knew what was there. Fear. Old fear, and new fear, for the next time.

The last of the nobles forced their way from the Grand Hall, without anyone being trampled. Sending Aram off to tell Dannil to bring the Two Rivers men into the city – and wondering how he was going to feed them – Perrin offered Faile his arm and led her out, leaving Dobraine with Colavaere, who was finally showing signs of awakening. He had no wish to be around when she woke, and Faile, with her hand on his wrist, seemed not to either. They walked quickly, eager to reach their rooms, if not necessarily for the same reasons.

The nobles apparently had not stopped their flight once they were out of the Grand Hall. The corridors were empty except for servants who kept their eyes down and moved at a silent rush, but before they had gone very far, Perrin caught the sound of footsteps and realized they were being followed. It seemed unlikely that Colavaere had any open supporters still, but if there were any, they might think to strike at Rand through his friend, walking alone with his wife while the Dragon Reborn was elsewhere.

Only, when Perrin spun about, hand to his axe, he stared instead of drawing the weapon. It was Selande and her friends from the entry hall, with eight or nine new faces. They gave a start when he turned, and exchanged abashed glances. Some were Tairens, including a woman who stood taller than all but one of the Cairhienin men. She wore a man's coat and tight breeches, just like Selande and the rest of the women, with a sword on her hip. He had not heard that this nonsense had spread to the Tairens.

'Why are you following us?' he demanded. 'If you try to make me any of your woolhead trouble, I vow I'll kick the lot of you from here to Bel Tine!' He had had problems before with these idiots, or some just like them, anyway. All they thought about was their honor, and fighting duels, and taking one another *gai'shain*. That last really set the Aiel's teeth on edge.

'Attend my husband and obey,' Faile put in sharply. 'He is not a man to be trifled with.' Gawking stares vanished, and they backed away, bowing, competing over flourishes. They were still at it when they vanished around a turn.

'Bloody young buffoons,' Perrin muttered, offering Faile his wrist again.

'My husband is wise in his years,' she murmured. Her tone was utterly serious; her smell was something else again.

Perrin managed not to snort. True, a few of them might be a year or two older than he, but they all were like children with their playing at Aiel. Now, with Faile in a good mood, seemed as good a time as any to begin what they had to talk about. What he had to talk about. 'Faile, how did you come to be one of Colavaere's attendants?'

'The servants, Perrin.' She spoke softly; nobody two steps away could have heard a word. She knew all about his hearing, and the wolves. That was nothing a man could keep from his wife. Her fan touched her ear, admonishing caution in speech. 'Too many people forget servants are there, but servants listen too. In Cairhien, they listen far too much.'

None of the liveried people he saw were doing any listening. The few who did not duck down side corridors when they saw him and Faile went by at a near run, gazes on the floor and gathered in on themselves. Any sort of news spread quickly in Cairhien. Events in the Grand Hall would have flown. The word was in the streets by now, probably on its way out of the city already. Without any doubt there were eyes-and-ears in Cairhien for the Aes Sedai, and the Whitecloaks, and likely more thrones than not.

In that hushed voice, she went on despite her caution to him. 'Colavaere could not be fast enough to take me in, once she learned who I am. My father's name impressed her as much as my cousin's.' She finished with a little nod, as if she had answered everything.

It was a good enough answer. Almost. Her father was Davram, High Seat of House Bashere, Lord of Bashere, Tyr and Sidona, Guardian of the Blightborder, Defender of the Heartland, and Marshal-General to Queen Tenobia of Saldaea. Faile's cousin was Tenobia herself. More than reason for Colavaere to leap at Faile for one of her attendants. But he had had time to mull things over now, and he prided himself that he was becoming used to her ways. Married life taught a man about women; or about one woman, anyway. The answer she had not given, confirmed something. Faile had no concept of danger, not where she herself was concerned.

He could not speak of it there in the corridor, of course. Whisper how he would, she did not have his ears, and doubtless she would insist every servant within fifty paces was listening. Holding his patience, he walked on with her until they reached the rooms that had been set aside for them what seemed an age ago now. The lamps had been lit, making shimmers on the dark polished walls, each tall wooden panel carved in concentric rectangles. In the square stone fireplace the hearth was swept bare and laid with a few pitiful branches of leatherleaf. They were almost green.

Faile went straight to a small table where two golden pitchers stood beaded with moisture on a tray. 'They have left us blueberry tea, my husband, and wine punch. The wine is from Tharon, I think. They cool the punch in the cisterns beneath the palace. Which would you prefer?'

Perrin unbuckled his belt and tossed belt and axe on a chair. He had planned out what he had to say very carefully on the way here. She could be a prickly woman. 'Faile, I missed you more than I can say, and worried about you, but—'

'Worried about me!' she snapped, spinning to face him. She stood straight and tall, eyes fierce as those of her falcon namesake, and her fan made a coring motion toward his middle. Not part of the language of fans; she made the same gesture with a knife sometimes. 'When almost the first words from your mouth were to ask after that . . . that *woman*!'

His jaw dropped. How could he have forgotten the smell filling his nostrils? He nearly put a hand up to see whether his nose was bleeding. 'Faile, I wanted her thief-catchers. Be—' No, he was not stupid enough to repeat that name. 'She said she had proof of the poison before I left. You heard her! I just wanted the proof, Faile.'

It did no good. That spiky stench softened not a whit, and the thin, sour smell of hurt joined it. What under the Light had he said to hurt her?

'*Her* proof! What *I* gathered went for nothing, but *her* proof put Colavaere's head on the block. Or should have.' That was his opening, but she was not about to let him push a word in edgewise. She advanced on him, looking daggers, her fan darting like one. All he could do was back away. 'Do you know what story that woman put about?' Faile almost hissed. A black viper could not have dripped so much venom. 'Do you? She said the reason you were not here was that you were at a manor not far from the city. Where she could *visit* you! I told the story I prepared – that you were hunting, and the

Light knows you spent enough days hunting! – but everyone believed I was putting a good face on you and her! Together! Colavaere delighted in it. I could believe she only took that Mayener strumpet as an attendant to throw the two of us together. "Faile, Berelain, come lace my gown." "Faile, Berelain, come hold the mirror for the hairdresser." "Faile, Berelain, come wash my back." So she could amuse herself waiting for us to claw one another's eyes out! That is what I have put up with! For you, you hairy-eared—!'

His back thumped against the wall. And something snapped inside him. He had been frightened spitless for her, terrified, ready to face down Rand or the Dark One himself. And he had done nothing, had never encouraged Berelain, had done everything in his wits to chase the woman away. For which his thanks was this.

Gently he took her by the shoulders and lifted her until those big tilted eyes were level with his. 'You listen to me,' he said calmly. He tried to make his voice calm, at least; it came out more of a growl in his throat. 'How dare you speak to me like that? How *dare* you? I worried myself near to death for fear you'd been hurt. I love you, and nobody else but you. I want no other woman but you. Do you hear me? Do you?' Crushing her to his chest, he held her, wanting to never let her go. Light, he had been so afraid. He shook even now, for what might have been. 'If anything happened to you, I'd die, Faile. I would lie down on your grave and die! Do you think I don't know how Colavaere found out who you are? You made sure she found out.' Spying, she had told him once, was a wife's work. 'Light, woman, you could have ended like Maire. Colavaere knows you're my wife. *My* wife. Perrin Aybara, Rand al'Thor's friend. Did it ever occur to you she might be suspicious? She could have ... Light, Faile, she could have ... '

Abruptly he realized what he was doing. She was making sounds against his chest, but no words he could recognize. He wondered that he did not hear her ribs creaking. Berating himself for being an oaf, he let her go, arms springing apart, but before he could apologize, her fingers clutched his beard.

'So you love me?' she said softly. Very softly. Very warmly. She was smiling, too. 'A woman likes to hear that said the right way.'

She had dropped the fan, and her free hand drew fingernails down his cheek, not far from hard enough to draw blood, but her throaty laugh held heat, and the smoldering in her eyes was as far from anger as possible. 'A good thing you didn't say you never looked at another woman, or I would think you had gone blind.'

He was too stunned for words, too stunned even to gape. Rand understood women, Mat understood women, but Perrin knew he never would. She was always as much kingfisher as falcon, changing direction faster than he could think, yet this . . . That thorny scent was gone completely, and in its place was another smell of her he knew well. A smell that *was* her, pure and strong and clean. Add that to her eyes, and any moment she was going to say something about farmgirls at harvest. They were notorious, apparently, Saldaean farmgirls.

'As for you lying down on my grave,' she went on, 'if you do, my soul will haunt yours, I promise you. You will mourn me a decent time, and then you'll find yourself another wife. Someone I'd approve of, I hope.' With a soft laugh, she stroked his beard. 'You really aren't fit to take care of yourself, you know. I want your promise.'

Best not to crack his teeth on that. Say he would not, and this wonderful mood might be swallowed in a firestorm. Quicksilver was not in it, really. Say he would . . . By the smell of her, every word was the Light's pure truth, but he would believe that when horses roosted in trees. He cleared his throat. 'I need to bathe. I haven't seen soap in I don't know how long. I must smell like an old barn.'

Leaning against his chest, she drew a deep breath. 'You smell wonderful. Like you.' Her hands moved on his shoulders. 'I feel as—' The door banged open.

'Perrin, Berelain isn't— I'm sorry. Forgive me.' Rand stood shifting his feet, not at all like the Dragon Reborn. There were Maidens in the hallway outside. Min put her head around the doorframe, took one look, grinned at Perrin and ducked back out of sight.

Faile stepped away so smoothly, so stately, that no one would ever have guessed what she had been saying a moment before. Or what she had been about to say. There were spots of color in her cheeks, though, bright and hot. 'So kind of you, my Lord Dragon,' she said coolly, 'to drop in so unexpectedly. I apologize for not hearing your knock.' Maybe those blushes were as much anger as embarrassment.

It was Rand's turn to blush, and scrub a hand through his hair. 'Berelain isn't in the palace. She's spending the night on that Sea Folk ship anchored in the river, of all things. Annoura didn't tell me till I was nearly to Berelain's apartments.'

Perrin tried very hard not to wince. Why did he have to keep saying the woman's name? 'You wanted to talk to me about something else, Rand?' He hoped he had not put too much emphasis in that, yet he hoped Rand caught it. He did not look at Faile, but he tested the air gingerly. No jealousy, not yet. A good deal of anger, however.

For a moment Rand stared at him, looked through him. Listening to something else. Perrin folded his arms to stop from shuddering.

'I need to know,' Rand said finally. 'Are you still unwilling to command the army against Illian? I have to know now.'

'I'm no general,' Perrin said raggedly. There would be battles in Illian. Images flashed in his head. Men all around him, and the axe in his hands spinning, hewing his way through. Always more men, however many he cut down, in endless ranks. And in his heart, a seed growing. He could not face that again. He would not. 'Besides, I thought I was supposed to stay close to you.' That was what Min had said, from one of her viewings. Twice Perrin had to be there, or Rand would go down to disaster. Once had been Dumai's Wells, maybe, but there was still another to come.

'We all must take risks.' Rand's voice was very quiet. And very hard. Min peered around the doorframe again, looking as if she wanted to come to him, but she glanced at Faile and stayed outside.

'Rand, the Aes Sedai . . . ' A smart man would let this lie, probably. He had never claimed to be particularly smart, though. 'The Wise Ones are ready to skin them alive, or near enough. You can't let them be harmed, Rand.' In the corridor, Sulin turned to study him through the doorway.

The man he thought he knew laughed, a wheezing sound. 'We all have to take risks,' he repeated.

'I won't let them be hurt, Rand.'

Cold blue eyes met his gaze. '*You* won't let it?'

'*I* won't,' Perrin told him levelly. He did not flinch from that stare, either. 'They are prisoners, and no threat. They're women.'

'They are Aes Sedai.' Rand's voice was so like Aram's back at Dumai's Wells that it nearly took Perrin's breath.

'Rand—'

'I do what I have to do, Perrin.' For a moment he was the old Rand, not liking what was happening. For a moment he looked tired to death. A moment only. Then he was the new Rand again, hard enough to mark steel. 'I won't harm any Aes Sedai who doesn't deserve it, Perrin. I can't promise more. Since you don't want the army, I can use you elsewhere. Just as well, really. I wish I could let you rest longer than a day or two, but I can't. There's no time. No time, and we must do what we must. Forgive me for interrupting you.' He sketched a bow, one hand on the hilt of his sword. 'Faile.'

Perrin tried to catch his arm, but he was out of the room, the door closing behind him, before Perrin could move. Rand was not really Rand anymore, it seemed. A day or two? Where in the Light did Rand mean him to go, if not to the army gathering down on the Plains of Maredo?

'My husband,' Faile breathed, 'you have the courage of three men. And the sense of a child on leading strings. Why is it that as a man's courage goes up, his sense goes down?'

Perrin grunted indignantly. He refrained from mentioning women who set themselves to spy on people who had committed murders and almost certainly knew they were spying. Women always talked about how logical they were compared to men, but for himself, he had seen precious little of it.

'Well, perhaps I don't really want the answer even if you know it.' Stretching with her arms over her head, she gave a throaty laugh. 'Besides, I don't mean to let him spoil the mood. I still feel as forward as a farmgirl at— Why are you laughing? Stop laughing at me, Perrin t'Bashere Aybara! Stop it, I say, you uncouth oaf! If you don't—'

The only way to put an end to it was to kiss her. In her arms he forgot Rand and Aes Sedai and battles. Where Faile was, was home.

Chapter 7

Pitfalls and Tripwires

Rand felt the Dragon Scepter in his hand, felt every line of the carved Dragons against his heron-branded palm as clearly as if he were running his fingers over them, yet it seemed someone else's hand. If a blade cut it off, he would feel the pain – and keep going. It would be another's pain.

He floated in the Void, surrounded by emptiness beyond knowing, and *saidin* filled him, trying to grind him to dust beneath steel-shattering cold and heat where stone would flash to flame, carrying the Dark One's taint on its flow, forcing corruption into his bones. Into his soul, he feared sometimes. It did not make him feel so sick to his stomach as it once had. He feared that even more. And larded through that torrent of fire, ice and filth – life. That was the best word. *Saidin* tried to destroy him. *Saidin* filled him to overflowing with vitality. It threatened to bury him, and it enticed him. The war for survival, the struggle to avoid being consumed, magnified the joy of pure life. So sweet even with the foulness. What would it be like, clean? Beyond imagining. He wanted to draw more, draw all there was.

There lay the deadly seduction. One slip, and the ability to channel would be seared out of him forever. One slip and his mind was gone, if he was not simply destroyed on the spot, and maybe everything around him too. It was not madness, focusing on the fight for existence; it was like highwalking blindfolded over a pit full of sharpened stakes, basking in so pure a sense of life that thinking of giving it up was like thinking of a world forever in shades of gray. Not madness.

His thoughts whirled through his dance with *saidin*, slid across the Void. Annoura, peering at him with that Aes Sedai gaze. What was Berelain playing at? She had never mentioned an Aes Sedai advisor. And those other Aes Sedai in Cairhien. Where had they come from, and why? The rebels outside the city. What had emboldened them to move? What did they intend now? How could he stop them, or use them? He was becoming good at using people; sometimes he made himself sick. Sevanna and the Shaido. Rhuarc already had scouts on the way to Kinslayer's Dagger, but at best they could only find out where and when. The Wise Ones who could find out why, would not. There were a lot of why's connected to Sevanna. Elayne, and Aviendha. No, he would not think of them. No thoughts of them. None. Perrin, and Faile. A fierce woman, falcon by name and nature. Had she really attached herself to Colavaere just to gather evidence? She would try to protect Perrin if the Dragon Reborn fell. Protect him from the Dragon Reborn, should she decide it necessary; her loyalties were to Perrin, but she would decide for herself how to meet them. Faile was no woman to do meekly as her husband told her, if such a woman existed. Golden eyes, staring challenge and defiance. Why was Perrin so vehement about the Aes Sedai? He had been a long time with Kiruna and her companions on the road to Dumai's Wells. Could Aes Sedai really do with him what everybody feared? Aes Sedai. He shook his head without being aware. Never again. Never! To trust was to be betrayed; trust was pain.

He tried to push that thought away. It came a little too close to raving. Nobody could live without giving trust somewhere. Just not to Aes Sedai. Mat, Perrin. If he could not trust them ... Min. Never a thought of not trusting Min. He wished she were with him, instead of snugged in her bed. All those days a prisoner, days of worry – more for him than herself, if he knew her – days of being questioned by Galina and ill-treated when her answers failed to please – unconsciously he ground his teeth – all of that, and the strain of being Healed on top of it, had caught up with her at last. She had stayed by his side until her legs gave way, and he had to carry her to her bedchamber, with her sleepily protesting all the way that he needed her with him. No Min here, no comforting presence to make him laugh, make him forget the Dragon Reborn. Only the war with *saidin*, and the whirlwind of his thoughts, and ...

They must be done away with. You must do it. Don't you remember the last time? That place by the wells was a pittance. Cities burned whole out of the earth were nothing. We destroyed the world! DO YOU HEAR ME? THEY HAVE TO BE KILLED, WIPED FROM THE FACE ... !

Not his, that voice shouting inside his skull. Not Rand al'Thor. Lews Therin Telamon, more than three thousand years dead. And talking in Rand al'Thor's head. The Power often drew him out of his hiding place in the shadows of Rand's mind. Sometimes Rand wondered how that could be. He *was* Lews Therin reborn, the Dragon Reborn, no denying that, but everybody was someone reborn, a hundred someones, a thousand, more. That was how the Pattern worked; everyone died and was reborn, again and again as the Wheel turned, forever without end. But nobody else talked with who they used to be. Nobody else had voices in their heads. Except madmen.

What about me, Rand thought. One hand tightened on the Dragon Scepter, the other on his sword hilt. *What about you? How are we different from them?*

There was only silence. Often enough, Lews Therin did not answer. Maybe it had been better when he never had.

Are you real? the voice said at last, wonderingly. That denial of Rand's existence was as usual as refusing to answer. *Am I? I spoke to someone. I think I did. Inside a box. A chest.* Wheezing laughter, soft. *Am I dead, or mad, or both? No matter. I am surely damned. I am damned, and this is the Pit of Doom. I am ... d-damned,* wild, that laughing, now, *and t-this – is the P-Pit of—*

Rand muted the voice to an insect's buzz, something he had learned while cramped into that chest. Alone, in the dark. Just him, and the pain, and the thirst, and the voice of a long-dead madman. The voice had been a comfort sometimes, his only companion. His friend. Something flashed in his mind. Not images, just flickers of color and motion. For some reason they made him think of Mat, and Perrin. The flashes had begun inside the chest, them and a thousand more hallucinations. In the chest, where Galina and Erian and Katerine and the rest stuffed him every day after he was beaten. He shook his head. No. He was not in the chest anymore. His fingers ached, clenched around scepter and hilt. Only memories remained, and memories had no force. He was not—

'If we must make this journey before you eat, let us make it. The evening meal is long finished for everyone else.'

Rand blinked, and Sulin stepped back from his stare. Sulin, who would stand eye-to-eye with a leopard. He smoothed his face, tried to. It felt a mask, somebody else's face.

'Are you well?' she asked.

'I was thinking.' He made his hands unknot, shrugged inside his coat. A better-fitting coat than the one he had worn from Dumai's Wells, dark blue and plain. Even after a bath he did not feel clean, not with *saidin* in him. 'Sometimes I think too much.'

Nearly twenty more Maidens clustered at one end of the windowless, dark-paneled room. Eight gilded stand-lamps against the walls, mirrored to increase the light, provided illumination. He was glad of that; he did not like dark places anymore. Three of the Asha'man were there, too, the Aiel women to one side of the chamber, the Asha'man to the other. Jonan Adley, an Altaran despite his name, stood with his arms folded, working eyebrows like black caterpillars in deep thought. Perhaps four years older than Rand, he was intent on earning the silver sword of the Dedicated. Eben Hopwil carried more flesh on his bones and fewer blotches on his face than when Rand had first seen him, though his nose and ears still seemed the biggest part of him. He fingered the sword pin on his collar as if surprised to find it there. Fedwin Morr would have worn the sword as well, had he not been in a green coat suitable for a well-to-do merchant or a minor noble, with a little silver embroidery on cuffs and lapels. Of an age with Eben, but stockier and with almost no blotches, he did not look happy that his black coat was stuffed into the leather scrip by his feet. They were the ones Lews Therin had been raving about, them and all the rest of the Asha'man. Asha'man, Aes Sedai, anyone who could channel set him off, often as not.

'Think too much, Rand al'Thor?' Enaila gripped a short spear in one hand and her buckler and three more spears in the other, yet she sounded as if she were shaking a finger at him. The Asha'man frowned at her. 'Your trouble is, you do not think at all.' Some of the other Maidens laughed softly, but she was not making a joke. Shorter than any other Maiden there by at least a hand, she had hair as fiery as her temper, and an odd view of her relationship to him. Her flaxen-haired friend Somara, who stood head and shoulders taller, nodded agreement; she held the same peculiar view.

He ignored the comment, but could not stop a sigh. Somara and Enaila were the worst, yet none of the Maidens could decide whether he was the *Car'a'carn*, to be obeyed, or the only child of a Maiden ever known to the Maidens, to be cared for as a brother, bullied as a son for a few. Even Jalani there, not many years from playing with dolls, seemed to think he was her *younger* brother, while Corana, graying and nearly as leather-faced as Sulin, treated him like an older. At least they only did that around themselves, not often where other Aiel could hear. When it counted, he would be the *Car'a'carn.* And he owed it to them. They died for him. He owed them whatever they wanted.

'I don't intend to spend all night here while you lot play Kiss the Daisies,' he said. Sulin gave him one of those looks – in dresses or in *cadin'sor*, women tossed those looks about like farmers scattering seed – but the Asha'man abandoned staring at the Maidens and slung the straps of their scrips over their shoulders. Push them hard, he had told Taim, make them weapons, and Taim had delivered. A good weapon moved as the man who held it directed. If only he could be sure it would not turn in his hand.

He had three destinations tonight, but one of those the Maidens could not be allowed to know. No one but himself. Which of the other two came first he had decided earlier, yet he hesitated. The journey would be known soon enough, yet there were reasons to keep it secret as he could.

When the gateway opened there in the middle of the room, a sweetish smell familiar to any farmer drifted through. Horse dung. Wrinkling her nose as she veiled, Sulin led half the Maidens through at a trot. After a glance to him, the Asha'man followed, drawing deeply on the True Source as they went, as much as they could hold.

Because of that, he could feel their strength as they passed him. Without that, it took some effort to tell a man could channel, longer still unless he cooperated. None were near as strong as he. Not yet, anyway; there was no saying how strong a man would be until he stopped growing stronger. Fedwin stood highest of the three, but he had what Taim called a bar. Fedwin did not really believe he could affect anything at a distance with the Power. The result was that at fifty paces his ability began to fade, and at a hundred he could not weave even a thread of *saidin*. Men gained strength faster than women, it seemed, and a good thing. These three were all strong enough to make a gateway of useful size, if just barely in Jonan's case. Every Asha'man he had kept was that.

Kill them before it is too late, before they go mad, Lews Therin whispered. *Kill them, hunt down Sammael, and Demandred, and all the Forsaken. I have to kill them all, before it is too late!* A moment of struggle as he attempted to wrest the Power away from Rand and failed. He seemed to try that more often of late, or to seize *saidin* on his own. The second was a bigger danger than the first. Rand doubted that Lews Therin could take the True Source away once Rand held it; he was not certain he could take it from Lews Therin, either, if the other reached it first.

What about me? Rand thought again. It was nearly a snarl, and no less vicious for falling short. Wrapped in the Power as he was, anger spiderwebbed across the outside of the Void, a fiery lace. *I can channel, too. Madness waits for me, but it already has you! You killed yourself, Kinslayer, after you murdered your wife and your children and the Light alone knows how many others. I won't kill where I don't have to! Do you hear me, Kinslayer?* Silence answered.

He drew a deep, uneven breath. That web of fire flickered, lightning in the distance. He had never spoken to the man – it was the man, not just a voice; a man, entire with memories – never spoken to him like that before. Perhaps it might drive Lews Therin away for good. Half the man's mad rantings were tears over his dead wife. Did he want to drive Lews Therin away? His only friend in that chest.

He had promised Sulin to count to one hundred before following, but he did it by fives, then stepped more than a hundred and fifty leagues to Caemlyn.

Night had closed down on the Royal Palace of Andor, moon-shadows cloaking delicate spires and golden domes, but a gentle breeze did nothing to break the heat. The moon hung above, still almost full, giving some light. Veiled Maidens scurried around the wagons lined up behind the largest of the palace stables. The odor of the stable muck the wagons hauled away every day had long since soaked into the wood. The Asha'man had hands to their faces, Eben actually pinching his nose shut.

'The *Car'a'carn* counts quickly,' Sulin muttered, but she lowered her veil. There would be no surprises here. No one would stay near those wagons who did not have to.

Rand let the gateway close as soon as the remaining Maidens came through, right behind him, and as it winked out of existence, Lews Therin whispered, *She is gone. Almost gone.* There was relief in his voice; the bond of Warder and Aes Sedai had not existed in the Age of Legends.

Alanna was not really gone, no more than she had been any time since bonding Rand against his will, but her presence had lessened, and it was the lessening that made Rand truly aware. You could become used to anything, begin taking it for granted. Near to her, he walked around with her emotions nestled in the back of his head, her physical condition as well, if he thought about it, and he knew exactly where she was as well as he knew his own hand's place, but just as with his hand, unless he thought about it, it just was. Only distance had any effect, but he could still *feel* that she was somewhere east of him. He wanted to be aware of her. Should Lews Therin fall silent and all the memories of the chest somehow be wiped from his head, he would still have the bond to remind him, 'Never trust Aes Sedai.'

Abruptly he realized that Jonan and Eben still held *saidin* too. 'Release,' he said sharply – that was the command Taim used – and he felt the Power vanish from them. Good weapons. So far. *Kill them before it's too late*, Lews Therin murmured. Rand released the Source deliberately, and reluctantly. He always hated letting go of the life, the enhanced senses. Of the struggle. Inside, though, he was tense, a jumper ready to leap, ready to seize it once more. He always was, now.

I have to kill them, Lews Therin whispered.

Shoving the voice back, Rand sent one of the Maidens, Nerilea, a square-faced woman, into the palace and began pacing alongside the wagons, thoughts spinning again, faster than before. He should not have come here. He should have sent Fedwin, with a letter. Spinning. Elayne. Aviendha. Perrin. Faile. Annoura. Berelain. Mat. Light, he should not have come. Elayne and Aviendha. Annoura and Berelain. Faile and Perrin and Mat. Flashes of color, quick motion just out of sight. A madman muttering angrily in the distance.

Slowly he became aware of the Maidens talking among themselves. About the smell. Implying that it came from the Asha'man. They wanted to be heard, or they would have been using handtalk; there was moonlight enough for that. Moonlight enough to see the color in Eben's face, too, and how Fedwin's jaw was set. Maybe they were not boys any longer, not since Dumai's Wells certainly, but they were still only fifteen or sixteen. Jonan's eyebrows had drawn down so far they seemed to be sitting on his cheeks. At least nobody had seized *saidin* again. Yet.

He started to step over to the three men, then raised his voice instead. Let them all hear. 'If I can put up with foolishness from Maidens, so can you.'

If anything, the color in Eben's face deepened. Jonan grunted. All three saluted Rand with fist to chest, then they turned to one another. Jonan said something in a low voice, glancing at the Maidens, and Fedwin and Eben laughed. The first time they saw Maidens they had stumbled between wanting to goggle at these exotic creatures they had only read about and wanting to run before the murderous Aiel of the stories killed them. Nothing much frightened them anymore. They needed to relearn fear.

The Maidens stared at Rand, and began talking with their hands, sometimes laughing softly. Wary of the Asha'man they might be, yet Maidens being Maidens – Aiel being Aiel – risk only made taunts more fun. Somara murmured aloud about Aviendha settling him down, which earned firm nods of approval. Nobody's life was ever this tangled in the stories.

As soon as Nerilea returned saying that she had found Davram Bashere and Bael, the clan chief leading the Aiel here in Caemlyn, Rand took off his sword belt, and so did Fedwin. Jalani produced a large leather bag for the swords and the Dragon Scepter, holding it as if the swords were poisonous snakes, or perhaps long dead and rotten. Though in truth she would not have held it so gingerly in either case. Putting on a hooded cloak that Corana handed him, Rand held his wrists together behind his back, and Sulin bound them with a cord. Tightly, muttering to herself.

'This is nonsense. Even wetlanders would call it nonsense.'

He tried not to wince. She was strong, and using every ounce of it. 'You have run away from us too often, Rand al'Thor. You have no care for yourself.' She considered him a brother of an age with herself, but irresponsible at times. '*Far Dareis Mai* carries your honor, and you have no care.'

Fedwin glowered while his own wrists were tied, though the Maiden binding him hardly put out much effort. Watching, Jonan and Eben frowned deeply. They disliked this plan as much as Sulin did. And understood it as little. The Dragon Reborn did not have to explain himself, and the *Car'a'carn* seldom did. No one said anything, though. A weapon did not complain.

When Sulin stepped around in front of Rand, she took one look at his face, and her breath caught. 'They did this to you,' she said softly, and reached for her heavy-bladed belt knife. A foot or more of steel, it was almost a short-sword, though none but a fool would say that to an Aiel.

'Pull up the hood,' Rand told her roughly. 'The whole point of this is that no one recognize me before I reach Bael and Bashere.' She hesitated, peering into his eyes. 'I said, pull it up,' he growled. Sulin could kill most men with her bare hands, but her fingers were gentle settling the hood around his face.

With a laugh, Jalani snatched the hood down over his eyes. 'Now you can be sure no one will know you, Rand al'Thor. You must trust us to guide your feet.' Several Maidens laughed.

Stiffening, he barely stopped short of seizing *saidin*. Barely. Lews Therin snarled and gibbered. Rand forced himself to breathe normally. It was not total darkness. He could see moonlight below the edge of the hood. Even so, he stumbled when Sulin and Enaila took his arms and led him forward.

'I thought you were old enough to walk better than that,' Enaila murmured in mock surprise. Sulin's hand moved. It took him a moment to realize she was stroking his arm.

All he could see was what lay just before him, the moonlit flagstones of the stableyard, then stone steps, floors of marble by lamplight, sometimes with a long runner of carpet. He strained his eyes at the movement of shadows, felt for the telltale presence of *saidin*, or worse, the prickling that announced a woman holding *saidar*. Blind like this, he might not know he was under attack until too late. He could hear the whisper of a few servants' feet as they hurried on nighttime chores, but no one challenged five Maidens apparently escorting two hooded prisoners. With Bael and Bashere living in the palace and policing Caemlyn with their men, doubtless stranger sights had been seen in these corridors. It was like walking a maze. But then he had been in one maze or another since leaving Emond's Field, even when he had thought that he walked a clear path.

Would I know a clear path if I saw one? he wondered. *Or have I been at this so long I'd think it was a trap?*

There are no clear paths. Only pitfalls and tripwires and darkness. Lews Therin's snarl sounded sweaty, desperate. The way Rand felt.

When Sulin finally led them into a room and shut the door, Rand tossed his head violently to throw back the hood – and stared. Bael and Davram he had expected, but not Davram's wife, Deira, nor Melaine, nor Dorindha.

'I see you, *Car'a'carn*.' Bael, the tallest man Rand had ever seen, sat cross-legged on the green-and-white floor tiles in his *cadin'sor*, an air about him even at ease that said he was ready to move in a heartbeat. The clan chief of the Goshien Aiel was not young – no clan chief was – and there was gray in his dark reddish hair, but anyone who thought him soft with age was in for a sad surprise. 'May you always find water and shade. I stand with the *Car'a'carn*, and my spears stand with me.'

'Water and shade may be all very well,' Davram Bashere said, hooking a leg over the gilded arm of his chair, 'but myself I would settle for chilled wine.' Little taller than Enaila, he had his short blue coat undone, and sweat glistened on his dark face. Despite his apparent indolence, he looked even harder than Bael, with his fierce tilted eyes, and his eagle's beak of a nose above thick gray-streaked mustaches. 'I offer congratulations on your escape, and your victory. But why do you come disguised as a prisoner?'

'I prefer to know whether he is bringing Aes Sedai down on us,' Deira put in. A large woman gowned in gold-worked green silk, Faile's mother stood as tall as any Maiden there except Somara, long black hair slashed with white at the temples, her nose only a little less bold than her husband's. Truth, she could give him lessons in looking fierce, and she was very like her daughter in one respect. Her loyalty was to her husband, not Rand. 'You've taken Aes Sedai *prisoner*! Are we now to expect the entire White Tower to descend upon our heads?'

'If they do,' Melaine said sharply, adjusting her shawl, 'they will be dealt with as they deserve.' Sun-haired, green-eyed and beautiful, no more than a handful of years older than Rand by her face, she was a Wise One, and married to Bael. Whatever had caused the Wise Ones to change their view of Aes Sedai, Melaine, Amys and Bair had changed the most.

'What I wish to know,' the third woman said, 'is what you will do about Colavaere Saighan.' While Deira and Melaine had presence, great presence, Dorindha outshone both, though it was difficult to see how exactly. The roofmistress of Smoke Springs Hold was a solid, motherly woman, much nearer handsome than pretty, with creases at the corners of her blue eyes and as much white in her pale red hair as Bael had gray, yet of the three women, any eye with a brain behind it would have said she held sway. 'Melaine says that Bair considers Colavaere Saighan of little importance,' Dorindha went on, 'but Wise Ones can be as blind as any man when it comes to seeing the battle ahead and missing the scorpion underfoot.' A smile for Melaine robbed the words of their sting; Melaine's answering smile certainly said she took none. 'A roofmistress's work is finding those scorpions before anyone is stung.' She also was Bael's wife, a fact that still disconcerted Rand, for all it had been her choice and Melaine's. Perhaps partly *because* it had been theirs;

among Aiel, a man had little say if his wife chose a sister-wife. It was not a common arrangement even among them.

'Colavaere has taken up farming,' Rand growled. They blinked at him, wondering whether that was a joke. 'The Sun Throne is empty again, and waiting for Elayne.' He had considered weaving a ward against listeners, but a ward could be detected by anyone searching, man or woman, and its presence would announce that something interesting was being said. Well, everything said here would be known from the Dragonwall to the sea soon enough.

Fedwin was already rubbing his wrists, while Jalani sheathed her knife. No one looked at them twice; all eyes were on Rand. Frowning at Nerilea, he waggled his bound hands until Sulin sliced the cords. 'I didn't realize this was to be a family gathering.' Nerilea looked a trifle abashed, maybe, but no one else did.

'After you marry,' Davram murmured with a smile, 'you will learn you must choose very carefully what to keep from your wife.' Deira glanced down at him, pursing her lips.

'Wives are a great comfort,' Bael laughed, 'if a man does not tell them too much.' Smiling, Dorindha ran her fingers into his hair — and gripped for a moment as though she meant to tug his head off. Bael grunted, but not for Dorindha's fingers alone. Melaine wiped her small belt knife on her heavy skirt and sheathed it. The two women grinned at one another over his head while he rubbed at his shoulder, where a small spot of blood stained his *cadin'sor*. Deira nodded thoughtfully; it seemed she had just gotten an idea.

'What woman could I hate enough to marry her to the Dragon Reborn?' Rand said coldly. That caused a silence solid enough to touch.

He tried to take rein on his anger. He should have expected this. Melaine was not just a Wise One, she was a dreamwalker, as were Amys and Bair. Among other things, they could talk to one another in their dreams, and to others; a useful skill, though they had only used it for him once. It was Wise Ones' business. No wonder at all that Melaine was abreast of everything that had happened. No wonder that she told Dorindha everything, Wise Ones' business or no; the two women were best friends and sisters rolled into one. Once Melaine let Bael know of the kidnapping, of course he had told Bashere; expecting Bashere to keep that from his wife was like expecting him to keep it secret that the house was on fire. Inch by inch he drew the anger in, forced it down.

'Has Elayne arrived?' He tried to make his voice casual, and missed. No matter. There were reasons everyone knew for him to be anxious. Andor might not be as unquiet as Cairhien, but Elayne on the throne was the fastest way to settle both lands. Maybe the only way.

'Not yet.' Bashere shrugged. 'But tales have come north of Aes Sedai with an army somewhere in Murandy, or maybe Altara. That could be young Mat and his Band of the Red Hand, with the Daughter-Heir and the sisters who fled the Tower when Siuan Sanche was deposed.'

Rand rubbed his wrists where the cords had chafed. All that 'captive' rigmarole had been on the chance Elayne was here already. Elayne, and Aviendha. So he could come and go without them learning of it till he was gone. Maybe he would have found a way to peek at them. Maybe ... He was a fool, and no maybe about that.

'Do you mean those sisters to swear oath to you, too?' Deira's tone was icy as her face. She did not like him; as she saw it, her husband had set off down a road that likely would end with his head on a pike over a gate in Tar Valon, and Rand had put his feet on that road. 'The White Tower will not hold still for your coercing Aes Sedai.'

Rand made her a small bow, and burn her if she took it for mocking. Deira ni Ghaline t'Bashere never gave him a title, never even used his name; she could as well have been talking to a footman, and not a very intelligent or trustworthy one. 'Should they choose to swear, I'll accept their oaths. I doubt many are exactly eager to return to Tar Valon. If they choose otherwise, they can go their own way, so long as they don't put themselves against me.'

'The White Tower has put itself against you,' Bael said, leaning forward with his fists on his knees. His blue eyes made Deira's voice seem warm. 'An enemy who comes once, will come again. Unless they are stopped. My spears will follow wherever the *Car'a'carn* leads.' Melaine nodded, of course; she very likely wanted every last Aes Sedai shielded and kneeling under guard if not bound hand and foot. But Dorindha nodded as well, and Sulin, and Bashere knuckled his mustaches thoughtfully. Rand did not know whether to laugh or weep.

'Don't you think I've enough on my plate without a war against the White Tower? Elaida grabbed my throat and was slapped down.' The ground erupting in fire and torn flesh. Ravens and vultures gorging. How many dead? 'If she has sense enough to stop there, I will too.' So long as they did not ask him to trust. The chest. He was shaking his head, half-aware of Lews Therin suddenly moaning about the dark and the thirst. He could ignore, he had to ignore, but not forget, or trust.

Leaving Bael and Bashere arguing over whether Elaida did have sense enough to stop, now that she had begun, he moved to a map-covered table against the wall, beneath a tapestry of some battle where the White Lion of Andor stood prominent. Apparently Bael and Bashere used this room for their planning. A little rooting around found the map he needed, a large roll displaying all of Andor from the Mountains of Mist to the River Erinin, and parts of the lands to the south as well, Ghealdan and Altara and Murandy.

'The women held captive in the treekiller's lands are allowed to cause no trouble, so why should any others?' Melaine said, apparently in answer to something he had not heard. She sounded angry.

'We will do what we must, Deira t'Bashere,' Dorindha said calmly; she was seldom anything but. 'Hold to your courage, and we will arrive where we must go.'

'When you leap from a cliff,' Deira replied, 'it is too late for anything but holding to your courage. And hoping there's a haywain at the bottom to land in.' Her husband chuckled as though she was making a joke. She did not sound it.

Spreading the map out and weighting the corners with ink jars and sand bottles, Rand measured off distances with his fingers. Mat was not moving very fast if rumor placed him in Altara or Murandy. He took pride in how fast the Band could march. Maybe the Aes Sedai were slowing him, with servants and wagons. Maybe there were more sisters than he had thought. Rand realized his hands were clenched into fists and made them straighten. He needed Elayne. To take the throne here and in Cairhien; that was why he needed her.

Just that. Aviendha ... He did not need her, not at all, and she had made it clear she had no need for him. She was safe, away from him. He could keep them both safe by keeping them as far from him as possible. Light, if he could only look at them. He needed Mat, though, with Perrin being stubborn. He was not sure how Mat had suddenly become expert on everything to do with battle, but even Bashere respected Mat's opinions. About war, anyway.

'They treated him as *da'tsang*,' Sulin growled, and some of the other Maidens growled wordlessly in echo.

'We know,' Melaine said grimly. 'They have no honor.'

'Will he truly hold back after what you describe?' Deira demanded in disbelieving tones.

The map did not extend far enough south to show Illian – no map on the table showed any part of that country – but Rand's hand drifted down across Murandy, and he could imagine the Doirlon Hills, not far inside Illian's borders, with a line of hillforts no invading army could afford to ignore. And some two hundred and fifty miles to the east, across the Plains of Maredo, an army such as had not been seen since the nations gathered before Tar Valon in the Aiel War, maybe not since Artur Hawkwing's day. Tairen, Cairhienin, Aiel, all poised to smash into Illian. If Perrin would not lead, then Mat must. Only there was not enough time. There was never enough time.

'Burn my eyes,' Davram muttered. 'You never mentioned that, Melaine. Lady Caraline and Lord Toram camped right outside the city, and High Lord Darlin as well? They didn't come together by chance, now right at this time, they did not. That's a pit of vipers to have on your doorstep, whoever you are.'

'Let the *algai'd'siswai* dance,' Bael replied. 'Dead vipers bite no one.'

Sammael had always been at his best defending. That was Lews Therin's memory, from the War of the Shadow. With two men inside one skull, maybe it was to be expected that memories would drift between them. Had Lews Therin suddenly found himself recalling herding sheep, or cutting firewood, or feeding the chickens? Rand could hear him faintly, raging to kill, to destroy; thoughts of the Forsaken almost always drove Lews Therin over the brink.

'Deira t'Bashere speaks truly,' Bael said. 'We must stay on the path we have begun until our enemies are destroyed, or we are.'

'That was not how I meant it,' Deira said dryly. 'But you are right. We have no choice, now. Until our enemies are destroyed, or we are.'

Death, destruction and madness floated in Rand's head as he studied the map. Sammael would be at those forts soon after the army struck, Sammael with the strength of a Forsaken and the knowledge of the Age of Legends. Lord Brend, he called himself, one of the Council of Nine, and Lord Brend they called him who refused to admit the Forsaken were loose, but Rand knew him. With Lews Therin's memory, he knew Sammael's face, knew him to the bone.

'What does Dyelin Taravin intend with Naean Arawn and Elenia Sarand?' Dorindha asked. 'I confess I do not understand this shutting people away.'

'What she does there is hardly important,' Davram said. 'It is her meetings with those Aes Sedai that concern me.'

'Dyelin Taravin is a fool,' Melaine muttered. 'She believes the rumors about the *Car'a'carn* kneeling to the Amyrlin Seat. She will not brush her hair unless those Aes Sedai give her permission.'

'You mistake her,' Deira said firmly. 'Dyelin is strong enough to rule Andor; she proved that at Aringill. Of course she listens to the Aes Sedai – only a fool ignores Aes Sedai – but to listen is not to obey.'

The wagons that had been brought from Dumai's Wells would have to be searched again. The fat-little-man *angreal* had to be there somewhere. None of the sisters who escaped could have had a clue what it was. Unless, perhaps, one had stuck a souvenir of the Dragon Reborn in her pouch. No. It had to be in the wagons somewhere. With that, he was more than a match for any of the Forsaken. Without it ... Death, destruction and madness.

Suddenly what he had been hearing rushed forward. 'What was that?' he demanded, turning from the ivory-inlaid table.

Surprised faces turned toward him. Jonan straightened from where he had been slouching against the doorframe. The Maidens, squatting easily on their heels, suddenly appeared alert. They had been talking idly among themselves; even they were wary around him now.

Fingering one of her ivory necklaces, Melaine shared a decided look between Bael and Davram, then spoke before anyone else. 'There are nine Aes Sedai at an inn called The Silver Swan, in what Davram Bashere calls the New City.' She said the word 'inn' in an odd way, and 'city' as well; she had only known them from books before coming across the Dragonwall. 'He and Bael say we must leave them alone unless they do something against you. I think you have learned about waiting for Aes Sedai, Rand al'Thor.'

'My fault,' Bashere sighed, 'if fault there is. Though what Melaine expects to do, I can't say. Eight sisters stopped at The Silver Swan almost a month ago, just after you left. Now and then a few more come or go, but there are never more than ten at one time. They keep to themselves, cause no trouble, and ask no questions that Bael or I can learn. A few Red sisters have come into the city, as well; twice. Those at The Silver Swan all have Warders, but these never do. I'm sure they are Reds. Two or three appear, ask after men heading for the Black Tower, and after a day or so, they leave. Without learning much, I'd say. That Black Tower is as good as a fortress for holding in secrets. None of them has made trouble, and I would rather not trouble them until I know it is necessary.'

'I didn't mean that,' Rand said slowly. He sat down in a chair opposite Bashere, gripping the carved arms till his knuckles hurt. Aes Sedai gathering here, Aes Sedai gathering in Cairhien. Happenstance? Lews Therin rumbled like thunder on the horizon about death and betrayal. He would have to warn Taim. Not about the Aes Sedai at The Silver Swan – Taim certainly knew already; why had he not mentioned it? – about staying away from them, keeping the Asha'man away. If Dumai's Wells was to be an end, there could be no new beginnings here. Too many things seemed to be spinning out of control. The harder he tried to gather them all in, the more there were and the faster they spun. Sooner or later, everything was going to fall, and shatter. The thought dried his throat. Thom Merrilin had taught him to juggle a little, but he had never been very good. Now he had to be very good indeed. He wished he had something to wet his throat.

He did not realize he had spoken that last aloud until Jalani straightened from her crouch and strutted across the room to where a tall silver pitcher stood on a small table. Filling a hammered silver goblet, she brought it back to Rand with a smile, her mouth opening as she proffered it. He expected something rude, but a change came over her face. All she said was, '*Car'a'carn*,' then went back to her place with the other Maidens, so dignified it seemed she was imitating Dorindha, or maybe Deira. Somara gestured in handtalk, and suddenly every Maiden was red-faced and biting her lips to keep from laughing. Every Maiden but Jalani, who was just red-faced.

The wine punch tasted of plums. Rand could remember fat sweet plums from the orchards across the river when he was young, climbing the trees to pick them himself . . . Tilting his head back, he drained the goblet. There were plum trees in the Two Rivers, but no orchards of them, and certainly not across any river. *Keep your bloody memories to yourself*, he snarled at Lews Therin. The man in his head laughed at something, giggling quietly to himself.

Bashere frowned at the Maidens, then glanced at Bael and his wives, all impassive as stone, and shook his head. He got on well with Bael, but Aiel in general mystified him. 'Since no one is bringing me any drink,' he said, rising, and went to pour his own. He took a long swallow that wet his heavy mustaches. 'Now, that's cooling. Taim's way of enrolling men seems to sweep up every fellow who'd like to follow the Dragon Reborn. He has delivered a goodly army to me, men who lack whatever it is your Asha'man need. They all talk wide-eyed about walking through holes in the air, but none has been anywhere near the Black Tower. I'm trying out a few thoughts young Mat had.'

Rand waved that away with the empty goblet. 'Tell me about Dyelin.' Dyelin of House Taravin would be next in line for the throne should anything happen to Elayne, but he had told her he was having Elayne brought to Caemlyn. 'If she thinks she can take the Lion Throne, I can find a farm for her, too.'

'Take the throne?' Deira said incredulously, and her husband laughed out loud.

'I have no understanding of wetlander ways,' Bael said, 'but I do not think that is what she has done.'

'Far from it.' Davram carried the pitcher over to pour more punch for Rand. 'Some lesser lords and ladies who thought to curry favor proclaimed for her at Aringill. She moves quickly, Lady Dyelin. Within four days she had the two leaders hanged, for treason to the Daughter-Heir Elayne, and ordered another twenty flogged.' He chuckled approvingly. His wife sniffed. Likely she would have had the road lined with gibbets all the way from Aringill to Caemlyn.

'Then what was that about her ruling Andor?' Rand demanded. 'And imprisoning Elenia and Naean.'

'They are the ones who tried to claim the throne,' Deira said, dark eyes sparkling angrily.

Bashere nodded. He was much calmer. 'Only three days ago. When word arrived of Colavaere's coronation, and the rumors from Cairhien that you had gone to Tar Valon began to sound more real. With trade beginning again, there are so many pigeons in the air between Cairhien and Caemlyn, you could walk on their backs.' Putting the pitcher back, he returned to his chair. 'Naean proclaimed for the Lion Throne in the morning, Elenia before midday, and by sunset Dyelin, Pelivar and Luan had arrested them both. They announced Dyelin as Regent the next morning. In Elayne's name, until Elayne returns. Most of the Houses of Andor have declared support for Dyelin. I think some would like her to take the throne herself, but Aringill keeps even the most powerful careful of their tongues.' Closing one eye, Bashere pointed at Rand. 'You, they do not mention at all. Whether that is good or bad, it will take a wiser head than mine to say.'

Deira offered a cool smile, looking down that nose of hers. 'Those ... lickspittles ... you allowed to make free of the palace have all fled the city, it seems. Fled Andor, some of them, according to rumor. You should know, they were all behind either Elenia or Naean.'

Rand carefully set his full goblet on the floor beside his chair. He had only let Lir and Arymilla and the rest remain in order to try pushing Dyelin and those who supported her into cooperation with him. They would never have left Andor to the likes of Lord Lir. With time and Elayne's return, it might yet work. But everything was whirling faster and faster, whirling away from his fingers. There were a few things he could control, though.

'Fedwin, there, is an Asha'man,' he said. 'He can bring messages to me in Cairhien, if there's need.' That with a glare for Melaine, who returned the blandest sort of look. Deira studied Fedwin as she might a dead rat some over-eager dog had dropped on her rug. Davram and Bael were more considering; Fedwin tried to stand straighter under their gaze. 'Don't let anyone know who he is,' Rand went on. 'No one. That's why he isn't wearing black. I am taking two more to Lord Semaradrid and High Lord Weiramon tonight. They'll have need when they face Sammael in the Doirlon Hills. I will be busy chewing on Cairhien for a while yet, it seems.' And maybe Andor, too.

'Does this mean you will send the spears forward at last?' Bael said. 'You give the orders tonight?'

Rand nodded, and Bashere gave a great hoot of laughter. 'Now, that calls for a good wine. Or it would if it wasn't hot enough to make a man's blood thick as porridge.' Laughter slid into a grimace. 'Burn me, but I wish I could be there. Still, I suppose holding Caemlyn for the Dragon Reborn is no small thing.'

'You always want to be where the swords are bared, my husband.' Deira sounded quite fond.

'The fifth,' Bael said. 'You will allow the fifth in Illian, when Sammael has fallen?' Aiel custom allowed taking the fifth part of all that was in a place taken by force of arms. Rand had forbidden it here in Caemlyn; he would not give Elayne a city looted even that much.

'They will have the fifth,' Rand said, but it was not of Sammael or Illian that he thought. *Bring Elayne quickly, Mat.* It ran wild in his head, across Lews Therin's cackling. *Bring her quickly, before Andor and Cairhien both erupt in my face.*

CHAPTER 8

The Figurehead

'We must stop here tomorrow.' Egwene shifted carefully on her folding chair; it had a tendency to fold on its own, sometimes. 'Lord Bryne says the army is running short of food. Our camp is certainly short of everything.'

Two stubby tallow candles burned on the wooden table in front of her. That folded, too, for easy packing, but it was sturdier than the chair. The candles in the tent that served as her study were supplemented by an oil lantern hanging from the centerpole up near the peak. The dim yellow light flickered, making faint shadows dance on patched canvas walls that were a far cry from the grandeur of the Amyrlin's study in the White Tower, but that did not upset her. Truth be known, she herself was some considerable distance short of the grandeur normally associated with the Amyrlin Seat. She knew very well that the seven-striped stole on her shoulders was the only reason any stranger would believe her Amyrlin. If they did not think it an extremely foolish joke. Odd things had happened in the White Tower's history – Siuan had told her secret details of some of them – yet surely nothing so odd as her.

'Four or five days would be better,' Sheriam mused, studying the sheaf of papers in her lap. Slightly plump, with high cheekbones and tilted green eyes, in her dark green riding dress she managed to look elegant and commanding despite her perch on one of the two precarious stools in front of the table. Exchange her narrow blue stole of the Keeper of the Chronicles for the Amyrlin's, and anyone would think she wore it by right. Sometimes she certainly seemed to believe the striped stole rested on her own shoulders. 'Or perhaps longer. It would not hurt to build our stores up once more.'

Siuan, atop the other rickety stool, shook her head slightly, but Egwene did not need the hint. 'One day.' She might be just eighteen and well short of a true Amyrlin's grandeur, but she was no fool. Too many of the sisters seized on any excuse for a halt – too many of the Sitters, as well – and if they stopped too long, it might be impossible to start them moving again. Sheriam opened her mouth.

'One, daughter,' Egwene said firmly. Whatever Sheriam thought, the fact was that Sheriam Bayanar was the Keeper and Egwene al'Vere the Amyrlin. If only Sheriam could be brought to realize that. And the Hall of the Tower; they were worse. She wanted to snarl or snap or maybe throw something, but after close to a month and a half, she already had a lifetime's practice in keeping her face and voice smooth at far greater provocation than this. 'Any longer, and we'll begin to strip the countryside bare. I won't leave people to starve. On the practical side, if we take too much from them, even paid for, they'll give us a hundred problems in return.'

'Raids on the herds and flocks and thieves at the storewagons,' Siuan murmured. Studying her divided gray skirts, not looking at anyone, she seemed to be thinking aloud. 'Men shooting at our guards at night, maybe setting fire to whatever they can reach. A bad business. Hungry people become desperate in a hurry.' Those were the same reasons Lord Bryne had given Egwene, in very nearly the same words.

The fiery-haired woman shot Siuan a hard look. Many sisters had a difficult time with Siuan. Her face was probably the best known in the camp, young enough to have looked proper above an Accepted's dress, or a novice's for that matter. That was a side effect of being stilled, though not many had known it; Siuan could hardly walk a step without sisters staring at her, the once Amyrlin Seat, deposed and cut off from *saidar*, then Healed and restored to at least some ability, when everyone knew that was impossible. Many welcomed her back warmly as a sister once more, for herself and for the miracle that held out hope against what every Aes Sedai feared beyond death, but just as many or more offered lukewarm toleration or condescension or both, blaming her for their present situation.

Sheriam was one of those who thought Siuan should instruct the new young Amyrlin in protocol and the like, which everyone believed she hated, and keep her mouth closed unless she was called upon. She was less than she had been, no longer Amyrlin and no longer anywhere near so strong in the Power. It was not cruelty as Aes Sedai saw it. The past was past; what was now, was, and must be accepted. Anything else only brought greater pain. By and large, Aes Sedai admitted change slowly, but once they did, for most it was as if things had always been that way.

'One day, Mother, as you say,' Sheriam sighed at last, bowing her head slightly. Less in submission, Egwene was sure, than to hide a grimace over her stubbornness. She would accept the grimace if the acquiescence came with it. For the time being, she had to.

Siuan bowed her head, too. To hide a smile. Any sister might be appointed to any post, but the social pecking order was quite rigid, and Siuan stood a long way further down than she had. That was one reason.

The papers on Sheriam's lap were duplicated on Siuan's, and on the table in front of Egwene. Reports on everything from the number of candles and sacks of beans remaining in the camp to the state of the horses, and the same for Lord Bryne's army. The army's camp encircled the Aes Sedai's, with a ring perhaps twenty steps wide between, but in many ways they might as well have been a mile apart. Surprisingly, Lord Bryne insisted on that as much as the sisters. The Aes Sedai did not want soldiers wandering among their tents, a lot of unwashed, illiterate ruffians with light fingers often as not, and it seemed the soldiers did not want Aes Sedai wandering among them either – though, perhaps wisely, they held their reasons close. They marched toward Tar Valon to pull down a usurper to the Amyrlin Seat and raise Egwene in her place, yet few men were truly comfortable around Aes Sedai. Few enough women, either.

As Keeper, Sheriam would have been all too happy to take these minor matters out of Egwene's hands. She had said as much, explaining how minor they were, how the Amyrlin Seat should not be burdened with day-to-day trifles. Siuan, on the other hand, said a good Amyrlin paid attention to just those, not trying to duplicate the work of dozens of sisters and clerks, yet checking on something different every day. That way she had a good idea of what was happening and what needed doing before someone came running to her with a crisis already breaking into shards. A feel for how the wind was blowing, Siuan called it. Making sure these reports reached her had required weeks, and Egwene was sure that once she let them pass to Sheriam's control, she would never again learn anything until it was long dealt with. If then.

A silence stretched as they began reading the next paper in each stack.

They were not alone. Chesa, seated on cushions to one side of the tent, spoke. 'Too little light is bad for the eyes,' she murmured almost to herself, holding up one of Egwene's silk stockings that she was darning. 'You'll never catch me ruining my eyes over words in this little light.' Just short of stout, with a twinkle in her eyes and a merry smile, Egwene's maid was always trying to slip advice to the Amyrlin as though talking about herself. She could have been in Egwene's service twenty years instead of less than two months, and three times as old as Egwene instead of barely twice. Tonight, Egwene suspected that she talked to fill silences. There was a tension in the camp since Logain had escaped. A man who could channel, shielded and under close guard, yet he had slipped away like fog. Everyone walked on edge wondering how, wondering where he was, what he intended to do now. Egwene wished harder than most that she could be sure she knew where Logain Ablar was.

Giving her papers a firm snap of her wrists, Sheriam frowned at Chesa; she did not understand why Egwene let her maid be present at these meetings, much less let her chatter away freely. It probably never occurred to her that Chesa's presence and her unexpected chatter frequently unsettled her just enough to help Egwene sidestep advice she did not want to take and postpone decisions she did not want to make, at least not the way Sheriam wanted them made. Certainly the notion had never occurred to Chesa; she smiled apologetically and returned to her darning, occasionally murmuring to herself.

'If we continue, Mother,' Sheriam said coolly, 'we may finish before dawn.'

Staring at the next page, Egwene rubbed her temples. Chesa might be right about the light. She had another headache coming on. Then again, it might be the page, detailing what money was left. The stories she had read never mentioned how much coin was required to keep an army. Pinned to the sheet were notes from two of the Sitters, Romanda and Lelaine, suggesting the soldiers be paid less frequently, paid less in fact. More than suggesting, really, just as Romanda and Lelaine were more than simply two Sitters in the Hall. Other Sitters followed where they led, if not all by any means, while the only Sitter Egwene could count on was Delana, and her not far. It was rare that Lelaine and Romanda agreed on anything, and they could hardly have chosen a worse. Some of the soldiers had sworn oaths, yet most were there for their pay, and maybe the hope of loot.

'The soldiers are to be paid as before,' Egwene muttered, crumpling the two notes. She was not going to let her army melt away, any more than she would allow looting.

'As you command, Mother.' Sheriam's eyes sparkled with pleasure. The difficulties must be clear to her – anyone who thought her less than very intelligent was in deep trouble – but she did have a blind spot. If Romanda or Lelaine said the sun was coming up, Sheriam most likely would claim it was going down; she had had almost as much sway with the Hall as they did now, perhaps more, until they put a halt to it between them. The opposite was true, as well; those two would speak against anything Sheriam wanted before they stopped to think. Which had its uses, all in all.

Egwene's fingers tapped on the tabletop, but she made them stop. The money had to be found – somewhere, somehow – but she did not have to let Sheriam see her worry.

'That new woman will work out,' Chesa murmured over her sewing. 'Tairens always carry their noses high, of course, but Selame does know what's required of a lady's maid. Meri and I will settle her down soon enough.' Sheriam rolled her eyes irritably.

Egwene smiled to herself. Egwene al'Vere with three maids waiting on her; as unbelievable as the stole itself. But the smile lasted only a heartbeat. Maids had to be paid, too. A tiny sum, balanced against thirty thousand soldiers, and the Amyrlin could hardly do her own laundry or mend her own shifts, but she could have managed splendidly with Chesa alone. And would have, had she any choice in it. Less than a week earlier Romanda had decided that the Amyrlin needed another servant and found Meri among the refugees who huddled in every village until they were chased away, and not to be outdone, Lelaine produced Selame from the same source. The two women were crowded into Chesa's small tent before Egwene knew either existed.

The principle of the thing was wrong: *three* maids when there was not enough silver to pay the army halfway to Tar Valon, servants chosen for her without any say; and then there was the fact that she had yet another, if one who received not a copper. Everyone believed Marigan was the Amyrlin's maidservant, anyway.

Beneath the edge of the table she felt her belt pouch, felt the bracelet inside. She should wear it more; it was a duty. Keeping her hands low, she dug the bracelet out and slipped it around her wrist, a band of silver made so the catch was invisible once closed. Made with the One Power, the bracelet snapped shut beneath the table, and she very nearly snatched it off again.

Emotion flooded into a corner of her mind, emotion and awareness, a little pocket, as if she were imagining it. Not imagination, though; all too real. Half of an *a'dam*, the bracelet created a link between her and the woman who wore the other half, a silver necklace the wearer could not remove herself. They were a circle of two without embracing *saidar*, Egwene always leading by virtue of the bracelet. 'Marigan' was asleep now, her feet sore from walking all day and days past, but even sleeping, fear oozed through most strongly; only hate ever came near fear in the stream that flowed through the *a'dam*. Egwene's reluctance came from the constant gnawing of the other woman's terror, from having worn the necklace end of an *a'dam* once, and from knowing the woman on the far end. She hated sharing any part of her.

Only three women in the camp knew that Moghedien was a prisoner, hidden in the midst of Aes Sedai. If it came out, Moghedien would be tried, stilled and executed in short order. If it came out,

Egwene might not be far behind her, and Siuan and Leane, as well. They were the other two who knew. At best she would have the stole stripped away.

For hiding one of the Forsaken from justice, she thought grimly, *I'll be lucky if they just stick me back with the Accepted.* Unconsciously she thumbed the golden Great Serpent ring on the first finger of her right hand.

Then again, however just such a punishment might be, it was unlikely. She had been taught that the wisest of the sisters was chosen Amyrlin Seat, yet she had learned better. The choosing of an Amyrlin was as hotly contested as electing a mayor in the Two Rivers, and maybe more; no one bothered to stand against her father in Emond's Field, but she had heard about elections in Deven Ride and Taren Ferry. Siuan had only been raised Amyrlin because the three before her each had died after just a few years on the Amyrlin Seat. The Hall had wanted someone young. Speaking of age to a sister was at least as rude as slapping her face, yet she had begun to get some idea how long Aes Sedai lived. Rarely was anyone chosen Sitter before she had worn the shawl seventy or eighty years at least, and Amyrlins generally longer. Often *much* longer. So when the Hall deadlocked between four sisters raised Aes Sedai less than fifty years before, and Seaine Herimon of the White suggested a woman who had worn the shawl only *ten* years, it might have been as much exhaustion as Siuan's qualifications in administration that brought the Sitters to stand for her.

And Egwene al'Vere, who in many eyes should still have been a novice? A figurehead, easily directed, a *child* who had grown up in the same village with Rand al'Thor. That last definitely had its part in the decision. They would not take back the stole, but she would find the little authority she had managed to accumulate gone. Romanda, Lelaine and Sheriam might actually come to blows over which would march her about by the scruff of her neck.

'That looks much like a bracelet I saw Elayne wearing.' The papers on Sheriam's lap crackled as she leaned forward for a better look. 'And Nynaeve. They shared it, as I recall.'

Egwene gave a start. She had been careless. 'It's the same. A remembrance gift, when they left.' Twisting the silver circlet around her wrist, she felt a stab of guilt that was all her own. The bracelet appeared segmented, but so cunningly you could not see how exactly. She had hardly thought of Nynaeve and Elayne since their departure for Ebou Dar. Perhaps she should call them back. Their search was not going well, it seemed, though they denied it. Still, if they could find what they were after . . .

Sheriam was frowning, whether or not at the bracelet, Egwene could not say. She could not allow Sheriam to start thinking too much on that bracelet, though; if she ever noticed that the necklace 'Marigan' wore was a match, there might be painfully awkward questions.

Rising, Egwene smoothed her skirt as she moved around the table. Siuan had acquired several pieces of information today; one could be put to good use now. She was not the only one with secrets. Sheriam looked surprised when she stopped too close for the other woman to stand.

'Daughter, I've learned that a few days after Siuan and Leane arrived in Salidar, ten sisters left, two from each Ajah there except the Blue. Where did they go, and why?'

Sheriam's eyes narrowed a fraction, but she wore serenity as comfortably as her dress. 'Mother, I can hardly recall every—'

'No dancing around, Sheriam.' Egwene moved a little closer, until their knees almost touched. 'No lies by omission. The truth.'

A frown creased Sheriam's smooth forehead. 'Mother, even if I knew, you cannot trouble yourself with every little—'

'The truth, Sheriam. The whole truth. Must I ask before the entire Hall why I cannot have the truth from my Keeper? I will have it, daughter, one way or another. I *will* have it.'

Sheriam's head swiveled as though she was looking for a way to escape. Her eyes fell on Chesa, hunched over her sewing, and she all but gasped with relief. 'Mother, tomorrow, when we are alone, I am sure I can explain everything to your satisfaction. I must speak with a few of the sisters first.'

So they could work up what Sheriam was to tell her tomorrow. 'Chesa,' Egwene said, 'wait outside, please.' For all that she seemed focused on her work to the exclusion of everything else, Chesa bounded to her feet in a flash and very nearly ran from the tent.

When Aes Sedai were at odds, anyone with half a brain went elsewhere. 'Now, daughter,' Egwene said. 'The truth. All that you know. This is as private as you will be,' she added when Sheriam glanced at Siuan.

For a moment Sheriam adjusted her skirts, plucking at them really, avoiding Egwene's eyes, no doubt still working out evasions. But the Three Oaths trapped her. She could not speak an untrue word, and whatever she thought Egwene's true position, slipping behind her back was a long way from denying her authority to her face. Even Romanda maintained the proper courtesies, if only by a hair at times.

Drawing a deep breath, Sheriam folded her hands in her lap and spoke to Egwene's chest, matter-of-fact. 'When we learned the Red Ajah was responsible for setting Logain up as a false Dragon, we felt something had to be done.' 'We' certainly meant the small coterie of sisters she had gathered around her; Carlinya and Beonin and the rest held as much real sway as most Sitters, if not actually in the Hall. 'Elaida was sending out demands for every sister to return to the Tower, so we chose ten sisters to do just that, by the fastest means they could manage. They all should be there long since. Quietly making sure that every sister in the Tower understands the truth of what the Reds did with Logain. Not—' She hesitated, then finished in a rush. 'Not even the Hall knows of them.'

Egwene stepped away, rubbing her temples again. Quietly making sure. In the hope that Elaida would be deposed. Not exactly a bad scheme, really; it might even work, eventually. It might take years, too. But then, for most sisters, the longer they could go without truly *doing* anything, the better. With enough time, they could convince the world that the White Tower had never really broken. It had been broken before, even if only a handful knew it. Maybe, with enough time, they could find a way to adjust everything so it had not, really. 'Why keep it from the Hall, Sheriam? Surely you don't think any of them would betray your plan to Elaida.' Half the sisters eyed the other half askance for fear of Elaida's sympathizers. Partly for fear of that.

'Mother, a sister who decided that what we do is a mistake would hardly let herself be chosen a Sitter. Any such would have taken herself away long since.' Sheriam had not relaxed, but her voice took on the patient, instructing tone she seemed to think had the greatest effect on Egwene. Usually, though, she was more adroit at changing the subject. 'Those suspicions are the worst problem we face for the time being. No one really trusts anyone. If we could only see how to—'

'The Black Ajah,' Siuan cut in quietly. 'That's what chills your blood like a silverpike up your skirts. Who can say for sure who is Black, and who can say what a Black sister might do?'

Sheriam darted another hard look at Siuan, but after a moment the force went out of her. Or rather, one sort of tension replaced another. She glanced at Egwene, then nodded, reluctantly. By the sour twist to her mouth, she would have made another evasion had it not been plain Egwene would not stand for it. Most sisters in the camp believed now, but after more than three thousand years denying the Black Ajah's existence, it was a queasy belief. Almost no one would open her mouth on that topic, no matter what they believed.

'The question, Mother,' Siuan went on, 'is what happens when the Hall does find out.' She seemed to be thinking aloud again. 'I can't see any Sitter accepting the excuse that she couldn't be told because she might be on Elaida's side. And as for the possibility she might be Black Ajah ... Yes, I think they will be quite upset.'

Sheriam's face paled slightly. It was a wonder she did not go dead white. 'Upset' did not begin to cover it. Yes, Sheriam would face *much* more than upset if this came out.

Now was the time to drive home her advantage, but another question occurred to Egwene. If Sheriam and her friends had sent – what were they? Not spies. Ferrets, maybe, sent into the walls after rats – if Sheriam had sent ferrets into the White Tower, could ... ?

A sudden stab of pain through that pocket of sensations in the back of her head sent everything else flying. Had she felt it directly, it would have been numbing. As it was, her eyes bulged in shock. A man who could channel was touching the necklace around Moghedien's neck; this was one link no man could be brought into. Pain, and something unheard of from Moghedien. Hope. And then it was all gone, the awareness, the emotions. The necklace was off.

'I ... need some fresh air,' she managed. Sheriam started to rise, and Siuan, but she waved them back down. 'No, I want to be alone,' she said hastily. 'Siuan, find out everything Sheriam knows about the ferrets. Light, I mean the ten sisters.' They both stared at her, but thank the Light, neither followed as she snatched the lantern from its hook and hurried out.

It would not do for the Amyrlin to be seen running, yet she came close, hoisting her divided skirts as well as she could with her free hand and very nearly trotting. A cloudless sky made the moonlight bright, dappling the tents and wagons with shadows. Most people in the camp were asleep, but low fires still burned here and there. A handful of Warders were about, a few servants. Too many eyes to see if she ran. The last thing she wanted was someone offering help. She realized she was panting, but from alarm, not exertion.

Thrusting her head and the lantern into 'Marigan's' tiny tent, she found it empty. The blankets that made up the pallet on the ground lay in a sprawl, tossed aside by someone in a hurry.

And what if she had still been here? she wondered. *With the necklace off, and maybe whoever freed her?* Shivering, she withdrew slowly. Moghedien had good reason to dislike her, very personally, and the only sister who could match one of the Forsaken alone, when she could channel at all, was in Ebou Dar. Moghedien could have killed Egwene without anyone noticing; even had a sister felt her channel, there would be nothing remarkable in that. Worse, Moghedien might not have killed her. And no one would have known anything until they found the pair of them gone.

'Mother,' Chesa fussed behind her, 'you should not be out in the night air. Night air is bad air. If you wanted Marigan, I could have fetched her.'

Egwene very nearly jumped. She had not been aware of Chesa following her. She studied the people at the nearest fires. They had gathered for companionship, not warmth in this unholy heat, and they were not close, but maybe someone had seen who went into 'Marigan's' tent. She certainly had few visitors. And no men among them. A man might well have been remarked. 'I think she has run away, Chesa.'

'Why, that wicked woman!' Chesa exclaimed. 'I always said she had a mean mouth and a sneaking eye. Slinking away like a thief after you took her in. She'd be starving by a road, if not for you. No gratitude at all!'

She followed all the way back to the tent where Egwene slept, nattering on about wickedness in general, the thanklessness of 'Marigan' in particular, and how that sort should be handled, which seemed to jump between switching them till they settled down and tossing them out before they could run away, tucked around cautions that Egwene check her jewelry to be sure it was all still there.

Egwene barely heard. Her mind spun. It could not have been Logain, could it? He could not have known about Moghedien, must less come back to rescue her. Could he? Those men Rand was gathering, those Asha'man. Rumor in every village carried whispers of Asha'man and the Black Tower. Most of the sisters tried to pretend they were unaffected by dozens of men who could channel gathering in one spot – the worst of the tales had to be inflated; rumor always exaggerated – but Egwene's toes wanted to curl under with fright whenever she thought of them. An Asha'man could have . . . But why? How would he have known, any more than Logain?

She was trying to avoid the only reasonable conclusion. Something far worse than Logain come back, or even Asha'man. One of the Forsaken had freed Moghedien. Rahvin was dead by Rand's hand, according to Nynaeve, and he had killed Ishamael as well, or so it seemed. And Aginor and Balthamel. Moiraine had killed Be'lal. That left only Asmodean, Demandred and Sammael among the men. Sammael was in Illian. No one knew where the others were, or any of the women who survived. Moiraine had done for Lanfear too, or they had done for each other, but all the other women were still alive, so far as anyone knew. Forget the women. It had been a man. Which? Plans had been laid long since in case one of the Forsaken struck at the camp. No one sister here could equal any of the Forsaken by herself, but linked in circles was another matter, and any Forsaken who stepped into their camp would find circles forming on every side of him. Or her. Once they realized who she was. The Forsaken showed no signs of agelessness, for some reason. Maybe it was some effect of being connected to the Dark One. They . . .

This was dithering. She had to start thinking clearly.

'Chesa?'

'... look like you need your head rubbed for the ache again is what, is what you ... Yes, Mother?'

'Find Siuan and Leane. Tell them to come to me. But don't let anyone hear you.'

Grinning, Chesa dropped a curtsy and scampered out. She could hardly avoid knowing the currents that swirled around Egwene, yet she found all the plotting and scheming fun. Not that she knew more than surface, and little enough of that. Egwene did not doubt her loyalty, but Chesa's opinion of what was exciting might change if she learned the depth of those swirls.

Channeling the oil lamps inside the tent alight, Egwene blew out the lantern and set it carefully in a corner. Maybe she had to think clearly, but she still felt as if she was stumbling in the dark.

CHAPTER 9

A Pair of Silverpike

Egwene was sitting in her chair – one of the few real chairs in the camp, with a little plain carving like a farmer's best armchair, roomy and comfortable enough that she felt only a touch of guilt about taking up valuable wagon space for it – she was sitting there trying to pull her thoughts together when Siuan swept aside the entry flaps and ducked into the tent. Siuan was not happy.

'Why in the Light did you run off?' Her voice had not changed with her face, and she chided with the best even when she did it in respectful tones. Barely respectful. Her blue eyes remained the same, too; they could have done for a saddlemaker's awls. 'Sheriam brushed me aside like a fly.' That surprisingly delicate mouth twisted bitterly. 'She was gone almost as soon as you were. Don't you realize she handed herself to you? She certainly does. Her, and Anaiya and Morvrin and the lot of them. You can be sure they'll spend tonight trying to bail water and patch holes. They could manage it. I don't see how, but they might.'

Almost as the last word left her mouth, Leane entered. A tall, willowy woman, her coppery face was as youthful as Siuan's, and for the same reason; she also was more than old enough to be Egwene's mother, in truth. Leane took one look at Siuan and threw up her hands as much as the roof of the tent would allow. 'Mother, this is a foolish risk.' Her dark eyes went from dreamy to flashing, but her voice had a languorous quality even when she was irritated. Once, it had been brisk. 'If anyone sees Siuan and me together this way—'

'I don't care if the whole camp learns your squabbling is a fraud,' Egwene broke in sharply, weaving a small barrier against eavesdropping around the three of them. It could be worked through with time, but not without detection, not so long as she held the weave instead of tying it off.

She did care, and perhaps she should not have called them both, but her first half-coherent thought had been to summon the two sisters she could count on. No one in the camp so much as suspected. Everyone knew the former Amyrlin and her former Keeper detested one another every bit as much as Siuan detested being tutor to her successor. Should any sister uncover the truth, they might well find themselves doing penance for a long time to come, and not an easy one – Aes Sedai appreciated being made fools of even less than other people; *kings* had been made to pay for that – but in the meanwhile their supposed animosity resulted in a certain leverage with the other sisters, including Sitters. If *they* both said the same thing, it must be so. Another incidental effect of being stilled was very useful, one no one else knew about. The Three Oaths no longer held them; they could lie like wool merchants, now.

Schemes and deceptions on every side. The camp was like some fetid swamp where strange growths sprouted unseen in mists. Maybe anywhere Aes Sedai gathered was like that. After three thousand years of plotting, however necessary, it was hardly surprising that scheming had become second nature to most sisters and only a breath away for the rest. The truly horrible thing, was that she found herself beginning to enjoy all the machinations. Not for their own sake, but as puzzles, though no twisted bits of iron could intrigue her a quarter so much. What that said about her, she did not want to know. Well, she *was* Aes Sedai, whatever anyone thought, and she had to take the bad of it with the good.

'Moghedien has escaped,' she went on without pause. 'A man removed the *a'dam* from her. A man who can channel. I think one of them took the necklace away; it wasn't in her tent, that I saw. There might be some way to find it using the bracelet, but if there is, I don't know it.'

That took the starch right out of them. Leane's legs gave way, and she dropped like a sack onto the stool Chesa sometimes used. Siuan sat down on the cot slowly, back very straight, hands very still on her knees. Incongruously, Egwene noticed that her dress had tiny blue flowers embroidered in a wide Tairen maze around the bottom, a band that made the divided skirts seem one when she was still. Another band curved becomingly across the bodice. Concern for her clothes, that they be pretty instead of just suitable, was certainly a small change, looking at it one way – she never took it to extremes – yet in another, it was as drastic as her face. And a puzzle. Siuan resented the changes, and resisted them. Except for this one.

Leane, on the other hand, in true Aes Sedai fashion embraced what had changed. A young woman again – Egwene had overheard a Yellow exclaiming in wonder that both were prime childbearing age, by everything she could find – she might never have been Keeper, never have had any other face. The very image of practicality and efficiency became the ideal of an indolent and alluring Domani woman. Even her riding dress was cut in the style of her native land, and no matter that its silk, so thin it barely seemed opaque, was as impractical as the pale green color for traveling dusty roads. Told that having been stilled had broken all ties and associations, Leane had chosen the Green Ajah over a return to the

Blue. Changing Ajahs was not done, but then, no one had been stilled and then Healed before, either. Siuan had gone right back into the Blue, grumbling over the idiotic need to 'entreat and appeal for acceptance' as the formal phrase went.

'Oh, Light!' Leane breathed as she thumped onto the stool with considerably less than her usual grace. 'We should have turned her over for trial the first day. Nothing we've learned from her is worth letting her loose on the world again. Nothing!' It was a measure of her shock; she did not normally go about stating the obvious. Her brain had not grown indolent, whatever her outward demeanor. Languid and seductive Domani women might be on the outside, but they were still known as the sharpest traders anywhere.

'Blood and bloody—! We should have had her watched,' Siuan growled through her teeth.

Egwene's eyebrows rose. Siuan must be as shaken as Leane. 'By who, Siuan? Faolain? Theodrin? They don't even know you two are of my party.' A party? Five women. And Faolain and Theodrin were hardly eager adherents, especially Faolain. Nynaeve and Elayne could be counted too, of course, and Birgitte certainly, even if she was not Aes Sedai, but they were a long way off. Stealth and cunning were still her major strengths. Plus the fact that no one expected them of her. 'How should I have explained to *anyone* why they were supposed to watch my serving woman? For that matter, what good would it have done? It had to be one of the Forsaken. Do you really think Faolain and Theodrin together could have stopped him? I'm not sure *I* could have, even linked with Romanda and Lelaine.' They were the next two strongest women in the camp, as strong in the Power as Siuan used to be.

Siuan visibly forced a scowl from her face, but even so, she snorted. She often said that if she could no longer be Amyrlin, then she would teach Egwene how to be the best Amyrlin ever, yet the transition from lion on a hill to mouse underfoot was difficult. Egwene allowed her no little latitude because of that.

'I want the two of you to ask about among those near the tent Moghedien was sleeping in. Someone must have seen the man. He had to come afoot. Anybody opening a gateway inside a space that little risked cutting her in two, however small he wove it.'

Siuan snorted, louder than the first time. 'Why bother?' she growled. 'Do you mean to go chasing after her like some fool hero in a gleeman's fool story and bring her back? Maybe tie up all the Forsaken at one go? Win the Last Battle while you're at it? Even if we get a description head to toe, nobody knows one Forsaken from another. Nobody here, anyway. It's the most bloody useless barrel of fish guts I ever—!'

'Siuan!' Egwene said sharply, sitting up straighter. Latitude was one thing, but there were limits. She did not put up with this even from Romanda.

Color bloomed slowly in Siuan's cheeks. Struggling to master herself, she kneaded her skirts and avoided Egwene's eyes. 'Forgive me, Mother,' she said finally. She almost sounded as if she meant it.

'It has been a difficult day for her, Mother,' Leane put in with an impish smile. She was very good at those, though she generally used them to set some man's heart racing. Not promiscuously, of course; she possessed discrimination and discretion in ample supply. 'But then, most are. If she could only learn not to throw things at Gareth Bryne every time she gets angry—'

'Enough!' Egwene snapped. Leane was only trying to take a little of the pressure from Siuan, but she was in no mood for it. 'I want to know anything I can learn about whoever freed Moghedien, even if it's just whether he was short or tall. Any scrap that makes him less a shadow creeping in the dark. If that's not more than I have a right to ask.' Leane sat quite still, staring at the flowers in the carpet in front of her toes.

The redness spread to cover nearly Siuan's whole face; with her fair skin, it made her look like a sunset. 'I ... humbly beg your pardon, Mother.' This time, she did sound penitent. Her difficulty meeting Egwene's gaze was obvious. 'Sometimes it's hard to ... No, no excuses. I humbly beg pardon.'

Egwene fingered her stole, letting the moment set itself as she looked at Siuan without blinking. That was something Siuan herself had taught her, but after a bit she shifted uneasily on the cot. When you knew you were in the wrong, silence pricked, and the pricks drove home that you *were* wrong. Silence was a very useful tool in a number of situations. 'Since I can't recall what I should forgive,' she said at last, quietly, 'there seems to be no need. But, Siuan ... Don't let it happen again.'

'Thank you, Mother.' A hint of wry laughter curled the corners of Siuan's mouth. 'If I may say so, I seem to have taught you very well. But if I may suggest ... ?' She waited for Egwene's impatient nod. 'One of us should carry your order to Faolain or Theodrin to ask the questions, very sulky at being made a messenger. They'll occasion a deal less comment than Leane or I. Everyone knows you are their patron.'

Egwene agreed immediately. She still was not thinking clearly, or she would have seen that for herself. The headachy feeling was back again. Chesa claimed it came from too little sleep, but sleeping was difficult when your head felt taut as a drumhead. It would take a larger head than hers not to feel tight, stuffed with as many worries as she had. Well, at least now she could pass on the secrets that had kept Moghedien hidden, how to weave disguises with the Power and how to mask your ability from other women who could channel. Revealing those had been too risky when they might have led to unmasking Moghedien.

A bit more acclaim, she thought wryly. There had been great petting and exclaiming when she announced the once-lost secret of Traveling, which at least had been her own, and more praise since for every one of the secrets she had wrenched out of Moghedien, like pulling a back tooth each time. None of the acclaim made an ounce of difference in her position, though. You could pat a talented child on the head without forgetting she was a child.

Leane departed with a curtsy and a dry comment that she was not sorry somebody else would have less than a full night's rest for once. Siuan waited; no one could be allowed to see her and Leane leaving together. For a time Egwene merely studied the other woman. Neither spoke; Siuan seemed lost in thought. Finally she gave a start and stood, straightening her dress, plainly preparing to go.

'Siuan,' Egwene began slowly, and found herself uncertain how to continue.

Siuan thought she understood. 'You were not only right, Mother,' she said, looking Egwene straight in the eye, 'you were lenient. Too lenient, though I say it who shouldn't. You are the

Amyrlin Seat, and *no one* may be insolent or impertinent to you. If you'd given me a penance that made even Romanda feel sorry for me, it would have been no more than I deserved.'

'I will remember that next time,' Egwene said, and Siuan bowed her head as if in acceptance. Maybe it was. Unless the changes in her ran deeper than seemed possible, there almost certainly would be a next time, and more after that. 'But what I want to ask about is Lord Bryne.' All expression vanished from Siuan's face. 'Are you sure you wouldn't like me to . . . intervene?'

'Why would I want that, Mother?' Siuan's voice was blander than cold water soup. 'The only duties I have are teaching you the etiquette of your office and handing Sheriam reports from my eyes-and-ears.' She still retained some of her former network, though it was doubtful any knew who their reports went to now. 'Gareth Bryne hardly requires enough of my time to interfere with that.' She almost always referred to him that way, and even when she used his title, she put a bite into it.

'Siuan, a burned barn and a few cows couldn't cost that much.' Not compared with paying and feeding all those soldiers, certainly. But she had offered before, and the stiff reply was the same.

'I thank you, Mother, but no. I won't have him saying I break my word, and I swore to *work* the debt off.' Abruptly, Siuan's stiffness dissolved in laughter, rare when she spoke about Lord Bryne. Scowls were much more common. 'If you need to worry about somebody, worry about him, not me. I need no help handling Gareth Bryne.'

And that was the strange part. Weak she might be in the One Power, now, but not so weak that Siuan had to keep on as his servant, spending hours up to her elbows in hot soapy water with his shirts and smallclothes. Perhaps she did so in order to have someone at hand on whom she could loose the temper she was otherwise forced to keep in a sack. Whatever the reason, it occasioned no little talk, and confirmed her oddness in many eyes; she *was* Aes Sedai, after all, if rather far down. His methods of dealing with her temper – once she threw plates and boots, anyway – outraged her and provoked threats of dire consequences, yet though she could have wrapped him up unable to stir a finger, Siuan never touched *saidar* around him, not to do his chores and not even when it meant being turned over his knee. That fact she had kept hidden from most so far, but some things slipped out when she was in a rage, or when Leane was in a humor. There seemed to *be* no explanation. Siuan was not weak-spirited or a fool, she was neither meek nor afraid, she was not . . .

'You might as well be on your way, Siuan.' Clearly, some secrets were not going to be revealed tonight. 'It's late, and I know you want your bed.'

'Yes, Mother. And, thank you,' she added, though Egwene could not have said for what.

After Siuan left, Egwene rubbed her temples once more. She wanted to pace. The tent would not do; it might be the largest in the camp occupied by just one person, but that meant less than two spans by two, and it was crowded with cot and chair and stool, washstand and stand-mirror and no fewer than three chests full of clothes. Chesa had seen to those last, and Sheriam, and Romanda and Lelaine and a dozen more Sitters. They kept seeing to them; a few more gifts of silk shifts or stockings, one more dress grand enough to receive a king, and there would be need for a fourth chest. Maybe Sheriam and the Sitters hoped all the fine dresses would blind her to anything else, but Chesa just thought the Amyrlin Seat had to be clothed suitably for her station. Servants, it seemed, believed in following the correct rituals as much as the Hall ever did. Shortly Selame would be there; it was her turn to undress Egwene for bed, another ritual. Only, between her head and her restless feet, she was not ready for bed yet.

Leaving the lamps burning, she hurried out before Selame could arrive. Walking would clear her head, and maybe tire her enough that she could sleep soundly. Putting herself to sleep would be no problem – the Wise One dreamwalkers had taught her that skill early on – yet finding any rest in it was another matter. Especially when her mind boiled with a list of worries that began with Romanda and Lelaine and Sheriam, then ran through Rand, Elaida, Moghedien, the weather and on out of sight.

She avoided the area near Moghedien's tent. If she asked questions herself, too much importance would be given to a servant running away. Discretion had become part of her. The game she played allowed few slips, and being careless where you knew it did not matter could lead to being careless where it did. Worse, you could discover you had been wrong about where it mattered. *The weak must be bold cautiously.* That was Siuan again; she truly did her best to teach, and she knew this particular game very well.

There were no more people out and about in the moon-shadowed camp than had been there before, handfuls slouched wearily around low fires, exhausted by their evening's labors after a hard day's journey. Those who saw her rose tiredly to make their courtesies as she passed, murmuring 'The Light shine on you, Mother' or something like, occasionally asking her blessing, which she gave with a simple 'The Light bless you, my child.' Men and women old enough to be her grandparents sat back down beaming from that, yet she wondered what they actually believed about her, what they knew. All the Aes Sedai presented an unbroken front to the outside world, including their own servants. But Siuan said that if you believed a servant knew twice what he should, you only knew half the truth. Still, those bows and curtsies and murmurs followed her from one clump of people to the next, comforting her with the possibility that there were some at least who did not see her as a child the Hall brought out when they needed her.

As she passed an open area surrounded by ropes tied to posts driven into the ground, a gateway's silver slash of light flashed vivid in the darkness as it rotated open. It was not really light, though; it cast no shadows. She paused to watch beside a corner post. No one at the nearby fires even looked up; they were used to this by now. A dozen or more sisters, twice as many servants and a number of Warders bustled out, returning with messages and wicker cages of pigeons from the dovecotes in Salidar, a good five hundred miles west and south as the goose flew.

They began scattering before the gateway closed, carrying their burdens to Sitters, to their Ajahs, a few back to their own tents. Most nights, Siuan would have been with them; she seldom trusted anyone else to fetch messages destined for her even if most were in codes or ciphers. Sometimes the world seemed to hold more networks of eyes-and-ears than it did Aes Sedai, though most were severely truncated by circumstance. The majority of agents for the various Ajahs seemed to be lying low until the 'difficulties' in the White Tower subsided, and a good many of the individual sisters' eyes-and-ears had no idea where the woman they served was at present.

Several of the Warders saw Egwene and made careful bows, with a respect proper to the stole; sisters might eye her askance, but the Hall had raised her Amyrlin and the Gaidin needed no more. A number of the servants offered bows or curtsies, too. Not one of the Aes Sedai hurrying away from the gateway so much as glanced in her direction. Perhaps they did not notice her. Perhaps.

In a way, that anybody could still hear from any of their eyes-and-ears at all was one of Moghedien's 'gifts.' The sisters with the strength to make gateways had all been in Salidar long enough to know it well. Those who could weave a gateway of useful size were able to Travel almost anywhere from there, and land right on the spot. Trying to Travel *to* Salidar, however, would have meant spending half of each night learning the new roped-off patch of ground, more for some, every time they made camp. What Egwene had pried from Moghedien was a way to journey from a place you did not know well to one you did. Slower than Traveling, Skimming was not one of the lost Talents – no one had ever heard of it – so even the name was credited to Egwene. Anyone who could Travel could Skim, so every night sisters Skimmed to Salidar, checking the dovecotes for birds that had returned to where they had been hatched, then Traveled back.

The sight should have pleased her – the rebel Aes Sedai had gained Talents the White Tower thought lost forever, as well as learned new ones, and those abilities would help cost Elaida the Amyrlin Seat before all was done – yet instead of pleasure, Egwene felt sourness. Being snubbed had nothing to do with it, or not much, anyway. As she walked on, the fires grew farther between, then faded behind; all around her lay the dark shapes of wagons, most with canvas tops stretched over iron hoops, and tents glowing palely in the moonlight. Beyond, the army's campfires climbed the surrounding hills all around, the stars brought to ground. The silence from Caemlyn tied her middle into knots, whatever anyone else thought.

The very day they left Salidar a message had arrived, though Sheriam had not bothered to show it to her until a few days ago, and then with repeated warnings on the need to keep the contents secret. The Hall knew, but no one else must. More of the ten thousand secrets that infested the camp. Egwene was sure she never would have seen it if she had not kept going on about Rand. She could recall every carefully chosen word, written in a tiny hand on paper so thin it was a wonder the pen had not torn through.

We are well settled at the inn of which we spoke, and we have met with the wool merchant. He is a very remarkable young man, everything that Nynaeve told us. Still, he was courteous. I think he is somewhat afraid of us, which is to the good. It will go well.

You may have heard rumors about men here, including a fellow from Saldaea. The rumors are all too true, I fear, but we have seen none of them and will avoid them if we can. If you pursue two hares, both will escape you.

Verin and Alanna are here, with a number of young women from the same region as the wool merchant. I will try to send them on to you for training. Alanna has formed an attachment to the wool merchant which may prove useful, though it is troubling too. All will go well, I am sure.

Merana

Sheriam emphasized the good news, as she saw it. Merana, an experienced negotiator, had reached Caemlyn and been well received by Rand, the 'wool merchant.' Wonderful news, to Sheriam. And Verin and Alanna would be bringing Two Rivers girls to become novices. Sheriam was sure they must be coming down the same road they themselves were headed up. She seemed to think Egwene would be all aglow at the expectation of seeing faces from home. Merana would handle everything. Merana knew what she was doing.

'That's a bucket of horse sweat,' Egwene muttered at the night. A gap-toothed fellow carrying a large wooden bucket gave a start and gaped at her, so amazed he forgot to bow.

Rand, *courteous*? She had seen his first meeting with Coiren

Saeldain, Elaida's emissary. 'Overbearing' summed it up nicely. Why should he be different with Merana? And Merana thought he was afraid, thought that was good. Rand was seldom afraid even when he should be, and if he was now, Merana should remember that fear could make the mildest man dangerous, remember that Rand was dangerous just being who he was. And what was this attachment Alanna had formed? Egwene did not entirely trust Alanna. The woman did extremely odd things at times, maybe impetuously and maybe with some deeper motive. Egwene would not put it past her to find a way into Rand's bed; he would be clay in the hands of a woman like her. Elayne would break Alanna's neck if that was so, but that was the least of it. Worst of all, no more of the pigeons Merana had taken with her had appeared in the Salidar dovecotes.

Merana should have had some word to send, if only that she and the rest of the embassy had gone to Cairhien. Lately the Wise Ones did little more than acknowledge Rand was alive, yet it seemed he was there, sitting on his hands as far as she could make out. Which should have been a warning beacon. Sheriam saw it differently. Who could say why any man did what he did? Probably not even the man himself, most of the time, and when it came to one who could channel . . . Silence proved all was well; Merana surely would have reported any real difficulty. She must be on her way to Cairhien, if not there already, and there was no need to report further until she could send word of success. For that matter, Rand in Cairhien *was* success of a sort. One of Merana's goals, if not the most important, had been to ease him out of Caemlyn so that Elayne could return there safely and take the Lion Throne, and the dangers of Cairhien had dissipated. Incredible as it seemed, the Wise Ones said Coiren and her embassy had left the city on their way back to Tar Valon. Or maybe not so incredible. It all made a sort of sense, given Rand, given the way Aes Sedai did things. Even so, to Egwene, it all felt . . . wrong.

'I have to go to him,' she muttered. One hour, and she could straighten everything out. Underneath, he was still Rand. 'That's all there is to it. I have to go to him.'

'That isn't possible, and you know it.'

If Egwene had not had herself on a tight rein, she would have jumped a foot. As it was, her heart pounded even after she made out Leane by the light of the moon. 'I thought you were . . .' she said before she could stop herself, and only just managed not to say Moghedien's name.

The taller woman fell in beside her, keeping a careful watch for other sisters as they walked. Leane did not have Siuan's excuse for spending time with her. Not that being seen together once should cause any harm, but . . .

'Should not' isn't always 'will not', Egwene reminded herself. Slipping the stole from her shoulders, she folded it to carry in one hand. At a glance, from a distance, Leane might well be taken for an Accepted despite her dress; many Accepted lacked enough of the banded white dresses to wear one all the time. From a distance, Egwene might be taken for one, too. Not the most pacifying thought.

'Theodrin and Faolain are asking around near Marigan's tent, Mother. They weren't especially pleased. I did a fine sulk over carrying messages, if I do say so. Theodrin had to stop Faolain dressing me down for it.' Leane's laughter was quiet and breathy. Situations that grated Siuan's teeth usually amused her. She was cosseted by most of the other sisters for how well she had adjusted.

'Good, good,' Egwene said absently. 'Merana misstepped somehow, Leane, or he wouldn't be staying in Cairhien, and she wouldn't be keeping quiet.' Off in the distance, a dog bayed at the moon, then others, until they were abruptly silenced by shouts that, perhaps luckily, she could not quite understand. A number of the soldiers had dogs tagging along; there were none in the Aes Sedai camp. Any number of cats, but no dogs.

'Merana does know what she is doing, Mother.' It sounded very like a sigh. Leane and Siuan both agreed with Sheriam. Everyone did, except her. 'When you give someone a task, you have to trust it to them.'

Egwene sniffed and folded her arms. 'Leane, that man could strike sparks from a damp cloth, if it wore the shawl. I don't know Merana, but I've never seen an Aes Sedai who qualified as a damp cloth.'

'I've met one or two,' Leane chuckled. This time her sigh was plain. 'But not Merana, true. Does he really believe he has friends inside the Tower? Alviarin? That might make him difficult for Merana, I suppose, but I can hardly see Alviarin doing anything to risk her place. She was always ambitious enough for three.'

'He has a letter supposedly from her.' She could still see Rand gloating over receiving letters from Elaida and Alviarin both, back before she herself left Cairhien. 'Maybe her ambitions make her think *she* can replace Elaida with him on her side. That's if she really wrote it. He thinks he's clever, Leane – maybe he is – but he doesn't believe he needs anyone.' Rand would go on thinking he could handle anything by himself right up until one of those anythings crushed him. 'I know him inside and out, Leane. Being around the Wise Ones seems to have infected him, or maybe he infected them. Whatever the Sitters think, whatever any of you think, an Aes Sedai's shawl doesn't impress him any more than it does the Wise Ones. Sooner or later he'll exasperate a sister until she does something about it, or one of them will push him the wrong way, not realizing how strong he is, and what his temper is now. After that there might be no going back. I'm the only one who can deal with him safely. The only one.'

'He can hardly be as ... irritating ... as those Aiel women,' Leane murmured wryly. Even she found it difficult to be amused by her experiences with the Wise Ones. 'But it hardly matters. "The Amyrlin Seat being valued with the White Tower itself..."'

A pair of women appeared between the tents ahead, moving slowly as they talked. Distance and shadows obscured their faces, yet it was clear they were Aes Sedai from the way they carried themselves, an assurance that nothing hiding in any darkness could harm them. No Accepted on the brink of the shawl could manage quite that degree of confidence. A queen with an army at her back might not. They were coming toward her and Leane. Leane quickly turned in to the deeper dimness between two wagons.

Scowling with frustration, Egwene nearly pulled her out again and marched on. Let it all come into the open. She would stand before the Hall and tell them it was time they realized the Amyrlin's stole was more than a pretty scarf. She would ...

Following Leane, she motioned the other woman to walk on. What she would not do was throw everything on the midden heap in a fit of pique.

Only one Tower law specifically limited the power of the Amyrlin Seat. A fistful of irritating customs and a barrel full of inconvenient realities, but only one law, yet it could not have been a worse for her purposes. 'The Amyrlin Seat being valued with the White Tower itself, as the very heart of the White Tower, she must not be endangered without dire necessity, therefore unless the White Tower be at war by declaration of the Hall of the Tower, the Amyrlin Seat shall seek the lesser consensus of the Hall of the Tower before deliberately placing herself in the way of any danger, and she shall abide by the consensus that stands.' What rash incident by an Amyrlin had inspired that, Egwene did not know, but it had been law for something over two thousand years. To most Aes Sedai, any law that old attained an aura of holiness; changing it was unthinkable.

Romanda had quoted that ... that *bloody* law as though lecturing a half-wit. If the Daughter-Heir of Andor could not be allowed within a hundred miles of the Dragon Reborn, how much more they must preserve the Amyrlin Seat. Lelaine sounded almost regretful, most likely because she was agreeing with Romanda. That had nearly curdled both their tongues. Without them, both of them, the lesser consensus lay as far out of reach as the greater. Light, even that declaration of war only required the lesser consensus! So if she could not obtain permission ...

Leane cleared her throat. 'You can hardly do much if you go in secret, Mother, and the Hall will find out, soon or late. I think you would find it difficult to have an hour to yourself after that. Not that they'd dare put a guard on you, precisely, but there are ways. I can quote examples from ... certain sources.' She never mentioned the hidden records directly unless they were behind a ward.

'Am I so transparent?' Egwene asked after a moment. There were only wagons around them here, and beneath the wagons the dark mounds of sleeping wagon drivers and horse handlers and all the rest needed to keep so many vehicles moving. It was remarkable just how many conveyances over three hundred Aes Sedai required, when few would condescend to ride even a mile in wagon or cart. But there were tents and furnishings and foodstuffs, and a thousand things needed to keep the sisters and those who served them. The loudest sounds here were snores, a chorus of frogs.

'No, Mother,' Leane laughed softly. 'I just thought what I would do. But it's well known I've lost all my dignity and sense; the Amyrlin Seat can hardly take me for a model. I think you must let young Master al'Thor go as he will, for a time anyway, while you pluck the goose that's in front of you.'

'His way may lead us all to the Pit of Doom,' Egwene muttered, but it was not an argument. There had to be a way to pluck that goose and still keep Rand from making dangerous mistakes, but she could not see it now. Not frogs; those snores sounded like a hundred saws cutting logs full of knots. 'This is as bad a spot for a soothing walk as I've ever visited. I think I might as well go to bed.'

Leane tilted her head. 'In that case, Mother, if you will forgive me, there's a man in Lord Bryne's camp . . . After all, whoever heard of a Green without even one Warder?' From the sudden quickening in her voice, you might have thought she was off to meet a lover. Considering what Egwene had heard about Greens, perhaps there was not that much difference.

Back among the tents, the last of the fires had been doused with dirt; no one took risks with fire when the countryside was tinder dry. A few tendrils of smoke rose lazily in the moonlight where the job had not been well done. A man murmured drowsily in his sleep inside a tent, and here and there a cough drifted out or a rasping snore, but otherwise the camp lay silent and still. Which was why Egwene was surprised when someone stepped from the shadows in front of her, especially someone wearing the simple white dress of a novice.

'Mother, I need to speak to you.'

'Nicola?' Egwene had made a point of fixing name to face for every novice, no easy chore given how sisters hunted all along the army's path for girls and young women who could learn. Active search was still not well thought of – custom was to wait for the girl to ask, best of all to wait for her to come to the Tower – but ten times as many novices studied in the camp now as the White Tower had held in years. Nicola was one to be remembered, though, and besides, Egwene had often noticed the young woman staring at her. 'Tiana won't be pleased if she finds you up this late.' Tiana Noselle was the Mistress of Novices, known equally for a comforting shoulder when a novice needed to cry and an unyielding stance when it came to rules.

The other woman shifted as if to hurry away, then straightened her back. Sweat glistened on her cheeks. The darkness was cooler than the light had been, but not what anyone would call cool, and the simple trick of ignoring heat or cold came only with the shawl. 'I know I'm supposed to ask to see Tiana Sedai and then ask her to see you, Mother, but she'd never let a novice approach the Amyrlin Seat.'

'About what, child?' Egwene asked. The woman was older by six or seven years at least, but that was the proper address for a novice.

Fidgeting with her skirt, Nicola stepped closer. Large eyes met Egwene's perhaps more directly than a novice's should have. 'Mother, I want to go as far as I can.' Her hands plucked at her dress, but her voice was cool and self-possessed, fit for an Aes Sedai. 'I won't say they are holding me back, but I am sure I can become stronger than they say. I just know I can. You were never held back, Mother. No one has ever gained so much of her strength as fast as you. All I ask is the same chance.'

Movement in the shadow behind Nicola turned into another sweaty-faced woman, this one in short coat and wide trousers, carrying a bow. Her hair hung to her waist in a braid tied with six ribbons, and she wore short boots with raised heels.

Nicola Treehill and Areina Nermasiv seemed an odd pair to be friends. Like many of the older novices – women with nearly ten years on Egwene were tested now, though many sisters still grumbled that they were ten years too old to accept novice discipline – like many of those older women, Nicola was ferocious in her desire to learn, by all reports, and she had a potential bettered only by Nynaeve, Elayne and Egwene herself among living Aes Sedai. In fact, Nicola apparently was making great strides, often great enough that her teachers had to slow her down. Some said she had begun picking up weaves as if she already knew them. Not only that, but she already demonstrated two Talents, although the ability to 'see' *ta'veren* was minor, while the major Talent, Foretelling, emerged so that no one understood what she had Foretold. She herself did not remember a word she said. All in all, Nicola was already marked by the sisters as someone to watch despite her late start. The begrudging agreement to test women older than seventeen or eighteen probably could be laid at Nicola's feet.

Areina, on the other hand, was a Hunter for the Horn who swaggered as much as a man and sat around talking of adventures, those she had had and those she would, when she was not practicing with her bow. Very likely she had picked that weapon up from Birgitte, along with her manner of dress. She certainly seemed to have no interest in anything beside the bow, except flirting occasionally, in a rather forward manner, though not lately. Perhaps long days on the road left her too tired for it, if not for archery. Why she was still traveling with them, Egwene could not understand; it was hardly likely that Areina believed the Horn of Valere would turn up along their march, and impossible that she even suspected it was hidden away inside the White Tower. *Very* few people knew that. Egwene was not certain even Elaida did.

Areina seemed a posturing fool, but Egwene felt a certain sympathy for Nicola. She understood the woman's discontent, understood wanting to know it all now. She had been that way, too. Maybe she still was. 'Nicola,' she said gently, 'we all have limits. I'll never match Nynaeve Sedai, for example, whatever I do.'

'But if I could only have the chance, Mother.' Nicola actually wrung her hands in pleading, and there was a touch of it in her voice, yet her eyes still met Egwene's levelly. 'The chance you had.'

'What I did – because I had no choice, because I didn't know better – is called forcing, Nicola, and it is dangerous.' She had not heard that term until Siuan apologized for doing it to her; that was one time Siuan truly had seemed repentant. 'You know if you try to channel more of *saidar* than you're ready to handle, you risk burning yourself out before you ever come close to your full strength. Best you learn to be patient. The sisters won't let you be anything else until you are ready, anyway.'

'We came to Salidar on the same riverboat as Nynaeve and

Elayne,' Areina said suddenly. Her gaze was more than direct; it was challenging. 'And Birgitte.' For some reason, she said the name bitterly.

Nicola made shushing motions. 'There's no need to bring that up.' Oddly, she did not sound as if she meant it.

Hoping she was keeping her face half so smooth as Nicola's, Egwene tried to quell a sudden uneasiness. 'Marigan' had come to Salidar on that boat, too. An owl hooted, and she shivered. Some people thought hearing an owl in moonlight meant bad news was coming. She was not superstitious, but ... 'No need to bring up what?'

The other two women exchanged looks, and Areina nodded.

'It was on the walk from the river to the village.' For all her supposed reluctance, Nicola peered straight into Egwene's eyes. 'Areina and I heard Thom Merrilin and Juilin Sandar talking. The gleeman, and the thief-taker? Juilin said if there were Aes Sedai in the village — we weren't sure, yet — and they learned Nynaeve and Elayne had been pretending to be Aes Sedai, then we were all jumping into a school of silverpike, which I take it isn't very safe.'

'The gleeman saw us and hushed him,' Areina put in, fingering the quiver at her waist, 'but we heard.' Her voice was hard as her stare.

'I know they're both Aes Sedai now, Mother, but wouldn't they still be in trouble if anyone found out? The sisters, I mean? Anybody who pretends to be a sister is in trouble if they find out, even years later.' Nicola's face did not change, but her gaze suddenly seemed to be trying to fix Egwene's. She leaned a little forward, intent. 'Anybody at all. Isn't that so?'

Emboldened by Egwene's silence, Areina grinned. An unpleasant grin in the night. 'I hear Nynaeve and Elayne were sent out of the Tower on some task by the Sanche woman back when she was Amyrlin. I hear you were sent off by her, too, at the same time. Got into all sorts of trouble when you came back.' Sly insinuation slithered into her voice. 'Do you remember them playing at Aes Sedai?'

They stood there looking at her, Areina leaning insolently on her bow, Nicola so expectant the air should have crackled.

'Siuan Sanche is Aes Sedai,' Egwene said coldly, 'and so are

Nynaeve al'Meara and Elayne Trakand. You will show them proper respect. To you, they are Siuan Sedai, Nynaeve Sedai and Elayne Sedai.' The pair blinked in surprise. Inside, her stomach quivered. With outrage. After everything she had been through tonight, she was confronted with *blackmail* from these . . . ? She could not think of a word bad enough. Elayne could have; Elayne listened to stablemen and wagon drivers and every sort, memorizing the words she should have refused to hear. Unfolding the striped stole, Egwene draped it carefully across her shoulders.

'I don't think you understand, Mother,' Nicola said hastily. Not fearfully, however; just attempting to force her point. 'I merely worried that if anyone found out that you had—' Egwene gave her no chance to go further.

'Oh, I understand, child.' The fool woman *was* a child, however old she was. Any number of the older novices gave trouble, usually in the form of insolence toward Accepted set to teach them, but even the silliest had sense enough to avoid impertinence to the sisters. It fanned her anger to white heat, that the woman had the gall to try this on with her. They were both taller than she, if not by much, but she planted her fists on her hips and drew herself up, and they shrank away as though she loomed. 'Do you have any notion how serious it is to bring charges against a sister, especially for a novice? Charges based on a conversation you claim to have heard between men now a thousand miles away. Tiana would skin you alive and put you to scrubbing pots the rest of your natural life.' Nicola kept trying to push a word in – apologies, they sounded like this time, and more protests that Egwene did not understand, frantic attempts to change everything – but Egwene ignored her and rounded on Areina. The Hunter took another step back, wetting her lips and looking remarkably uncertain. 'You needn't think you would walk away clear, either. Even a Hunter could be hauled to Tiana for a thing like this. If you're lucky enough not to be flogged at a wagon tongue, the way they do soldiers caught stealing. Either way, you'll be tossed out by the road with your welts for company.'

Drawing a deep breath, Egwene folded her hands at her waist. Clutched together, they would not tremble. All but cowering, the pair looked suitably chastened. She hoped those downcast eyes and slumped shoulders and shifting feet were not feigned. By rights, she should send them to Tiana right now. She had no idea what the penalty might be for trying to blackmail the Amyrlin Seat, but it seemed likely that being turned out of the camp would be the least of it. In Nicola's case, the turning out would have to wait until her teachers were satisfied she knew enough of channeling not to hurt herself or others by accident. Nicola Treehill would never be Aes Sedai, though, once that charge was laid against her; all that potential would go for nothing.

Except ... Any woman caught pretending to be Aes Sedai was set down so hard she would still be whimpering years later, and an Accepted caught might very well consider the other woman fortunate, but surely Nynaeve and Elayne were safe now they really were sisters. Herself, as well. Only, it might take no more than a whisper of this to erase any chance of making the Hall acknowledge her truly the Amyrlin Seat. As well jaunt off to Rand, and then tell the Hall to their faces. She dared not allow these two to see her doubt, or even suspect.

'I will forget this,' she said sharply. 'But if I hear so much as a whisper of it again, from anyone ... ' She drew a ragged breath – if she heard *shouts* of it, there might be little she could do – but by the way they jumped, they read a threat that pricked deep. 'Get to your beds before I change my mind.'

In an instant they became a flurry of curtsies, of 'Yes, Mother' and 'No, Mother' and 'As you command, Mother.' They scurried away looking back over their shoulders at her, every step faster than the last, until they were running. She had to walk on sedately, but she wanted to run too.

Chapter 10

Unseen Eyes

Selame was waiting when Egwene got back to her tent, a rail-thin woman with dark Tairen coloring and a nearly impervious self-assurance. Chesa was right; she did carry her long nose raised, as though recoiling from a bad smell. Yet if her manner with the other maids was arrogant, she was in reality quite different around her patroness. As Egwene entered, Selame folded herself into a curtsy so deep her head nearly brushed the carpet, skirts spread as wide as they would go in the cramped quarters. Before Egwene had taken her second step inside, the woman leaped up into fussing over her buttons. And fussing over her, too. Selame had very little sense.

'Oh, Mother, you went out with your head uncovered again.' As if she had ever worn any of those beaded caps the woman favored, or the embroidered velvet things Meri favored, or Chesa's plumed hats. 'Why, you're shivering. You should never go walking out-of-doors without a shawl and parasol, Mother.' How was a parasol supposed to stop shivering? With sweat trickling down her own cheeks however fast she dabbed with her handkerchief, Selame never thought to ask *why* she shivered, which was perhaps just as well. 'And you went alone, in the night. It just isn't proper, Mother. Besides, there are all those soldiers, rough men, with no decent respect for any woman, even Aes Sedai. Mother, you simply mustn't . . .'

Egwene let the foolish words wash over her in the same way she let the woman undress her, paying less than half a mind. Ordering her to be quiet would only produce so many hurt looks and abused sighs that it made little difference. Except for the brainless chatter, Selame performed her duties diligently, if with so many flourishes they became a dance of grand gestures and obsequious curtsies. It seemed impossible that anyone could be as silly as Selame, always concerned with appearances, always worrying over what people would think. To her, people were Aes Sedai and the nobility, and their upper servants. By her book, no one else mattered; perhaps no one else thought, by her book. It probably *was* impossible. Egwene was not about to forget who had found Selame in the first place, any more than she did who had found Meri. True, Chesa was a gift from Sheriam, but Chesa had shown her loyalties to Egwene more than once.

Egwene wanted to tell herself the tremors that the other woman took for shivers were quivers of rage, yet she knew a worm of fear writhed in her belly. She had come too far, had too much to do yet, to allow Nicola and Areina to put a spoke through her wheels.

As her head popped through the top of a clean shift, she caught a bit of the skinny woman's prattle and stared. 'Did you say ewe's milk?'

'Oh, yes, Mother. Your skin is so soft, and nothing will keep it that way like bathing in ewe's milk.'

Maybe she really was an idiot. Hustling a protesting Selame out, Egwene brushed her own hair, turned down her own cot, placed the now useless *a'dam* bracelet in the small carved ivory box where she kept her few pieces of jewelry, then extinguished the lamps. *All by myself*, she though sarcastically in the darkness. *Selame and Meri will have conniptions.*

Before retiring, however, she padded to the entrance and opened a small gap in the doorflaps. Outside was moonlit stillness and silence, broken by a night heron's cry that suddenly cut off in a shriek. There were hunters abroad in the darkness. After a moment something moved in the shadows beside a tent across the way. It looked like a woman.

Perhaps idiocy did not disqualify Selame any more than dour-faced gloom eliminated Meri. It could be either one. Or someone else entirely. Even Nicola or Areina, however unlikely. She let the tentflap fall shut with a smile. Whoever the watcher was would not see where she went tonight.

The way the Wise Ones had taught her to put herself to sleep was simple. Eyes closed, feeling each part of the body relax in turn, breathing in time with her heartbeat, mind unfocused and drifting, all but one tiny corner, drifting. Sleep swept over her in moments, but it was the sleep of a dreamwalker.

Formless, she floated deep within an ocean of stars, infinite points of light glimmering in an infinite sea of darkness, fireflies beyond counting flickering in an endless night. Those were dreams, the dreams of everyone sleeping anywhere in the world, maybe of everyone in all possible worlds, and this was the gap between reality and *Tel'aran'rhiod*, the space separating the waking world from the World of Dreams. Wherever she looked ten thousand fireflies vanished as people woke, and ten thousand new were born to replace them. A vast ever-changing array of sparkling beauty.

She did not waste time in admiration, though. This place held dangers, some deadly. She was sure she knew how to avoid those, but one peril in this place aimed straight at her if she lingered too long, and being caught in it would be embarrassing to say the least. Keeping a wary eye out – well, it would have been a wary eye had she had eyes here – she moved. She had no sense of motion. It seemed she stood still and that glittering ocean swirled around her until one light settled before her. Every twinkling star looked exactly like every other, yet she knew this was Nynaeve's dream. *How* she knew was another matter; not even the Wise Ones understood that recognition.

She had considered trying to find Nicola's dreams, and Areina's. Once she unearthed them, she knew exactly how to sink the fear of the Light into their bones, and she did not give a fig that every bit of it was proscribed. Practicality sent her here instead, not fear of the forbidden. She had done what was not done before, and she was certain she would again should it become necessary. Do what you must, then pay the price for it, was what she had been taught, by the same women who had marked off those forbidden areas. It was refusal to admit the debt, refusal to pay, that often turned necessity to evil. But even if that pair were asleep, locating someone's dreams the first time was arduous at best, without guarantees. Days of effort – nights of it, rather – were more likely to deliver utter nothing. This was at least sure.

Slowly she moved closer through everlasting darkness, though once again it seemed that she stayed still and the pinpoint of light grew, to a glowing pearl, an iridescent apple, a full moon, until it filled her vision entirely with brightness, all the world. She did not touch it, though, not yet. A space finer than a hair remained between. Ever so gently, she reached across that gap. With what, lacking a body, was as much a mystery as how she knew one dream from another. Her will, the Wise Ones said, but she still did not understand how that could be. As though laying a finger to a soap bubble, she kept her touch very delicate indeed. The shining wall shimmered like spun glass, pulsed like a heart, delicate and alive. A little firmer touch, and she would be able to 'see' inside, 'see' what Nynaeve was dreaming. A bit firmer still, and she could actually step inside and be a part of the dream. That carried hazards, especially with anyone of a strong mind, but either looking in or stepping in could be mortifying. For example, if the dreamer happened to be dreaming of a man she was particularly interested in. Apologies alone took half the night when you did that. Or, with a hooking sort of motion, like rolling a fragile bead across a tabletop, she could snatch Nynaeve out, into a dream of her own making, a part of *Tel'aran'rhiod* itself, where she was in complete control. She was sure that would work. Of course, that was one of the forbidden things, and she did not think Nynaeve would appreciate it.

NYNAEVE, THIS IS EGWENE. UNDER NO CIRCUMSTANCES ARE YOU TO RETURN UNTIL YOU FIND THE BOWL, NOT UNTIL I CAN SETTLE A PROBLEM WITH AREINA AND NICOLA. THEY KNOW YOU WERE PRETENDING. I WILL EXPLAIN MORE WHEN I SEE YOU NEXT IN THE LITTLE TOWER. BE CAREFUL. MOGHEDIEN HAS ESCAPED.

The dream winked out, the soap bubble pricked. Despite the message, she would have giggled had she possessed a throat. A disembodied voice in your dream could have a startling effect. Especially if you were afraid the speaker might be peeking. Nynaeve was not one to forget even when it was an accident.

That light-spangled sea whirled about her once more until she settled on another sparkling pinpoint. Elayne. The two women very likely slept no more than a dozen paces apart in Ebou Dar, but distance had no meaning here. Or perhaps it had a different meaning.

This time when she delivered her message, the dream pulsed and changed. It still appeared exactly the same as every other, but even so, to her it was transformed. Had the words drawn Elayne into another dream? They would remain, however, and she would remember on waking.

With Nicola and Areina's bowstrings dampened a little more, it was time to turn her attention to Rand. Unfortunately, finding his dreams would be as useless as finding an Aes Sedai's. He shielded his somewhat as they did theirs, although apparently a man's shield differed from a woman's. An Aes Sedai's shield was a crystal carapace, a seamless sphere woven of Spirit, but however transparent it appeared, it might as well have been steel. She could not recall how many fruitless hours she had frittered away trying to peer through his. Where a sister's shielded dream seemed brighter, close up, his were dimmer. It was like staring into muddy water; sometimes you had the impression that something had moved deep in those gray-brown swirls, but you could never tell what.

Again the endless array of lights spun and settled, and she approached a third woman's dream. Gingerly. So much lay between her and Amys that it seemed akin to approaching her mother's dreams. In truth, she had to admit, she wanted to emulate Amys in many ways. She desired Amys' respect every bit as greatly as she did the Hall's. Maybe, if she had to choose, she would choose Amys'. Certainly, there was no Sitter she esteemed as highly as she did Amys. Pushing away a sudden diffidence, she tried to make her 'voice' softer, to no avail. AMYS, THIS IS EGWENE. I MUST SPEAK WITH YOU.

We will come, a voice murmured to her. Amys' voice.

Startled, Egwene backed away. She felt like laughing at herself. Perhaps it was just as well to be reminded that the Wise Ones had long years' more experience at this. There were times she was afraid she might have been spoiled by not having to work harder for her abilities with the One Power. Then again, as if to make up for it, sometimes everything else seemed like trying to climb a cliff in a rainstorm.

Abruptly she caught movement at the very edge of her field of vision. One of those points of light slid through the sea of stars, drifting toward her of its own volition, growing larger. Only one dream would do that, one dreamer. In a panic, she fled, wishing she had a throat to scream, or curse, or just shout. Especially at the tiny corner of her that wanted to stay where she was and wait.

Not even the stars moved this time. They simply disappeared, and she was leaning against a thick redstone column, panting as though she had sprinted a mile, heart beating fit to burst. After a moment, she looked down at herself and began to laugh a trifle unsteadily, trying to catch her breath. She had on a full-skirted gown of shimmering green silk, worked in thread-of-gold in wide, ornate bands across the bodice and along the hem. That bodice also showed *considerably* more bosom than she ever would waking, and a broad cinched belt of woven gold made her waist seem smaller than it really was. Then again, maybe it was smaller. Here in *Tel'aran'rhiod*, you could be however you wanted, whatever you wanted. Even when the wanting was unconscious, if you were not careful. Gawyn Trakand had unfortunate effects on her, *very* unfortunate.

That tiny part of her still wished she had waited to be overtaken by his dream. Overtaken and absorbed by it. If a dreamwalker loved somebody to distraction, or hated them beyond reason, most especially if the emotion was returned, she could be pulled into that person's dream; she drew the dream, or it drew her, as a lodestone drew iron filings. She certainly did not hate Gawyn, but she could not afford to be trapped in his dream, not tonight, trapped until he wakened, being as he saw her. Which was a good deal more beautiful than she truly was; oddly, *he* appeared less beautiful than he was in life. There was no question of a strong mind or concentration when love or hate that strong was involved. Once you were in that dream, there you remained until the other person stopped dreaming about you. Remembering what he dreamed of doing with her, what they had done in his dreams, she felt a fiery blush suffusing her face.

'A good thing none of the Sitters can see me now,' she muttered.

'They'd never take me for anything but a girl, then.' Grown women did not flutter and moon over a man this way; she was certain of that. Not women with any sense, anyway. What he dreamed of would come, but at a time of her choosing. Obtaining her mother's permission might be difficult, yet surely she would not withhold it even if she had never laid eyes on Gawyn. Marin al'Vere trusted her daughters' judgment. Now it was time for her youngest daughter to show a little of that judgment and put these fancies away until a better time.

Looking around, she almost wished she could go on letting Gawyn fill her thoughts. More massive columns ran in every direction, supporting a soaring, vaulted ceiling and a great dome. None of the gilded lamps hanging from golden chains overhead was lit, yet there was light of a sort, light that was just there, without source, neither bright nor dim. The Heart of the Stone, inside the great fortress called the Stone of Tear. Or rather its image in *Tel'aran'rhiod*, an image as real as the original in many ways. This was where she had met the Wise Ones before, their choice. A strange one for Aiel, it seemed to her. She would have expected Rhuidean, now that it was open, or somewhere else in the Aiel Waste, or simply wherever the Wise Ones happened to be. Every place except Ogier *stedding* had its reflection in the World of Dreams – even the *stedding* did, really; but they could not be entered, just as Rhuidean had once been closed. The Aes Sedai camp was out of the question, of course. A number of the sisters now had access to *ter'angreal* that allowed them to enter the World of Dreams, and since none really knew what they were doing, they often began their ventures by appearing in the camp of *Tel'aran'rhiod* as though setting out on a normal journey.

Like *angreal* and *sa'angreal*, by Tower law *ter'angreal* were the property of the White Tower, no matter who happened to possess them for the present. Very seldom did the Tower insist, at least when possession lay somewhere like the so-called Great Holding in this very Stone of Tear – eventually they would come to the Aes Sedai, and the White Tower had always been good at waiting when it needed to – but those actually in Aes Sedai hands were in the gift of the Hall, of individual Sitters. The loan, really; they were almost never given. Elayne had learned to duplicate dream *ter'angreal*, and she and Nynaeve had taken two with them, but the rest were in the Hall's possession now, along with the other sorts Elayne had made. Which meant that Sheriam and her little circle could use them whenever they wished, and most assuredly Lelaine and Romanda, though it was likely those two sent others instead of entering *Tel'aran'rhiod* themselves. Until quite recently, no Aes Sedai had walked the dream in centuries, and they still had considerable difficulties, most of which stemmed from a belief that they could learn by themselves. Even so, the last thing Egwene wanted was any of *their* followers spying on this meeting tonight.

As though the thought of spies had made her more sensitive, she became aware of being watched by unseen eyes. That sensation was always present in *Tel'aran'rhiod*, and not even the Wise Ones knew why, but although hidden eyes always seemed to be there, actual watchers might be present as well. It was not Romanda or Lelaine on her mind, now.

Trailing her hand against the column, she walked all the way around it slowly, studying the redstone forest as it ran away in deepening shadows. The light surrounding her was not real; anybody in one of those shadows would see the same light around them while shadows hid her. People did appear, men and women, flickering images that rarely lasted more than a few heartbeats. She had no interest in those who touched the World of Dreams in their sleep; anyone might do that by happenstance, but luckily for them, only for moments, seldom long enough to face any of the dangers. The Black Ajah possessed dream *ter'angreal*, too, stolen from the Tower. Worse, Moghedien knew *Tel'aran'rhiod* as well as any dreamwalker. Perhaps better. She could control this place and anyone in it as easily as turning her hand.

For a moment Egwene wished she had spied on Moghedien's dreams while the woman was prisoner, just once, just enough to be able to distinguish them. But even identifying her dreams would not reveal where she was now. And there had been the possibility of being drawn in against her will. She certainly despised Moghedien enough, and the Forsaken most assuredly hated her without bounds. What happened in there was not real, not even as real as in *Tel'aran'rhiod*, but you remembered it as if it was. A night in Moghedien's power would have been a nightmare she likely would have relived every time she went to sleep for the rest of her life. Maybe awake, too.

Another circuit. What was that? A dark, regally beautiful woman in pearl-covered cap and lace-ruffed gown strode from the shadows and vanished. A Tairen woman dreaming, a High Lady or dreaming herself as one. She might be plain and dumpy, a farmwife or a merchant, awake.

Better to have spied on Logain than Moghedien. She still would not know where he was, but she might have some idea of his plans. Of course, being pulled into his dream might not have been much more pleasant than being drawn into Moghedien's. He hated all Aes Sedai. Arranging his escape had been one of those necessary things; she just hoped the price would not be too high. Forget Logain. Moghedien was the danger, Moghedien who might come after her, even here, especially here, Moghedien who . . .

Suddenly she became aware of how heavily she was moving, and made a vexed sound in her throat, very nearly a groan. The beautiful gown had become a full set of plate-and-mail armor like that of Gareth Bryne's heavy cavalry. An open-faced helmet rested on her head, with a crest in the shape of the Flame of Tar Valon, by the feel. It was very irritating. She was beyond this sort of lack of control.

Firmly she changed the armor to what she had worn meeting the Wise Ones before. It was just a matter of thought. Full skirt of dark wool and loose white *algode* blouse, just as she had worn while studying with them, complete with a fringed shawl so green it was nearly black and a folded head scarf to hold her hair back. She did not duplicate their jewelry, of course, all the multitudes of necklaces and bracelets. They would laugh at her for that. A woman built her collection over the years, not in the blink of a dream.

'Logain is on his way to the Black Tower,' she said aloud; she certainly hoped he was; at least there would be some check on him then, or so she hoped, and if he was caught and gentled again, Rand could not blame any sister following her, 'and Moghedien has no way of knowing where I am.' That, she tried to make sound a certainty.

'Why should you fear the Shadowsouled?' asked a voice behind her, and Egwene tried to climb into the air. This being *Tel'aran'rhiod*, and she a dreamwalker, she was more than her own height above the floorstones before she came to herself. *Oh, yes,* she thought, floating, *I'm far beyond all those beginner's mistakes.* If this went on, next she would be jumping when Chesa gave her good morning.

Hoping she was not blushing too badly, she let herself settle slowly; perhaps she could retain a little dignity.

Perhaps, yet Bair's aged face had more creases than usual from a grin that seemed nearly to touch her ears. Unlike the other two women with her, she could not channel, but that had nothing to do with dreamwalking. She was as skilled as either, more in some areas. Amys was smiling too, if not so broadly, but sun-haired Melaine threw back her head and roared.

'I have never seen anyone . . .' Melaine just managed to get out. 'Like a rabbit.' She gave a little hop and lifted a full pace into the air.

'I recently caused Moghedien some hurt.' Egwene was quite proud of her poise. She liked Melaine – the woman was much less thorny since she was with child; with twins, actually – but at the moment Egwene could have strangled her cheerfully. 'Some friends and I damaged her pride, if not much more. I think she would like the opportunity to repay me.' On impulse, she changed her clothes once more, to the sort of riding dress she wore every day now, in lustrous green silk. The Great Serpent encircled her finger with gold. She could not tell them everything, but these women were friends too, and they deserved to know what she could tell.

'Wounds to the pride are remembered long after wounds to the flesh.' Bair's voice was thin and high, yet strong, a reed of iron.

'Tell us about it,' Melaine said, with an eager smile. 'How did you shame her?' Bair's was just as enthusiastic. In a cruel land, you either learned to laugh at cruelty or spent your life weeping; in the Three-fold Land, the Aiel had learned to laugh long since. Besides, shaming an enemy was considered an art.

Amys studied Egwene's new clothes for a moment, then said, 'That can come later, I think. We are to talk, you said.' She gestured to where the Wise Ones liked to talk, out beneath the vast dome at the heart of the chamber.

Why they chose that spot was another mystery Egwene could not puzzle out. The three women settled themselves cross-legged, spreading their skirts neatly, only a few paces from what seemed to be a sword made of gleaming crystal, rising hilt-first from where it had been driven into the floorstones. They paid it no mind whatsoever – it was no part of their prophecies – any more than they did the people who flashed into existence around the great chamber, but here was always where they came.

Fabled *Callandor* would indeed function as a sword despite its appearance, but in truth it was a male *sa'angreal*, one of the most powerful ever made in the Age of Legends. She felt a little shiver, thinking of male *sa'angreal*. It had been different when there was only Rand. And the Forsaken, of course. But now there were these Asha'man. With *Callandor*, a man could draw enough of the One Power to level a city in a heartbeat and devastate everything for miles. She walked wide around it, holding her skirts aside reflexively. From the Heart of the Stone Rand had drawn *Callandor* in fulfillment of the Prophecies, then returned it for his own reasons. Returned it, and snared it round with traps woven in *saidin*. They would have their reflection, too, one that might trigger as decisively as the original should the wrong weaves be tried nearby. Some things in *Tel'aran'rhiod* were all too real.

Trying not to think of the Sword That Is Not a Sword, Egwene placed herself before the three Wise Ones. Fastening their shawls around their waists, they unlaced their blouses. That was how Aiel women sat with friends, in their tents beneath a hot sun. She did not sit, and if that made her seem a supplicant or on trial, so be it. In a way, in her heart, she was. 'I've not told you why I was summoned away from you, and you have not asked.'

'You will tell us when you are ready,' Amys said complacently. She looked of an age with Melaine despite hair white as Bair's tumbling to her waist – her hair had begun turning when she was little older than Egwene – but she was the leader among the three, not Bair. For the first time, Egwene wondered just how old she was. Not a question you asked a Wise One, any more than an Aes Sedai.

'When I left you, I was one of the Accepted. You know about the division in the White Tower.' Bair shook her head and grimaced; she knew, but she did not understand. None of them did. To Aiel, it was as unreal as clan or warrior society dividing against itself. Perhaps it was also affirmation in their eyes that Aes Sedai were less than they should be. Egwene went on, surprised that her voice was collected, steady. 'The sisters who oppose Elaida have raised me as their Amyrlin. When Elaida is pulled down, I will sit on the Amyrlin Seat, in the White Tower.' She added the striped stole to her clothes and waited. Once she had lied to them, a serious transgression under *ji'e'toh*, and she was not sure how they would react to learning this truth she had hidden. If only they believed, at least. They merely looked at her.

'There is a thing children do,' Melaine said carefully after a time. Her pregnancy did not show yet, but already she had the inner radiance, making her even more beautiful than usual, and an inward, unshakable calm. 'Children all want to push spears, and they all want to be the clan chief, but eventually they realize that the clan chief seldom dances the spears himself. So they make a figure and set it on a rise.' Off to one side the floor suddenly mounded up, no longer stone tiles but a ridge of sun-baked brown rock. Atop it stood a shape vaguely like a man, made of twisted twigs and bits of cloth. 'This is the clan chief who commands them to dance the spears from the hill where he can see the battle. But the children run where they will, and their clan chief is only a figure of sticks and rags.' A wind whipped the cloth strips, emphasizing the hollowness of the shape, and then ridge and figure were gone.

Egwene drew a deep breath. Of course. She had atoned for her lie according to *ji'e'toh*, by her own choice, and that meant it was as if the lie had never been spoken. She should have known better. But they had struck to the heart of her situation as though they had been weeks in the Aes Sedai camp. Bair studied the floor, not wanting to witness her shame. Amys sat with chin in hand, sharp blue gaze trying to dig to her heart.

'Some see me so.' Another deep breath, and she pushed the truth out. 'All but a handful do. Now. By the time we finish our battle, they will know I *am* their chief, and they will run as *I* say.'

'Return to us,' Bair said. 'You have too much honor for these women. Sorilea already has a dozen young men picked out for you to view in the sweat tents. She has a great desire to see you make a bridal wreath.'

'I hope she will be there when I wed, Bair' – to Gawyn, she hoped; that she would bond him, she knew from interpreting her dreams, but only hope and the certainty of love said they would wed – 'I hope all of you will, but I've made my choice.'

Bair would have argued further, and Melaine too, but Amys raised a hand, and they fell silent, if not pleased. 'There is much *ji* in her decision. She will bend her enemies to her will, not run from them. I wish you well in your dance, Egwene al'Vere.' She had been a Maiden of the Spear, and often thought as one still. 'Sit. Sit.'

'Her honor is her own,' Bair said, frowning at Amys, 'but I have another question.' Her eyes were an almost watery blue, yet when they turned on Egwene, they were sharp as ever Amys' had been. 'Will you bring these Aes Sedai to kneel to the *Car'a'carn*?'

Startled, Egwene nearly fell the last foot to the floorstones rather than sitting. There was no hesitation in her answer, though. 'I can't do that, Bair. And would not if I could. Our loyalty is to the Tower, to the Aes Sedai as a whole, above even the lands we were born in.' That was true, or was supposed to be, though she wondered how the claim squared in their minds with her and the others' rebellion. 'Aes Sedai don't even swear fealty to the Amyrlin, and certainly not to any man. That would be like one of you kneeling to a clan chief.' She made an illustration the way Melaine had, by concentrating on its reality; *Tel'aran'rhiod* was infinitely malleable if you knew how. Beyond *Callandor* three Wise Ones dropped to their knees before a clan chief. The man strongly resembled Rhuarc, the women the three in front of her. She only held it for an instant, but Bair glanced at it and sniffed loudly. The notion *was* preposterous.

'Do not compare those women to us.' Melaine's green eyes sparkled with something very like their old sharpness; her tone was honed like a razor.

Egwene held her tongue. The Wise Ones seemed to despise Aes Sedai, all except her, or perhaps better to say they were contemptuous. She thought they might actually resent the prophecies that linked them to Aes Sedai. Before she had been summoned by the Hall to be raised Amyrlin, Sheriam and her circle of friends had met here regularly with these three, but that had ended as much because the Wise Ones refused to hide their contempt as because Egwene finally had been called. In *Tel'aran'rhiod*, a confrontation with someone more familiar with the place could be mortifying in the extreme. Even with Egwene, there was a distance now, and certain matters they would not discuss, such as whatever they knew of Rand's plans. Before, she had been one with them, a student in dreamwalking; after, she was Aes Sedai, even before they learned what she had just told them.

'Egwene al'Vere will do as she must,' Amys said. Melaine gave her a long look and rearranged her shawl ostentatiously, shifted several long necklaces in a clatter of ivory and gold, but said nothing. Amys seemed even more the leader than she had been. The only Wise One Egwene had ever seen make other Wise Ones defer to her so easily was Sorilea.

Bair had imagined tea before her, as it might be in the tents, a golden teapot worked with lions from one country, a silver tray edged in ropework from another, tiny green cups of delicate Sea Folk porcelain. The tea tasted real, of course, felt real going down. Despite a hint of some sweet berry or herb she did not recognize, it was too bitter for Egwene's tongue. She imagined a little honey in it and took another sip. Too sweet. A touch less honey. Now it tasted right. That was something you could not do with the Power. Egwene doubted that anyone had the skill to weave threads of *saidar* fine enough to remove honey from tea.

For a moment she sat peering into her teacup, thinking about honey and tea and fine threads of *saidar*, but that was not what held her silent. The Wise Ones wanted to guide Rand no less than Elaida or Romanda or Lelaine, or very likely any other Aes Sedai. Of course, they only wanted to direct the *Car'a'carn* in a way that was best for the Aiel, yet those sisters wanted to direct the Dragon Reborn toward what was best for the world, as they saw it. She did not spare herself. Helping Rand, keeping him from putting himself at odds with Aes Sedai beyond recovery, those meant guiding him, too. *Only, I'm right*, she reminded herself. *Whatever I do is as much for his own good as for anybody else's. None of the others ever think about what's right for him.* But it was best to remember that these women were more than simply her friends and followers of the *Car'a'carn*. No one was ever simply anything, she was learning.

'I do not think you wished only to tell us you are now a woman chief among the wetlanders,' Amys said over her teacup. 'What troubles your mind, Egwene al'Vere?'

'What troubles me is what always does.' She smiled to lighten the mood. 'Sometimes I think Rand is going to give me gray hairs before my time.'

'Without men, no woman would have gray hairs.' Normally, that would have been a joke on Melaine's tongue, and Bair would have made another over the vast knowledge of men Melaine had gained in just a few months of marriage, but not this time. All three women simply watched Egwene and waited.

So. They wished to be serious. Well, Rand was serious business. She just wished she could be sure they saw it anything at all the way she did. Balancing her cup on her fingertips, she told them everything. About Rand, anyway, and her fears since learning of the silence from Caemlyn. 'I don't know what he's done – or what she has; everybody tells me how experienced Merana is, but she's had none with the likes of him. When it comes to Aes Sedai, if you hid this cup in a meadow, he'd still manage to step on it inside three paces. I know I could do better than Merana, but . . .'

'You could return,' Bair suggested again, and Egwene shook her head firmly.

'I can do more where I am, as Amyrlin. And there are rules even for the Amyrlin Seat.' Her mouth twisted for an instant. She did not like admitting that, especially not to these women. 'I can't even visit him without the Hall's permission. I'm Aes Sedai now, and I have to obey our laws.' That came out more fiercely than she intended. It was a stupid law, but she had not yet found a way around it. Besides, they wore so little expression she was sure they were snickering incredulously inside. Not even a clan chief had the right to say when or where a Wise One could go.

The three women across from her exchanged long looks. Then Amys set her teacup down and said, 'Merana Ambrey and other Aes Sedai followed the *Car'a'carn* to the treekillers' city. You need have no fear he will put his foot wrong with her, or any of your sisters with her. We will see that there is no difficulty between him and any Aes Sedai.'

'That hardly sounds like Rand,' Egwene said doubtfully. So Sheriam had been right about Merana. But why was she still silent?

Bair cackled with laughter. 'Most parents have more trouble with their children than lies between the *Car'a'carn* and the women who came with Merana Ambrey.'

'So long as he isn't the child,' Egwene chuckled, relieved that someone was amused at something. The way these women felt about Aes Sedai, they would have been spitting nails if they thought any sister was gaining influence with him. On the other hand, Merana had to gain some, or she might as well leave now. 'But Merana should have sent a report. I don't understand why she hasn't. You're certain there isn't any—?' She could not think of how to finish. There was no way that Rand could have stopped Merana from sending off a pigeon.

'Perhaps she sent a man on a horse.' Amys grimaced faintly; as much as any Aiel, she found riding repugnant. Your own legs were good enough. 'She brought none of the birds that wetlanders use.'

'That was foolish of her,' Egwene muttered. Foolish did not come close. Merana's dreams would be shielded, so there was no point trying to talk to her there. Even if they could be found. Light, but it was vexing! She leaned forward intently. 'Amys, promise me you won't try to stop him from talking with her, or make her so angry she does something foolish.' They were quite capable of that; more than capable. They had putting an Aes Sedai's back up perfected to a Talent. 'She's just supposed to convince him that we mean him no harm. I'm sure Elaida has some nasty surprise hidden behind her skirts, but we don't.' She would see to that, if anyone had different notions. Somehow, she would. 'Promise me?'

They passed unreadable looks back and forth. They could not like the idea of letting a sister near Rand, certainly not unhindered. Doubtless one of them would contrive to be present whenever Merana was, but she could live with that so long as they didn't hinder too much.

'I promise, Egwene al'Vere,' Amys said finally, in a voice flat as worked stone.

Probably she was offended that Egwene had required a pledge, but Egwene felt as though a weight had lifted. Two weights. Rand

and Merana were not at each other's throats, and Merana would have a chance to do what she had been sent to do. 'I knew I'd have the unvarnished truth from you, Amys. I can't tell you how glad I am to hear it. If anything were wrong between Rand and Merana . . . Thank you.'

Startled, she blinked. For an instant, Amys wore *cadin'sor*. She made some sort of small gesture, too. Maiden handtalk, perhaps. Neither Bair nor Melaine, sipping their tea, gave any sign that they had noticed. Amys must have been wishing she were somewhere else, away from the tangle Rand had made of everybody's life. It would be embarrassing, shaming, for a Wise One dreamwalker to lose control of herself in *Tel'aran'rhiod* even for an instant. To the Aiel, shame hurt far worse than pain, but it had to be witnessed to *be* shame. If it was not seen, or those who saw refused to admit it, then it might as well never have happened. A strange people, but she certainly did not want to shame Amys. Composing her face, she went on as if nothing had happened.

'I must ask a favor. An important favor. Don't tell Rand – or anybody – about me. About this, I mean to say.' She lifted an end of her stole. Their faces made an Aes Sedai's best calm look maniacal. Stone was not in it. 'I don't mean lie,' she added hastily. Under *ji'e'toh*, asking someone to lie was little better than telling one yourself. 'Just don't bring it up. He's already sent somebody to "rescue" me.' *And won't he be furious when he finds out I shuffled Mat off to Ebou Dar with Nynaeve and Elayne*, she thought. She had had to do it, though. 'I don't need rescuing, and I don't want it, but he thinks he knows better than everybody. I'm afraid he might come hunting for me himself.' Which frightened her more – that he might appear in the camp alone, raging, with three hundred or so Aes Sedai around him? Or that he might come with some of the Asha'man? Either way, a disaster.

'That would be . . . unfortunate,' Melaine murmured, though she was seldom one for understatement, and Bair muttered, 'The *Car'a'carn* is headstrong. As bad as any man I have ever known. And a few women, for that matter.'

'We will hold your confidence close, Egwene al'Vere,' Amys said gravely.

Egwene blinked at the quick agreement. But perhaps it was not so surprising. To them, the *Car'a'carn* was only another chief, just more so, and Wise Ones had certainly been known to keep things from a chief they thought he should not know.

After that there was not much to say, though they talked a while longer over more cups of tea. She longed for a lesson in walking the dream, but could not ask with Amys there. Amys would go, and she wanted her company more than learning. The closest the Wise Ones came to telling her anything Rand was actually doing was when Melaine grumbled that he should finish the Shaido and Sevanna now, and both Bair and Amys frowned at her so, she turned bright red. After all, Sevanna was a Wise One, as Egwene knew quite bitterly. Not even the *Car'a'carn* would be allowed to interfere with even a Shaido Wise One. And she could not give them details of her own circumstances. That they had leaped right to the most shaming part did nothing to lessen the shame she would feel talking about it – it was very hard not to drop back into behaving, even thinking, as the Aiel did when she was around them; for that matter, she thought it might have shamed her had she never met an Aiel – and the only sort of advice they had about dealing with Aes Sedai lately was of a nature that Elaida herself would not try to follow. An Aes Sedai riot, unlikely as it sounded, might result. Worse, they already thought badly enough of Aes Sedai without her adding wood to the fire. Some day she wanted to forge a link between the Wise Ones and the White Tower, but that would never happen unless she managed to dampen that fire down. Another thing she had no idea how to do, as yet.

'I must go,' she said at last, standing. Her body lay asleep in her tent, but there was never quite enough rest in sleep while you were in *Tel'aran'rhiod*. The others rose with her. 'I hope you will all be very careful. Moghedien hates me, and she would certainly try to hurt anyone who's my friend. She knows a great deal about the World of Dreams. At least as much as Lanfear did.' That was as close as she could come to warning them without saying right out that Moghedien might know more than they. Aiel pride could be prickly. They took her meaning, though, and without offense.

'If the Shadowsouled meant to threaten us,' Melaine said, 'I think they would have by now. Perhaps they believe we are no threat to them.'

'We have glimpsed those who must be dreamwalkers, including men.' Bair shook her head incredulously; no matter what she knew about the Forsaken, she considered male dreamwalkers about as common as legs on snakes. 'They avoid us. All of them.'

'I think we are as strong as they,' Amys added. In the One Power, she and Melaine were no stronger than Theodrin and Faolain – far from weak, indeed stronger than most Aes Sedai, but far from a Forsaken's strength, too – yet in the World of Dreams, knowledge of *Tel'aran'rhiod* was often as powerful as *saidar*, more at times. Here, Bair was the equal of any sister. 'But we will take care. It is the enemy you underestimate who kills you.'

Egwene took Amys' hand and Melaine's, and would have Bair's had there been a way. Instead, she included her with a smile. 'I'll never be able to tell you what your friendship means to me, what you mean to me.' Despite everything, that was simple truth. 'The whole world seems to be changing every time I blink. You three are one of the few firm spots in it.'

'The world does change,' Amys said, sadly. 'Even mountains are worn away by the wind, and no one can climb the same hill twice. I hope we will always be friends in your eyes, Egwene al'Vere. May you always find water and shade.' And with that, they were gone, back to their own bodies.

For a time she stood frowning at *Callandor* but not seeing it, until suddenly she gave herself an exasperated shake. She had been thinking about that endless field of stars. If she waited there long, Gawyn's dream would find her again, swallow her the way his arms would shortly thereafter. A pleasant way to spend the rest of the night. And a childish waste of time.

Firmly she made herself step back to her sleeping body, but not to ordinary sleep. She never did that anymore. That one corner of her brain remained fully aware, cataloging her dreams, filing away those that foretold the future, or at any rate gave glimpses of the possible course it might take. At least she could tell that much now, though the only one she had been able to interpret so far was the dream that told of Gawyn becoming her Warder. Aes Sedai called this Dreaming, and the women who could do it Dreamers, all long dead but her, yet it had no more to do with the One Power than dreamwalking did.

Perhaps it was inevitable she should dream first of Gawyn, because she had been thinking of him.

She stood in a vast, dim chamber where everything was indistinct. Everything except Gawyn, slowly coming toward her. A tall, beautiful man – had she ever thought his half-brother Galad was more beautiful? – with golden hair and eyes of the most wonderful deep blue. He had some distance to cover yet, but he could see her; his gaze was fixed on her like an archer's on the target. A faint sound of crunching and grating hung in the air. She looked down. And felt a scream building in her. On bare feet, Gawyn walked across a floor of broken glass, shards breaking at every slow step. Even in that faint light she could see the trail of blood left by his slashed feet. She flung out a hand, tried to shout for him to stop, tried to run to him, but just that quickly she was elsewhere.

In the way of dreams she floated above a long, straight road across a grassy plain, looking down upon a man riding a black stallion. Gawyn. Then she was standing in the road in front of him, and he reined in. Not because he saw her, this time, but the road that had been straight now forked right where she stood, running over tall hills so no one could see what lay beyond. She knew, though. Down one fork was his violent death, down the other, a long life and a death in bed. On one path, he would marry her, on the other, not. She knew what lay ahead, but not which way led to which. Suddenly he did see her, or seemed to, and smiled, and turned his horse along one of the forks ... And she was in another dream. And another. Another. And again.

Not all had any bearing on the future. Dreams of kissing Gawyn, of running in a cool spring meadow with her sisters the way they had as children, slid by along with nightmares where Aes Sedai with switches chased her through endless corridors, where misshapen things lurched through shadows all around, where a grinning Nicola denounced her to the Hall and Thom Merrilin came forward to give evidence. Those she discarded; the others she tucked away, to be prodded and poked later in the hope she might understand what they meant.

She stood before an immense wall, clawing at it, trying to tear it down with her bare hands. It was not made of brick or stone, but countless thousands of discs, each half white and half black, the ancient symbol of the Aes Sedai, like the seven seals that had once held the Dark One's prison shut. Some of those seals were broken now, though not even the One Power could break *cuendillar*, and the rest had weakened somehow, but the wall stood strong, however she beat at it. She could not tear it down. Maybe it was the symbol that was important. Maybe it was the Aes Sedai she was trying to tear down, the White Tower. Maybe ...

Mat sat on a night-shrouded hilltop, watching a grand Illuminator's display of fireworks, and suddenly his hand shot up, seized one of those bursting lights in the sky. Arrows of fire flashed from his clenched fist, and a sense of dread filled her. Men would die because of this. The world would change. But the world *was* changing; it always changed.

Straps at waist and shoulder held her tightly to the block, and the headsman's axe descended, but she knew that somewhere someone was running, and if they ran fast enough, the axe would stop. If not ... In that corner of her mind, she felt a chill.

Logain, laughing, stepped across something on the ground and mounted a black stone; when she looked down, she thought it was Rand's body he had stepped over, laid out on a funeral bier with his hands crossed at his breast, but when she touched his face, it broke apart like a paper puppet.

A golden hawk stretched out its wing and touched her, and she and the hawk were tied together somehow; all she knew was that the hawk was female. A man lay dying in a narrow bed, and it was important he not die, yet outside a funeral pyre was being built, and voices raised songs of joy and sadness. A dark young man held an object in his hand that shone so brightly she could not see what it was.

On and on they came, and she sorted feverishly, desperately tried to understand. There was no rest in it, but it must be done. She would do what must be done.

Chapter 11

An Oath

'You asked to be wakened before the sun, Mother.'

Egwene's eyes popped open – she had set herself a time to wake only moments from now – and despite herself she started back against her pillow from the face above her. Stern through a sheen of perspiration, it was not a pleasant sight first thing in the morning. Meri's manner was perfectly respectful, but a pinched nose, a permanently downturned mouth and dark eyes sharp with censure said she had never seen anyone half as good as they should be or pretended to be, and her flat tone turned every meaning head to heels.

'I hope you slept well, Mother,' she said, while her expression managed a fair accusation of sloth. Her black hair, in tight coils over her ears, seemed to pull her face painfully. The unrelieved drab dark gray she always wore, however it made her sweat, only added to the gloom.

It was a pity she had not managed a little real rest. Yawning, Egwene rose from her narrow cot and scrubbed her teeth with salt, washed her face and hands while Meri laid out her clothes for the day, donned stockings and a clean shift, then suffered herself to be dressed. 'Suffered' was the word.

'I fear some of these knots will pull, Mother,' the cheerless woman murmured, drawing the brush through Egwene's hair, and Egwene very nearly told her she had not deliberately tangled it in her sleep.

'I understand we will rest here today, Mother.' Bone idleness, seethed Meri's reflection in the stand-mirror.

'This shade of blue will set off your coloring nicely, Mother,' Meri said as she did up Egwene's buttons, her face an accusation of vanity.

Filled with relief that she would have Chesa tonight, Egwene donned the stole and fled almost before the woman finished.

Not even a rim of the sun showed above the hills to the east. The land humped up all around in long ridges and irregular mounds, sometimes hundreds of feet high, that often looked as though monstrous fingers had squeezed them. Shadows like twilight bathed the camp lying in one of the broad valleys between, but it was well awake in the heat that never really lifted. Smells of breakfast cooking filled the air, and people bustled about, though there was none of the rush that would have meant a day's marching ahead. White-clad novices darted about at a near run; a wise novice always carried out her chores as quickly as she could. Warders never seemed hurried, of course, but even servants carrying the morning meal to Aes Sedai appeared to stroll this morning. Well, almost. In comparison to the novices. The whole camp was taking advantage of the halt. A clatter and curses as a jack-lever slipped announced wagonwrights making repairs, and a distant tapping of hammers told of farriers reshoeing horses. A dozen candlemakers had their molds lined up already, and the kettles heating to melt the carefully hoarded drippings and tag-ends of every candle that had been burned. More big black kettles stood on fires to boil water for baths and laundry, and men and women were heaping clothes up nearby. Egwene gave little notice to any of the activity.

The thing of it was, she was certain Meri did not do it apurpose; she could not help her face. Even so, she was as bad as it would be to have Romanda for a maid. The thought made her laugh out loud. Romanda as lady's maid would have her mistress toeing the line in no time; no doubt as to who would run and fetch in *that* pair. A gray-haired cook paused in raking coals from atop an iron oven to give her a grin of shared amusement. For a moment, anyway. Then he realized he was grinning at the Amyrlin Seat, not just some young woman walking by, and the grin melted crookedly as he jerked a bow before bending back to his work.

If she sent Meri off, Romanda would only find a new spy. And

Meri would again be starving her way from village to village. Adjusting her dress – she really had gone before the woman was quite finished – Egwene's fingers found a small linen bag, the strings tucked behind her belt. She did not have to lift it all the way to her nose to smell rose petals and a blend of herbs with a cool scent. It made her sigh. A face like a headsman's, spying for Romanda without any doubt, and trying to perform her duties as well as she could. Why were these things never easy?

Approaching the tent she used as a study – many called it the Amyrlin's study, as if it were the rooms in the Tower – a solemn satisfaction replaced worry over Meri. Whenever they halted for a day, Sheriam would be there before her with fat sheaves of petitions. A laundress imploring clemency on a charge of theft when she had been caught with the jewelry sewn into her dress, or a blacksmith begging a testimonial for his work, which he could not use unless he intended to leave, and likely not then. A harness maker asking the Amyrlin's prayers for her to give birth to a daughter. One of Lord Bryne's soldiers requesting the Amyrlin's personal blessing to his wedding a seamstress. There was always a slew from older novices, appealing visits to Tiana and even extra chores. Anyone had the right to petition the Amyrlin, but those in service to the Tower seldom did, and never novices. Egwene suspected that Sheriam worked to dig up petitioners, something to butter the cat's paws, keep her out of Sheriam's hair while the Keeper took care of what she considered important. This morning, Egwene thought she might make Sheriam eat those petitions for her breakfast.

When she entered the tent, though, Sheriam was not there. Which perhaps should not have been a surprise, given the night before. The tent was not empty, however.

'The Light illumine you this morning, Mother,' Theodrin said, making a deep curtsy that set the brown fringe of her shawl swaying. She had all the fabled Domani grace, though her high-necked dress was really quite modest. Domani women were not known for modesty. 'We did as you commanded, but no one saw anybody near Marigan's tent last night.'

'Some of the men remembered seeing Halima,' Faolain added

sourly, with a much briefer bend of her knees, 'but aside from that, they hardly recalled whether they went to sleep.' Many women disapproved of Delana's secretary, but it was her next remark that made Faolain's round face darker than usual. 'We met Tiana while we were roaming about. She told us to go to bed and be quick about it.' Unconsciously she stroked the blue fringe on her shawl. New Aes Sedai almost always wore their shawls more often than they needed to, so Siuan said.

Giving them a smile she hoped was welcoming, Egwene took her place behind the small table. Carefully; the chair tilted for a moment anyway, until she reached down and pulled the leg straight. An edge of folded parchment peeked out from beneath the stone inkwell. Her hands twitched toward it, but she made them be still. Too many sisters saw little need for courtesy. She would not be one of those. Besides, these two had a claim on her.

'I am sorry for your difficulties, daughters.' Made Aes Sedai by her decree on being raised Amyrlin, they faced the same predicament as she, but lacking the added shield of the Amyrlin's stole, small shield that that had proved. Most sisters behaved as though they were still only Accepted. What went on inside the Ajahs was seldom known outside, but it was rumored that they truly had had to beg admittance, and that guardians had been named to oversee their behavior. No one had ever heard the like, but everyone took it for fact. She had done them no favor. Another thing that had been necessary, though. 'I will speak to Tiana.' It might do some good. For a day, or an hour.

'Thank you, Mother,' Theodrin said, 'but there is no need to bother yourself.' Still, she also touched her shawl, hands lingering. 'Tiana wanted to know why we were up so late,' she added after a moment, 'but we didn't tell her.'

'There was no need for secrecy, daughter.' A pity they had not found a witness, though. Moghedien's rescuer would remain a shadow half-glimpsed. Always the most frightening sort. She glanced at the tiny corner of parchment, itching to read it. Maybe Siuan had discovered something. 'Thank you both.' Theodrin recognized a dismissal and made her manners to go, but stopped when Faolain remained where she was.

'I wish I had held the Oath Rod already,' Faolain told Egwene in tones of frustration, 'so you could know what I say is true.'

'This isn't the time to bother the Amyrlin,' Theodrin began, then folded her hands and turned her attention to Egwene. Patience blended with something else on her face. Clearly the stronger of the two in the Power, she always took the lead, yet this time she was prepared to step back. In aid of what, Egwene wondered.

'It isn't the Oath Rod that makes a woman Aes Sedai, daughter.' Whatever some believed. 'Speak the truth to me, and I will believe it.'

'I don't like you.' Faolain's mop of dark curls swayed as she shook her head for emphasis. 'You must know that. You probably think I was mean when you were a novice, when you came back to the White Tower after running away, but I still believe you didn't get half the punishment you should have. Maybe my admitting it will help you know I speak the truth. It isn't as though we have no choice even now. Romanda offered to take us under her protection, and so did Lelaine. They said they'd see we were tested and raised properly as soon we return to the Tower.' Her face grew angrier, and Theodrin rolled her eyes and broke in.

'Mother, what Faolain is fumbling all around without getting to the point is that we didn't attach ourselves to you because we had no choice. And we didn't do it in gratitude for the shawl.' She pursed her lips as if thinking that raising them Aes Sedai in the manner Egwene had was not really a gift to inspire much gratitude.

'Then why?' Egwene asked, leaning back. The chair shifted, but held.

Faolain jumped in before Theodrin could more than open her mouth. 'Because you are the Amyrlin Seat.' She still sounded angry. 'We can see what happens. Some of the sisters think you're Sheriam's puppet, but most believe Romanda or Lelaine tell you where and when to step. It is not right.' Her face was twisted in a scowl. 'I left the Tower because what Elaida did wasn't right. They raised you Amyrlin. So I am yours. If you will have me. If you can trust me without the Oath Rod. You must believe me.'

'And you, Theodrin?' Egwene said quickly, schooling her face. Knowing how the sisters felt was bad enough; hearing it again was ... painful.

'I am yours, too,' Theodrin sighed, 'if you'll have me.' She spread her hands disparagingly. 'We are not much, I know, but it looks as though we are all you have. I must admit I was hesitant, Mother. Faolain is the one who kept insisting we do this. Frankly . . .' She settled her shawl again unnecessarily, and her voice firmed. 'Frankly, I do not see how you can win out over Romanda and Lelaine. But we are trying to behave as Aes Sedai, even though we aren't really, yet. We will not be that, Mother, whatever you say, until the other sisters see us as Aes Sedai, and that won't happen until we have been tested and have sworn the Three Oaths.'

Plucking the folded scrap of parchment out from under the inkwell, Egwene fingered it while she thought. Faolain was the driving force behind this? That seemed as unlikely as a wolf befriending the shepherd. She suspected 'dislike' was a mild word for what Faolain felt for her, and the woman must know Egwene hardly saw her as a potential friend. If they had accepted either Sitter's arrangement, mentioning the offer might be a good means of disarming her suspicions.

'Mother,' Faolain said, and stopped, looking surprised at herself. It was the first time she had addressed Egwene so. Drawing a deep breath, she went on. 'Mother, I know you must have a hard time believing us, since we've never held the Oath Rod, but—'

'I wish you would stop bringing that up,' Egwene said. It was well to be careful, but she could not afford to refuse every offer of help for fear of plots. 'Do you think everybody believes Aes Sedai because of the Three Oaths? People who know Aes Sedai know a sister can stand truth on its head and turn it inside out if she chooses to. Myself, I think the Three Oaths hurt as much as they help, maybe more. I will believe you until I learn you've lied to me, and I will trust you until you show you don't deserve it. The same way everybody else does with one another.' Come to think of it, the Oaths did not really change that. You still had to take a sister on trust most of the time. The Oaths just made people warier about it, wondering whether and how they were being manipulated. 'Another thing. You two *are* Aes Sedai. I don't want to hear any more about having to be tested, or hold the Oath Rod, or any of it. Bad enough you have to face that nonsense without parroting it yourselves. Have I made myself clear?'

The two women standing on the other side of the table murmured hastily that she had, then exchanged long looks. This time, it was Faolain who appeared indecisive. Finally, Theodrin glided around to kneel beside Egwene's chair and kiss her ring. 'Under the Light and by my hope of salvation and rebirth, I, Theodrin Dabei, swear fealty to you, Egwene al'Vere, to faithfully serve and obey on pain of my life and honor.' She looked at Egwene questioningly.

It was all Egwene could do to nod. This was no part of Aes Sedai ritual; this was how noble swore to ruler. Even some rulers did not receive so strong an oath. Yet no sooner had Theodrin risen with a relieved smile than Faolain took her place.

'Under the Light and by my hope of salvation and rebirth, I, Faolain Orande . . .'

All that she could have wished for and more. From any other sisters, at least, who were not just as likely to be sent to fetch another's dustcloak if the wind rose.

When Faolain finished, she remained kneeling, but stiffly upright. 'Mother, there is the matter of my penance. For what I said to you, about not liking you. I will set it myself, if you wish, but it is your right.' Her voice was as rigid as her posture, yet not at all fearful. She looked ready to stare down a lion. Eager to, in fact.

Biting her lip, Egwene nearly laughed aloud. Keeping her face smooth took effort; maybe they would take it for a hiccough. However much they claimed they were not really Aes Sedai, Faolain had just proved how much of one she was. Sometimes sisters set themselves penances, in order to maintain the proper balance between pride and humility – that balance was much prized, supposedly, and the only reason given usually – but certainly none sought to have one imposed. Penance set by another could be quite harsh, and the Amyrlin was supposed to be harder in this than the Ajahs. Either way, though, many sisters made a haughty display of submission to the greater will of the Aes Sedai, an arrogant showing of their lack of arrogance. The pride of humility, Siuan called it. She considered telling the woman to eat a handful of soap just to see her expression – Faolain had a mean tongue – but instead . . .

'I don't hand out penance for telling the truth, daughter. Or for not liking me. Dislike to your heart's content, so long as you keep your oath.' Not that anyone except a Darkfriend would break that particular oath. Still, there were ways around almost anything. But weak sticks were better than none, when you were fending off a bear.

Faolain's eyes widened, and Egwene sighed as she motioned the woman to rise. Had their positions been reversed, Faolain *would* have put her nose firmly in the dust.

'I'm setting you two tasks to begin, daughters,' she went on.

They listened carefully, Faolain not even blinking, Theodrin with a thoughtful finger to her lips, and this time when she dismissed them, they said, 'As you command, Mother,' in unison as they curtsied.

Egwene's good mood was fleeting, though. Meri arrived with her breakfast on a tray as Theodrin and Faolain departed, and when Egwene thanked her for the rose-petal pomander, she said, 'I had a few spare moments, Mother.' By her expression, that could have been an accusation that Egwene worked her too hard, or that she herself did not work hard enough. Not a pleasant spice for the stewed fruit. For that matter, the woman's face might sour the mint tea and turn the warm crusty bun hard as a rock. Egwene sent her away before eating. The tea was weak anyway. Tea was one of the things in short supply.

The note that had been under the inkwell proved no better seasoning. 'Nothing of interest in the dream,' said Siuan's fine script. So Siuan had been in *Tel'aran'rhiod* last night too; she did a good deal of spying there. It mattered little whether she had been hunting some sign of Moghedien, though that would have been insanely foolish, or something else; nothing was nothing.

Egwene grimaced, and not just for the 'nothing.' Siuan in *Tel'aran'rhiod* last night meant a visit from Leane sometime today, complaining. Siuan most definitely no longer was allowed any of the dream *ter'angreal*, not since she had tried to teach some of the other sisters about the World of Dreams. It was not so much that she knew little more than they, or even that few sisters believed they actually needed a teacher to learn anything, but Siuan possessed a tongue like a rasp and no patience. Usually she managed to hold her temper, but two outbursts of shouting and fist-shaking, and she had been fortunate just to find herself denied access to the *ter'angreal*. Leane was given one whenever she asked, though, and frequently Siuan used it in secret. That was one of the few real bones of contention between them; both would have been in *Tel'aran'rhiod* every night if they could.

With a grimace Egwene channeled the tiniest spark of Fire to set a corner of the parchment alight and held it until it burned nearly to her fingers. Nothing left to be found by anyone rooting through her belongings and reported where it would rouse suspicions.

Breakfast almost done, she was still alone, and that was not usual. Sheriam might well be avoiding her, but Siuan should have been there. Popping a last bit of the bun into her mouth and washing it down with a final swallow of tea, she rose to go find her, only to have the object of her intended search stalk into the tent. Had Siuan had a tail, she would have been lashing it.

'Where have you been?' Egwene demanded, weaving a ward against listeners.

'Aeldene pulled me out of my blankets first thing,' Siuan growled, dropping onto one of the stools. 'She still thinks she'll pump the Amyrlin's eyes-and-ears out of me. No one gets that! No one!'

When Siuan had first arrived in Salidar, a stilled woman on the run, a deposed Amyrlin the world thought dead, the sisters might well not have let her stay except that she knew not only the Amyrlin Seat's network of agents, but also that of the Blue Ajah, which she had run before being raised to the stole. That had given her a certain influence, just as Leane's agents inside Tar Valon had given her some. The arrival of Aeldene Stonebridge, who had taken her place with the Blue eyes-and-ears, had changed matters for Siuan. Aeldene had been outraged that reports from the handful of Blue agents Siuan had managed to reach had been handed to women outside the Ajah. That Aeldene's own position had been revealed – only two or three sisters were supposed to know, even within the Blue –infuriated her to near apoplexy. She not only snatched back control of the Blue network, not only upbraided Siuan in a voice that might have been heard a mile off, she very nearly went for Siuan's throat. Aeldene was from an Andoran mining village in the Mountains of Mist, and it was said her crooked nose came from fighting with her fists when she was a girl. Aeldene's actions had started others thinking.

Egwene returned to her unsteady chair and pushed her breakfast tray aside. 'Aeldene won't take it away from you, Siuan, and neither will anyone else.' When Aeldene reclaimed the Blue eyes-and-ears, others had begun thinking that the Blue should not have the Amyrlin's as well. No one suggested that it should be in Egwene's control. The Hall was to have it. So Romanda said, and Lelaine. Each intended to be the one in charge, of course, the one those reports came to first, for being first to know had advantages. Aeldene thought those agents should be added to the Blue network since Siuan was Blue. At least Sheriam was content simply to be handed all the reports Siuan received. Which she usually was. 'They can't make you give it up.'

Egwene filled her teacup again, setting it and the blue-glazed honeypot on the corner of the table nearest Siuan, but the other woman only stared at them. The anger had gone out of her. She slumped on the stool. 'You never really think about strength,' she said, half to herself. 'You're aware of it, whether you're stronger than somebody else, but you don't think about it. You just know that she defers to you, or you to her. There was no one stronger than me, before. No one, since . . .' Her eyes dropped to her hands, stirring uneasily on her lap. 'Sometimes, when Romanda is hammering at me, or Lelaine, it suddenly hits me like a gale. They're so far above me now, I should be holding my tongue until they give me permission to speak. Even Aeldene is, and she's no more than middling.' She forced her head upright, mouth tight and voice bitter. 'I suppose I'm adjusting to reality. That's ingrained in us, too, driven deep before you ever test for the shawl. But I don't like it. I don't!'

Egwene picked up her pen from beside the inkwell and the sand jar, fiddling with it while she chose words. 'Siuan, you know how I feel about what needs to be changed. There's too much we do because Aes Sedai have always done it that way. But things are changing, no matter who believes it will all go back to how it was. I doubt anyone else was ever raised Amyrlin without being Aes

Sedai first.' That should have elicited a comment on the White Tower's hidden records – Siuan often said there was *nothing* that had not occurred at least once in the Tower's history, though this did seem to be a first – but Siuan sat there disheartened, like a sack. 'Siuan, the Aes Sedai way isn't the only way, and not even always the best. I intend to make sure we follow the best way, and whoever can't learn to change, or won't, had better learn to live with it.' Leaning across the table, she tried to make her expression encouraging. 'I never did figure out how Wise Ones determine precedence, but it isn't strength in the Power. There are women who can channel who defer to women who can't. One, Sorilea, would never have made it to Accepted, yet even the strongest jump when she says toad.'

'Wilders,' Siuan said dismissively, but it lacked force.

'Aes Sedai, then. I wasn't raised Amyrlin because I am the strongest. The wisest women are chosen for the Hall or to be ambassadors or advisors, the most skillful anyway, not those with the most strength.' Best not to say skillful in what, though Siuan certainly possessed those particular skills too.

'The Hall? The Hall might send me for tea. They might have me sweep out when they've finished sitting.'

Sitting back, Egwene threw down the pen. She wanted to shake the woman. Siuan had kept going when she could not channel at all, and *now* her knees began to fold? Egwene was on the point of telling her about Theodrin and Faolain – that should get some rise, and approval – when she saw an olive-skinned woman ride past the open tent flaps looking lost in thought beneath the wide gray hat she wore to keep off the sun.

'Siuan, it's Myrelle.' Letting the ward go, she rushed outside. 'Myrelle,' she called. Siuan needed a victory to wash the taste of being bullied out of her mouth, and this might be just the thing. Myrelle was one of Sheriam's lot, and apparently with a secret all her own.

Reining in her sorrel gelding, Myrelle looked around, and gave a start when she saw Egwene. By her expression, the Green sister had not realized what part of the camp she was passing through. A thin dustcloak hung down the back of her pale gray riding dress. 'Mother,' she said hesitantly, 'if you will forgive me, I—'

'I will not forgive you,' Egwene cut in, making her flinch. Any doubt vanished that Myrelle had heard about last night from Sheriam. 'I will talk with you. Now.'

Siuan had come outside too, but instead of watching the sister climb uneasily from her saddle, she stared down the rows of tents toward a stocky, graying man with a battered breastplate strapped over his buff-colored coat, leading a tall bay in their direction. His presence was a surprise. Lord Bryne usually communicated with the Hall by messenger, and his rare visits mostly finished before Egwene learned he had come. Siuan assumed such a look of Aes Sedai serenity it nearly made you forget her youthful face.

Glancing briefly at Siuan, Bryne made a leg, handling his sword with a spare grace. A weathered man, he was only moderately tall, but the way he carried himself made him seem taller. There was nothing flashy about him; the sweat on his broad face made him seem to be about a job of work. 'Mother, may I speak with you? Alone?'

Myrelle turned as if to go, and Egwene snapped, 'You stay right there! Right where you are!' Myrelle's mouth dropped open. Her surprise seemed as much for her own obedience as Egwene's decisive tone, and it faded into bitter resignation that she quickly hid behind a cool façade. One belied by the way she twiddled her reins.

Bryne did not even blink, though Egwene was sure he at least had an inkling of her situation. She suspected that very little surprised him, or unsettled him. Just the sight of him had made Siuan ready to fight back, for all it was apparently she who started most of their arguments. Already her fists rested on her hips and her gaze was fixed on him, an auguring stare that should have made anyone uneasy even had it not come from an Aes Sedai. Myrelle offered more than helping Siuan, though. Perhaps. 'I intended to ask you to come this afternoon, Lord Bryne. I ask now.' She had questions to put to him. 'We can talk then. If you will forgive me.'

Instead of accepting her dismissal, he said, 'Mother, one of my patrols found something just before dawn, something I think you should see for yourself. I can have an escort ready in—'

'No need for that,' she broke in quickly. 'Myrelle, you will come with us. Siuan, would you ask someone to bring my horse, please? Without delay.'

Riding out with Myrelle would be better than confronting her here, if Siuan's patched-together clues really pointed at anything, and on a ride she could ask Bryne her questions, but neither fueled her haste. She had just spotted Lelaine striding toward her through the tentrows, Takima at her side. With one exception, all the women who had been Sitters before Siuan was deposed had drifted to either Lelaine or Romanda. Most of the newly chosen Sitters went their own way, which was slightly better in Egwene's view. Just slightly.

Even at a little distance the set of Lelaine's shoulders was evident. She looked ready to walk through whatever got in her way. Siuan saw her as well and darted off without pausing for so much as a curtsy, yet there was no time to make a clean escape short of leaping onto Lord Bryne's horse.

Lelaine planted herself in front of Egwene, but it was Bryne she fixed with eyes sharp as tacks, considering, calculating what he was doing there. She had larger fish to put on the fire, though. 'I must speak with the Amyrlin,' she said peremptorily, pointing toward Myrelle. 'You will wait; I will talk to you after.' Bryne bowed, not too deeply, and led his horse where she pointed. Men who had any brains at all soon learned arguments did little good with Aes Sedai, and with Sitters the tally was usually none.

Before Lelaine could open her mouth, Romanda was suddenly there, radiating command so strongly that at first Egwene did not even notice Varilin with her, and the slender, red-haired Sitter for the Gray was inches taller than most men. The only surprise was that Romanda had not appeared sooner. She and Lelaine watched one another like hawks, neither allowing the other near Egwene alone. The glow of *saidar* surrounded both women at the same instant, and each wove a ward around the five of them to stop eavesdropping. Their eyes clashed, challenging in faces utterly cool and collected, but neither let her ward drop.

Egwene bit her tongue. In a public place, it was up to the strongest sister present to decide whether a conversation should be warded, and protocol said the Amyrlin made that decision whenever she was present. She had no desire for the not-quite apologies mentioning it would bring, though. If she pressed, they would accede, of course. While behaving as though soothing a petulant toddler. She bit her tongue, and boiled inside. Where *was* Siuan? That was not fair – getting horses saddled required more than moments – but she wanted to grip her skirts to keep her hands away from her head.

Romanda dropped the staring match first, though not in defeat. She rounded on Egwene so suddenly that Lelaine was left staring past her and looking foolish. 'Delana is making trouble again.' Her high-pitched voice was almost sweet, but it held a sharpness that emphasized the lack of any title of respect. Romanda's hair was completely gray, gathered in a neat bun on the nape of her neck, but age had certainly not softened her. Takima, with her long black hair and aged ivory complexion, had been almost nine years a Brown Sitter, as forceful in the Hall as in the classroom, yet she stood a meek pace back, hands folded at her waist. Romanda led her faction as firmly as Sorilea. She was one to whom strength was indeed all-important, and in truth, Lelaine seemed not far behind.

'She plans to lay a proposal before the Hall,' Lelaine put in sourly, refusing to look at Romanda at all, now. Agreeing with the other woman certainly pleased her as little as speaking second. Aware that she had gained an edge, Romanda smiled, a faint curving of her lips.

'About what?' Egwene asked, playing for time. She was certain she knew. It was very hard not to sigh. It was very hard not to rub her temples.

'Why the Black Ajah, of course, Mother,' Varilin replied, lifting her head as if surprised at the question. Well she might be; Delana was rabid on the subject. 'She wants the Hall to condemn Elaida openly as Black.' She stopped abruptly when Lelaine raised a hand. Lelaine allowed her followers more leeway than Romanda, or maybe she just did not have as tight a grip, but it was tight enough.

'You must speak with her, Mother.' Lelaine had a warm smile when she chose to use it. Siuan said they had been friends once – Lelaine had accepted her back with some version of welcome – yet Egwene thought that smile a practiced tool.

'And say what?' Her hands ached to soothe her head. These two each made sure the Hall passed only what she wanted, certainly little that Egwene suggested, with the result that nothing much at all was passed, and they wanted *her* to intercede with a Sitter? Delana did support her proposals, true – when they suited her. Delana was a weathervane, turning with the last breath of air to pass, and if she turned in Egwene's direction a great deal of late, it did not mean very much. The Black Ajah seemed her only fixed point. What was keeping Siuan?

'Tell her she must stop, Mother.' Lelaine's smile and tone made her seem to be counseling a daughter. 'This foolishness – worse than foolishness – has everyone at daggers' points. Some of the sisters are even beginning to believe, Mother. It will not be long before the notion spreads to the servants, and the soldiers.' The look she directed toward Bryne was full of doubt. Bryne appeared to be attempting to chat with Myrelle, who was staring at the warded group and running her reins uneasily through her gloved hands.

'Believing what is plain is hardly foolish,' Romanda barked. 'Mother . . .' In her mouth, that sounded entirely too much like 'girl' '. . . the reason Delana must be stopped is she does no good and considerable harm. Perhaps Elaida is Black – though I have strong doubts, whatever secondhand gossip that trollop Halima brought; Elaida is wrongheaded to a fault, but I cannot believe her evil – yet even if she is, trumpeting it will make outsiders suspicious of every Aes Sedai and drive the Black into deeper hiding. There are methods to dig them out, if we don't frighten them into flight.'

Lelaine's sniff bordered on a snort. 'Even were this nonsense true, no self-respecting sister would submit to your *methods*, Romanda. What you've suggested is close to being put to the question.' Egwene blinked in confusion; neither Siuan nor Leane had brought her a whisper of this. Luckily, the Sitters were not paying her enough mind to notice. As usual.

Planting her fists on her hips, Romanda squared around on Lelaine. 'Desperate days demand desperate actions. Some might ask why anyone would put her dignity ahead of exposing the Dark One's servants.'

'That sounds dangerously near an accusation,' Lelaine said, eyes narrowing.

Romanda was the one smiling now, a cold flinty smile. 'I will be the first to submit to my *methods*, Lelaine, if you are the second.'

Lelaine actually growled, taking half a step toward the other woman, and Romanda leaned toward her, chin thrust out. They looked ready to begin pulling hair and rolling in the dirt, and Aes Sedai dignity be hanged. Varilin and Takima glared at one another like two maidservants supporting their mistresses, a long-legged wading bird in a scowling match with a wren. The whole lot of them seemed to have forgotten Egwene entirely.

Siuan came running up in a broad straw hat, leading a fat dun mare with white-stockinged hind legs, and skidded to a halt when she saw the warded gathering. One of the grooms was with her, a lanky fellow in a long, frayed vest and a patched shirt, holding the reins of a tall roan. The wards were invisible to him, but *saidar* did not hide the faces. His eyes went very wide, and he began licking his lips. For that matter, passersby walked wide around the tent and pretended to see nothing, Aes Sedai, Warders and servants alike. Bryne alone frowned and studied them as though wondering what was hidden from his ears. Myrelle was retying her saddlebags, plainly on the point of leaving.

'When you have decided what I should say,' Egwene announced, 'then I can decide what to do.' They really had forgotten her. All four stared at her in amazement as she walked between Romanda and Lelaine and out through the doubled wards. There was nothing to feel as she brushed by the weave, of course; they had never been made to stop anything as solid as a human body.

When she scrambled onto the roan, Myrelle drew a deep breath and emulated her in resignation. The wards had vanished, though the glow still enveloped the two Sitters, each more the image of frustration than the other as they stood watching. Hurriedly Egwene donned the thin linen dustcloak that had been draped in front of her gelding's saddle, and the riding gloves that were tucked into a small pocket in the cloak. A wide-brimmed hat hung from the saddle's high pommel, deep blue to match her dress, with a spray of white plumes pinned slanting across the front that shouted of Chesa's hand. Heat she could ignore, but the glare of the sun was another matter. Removing plumes and pin, she tucked them into the saddlebags, put the hat on her head and tied the ribbons beneath her chin.

'Shall we go, Mother?' Bryne asked. He was already mounted, the helmet that had been hanging from his saddle now obscuring his face behind steel bars. It looked quite natural on him, as though he had been born for armor.

She nodded. There was no attempt to stop them. Lelaine would not stoop to shouting halt in public, of course, but Romanda ... Egwene felt a sense of relief as they rode away, yet her head seemed to be splitting. What *was* she to do about Delana? What could she do?

The main road in this area, a wide stretch of dirt packed so hard nothing could raise dust from it, ran through the army's camp and along the gap between that and the Aes Sedai's. Bryne angled across it, through the rest of the army on the other side.

Although the army camp held thirty times or more as many people as the Aes Sedai camp, there seemed to be few more tents than for the sisters and those who served them, all scattered out across the flats and up the hillsides. Most of the soldiers slept in the open. But then, it was hard to remember the last time rain had fallen, and there certainly was not a cloud to be seen. Strangely, there were more women than in the sisters' camp, though they seemed fewer at first glance, among so many men. Cooks tended kettles and laundresses attacked great heaps of clothing, while some worked with the horses or wagons. A fair number appeared to be wives; at least, they sat about knitting or darning dresses or shirts or stirring small cookpots. Armorers had set up almost anywhere she looked, hammers making steel ring on their anvils, and fletchers adding arrows to bundles by their feet, and farriers checking horses. Wagons of every sort and size stood everywhere, hundreds, perhaps thousands; the army seemed to scoop up every one it found along its path. Most of the foragers were already out, but a few high-wheeled carts and lumbering wagons still trundled away in search of farms and villages. Here and there soldiers raised a cheer as they rode by. 'Lord Bryne!' and 'The Bull! The Bull!' That was his sigil. Nothing about Aes Sedai or the Amyrlin Seat.

Egwene twisted around in her saddle to make sure Myrelle was still close behind. She was, letting her horse follow on its own, a far-off, slightly sickly expression on her face. Siuan had taken a position at the rear, shepherd to their lone sheep. Then again, she might just have been afraid to urge her mount ahead. The dun was positively a butterball, but Siuan would probably treat a pony like a warhorse.

Egwene felt a stab of irritation at her own animal. His name was Daishar; Glory, in the Old Tongue. She would much rather be riding Bela, a shaggy little mare not much slimmer than Siuan's dun that she had ridden out of the Two Rivers. Sometimes she thought she must look a doll, perched atop a gelding that could be taken for a warhorse, but the Amyrlin had to have a proper mount. No shaggy cart horses. Even if this rule was of her own making, she felt as confined as a novice.

Turning in the saddle, she said, 'Do you expect any opposition ahead, Lord Bryne?'

He glanced at her sideways. She had asked the same once before leaving Salidar and twice while crossing Altara. Not enough to rouse suspicions, she thought.

'Murandy is like Altara, Mother. Neighbor too busy scheming against neighbor, or outright fighting him, to band together for anything short of a war, and not to any great degree then.' His tone was very dry. He had been Captain-General of the Queen's Guards in Andor, with years of border skirmishes against the Murandians behind him. 'Andor will be another matter, I fear. I am not looking forward to that.' He turned another way, climbing a gentle slope to avoid three wagons rumbling over rocks in the same direction.

Egwene tried not to grimace. Andor. Before, he had just said no. These were the tail end of the Cumbar Hills, somewhat south of Lugard, the capital of Murandy. Even if they were lucky, the border of Andor lay at least ten days ahead.

'And when we reach Tar Valon, Lord Bryne. How do you plan to take the city?'

'No one has asked me that yet, Mother.' She had only thought his voice was dry before; *now* it was dry. 'By the time we reach Tar Valon, the Light willing, I'll have two or three times as many men as I do now.' Egwene winced at the idea of paying so many soldiers; he did not seem to notice. 'With that, I will lay siege. The hardest part will be finding ships, and sinking them to block Northharbor and Southharbor. The harbors are as much the key as holding the bridge towns, Mother. Tar Valon is larger than Cairhien and Caemlyn together. Once food stops going in ...' He shrugged. 'Most of soldiering is waiting, when it isn't marching.'

'And if you don't have that many soldiers?' She had never thought of all those people going hungry, women and children. She had never really thought of anyone being involved except the Aes Sedai, and the soldiers. How could she have been so foolish? She had seen the results of war in Cairhien. Bryne seemed to take it so lightly. But then, he was a soldier; privation and death must be everyday to soldiers. 'What if you only have ... say ... what you do now?'

'Siege?' Apparently some of what they had been saying had finally broken into whatever Myrelle was thinking. She booted the sorrel forward, making a number of men jump aside, some falling on their faces. A few opened their mouths angrily, then saw her ageless features and shut their jaws again, glowering. They might as well not have existed for all of her. 'Artur Hawkwing besieged Tar Valon for twenty years and failed.' Abruptly she realized ears were about and lowered her voice, but it was still acid. 'Do you expect us to wait twenty years?'

That acid washed over Gareth Bryne without leaving a stain. 'Would you prefer a direct assault right off, Myrelle Sedai?' He could have been asking whether she wanted her tea sweet or bitter. 'Several of Hawkwing's generals tried, and their men were slaughtered. No army has ever managed to breach Tar Valon's walls.'

That was not strictly true, Egwene knew. In the Trolloc Wars, an army of Dreadlord-led Trollocs had actually plundered and burned a part of the White Tower itself. At the end of the War of the Second Dragon, an army trying to rescue Guaire Amalasan before he was gentled had reached the Tower, too. Myrelle could not know, though, much less Bryne. Access to those secret histories, hidden deep in the Tower library, was set out in a law that was itself secret, and revealing the existence of either records or law was treason. Siuan said if you read between the lines, you found hints of things that had not been recorded even there. Aes Sedai were very good at hiding truth when they thought it necessary, even from themselves.

'With a hundred thousand or what I have now,' Bryne continued, 'I will be the first. If I can block the harbors. Hawkwing's generals never managed that. The Aes Sedai always raised those iron chains in time to stop the ships getting into the harbor mouth and sank them before they could be placed to hinder trade. Food and supplies got in. It will come to your assault eventually, but not until the city's weakened, if I have my way.' His voice was still . . . ordinary. A man discussing an outing. His head turned toward Myrelle, and though his tone did not change, the intensity in his eyes was evident even behind his faceguard. 'And you all agreed I would, when it came to the army. I won't throw men away.'

Myrelle opened her mouth, then closed it slowly. Plainly she wanted to say something but did not know what. They *had* given their word, her and Sheriam and those who had been running things when he appeared in Salidar, however much giving it galled. However much the Sitters tried to get round it. *They* had given no word. Bryne acted as though they had, though, and so far he had managed to get away with it. So far.

Egwene felt ill. She *had* seen war. Images flashed in her head, men fighting, killing their way through the streets of Tar Valon, dying. Her eyes fell on a square-jawed fellow chewing his tongue while he sharpened a pikehead. Would he die in those streets? The grizzled, balding man running his fingers so carefully down each arrow before sliding the shaft into his quiver? And there. That lad swaggering in his high riding boots. He looked too young to shave. Light, so many were boys. How many would die? For her. For justice, for the right, for the world, but at the heart, for her. Siuan raised her hand, but did not complete the gesture. Had she been close enough, she could not pat the Amyrlin Seat on the shoulder where everyone could see.

Egwene straightened her back. 'Lord Bryne,' she said in a tight voice, 'what is it you want me to see?' She thought he half glanced at Myrelle before answering.

'Better you see it for yourself, Mother.'

Egwene thought her head might break open. If Siuan's clues led to anything at all, she might just skin Myrelle. If they did not, she might skin Siuan. And she might throw Gareth Bryne in for good measure.

Chapter 12

A Morning of Victory

The crooked hills and ridges surrounding the camp showed every sign of the drought and unseasonable heat. The unholy heat in truth; even the dullest scullion scrubbing pots saw the Dark One's touch on the world. The true forest lay behind them to the west, but twisted oaks grew out of the rocky slopes, sourgums and pines of unfamiliar shape, and trees Egwene had no names for, brown and yellow and bare-branched. Not winter bare or brown. Starved for moisture and coolness. Dying, if the weather did not change soon. Beyond the last of the soldiers a river ran off south and west, the Reisendrelle, twenty paces wide and flanked on either side by hard-baked mud studded with stones. Swirling around rocks that might have made crossing hazardous in other days, the water rose short of the horses' knees as they forded. Egwene felt her own problems dwindle in size. Despite her head, she offered a small prayer for Nynaeve and Elayne. Their search was as important as anything she did. More. The world would live if she failed, but they had to succeed.

They traveled southward at an easy canter, slowing when the hillside slant of the land grew too great or the horses had to climb any distance through trees and sparse scrub, but keeping to the lowland as much as possible and covering ground quickly. Bryne's big-nosed gelding, surefooted and strong, hardly seeming to mind which way the ground tilted or whether smooth or rough, yet Daishar kept pace easily. Sometimes Siuan's plump animal labored, though she might just have been picking up her rider's anxiety. No amount of practice could make Siuan anything but a terrible rider, nearly throwing her arms around the mare's neck climbing upslope, almost falling from the saddle going down, awkward as a duck afoot on the flats and not far from wide-eyed as the horse. Myrelle actually regained some of her humor watching Siuan. Her own white-footed sorrel picked her way in delicate swoops like a swallow, and Myrelle rode with an assurance and flair that made Bryne appear stolid and workmanlike.

Before they had gone very far, riders appeared atop a high ridge to the west, perhaps a hundred men in column, the rising sun glinting off breastplates and helmets and lance points. At their head streamed a long white pennant Egwene could not make out, but she knew it bore the Red Hand. She had not expected to see them so close to the Aes Sedai camp.

'Dragonsworn animals,' Myrelle muttered, watching the horsemen parallel their route. Her gloved hands tightened on her reins — with fury not fear.

'The Band of the Red Hand puts out patrols,' Bryne said placidly. With a glance at Egwene, he added, 'Lord Talmanes seems concerned about you, Mother, last I spoke to him.' He put no more emphasis on that than the other.

'You've *spoken* with him?' Every vestige of Myrelle's serenity vanished. The anger she had to hold in with Egwene, she could safely unleash on him. She all but shook with it. 'That is very close to treason, Lord Bryne. It might well *be* treason!' Siuan had been dividing her attention between her horse and the men on the ridge, and she did not look at Myrelle, but she stiffened. No one had tied the Band and treason together before.

They rounded a bend in the hill valley. A farm clung to a hillside, or what had been a farm once. One wall of the small stone house had collapsed, and a few charred timbers stuck up beside the soot-coated chimney like grimy fingers. The roofless barn was a blackened hollow box of stone, and scattered ash marked where sheds might once have stood. All across Altara they had seen as bad and worse, entire villages sometimes, the dead lying in the streets, food for ravens and foxes and feral dogs that fled when people came close. Stories of anarchy and murder in Tarabon and Arad Doman suddenly had flesh and bones. Many men seized any excuse to turn bandit or settle old grudges – Egwene hoped fervently it was so – but the name on every survivor's lips was Dragonsworn, and the sisters blamed Rand as surely as if he had carried the torches himself. They would use him still if they could, though, control him if they found a way. She was not the only Aes Sedai to believe in doing what she must even when she had to hold her nose.

Myrelle's anger affected Bryne as little as rain affected a boulder. Egwene had a sudden image of storms whirling about his head and floodwaters swirling around his knees while he just kept striding ahead. 'Myrelle Sedai,' he said with the calm she should have shown, 'when ten thousand men or more are shadowing my backtrail, I want to know what their intentions are. Especially this particular ten thousand or more.'

This was a dangerous topic. However happy Egwene was that they were past questions of Talmanes' concern over her, she should have been grinding her teeth that he had mentioned her at all, but she was so startled she sat bolt upright in her saddle. 'Ten thousand? Are you sure?' The Band had had little more than half that when Mat brought it to Salidar hunting her and Elayne.

Bryne merely shrugged. 'I gather recruits as I go, and so does he. Not as many, but some men have notions about serving Aes Sedai.' More people than not would have been distinctly uneasy, saying that to three sisters; he said it with a wry smile. 'Besides, it seems the Band has a certain reputation from the fighting in Cairhien. The tale is, *Shen an Calhar* never loses, whatever the odds.' That was what drove men to join, here as back in Altara, the thought that two armies must mean a battle. Trying to stand aside might end as hard as choosing the wrong side; at best there would be no pickings for neutrals. 'I've had a few deserters to my ranks from Talmanes' newlings. Some seem to think the Band's luck is tied up in Mat Cauthon and can't be there without him.'

Something close to a sneer twisted Myrelle's lips. 'These fool Murandians' fears are certainly useful, but I did not think you were a fool, too. Talmanes follows us because he fears we might turn against his precious Lord Dragon, but if he truly intended to attack, don't you think he would have by now? These Dragonsworn can be dealt with once more important matters are done. Communicating with him, however . . . !' Giving herself a shake, she managed to regain her serenity. On the surface, at least. Her tone could still have scorched wood. 'You mark me, Lord Bryne . . .'

Egwene let Myrelle's words pass her by. Bryne had looked at her when he mentioned Mat. The sisters thought they knew the situation with the Band, and Mat, and did not think on it much, but Bryne apparently did. Tilting her head so the brim of her hat obscured her face, she studied him from the corner of her eye. He was oathbound to build the army and lead it until Elaida was brought down, but why had he sworn? Surely he could have found some lesser oath, and it surely would have been accepted by sisters who only thought to use all those soldiers as a Foolday mask to frighten Elaida. Having him on their side was comforting; even the other Aes Sedai seemed to feel that. Like her father, he was the sort of man who made you believe there was no cause for panic whatever the situation. Having him oppose her, she realized suddenly, might be as bad as having the Hall against her, and never mind the army. The one approving comment Siuan had ever had of him was that he was formidable, even if she did try to change her remark immediately to mean something else. Any man Siuan Sanche thought formidable was one to be mindful of.

They splashed across a tiny stream, a rivulet that barely wet the horses' hooves. A bedraggled crow, feeding on a fish that had stranded itself in water too shallow to swim, fluttered its tattered wings on the edge of flight, then settled back to its meal.

Siuan also was studying Bryne – the mare made much easier going when she forgot to saw at the reins or dig her heels in at just the wrong moment. Egwene had asked her about Lord Bryne's motives, but Siuan's own tangled connection to the man left her little except acid when it came to him. She either hated Gareth Bryne to his bootsoles or loved him, and imagining Siuan in love was like imagining that crow swimming.

The ridgeline where the Band's soldiers had been showed only cockeyed lines of dead conifers now. She had not noticed them going. Mat had a reputation as a *soldier*? Crows swimming did not come close. She had believed he commanded only because of Rand, and that had been hard enough to swallow. *Believing because you think you know is dangerous*, she reminded herself, eyeing Bryne.

'... should be flogged!' Myrelle's voice still burned. 'I warn you, if I hear that you've met with this Dragonsworn again ...!'

Rain washing over that boulder as far as Bryne was concerned, or so it seemed. He rode easily, occasionally murmuring 'Yes, Myrelle Sedai' or 'No, Myrelle Sedai' without any hint of distress and without lessening the watch he kept on the countryside. No doubt *he* had seen the soldiers leave. However he mustered the patience – Egwene was sure fear was no part of it – she was in no mood to listen to that.

'Be quiet, Myrelle! No one is going to do anything to Lord Bryne.' Rubbing her temple, she thought of asking one of the sisters back in the camp for Healing. Neither Siuan nor Myrelle had much ability there. Not that Healing would do any good if it was just lack of sleep and worry. Not that she wanted whispers spreading that the strain was growing too great for her. Besides, there were other ways to deal with headaches than Healing, although not here.

Myrelle's mouth tightened, only for an instant. With a toss of her head, she turned her face away, color in her cheeks, and Bryne suddenly appeared absorbed in examining a red-winged hawk wheeling off to their left. Even a brave man could know when to be discreet. Folding its wings, the hawk plummeted toward unseen prey behind a stand of bedraggled leatherleafs. Egwene felt that way, stooping on targets she could not see, hoping she had chosen the right one, hoping there was a target there.

She drew breath, wishing it were steadier. 'Just the same, Lord Bryne, I think it's best you don't meet Talmanes again. Surely you know as much of his intentions as you need by this time.' Light send Talmanes had not said too much already. A pity she could not send Siuan or Leane to caution him, if he would take it, but given feelings among the sisters, she might as well risk going to see Rand.

Bryne bowed in his saddle. 'As you command, Mother.' There was no mockery in his tone; there never was. He had obviously learned to school his voice around Aes Sedai. Siuan hung back, frowning at him. Perhaps she could dig out where his loyalties lay. For all her animosity, she spent a great deal of time in his company, much more than she absolutely had to.

With an effort, Egwene kept her hands on Daishar's reins, away from her head. 'How much further, Lord Bryne?' Keeping impatience from her voice was more difficult.

'Just a little way, Mother.' For some reason, he halfway turned his head to look at Myrelle. 'Not far, now.'

Increasingly, farms dotted the region, as many clinging to hillsides as on the flats, though the Emond's Fielder in Egwene said that made no sense, low gray stone houses and barns, and unfenced pastures with a few slat-ribbed cows and sad-looking black-tailed sheep. Not all had been burned by far, only one here and one there. Supposedly the burnings were to let the others know what would happen if they did not declare for the Dragon Reborn.

At one farm, she saw some of Lord Bryne's foragers with a wagon. That they were his was plain as much by the way he eyed them and nodded as by the lack of a white pennant. The Band always flaunted itself; aside from the banners, some had of late taken to wearing a red scarf tied around the arm. Half a dozen cattle and maybe two dozen sheep lowed and baaed under the guard of men on horseback, and other men toted sacks from barn to wagon past a slump-shouldered farmer and his family, a sullen lot in dark rough woolens. One of the little girls, wearing a deep bonnet like the others, had her face pressed to her mother's skirts, apparently crying. Some of the boys had their fists clenched, as if they wanted to fight. The farmer would be paid, but if he could not really spare what was taken, if he had had a mind to resist close on twenty men in breastplates and helmets, those burned farms would have given him pause. Quite often Bryne's soldiers found charred corpses in the ruins, men and women and children who had died trying to get out. Sometimes the doors and windows had been sealed up from outside.

Egwene wondered whether there was any way to convince the farmers and villagers that there was a difference between the brigands and the army. She wanted to, very much, but she did not see how, short of letting her own soldiers go hungry until they deserted. If the sisters could see no difference between the brigands and the Band, there seemed no hope for the country folk. As the farm dwindled behind them, she resisted the urge to twist around in her saddle and look back. Looking would change nothing.

Lord Bryne was as good as his word. Perhaps three or four miles from the camp – three or four in a straight line; twice that over the country they had crossed – they rounded the shoulder of a hill spotted with brush and trees, and he drew rein. The sun stood almost halfway to its crest, now. Another road ran below, narrower and much more winding than the one through the camp. 'They had the idea traveling by night would take them safe past the bandits,' he said. 'Not a bad notion, as it turns out, or else they've just had the Dark One's own luck. They've come from Caemlyn.'

A merchant train of some fifty large wagons behind teams of ten or so lay stretched out along the road, halted under the eyes of more of Bryne's soldiers. A few of the soldiers were afoot, supervising the transfer of barrels and bags from the merchants' wagons to half a dozen of their own. One woman in a plain dark dress waved her arms and pointed vigorously to this item or that, either protesting or bargaining, but her fellows stood in a glum silent knot. A short way farther up the road, grim fruit decorated the spreading limbs of an oak, men hanging by the neck from every bare branch. Bare except for crows, almost enough to make the tree seem leaved in black. They had larger than fish to feed on, these birds. Even at a distance it was not a sight to ease Egwene's head, or her stomach.

'This what you wanted me to see? The merchants, or the bandits?' She could not see a dress on any of those dangling corpses and, when the bandits hanged people, they included women and children. Anyone could have put the corpses there, Bryne's soldiers, the Band – that the Band hanged any of the so-called Dragonsworn they caught made little difference to the sisters – or even some local lord or lady. Had the Murandian nobles worked together, all the brigands might have hung from trees by now, but that was like asking cats to dance. Wait. He had said Caemlyn. 'Is it something to do with Rand? Or the Asha'man?'

This time he looked from her to Myrelle and back quite openly. Myrelle's hat cast shadows on her face. She appeared sunk in gloom, sagging in her saddle and not at all the confident rider she had been earlier. He seemed to reach a decision. 'I thought you should hear before anybody else did, but perhaps I misunderstood . . . ' He eyed Myrelle again.

'Hear what, you hairy-eared lump?' Siuan growled, thumping the fat mare closer with her heels.

Egwene made a soothing gesture toward her. 'Myrelle can hear anything I do, Lord Bryne. She has my complete trust.' The Green sister's head jerked around. From her stricken look, anyone would doubt they had heard Egwene correctly, but after a moment Bryne nodded.

'I see that matters have . . . changed. Yes, Mother.' Removing his helmet, he set it on the pommel of his saddle. He still seemed reluctant, picking his words with care. 'Merchants carry rumors the way dogs do fleas, and that lot down there has a fine crop. I don't say any of it is true, of course, but . . . ' It was odd, seeing him so hesitant. 'Mother, one tale that caught them up on the road is that Rand al'Thor has gone to the White Tower and sworn fealty to Elaida.'

For a moment Myrelle and Siuan looked much alike, blood draining from their faces as they envisioned catastrophe. Myrelle actually swayed in her saddle. For a moment Egwene could only stare at him. Then she startled herself, and the others, by bursting out laughing. Daishar danced in surprise, and settling him on the rocky slope settled her nerves as well. 'Lord Bryne,' she said, patting the gelding's neck, 'that isn't so, believe me. I know it for a fact, as of last night.'

Siuan heaved an instant sigh, and Myrelle was only a heartbeat behind. Egwene felt like laughing again, at their expressions. So incredibly relieved they were wide-eyed. Children who had been told the Shadowman was *not* under the bed. Aes Sedai calm indeed.

'That's good to hear,' Bryne said flatly, 'but even if I sent away every man down there, the tale will still reach my ranks. It will go through the army like wildfire crossing these hills.' That cut her mirth short. That could be disaster, left alone.

'I will have sisters announce the truth to your soldiers tomorrow. Will six Aes Sedai who know of themselves be enough? Myrelle, here, and Sheriam. Carlinya and Beonin, Anaiya and Morvrin.'

Those sisters would not like having to meet with the Wise Ones, but they would not be able to refuse her, either. Would not want to, really, to stop this tale spreading. Should not want to, at least. Myrelle's tiny wince was followed by a resigned twist of her mouth.

Leaning an elbow on his helmet, Bryne studied Egwene and Myrelle. He never so much as peeked at Siuan. His bay stamped a hoof on the rocks, and a covey of some sort of dove with bright blue wings whirred into the air from beneath bushes a few paces away, making Daishar and Myrelle's roan start skittishly. Bryne's mount did not stir. He had heard of the gateways, without doubt, though he surely knew nothing of what they were – Aes Sedai did keep secrets by habit, and had some hope of keeping that one from Elaida – and he certainly knew nothing at all about *Tel'aran'rhiod* – that vital secret was easier to guard, with no manifestations anyone could see – yet he did not ask how. Perhaps he was accustomed to Aes Sedai and secrets by now.

'So long as they say the words straight,' he said at last. 'If they hedge even a hair . . . ' His stare was not an attempt to intimidate, just to drive the point home. He seemed satisfied by what he saw in her face. 'You do very well, it appears, Mother. I wish you continued success. Set your time for this afternoon, and I will come. We should confer regularly. I will come whenever you send for me. We should begin making firm plans how to put you on the Amyrlin Seat once we reach Tar Valon.'

His tone was guarded – very likely he still was not entirely sure what was going on, or how far he could trust Myrelle – and it took her a moment to realize what he had done. It made her breath catch. Maybe she was just becoming too used to the way Aes Sedai shaded words, but . . . Bryne had just said the army was hers. She was sure of it. Not the Hall's, and not Sheriam's; hers.

'Thank you, Lord Bryne.' That seemed little enough, especially when his careful nod, his eyes steady on hers, seemed to confirm her belief. Suddenly she had a thousand more questions. Most of which she could not ask even were they alone. A pity she could not take him into her confidence completely. *Caution until you're sure, and then a little more caution.* An old saying that applied very well to any dealings that brushed against Aes Sedai. And even the best men would talk things over with their friends, perhaps especially when things were supposed to be secret. 'I'm sure you have a thousand details to see to, what's left of the morning,' she said, gathering her reins. 'You go on back. We will ride a little more.'

Bryne protested, of course. He almost sounded like a Warder, talking of the impossibility of watching every way at once and how an arrow in the back could kill an Aes Sedai as quickly as it could anyone else. The next man who told her that, she decided, was going to pay for it. Three Aes Sedai were surely the equal of three hundred men. In the end, for all his grumbles and grimaces, he had no choice but to obey. Donning his helmet, he started his horse down the uneven slope toward the merchant train, instead of back the way they had come, but that was even better from her point of view.

'Will you lead the way, Siuan,' she said when he was a dozen strides below.

Siuan glared after him as though he had been badgering her the whole time. With a snort, she tugged her straw hat straight, wheeled her mare around – well, dragged her around – and heeled the stout animal to a walk. Egwene motioned Myrelle to follow. Like Bryne, the woman had no choice.

At first Myrelle directed sidelong glances at her, plainly expecting her to bring up the sisters sent to the White Tower, plainly gathering excuses for why they had to be kept secret even from the Hall. The longer Egwene rode in silence, the more uneasily the other shifted in her saddle. Myrelle began wetting her lips, fine cracks spreading in that Aes Sedai calm. A *very* useful tool, silence.

For a time the only sounds were their horses' hooves and the occasional cry of a bird in the brush, but as Siuan's direction became clear, angling a little west from the path back to the camp, Myrelle's shifting increased until she might have been sitting on nettles. Maybe there was something to those bits and pieces Siuan had gathered after all.

When Siuan took another turn westward, between two misshapen hills that bent toward each other, Myrelle drew rein. 'There ... There is a waterfall in that direction,' she said, pointing east. 'Not very large, even before the drought, but quite pretty even now.' Siuan stopped too, looking back with a small smile.

What could Myrelle be hiding? Egwene was curious. Glancing at the Green sister, she gave a start at a single bead of perspiration on the woman's forehead, glistening in the shadow just at the edge of her wide gray hat. She most certainly wanted to know what could shake an Aes Sedai enough to make her sweat.

'I think Siuan's way will offer even more interesting sights, don't you?' Egwene said, turning Daishar, and Myrelle seemed to fold in on herself. 'Come along.'

'You know everything, don't you?' Myrelle muttered unsteadily as they rode between the leaning hills. More than one drop of sweat decorated her face now. She was shaken to her core. 'Everything. How could you . . . ?' Suddenly she jerked upright in her saddle, staring at Siuan's back. 'Her! Siuan's been your creature from the beginning!' She sounded almost indignant. 'How could we have been so blind? But I still don't understand. We were so circumspect.'

'If you want to keep something hidden,' Siuan said contemptuously over her shoulder, 'don't try to buy coin peppers this far south.'

What in the world were coin peppers? And what were they talking about? Myrelle shuddered. It was a measure of how upset she was that Siuan's tone brought no quick snap to put the other woman in her place. Instead, she licked her lips as though they were suddenly very dry.

'Mother, you have to understand why I did it, why we did it.' The frantic edge to her voice was fit for confronting half the Forsaken, and her in her shift. 'Not just because Moiraine asked, not just because she was my friend. I hate letting them die. I hate it! The bargain we make is hard on us, sometimes, but harder on them. You must understand. You must!'

Just when Egwene thought she was about to reveal everything, Siuan halted her round mare again and faced them. Egwene could have slapped her. 'It might go easier with you, Myrelle, if you lead the rest of the way,' she said coldly. Disgustedly, in fact. 'Cooperation might mean mitigation. A little.'

'Yes.' Myrelle nodded, hands working incessantly on the reins. 'Yes, of course.'

She looked on the point of tears as she took the lead. Siuan, falling in behind, appeared relieved for just an instant. Egwene thought she herself was going to burst. What bargain? With whom? Letting who die? And who was 'we'? Sheriam and the others? But Myrelle would have heard, and exposing her own ignorance hardly seemed advisable at this point. *An ignorant woman who keeps her mouth shut will be thought wise*, the saying went. And there was another: *Keeping the first secret always means keeping ten more.* There was nothing for it but to follow, holding everything in. Siuan was going to get a talking-to, though. The woman was *not* supposed to be keeping secrets from *her*. Grinding her teeth, Egwene tried to appear patient, unconcerned. Wise.

Almost back to the road the camp was on, a few miles to the west, Myrelle led the way up a low flat-topped hill covered with pine and leatherleaf. Two huge oaks kept anything else from growing in the wide depression on the crown. Beneath thick intertwined branches stood three peaked tents of patched canvas, and a picket line of horses, with a cart nearby, and five tall warhorses each carefully picketed away from the others. Nisao Dachen, in a simply cut bronze-colored riding dress, waited under the awning in front of one of the tents as if to welcome guests, with Sarin Hoigan at her side in the olive green coat so many of the Gaidin wore. A bald-headed stump of a man with a thick black beard, Nisao's Warder still stood taller than she. A few paces away, two of Myrelle's three Gaidin warily watched them descend into the hollow, Croi Makin, slender and yellow-haired, and Nuhel Dromand, dark and bulky, with a beard that left his upper lip bare. No one looked surprised in the least. Obviously one of the Warders had been keeping guard and given warning. Nothing in sight warranted all the secrecy, though, or Myrelle's lip-licking. For that matter, if Nisao waited in welcome, why did her hands keep stroking her divided skirts? She looked as if she would rather face Elaida while shielded.

Two women peering around a corner of one of the tents ducked back hurriedly, but not before Egwene recognized them. Nicola and Areina. Suddenly she felt very uneasy. What had Siuan brought her to?

Siuan showed no nervousness at all as she dismounted. 'Bring him out, Myrelle. Now.' She was getting her own back with a vengeance; her tone made a file seem smooth. 'It's too late for hiding.'

Myrelle barely managed a frown at being addressed so, and it appeared an effort. Visibly pulling herself together, she jerked her hat from her head and climbed down without a word, glided to one of the tents and vanished inside. Nisao's already big eyes followed her, growing wider by the moment. She seemed frozen to the spot.

No one but Siuan was near enough to overhear. 'Why did you break in?' Egwene demanded softly as she got down. 'I'm sure she was about to confess ... whatever it is ... and I still don't have a clue. Coin peppers?'

'Very popular in Shienar, and Malkier,' Siuan said just as quietly. 'I only heard that after I left Aeldene this morning. I had to make her lead the way; I didn't know it, not exactly. It would hardly have done much good to let her discover that, now would it? I didn't know about Nisao, either. I thought they hardly ever spoke to one another.' She glanced at the Yellow sister and gave her head an irritated shake. A failure to learn something was a failure Siuan did not tolerate well in herself. 'Unless I've gone blind *and* stupid, what these two ... ' Grimacing as though she had a mouthful of something rotten, she spluttered trying to find a name to fit. Abruptly she caught Egwene's sleeve. 'Here they come. Now you'll see for yourself.'

Myrelle left the tent first, then a man in just boots and breeches who had to duck low through the doorflaps, a bared sword in his hand and scars crisscrossing his lightly furred chest. He was head and shoulders and more taller than her, taller than any of the other Warders. His long dark hair, held by a braided leather cord around his temples, was more streaked with gray than when Egwene has seen him last, but there was nothing at all soft in Lan Mandragoran. Pieces of the puzzle suddenly clicked into place, yet it still would not come apart for her. He had been Warder to Moiraine, the Aes Sedai who had brought her and Rand and the rest out of the Two Rivers what seemed an Age ago, but Moiraine was dead killing Lanfear, and Lan had gone missing in Cairhien right after. Maybe it was all clear to Siuan; to her, it was mostly mud.

Murmuring something to Lan, Myrelle touched his arm. He flinched slightly, like a nervous horse, but his hard face never turned from Egwene. Finally, though, he nodded and pivoted on his heel, strode farther away beneath the branches of the oaks. Gripping the sword hilt in both hands above his head, blade slanted down, he rose onto the ball of one booted foot and stood motionless.

For a moment, Nisao frowned at him as though she, too, saw a puzzle. Then her gaze met Myrelle's, and together their eyes swept to Egwene. Instead of coming to her, they went to each other, exchanging hasty whispers. At least, it was an exchange at first. Then Nisao merely stood there, shaking her head in disbelief or denial. 'You dropped me into this,' she groaned aloud at last. 'I was a blind fool to listen to you.'

'This should be ... interesting,' Siuan said as they finally turned toward her and Egwene. The twist she gave the word made it sound decidedly unpleasant.

Myrelle and Nisao hurriedly touched hair and dresses as they crossed the short distance, making certain everything was in order. Perhaps they had been caught out – *In what?* Egwene wondered – but apparently they intended to put the best face they could on matters.

'If you will step inside, Mother,' Myrelle said, gesturing to the nearest tent. Only the slightest tremor in her voice betrayed her cool face. The sweat was gone. Wiped away, of course, but it had not returned.

'Thank you, no, daughter.'

'Some wine punch?' Nisao asked with a smile. Hands clasped at her breast, she looked anxious anyway. 'Siuan, go tell Nicola to bring the punch.' Siuan did not move, and Nisao blinked in surprise, her mouth thinning. The smile returned in an instant, though, and she raised her voice a little. 'Nicola? Child, bring the punch. Made with dried blackberries, I fear,' she confided to Egwene, 'but quite restorative.'

'I don't want punch,' Egwene said curtly. Nicola emerged from behind the tent, yet she showed no sign of running to obey. Instead, she stood staring at the four Aes Sedai, chewing her underlip. Nisao flashed a glare of what could only be called distaste, but said nothing. Another piece of the puzzle snapped into place, and Egwene breathed a trifle easier. 'What I want, daughter, what I require, is an explanation.'

Best face or no, it was a thin veneer. Myrelle stretched out a pleading hand. 'Mother, Moiraine did not choose me just because we were friends. Two of my Warders belonged first to sisters who died. Avar and Nuhel. No other sister has saved more than one in centuries.'

'I only became involved because of his mind,' Nisao said hastily. 'I have some interest in diseases of the mind, and this must rightly be called one. Myrelle practically dragged me into it.'

Smoothing her skirts, Myrelle directed a dark look at the Yellow that was returned with interest. 'Mother, when a Warder's Aes Sedai dies, it is as though he swallows her death and is consumed by it from the inside. He—'

'I know that, Myrelle,' Egwene broke in sharply. Siuan and Leane had told her a good bit, though neither knew she had asked because she wanted to know what to expect with Gawyn. A poor bargain, Myrelle had called it, and perhaps it was. When a sister's Warder died, grief enveloped her; she could control it somewhat, sometimes, hold it in, but sooner or later it gnawed a way out. However well Siuan managed when others were around, she still wept alone many nights for her Alric, killed the day she was deposed. Yet what were even months of tears, compared with death itself? The stories were full of Warders dying to avenge their Aes Sedai, and indeed it was very often the case. A man who wanted to die, a man looking for what could kill him, took risks not even a Warder could survive. Perhaps the most horrible part of it, to her, was that they knew. Knew what their fate would be if their Aes Sedai died, knew what drove them when she did, knew nothing they did could change it. She could not imagine the courage required to accept the bargain, knowing.

She stepped aside, so she could see Lan clearly. He still stood motionless, not even seeming to breathe. Apparently forgetting the tea, Nicola had seated herself cross-legged on the ground to watch him. Areina squatted on her heels at Nicola's side with her braid pulled over her shoulder, staring even more avidly. Much more avidly, actually, since Nicola sometimes darted furtive glances at Egwene and the others. The rest of the Warders made a small cluster, pretending to watch him too while keeping a close eye on their Aes Sedai.

A more than warm breeze stirred, ruffling the dead leaves that carpeted the ground, and with shocking suddenness, Lan was moving, shifting from stance to stance, blade a whirling blur in his hands. Faster and faster, till he seemed to sprint from one to the next, yet all as precise as the movements of a clock. She waited for him to stop, or at least slow, but he did not. Faster. Areina's mouth slowly dropped open, eyes going wide with awe, and for that matter, so did Nicola's. They leaned forward, children watching candy set to dry on the kitchen table. Even the other Warders really divided their attention between their Aes Sedai and him now, but in contrast to the two women, they watched a lion that might charge any moment.

'I see you are working him hard,' Egwene said. That was part of the method for saving a Warder. Few sisters were willing to make the attempt, given the rate of failure, and the cost of it to themselves. Keeping him from risks was another. And bonding him again; that was the first step. Without doubt Myrelle had taken care of that little detail. Poor Nynaeve. She might well strangle Myrelle, when she learned. Then again, she might countenance anything that kept Lan alive. Maybe. For Lan's part, he deserved the worst he received, letting himself be bonded by another woman when he knew Nynaeve was pining for him.

She thought she had kept her voice clear, but something of what she felt must have crept through, because Myrelle began trying to explain again.

'Mother, passing a bond is not that bad. Why, in point of fact, it's no more than a woman deciding who should have her husband if she dies, to see he is in the right hands.'

Egwene stared at her so hard that she stepped back, almost tripping over her skirts. It was only shock, though. Every time she thought she had heard of the strangest possible custom, another popped up stranger still.

'We aren't all Ebou Dari, Myrelle,' Siuan said dryly, 'and a

Warder isn't a husband. For most of us.' Myrelle's head came up defiantly. Some sisters did marry a Warder, a handful; not many married at all. No one inquired too closely, but rumor said she had married all three of hers, which surely violated custom and law even in Ebou Dar. 'Not that bad, you say, Myrelle? Not that bad?' Siuan's scowl matched her tone; she sounded as if she had a vile taste in her mouth.

'There is no law against it,' Nisao protested. To Egwene, not Siuan. 'No law against passing a bond.' Siuan received a frown that should have made her step back and shut her mouth. She was having none of it, though.

'That's not the point, is it?' she demanded. 'Even if it hasn't been done in – what? four hundred years or more? – even if customs *have* changed, you might have escaped with a few stares and a little censure if all you and Moiraine had done was pass his bond between you. But he wasn't asked, was he? He was given no choice. You might as well have bonded him against his will. In fact, you bloody well did!'

At last the puzzle came clear for Egwene. She knew she should feel the same disgust as Siuan. Aes Sedai put bonding a man against his will on a level with rape. He had as much chance to resist as a farmgirl would if a man the size of Lan cornered her in a barn. If three men the size of Lan did. Sisters had not always been so particular, though – a thousand years earlier, it would hardly have been remarked – and even today an argument could sometimes be made as to whether a man had actually known what he was agreeing to. Hypocrisy was a fine art among Aes Sedai sometimes, like scheming or keeping secrets. The thing was, she knew he had resisted admitting his love for Nynaeve. Some nonsense about how he was bound to be killed sooner or later and did not want to leave her a widow; men always did spout drivel when they thought they were being logical and practical. Would Nynaeve have let him walk away unbonded, had she had the chance, whatever he said? Would she herself let Gawyn? He had said he would accept, yet if he changed his mind?

Nisao's mouth worked, but she could not find the words she wanted. She glared at Siuan as though it were all her fault, yet that was nothing alongside the scowl she directed at Myrelle. 'I should *never* have listened to you,' she growled. 'I must have been *mad*!'

Somehow, Myrelle still managed to maintain a smooth face, but she wavered a little, as though her knees had gone weak. 'I did not do it for myself, Mother. You must believe that. It was to save him. As soon as he is safe, I will pass him on to Nynaeve, the way Moiraine wanted, just as soon as she's—'

Egwene flung up a hand, and Myrelle stopped as if she had clapped it over her mouth. 'You mean to pass his bond to Nynaeve?'

Myrelle nodded uncertainly, Nisao much more vigorously. Scowling, Siuan muttered something about doubling a wrong making it three times as bad. Lan *still* had not slowed. Two grasshoppers whirred up from the leaves behind him, and he spun, sword flicking them out of the air without a pause.

'Are your efforts succeeding? Is he any better? How long have you had him, exactly?'

'Only two weeks,' Myrelle replied. 'Today is the twentieth. Mother, it could require months, and there is no guarantee.'

'Perhaps it is time to try something different,' Egwene said, more to herself than anyone else. More to convince herself than for any other reason. In his circumstances, Lan was hardly an easy present to hand anyone, but bond or no bond, he belonged to Nynaeve more than he ever would to Myrelle.

When she crossed the hollow to him, though, doubts sprang up strong. He whirled to face her in his dance, sword streaking toward her. Someone gasped as the blade halted abruptly only inches from her head. She was relieved that it had not been her.

Brilliant blue eyes regarded her intently from beneath lowered brows, in a face all planes and angles that might have been carved from stone. Lan lowered his sword slowly. Sweat coated him, yet he was not even breathing hard. 'So you are the Amyrlin now. Myrelle told me they had raised one, but not who. It seems you and I have a good deal in common.' His smile was as cold as his voice, as cold as his eyes.

Egwene stopped herself from adjusting her stole, reminding herself that she was Amyrlin and Aes Sedai. She wanted to embrace *saidar*. Until this moment, she had not realized exactly how dangerous he was. 'Nynaeve is Aes Sedai now, too, Lan. She's in need of a good Warder.' One of the other women made a noise, but Egwene held her gaze on him.

'I hope she finds a hero out of legend.' He barked a laugh. 'She'll need the hero just to face her temper.'

The laugh convinced her, icy hard as it was. 'Nynaeve is in Ebou Dar, Lan. You know what a dangerous city that is. She is searching for something we need desperately. If the Black Ajah learns of it, they'll kill her to get it. If the Forsaken find out ...' She had thought his face bleak before, but the pain that tightened his eyes at Nynaeve's danger confirmed her plan. Nynaeve, not Myrelle, had the right. 'I am sending you to her, to act as her Warder.'

'Mother,' Myrelle said urgently behind her.

Egwene flung out a hand to silence her. 'Nynaeve's safety will be in your hands, Lan.'

He did not hesitate. Or even glance at Myrelle. 'It will take at least a month to reach Ebou Dar. Areina, saddle Mandarb!' On the point of turning away, he paused, lifting his free hand as if to touch her stole. 'I apologize for ever helping you leave the Two Rivers. You, or Nynaeve.' Striding away, he vanished into the tent he had come out of earlier, but before he had gone two steps, Myrelle and Nisao and Siuan were all clustered around her.

'Mother, you don't understand what you are proposing,' Myrelle said breathlessly. 'You might as well give a child a lighted lantern to play with in a haybarn. I began readying Nynaeve as soon as I felt his bond pass to me. I thought I had time. But she was raised to the shawl in a blink. She isn't ready to handle him, Mother. Not him, not the way he is.'

With an effort Egwene made herself be patient. They still did not understand. 'Myrelle, even if Nynaeve could not channel a lick.' She could not, actually, unless she was angry '... that would make no difference, and you know it. Not in whether she can handle him. There's one thing you haven't been able to do. Give him a task so important that he has to stay alive to carry it out.' That was the final element. Supposedly it worked better than the rest. 'To him, Nynaeve's safety is that important. He loves her, Myrelle, and she loves him.'

'That explains ...' Myrelle began softly, but Nisao burst out incredulously atop her.

'Oh, surely not. Not him. She might love him, I suppose, or think she does, but women have been chasing Lan since he was a beardless boy. And catching him, for a day or a month. He was quite a beautiful boy, however hard that might be to believe now. Still, he does appear to have his attractions.' She glanced sideways at Myrelle, who frowned slightly, tiny spots of color blooming in her cheeks. She did not react any further, but that was more than enough. 'No, Mother. Any woman who thinks she has leashed Lan Mandragoran will find she has collared only air.'

Egwene sighed in spite of herself. Some sisters believed there was one more part of saving a Warder whose bond was broken by death; putting him into the arms – into the bed – of a woman. No man could focus on death then, the belief ran. Myrelle, it seemed, had taken care of that herself, too. At least she had not actually married him, not if she meant to pass him on. It would be just as well if Nynaeve never found out.

'Be that as it may,' she told Nisao absently. Areina was fastening the girths on Mandarb's saddle with a brisk competence, the tall black stallion standing with head high but allowing it. Plainly this was not the first time she had been around the animal. Nicola stood close by the thick bole of the farther oak, arms crossed beneath her breasts, staring at Egwene and the others. She looked ready to run. 'I don't know what Areina has squeezed out of you,' Egwene said quietly, 'but the extra lessons for Nicola stop now.'

Myrelle and Nisao jumped, mirror images of surprise. Siuan's eyes grew to the size of teacups, but luckily she recovered before anyone noticed. 'You really do know everything,' Myrelle whispered. 'All Areina wants is to be around Lan. I think she believes he'll teach her things she can use as a Hunter. Or maybe that he'll go off on the Hunt with her.'

'Nicola wants to be another Caraighan,' Nisao muttered caustically. 'Or another Moiraine. I think she had some notion she could make Myrelle give Lan's bond to her. Well! At least we can deal with that pair as they deserve, now that he's out in the open. Whatever happens to me, it will be a joy to know they'll be squealing from here to year's end.'

Siuan finally realized what had been going on, and outrage

warred on her face with the wondering looks she directed at Egwene. That someone else had puzzled matters out first probably upset her as much as Nicola and Areina blackmailing Aes Sedai. Or perhaps not. Nicola and Areina were not Aes Sedai themselves, after all. That drastically changed Siuan's view of what was allowed. But then, it did the same for any sister.

With so many eyes turned her way, and not a friendly gaze in the lot, Nicola backed up against the oak tree and seemed to be trying to back further. Stains on that white dress would put her in hot water when she returned to the camp. Areina was still absorbed in Lan's horse, unaware of what was crashing down on her head.

'That would be justice,' Egwene agreed, 'but not unless you two face full justice yourselves.'

Nobody was looking at Nicola anymore. Myrelle's eyes filled her face, and Nisao's opened wider yet. Neither seemed to dare crack her teeth. Siuan wore grim satisfaction like another skin; by her lights, they deserved no mercy at all. Not that Egwene intended to give much.

'We will speak further when I come back,' she told them as Lan reappeared, his sword buckled on over a green coat undone to reveal an unlaced shirt, bulging saddlebags draped over his shoulder. The color-shifting Warder cloak hanging down his back wrenched the eye as it swirled behind him.

Leaving the stunned sisters to stew in their own juices, Egwene went to meet him. Siuan would keep them on a fine simmer, should they show any sign of falling off. 'I can have you in Ebou Dar sooner than a month,' she said. He only nodded impatiently and called for Areina to bring Mandarb. His intensity was unnerving, an avalanche poised to fall, held back by a thread.

Weaving a gateway where he had been practicing the sword, a good eight feet by eight, she stepped though onto what seemed to be a ferry, floating in darkness that stretched forever. Skimming required a platform, and though it could be anything you chose to imagine, every sister seemed to have one she preferred. For her that was this wooden barge, with stout railings. If she fell off, she could make another barge beneath her, although where she came out then would be something of a question, but for anyone who could not channel, that fall would be as endless as the black that ran off in every direction. Only at the near end of the barge was there any light, the gateway giving a constricted view of the hollow. That light did not penetrate the darkness at all, yet there was light of a sort. At least, she could see quite clearly, as in *Tel'aran'rhiod*. Not for the first time she wondered whether this actually was some part of the World of Dreams.

Lan followed without needing to be told, leading his horse. He examined the gateway as he came through, studied the darkness as his boots and the stallion's hooves thudded across the deck planks to her. The only question he asked was 'How quickly will this take me to Ebou Dar?'

'It won't,' she said, channeling to swing the gate shut, then closing the gateway. 'Not right to the city.' Nothing moved that anyone could have seen; there was no wind or breeze, nothing to feel. They were in motion, though. And fast; faster than she could imagine anything moving. It must be six hundred miles or more they had to go. 'I can put you out five, maybe six days north of Ebou Dar.' She had seen the gateway woven when Nynaeve and Elayne Traveled south, and she remembered enough for Skimming to the same place.

He nodded, peering ahead as though he could see their destination. He reminded her of an arrow in a drawn bow.

'Lan, Nynaeve is staying at the Tarasin Palace, a guest of Queen Tylin. She might deny she's in any danger.' Which she certainly would, indignantly if Egwene knew Nynaeve, and rightfully so. 'Try not to make a point of it – you know how stubborn she is – but you mustn't pay that any mind. If necessary, just protect her without letting her know.' He said nothing, did not glance at her. She would have had a hundred questions in his place. 'Lan, when you find her, you must tell her that Myrelle will give your bond to her as soon as you three can be together.' She had thought of passing that information along herself, but it seemed better not to let Nynaeve know he was coming. She was as besotted with him as . . . as . . . *As I am with Gawyn*, she thought ruefully. If Nynaeve knew he was on his way, there would be little room in her head for anything else. With the best will in the world, she would let the search fall on Elayne. Not that she would curl up and daydream, but any searching she did would be with dazzled eyes. 'Are you listening to me, Lan?'

'Tarasin Palace,' he said in a flat voice, without shifting his gaze. 'Guest of Queen Tylin. Might deny she's in danger. Stubborn, as if I didn't know already.' He looked at her then, and she almost wished he had not. She was full of *saidar*, full of the warmth and the joy and the power, the sheer life, but something stark and primal raged in those cold blue eyes, a denial of life. His eyes were terrifying; that was all there was to it. 'I will tell her everything she needs to know. You see, I listen.'

She made herself meet his stare without flinching, but he only turned away again. There was a mark on his neck, a bruise. It might – just might – be a bite. Perhaps she should caution him, tell him he did not have to be too ... detailed ... in any explanations about himself and Myrelle. The thought made her blush. She tried not to see the bruise, but now she had noticed it, she could not seem to see anything else. Anyway, he would not be that foolish. You could not expect a man to be sensible, but even men were not that scatterbrained.

In silence they floated, moving without moving. She had no fears of the Forsaken suddenly appearing here, or anyone else. Skimming had its oddities, some of which made for safety, and privacy. If two sisters wove gateways on the same spot only moments apart, aiming to Skim to the same place, they would not see one another, not unless it was *exactly* the same spot, with the weaves *exactly* identical, and neither precision was as easy to achieve as it might seem.

After a time – it was hard to tell how long exactly, but she thought well under half an hour – the barge stopped suddenly. Nothing altered in the feel, nor in the weaves she held. She simply knew that one moment they were speeding through the blackness, and the next standing still. Opening a gateway just at the barge's bow – she was not sure where one opened at the stern would lead, and not anxious to find out, frankly; Moghedien had found the very idea frightening – she motioned Lan to go ahead. The barge only existed so long as she was present, another thing like *Tel'aran'rhiod*.

He swung back the ferry gate, leading Mandarb out, and when

she followed, he was already in the saddle. She left the gateway open for her return. Low rolling hills ran off in every direction, covered in withered grass. There was not a tree to be seen, nothing more than patches of shriveled scrub brush. The stallion's hooves kicked up little spurts of dust. The morning sun in that cloudless sky baked even hotter here than in Murandy. Long-winged vultures circled over something to the south, and in another place to the west.

'Lan,' she began, meaning to make sure he understood what he was to tell Nynaeve, but he forestalled her.

'Five or six days, you said,' he said, peering south. 'I can make it faster. She will be safe, I promise.' Mandarb danced, impatient as his rider, but Lan held him easily. 'You've come a very long way since Emond's Field.' Looking down at her, he smiled. Any warmth in it was swallowed by his eyes. 'You have a hold on Myrelle and Nisao, now. Don't let them argue with you again. By your command, Mother. The watch is not done.' With a small bow, he dug in his heels, walking Mandarb just far enough to put her clear of the dust before setting the horse to a gallop.

Watching him speed southward, she closed her mouth. Well. He had noticed in the middle of all that sword practice, noticed and done the sums correctly. Apparently including sums he could not have suspected before seeing her with the stole. Nynaeve had better take care; she always did think men were dimmer than they actually were.

'At least they can't get into any real trouble,' she told herself aloud. Lan topped a hill and vanished over the other side. Had there been any real danger in Ebou Dar, Elayne or Nynaeve would have said something. They did not meet often – she just had too much to do – but they had worked out a way to leave messages in the Salidar of *Tel'aran'rhiod* whenever there was need for one.

A wind that might have come from an open oven gusted up sheets of dust. Coughing, she covered her mouth and nose with a corner of the Amyrlin's striped stole and hurriedly retreated through the gateway to her ferry. The journey back was silent and boring, leaving her to worry whether she had done the right thing sending Lan, whether it was right to keep Nynaeve in the dark. *It's done*, she kept telling herself, but that did not help.

When she stepped once more into the hilltop hollow beneath the oak trees, Myrelle's third Warder, Avar Hachami, had joined the others, a hawk-nosed man with thick, gray-streaked mustaches like down-curving horns. All four Gaidin were hard at work, the tents down and neatly folded. Nicola and Areina trotted back and forth loading all the camp paraphernalia into the cart, everything from blankets to cookpots and black iron washkettle. They really did trot, not pausing, but at least half their attention was on Siuan and the other two sisters, over near the treeline. For that matter, the Warders gave the three Aes Sedai much more than half their consideration. Their ears might as well have been up in points. Who was simmering who seemed to be a question.

'... not speak to me in that manner, Siuan,' Myrelle was saying. Not only loud enough to be heard across the clearing, but cold enough to take the edge off the weather. Arms folded tightly beneath her breasts, she was drawn up to every inch of height, imperious to the point of bursting. 'Do you hear me? You will not!'

'Are you lost to all propriety, Siuan?' Nisao's hands were knotted in her skirts in a vain attempt to keep herself from quivering, and the heat in her voice easily matched the ice in Myrelle's. 'If you've forgotten simple manners completely, you can be taught again!'

Facing them with her hands on her hips, Siuan moved her head jerkily, struggling, both to keep a glare on her face and to keep it fixed on the other two. 'I ... I am only ...' When she saw Egwene approaching, her relief bloomed like a flower in spring. 'Mother ...' That was almost a gasp. '... I was explaining possible penalties.' She drew a long breath, and went on more definitely. 'The Hall will have to invent them as they go, of course, but I think they might well start with making these two pass their Warders to others, since they seem so fond of it.'

Myrelle squeezed her eyes shut, and Nisao turned to look at the Warders. Her expression never changed, calm if a touch flushed, but Sarin stumbled to his feet and took three quick steps toward her before she raised a hand to stop him. A Warder could sense his Aes Sedai's presence, her pain, her fear and anger, every bit as much as Egwene could feel Moghedien's when she wore the *a'dam*. No wonder all the Gaidin moved on their toes and looked ready to spring at something; they might not know what had driven their Aes Sedai to the brink of despair, but they knew the two women were at that brink.

Which was exactly where Egwene wanted them. She did not like this part of it. All the maneuvering was like a game, but this . . . *I do what I must*, she thought, unsure whether that was an attempt to stiffen her backbone or an attempt to excuse what she was about to do. 'Siuan, please send Nicola and Areina back to the camp.' What they did not see, they could not tell. 'We can't have their tongues flapping, so make sure they know what will happen to them. Tell them they have one more chance, because the Amyrlin is feeling merciful, but they'll never get another.'

'I think I can manage that much,' Siuan replied, and gathering her skirts, she stalked off. No one could stalk like Siuan, yet she seemed more eager to be away from Myrelle and Nisao than anything else.

'Mother,' Nisao said, choosing her words, 'before you left, you said something — indicated there might be some way — for us to avoid — some way we might not have to—' She glanced at Sarin again. Myrelle would have been a study in Aes Sedai serenity as she examined Egwene, except that her fingers were laced together so tightly that her knuckles strained the thin leather of her gloves. Egwene motioned them to wait.

Nicola and Areina, turning away from the cart, saw Siuan coming and went stiff as posts. Which was no wonder, considering that Siuan advanced as though she intended to walk right over them *and* the cart. Areina's head swiveled, searching, but before she could think to actually run, Siuan's hands darted out and caught each of them by an ear. What she said was too low to carry, yet Areina stopped trying to pry her ear free. Her hands stayed on Siuan's wrist, but she almost seemed to be using it to hold herself up. A look of such horror oozed across Nicola's face that Egwene wondered whether Siuan might be going too far. But then, maybe not, under the circumstances; they *were* going to walk free of their crime. A pity she could not find a way to harness such a talent for ferreting out what was hidden. A way to harness it safely.

Whatever Siuan said, when she loosed their ears, the pair immediately turned toward Egwene and dropped into curtsies. Nicola's was so low it nearly put her face on the ground, and Areina came close to falling on hers. Siuan clapped hands sharply, and the two women bounded to their feet, scrambled to untie a pair of shaggy wagon horses from the picket line. They were astride bareback and galloping out of the hollow so quickly, it was a wonder they did not have wings.

'They won't even talk in their sleep,' Siuan said sourly when she returned. 'I can still handle novices and scoundrels, at least.' Her eyes stayed on Egwene's face, avoiding the other two sisters entirely.

Suppressing a sigh, Egwene turned to Myrelle and Nisao. She had to do something about Siuan, but first things first. The Green sister and the Yellow eyed her warily. 'It is very simple,' she said in a firm voice. 'Without my protection, you will very likely lose your Warders, and almost certainly wish you'd been skinned alive by the time the Hall finishes with you. Your own Ajahs may have a few choice words for you, as well. It may be years before you can hold your heads up again, years before you don't have sisters looking over your shoulder every minute. But why should I protect you from justice? It puts me under an obligation; you might do the same again, or worse.' The Wise Ones had their part in this, though it was not exactly *ji'e'toh*. 'If I'm to take on that responsibility, then you must have an obligation too. I must be able to trust you utterly, and I can only see one way to do that.' The Wise Ones, and then Faolain and Theodrin. 'You must swear fealty.'

They had been frowning, wondering where she was headed, but wherever they thought, it was not where she ended. Their faces were a study. Nisao's jaw dropped, and Myrelle looked as though she had been hit between the eyes with a hammer. Even Siuan gaped in disbelief.

'Im-p-possible,' Myrelle spluttered. 'No sister has ever—! No Amyrlin has required—! You can't really think—!'

'Oh, do be quiet, Myrelle,' Nisao snapped. 'This is all your fault! I should never have listened—! Well. Done is done. And what is, is.' Peering at Egwene from beneath lowered brows, she muttered, 'You are a dangerous young woman, Mother. A very dangerous woman. You may break the Tower more than it already is, before you're done. If I was sure of that, if I had the courage to do my duty and face whatever comes—' Yet she knelt smoothly, pressing her lips to the Great Serpent ring on Egwene's finger. 'Beneath the Light and by my hope of rebirth and salvation . . .' Not the same wording as Faolain and Theodrin, but every scrap as strong. More. By the Three Oaths, no Aes Sedai could speak a vow she did not mean. Except the Black Ajah, of course; it seemed obvious they must have found a way to lie. Whether either of these women was Black was a problem for another time, though. Siuan, eyes popping and mouth working without sound, looked like a fish stranded on a mudbank.

Myrelle tried another protest, but Egwene just thrust out her right hand with the ring, and Myrelle's knees folded in jerks. She gave the oath in bitter tones, then looked up. 'You've done what has never been done before, Mother. That is always dangerous.'

'It won't be the last time,' Egwene told her. 'In fact . . . My first order to you is that you will tell no one that Siuan is anything but what everybody thinks. My second is, you will obey any order she gives as if it came from me.'

Their heads turned toward Siuan, faces unruffled. 'As you command, Mother,' they murmured together. It was Siuan who looked ready to faint.

She was still staring at nothing when they reached the road and turned their horses east toward the Aes Sedai camp and the army. The sun still climbed toward its zenith, still well short. It had been a morning eventful as most days. Most weeks, for that matter. Egwene let Daishar amble.

'Myrelle was right,' Siuan mumbled finally. With her rider's mind elsewhere, the mare moved with something close to a smooth gait; she actually made Siuan appear a competent rider. 'Fealty. No one has ever done that. No one. There isn't so much as a hint in the secret histories. And *them*, obeying *me*. You aren't just changing a few things, you're rebuilding the boat while sailing a storm! *Everything* is changing. And Nicola! In my day, a novice would have wet herself if she even thought of blackmailing a sister!'

'Not their first attempt,' Egwene told her, relating the facts in as few words as possible.

She expected Siuan to explode in a fury at the pair, but instead the woman said, quite calmly, 'I fear our two adventurous lasses are about to meet with accidents.'

'No!' Egwene reined in so suddenly that Siuan's mare ambled another half-dozen paces before she could bring the animal under control and turn her, all the while muttering imprecations under her breath. She sat there giving Egwene a patient look that outdid Lelaine at her worst.

'Mother, they have a club over your head, if they're ever smart enough to think it out. Even if the Hall doesn't force you into a penance, you can watch any hope you have with them sail right over the horizon.' She shook her head disgustedly. 'I knew you would do it when I sent you out – I knew you'd have to – but I never thought Elayne and Nynaeve were witless enough to bring back anyone who knew. Those two girls deserve all they'll catch if this gets out. But you can't afford to let it out.'

'Nothing is to happen to Nicola or Areina, Siuan! If I approve killing them for what they know, who's next? Romanda and Lelaine, for not agreeing with me? Where does it stop?' In a way, she felt disgusted with herself. Once, she would not have understood what Siuan meant. It was always better to know than to be ignorant, but sometimes ignorance was much more comfortable. Heeling Daishar on, she said, 'I won't have a day of victory spoiled with talk of murder. Myrelle wasn't even the beginning, Siuan. This morning, Faolain and Theodrin were waiting ...' Siuan brought the plump mare in closer to listen as they rode.

The news did not relieve Siuan's concern over Nicola and Areina, but Egwene's plans certainly put a sparkle in her eye and a smile of anticipation on her lips. By the time they reached the Aes Sedai camp, she was eager to take on her next task. Which was to tell Sheriam and the rest of Myrelle's friends that they were expected in the Amyrlin's study at midday. She could even say quite truthfully that nothing would be required of them that other sisters had not done before.

For all her talk of victory, Egwene did not feel so zestful. She barely heard blessings and calls for blessings, acknowledging them with only a wave of her hand, and was sure she missed more than she did hear. She could not countenance murder, but Nicola and Areina would bear watching. *Will I ever reach a place where the difficulties don't keep piling up?* she wondered. Somewhere a victory did not seem to have to be matched by a new danger.

When she walked into her tent, her mood sank right to her feet. Her head throbbed. She was beginning to think she should just stay away from the tent altogether.

Two carefully folded sheets of parchment sat neatly atop the writing table, each sealed with wax and each bearing the words 'Sealed to the Flame.' For anyone other than the Amyrlin, breaking that seal was accounted as serious as assaulting the Amyrlin's person. She wished she did not have to break them. There was no doubt in her mind who had written those words. Unfortunately, she was right.

Romanda suggested – 'demanded' was a better word – that the Amyrlin issue an edict 'Sealed to the Hall,' known only to the Sitters. The sisters were all to be summoned one by one, and any who refused was to be shielded and confined as a suspected member of the Black Ajah. What they were to be summoned for was left rather vague, but Lelaine had more than hinted this morning. Lelaine's own missive bore her manner all over it, mother to child, what should be done for Egwene's own good and everyone's. The edict she wanted was only to be 'Sealed to the Ring'; any sister could know, and in fact, in this case they would have to. Mention of the Black Ajah was to be forbidden as fomenting discord, a serious charge under Tower law, with appropriate penalties.

Egwene dropped onto her folding chair with a groan, and of course the legs shifted and nearly deposited her on the carpet. She could delay and sidestep, but they would keep coming back with these idiocies. Sooner or later one would introduce her modest proposal to the Hall, and that would put the fox in the henyard. Were they blind? Fomenting *discord*? Lelaine would have every sister convinced not just that there was a Black Ajah, but that Egwene was part of it. The stampede of Aes Sedai back to Tar Valon and Elaida could not be far behind. Romanda just meant to set off a mutiny. There were six of those hidden in the secret histories. Half a dozen in more than three thousand years might not be very many, but each had resulted in an Amyrlin resigning, and the entire Hall as well. Lelaine knew that, and Romanda. Lelaine had been a Sitter for nearly forty years, with access to all the hidden records. Before resigning to go into a country retreat, as many sisters did in age, Romanda had held a chair for the Yellow so long that some said she had had as much power as any Amyrlin she sat under. Being chosen to sit a second time was nearly unheard of, but Romanda was not one to let power reside anywhere outside her own hands if she could manage.

No, they were not blind; just afraid. Everybody was, including her, and even Aes Sedai did not always think clearly when they were afraid. She refolded the pages, wanting to crumple them up and stamp her feet on them. Her head *was* going to burst.

'May I come in, Mother?' Halima Saranov swayed into the tent without waiting for an answer. The way Halima moved always drew every male eye from age twelve to two days past the grave, but then, if she hid herself in a heavy cloak from the shoulders down, men still would stare. Long black hair, glistening as if she washed it every day in fresh rainwater, framed a face that made sure of that. 'Delana Sedai thought you might want to see this. She's putting it before the Hall this morning.'

The Hall was sitting without so much as informing her? Well, she had been away, but custom if not law said the Amyrlin must be informed before the Hall *could* sit. Unless they were sitting to depose her, anyway. At that moment, she would almost have taken it as a blessing. She eyed the folded sheet of paper Halima laid on her table much as she would a poisonous snake. Not sealed; the newest novice could read it, so far as Delana was concerned. The declaration that Elaida was a Darkfriend, of course. Not quite as bad as Romanda or Lelaine, but if she heard the Hall had broken up in a riot, she would hardly blink.

'Halima, I could wish you'd gone home when Cabriana died.' Or at least that Delana had had the sense to seal the woman's information to the Hall. Or even to the Flame. Instead of telling every sister she could collar.

'I could hardly do that, Mother.' Halima's green eyes flashed with what seemed challenge or defiance, but she only had two ways to look at anyone, a wide, direct stare that dared and a lidded gaze that smoldered. Her eyes caused a lot of misunderstanding. 'After Cabriana Sedai told me what she'd learned about Elaida? And her plans? Cabriana was my friend, and friend to you, to all of you opposing Elaida, so I had no choice. I only thank the Light she mentioned Salidar, so I knew where to come.' She put her hands on a waist as small as Egwene's had been in *Tel'aran'rhiod* and tilted her head to one side, studying Egwene intently. 'Your brain is hurting again, isn't it? Cabriana used to have such pains, so bad they made her toes cramp. She had to soak in hot water till she could bear to put on clothes. It took days, sometimes. If I hadn't come, yours could have gotten that bad eventually.' Moving around behind the chair, she began kneading Egwene's scalp. Halima's fingers possessed a skill that melted pain away. 'You could hardly ask another sister for Healing as often as you have these aches. It's just tightness, anyway. I can feel it.'

'I suppose I couldn't,' Egwene murmured. She rather liked the woman, whatever anyone said, and not just for her talent in smoothing away headaches. Halima was earthy and open, a country woman however much time she had spent gaining a skim of city sophistication, balancing respect for the Amyrlin with a sort of neighborliness in a way Egwene found refreshing. Startling, sometimes, but enlivening. Even Chesa did not do better, but Chesa was always the servant, even if friendly, while Halima never showed the slightest obsequiousness. Yet Egwene really did wish she had gone back to her home when Cabriana fell from that horse and broke her neck.

It might have been useful had the sisters accepted Cabriana's belief that Elaida intended to still half of them and break the rest, but everyone was sure Halima had garbled that somehow. It was the Black Ajah they latched on to. Women unused to being afraid of anything had taken what they had always denied existed and terrified themselves half-witless with it. How was she to root the Darkfriends out without scattering the other sisters like a frightened covey of quail? How to stop them scattering sooner or later anyway? Light, how?

'Think on looseness,' Halima said softly. 'Your face is loose. Your neck is loose. Your shoulders . . . ' Her voice was almost hypnotic, a drone that seemed to caress each part of Egwene's body she wanted to relax.

Some women disliked her just for the way she looked, of course, as though a particularly lascivious man had dreamed her, and a good many claimed she flirted with anything in breeches, which Egwene could not have approved of, but Halima admitted she liked looking at men. Her worst critics never claimed she had done more than flirt, and she herself became indignant at the suggestion. She was no fool – Egwene had known that at their first conversation, the day after Logain escaped, when the headaches had begun – not at all the brainless flipskirt. Egwene suspected it was much as with Meri. Halima could not help her face or her manner. Her smile seemed inviting or teasing because of the shape of her mouth; she smiled the same at man or woman or child. It was hardly her fault that people thought she was flirting when she was only looking. Besides, she had never mentioned the headaches to anyone. If she had, every Yellow sister in the camp would be laying siege. That indicated friendship, if not loyalty.

Egwene's eyes fell on the papers on the writing table, and her thoughts drifted under Halima's stroking fingers. Torches ready to be tossed into the haystack. Ten days to the border of Andor, unless Lord Bryne was willing to push without knowing why, and no opposition before. Could she hold those torches back ten days? Southharbor. Northharbor. The keys to Tar Valon. How could she be sure of Nicola and Areina, short of Siuan's suggestion? She needed to arrange for every sister to be tested before they reached Andor. She had the Talent for working with metals and ores, but it was rare among Aes Sedai. Nicola. Areina. The Black Ajah.

'You're tensing again. Stop worrying over the Hall.' Those soothing fingers paused, then began once more. 'This would do better tonight, after you've had a hot bath. I could work your shoulders and back, everywhere. We haven't tried that, yet. You're stiff as a stake; you should be supple enough to bend backwards and put your head between your ankles. Mind and body. One can't be limber without the other. Just put yourself in my hands.'

Egwene teetered on the brink of sleep. Not a dreamwalker's

sleep; just sleep. How long since she had done that? The camp would be in an uproar once Delana's proposal got out, which it would soon enough, and that was before she had to tell Romanda and Lelaine she had no intention of issuing their edicts. But there was one thing yet today to look forward to, a reason to remain awake. 'That will be nice,' she murmured, meaning more than the promised massage. Long ago she had pledged that one day she would bring Sheriam to heel, and today was the day. At last she was beginning to *be* the Amyrlin, in control. 'Very nice.'

Chapter 13

The Bowl of the Winds

Aviendha would have sat on the floor, but three other women occupying the boat's small room left not quite enough space, so she had to be content with folding her legs atop one of the carved wooden benches built against the walls. That way, it was not so much like sitting in a chair. At least the door was shut, and there were no windows, only fanciful carved scrollwork piercing the walls near the ceiling. She could not see the water outside, but the piercings let in the smell of salt and the slap of waves against the hull and the splash of the oars. Even the shrill hollow cries of some sort of birds shouted of vast expanses of water. She had seen men die for a pool they might have stepped across, but this water was bitter beyond belief. Reading of it was not at all the same as tasting it. And the river had been at least half a mile wide where they boarded

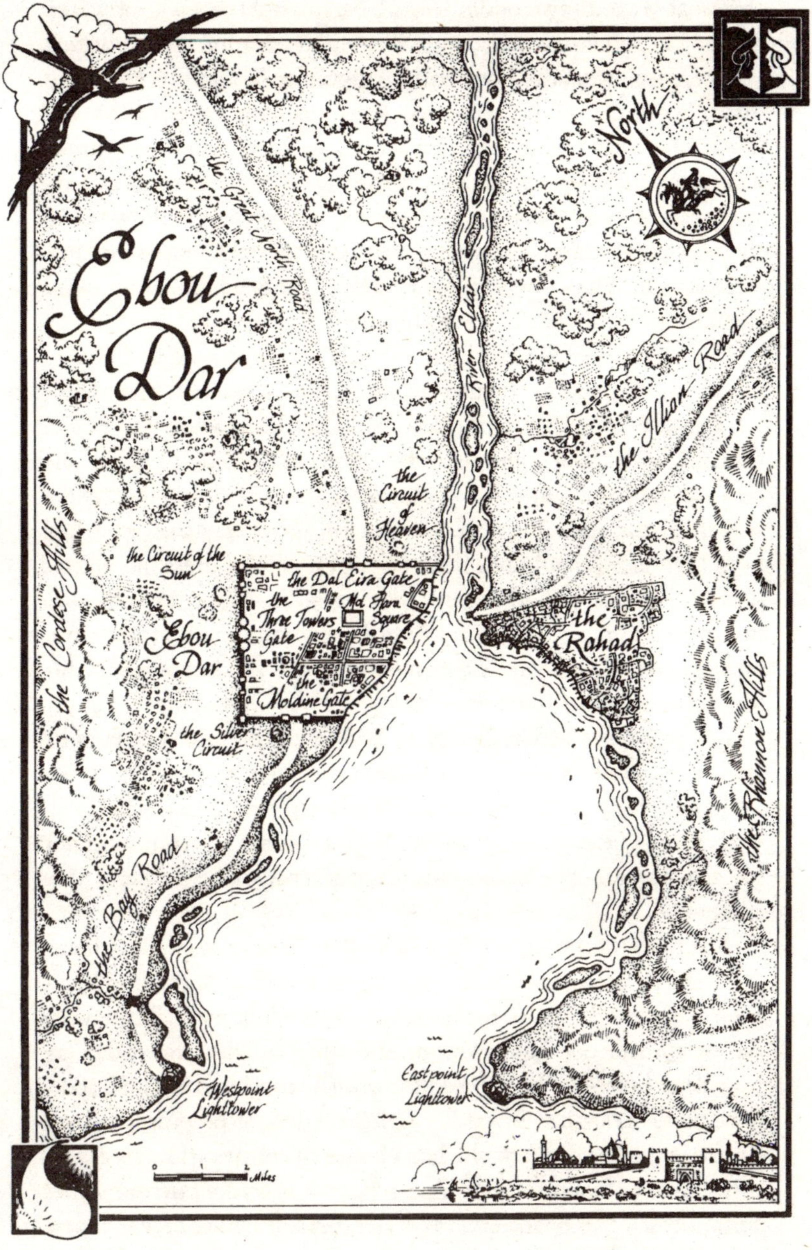

Ebou Dar
North
the Great North Road
River Eldar
the Illian Road
the Circuit of Heaven
the Circuit of the Sun
the Dal Eira Gate
Mol Hara Square
the Three Towers Gate
Ebou Dar
the Moldine Gate
the Rahad
the Cordese Hills
the Silver Circuit
the Rhannon Hills
the Bay Road
Westpoint Lighttower
Eastpoint Lighttower
0
1
2
Miles

this boat with its two oddly leering oarsmen. Half a *mile* of water, and not a drop fit for drinking. Who could imagine useless water?

The motion of the boat had changed, to a rocking back and forth. Were they out of the river, yet? Into what was called 'the bay'? That was wider still, far wider, so Elayne said. Aviendha locked her hands on her knees and tried desperately to think of anything else. If the others saw her fear, the shame would follow her to the end of her days. The worst of it was, she had suggested this, after hearing Elayne and Nynaeve talk of the Sea Folk. How could she have known what it would be like?

The blue silk of her dress felt incredibly smooth, and she latched on to that. She was barely used to skirts at all – she still yearned for the *cadin'sor* the Wise Ones had made her burn when she began training with them – and here she wore a *silk* dress – of which she now owned four! – and silk stockings instead of stout wool, and a silk shift that made her aware of her skin in a way she never had been before. She could not deny the beauty of the dress, no matter how odd it was to find herself wearing such things, but silk was precious, and rare. A woman might have a scarf of silk, to be worn on feastdays and envied by others. Few women had two. It was different among these wetlanders, though. Not everyone wore silk, yet sometimes it seemed to her every second person did. Great bolts and even bales of it came by ship from the lands beyond the Threefold Land. By ship. On the ocean. Water stretching to the horizon, with many places where, if she understood correctly, you could not see land at all. She came close to shivering at the impossible thought.

None of the others looked as if they wished to talk. Elayne absently twisted the Great Serpent ring on her right hand and peered at something not to be seen inside the four walls. These worries often overtook her. Two duties confronted her, and if one lay nearer her heart, she had chosen the one she considered more important, more honorable. It was her right and duty to become the chief, the queen, of Andor, but she had chosen to continue hunting. In a way, however important their search, that was like putting something before clan or society, yet Aviendha felt pride. Elayne's view of honor was as peculiar at times as the notion of a woman being a chief, or her becoming chief just because her mother had been, but she followed it admirably. Birgitte, in the wide red trousers and short yellow coat Aviendha envied, sat toying with her waist-long braid, lost in thought as well. Or maybe sharing part of Elayne's worries. She was Elayne's first Warder, which upset the Aes Sedai back in the Tarasin Palace no end, though it did not seem to bother their Warders. Wetlander customs were so curious they hardly bore thinking about.

If Elayne and Birgitte seemed to deflect any thought of talk, Nynaeve al'Meara, directly opposite Aviendha by the door, rebuffed it firmly. Nynaeve; not Nynaeve al'Meara. Wetlanders liked to be called by only half their names, and Aviendha was trying to remember, however much it felt like using a honey-name. Rand al'Thor was the only lover she had ever had, and she did not think even of him so intimately, but she had to learn their ways if she was to wed one of them.

Nynaeve's deep brown eyes stared through her. Her knuckles were white on a thick braid as dark as Birgitte's was golden, and her face had gone beyond pale to a faint green. From time to time she emitted a tiny muted groan. She did not usually sweat; she and Elayne had taught Aviendha the trick. Nynaeve was a puzzle. Brave to the point of madness sometimes, she moaned over her supposed cowardice, and here she displayed her shame for all to see without a care. How could the *motion* disturb her so, when all that water did not?

Water again. Aviendha shut her eyes to avoid seeing Nynaeve's face, but that only made the sounds of the birds and the lapping water fill her head.

'I have been thinking,' Elayne said suddenly, then paused. 'Are you all right, Aviendha? You ... ' Aviendha's cheeks reddened, but at least Elayne did not say aloud that she had jumped like a rabbit at the sound of her voice. Elayne seemed to realize how close she had come to revealing Aviendha's dishonor; color flushed her own cheeks as she continued. 'I was thinking about Nicola, and Areina. About what Egwene told us last night. You don't suppose they can cause *her* any trouble, do you? What is she to do?'

'Rid herself of them,' Aviendha said, drawing a thumb across her neck. The relief of speaking, of hearing voices, was so great that she almost gasped. Elayne appeared shocked. She was remarkably soft-hearted at times.

'It might be for the best,' Birgitte said. She had revealed no more name than that. Aviendha thought her a woman with secrets. 'Areina could have made something of herself with time, but— Don't look at me that way, Elayne, and stop going all prim and indignant in your head.' Birgitte often slipped back and forth between the Warder who obeyed and the older first-sister who instructed whether or not you wished to learn. Right then, waving an admonishing finger, she was the first-sister. 'You two wouldn't have been warned to stay away if it was a difficulty the Amyrlin could solve by having them set to work with the laundresses or the like.'

Elayne gave a sharp sniff in the face of what she could not deny, and adjusted her green silk skirts where they were drawn up in front to expose layers of blue and white petticoats. She was wearing the local fashion, complete with creamy lace at her wrists and around her neck, a gift from Tylin Quintara, as was the close-fitting necklace of woven gold. Aviendha did not approve. The upper half of the dress, the bodice, fitted as snugly as that necklace, and a missing narrow oval of cloth revealed the inner slopes of her breasts. Walking about where all could see was not the same as the sweat tents; people in the streets of the city were not *gai'shain*. Her own dress had a high neck that brushed her chin with lace, and no parts of it missing.

'Beside,' Birgitte went on, 'I would think *Marigan* would worry you more. She frightens me spitless.'

That name got through to Nynaeve, as well it might. Her groaning ceased, and she sat up straight. 'If she comes after us, we will just settle for her again. We'll ... we'll ...' Drawing breath, she stared at them pointedly, as if they were arguing with her. What she said, in a faint voice, was 'Do you think she will?'

'Fretting will do no good,' Elayne told her, much more calmly than Aviendha could have managed if she thought one of the Shadowsouled had marked her out. 'We will just have to do as Egwene said and be careful.' Nynaeve muttered something inaudible, which was probably just as well.

Silence descended again, Elayne settling to a browner study than before, Birgitte propping her chin on one hand as she frowned at nothing. Nynaeve kept right on grumbling under her breath, but she had both hands pressed to her middle now, and from time to time she paused to swallow. The splashing of water seemed louder than ever, and the cries of the birds.

'I have been thinking too, near-sister.' She and Elayne had not reached the point of adopting each other as first-sisters yet, but she was sure they would, now. Already they brushed each other's hair, and every night in the dark shared another secret never told to anyone else. This Min woman, though ... That was for later, when they were alone.

'About what?' Elayne asked absently.

'Our search. We prepare for success, but we are as far away as when we began. Does it make sense not to use every weapon at hand? Mat Cauthon is *ta'veren*, yet we work to avoid him. Why not take him with us? With him, we might find the bowl at last.'

'Mat?' Nynaeve exclaimed incredulously. 'As well stuff your shift full of nettles! I would not endure the man if he had the bowl in his coat pocket.'

'Oh, *do* be quiet, Nynaeve,' Elayne murmured, without any heat. She shook her head wonderingly, taking no notice of the other's sudden glower. 'Prickly' only began to describe Nynaeve, but they were all used to her ways. '*Why* didn't I think of that? It is so *obvious*!'

'Maybe,' Birgitte murmured dryly, 'you had Mat the scoundrel set so hard in your mind, you couldn't see he had any use.' Elayne gave her a cool stare, chin raised, then abruptly grimaced, and nodded reluctantly. She did not accept criticism easily.

'No,' Nynaeve said in a voice that somehow managed to be sharp and weak at the same time. The sickly cast of her face had deepened, but it no longer seemed caused by the boat's heaving. 'You cannot possibly mean it! Elayne, you know what a torment he can be, how stubborn he is. He'll insist on bringing those soldiers of his like a feastday parade. Try finding anything in the Rahad with soldiers at your shoulder. Just try! Inside two steps, he'll try to take charge, flaunting that *ter'angreal* at us. He's a thousand times worse than

Vandene or Adeleas, or even Merilille. The way he behaves, you would think we'd walk into a bear's den just to see the bear!'

Birgitte made a noise in her throat that might have been amusement, and received a darted glare. She returned such a look of bland innocence that Nynaeve began to sound as if she were choking.

Elayne was more soothing; she probably would try to make peace in a water-feud. 'He *is ta'veren*, Nynaeve. He alters the Pattern, alters *chance*, just being there. I'm ready to admit we need luck, and a *ta'veren* is more than luck. Besides, we can snare two birds at once. We should not have been letting him run loose all this time, no matter how busy we were. That's done no one any good, him least of all. He needs to be made fit for decent company. We will put him on a short rein from the start.'

Nynaeve smoothed her skirts with considerable vigor. She claimed to have no more interest in dresses than Aviendha – in what they looked like, anyway; she was always muttering about good plain wool being fine enough for anybody – yet her own blue dress was slashed with yellow on the skirts and sleeves, and she herself had chosen its design. Every stitch she owned was silk or embroidered or both, all cut with what Aviendha had learned to recognize as fine care.

For once Nynaeve appeared to understand she would not get her way. Sometimes she threw amazing tantrums until she did, not that she would admit that was what they were. The glower faded to a grumpy sulk. 'Who will ask him? Whoever does, he will make her beg. You know he will. I'd sooner marry him!'

Elayne hesitated, then said firmly, 'Birgitte will. And she won't beg; she will tell him. Most men will do as you say if you use a firm, confident voice.' Nynaeve looked doubtful, and Birgitte jerked erect on her bench, startled for the first time Aviendha had ever seen. With anyone else, Aviendha might have said she looked a little afraid, too. Birgitte would have done very well as *Far Dareis Mai*, for a wetlander. She had remarkable skill with a bow.

'You are the clear choice, Birgitte,' Elayne went on quickly. 'Nynaeve and I are Aes Sedai, and Aviendha might as well be. We cannot *possibly* do it. Not and maintain proper dignity. Not with him. You *know* what he is like.' What had happened to all that talk of a firm, confident voice? Not that Aviendha had ever noticed that working for anyone except Sorilea. It surely had not so far on Mat Cauthon that she had seen. 'Birgitte, he *can't* have recognized you. If he had, he would have said something by now.'

Whatever that meant, Birgitte leaned back against the wall and laced her fingers over her stomach. 'I should have known you'd get back at me ever since I said it was a good thing your bottom wasn't any—' She stopped, and a faint satisfied smile appeared on her lips. Nothing changed in Elayne's expression, but plainly Birgitte thought she had gained a measure of revenge. It must have been something felt through the Warder bond. How Elayne's bottom entered into anything, though, Aviendha could not puzzle out. Wetlanders were so ... *odd* ... at times. Birgitte continued, still wearing that smile. 'What I don't understand is why he starts chafing as soon as he sees you two. It can't be that you snagged him off here. Egwene was as deep in that as you, but I saw him treat her with more respect than most of the sisters do. Besides, the times I've glimpsed him coming out of The Wandering Woman, he looked to be enjoying himself.' Her smile became a grin that made Elayne sniff disapprovingly.

'That is one thing we need to change. A decent woman cannot be in the room with him. Oh, do wipe that smirk off your face, Birgitte. I vow, you are as bad as he, sometimes.'

'The man was born just to be a trial,' Nynaeve muttered sourly.

Suddenly Aviendha was forcibly reminded that she was on a boat as everything lurched, swaying and swinging around to a halt. Rising and straightening dresses, they gathered the light cloaks they had brought. She did not don hers; the sunlight here was not so bright that she needed the hood to keep it from her eyes. Birgitte only draped hers over one shoulder and pushed open the door, following up the three steps after Nynaeve had rushed past her with a hand clapped over her mouth.

Elayne paused to tie her cloak ribbons and arrange the hood around her face, red-gold curls peeking out all around. 'You did not say much, near-sister.'

'I said what I had to say. The decision was yours.'

'The key thought was yours, though. Sometimes I think the rest of us are turning into half-wits. Well.' Half turning to the steps, not quite looking at her, Elayne paused. 'Distances bother me, sometimes, over water. I think I will look only at the ship, myself. Nothing else.' Aviendha nodded – her near-sister had a fine delicacy – and they went up.

On the deck, Nynaeve was just shaking off Birgitte's offer of help and pushing herself up from the railing. The two oarsmen looked on in amusement as she wiped her mouth with the back of her hand. Shirtless fellows with a brass hoop in each ear, they must have had frequent use for the curved daggers shoved behind their sashes. Most of their attention went to working their pairs of long sweeps, though, walking back and forth on the deck to hold the heaving boat in place near a ship that almost took Aviendha's breath with its size, looming above their suddenly very tiny vessel, its three great masts reaching taller than most trees she had seen even here in the wetlands. They had chosen it because it was the largest of the hundreds of Sea Folk ships anchored in the bay. On a ship that big, surely it must be possible to forget all the surrounding water. Except . . .

Elayne had not really acknowledged her shame, and if she had, a near-sister could know your deepest humiliation without it mattering, but . . . Amys said she had too much pride. She made herself turn and look away from the boat.

She had never seen so much water in her life, not if every drop seen before had been gathered in one place, all of it rolling gray-green and here and there frothing white. Her eyes darted, trying to avoid taking it in. Even the sky seemed larger here, immense, with a liquid gold sun crawling up from the east. A gusting wind blew, somewhat cooler than on the land and never failing entirely. Clouds of birds flurried in the air, gray and white and sometimes splotched with black, giving those shrill cries. One, all black except for its head, skimmed along the surface with its long lower beak slicing through the water, and a slanted line of ungainly brown birds – pelicans, Elayne had named them – suddenly folded their wings one by one and plummeted with great splashes, bobbing back to the top, where they floated, tilting up beaks of incredible size. There were ships everywhere, many almost as large as the one behind her, not all belonging to the Atha'an Miere, and smaller vessels with one or two masts moving under triangular sails. Smaller ships still, mastless like the boat she was on, with a high sharp peak at the front and a low flat house at the back, spidered across the water on oars, one pair or two, or sometimes three. One long, narrow boat that must have had twenty to a side looked like a hundred-legs skittering along. And there was land. Maybe seven or eight miles distant, sunlight gleamed off the white-plastered buildings of the city. Seven or eight miles of water.

Swallowing, she turned back more swiftly than she had turned away. She thought her cheeks must be greener than Nynaeve's had been. Elayne was watching her, trying to keep a smooth face, but wetlanders showed their emotions so plainly her concern was visible. 'I am a fool, Elayne.' Even with her, using no more of her name made Aviendha feel uneasy; when they were first-sisters, when they were sister-wives, it would be easier. 'A wise woman listens to wise advice.'

'You are braver than I will ever be,' Elayne replied, quite seriously. She was another who kept denying that she had any courage. Maybe that was also a wetlander custom? No, Aviendha had heard wetlanders speak of their own bravery; these Ebou Dari, for one, seemed unable to utter three words without boasting. Elayne drew a deep breath, steeling herself. 'Tonight we will talk about Rand.'

Aviendha nodded, but she did not see how that followed from talk of courage. How could sister-wives manage a husband if they did not talk of him in detail? That was what the older women told her, anyway, and the Wise Ones. They were not always so forthcoming, of course. When she complained to Amys and Bair that she must be ill because she felt as though Rand al'Thor was carrying some part of her around with him, they had fallen down laughing. *You will learn*, they cackled at her, and, *You would have learned sooner had you grown up in skirts.* As if she had ever wanted any life but that of a Maiden, running with her spear-sisters. Maybe Elayne felt something of the same emptiness. Speaking of him did seem to make the hollowness grow even while filling it.

For some time she had been aware of voices rising, and now she heard the words.

'... you earringed buffoon!' Nynaeve was shaking her fist at a very dark man peering down at her from over the tall side of the ship. He looked calm, but then, he could not see the glow of *saidar* surrounding her. 'We are not after the gift of passage, so it doesn't matter whether you refuse it to Aes Sedai! You let down a ladder this instant!' The men at the oars were missing their grins. Apparently they had failed to see the serpent rings back at the stone landing, and they did not look pleased to learn they had Aes Sedai aboard.

'Oh, dear,' Elayne sighed. 'I must retrieve this, Aviendha, or we've wasted the morning just so she could lose her breakfast porridge.' Gliding across the *deck* – Aviendha was proud of knowing the proper names for things on boats – Elayne addressed the man up on the ship. 'I am Elayne Trakand, Daughter-Heir of Andor and Aes Sedai of the Green Ajah. My companion is quite truthful. We do not seek the gift of passage. But we must speak with your Windfinder on a matter of urgency. Tell her we know of the Weaving of Winds. Tell her we know of Windfinders.'

The man above frowned down at her, then abruptly vanished without a word.

'The woman will probably think you mean to blab her secrets,' Nynaeve muttered, jerking her cloak into place. She tied the ribbons fiercely. 'You know how afraid they are that Aes Sedai will haul them all off to the Tower, if it's known most can channel. Only a ninny thinks she can threaten people, Elayne, and still get anywhere.'

Aviendha burst out laughing. By the startled look Nynaeve gave her, she did not see the joke she had made on herself. Elayne's lips quivered, though, however she tried to hold them. You could never be sure about wetlander humor; they found strange things funny and missed the best.

Whether or not the Windfinder felt threatened, by the time Elayne had paid the boatmen and cautioned them to wait for their return – with Nynaeve grumbling over the amount and telling them she would box their ears if they left, and how she was to manage that nearly set Aviendha laughing again – by the time all that was done, it seemed a decision had been reached to allow them on. No ladder was lowered, but instead a flat piece of wood, the two ropes it hung from becoming one and running up to a thick pole swung out over the side from one of the masts. Nynaeve took her place sitting on the board with dire warnings for the boatmen if they even thought of trying to look up her skirts, and Elayne blushed and held hers tightly around her legs, hunched over so she appeared ready to fall off headfirst as she wobbled into the air and disappeared from sight onto the ship. One of the fellows looked upward anyway, until Birgitte struck him on the nose with her fist. They certainly did not watch *her* ascent.

Aviendha's belt knife was small, with a blade not half a foot long, but the oarsmen frowned worriedly when she drew it. Her arm went back, and they fell sprawling to the deck as the knife whirled over their heads to sink with a solid *thunk* into the thick wooden post at the front of the boat. Looping the cloak over her arms like a shawl, she hoisted her skirts well above her knees so she could climb over the oars and retrieve her blade, then took her place on the dangling board. She did not replace the knife in its sheath. For some reason the two men exchanged confused looks, but they kept their eyes down as she was lifted up. Perhaps she was beginning to get a feel for wetlander customs.

Settling onto the great ship's deck, she gaped, almost forgetting to climb off the narrow seat. She had read of the Atha'an Miere, but reading and seeing was as different as reading of salt water and tasting it. They were all dark, for one thing, much darker than the Ebou Dari, even darker than most Tairens, with straight black hair and black eyes and tattooed hands. Bare-chested, barefoot men with bright narrow sashes holding up baggy breeches of some dark cloth that had an oily look to it, and women in blouses as brilliantly colored as their sashes, all with a sway to their movements, gliding gracefully with the rocking of the ship. Sea Folk women had very strange customs when it came to men, according to what she had read, dancing with no more than a single scarf for covering and worse, but it was the earrings that made her stare. Most had three or four, often with polished stones, and some actually had a small ring in one side of their noses! The men did, too, the earrings at least, and just as many heavy gold and silver chains around their necks. Men! Some wetlander men wore rings in their ears, true – most Ebou Dari men seemed to – but so many! And necklaces! Wetlanders did have strange ways. The Sea Folk never left their ships – never – so she had read, and supposedly they ate their dead. She had not been quite able to credit that, but if the men wore necklaces, who could say what else they did?

The woman who came to meet them wore breeches and blouse and sash like the others, but hers were of brocaded yellow silk, the sash knotted intricately with ends trailing to her knee, and one of her necklaces bore a small golden box of intricate piercework. A sweetly musky scent surrounded her. Gray streaked her hair heavily, and she had a grave face. Five small fat golden rings decorated each of her ears, and a fine chain connected one to a similar ring in her nose. Tiny medallions of polished gold dangling from the chain flashed in the sunlight as she studied them.

Aviendha pulled her hand down from her own nose – to wear that chain, always tugging! – and barely managed to suppress a laugh. Wetlander customs were odd beyond belief, and surely no one deserved the name better than the Sea Folk.

'I am Malin din Toral Breaking Wave,' the woman said. 'A Wavemistress of Clan Somarin and Sailmistress of *Windrunner*.' A Wavemistress was important, like a clan chief, yet she seemed at a loss, looking from one face to the next, until her eye fell on the Great Serpent rings Elayne and Nynaeve wore, and then she exhaled in resignation. 'If it pleases you to come with me, Aes Sedai?' she said to Nynaeve.

The back of the ship was raised, and she led the way inside that by a door, then down a hallway to a large room – a *cabin* – with a low ceiling. Aviendha doubted Rand al'Thor would have been able to stand upright beneath one of the thick beams. Except for a few lacquered chests, everything seemed to have been built in place, cabinets along the walls, even the long table that ran half the length of the room and the armchairs that surrounded it. It was difficult to think of something the size of this ship being made of wood, and even after all her time in the wetlands, the sight of all that polished wood nearly made her gasp. It glowed almost as much as the gilded lamps, hanging unlit in some sort of cage so they remained upright as the ship moved with the waves. In truth, the ship hardly seemed to move at all, at least in comparison with the boat they had been on, but unfortunately the back of the cabin, of the ship, was a line of windows with the painted and gilded shutters standing open, giving a splendid view of the bay. Worse, there was no land in sight out those windows. No land at all! Her throat seized. She could not have spoken. She could not have screamed, although that was what she wanted to do.

Those windows and what they showed – what they did not show – had caught her eyes so quickly that it took her a moment to realize people were there already. A fine thing! Had they wished, they could have killed her before she knew. Not that they showed any sign of hostility, but you could never be too careful with wetlanders.

A spindly old man with deep-set eyes was sitting at his ease atop one of the chests; what little hair remained to him was white, and his dark face had a kindly look, though a full dozen earrings altogether and a number of thick gold chains around his neck gave his expression a strange twist in her eyes. Like the men above, he was barefoot and bare-chested, but his breeches were a dark blue silk, and his long sash a bright red. An ivory-hilted sword was thrust through that sash, she noted with disdain, as well as two curved daggers to match.

The slender, handsome woman with her arms folded and a grimly foreboding frown was more worthy of notice. She wore only four earrings in each ear, and fewer medallions on her chain than Malin din Toral, and her clothing was all in reddish-yellow silk. She could channel; Aviendha knew that, this close. She must be the woman they had come for, the Windfinder. And yet it was another who held Aviendha's eye. And for that matter, Elayne's and Nynaeve's and Birgitte's.

The woman who had looked up from an unrolled map on the table might have been as old as the man by her white hair. Short, no taller than Nynaeve, she looked like someone who had once been stocky and was beginning to go stout, but her jaw thrust forward like a hammer, and her black eyes spoke of intelligence. And power. Not the One Power, just that of someone who said 'go' and knew that people would go, yet she had it strongly. Her breeches were brocaded green silk, her blouse blue, and her sash red like the man's. The stout-bladed knife in a gilded sheath tucked behind that sash had a round pommel covered with red and green stones; firedrops and emeralds, Aviendha thought. Twice as many medallions hung from her nose chain as from Malin din Toral's, and another, thinner gold chain connected the six rings in each of her ears. Aviendha barely kept her hand from going to her own nose again.

Without a word the white-haired woman came to stand in front of Nynaeve, rudely examining her from head to toe, frowning in particular at Nynaeve's face and the Great Serpent ring on her right hand. She took no time about it, and with a grunt moved on from her ruffled object of study to give Elayne the same quick, intense scrutiny, and then Birgitte. At last she spoke. 'You are not an Aes Sedai.' Her voice sounded like rocks tumbling.

'By the nine winds and Stormbringer's beard, I am not,' Birgitte replied. Sometimes she said things even Elayne and Nynaeve seemed not to understand, but the white-haired woman jumped as if she had been goosed, and stared a long moment before turning to frown up at Aviendha.

'You are not Aes Sedai, either,' she grated after the examination.

Aviendha drew herself to her full height, feeling as though the woman had rummaged through her garments and twisted her about to look at her better. 'I am Aviendha, of the Nine Valleys sept of the Taardad Aiel.'

The woman gave twice the start she had for Birgitte, black eyes going wide. 'You are not garbed as I expected, girl' was all she said, though, and strode back to the far end of the table, where she planted her fists on her hips and studied them all again, much as she might have some strange animal she had never seen before. 'I am Nesta din Reas Two Moons,' she said at last, 'Mistress of the Ships to the Atha'an Miere. How do you know what you know?'

Nynaeve had been working on a scowl since the woman first looked at her, and now she snapped, 'Aes Sedai know what they know. And we expect more in the way of manners than I've seen so far! I certainly saw more the last time I was on a Sea Folk ship. Maybe we should find another, where the people don't all have sore teeth.' Nesta din Reas' face grew darker, but Elayne of course stepped into the breech, removing her cloak and laying it over the edge of the table.

'The Light illumine you and your vessels, Shipmistress, and send the winds to speed you all.' Her curtsy was moderately deep; Aviendha had become a judge of these things, for all she thought it looked the most awkward thing any woman could ever do. 'Forgive us if there have been words in haste. We mean no disrespect to one who is as a queen to the Atha'an Miere.' That with a speaking look for Nynaeve. Nynaeve only shrugged, though.

Elayne introduced herself again, and the rest of them, to strange reactions. That Elayne was Daughter-Heir produced none, though that was a high position among the wetlanders, and that she was Green Ajah and Nynaeve Yellow received sniffs from Nesta din Reas and sharp looks from the spindly old man. Elayne blinked, taken aback, but she went on smoothly. 'We have come for two reasons. The lesser is to ask how you mean to aid the Dragon Reborn, who according to the Jendai Prophecy you call the Coramoor. The greater is to request the help of this vessel's Windfinder. Whose name,' she added gently, 'I regret I do not yet know.'

The slender woman who could channel reddened. 'I am Dorile din Eiran Long Feather, Aes Sedai. I may help, if it pleases the Light.'

Malin din Toral looked abashed, too. 'The welcome of my ship to you,' she murmured, 'and the grace of the Light be upon you until you leave his decks.'

Not so Nesta din Reas. 'The Bargain is with the Coramoor,' she said in a hard voice, and made a sharp cutting gesture. 'The shorebound have no part of it, except where they tell of his coming. You, girl, Nynaeve. What ship gave you the gift of passage? Who was his Windfinder?'

'I can't recall.' Nynaeve's airy tone was at odds with the stony smile she wore. She had a deathgrip on her braid, too, but at least she had not embraced *saidar* again. 'And I am Nynaeve Sedai, Nynaeve Aes Sedai, not girl.'

Putting her hands flat on the table, Nesta din Reas directed a stare at her that reminded Aviendha of Sorilea. 'Perhaps you are, but

I will know who revealed what should not have been revealed. She has lessons of silence to learn.'

'A split sail is split, Nesta,' the old man said suddenly, in a deep voice much stronger than his bony limbs suggested. Aviendha had taken him for a guard, but his tone was that of an equal. 'It might be well to ask what aid Aes Sedai would have of us, in days when the Coramoor has come, and the seas rage in endless storms, and the doom of the Prophecy sails the oceans. If they are Aes Sedai?' That with a raised eyebrow to the Windfinder.

She answered quietly, in a respectful voice. 'Three can channel, including her.' She pointed at Aviendha. 'I have never met anyone so strong as they. They must be. Who else would dare wear the ring?'

Waving her to silence, Nesta din Reas turned that same iron gaze on the man. 'Aes Sedai never ask aid, Baroc,' she growled. 'Aes Sedai never *ask* anything.' He met her gaze mildly, but after a moment she sighed as though he had stared her down. The eyes she aimed at Elayne were no whit softer, though. 'What would you have of us . . .' She hesitated. '. . . Daughter-Heir of Andor?' Even that sounded skeptical.

Nynaeve gathered herself, ready to launch into an attack – Aviendha had had to listen to more than one tirade sparked by the Aes Sedai back in the Tarasin Palace and their habit of forgetting that she and Elayne were Aes Sedai too; someone not even Aes Sedai denying it might bring the shedding of blood – Nynaeve gathered herself up and opened her mouth . . . And Elayne silenced her with a touch on the arm and a whisper too low for Aviendha to hear. Nynaeve's face was still crimson, and she looked about to pull her braid out slowly by the roots, yet she held her tongue. Maybe Elayne *could* make peace in a water-feud.

Of course, Elayne could not be pleased, when not only her right to be called Aes Sedai but her right to the title of Daughter-Heir was doubted so openly. Most would have thought her quite calm, but Aviendha knew the signs. The raised chin spoke of anger; add eyes open as wide as they would go, and Elayne was a torch to overwhelm Nynaeve's ember. Besides, Birgitte was on her toes, face like stone and eyes like fire. She did not usually mirror Elayne's emotions, except when they were very strong. Wrapping her fingers around the hilt of her belt knife, Aviendha readied herself to embrace *saidar*. She would kill the Windfinder first; the woman was not weak in the Power, and she would be dangerous. They could find others with so many ships about.

'We seek a *ter'angreal*.' Except that her tone was cool, anyone who did not know her would think Elayne was absolutely serene. She faced Nesta din Reas, but she addressed everyone, perhaps especially the Windfinder. 'With it, we believe we can remedy the weather. It must trouble you as much as it does the land. Baroc spoke of endless storms. You must be able to see the Dark One's touch, the Father of Storms' touch, on the sea just as we do on the land. With this *ter'angreal*, we can change that, but we cannot do it alone. It will require many women working together, perhaps a full circle of thirteen. We think those women should include Windfinders. No one else knows so much of weather, not any Aes Sedai living. That is the aid we ask.'

Dead silence met her speech, until Dorile din Eiran said carefully, 'This *ter'angreal*, Aes Sedai. What is it called? How does it look?'

'It has no name, that I know,' Elayne told her. 'It is a thick crystal bowl, shallow but something over two feet across, and worked inside with clouds. When it is channeled into, the clouds move—'

'The Bowl of the Winds,' the Windfinder broke in excitedly, stepping toward Elayne as if she did not realize it. 'They have the Bowl of the Winds.'

'You truly have it?' The Wavemistress's eyes were fixed on Elayne eagerly, and she also took an involuntary step.

'We are *looking* for it,' Elayne said. 'But we know it is in Ebou Dar. If it is the same—'

'It must be,' Malin din Toral exclaimed. 'By your description, it must!'

'The Bowl of the Winds,' Dorile din Eiran breathed. 'To think it would be found again after two thousand years here! It must be the Coramoor. He must have—'

Nesta din Reas' hands slapped together loudly. 'Do I see a Wavemistress and her Windfinder, or two deckgirls at their first shipmeet?' Malin din Toral's cheeks reddened with a proud anger, and she bent her head stiffly, pride in that as well. Twice as flushed, Dorile din Eiran bowed, touching fingertips to forehead, lips and heart.

The Shipmistress frowned at them a moment, before going on. 'Baroc, summon the other Wavemistresses who hold this port, and the First Twelve as well. With their Windfinders. And let them know you will hoist them by their toes in their own rigging if they do not hurry.' As he rose, she added, 'Oh. And have tea sent down. Working out the terms of this bargain will be thirsty.'

The old man nodded; that he might dangle Wavemistresses by their toes and that he must send tea were accepted equally. Eyeing Aviendha and the others, he sauntered out with that rolling walk. She changed her opinion when she saw his eyes close up. It might have been a fatal mistake to kill the Windfinder first.

Someone must have been awaiting orders of the sort, because Baroc was only gone moments before a slim, pretty young man with a single thin ring in each ear entered carrying a wooden tray that bore a square blue-glazed teapot with a golden handle and large blue cups of thick pottery. Nesta din Reas waved him out – 'He will spread enough tales as it is, without hearing what he should not,' she said when he was gone – and directed Birgitte to pour. Which she did, to Aviendha's surprise, and maybe her own.

The Shipmistress settled Elayne and Nynaeve in chairs at one end of the table, apparently intent on beginning her bargaining. Aviendha refused a chair – at the other end of the table – but Birgitte took one, swinging the arm out, then latching it back when she was seated. The Wavemistress and the Windfinder were excluded from that discussion, too, if discussion it could be called. The words were too low to hear, but Nesta din Reas emphasized everything she said with a finger driven like a spear, Elayne had her chin so high she seemed to be looking down her nose, and if Nynaeve for once was managing to keep her face calm, she seemed to be trying to climb her own braid.

'If it pleases the Light, I will speak with both of you,' Malin din Toral said, looking from Aviendha to Birgitte, 'but I think I must hear your story first.' Birgitte began to look alarmed as the woman sat down across from her.

'Which means I can speak first with you, if it pleases the Light,' Dorile din Eiran told Aviendha. 'I have read of the Aiel. If it pleases you, tell me, if an Aielwoman must kill a man every day, how are there any men left among you?'

Aviendha did her best not to stare. How could the woman believe such nonsense?

'When did you live among us?' Malin din Toral said over her teacup at the near end of the table. Birgitte was leaning away from her as though she wanted to climb over the back of the chair.

At the far end of the table, Nesta din Reas' voice rose for a moment. ' . . . came to me, not I to you. *That* sets the basis for our bargain, even if you are Aes Sedai.'

Slipping into the room, Baroc paused between Aviendha and Birgitte. 'It seems your shoreboat departed as soon as you came below, but have no worry; *Windrunner* has boats to put you on the shore.' Walking on down the cabin, he took a chair below Elayne and Nynaeve and joined right in. When they looked at whichever was speaking, the other could observe them unnoticed. They had lost an advantage, one they needed. 'Of course the bargain is on our terms,' he said in tones of disbelief that it could be otherwise, while the Shipmistress studied Elayne and Nynaeve as a woman might two goats she meant to skin for a feast. Baroc's smile was almost fatherly. 'Who asks must of course pay highest.'

'But you must have lived among us to know those ancient oaths,' Malin din Toral insisted.

'Are you well, Aviendha?' Dorile din Eiran asked. 'Even here, the motion of a ship sometimes affects shorefolk – No? And my questions do not offend? Then tell me. Do Aiel women truly tie a man down before you – I mean, when you and he – when you—' Cheeks reddened, she broke off with a weak smile. 'Are many Aiel women as strong in the One Power as you?'

It was not the Windfinder's foolish fumbling about that had made the blood drain from Aviendha's face, or that Birgitte appeared ready to run once she could manage to unlatch the chair arm again, or even that Nynaeve and Elayne were apparently discovering they were two bright-eyed girls at a fair, in the hands of well-seasoned traders. They would all blame her, and rightly. She was the one who had said if they could not take the *ter'angreal* back to Egwene and the other Aes Sedai once found, why not secure these Sea Folk women they spoke of? Time could not be wasted, waiting for Egwene al'Vere to say they could return. They would blame her, and she would meet her *toh*, but she was remembering the boats she had seen on the deck, stacked upside down atop one another. Boats without any shelter on board. They would blame her, but whatever debt she owed she was going to repay a thousandfold in shame by the time she was taken across seven or eight miles of water in an open boat.

'Do you have a bucket?' she asked the Windfinder faintly.

CHAPTER 14

White Plumes

The Silver Circuit was misnamed at first glance, but Ebou Dar liked grand names, and sometimes it seemed that the worse they fit, the better. The grimiest tavern Mat had seen in the city, smelling of very old fish, bore the name of The Queen's Glory in Radiance, while The Golden Crown of Heaven graced a dim hole across the river in the Rahad with only a blue door to mark it, where black stains from old knife fights splotched the grimy floor. The Silver Circuit was for racing horses.

Removing his hat, he fanned himself with the broad brim, and went so far as to loosen the black silk scarf he wore to hide the scar around his neck. The morning air shimmered with heat already, yet crowds packed the two long earthen banks that flanked the course where the horse would run up and back. That was all there was to the Silver Circuit. The murmur of voices almost drowned out the cries of the gulls overhead. There was no charge to watch, so saltworkers in the white vest of their guild and gaunt-faced farmers who had fled from the Dragonsworn inland rubbed shoulders with ragged Taraboners wearing transparent veils across their thick mustaches, weavers in vests with vertical stripes, printers in horizontal stripes and dyers with hands stained to the elbow. The unrelieved black of Amadician countrymen, buttoned to the neck though the wearers seemed about to sweat to death, stood alongside Murandian village dresses with long colorful aprons so narrow they must be only for show, and even a handful of copper-skinned Domani, the men in short coats if they wore one, the women in wool or linen so thin it clung like silk. There were apprentices, and laborers from the docks and warehouses, tanners who had a small space around them in the crowd because of the smell of their work, and filthy-faced street children watched closely because they would steal whatever they could lay hand to. There was little silver among the working people, though.

All of them were above the thick hemp ropes strung on posts. Below was for those who did have silver, and gold; the well-born, the well-dressed and the well-to-do. Smug menservants poured punch into silver cups for their masters, fluttery maids waved feathered fans to cool their mistresses, and there was even a capering fool with white-painted face and jingling brass bells on his black-and-white hat and coat. Haughty men in high-crowned velvet hats strutted with slender swords on their hips, their hair brushing silk coats slung across their shoulders and held by gold or silver chains between the narrow, embroidered lapels. Some of the women had hair shorter than the men and some longer, arranged in as many ways as there were women; they wore wide hats with plumes or sometimes fine netting to obscure their faces, and gowns usually cut to show bosom whether in the local style or from elsewhere. The nobles, beneath brightly colored parasols, glittered with rings and earrings, necklaces and bracelets in gold and ivory and fine gems as they stared down their noses at everyone else. Well-fed merchants and moneylenders, with just a touch of lace and perhaps one pin or a ring bearing a fat polished stone, humbly bowed or curtsied to their betters, who very likely owed them vast sums. Fortunes changed hands at the Silver Circuit, and not just in wagers. It was said lives and honor changed hands, too, below the ropes.

Replacing his hat, Mat raised his hand, and one of the bookers came – a hatchet-faced woman with a nose like an awl – spreading bony hands as she bowed, murmuring the ritual 'As my Lord wishes to wager, so shall I write truly.' The Ebou Dari accent managed to be soft despite clipping the ends off some words. 'The book is open.' Like the saying, the open book embroidered on the breast of her red vest came from a time long past, when the wagers were written into a book, but he suspected he was the only one there who knew that. He remembered many things he had never seen, from times long gone to dust.

With a quick glance at the odds for the morning's fifth race, chalked on the slate the poleman held up behind the red-vested woman, he nodded. Wind was only the third favorite, despite his victories. He turned to his companion. 'Put it all on Wind, Nalesean.'

The Tairen hesitated, fingering the point of his oiled black beard. Sweat glistened on his face, yet he kept his coat with its fat, blue-striped sleeves fastened to the top and wore a square cap of blue velvet that did nothing to keep the sun off. 'All of it, Mat?' He spoke softly, trying to keep the woman from hearing. The odds could change any time until you actually offered your wager. 'Burn my soul, but that little piebald looks fast, and so does that pale dun gelding with the silvery mane.' They were the favorites today, new to the city and like all things new, of great expectation.

Mat did not bother to glance toward the ten horses entered in the next race that were parading at one end of the course. He had already taken a good look while putting Olver up on Wind. 'All of it. Some idiot clubbed the piebald's tail; he's already half mad from the flies. The dun is showy, but he has a bad angle to his fetlocks. He may have won some in the country, but he'll finish last today.' Horses were one thing he knew on his own; his father had taught him, and Abell Cauthon had a sharp eye for horseflesh.

'He looks more than showy to me,' Nalesean grumbled, but he was not arguing anymore.

The booker blinked as Nalesean, sighing, pulled purse after fat purse from his bulging coat pockets. At one point she opened her mouth to protest, but the Illustrious and Honored Guild of Bookers always claimed it would take any wager in any amount. They even wagered with shipowners and merchants as to whether a ship would sink or prices change; rather, the guild itself did, not individual bookers. The gold went into one of her iron-strapped chests, each carried by a pair of fellows with arms as thick as Mat's legs. Her guards, hard-eyed and bent-nosed in leather vests that showed arms still thicker, held long brass-bound cudgels. Another of her men handed her a white token bearing a detailed blue fish – every booker had a different sigil – and she wrote the wager, the name of the horse and a symbol indicating the race on the back with a fine brush that she took from a lacquered box held by a pretty girl. Slim, with big dark eyes, the girl directed a slow smile at Mat. The hatchet-faced woman certainly did not smile. Bowing again, she slapped the girl casually and walked off whispering to her poleman, who hastily wiped his slate with a cloth. When he held it up again, Wind was listed at the shortest odds. Rubbing her cheek surreptitiously, the girl scowled back at Mat as though the slap had been his fault.

'I hope your luck is in,' Nalesean said, holding the token carefully for the ink to dry. Bookers could be touchy about paying on a token with smeared ink, and no one was touchier than an Ebou Dari. 'I know you don't lose often, but I've seen it happen, burn me but I have. There's a lass I mean to step out with at the dancing tonight. Just a seamstress . . . ' He was a lord, though not a bad fellow really, and such things seemed important to him ' . . . but pretty enough to dry your mouth. She likes trinkets. Golden trinkets. She likes fireworks, too – I hear some Illuminators are setting up for tonight; you'll be interested in that – but it's trinkets make her smile. She won't be friendly if I cannot afford to make her smile, Mat.'

'You'll make her smile,' Mat said absently. The horses were still walking in a circle above the starting poles. Olver sat proudly on Wind's back, broad mouth grinning to split his more-than-plain face from jug-ear to jug-ear. In Ebou Dari races, all the riders were boys; a few miles inland, they used girls. Olver was the smallest here today, the lightest, not that the leggy gray gelding needed the advantage. 'You'll make her laugh till she can't stand up.' Nalesean gave him a frown he barely noticed. The man should know gold was one thing Mat never had to worry about. He might not always win, but close enough. His luck had nothing to do with whether Wind won anyway. Of that he was sure.

Gold did not concern him, but Olver did. There was no rule against the boys using their switches on each other instead of their mounts. In every race so far, Wind had broken to the lead and stayed there, but if Olver took any hurt, even just a bruise, Mat would never hear the end. Not from Mistress Anan, his innkeeper, not from Nynaeve or Elayne, not from Aviendha or Birgitte. The onetime Maiden of the Spear and the peculiar woman Elayne had taken as a Warder were the last he would have expected to gush with maternal feelings, yet they had already tried to move the boy out of The Wandering Woman behind his back and into the Tarasin Palace. Anywhere with so many Aes Sedai was the last place for Olver, or for anybody, but one bump and instead of telling Birgitte and Aviendha they had no right to take the boy, Setalle Anan would likely hustle him off there herself. Olver would probably cry himself to sleep if he was not allowed to race any more, but women never understood these things. For about the thousandth time, Mat cursed Nalesean for sneaking Olver and Wind to those first races. Of course, they had to find something to fill all the idle hours on their hands, but they could have found something else. Cutting purses could have been no worse in the women's eyes.

'Here's the thief-catcher,' Nalesean said, stuffing the token into his coat. He did not quite sneer. 'Much good he's done so far. We'd have done better to bring another fifty soldiers instead.'

Juilin strode through the crowd purposefully, a dark, hard man using a slender bamboo staff as tall as himself for a walking stick. With a flat-topped conical red Taraboner cap on his head and a plain coat, tight to the waist then flaring to his boot tops, well-worn and plainly not the coat of someone rich, he normally would not have been allowed below the ropes, but he made out to study the horses and ostentatiously bounced a fat coin on his palm. Several of the bookers' guards looked at him suspiciously, but the gold crown let him pass.

'Well?' Mat said sourly, tugging his hat low, once the thief-catcher reached him. 'No, let me tell you. They slipped out of the palace again. No one saw them go, again. Nobody has any bloody idea where they are, again.'

Juilin tucked the coin carefully into his coat pocket. He would make no wager; he seemed to save every copper that came into his hands. 'All four of them took a closed coach from the palace to a landing on the river, where they hired a boat. Thom hired another to follow and see where they're going. Nowhere dark or unpleasant, I'd say, by their clothes. But it is true, nobles wear silk to crawl in the mud.' He grinned at Nalesean, who folded his arms and pretended to be engrossed in the horses. The grin was a mere baring of teeth. They were both Tairen, but the gap between noble and common stood wide in Tear, and neither man liked the other's company.

'Women!' Several finely dressed specimens nearby turned to eye Mat askance from beneath bright parasols. He frowned right back, though two were pretty, and they set to laughing and chattering among themselves as though he had done something amusing. A woman would do a thing until you were sure she always would, then do something else just to fuddle you. But he had promised Rand to see Elayne safely to Caemlyn, and Nynaeve and Egwene with her. And he had promised Egwene to see the other two safe on this trip to Ebou Dar, not to mention Aviendha; that was the price of getting Elayne to Caemlyn. Not that they had told him why they needed to be here; oh, no. Not that they had spoken twenty words to him since arriving in the bloody city!

'I'll see them safe,' he muttered under his breath, 'if I have to stuff them into barrels and haul them to Caemlyn in a cart.' He might be the only man in the world who could say that about Aes Sedai without looking over his shoulder, maybe even including Rand and those fellows he was gathering. He touched the foxhead medallion hanging under his shirt to make sure it was there, though he never took it off, even to bathe. It did have flaws, but a man liked to be reminded.

'Tarabon must be terrible now for a woman not used to taking care of herself,' Juilin murmured. He was watching three veiled men in tattered coats and baggy once-white trousers scramble up the bank ahead of a pair of bookers' guards waving their clubs. No rule said the poor could not come below the ropes, but the bookers' guards did. The two pretty women who had eyed Mat appeared to be making a private wager on whether the Taraboners would outrun the guards.

'We've more than enough women right here without sense to come in out of the rain,' Mat told him. 'Go back to that boat landing and wait for Thom. Tell him I need him as soon as possible. I want to know what those fool bloody women are up to.'

Juilin's look did not quite call *him* a fool. They had, after all, been trying to find out exactly that for over a month now, ever since coming here. With a last glance at the fleeing men, he sauntered back the way he had come, once more bouncing the coin in his hand.

Frowning, Mat peered across the race course. It was barely fifty paces to the crowd on the other side, and faces leaped out at him — a bent, white-haired old man with a hooked nose, a sharp-faced woman under a hat that seemed mostly plumes, a tall fellow who looked like a stork in green silk and gold braid, a nicely plump, full-mouthed young woman who appeared about to come out of her dress at the top. The longer the heat continued, the fewer and thinner garments women in Ebou Dar wore, but for once he hardly gave them any notice. Weeks had gone by since he so much as glimpsed the women who concerned him now.

Birgitte certainly needed no one to hold her hand; a Hunter for the Horn, anyone who troubled her would be in a deep hole by his estimation. And Aviendha . . . All she needed was someone to keep her from stabbing everybody who looked at her crossways. As far as he was concerned, she could knife whoever she wanted so long as it was not Elayne. For all the bloody Daughter-Heir walked about with her nose in the air, she turned moon-eyed around Rand, and for all Aviendha behaved as if she would stab any man who glanced her way, she did the same. Rand usually knew how to deal with women, but he had jumped into a bear pit letting that pair come together. It was a short road to disaster, and why ruin had not happened was beyond Mat.

For some reason his eyes drifted back to the sharp-faced woman. She was pretty, if vulpine. About Nynaeve's age, he estimated; it was hard to tell at the distance, but he could judge women as well as he could horses. Of course, women could fool you faster than any horse. Slim. Why did she make him think of straw? What he could see of her hair beneath the plumed hat was dark. No matter.

Birgitte and Aviendha could do without his shepherding, and normally he would have said the same of Elayne and Nynaeve, however wrongheaded, conceited and downright pushy they could be. That they had been sneaking out all this time said differently, though. Wrongheadedness was the key. They were the sort who berated a man for meddling and chased him away, then berated him again for not being there when he was needed. Not that they would admit he was needed, even then, not them. Raise a hand to help and you were interfering, do nothing and you were an untrustworthy wastrel.

The fox-faced woman across the way popped into his view again. Not straw; a stable. Which made no more sense. He had had fine times in stables with many a young woman and some not so young, but she wore modestly cut blue silk with a high neck right under her chin trimmed in snowy lace, and more spilling over her hands. A lady, and he avoided noblewomen like death. Playing haughty like a harp, expecting a man always to be at their beck and call. Not Mat Cauthon. Strangely, she was fanning herself with a spray of white plumes. Where was her maid? A knife. Why should she make him think of a knife? And ... fire? Something burning, anyway.

Shaking his head, he tried to focus on what was important. Other men's memories, of battles and courts and lands vanished centuries ago, filled holes in his own, places where his own life suddenly went thin or was not there at all. He could remember fleeing the Two Rivers with Moiraine and Lan quite clearly for example, but almost nothing more until reaching Caemlyn, and there were gaps before and after, as well. If whole years of his own growing up lay beyond recall, why should he expect to recollect every woman he had met? Maybe she reminded him of some woman dead a thousand years or more; the Light knew that happened often enough.

Even Birgitte sometimes tickled his memory. Well, there were four women here and now who had his brain tied in knots. They were what was important.

Nynaeve and the others were avoiding him as if he had fleas. Five times he had been to the palace, and the once they would see him, it was to say they were too busy for him and send him away like an errand boy. It all added up to one thing. They thought he would interfere with whatever they were up to, and the only reason he would do that was if they were putting themselves in danger. They were not complete fools; idiots often, but not complete fools. If they saw danger, there was danger. Some places in this city, being a stranger or showing a coin could bring a knife in your ribs, and not even channeling would stop it if they did not see in time. And here he was, with Nalesean and a dozen good men from the Band, not to mention Thom and Juilin, who actually had rooms in the servants' quarters of the palace, all left to twiddle their thumbs. Those thick-skulled women were going to get their throats cut yet. 'Not if I can help it,' he growled.

'What?' Nalesean said. 'Look. They're lining up, Mat. The Light burn my soul, I hope you're right. That piebald doesn't look half-crazed to me; he looks eager.'

The horses were prancing, taking their places between tall poles stuck in the ground, with streamers trailing from the tops of them in a warm breeze, blue and green and every color, some striped. Five hundred paces down the track of hard-beaten red clay an identical number of streamered poles made another row. Each rider had to round the same-colored streamer as floated to his right at the start and then return. A booker stood at either end of the line of horses, just to the front, a round woman and a rounder man, each with a white scarf held overhead. The bookers took turns at this, and were not allowed to accept wagers on a race they started.

'Burn me,' Nalesean muttered.

'Light, man, be easy. You'll tickle your seamstress under the chin yet.' A roar drowned the last word as the scarves came down, and the horses surged forward, even the sound of their hooves submerged in the noise of the crowd. In ten strides Wind had the lead, Olver lying close on his neck, with the silver-maned dun only a head back. The piebald trailed in the pack, where the riders' switches already rose and fell frantically.

'I told you the dun was dangerous,' Nalesean moaned. 'We shouldn't have wagered everything.'

Mat did not bother to answer. He had another purse in his pocket and loose coins besides. He called the purse his seed; with that, with even a few of the coins in it, and a game of dice, he could repair his fortunes whatever happened this morning. Halfway down the course, Wind still held the lead, the dun clinging close a full length ahead of the next horse. The piebald was running fifth. After the turn would come the hazard; boys on trailing animals were known to slash at those who rounded the stakes ahead of them.

Following the horses, Mat's eyes swept across the sharp-faced woman again ... and snapped back. The shouts and screams of the crowd faded. The woman was shaking her fan at the horses and jumping excitedly, but suddenly he saw her in pale green and a rich gray cloak, her hair caught in a frothy net of lace, skirts held up delicately as she picked her way across a stable not far from Caemlyn.

Rand still lay there moaning in the straw, even if the fever seemed gone; at least he was not shouting anymore at people who were not there. Mat eyed the woman suspiciously as she knelt beside Rand. Maybe she could help as she claimed, but Mat did not trust as he once had. What was a fine lady like this doing in a village stable? Caressing the ruby-tipped hilt of the dagger hidden by his coat, he wondered why he had ever trusted. It never paid. Never.

'... weak as a day-old kitten,' she was saying as she reached beneath her cloak. 'I think ...'

A knife appeared in her hand so suddenly, streaking for Mat's throat, that he would have been dead if he had not been ready. Dropping flat, he seized her wrist, just pushing it away from him, the curved Shadar Logoth blade sweeping out to lie against her slim white neck. The woman froze, trying to look down at the sharp edge dimpling her skin. He wanted to slice. Especially when he saw where her own dagger had stabbed into the stable wall. Around the slim blade a black circle of char grew, and a thin gray tendril of smoke rose from wood about to burst into flame.

Shivering, Mat rubbed a hand across his eyes. Just carrying that Shadar Logoth knife had nearly killed him, eating those holes in his memories, but how could he forget a woman who tried to kill him? A Darkfriend – she had admitted as much – who tried to kill him with a dagger that set a bucket of water near boiling when they tossed it in after securing her in the tackroom. A Darkfriend who had been hunting Rand and him. What chance she was in Ebou Dar when he was, at the races on the same day? *Ta'veren* might be the answer – he liked thinking of that about as much as he did the Horn of bloody Valere – but the fact was, the Forsaken knew his name. That stable had not been the last time Darkfriends tried putting an end to Mat Cauthon.

He staggered as Nalesean suddenly began pounding his back. 'Look at him, Mat! Light of heaven, look at him!'

The horses had rounded the far poles and were well on their way back. Head stretched out, mane and tail flying behind, Wind streaked down the course with Olver clinging to his back like a part of the saddle. The boy rode as if he had been born there. Four lengths behind, the piebald pounded furiously, rider working his switch in a futile effort to close. Just like that they slashed across the finish line, with the next nearest horse another three lengths back. The white-maned dun came last. The moans and mutters of losing bettors overwhelmed the shouts of winners. Losing tokens made a shower of white onto the track, and dozens of bookers' servants rushed out to clear them away before the next race.

'We have to find that woman, Mat. I'd not put it past her to run off without paying out so much as she owes us.' From what Mat had heard, the bookers' guild was more than harsh the first time one of its members tried anything of the sort, and deadly the second, but they were commoners, and that was enough for Nalesean.

'She's standing right over there in plain view.' Mat gestured without taking his eyes from the fox-faced Darkfriend. Glaring at a token, she hurled it to the ground, and even lifted her skirts to stamp on it. Plainly not a wager on Wind. Still grimacing, she began threading her way through the crowd. Mat stiffened. She was leaving. 'Gather our winnings, Nalesean, then take Olver back to the inn. If he misses his reading lesson, you'll kiss the Dark One's sister before Mistress Anan lets him out for another race.'

'Where are you going?'

'I saw a woman who tried to kill me,' Mat said over his shoulder.

'Give her a trinket next time,' Nalesean shouted after him.

Following the woman was no trouble, with that white-plumed hat for a banner bobbing through the crowd on the other side. The earthen banks gave way to a large open area where brightly lacquered coaches and sedan chairs waited under the watchful eyes of drivers and bearers. Mat's horse Pips was one of scores being guarded by members of the Ancient and Worshipful Guild of Stablemen. There was a guild for most things in Ebou Dar, and woe to anyone who trespassed on their ground. He paused, but she walked on by the conveyances that had brought those with position or money. No maid, and now not even a chair. No one walked in this heat who had money to ride. *Had my Lady come on hard times?*

The Silver Circuit lay just south of the tall white-plastered city wall, and she strolled up the hundred paces or so of road to the broad pointed arch of the Moldine Gate and in. Trying to appear casual, Mat followed. The gateway was ten spans of dim tunnel, but her hat stood out among the folk passing through. People who had to walk seldom wore plumes. She seemed to know where she was going on the other side. The plumes wove through the crowds ahead of him, unhurried but always moving forward.

Ebou Dar shone white in the morning sun. White palaces with white columns and screened wrought-iron balconies cheek-by-jowl with white-plastered weavers' shops and fishmongers and stables, great white houses with louvered shutters hiding their arched windows beside white inns with painted signs hanging in front and open markets under long roofs where live sheep and chickens, calves and geese and ducks made a barnyard din alongside their fellows already butchered and hanging. All white, stone or plaster, except here and there bands of red or blue or gold on turnip-shaped domes and pointed spires that had balconies running around them. There were squares everywhere, always with a statue larger than life on a pedestal or a splashing fountain that only emphasized the heat, always packed with people. Refugees filled the city, and merchants and traders of every sort. Never a trouble but brought profit to somebody. What Saldaea had once sent into Arad Doman now came downriver to Ebou Dar, and so did what Amadicia had traded into Tarabon. Everyone scurried, for a coin or a thousand, for a bite to eat today. The aroma that hung in the air was equal parts perfume, dust and sweat. Somehow, it all smelled desperate.

Barge-filled canals sliced through the city, crossed by dozens of bridges, some so narrow that two people would have to squeeze past one another, others large enough that shops actually lined them, hanging out over the water. On one of those, he suddenly realized that the white-plumed hat had stopped. People flowed around him as he did, too. The shops here were really just open wooden nooks, with heavy plank shutters that could be let down to close them off at night. Raised overhead now, the shutters displayed signs for the shops. The one above the plumed hat showed a golden scale and hammer, sign of the goldsmiths' guild, though plainly not of a particularly prosperous member. Through a momentary gap in the crowd, he saw her look back, and turned hurriedly to the narrow stall to his right. On the wall at the back hung finger rings, and boards displaying stones cut in all sorts of designs.

'My Lord wishes a new signet ring?' the birdlike fellow behind the counter asked, bowing and dry-washing his hands. Skinny as a rail, he had no worry of anyone stealing his goods. Cramped into a corner on a stool sat a one-eyed fellow who might have had trouble standing upright inside the cubicle, with a long cudgel studded with nail heads propped between his massive knees. 'I can cut any design, as my Lord can see, and I have try-rings for the size, of course.'

'Let me see that one.' Mat pointed at random; he needed some reason to stand here until she went on. It might be a good time to decide exactly what he was going to do.

'A fine example of the long style, my Lord, much in favor now. Gold, but I work in silver, as well. Why, I think the size is right. If my Lord would care to try it on? My Lord may wish to examine the fine detail of the carving? Does my Lord prefer gold or silver?'

With a grunt that he hoped might be taken for answer to some of that, Mat shoved the proffered ring onto the second finger of his left hand and pretended to examine the dark oval of carved stone. All he really saw was that it was as long as the joint of his finger. Head down, he studied the woman from the corner of his eye the best he could through gaps that opened in the throng. She was holding a wide, flat gold necklace up to the light.

There was a Civil Guard in Ebou Dar, but not a very efficient one, seldom to be seen on the streets. If he denounced her, it would be his word against hers, and even if he was believed, a few coins might let her walk free even on that charge. The Civil Guard was cheaper than a magistrate, but either could be bought unless someone powerful was watching, and then if enough gold lay in the offer.

A swirl in the crowd suddenly turned into a Whitecloak, conical helmet and long mail shirt gleaming like silver, snowy cloak with the flaring golden sun billowing as he strode along confident that a path would clear for him. Which it certainly did; few were willing to put themselves in the way of the Children of the Light. Yet, for every eye that slid away from the stone-faced man, another beamed on him approvingly. The sharp-faced woman not only looked at him openly, she smiled. A charge laid against her might or might not put her in prison, but it could be the spark to ignite a city full of tales about Darkfriends in the Tarasin Palace. Whitecloaks were good at whipping up mobs, and to them, Aes Sedai were Darkfriends. As the Child of the Light passed her, she laid down the necklace, apparently regretful, and turned to go.

'Does the style suit my Lord?'

Mat gave a start. He had forgotten the skinny man and the ring, too. 'No, I don't want—' Frowning, he tugged at the ring again. It would not budge!

'No need to pull; you might crack the stone.' Now that he was no longer a potential customer, Mat was no longer my Lord, either. Sniffing, the fellow kept a sharp eye on him lest he try to run. 'I have some grease. Deryl, where's that grease-pot?' The guard blinked and scratched his head as if wondering what a grease-pot was. The white-plumed hat was halfway to the end of the bridge already.

'I'll take it,' Mat snapped. No time for haggling. Hauling a fistful of coins from his coat pocket, he slapped them down on the counter, mostly gold and a little silver. 'Enough?'

The ringmaker's eyes bulged. 'A little too much,' he quavered uncertainly. His hands hesitated above the coins, then two fingers pushed a pair of silver pennies toward Mat. 'So much?'

'Give them to Deryl,' Mat growled as the bloody ring slipped from his finger. The skinny man was hurriedly raking up the rest of the coins. Too late to try backing out of the purchase. Mat wondered by just how much he had overpaid. Stuffing the ring into his pocket, he hastened after the Darkfriend. The hat was nowhere to be seen.

Twinned statues decorated the end of the bridge, pale marble women over a span tall, each with one breast bared and a hand raised to point toward something in the sky. In Ebou Dar, a bare chest symbolized openness and honesty. Ignoring stares, he climbed up beside one of the women, steadying himself with an arm around her waist. A street ran along the canal, and two more split off at angles ahead, all full of people and carts, sedan chairs and wagons and coaches. Someone shouted in a rough voice about real women being warmer, and a number in the crowd laughed. White plumes appeared from behind a blue-lacquered coach on the left-hand fork.

Leaping down, he pushed up the street after her, ignoring the curses of those he bumped. It was an odd chase. In the mass of people, with wagons and coaches constantly getting in his way, he could not keep a clear sight of the hat from the street. Scampering up the broad marble steps of a palace, he got another glimpse, then scurried back down to shove ahead. The rim of a tall fountain gave him yet another view, then an upended barrel against a wall, and a crate that had just been unloaded from an ox-cart. Once he clung to the side of a wagon until the driver threatened him with her whip. With all the climbing and looking, he did not narrow the Darkfriend's lead very much. But then, he still had no notion what to do if he caught her. Suddenly, when he hoisted himself up onto the narrow coping along the face of one of the big houses, she was not there anymore.

Frantically he looked up and down the street. The white plumes no longer waved through the crowd. In easy sight were half a dozen houses much like the one he was clinging to, several palaces of various sizes, two inns, three taverns, a cutler's shop with a knife and a pair of scissors on its sign, a fishmonger with a board painted in fifty kinds of fish, two rugweavers with unrolled carpets spread on tables beneath awnings, a tailor's shop and four cloth sellers, two shops displaying lacquerware, a goldsmith, a silversmith, a livery stable . . . The list was too long. She could have gone into any of them. Or none. She might have taken a turn he had not seen.

Jumping down, he settled his hat, muttering under his breath . . . and saw her, almost at the top of the wide stairs leading to a palace nearly across from him, already half-hidden by the tall fluted columns out front. The palace was not large, with only two slim spires and a single pear-shaped dome banded in red, but Ebou Dari palaces always gave the ground floor to servants and kitchens and the like. The better rooms were high, to catch the breezes. Doormen liveried in black and yellow bowed deeply and swung the carved doors wide before she reached them. A servant inside curtsied, apparently saying something, and immediately turned to lead her deeper. She was known. He would have wagered everything on it.

For a while after the doors closed, he stood there studying the palace. Not the richest in the city by far, but only a noble would dare build its like. 'But who in the Pit of Doom lives there?' he muttered finally, plucking off his hat to fan himself. Not her, not when she had to walk. A few questions in the taverns along the street would tell him. And word of his queries would seep to the palace, sure as dirt soiled your hands.

Someone said, 'Carridin.' It was a scrawny, white-haired fellow lounging nearby in the shade. Mat looked at him questioningly, and he grinned, showing gaps in his teeth. His stooped shoulders and sad weathered face did not fit his fine gray coat. Despite a bit of lace at his neck, he was the very picture of hard times. 'You asked who lived there. The Chelsaine Palace is let to Jaichim Carridin.'

Mat's hat paused. 'You mean the Whitecloak ambassador?'

'Aye. And Inquisitor of the Hand of the Light.' The old man tapped a gnarled finger against the side of his beak of a nose. Both looked to have been broken several times. 'Not a man to bother unless you must, and then I'd think three times.'

Unconsciously Mat hummed a bit of 'Storm from the Mountains.' Not a man to bother indeed. Questioners were the nastiest of the Whitecloaks. A Whitecloak Inquisitor who had a Darkfriend come to call.

'Thank you—' Mat gave a start. The fellow was gone, swallowed up in the crowd. Strange, but he had looked familiar. Maybe another long-dead acquaintance drifting out of those old memories. Maybe... It hit him like an Illuminator's nightflower exploding inside his head. A white-haired man with a hooked nose. That old man had been at the Silver Circuit, standing not far from the woman who had just gone into Carridin's rented palace. Turning his hat in his hands, he frowned uneasily at the palace. The Mire never held a bog like this one. He could feel the dice tumbling in his head suddenly, and that was always a bad sign.

Chapter 15

Insects

Carridin did not look up immediately from the letter he was writing when the Lady Shiaine, as she called herself, was shown in. Three ants struggled futilely in the wet ink, trapped. Everything else might be dying, but ants and cockroaches and every sort of vermin seemed to thrive. Carefully he pressed the blotter down. He was not about to begin again for a few ants. A failure to send this report, or a report of failure, might doom him as surely as those mired insects, yet it was fear of a different failure that tightened his guts.

He had no worry of Shiaine reading what he wrote. It was in a cipher known to only two men beside himself. So many bands of 'Dragonsworn' at work, each stiffened by a core of his most trusted men, so many more who might be bandits or even truly sworn to that filth, al'Thor. Pedron Niall might not like that last, but his command had been to plunge Altara and Murandy into blood and chaos from which only Niall and the Children of the Light could rescue them, a madness clearly to be laid at the feet of this so-called Dragon Reborn, and that he had done. Fear held both countries by the throat. Tales that the witches marched across the same country were an added reward. Tar Valon witches and Dragonsworn, Aes Sedai carrying off young women and setting up false Dragons, villages in flames and men nailed to the doors of their barns – it was all one in half the street rumors, now. Niall would be pleased. And send more orders. How he expected Carridin to snatch Elayne Trakand out of the Tarasin Palace was beyond reason.

Another ant skittered across the ivory-inlaid table onto the page, and his thumb stabbed down, destroying it. And smearing a word to illegibility. The entire report would need to be redone. He wanted a drink very badly. There was brandy in a crystal flask on the table by the door, but he did not want the woman to see him drinking. Suppressing a sigh, he shoved the letter aside and pulled a kerchief from his sleeve to wipe his hand. 'So, Shiaine, do you finally have progress to report? Or have you just come for more money?'

She smiled at him lazily from a tall carved armchair. 'There are expenses associated with a search,' she said in almost the accents of an Andoran noble. 'Especially when we want no questions asked.'

Most people would have been unsettled by the sight of Jaichim Carridin, even cleaning a pen nib, with his steely face and deep-set eyes, the white tabard over his coat bearing the golden sunburst of the Children of the Light impressed upon the crimson shepherd's crook of the Hand. Not Mili Skane. That was her real name, though she did not know he knew. A saddler's daughter from a village near Whitebridge, she had gone to the White Tower at fifteen, another thing she thought secret. It was hardly the best start, becoming a Friend of the Dark because the witches told her she could not learn to channel, but before that year was out she had not only found a circle in Caemlyn but made her first kill. In the seven years since, she had added nineteen more. She was one of the best assassins available, and a hunter who could find anyone or anything. That much he had been told when she was sent to him. A circle that reported to her now. Several of them actually were nobles and almost all were older, but neither thing mattered among those who served the Great Lord. Another circle working for Carridin was led by a gnarled beggar with one eye, no teeth and a habit of bathing only once in the year. Had circumstances been different, Carridin himself would have knelt to Old Cully, the only name the stinking villain admitted to. Mili Skane surely groveled for Old Cully, and so did every last companion of her circle, noble or not. It irritated Carridin that 'Lady Shiaine' would be on her knees in a flash if the straggly-haired old beggar entered the room, but for him sat with her legs crossed, smiling and twitching her slippered foot as if impatient to be done. She had been ordered to obey him absolutely, by one even Old Cully would grovel for, and besides, he had a desperate need of success. Niall's schemes could go to dust, but not this.

'Many things can be excused,' he said, laying the pen on its ivory stand and shoving back his chair, 'for those who accomplish the tasks they are given.' He was a tall man, and he loomed threateningly. He was well aware that the gilt-framed mirrors on the wall showed a figure of strength, a dangerous man. 'Even dresses and baubles and gambling, paid for with coin that was to go for information.' That twitching foot froze for an instant, then began again, but her smile was forced, her face pale. Her circle obeyed her instantly, but they would string her up by the heels and skin her alive if he spoke the word. 'You have not accomplished very much, have you? In fact, you do not seem to have accomplished anything.'

'There are difficulties, as you well know,' she said breathily. She managed to meet his eyes squarely, though.

'Excuses. Tell me of difficulties surmounted, not those you stumble over and fall. You can fall a long way if you fail in this.' Turning his back, he strode to the nearest window. He could fall a long way, too, and he did not want to risk her seeing anything in his eyes. Sunlight slanted through the ornate stone screen. The high-ceilinged room, with its green-and-white-tiled floor and bright blue walls, stayed comparatively cool behind the thick walls of the palace, but the heat outside seeped in near the windows. He could almost feel the brandy across the room. He could not wait for her to be gone.

'My Lord Carridin, how can I have anyone ask too openly about objects of the Power? That *will* cause questions, and there are Aes Sedai in the city, you will recall.'

Peering down at the street through the scroll-carvings, he wrinkled his nose at the smell. Every sort was jammed together down there. An Arafellin with his hair in two long braids and a curved sword on his back tossed a coin to a one-armed beggar, who scowled at the gift before tucking it under his rags and resuming his piteous cries to the passersby. A fellow in a torn, bright red coat and even brighter yellow breeches came running from a shop clutching a bolt of cloth to his chest, pursued by a shouting pale-haired woman who had her skirts pulled above her knees and was outpacing the burly guard who lumbered behind her waving his truncheon. The driver of a red-lacquered coach with the moneylenders' gold coins and open hand on the door shook his whip at the driver of a canvas-covered wagon whose team had become entangled with the coach's, the pair filling the street with curses. Grimy street urchins crouched behind a dilapidated cart while they snatched puny, shriveled fruit brought in from the country. A Taraboner woman pushed her way through the crowd, veiled, her dark hair in thin braids, drawing every male eye in her dusty red dress that shaped itself to her form shamelessly.

'My Lord, I must have time. I *must*! I cannot do the impossible, certainly not in days.'

Trash, all of them. Grubbers for gold and Hunters for the Horn, thieves, refugees, even Tinkers. Scum. Riots would be easy to start, a purge for all this filth. Outlanders were always the first targets, always to blame for whatever was wrong, along with neighbors who had the misfortune to be on the wrong side of grudges, women who peddled herbs and cures, and folk with no friends, especially if they lived alone. Properly guided, as carefully as such things could be, a good riot might well burn the Tarasin Palace down around that useless jade Tylin and the witches as well. He glared at the swarm below. Riots did tend to get out of hand; the Civil Guard might stir itself, and inevitably a handful of true Friends would be snapped up.

He could not afford the chance that some of those might be from the circles he had hunting. For that matter, even a few days of rioting would disrupt their work. Tylin was not important enough for that; she did not matter at all, in truth. No, not yet. Niall, he could afford to disappoint, but not his true master.

'My Lord Carridin . . .' A note of defiance had entered Shiaine's voice. He had let her stew too long. 'My Lord Carridin, some of my circle question why we are looking for . . .'

He started to turn, to put her down hard – he needed success, not excuses, not questions! – but her voice dwindled to nothing as his eyes fell on a young man standing diagonally across the street, in a blue coat with enough red-and-gold embroidery on the sleeves and lapels for two nobles. Taller than most, he was fanning himself with a broad-brimmed black hat and adjusting his neck scarf as he spoke to a stooped, white-haired man. Carridin recognized the young man.

Suddenly he felt as though a knotted rope had been fastened around his head and was being drawn ever tighter. For an instant a face hidden behind a red mask filled his vision. Night-dark eyes stared at him, and then there were endless caverns of flame, and still staring. Within his head, the world exploded in fire, cascading images that battered him and swept him beyond screaming. The forms of three young men stood unsupported in air, and one of them began to glow, the form of the man in the street, brighter and brighter till it must have seared any living eyes to ash, brighter still, burning. A curled golden horn sped toward him, its cry pulling his soul, then flashed into a ring of golden light, swallowing him, chilling him until the last fragment of him that recalled his name was sure his bones must splinter. A ruby-tipped dagger hurtled straight at him, curved blade striking him between the eyes and sinking in, in, until gold-wrapped hilt and all was gone, and he knew agony that washed away all thought that what had gone before was pain. He would have prayed to a Creator he had long abandoned if he remembered how. He would have shrieked if he remembered how, if he remembered that humans shrieked, that he was human. On and on, more and more . . .

Raising a hand to his forehead, he wondered why it trembled.

His head ached, too. There had been something ... He gave a start at the street below. Everything was changed in the blink of an eye, the people different, wagons moved, colorful coaches and chairs replaced by others. Worse, Cauthon was gone. He wanted to swallow that whole flask of brandy in one gulp.

Suddenly he realized that Shiaine had stopped talking. He turned, ready to continue putting her in her place.

She was leaning forward in the act of rising, one hand on the arm of her chair, the other raised in a gesture. Her narrow face was fixed in petulant defiance, but not at Carridin. She did not move. She did not blink. He was not sure she breathed. He barely noticed her.

'Ruminating?' Sammael said. 'Can I at least hope that it is about what you are here to find for me?' He stood only a little taller than average, a muscular, solid man in a coat of the high-collared Illianer style, so covered with gold-work it was hard to tell the cloth was green, but more than being one of the Chosen gave him stature. His blue eyes were colder than winter's heart. A livid scar burned down his face from golden hairline to the edge of golden, square-cut beard, and it seemed a suitable decoration. Whatever got in his way was brushed aside, trampled or obliterated. Carridin knew Sammael would have turned his bowels to water if the man had been just someone met by chance.

Hurriedly moving from the window, he dropped to his knees before the Chosen. He despised the Tar Valon witches; indeed, he despised anyone who used the One Power, meddling with what had broken the world once, wielding what mere mortals should not touch. This man used the Power, too, but the Chosen could not be called mere mortals. Perhaps not mortals at all. And if he served well, neither would he be. 'Great Master, I saw Mat Cauthon.'

'Here?' Oddly, for a moment, Sammael seemed taken aback. He murmured something under his breath, and the blood drained from Carridin's face at one caught word.

'Great Lord, you know I would never betray—'

'You? Fool! You haven't the stomach. Are you certain it was Cauthon you saw?'

'Yes, Great Master. In the street. I know I can find him again.'

Sammael frowned down at him, stroking his beard, looking

through and beyond Jaichim Carridin. Carridin did not like feeling insignificant, especially when he knew it was true.

'No,' Sammael said finally. 'Your search is the most important thing, the *only* thing, so far as you are concerned. Cauthon's death would be convenient, certainly, but not if it draws attention here. If it appears that attention is already here, should he take an interest in your search, then he dies, but otherwise, he can wait.'

'But—'

'Did you mishear me?' Sammael's scar pulled his smile into a snarl on one side. 'I saw your sister Vanora recently. She did not look well, at first. Screaming and weeping, twitching constantly and pulling at her hair. Women do suffer worse than men from the attentions of Myrddraal, but even Myrddraal must find their pleasures somewhere. Don't worry that she suffered too long. The Trollocs are always hungry.' The smile faded; his voice was stone. 'Those who disobey can find themselves over a cookfire, too. Vanora seemed to be smiling, Carridin. Do you think you would smile, turning on a spit?'

Carridin swallowed in spite of himself, and quelled a pang for Vanora, with her ready laugh and her skill with horses, daring to gallop where others feared to walk. She had been his favorite sister, yet she was dead and he was not. If there were any mercies in the world, she had not learned why. 'I live to serve and obey, Great Master.' He did not believe he was a coward, but no one disobeyed one of the Chosen. Not more than once.

'Then find what I want!' Sammael roared. 'I know it's hidden somewhere in this *kjasic* flyspeck of a city! *Ter'angreal, angreal,* even *sa'angreal*! I have tracked them, traced them! Now you find them, Carridin. Do not make me grow impatient.'

'Great Master . . .' He worked his mouth to find moisture. 'Great Master, there are witches . . . Aes Sedai . . . here. I cannot be sure how many. If they hear a whisper . . .'

Waving him to silence, Sammael paced a few quick steps, three times up and back, hands clasped behind his back. He did not look worried, only . . . considering. Finally he nodded. 'I will send you . . . someone . . . to deal with these *Aes Sedai*.' He barked a short laugh. 'I almost wish I could see their faces. Very well. You have a little while longer. Then perhaps someone else will have a chance.' He lifted a strand of Shiaine's hair with a finger; she still did not move; her eyes stared unblinking. 'This child would certainly leap at the opportunity.'

Carridin fought down a stab of fear. The Chosen cast down as quickly as they raised up, and as often. Failure never went unpunished. 'Great Master, the favor I asked of you. If I might know . . . Have you . . . will you—?'

'There is very little luck in you, Carridin,' Sammael said with another smile. 'You had better hope you have more carrying out my orders. It seems that someone is making sure at least some of Ishamael's commands are still carried out.' He was smiling, but he seemed far from amused. Or perhaps it was just the scar. 'You failed him, and you've lost your entire family for it. Only my hand protects you, now. Once, long ago, I saw three Myrddraal make a man give them his wife and his daughters one by one, then beg them to cut off his right leg, then the left, then his arms, and burn out his eyes.' The perfectly ordinary conversational tone made the recitation worse than any shouts or snarls ever could have. 'It was a game with them, you understand, to see how much they could make him beg them to take. They left his tongue for last, of course, but there wasn't a great deal of him remaining by then. He had been quite powerful, handsome and famous. Envied. No one would ever envy what they finally tossed to the Trollocs. You wouldn't believe the sounds it made. Find what I want, Carridin. You will not like it if I withdraw my hand.'

Abruptly there was a vertical line of light in the air before the Chosen. It seemed to turn in some fashion, widening as it did into a square . . . hole. Carridin gaped. He was staring through a hole in the air, at somewhere full of gray columns and thick mist. Sammael stepped through, and the opening snapped shut, a brilliant bar of light that vanished, leaving only a purple afterimage glowing in Carridin's eyes.

Unsteadily, he pushed himself to his feet. Failure was always punished, but no one survived disobeying one of the Chosen.

Suddenly Shiaine moved, completing her halted rise from the chair. 'You mark me, *Bors*,' she began, then cut off, staring at the window where he had been standing. Her eyes darted, found him, and she jumped. He could have been one of the Chosen himself from the way those eyes bulged.

No one survived disobeying the Chosen. He pressed his hands against his temples. His head felt tight to bursting. 'There is a man in the city, Mat Cauthon. You will—' She gave a small start, and he frowned. 'You know him?'

'I have heard the name,' she said warily. And angrily, he would have said. 'Few linked to al'Thor remain unknown for long.' As he stepped closer, she crossed her arms protectively in front of herself, and held her place with an obvious effort. 'What is a seedy farmboy doing in Ebou Dar? How did he—?'

'Don't bother me with foolish questions, Shiaine.' His head had never hurt like this; never. It felt as though a dagger was being driven into his skull between his eyes. No one survived... 'You will put your circle to locating Cauthon immediately. All of them.' Old Cully was coming tonight, slipping in through the back of the stables; she did not need to know there would be others. 'Nothing else is to get in the way.'

'But I thought—'

She broke off with a gasp as he seized her neck. A slim dagger appeared in her hand, but he wrenched it away. She twisted and jerked, but he drove her face down onto the table, her cheek smudging still-damp ink on the discarded letter to Pedron Niall. The dagger, stabbing down just in front of her eyes, froze her. By chance, the blade piercing the paper had caught an ant by the tip of one leg. It struggled as vainly as she had.

'You are an insect, Mili.' The pain in his head made his voice rasp. 'It is time you understand that. One insect is much like another, and if one won't do...' Her eyes followed his thumb down, and when it flattened on the ant, she flinched.

'I live to serve and obey, master,' she breathed. She had said that to Old Cully every time he saw them together, but never before to him.

'And this is how you will obey...' No one survived disobedience. No one.

Chapter 16

A Touch on the Cheek

The Tarasin Palace was a mass of shining marble and white plaster, with screened balconies of white-painted wrought iron and columned walks as much as four stories above the ground. Pigeons wheeled around pointed domes and tall, balcony-wreathed spires banded in red and green tiles, glittering in the sun. Sharp-arched gates in the palace itself led to various courtyards, and more pierced the high wall hiding the gardens, but deep, snowy white steps ten spans wide climbed on the side facing Mol Hara Square to great doors carved in coiling patterns like the balcony screens and covered with beaten gold.

The dozen or so guards lined up before those doors, sweating in the sun, wore gilded breastplates over green coats and baggy white trousers stuffed into dark green boots. Green cords secured thick twists of white cloth around glittering golden helmets, with the long ends hanging down their backs. Even their halberds and the scabbards of their daggers and short swords shone with gold. Guards for being looked at, not fighting. But then, when Mat reached the top, he could see swordsmen's calluses on their hands. Always before he had entered through one of the stableyards, to peruse the palace horses in passing, but this time he was going in the way a lord would.

'The Light's blessing on all here,' he said to their officer, a man not much older than he. Ebou Dari were polite people. 'I've come to leave a message for Nynaeve Sedai and Elayne Sedai. Or to give it to them, if they've returned.'

The officer stared at him, looked at the stairs in consternation. Gold cord as well as green on his pointed helmet signified some rank Mat did not know, and he carried a gilded rod instead of a halberd, with a sharp end and a hook like an ox-goad. By his expression, no one had ever come up that way before. Studying Mat's coat, he mulled it over visibly, and at last decided he could not tell him to go away. With a sigh, the man murmured a benison in return and asked Mat's name, pushed open a small door in one of the larger and ushered him into a grand entry hall encircled by five stone-railed balconies beneath a domed ceiling painted like the sky, complete with clouds and a sun.

The guard's snapping fingers summoned a slim young serving woman in a white dress, sewn up on the left to show green petticoats and embroidered on the left breast with a green Anchor and Sword. She scurried across the red-and-blue marble floor looking startled, curtsying to Mat and the officer each. Short black hair framed a sweetly pretty face, with silken olive skin, and her livery had the deep narrow neckline common to all women except nobles in Ebou Dar. For once, Mat did not really notice. When she heard what he wanted, her big black eyes widened even more. Aes Sedai were not unpopular in Ebou Dar, exactly, but most Ebou Dari would go a long distance out of their way to avoid one.

'Yes, Sword-Lieutenant,' she said, bobbing again. 'Of course, Sword-Lieutenant. May it please you to follow me, my Lord?' It did.

Outside, Ebou Dar sparkled white, but inside, color ran wild. There seemed to be miles of broad corridor in the palace, and here the high ceiling was blue and the walls yellow, there the walls pale red and the ceiling green, changing with every turn, combinations to jar any eye but a Tinker's. Mat's boots sounded loud on floor tiles that made patterns of two or three or sometimes four colors in diamonds or stars or triangles. Wherever hallways crossed the floor was a mosaic of tiny tiles, intricate swirls and scrolls and loops. A few silk tapestries displayed scenes of the sea, and arched niches held carved crystal bowls and small statues and yellow Sea Folk porcelain that would fetch a fine penny anywhere. Occasionally a liveried servant hurried along silently, often as not carrying a silver tray, or a golden.

Normally, displays of wealth made Mat feel comfortable. For one thing, where there was money, some might stick to his fingers. This time he felt impatient, more so by the step. And anxious. The last time he had felt the dice rolling so hard in his head was just before he found himself with three hundred of the Band, a thousand of Gaebril's White Lions on a ridge to his front and another thousand coming hard up the road behind him, when all he had been trying to do was ride away from the entire mess. That time he had avoided the chop by the grace of other men's memories and more luck than he had a right to. The dice almost always meant danger, and something else he had not figured out yet. The prospect of having his skull cracked was not enough, and once or twice there had been no possibility of such, yet the upcoming likelihood of Mat Cauthon dead in some spectacular fashion seemed the most usual cause. Unlikely, maybe, in the Tarasin Palace, but unlikely did not make the dice go away. He was going to leave his message, grab Nynaeve and Elayne by the scruff of the neck if he had an opportunity, give them a talking-to that made their ears glow, and then get out.

The young woman glided ahead of him until they reached a short, bullish man a little older than she, another servant, in tight white breeches, a white shirt with wide sleeves, and a long green vest with the Anchor and Sword of House Mitsobar in a white disc. 'Master Jen,' she said, curtsying once more, 'this is Lord Mat Cauthon, who wishes to leave a message for the honored Elayne Aes Sedai and the honored Nynaeve Aes Sedai.'

'Very good, Haesel. You may go.' He bowed to Mat. 'May it please you to follow me, my Lord?'

Jen led him as far as a dark, grim-faced woman short of her middle years, and bowed. 'Mistress Carin, this is Lord Mat Cauthon, who wishes to leave a message for the honored Elayne Aes Sedai and the honored Nynaeve Aes Sedai.'

'Very good, Jen. You may go. May it please you to follow me, my Lord?'

Carin took him up a sweeping flight of marble stairs, the risers painted yellow and red, to a skinny woman named Matilde, who handed him over to a stout fellow named Bren, who led him to a balding man named Madic, each a little older than the one before. Where five corridors met like the spokes of a wheel, Madic left him with a round woman called Laren, who had a touch of gray at her temples and a stately carriage. Like Carin and Matilde, she wore what the Ebou Dari called a marriage knife, hanging hilt down from a close-fitting silver necklace between more than plump breasts. Five white stones in the hilt, two set in red, and four red stones, one surrounded by black, said three of her nine children were dead, two sons in duels. Rising out of her curtsy to Mat, Laren began to float up one of the hallways, but he hurried to catch her arm.

Dark eyebrows rose slightly as she glanced at his hand. She had no dagger except the marriage knife, but he released her immediately. Custom said she could only use that on her husband, yet there was no point in pushing. He did not soften his voice, though. 'How far do I have to go to leave a note? Show me to their rooms. A pair of Aes Sedai shouldn't be that hard to find. This isn't the bloody White Tower.'

'Aes Sedai?' a woman said behind him in a heavy Illianer accent. 'If you do seek two Aes Sedai, you have found two.'

Laren's face did not change, or almost not. Her nearly black eyes darted past him, and he was sure they tightened with worry.

Doffing his hat, Mat turned wearing an easy smile. With that silver foxhead around his neck, Aes Sedai did not put him off at all. Well, not very much. It had those flaws. Maybe the smile was not that easy.

The two women confronting him could not have been more different. One was slender, with a fetching smile, in a green-and-gold dress that showed a hint of what he judged to be a fine bosom. Except for that ageless face, he might have thought to strike up a conversation. It was a pretty face, with eyes large enough for a man to sink into. A pity. The other had the agelessness too, but seeing it took him a moment. He thought she was scowling until he realized that must be her normal expression. Her dark, almost black, dress covered her to the wrists and chin, for which he was grateful. She looked scrawny as an old bramble. She looked as if she ate brambles for breakfast.

'I'm trying to leave a message for Nynaeve and Elayne,' he told them. 'This woman—' He blinked, looking down each of the corridors. Servants hurried by, but Laren was nowhere in sight. He would not have thought she could move so fast. 'Anyway, I want to leave a note.' Suddenly cautious, he added, 'Are you friends of theirs?'

'Not exactly,' the pretty one said. 'I am Joline, and this is Teslyn. And you are Mat Cauthon.' Mat's stomach tightened. Nine Aes Sedai in the palace, and he had to walk into the two who followed Elaida. And one of them Red. Not that he had anything to fear. He lowered his hand to his side before it could touch the foxhead under his clothes.

The one who ate brambles – Teslyn – stepped closer. She was a Sitter, according to Thom, though what a Sitter was doing here even Thom did not understand. 'We would be their friends if we could. They do need friends, Master Cauthon, as do you.' Her eyes tried to dig holes in his head.

Joline moved to flank him, laying a hand on his lapel. He would have considered that smile inviting from another woman. She was Green Ajah. 'They are on dangerous ground and blind to what lies beneath their feet. I know you are their friend. You might show it by telling them to abandon this nonsense before it is too late. Foolish children who go too far can find themselves punished quite severely.'

Mat wanted to back away; even Teslyn stood close enough to be almost touching him. Instead he put on his most insolent grin. It had always landed him in trouble back home, but it seemed appropriate. Those dice in his head could have nothing to do with this pair, or they would have stopped spinning. And he did have the medallion. 'They see pretty well, I'd say.' Nynaeve badly needed to be snatched down a peg or six, and Elayne even more, but he was not about to stand by and listen to this woman talk Nynaeve down. If that meant defending Elayne too, so be it. 'Maybe you should abandon your nonsense.' Joline's smile vanished, but Teslyn replaced it with one of her own, a razored smile.

'We do know about you, Master Cauthon.' She looked a woman who wanted to skin something, and whoever was handy would do.

'*Ta'veren*, it do be said. With dangerous associations of your own. That do be more than hearsay.'

Joline's face was ice. 'A young man in your position who wished to be assured of his future could do much worse than seek the protection of the Tower. You should never have left it.'

His stomach clenched tighter. What else did they know? Surely not about the medallion. Nynaeve and Elayne knew, and Adeleas and Vandene, and the Light only knew who they had told, but surely not this pair. There was worse than *ta'veren* or the foxhead, though, or even Rand, as far as he was concerned. If they knew about the bloody Horn ...

Abruptly he was yanked away from them so hard that he stumbled and nearly dropped his hat. A slender woman with a smooth face and nearly white hair gathered at the back of her neck had him by sleeve and lapel. Reflexively Teslyn seized him the same way on the other side. He recognized the straight-backed newcomer in her plain gray dress, in a way. She was either Adeleas or Vandene, two sisters — real sisters, not just Aes Sedai — who might as well have been twins; he never could tell them apart for certain. She and Teslyn stared at one another, chill and serene, two cats with a paw on the same mouse.

'No need to tear my coat off,' he growled, trying to shrug free. 'My coat?' He was not sure they heard. Even wearing the foxhead he was not prepared to go as far as prying their fingers free — unless he had to.

Two other Aes Sedai accompanied whichever sister it was, though one, a dark, stocky woman with inquisitive eyes, was marked by no more than the Great Serpent ring and the brown-fringed shawl she wore, displaying the white Flame of Tar Valon among vines on her back. She appeared to be just a little older than Nynaeve, which made her Sareitha Tomares, only two years or so Aes Sedai.

'Do you stoop to kidnapping men in the halls now, Teslyn?' the other said. 'A man who cannot channel can hardly be of interest to you.' Short and pale in lace-trimmed gray slashed with blue, she was all cool ageless elegance and confident smile. A Cairhienin accent identified her. He had certainly attracted the top dogs in the yard. Thom had not been sure whether Joline or Teslyn was in charge of Elaida's embassy, but Merilille led the one from those idiots who had tricked Egwene into becoming their Amyrlin.

Mat could have shaved with Teslyn's return smile. 'Do no dissemble with me, Merilille. Mat Cauthon do be of considerable interest. He should no be running loose.' As if he was not standing there listening!

'Don't fight over me,' he said. Tugging his coat was not making anyone let go. 'There's enough to go around.'

Five sets of eyes made him wish he had kept his mouth shut. Aes Sedai had no sense of humor. He pulled a little harder, and Vandene – or Adeleas – jerked back hard enough to pull the coat out of *his* hand. Vandene, he decided. She was Green, and he had always thought she wanted to turn him upside down and shake the secret of the medallion out of him. Whichever she was, she smiled, part knowing, part amused. He saw nothing funny. The others did not look at him long. He might as well have vanished.

'What he needs,' Joline said firmly, 'is to be taken into custody. For his own protection, and more. Three *ta'veren* coming out of a single village? And one of them the Dragon Reborn? Master Cauthon should be sent to the White Tower immediately.' And he had thought her pretty.

Merilille only shook her head. 'You overestimate your situation here, Joline, if you think I will simply allow you to take the boy.'

'You overestimate yours, Merilille.' Joline stepped closer, until she was looking down at the other woman. Her lips curved, superior and condescending. 'Or do you understand that it's only a wish not to offend Tylin that keeps us from confining all of you on bread and water until *you* can be returned to the Tower?'

Mat expected Merilille to laugh in her face, but she shifted her head slightly as if she really wanted to break away from Joline's gaze.

'You would not dare.' Sareitha wore Aes Sedai tranquility like a mask, face smooth and hands calmly adjusting her shawl, but her breathy voice shouted that it was a mask.

'These are children's games, Joline,' Vandene murmured dryly. Surely that was who she was. She was the only one of the three who really did appear unruffled.

Faint splashes of color blossomed on Merilille's cheeks as if the white-haired woman had spoken to her, but her own gaze steadied. 'You can hardly expect us to go meekly,' she told Joline firmly, 'and there are five of us. Seven, counting Nynaeve and Elayne.' The last was a clear afterthought, and reluctant at that.

Joline arched an eyebrow. Teslyn's bony fingers did not loosen their grip any more than Vandene's, but she studied Joline and Merilille with an unreadable expression. Aes Sedai were a country of strangers, where you never knew what to expect until it was too late. There were deep currents here. Deep currents around Aes Sedai could snatch a man to his death without them so much as noticing. Maybe it was time to start prying at fingers.

Laren's sudden reappearance saved him the effort. Struggling to control her breath as if she had been running, the plump woman spread her skirts in a curtsy markedly deeper than she had given him. 'Forgiveness for disturbing you, Aes Sedai, but the Queen summons Lord Cauthon. Forgiveness, please. It's more than my ears are worth if I don't bring him straight away.'

The Aes Sedai looked at her, all of them, till she began to fidget; then the two groups stared at one another as if trying to see who could out-Aes Sedai who. And then they looked at him. He wondered whether anybody was going to move.

'I can't keep the Queen waiting, now can I?' he said cheerily. From the sniffs, you would have thought he had pinched somebody's bottom. Even Laren's brows drew down in disapproval.

'Release him, Adeleas,' Merilille said finally.

He frowned as the white-haired woman complied. Those two ought to wear little signs with their names, or different-color hair ribbons or something. She gave him another of those amused, knowing smiles. He hated that. It was a woman's trick, not just Aes Sedai, and they usually did not know anything at all like what they wanted you to believe. 'Teslyn?' he said. The grim Red still had hold of his coat with both hands. She peered up at him, ignoring everyone else. 'The Queen?'

Merilille opened her mouth and hesitated, obviously changing what she had been going to say. 'How long do you intend to stand here holding him, Teslyn? Perhaps you will explain to Tylin why her summons is disregarded.'

'Consider well who you do tie yourself to, Master Cauthon,' Teslyn said, still looking only at him. 'Wrong choices can lead to an unpleasant future, even for a *ta'veren*. Consider well.' Then she let go.

As he followed Laren, he did not allow himself to show his eagerness to be away, but he did wish the woman would walk a little faster. She glided along ahead of him, regal as any queen. Regal as any Aes Sedai. When they reached the first turning, he looked over his shoulder. The five Aes Sedai were still standing there, staring after him. As if his look had been a signal, they exchanged silent glances and went, each in a different direction. Adeleas came toward him but a dozen steps before reaching him she smiled at him again and disappeared through a doorway. Deep currents. He preferred swimming where his feet could touch the bottom of the pond.

Laren was waiting around the corner, hands on broad hips and her face much too smooth. Beneath her skirts, he suspected, her foot was tapping impatiently. He gave her his most winning smile. Giggling girls or gray-haired grandmothers, women softened for that one; it had won him kisses and eased him out of predicaments more often than he could count. It was almost as good as flowers. 'That was neatly done, and I thank you. I'm sure the Queen doesn't really want to see me.' If she did, he did not want to see her. Everything he thought about nobles was tripled for royalty. Nothing he had found in those old memories changed that, and some of those fellows had spent considerable time around kings and queens and the like. 'Now, if you will just show me where Nynaeve and Elayne stay . . .'

Strangely, the smile did not seem to have any effect. 'I would not lie, Lord Cauthon. It would be more than my ears are worth. The Queen is waiting, my Lord. You are a very brave man,' she added, turning, then said something more under her breath. 'Or a very great fool.' He doubted he had been supposed to hear that.

A choice between going to see the Queen and wandering miles of corridor until he stumbled on somebody who would tell him what he wanted to know? He went to see the Queen.

Tylin Quintara, by the Grace of the Light, Queen of Altara, Mistress of the Four Winds, Guardian of the Sea of Storms, High

Seat of House Mitsobar, awaited him in a room with yellow walls and a pale blue ceiling, standing before a huge white fireplace with a stone lintel carved into a stormy sea. She was well worth seeing, he decided. Tylin was not young – the shiny black hair cascading over her shoulders had gray at the temples, and faint lines webbed the corners of her eyes – nor was she exactly pretty, though the two thin scars on her cheeks had nearly vanished with age. Handsome came closer. But she was ... imposing. Large dark eyes regarded him majestically, an eagle's eyes. She had little real power – a man could ride beyond her writ in two or three days and still have a lot of Altara ahead – but he thought she might make even an Aes Sedai step back. Like Isebele of Dal Calain, who had made the Amyrlin Anghara come to her. That was one of the old memories; Dal Calain had vanished in the Trolloc Wars.

'Majesty,' he said, sweeping his hat wide in a bow and flourishing an imaginary cloak, 'by your summons do I come.' Imposing or not, it was hard to keep his eyes away from the not small lace-trimmed oval where her white-sheathed marriage knife hung. A very nicely rounded sight indeed, yet the more bosom a woman displayed, the less she wanted you to look. Openly, at least. White-sheathed; but he already knew she was a widow. Not that it mattered. He would as soon tangle himself with that fox-faced Darkfriend as with a queen. Not looking at all was difficult, but he managed. Most likely she would call guards rather than draw the gem-encrusted dagger thrust behind a woven-gold belt to match the collar her marriage knife hung from. Maybe that was why the dice were still rolling in his head. The possibility of an encounter with the headsman would set them spinning if anything did.

Layered silk petticoats rippled white and yellow as she crossed the room and walked slowly all the way around him. 'You speak the Old Tongue,' she said once she stood in front of him again. Her voice was low-pitched and musical. Without waiting for a reply, she glided to a chair and sat, adjusting her green skirts. An unconscious gesture; her gaze remained fixed on him. He thought she could probably tell when his smallclothes had been washed last. 'You wish to leave a message. I have what is necessary.' A lace fall at her wrist swayed as she gestured to a small writing table standing beneath a gilt-framed mirror. All the furnishings were gilded and carved like bamboo.

Tall triple-arched windows opening onto a wrought-iron balcony admitted a sea breeze that was surprisingly pleasant, if not exactly cool, yet Mat felt hotter than in the street, and it had nothing to do with her stare. *Deyeniye, dyu ninte concion ca'lyet ye.* That was what he had said. The bloody Old Tongue popping out of his mouth again without him knowing it. He had thought he had that little bother under control. No telling when those bloody dice would stop or for what. Best to keep his eyes to himself and his mouth shut as much as possible. 'I thank you, Majesty.' He made very sure of those words.

Thick sheets of pale paper already waited on the slanted table, at a comfortable height for writing. He propped his hat against the table leg. He could see her in the mirror. Watching. Why had he let his tongue run loose? Dipping a golden pen – what else would a queen have? – he composed what he wanted to write in his head before bending over the paper with an arm curled around it. His hand was awkward and square. He had no love of writing.

I followed a Darkfriend to the palace Jaichim Carridin is renting. She tried to kill me once, and maybe Rand as well. She was greeted like an old friend of the house.

For a moment he studied that, biting the end of the pen before realizing he was scoring the soft gold. Maybe Tylin would not notice. They needed to know about Carridin. What else? He added a few more reasonably worded lines. The last thing he wanted was to put their backs up.

Be sensible. If you have to go traipsing around, let me send a few men along to keep you from having your heads split open. Anyway, isn't it about time I took you back to Egwene? There's nothing here but heat and flies, and we can find plenty of those in Caemlyn.

There. They could not ask for pleasanter than that.
Blotting the page carefully, he folded it four times. Sand in a

small golden bowl covered a coal. He puffed on it till it glowed, then used it to light a candle and picked up the stick of red wax. As the sealing wax dripped onto the edges of the paper, it suddenly struck him that he had a signet ring in his pocket. Just something the ringmaker had carved to show his skill, but better than a plain lump. The ring was slightly longer than the pool of solidifying wax, yet most of the sigil took.

For the first time he got a good look at what he had bought. Inside a border of large crescents, a running fox seemed to have startled two birds into flight. That made him grin. Too bad it was not a hand, for the Band, but appropriate enough. He certainly needed to be crafty as a fox to keep up with Nynaeve and Elayne, and if they were not exactly flighty, well ... Besides, the medallion had made him fond of foxes. He scrawled Nynaeve's name on the outside, and then Elayne's, as an afterthought. One or the other, they should see it soon.

Turning with the sealed letter held in front of him, he gave a start as his knuckles brushed against Tylin's bosom. He stumbled back against the writing table, staring and trying not to turn red. Staring at her face; just her face. He had not heard her approach. Best to simply ignore the brushing, not embarrass her any further. She probably thought he was a clumsy lout as it was. 'There is something in this you should know, Majesty.' Insufficient room remained between them to lift the letter. 'Jaichim Carridin is entertaining Darkfriends, and I don't mean arresting them.'

'You are certain? Of course you are. No one would make that charge without being certain.' A furrow creased her forehead, but she gave her head a shake and the frown disappeared. 'Let us speak of more pleasant things.'

He could have yelped. He told her the Whitecloak ambassador to her court was a Darkfriend, and all she did was grimace.

'You are Lord Mat Cauthon?' There was just a hint of question in the title. Her eyes minded him more than ever of an eagle's. A queen could not like someone coming to her pretending to be a lord.

'Just Mat Cauthon.' Something told him she would hear a lie. Besides, letting people think he was a lord was just a ruse, one he would rather have managed without. In Ebou Dar you could find a duel any time you turned around, but few challenged lords except other lords. As it was, in the last month he had cracked a number of heads, bloodied four men and run half a mile to escape a woman. Tylin's stare made him nervous. And those dice still rattled about in his skull. He wanted out of there. 'If you'll tell me where to leave the letter, Majesty . . . ?'

'The Daughter-Heir and Nynaeve Sedai seldom mention you,' she said, 'but one learns to hear what is not said.' Casually she reached up and touched his cheek; he half-raised his own hand uncertainly. Had he smeared ink there, chewing the pen? Women did like to tidy things, including men. Maybe queens did, too. 'What they do not say, but I hear, is that you are an untamed rogue, a gambler and chaser after women.' Her eyes held his, expression never altering a hair, and her voice stayed firm and cool, but as she spoke, her fingers stroked his other cheek. 'Untamed men are often the most interesting. To talk to.' A finger outlined his lips. 'An untamed rogue who travels with Aes Sedai, a *ta'veren* who, I think, makes them a little afraid. Uneasy, at the least. It takes a man with a strong liver to make Aes Sedai uneasy. How will you bend the Pattern in Ebou Dar, just Mat Cauthon?' Her hand settled against his neck; he could feel his pulse throbbing against her fingers.

His mouth fell open. The writing table behind his back rattled against the wall as he tried to back away. The only way out was to push her aside or climb over her skirts. Women did not behave this way! Oh, some of those old memories suggested they did, but it was mainly memories of memories that that woman had done this or this woman had done that; the things he recalled clearly were battles for the most part, and no help here at all. She smiled, a faint curl of her lips that did not lessen the predatory gleam in her eyes. The hair on his head tried to stand up.

Her eyes flickered over his shoulder to the mirror, and she turned abruptly, leaving him gaping at her back as she moved away. 'I must arrange to speak with you again, Master Cauthon. I—' She cut off as the door swung all the way open, apparently surprised, but then he realized she had seen it begin moving in the mirror.

A slender young man entered, limping slightly, a dark lad with sharp eyes that flicked by Mat with barely a pause. Black hair hung to his shoulders, and he wore one of those coats that was never meant to be worn normally draped across his shoulders, green silk, with a gold chain across his chest and gold leopards worked on the lapels. 'Mother,' he said, bowing to Tylin and touching his lips with his fingers.

'Beslan.' She filled the name with warmth, and kissed him on both cheeks and his eyelids. The firm, even icy, tone she had used with Mat might as well have never been. 'It went well, I see.'

'Not as well as it might.' The boy sighed. Despite his eyes, he had a mild manner to him, and a soft voice. 'Nevin nicked my leg on the second pass, then slipped on the third so I ran him through the heart instead of his sword-arm. The offense was not worth killing, and now I must pay condolences to his widow.' He seemed to regret that as much as this Nevin's death.

Tylin's beaming face hardly seemed right on a woman whose son had just told her he had killed a man. 'Just be sure your visit is brief. Stab my eyes, but Davindra will be one of those widows who wants comforting, and then you will either have to marry her or kill her brothers.' By her tone, the first alternative was much the worse, the second merely a nuisance. 'This is Master Mat Cauthon, my son. He is *ta'veren*. I hope you will make a friend of him. Perhaps you two will go to the Swovan Night dances together.'

Mat jumped. The last thing he wanted was to go anywhere with a fellow who fought duels and whose mother wanted to stroke Mat Cauthon's cheek. 'I am not much for balls,' he said quickly. Ebou Dari liked festivals beyond reason. Here High Chasaline was just past, and they had five more in the next week, two all-day affairs, not just the simpler evening feasts. 'I do my dancing in taverns. The rougher sort, I'm afraid. Nothing you'd like.'

'I favor taverns of the rougher sort,' Beslan said with a smile, in that soft voice. 'The balls are for older people, and their pretties.'

After that, it was all downhill on crumpling shingle. Before Mat knew what was happening, Tylin had him sewed up in a sack. He and Beslan would be attending the festivals together. All of the festivals. Hunting, Beslan called it, and when Mat said hunting for girls without thinking — he would never have said that in front of somebody's mother had he thought – the boy laughed and said, 'A girl or a fight, pouting lips or a flashing blade. Whichever dance you're dancing at the moment is always the most fun. Wouldn't you say so, Mat?' Tylin smiled at Beslan fondly.

Mat managed a weak laugh. This Beslan was mad, him and his mother both.

CHAPTER 17

The Triumph of Logic

Mat stalked out of the palace when Tylin finally let him go, and had he thought it would do any good, he would have run. The skin between his shoulder blades prickled so, he almost forgot the dice dancing in his head. The worst moment – the very worst of a dozen bad – had been when Beslan teased his mother, saying she should find herself a pretty for the balls, and Tylin laughingly claimed a queen had no time for young men, all the while looking at Mat with those bloody eagle's eyes. Now he knew why rabbits ran so fast. He stumped across Mol Hara Square not seeing anything. Had Nynaeve and Elayne been cavorting with Jaichim Carridin and Elaida in the fountain beneath that statue of some long-dead queen, two spans or more tall and pointing to the sea, he would have passed by without a second look.

The common room of The Wandering Woman was dim and comparatively cool after the bright heat outside. He took off his hat gratefully. A faint haze of pipe smoke hung in the air, but the arabesque-carved shutters across the wide arched windows let in more than enough light. Some bedraggled pine branches had been tied above the windows for Swovan Night. In one corner, two women with flutes and a fellow with a small drum between his knees provided a shrill, pulsing sort of music that Mat had come to like. Even at this time of the day there were a few patrons, outland merchants in moderately plain woolens with a sprinkling of Ebou Dari, most in the vests of various guilds. No apprentices or even journeymen here; so close to the palace, The Wandering Woman was hardly an inexpensive place to drink or eat, much less sleep.

The rattle of dice at a table in the corner echoed the feeling in his head, but he turned the other way, to where three of his men sat on benches around another table. Corevin, a thickly muscled Cairhienin with a nose that made his eyes seem even smaller than they were, sat stripped to the waist, holding his tattooed arms over his head while Vanin wound strips of bandage around his middle. Vanin was three times Corevin's size, but he looked like a balding sack of suet overflowing his bench. His coat appeared to have been slept in for a week; it always did, even an hour after one of the serving women ironed it. Some of the merchants eyed the three uneasily, but none of the Ebou Dari; men or women, they had seen the same or worse, often.

Harnan, a lantern-jawed Tairen file leader with a crude tattoo of a hawk on his left cheek, was berating Corevin. '... don't care what the flaming fish-seller said, you goat-spawned toad, you use your bloody club and don't go accepting flaming challenges just because—' He cut off when he saw Mat, and tried to look as if he had not been saying what he had. He just looked as if he had a toothache.

If Mat asked, it would turn out Corevin had slipped and fallen on his own dagger or some such foolery Mat was supposed to pretend to believe. So he just leaned his fists on the table as if he saw nothing out of the ordinary. Truth to tell, it was not that out of the ordinary. Vanin was the only man who had not been in two dozen scrapes already; for some reason, men looking for trouble walked as wide of Vanin as they did Nalesean. The only difference was that Vanin seemed to like it that way. 'Has Thom or Juilin been here yet?'

Vanin did not look up from tying the bandages. 'Haven't seen hide, hair nor toenail. Nalesean was in for a bit, though.' There was no 'my lord' nonsense from Vanin. He made no bones about not liking nobles. With the unfortunate exception of Elayne. 'Left an iron-strapped chest up in your room, and went out babbling about trinkets.' He made as if to spit through the gap in his teeth, then glanced at one of the serving women and did not. Mistress Anan was death on anybody spitting on her floors, or tossing bones, or even tapping out a pipe. 'The boy's out back in the stable,' he went on before Mat could ask, 'with his book and one of the innkeeper's daughters. Another of the girls spanked his bottom for pinching hers.' Finishing the last knot, he gave Mat an accusatory look, as if it had been his fault in some way.

'Poor little mite,' Corevin muttered, twisting to see whether the bandages would stay in place. He had a leopard and a boar inked on one arm, a lion and a woman on the other. The woman did not seem to be wearing much except her hair. 'Sniveling, he was. Though he did brighten when Leral let him hold her hand.' The men all looked after Olver like a gaggle of uncles, though certainly the sort no mother would want near her son.

'He'll live,' Mat said dryly. The boy was probably picking up these habits from his 'uncles.' Next, they would give him a tattoo. At least Olver had not sneaked out to run with the street children; he seemed to enjoy that almost as much as he did making himself a nuisance to grown women. 'Harnan, you wait here, and if you see Thom or Juilin, collar them. Vanin, I want you to see what you can learn around the Chelsaine Palace, over near the Three Towers Gate.' Hesitating, he looked over the room. Serving women drifted in and out of the kitchens with food and, more often, drink. Most of the patrons seemed intent on their silver cups, though a pair of women in weaver's vests argued quietly, ignoring their wine punch and leaning across the table at one another. Some of the merchants appeared to be haggling, waving hands and dipping fingers in their drinks to scribble numbers on the table. The music should mask his words from eavesdroppers, but he lowered his voice anyway.

News that Jaichim Carridin had Darkfriends coming to call screwed Vanin's round face into a scowl, as if he might spit no matter who saw. Harnan muttered something about filthy Whitecloaks, and Corevin suggested denouncing Carridin to the Civil Guard. That got such disgusted looks from the other two that he buried his face in a cup of ale. He was one of the few men Mat knew who could drink Ebou Dari ale in this heat. Or drink it at all, for that matter.

'Be careful,' Mat warned when Vanin stood. It was not that he was worried, really. Vanin moved with surprising lightness for such a fat man. He was the best horsethief in two countries at the least, and could slip by even a Warder unseen, but . . . 'They're a nasty lot. Whitecloaks or Darkfriends, either one.' The man only grunted and motioned for Corevin to gather his shirt and coat and come along.

'My Lord?' Harnan said as they left. 'My Lord, I heard there was a fog in the Rahad yesterday.'

On the point of turning away, Mat stopped. Harnan looked worried, and nothing much worried him. 'What do you mean, a fog?' In this heat, fog thick as porridge would not last a heartbeat.

The file leader shrugged uncomfortably and peered into his mug. 'A fog. I heard there was . . . things . . . in it.' He looked up at Mat. 'I heard people just disappeared. And some was found eaten, parts of them.'

Mat managed not to shiver. 'The fog's gone, isn't it? You weren't in it. Worry when you are. That's all you can do.' Harnan frowned doubtfully, but that was the pure truth. These bubbles of evil – that was what Rand called them, what Moiraine had – burst where and when they chose, and there did not seem to be anything even Rand could do to stop them. Worrying about it did as much good as worrying whether a roof tile would fall on your head in the street tomorrow. Less, since you could decide to stay indoors.

There was something that was worth worrying over, though. Nalesean had left their winnings sitting upstairs. Bloody nobles tossed gold around like water. Leaving Harnan studying his mug, Mat headed for the railless stairs at the back of the room, but before he reached them, one of the serving women accosted him.

Caira was a slender, full-lipped girl with smoky eyes. 'A man came in looking for you, my Lord,' she said, twisting her skirts from side to side and looking up at him through long lashes. There was a certain smokiness in her voice, too. 'Said he was an Illuminator, but he looked seedy to me. He ordered a meal, and left when Mistress Anan wouldn't give it. He wanted you to pay.'

'Next time, pigeon, give the meal,' he told her, slipping a silver mark into the plunging neck of her dress. 'I'll speak to Mistress Anan.' He did want to find an Illuminator – a real one, not some fellow selling fireworks full of sawdust – but it hardly mattered now. Not with the gold lying unguarded. And fogs in the Rahad, and Darkfriends, and Aes Sedai, and bloody Tylin taking leave of her senses, and . . .

Caira giggled and twisted like a stroked cat. 'Would you like me to bring some punch to your room, my Lord? Or anything?' She smiled hopefully, invitingly.

'Maybe later,' he said, tapping her nose with a fingertip. She giggled again; she always did. Caira would have her skirt sewn to show petticoats to the middle of her thigh or higher had Mistress Anan allowed it, but the innkeeper looked after her serving women almost as closely as she did her daughters. Almost. 'Maybe later.'

Trotting up the wide stone stairs, he put Caira out of his mind. What was he to do about Olver? The boy would find himself in real trouble one day if he thought he could treat women that way. He was going to have to keep him away from Harnan and the others as much as possible, he supposed. They were a bad influence on a boy. To have this on top of everything else! He had to get Nynaeve and Elayne out of Ebou Dar before something worse went wrong.

His room was at the front, with windows overlooking the square, and as he reached for the door, the hallway floor behind him squeaked. In a hundred inns, it would not even have registered, but the floors in The Wandering Woman did not squeak.

He looked back – and spun just in time to drop his hat and catch the descending truncheon with his left hand instead of his skull. The blow stung his hand to numbness, but he held on desperately as thick fingers dug into his throat, forcing him back against the door to his room. His head hit with a thump. Silver-rimmed black spots danced in his vision, obscuring a sweating face. All he could really see was a big nose and yellow teeth, and those seemed hazy. Suddenly he realized he was on the far edge of consciousness; those fingers were closing off blood to his brain along with air. His free hand went beneath his coat, fumbling over the hilts of his knives as though his fingers no longer remembered what they were for. The cudgel wrenched free. He could see it rising, feel it rising to smash his skull. Focusing everything, he jerked a knife from its scabbard and thrust.

His attacker let out a high-pitched scream, and Mat was vaguely aware of the club bouncing off his shoulder as it fell to the floor, but the man did not let go of his throat. Stumbling, Mat drove him back, tearing at the clutching fingers with one hand, driving his knife repeatedly with the other.

Abruptly the fellow fell, sliding from Mat's blade. The knife nearly followed him to the floor. So did Mat. Gulping breath, sweet air, he clung to something, a doorway, to hold himself on his feet. From the floor a plain-faced man stared up at him with eyes that would never see anything again, a heavyset fellow with curled Murandian mustaches, in a dark blue coat fit for a small merchant or a prosperous shopkeeper. Not the look of a thief about him at all.

Abruptly he realized they had stumbled through an open door in their fight. It was a smaller room than Mat's, windowless, a pair of oil lamps on small tables beside the narrow bed providing a murky illumination. A lanky, pale-haired man straightened from a large open chest, staring oddly at the corpse. The chest took up most of the free space in the room.

Mat opened his mouth to apologize for intruding so roughly, and the lanky man snatched a long dagger from his belt, a cudgel from the bed, and leaped over the chest at him. That had not been the look you gave a dead stranger. Clinging unsteadily to the doorframe, Mat threw underhanded, the hilt no sooner leaving his hand than he was scrabbling under his coat for another. His knife stuck squarely in the other man's throat, and Mat almost fell again, this time from relief, as the man clutched himself, blood spurting between his fingers, and toppled backward into the open chest.

'It's good to be lucky,' Mat croaked.

Staggering, he retrieved his knife, wiping it clean on the fellow's gray coat. A better coat than the other; still wool, but of a better cut. A lesser lord would not have been ashamed to wear it.

Andoran, by the collar. He sank onto the bed, frowning at the man sprawled in the chest. A noise made him look up.

His manservant was in the doorway, trying unsuccessfully to hide a large black iron frying pan behind his back. Nerim kept a full set of pots, and everything else he thought a lord's servant might need traveling, in the small room he shared with Olver next to Mat's. He was short even for a Cairhienin, and skinny to boot. 'My Lord has blood on his coat again, I fear,' he murmured in melancholy tones. The day he sounded anything else, the sun would rise in the west. 'I do wish my Lord would be more careful of his clothes. It is so hard to remove blood without a stain, and the insects hardly need any encouragement to eat holes. This place has more insects than I have ever seen, my Lord.' No mention at all of two dead men, or what he had intended with the frying pan.

That scream had drawn other attention; The Wandering Woman was not the sort of inn where screams passed unremarked. Feet pounded in the hallway, and Mistress Anan pushed Nerim firmly out of her way and raised her skirts to step around the corpse on the floor. Her husband followed her in, a square-faced, gray-haired man with the double earring of the Ancient and Honorable League of the Nets dangling from his left ear. The two white stones on the lower hoop said he owned other boats beside the one he captained. Jasfer Anan was part of the reason Mat was careful not to smile too much at any of Mistress Anan's daughters. The man wore a work knife stuffed behind his belt and a longer, curved blade too, and his long blue-and-green vest revealed arms and chest crisscrossed with dueling scars. He was alive, though, and most of the men who had given those scars were not.

The other reason for caution was Setalle Anan herself. Mat had never before let himself be turned off a girl because of her mother, even if that mother owned the inn where he was staying, but Mistress Anan had a way about her. Large gold hoops in her ears swung as she surveyed the dead men without a flinch. She was pretty despite a touch of gray in her hair, and her marriage knife nestled in roundness that normally would have drawn his eyes like moths to a candle, yet looking at her that way would have been like looking at ... Not his mother. At an Aes Sedai, maybe – though he had done that, of course, just to look – or at Queen Tylin, the Light help him there. Putting a finger on why was not easy. She simply had a way about her. It was just difficult to think of doing anything that would offend Setalle Anan.

'One of them jumped me in the hall.' Mat kicked the chest lightly; it made a hollow sound despite the dead man slumped inside with his arms and legs dangling out. 'This is empty except for him. I think they meant to fill it with whatever they could steal.' The gold, perhaps? Not likely they could have heard of that, won only hours ago, but he would ask Mistress Anan about a safer place to keep it.

She nodded calmly, hazel eyes serene. Men knifed in her inn did not ruffle her feathers. 'They insisted on carrying it up themselves. Their stock, so they claimed. They took the room just before you came in. For a few hours, they said, to sleep before traveling on toward Nor Chasen.' That was a small village on the coast to the east, but it was unlikely they would have told the truth. Her tone implied as much. She frowned at the dead men as though wishing she could shake them alive to answer questions. 'They were picky about the room, though. The pale-haired man was in charge. He turned down the first three he was offered, then accepted this, that was meant for a single servant. I thought he was being stingy with a coin.'

'Even a thief can be tightfisted,' Mat said absently. This could have qualified to start those dice rolling in his head – a head that would have been cracked open for sure without the luck of that fellow stepping on the one board in the whole inn that would squeak – but the bloody things were still tumbling. He did not like it.

'You think it was chance then, my Lord?'

'What else?'

She had no answer, but she frowned at the corpses again. Maybe she was not so sanguine as he had thought. She was not native to Ebou Dar, after all.

'Too many roughs in the city of late.' Jasfer had a deep voice, and speaking normally he seemed to be barking commands on a fishing boat. 'Maybe you ought to think on hiring guards.' All Mistress

Anan did was lift an eyebrow at her husband, but his hands rose defensively. 'Peace be on you, wife. I spoke without thinking.' Ebou Dari women were known to express displeasure with a husband in a sharp fashion. It was not beyond possibility that a few of his scars came from her. The marriage knife had several uses.

Thanking the Light he was not married to an Ebou Dari, Mat replaced his own knife in its sheath alongside the others. Thank the Light he was not married at all. His fingers brushed paper.

Mistress Anan was not letting her husband off easily. 'You frequently do, husband,' she said, fingering the hilt between her breasts. 'Many women would not let it pass. Elynde always tells me I am not firm enough when you speak out of line. I need to provide a good example for my daughters.' Acerbity melted into a smile, if a small one. 'Consider yourself chastised. I will refrain from telling you who should haul which net on which boat.'

'You are too kind to me, wife,' he replied dryly. There was no guild for innkeepers in Ebou Dar, but every inn in the city was in the hands of a woman; to Ebou Dari, bad luck of the worst sort would dog any inn owned by a man or any vessel owned by a woman. There were no women in the fishermen's guild.

Mat pulled out the paper. It was snowy white, expensive and stiff, and folded small. The few lines on it were printed in square letters like those Olver might use. Or an adult who did not want the hand recognized.

ELAYNE AND NYNAEVE ARE PUSHING TOO FAR. REMIND THEM THEY ARE STILL IN DANGER FROM THE TOWER. WARN THEM TO BE CAREFUL, OR THEY WILL BE KNEELING TO ASK ELAIDA'S PARDON YET.

That was all; no signature. *Still* in danger? That suggested it was nothing new, and somehow it did not fit with them being snared up by the rebels. No, that was the wrong question. Who had slipped him this note? Obviously somebody who thought they could not simply hand it to him. Who had had the opportunity since he put the coat on this morning? It had not been there then, for sure. Somebody who had gotten close. Somebody ... Unbidden, he found himself humming a snatch of 'She Dazzles My Eyes and Clouds My Mind.' Around here the tune had different words; they called it 'Upside Down and 'Round and 'Round.' Only Teslyn or Joline fit, and that was impossible.

'Bad news, my Lord?' Mistress Anan asked.

Mat stuffed the note into his pocket. 'Does any man ever get to understand women? I don't mean just Aes Sedai. Any women.'

Jasfer roared, and when his wife directed a meaning gaze his way, he only laughed harder. The look she gave Mat would have shamed an Aes Sedai for its perfect serenity. 'Men have it quite easy, my Lord, if they only looked or listened. Women have the difficult task. We must try to understand men.' Jasfer took hold of the doorframe, tears rolling down his dark face. She eyed him sideways, tilting her head, then turned, all cool calmness – and punched him under the ribs with her fist so hard that his knees buckled. His laughter took on a wheeze without stopping. 'There is a saying in Ebou Dar, my Lord,' she said to Mat over her shoulder. '"A man is a maze of brambles in darkness, and even he does not know the way."'

Mat snorted. Fat lot of help she was. Well, Teslyn or Joline or somebody else – it must have been somebody else, if he could only think who – the White Tower was a long way away. Jaichim Carridin was right here. He frowned at the two corpses. And so were a hundred other scoundrels. Somehow he would see those two women safely out of Ebou Dar. The trouble was, he did not have a clue how. He wished those bloody dice would stop, and be done with it.

The apartments Joline shared with Teslyn were quite spacious, including a bedchamber for each of them, plus one apiece for their maids and another that would have done quite well for Blaeric and Fen, if Teslyn could have stood to have her Warders with them. The woman saw every man as a potentially rabid wolf, and there was no gainsaying her when she truly wanted something. As inexorable as Elaida, she ground down whatever lay in her path. They stood as equals in every real way, certainly, but not many managed to prevail over Teslyn without a clear advantage. She was at the writing table in the sitting room when Joline entered, her pen making an awful *scritch-scritch*. She was always parsimonious with the ink.

Without a word, Joline swept by her and out onto the balcony, a long cage of white-painted iron. The scrollwork was so tight that the men working in the garden three stories below would have a difficult time seeing that there was anyone within. Flowers in this region ordinarily thrived in heat, wild colors to outshine the interior of the palace, but nothing bloomed down there. Gardeners moved along the gravel walks with buckets of water, yet nearly every leaf was yellow or brown. She would not have admitted it under torture, but the heat made her afraid. The Dark One was touching the world, and their only hope a boy who was running wild.

'Bread and water?' Teslyn said suddenly. 'Send the Cauthon boy off to the Tower? If there do be changes in what we did plan, you will please inform me before telling others.'

Joline felt a touch of heat in her cheeks. 'Merilille needed to be set down. She lectured when I was a novice.' So had Teslyn; a severe teacher who held her classes with an iron grip. Just the way she spoke was a reminder, a marked warning not to go against her, equal or not. Merilille, though, stood lower. 'She used to make us stand in front of the class, and she would dig and dig for the answer she wanted, until we stood there in front of everyone, weeping with frustration. She pretended to sympathize, or perhaps she really did, but the more she patted us and told us not to cry, the worse it was.' She cut off abruptly. She had not intended to say all that. It was Teslyn's fault, always looking at her as if she were about to be upbraided for a spot on her dress. But she should understand; Merilille had taught her, too.

'You have remembered that all this time?' Stark incredulity painted Teslyn's voice. 'The sisters who did teach us did only do their duty. Sometimes I do think what Elaida did say of you do be right.' The annoying *scritch-scritch* resumed.

'It . . . simply came to mind when Merilille began as if she were truly an ambassador.' Instead of a rebel. Joline frowned at the garden. She despised every one of those women who had broken the White Tower, and flaunted the break before all the world. Them and anyone who aided them. But Elaida had blundered too, horribly. The sisters who were rebels now could have been reconciled, with a little effort. 'What did she say of me? Teslyn?' The sound of the pen continued, like fingernails scraping across a slate. Joline went back inside. 'What did Elaida say?'

Teslyn laid another sheet atop her letter, either to blot or to shield it from Joline's eyes, but she did not answer immediately. She scowled at Joline – or perhaps just looked; it was difficult to say with her at times – and at last sighed. 'Very well. If you must know. She did say you still do be a child.'

'A *child?*' Joline's shock had no effect on the other woman.

'Some,' Teslyn said calmly, 'do change little from the day they do put on novice white. Some do change no at all. Elaida does believe you have no grown up yet and never will.'

Joline tossed her head angrily, unwilling to let herself speak. To have that by someone whose *mother* had been a child when she herself gained the shawl! Elaida had been petted too much as a novice, made over too much for her strength and the remarkable speed of her learning. Joline suspected that was why she was in such a fury about Elayne and Egwene and the wilder Nynaeve; because they were stronger than she, because they had spent far less time as novices, no matter they had been pushed ahead too fast. Why, Nynaeve had never been a novice at all, and that was completely unheard of.

'Since you did bring it up,' Teslyn went on, 'perhaps we should try to take advantage of the situation.'

'What do you mean?' Embracing the True Source, Joline channeled Air to lift the silver pitcher on the turquoise-inlaid side table and fill a silver goblet with punch. As always, the joy of embracing *saidar* thrilled her, soothing even as it exhilarated.

'It do be obvious, I should think. Elaida's orders do still stand. Elayne and Nynaeve are to be returned to the Tower as soon as found. I did agree to wait, but perhaps we should wait no longer. A pity the al'Vere girl does no be with them. But two will put us back in Elaida's good graces, and if we can add the Cauthon boy . . . I do think those three will make her welcome us as if we did come with al'Thor himself. And this Aviendha will make a fine novice, wilder or no.'

The goblet floated into Joline's hand on Air, and she reluctantly released the Power. She had never lost the ardor she felt the first time she touched the Source. Dewmelon punch was a poor substitute for *saidar*. The worst part of her penance before leaving the Tower had been losing the right to touch *saidar*. Almost the worst part. She had set it all herself, but Elaida had made it clear that if she did not make it harsh, Elaida would. She had no doubt the result would have been much worse, then. 'Her good graces? Teslyn, she humiliated us for no more reason than to show the others that she could. She sent us to this fly-ridden hole as far from everything important as she could, short of the other side of the Aryth Ocean, ambassadors to a queen with less power than a dozen nobles, any one of whom could snatch the throne from her tomorrow if they could be bothered to. And you want to wheedle your way back into Elaida's favor?'

'She do be the Amyrlin Seat.' Teslyn touched the letter with the page lying atop it, moving the sheets a bit this way then a bit that, as if framing her thoughts. 'Remaining silent for a time did let her know we are no lapdogs, but remaining silent too long could be seen as treason.'

Joline sniffed. 'Ridiculous! When they're returned they'll only be punished for running away, and now for pretending to be full sisters.' Her mouth tightened. They were both guilty there, and those who allowed them to, as well, but it made a sharp difference when one of them claimed her own Ajah. By the time the Green Ajah finished with Elayne for that, it would be a very chastened young woman indeed who took the throne of Andor. Though it might be best if Elayne secured the Lion Throne first. Her training had to be completed, either way. Joline did not intend to see Elayne lost to the Tower, whatever she had done.

'Do no forget joining with the rebels.'

'Light, Teslyn, they were probably scooped up just like the girls the rebels took out of the Tower. Does it really matter a whit whether they begin mucking out stalls tomorrow or next year?' That was surely as much as the novices and Accepted with the rebels would have to face. 'Even the Ajahs can wait to have them in hand, really. It is not as if they aren't safe. They are Accepted, after all, and they certainly seem content to stay where we can reach them whenever we choose. I say, let us sit where Elaida put us, and continue to fold our hands and hold our tongues. Until she asks nicely to find out what we are doing.' She did not say that she was prepared to wait until Elaida found herself deposed as Siuan had been. The Hall surely would not put up with the bullying and bungling forever, but Teslyn *was* Red, after all, and would not appreciate hearing that.

'I suppose there do be no urgency,' Teslyn said slowly, the unspoken 'but' all but shouting itself.

Drawing a ball-footed chair to the table with another flow of Air, Joline settled herself to convincing her companion that silence remained the best policy. Still a child, was she? If she had her way, Elaida would not get so much as a word out of Ebou Dar until she begged for it.

The woman on the table arched up as far as her bonds would allow, eyes bulging, throat corded with a piercing scream that went on and on. Abruptly the scream was a loud choking rasp instead, and she convulsed, shaking from wrists to ankles, then collapsed in silence. Wider open eyes stared sightlessly at the cobwebbed basement ceiling.

Giving vent to curses was irrational, but Falion could have turned the air as blue as any stableman. Not for the first time she wished she had Temaile here instead of Ispan. Questions were answered eagerly for Temaile, and nobody died until she was ready. Of course, Temaile enjoyed the work entirely too much, but that was beside the point.

Channeling once more, Falion gathered the woman's clothes from the filthy floor and dropped them atop the body. The red leather belt fell off, and she snatched it up by hand and slapped it back onto the pile. Perhaps she should have used other methods, but straps and pincers and hot irons were so ... messy. 'Leave the body in an alley somewhere. Slit the throat so it looks as if she was robbed. You can keep the coins in her purse.'

The two men squatting on their heels against the stone wall exchanged looks. Arnin and Nad might have been brothers by their appearance, all black hair and beady eyes and scars, with more muscles than any three men could need, but they did have sufficient brains to carry out simple orders. Usually. 'Forgiveness, Mistress,' Arnin said hesitantly, 'but no one will believe—'

'Do as you are told!' she snapped, channeling to haul him to his feet and slam him back against the stones. His head bounced, yet that surely could do him no damage.

Nad rushed to the table, babbling, 'Yes, Mistress. As you command, Mistress.' When she released Arnin, he did not babble, but he staggered over without any more objections to help gather up the body like so much rubbish and carry it out. Well, it was so much rubbish, now. She regretted the outburst. Letting temper take control was irrational. It did seem to be effective at times, though. After all these years, that still surprised her.

'Moghedien, she will not like this,' Ispan said as soon as the men had gone. The blue and green beads that were worked into her many slim black braids clacked as she shook her head. She had remained in the shadows the whole time, in a corner, with a small ward woven so she could not hear.

Falion managed not to glare. Ispan was the last companion she would have chosen for herself. She was Blue, or had been. Perhaps she still was. Falion did not really think herself any less White Ajah because she had joined the Black. Blues were too fervent, tying emotion around what should be viewed with utter dispassion. Rianna, another White, would have been her choice. Though the woman did have odd, unsound notions on several points of logic. 'Moghedien has forgotten us, Ispan. Or have you received some private word from her? In any case, I am convinced this cache does not exist.'

'Moghedien, she says that it does.' Ispan began firmly, but her voice quickly grew warm. 'A store of *angreal*, and *sa'angreal*, and *ter'angreal*. We will have some part of them. *Angreal* of our very own, Falion. Perhaps even *sa'angreal*. She has promised.'

'Moghedien was wrong.' Falion watched shock widen the other woman's eyes. The Chosen were only people. Learning that lesson had stunned Falion too, but some refused to learn. The Chosen were vastly stronger, infinitely more knowledgeable, and quite possibly they had already received the reward of immortality, but by all evidence, they schemed and fought each other as hard as two Murandians with one blanket.

Ispan's shock quickly gave way to anger. 'There are others looking. Would they all look for nothing? There are Friends of the Dark looking; they must have been set by others of the Chosen. If the Chosen look, can you still say there is nothing?' She would not see. If a thing could not be found, the most obvious reason was that it was not there.

Falion waited. Ispan was not stupid, only awestruck, and Falion did believe in making people teach themselves what they should already be aware of. Lazy minds needed to be exercised.

Ispan paced, swishing her skirts and frowning at the dust and old cobwebs. 'This place smells. And it is filthy!' She shuddered as a large black cockroach went skittering up the wall. The glow surrounded her for a moment; a flow squashed the beetle with a popping sound. Making a face, Ispan wiped her hands on her skirts as if she had used them instead of the Power. She had a delicate stomach, though fortunately not when she could remove herself from the actual deed. 'I will not report the failure to one of the Chosen, Falion. She would make us envy Liandrin, yes?'

Falion did not quite shiver. She did, however, cross the basement and pour herself a cup of plum punch. The plums had been old, and the punch was too sweet, but her hands remained steady. Fear of Moghedien was perfectly sensible, but yielding to fear was not. Perhaps the woman was dead. Surely she would have summoned them by now, or snatched them sleeping into *Tel'aran'rhiod* again to tell her why they had not yet carried out her commands. Until she saw a body, though, the only logical choice was to continue as if Moghedien would appear any moment. 'There is a way.'

'How? Put every Wise Woman in Ebou Dar to the question? How many are there? A hundred? Two hundred perhaps? The sisters in the Tarasin Palace, they would notice this, I think.'

'Forget your dreams of owning a *sa'angreal*, Ispan. There is no long-hidden storehouse, no secret basement beneath a palace.' Falion spoke in cool, measured tones, perhaps more measured the more agitated Ispan became. She had always enjoyed mesmerizing a class of novices with the sound of her voice. 'Almost all of the

Wise Women are wilders, highly unlikely to know what we wish to learn. No wilder has ever been found keeping an *angreal*, much less a *sa'angreal*, and they surely would have been found. On the contrary, by every record, a wilder who discovers any object tied to the Power rids herself of it as soon as possible, for fear of attracting the wrath of the White Tower. Women who are put out of the Tower, on the other hand, seem not to have the same fear. As you well know, when they are searched before leaving, fully one in three has secreted something about her person, an actual object of the Power or something she believes is one. Of the few Wise Women who qualify at present, Callie was the perfect choice. When she was put out four years ago, she tried to steal a small *ter'angreal*. A useless thing that makes images of flowers and the sound of a waterfall, but still an object tied to *saidar*. And she tried to discover all the other novices' secrets, succeeding more often than not. If there was even a single *angreal* in Ebou Dar, not to speak of a vast storehouse, do you think she could have been four years here without locating it?'

'I *do* wear the shawl, Falion,' Ispan said with extraordinary asperity. 'And I *do* know all of that as well as you. You said there was another way. What way?' She simply would not apply her brain.

'What would please Moghedien as greatly as the cache?' Ispan simply stared at her, tapping her foot. 'Nynaeve al'Meara, Ispan. Moghedien abandoned us to go chasing after her, but obviously she escaped somehow. If we give Nynaeve – and the Trakand girl, for that matter – to Moghedien, she would forgive us a hundred *sa'angreal*.' Which clearly demonstrated that the Chosen could be irrational, of course. It was best, of course, to be extremely careful with those who were both irrational and more powerful than you. Ispan was not more powerful.

'We should have killed her as I wanted, when she first appeared,' she spat. Waving her hands, she stalked up and down, grime crunching loudly beneath her slippers. 'Yes, yes, I know. Our sisters in the palace, they might have become suspicious. We do not wish to draw their eyes. But have you forgotten Tanchico? And Tear? Where those two girls appear, disaster follows. Me, I think if we cannot kill them, we should remain as far from Nynaeve al'Meara and Elayne Trakand as we can. As far as we can!'

'Calm yourself, Ispan. Calm yourself.' If anything, Falion's soothing tone only seemed to agitate the other woman more, but Falion was confident. Logic must prevail over emotion.

Sitting on an upended barrel in the sparse coolness of a narrow, shaded alley, he studied the house across the busy street. Suddenly he realized he was touching his head again. He did not have a headache, but his head felt ... peculiar ... sometimes. Most often when he thought of what he could not remember.

Three stories of white plaster, the house belonged to a goldsmith who supposedly was being visited by two friends she had met on a journey north some years ago. The friends had only been glimpsed on arrival and not seen since. Finding that out had been easy, finding out they were Aes Sedai only a trifle more difficult.

A lean young man in a torn vest, whistling his way down the street with no good on his mind, paused when he glimpsed him sitting on the barrel. His coat and his location in the shadows – and the rest of him, he admitted ruefully – probably looked tempting. He reached under his coat. His hands no longer possessed the strength or flexibility for swordwork, but the two long knives he had carried for well over thirty years had surprised more than one swordsman. Maybe something showed in his eyes, because the lean young man thought better of it and whistled his way on.

Beside the house, the gate that led back to the goldsmith's stable swung open, and two burly men appeared pushing a barrow piled high with soiled straw and muck. What were they up to? Arnin and Nad were hardly the lads to be mucking out stables.

He would stay here until dark, he decided, then see whether he could find Carridin's pretty little killer again.

Once again he pulled his hand down from his head. Sooner or later, he would remember. He did not have much time left, but it was all he did have. He remembered that much.

Chapter 18

As the Plow Breaks the Earth

Seizing *saidin* long enough to unknot the ward he had woven across one corner of the anteroom, Rand raised his small silver-mounted cup and said, 'More tea.' Lews Therin muttered angrily in the back of his head.

Carved chairs heavy with gilt stood in paired lines to either side of a golden Rising Sun, two paces wide, set into the polished stone floor, and another tall chair so gilded it seemed entirely gold topped a small dais that was just as elaborate, but he sat cross-legged on a carpet spread for the occasion, green and gold and blue in a Tairen maze. The three clan chiefs seated across from him would have disliked him receiving them from a chair even if they were offered their own. They were another maze, to be trod warily. He was in his shirt, sleeves pushed up his forearms to expose the red-and-gold Dragon that curled around each, glittering metallically. The Aielmen's *cadin'sor* covered theirs, on the left arm alone. Perhaps the reminder of who he was – that he too had been to Rhuidean when the journey meant death for most men who entered – perhaps it was unnecessary. Perhaps.

Those three faces gave away little as they watched Merana come from the corner where she had been sealed off. Janwin's creased face could have been carved from old wood, but it always looked that way, and if his blue-gray eyes seemed stormy, so did they always too. Even his hair looked like storm clouds. He was an even-tempered man, though. Indirian and one-eyed Mandelain might have been thinking of something else, except that their unblinking gazes followed her. Lews Therin suddenly went silent, as if he too watched, through Rand's eyes.

Merana's ageless features revealed even less than the clan chiefs. Smoothing her pale gray skirts under, she knelt beside Rand and lifted the teapot. A massive ball of gold-washed silver, with leopards for feet and handle and another crouched on the lid, it required both of her hands and wavered a little as she carefully filled Rand's cup. Her manner seemed to say she did this because she wanted to, for reasons of her own that none of them could begin to understand; her manner shouted Aes Sedai louder than her face did. Was that to the good, or the bad?

'I do not allow them to channel without permission,' he said. The clan chiefs kept silent. Merana rose and moved to kneel beside each in turn. Mandelain covered his cup with a broad hand to indicate he wanted no more. The other two held out theirs, blue-gray eyes and green alike studying her. What did they see? What more could he do?

Replacing the heavy tea-pot on the thick leopard-handled tray, she remained on her knees. 'May I serve my Lord Dragon in any way else?'

Her voice was self-possession itself, but after he motioned her back to her corner, after she had risen and turned, slim hands clutched at her skirts for an instant. Yet that might have been because turning brought her to face Dashiva and Narishma. The two Asha'man – to be precise, Narishma was still only a soldier, the lowest level of Asha'man, with neither the sword nor the Dragon on his collar – the Asha'man stood impassively between two of the tall golden-framed mirrors that lined the walls. At least, the younger man looked impassive, at first glance. Thumbs tucked behind his sword belt, he ignored Merana and paid little more attention to Rand or the Aielmen, yet at a second glance you saw that his dark too-big eyes never rested, as if he expected the unexpected to leap out of the air any moment. And who could say it would not? Dashiva appeared to have his head in the clouds; his lips moved soundlessly, and he blinked and frowned at nothing.

Lews Therin snarled when Rand looked at the Asha'man, but it was Merana who occupied the dead man inside Rand's head. *Only a fool thinks a lion or a woman can truly be tamed.*

Irritably, Rand suppressed the voice to a muted buzz. Lews Therin could break through, but not without effort. Grabbing hold of *saidin*, he rewove the ward that shut Merana away from their voices. Releasing the Source again increased his irritation, the hissing in his head, the water drops on red coals. An echo pulsing in time with Lews Therin's mad, distant rage.

Merana stood behind the barrier she could neither see nor feel, head high and hands folded at her waist as if a shawl were looped over her arms. Aes Sedai to her toenails. She watched him and the clan chiefs with cool eyes, light brown flecked with yellow. *My sisters do not all realize how very much we need you,* she had told him this morning in this very room, *but all of us who swore will do whatever you ask that would not violate the Three Oaths.* He had just wakened when she came with Sorilea escorting her. Neither seemed to care at all that he was still in a robe, with only one bite taken from his breakfast bread. *I have more than a little skill in negotiation and mediation. My sisters have other skills. Let us serve you, as we pledged. Let me serve you. We need you, but you have some need of us, too.*

Ever present, Alanna lay nestled in a corner of his brain. She was weeping again. He could not understand why she wept so often. He had forbidden her to come near him unless summoned, or leave her room without an escort of Maidens – the sisters who had sworn to him had been found rooms last night, in the Palace where he could keep an eye on them – but he had sensed tears from the moment she bonded him, tears and a raw grief like being ripped by claws. Sometimes it was less, sometimes more, yet always there. Alanna also had told him he needed the sworn sisters, screamed it at him finally, with her face red and tears rolling down her cheeks, before literally running from his presence. And she had spoken of serving, too, though he doubted that Merana's present tasks were what either had in mind. Perhaps some sort of livery would make it clear?

The clan chiefs watched Merana watch them. Not so much as the flicker of an eyelash betrayed their thoughts.

'The Wise Ones have told you where the Aes Sedai stand,' Rand said bluntly. Sorilea had told him they knew, but the fact would have been clear from the lack of surprise when they first saw Merana fetch and curtsy. 'You've seen her bring the tray and pour your tea. You've seen her come and go as I say. If you want, I'll have her dance a jig.' Convincing the Aiel that he was not on the end of an Aes Sedai leash was the most needed service any of the sisters could do him right now. He would have them all doing jigs, if necessary.

Mandelain adjusted the gray-green patch over his right eye, the way he did when he wanted a moment to think. A thick puckered scar ran up his forehead from behind the leather patch and halfway across his mostly bald head. When he finally spoke, it was only a little less blunt than Rand. 'Some say an Aes Sedai will do anything to have what she wants.'

Indirian lowered heavy white eyebrows and peered down his long nose at his tea. Of only average height for an Aielman, he was shorter than Rand by half a hand, yet everything about him seemed long. The heat of the Waste appeared to have melted away every spare ounce of flesh and a few more besides. His cheekbones stood out sharp, and his eyes were emeralds set in caves. 'I do not like speaking of Aes Sedai.' His deep, rich voice was always a shock, coming from that gaunt face. 'What is done, is done. Let the Wise Ones deal with them.'

'Better to speak of the Shaido dogs,' Janwin said mildly. Which was almost as great a shock, coming from his fierce face. 'Within a few months, less than half a year at most, every Shaido who can be will be dead – or made *gai'shain*.' Just because his voice was soft did not mean he was. The other two nodded; Mandelain smiled eagerly.

They still seemed unconvinced. The Shaido had been the professed reason for this meeting, and no less important for not being the most important. Not unimportant – the Shaido had made trouble long enough – just not on the same page with the Aes Sedai in his book. They did present problems, though. Three clans joining Timolan's Miagoma, already near Kinslayer's Dagger, might well be able to do as Janwin said, but there were those who could not be made *gai'shain* and could not be killed. Some were more critical than others. 'What of the Wise Ones?' he asked.

For a moment their faces became unreadable; not even Aes Sedai could do that so well as Aiel. Facing the One Power did not frighten them, not where it showed, at least; no one could outrun death, so Aiel believed, and a hundred Aes Sedai in a rage could not make a lone Aiel lower the veil once raised. But learning that Wise Ones had taken part in the fighting at Dumai's Wells had hit them like watching the sun rise by night and the moon by day in a blood-red sky.

'Sarinde tells me almost all of the Wise Ones will run with the *algai'd'siswai*,' Indirian said at last, reluctantly. Sarinde was the Wise One who had followed him from Red Springs, clan hold of the Codarra. Or perhaps 'followed' was not the right word; Wise Ones seldom did. In any case, most of the Codarra Wise Ones, and the Shiande and the Daryne, would go north with the spears. 'The Shaido Wise Ones will be ... dealt with ... by Wise Ones.' His mouth twisted with disgust.

'All things change.' Janwin's voice was even softer than usual. He believed, but he did not want to. Wise Ones taking part in battle violated custom as old as the Aiel.

Mandelain set his cup down with exaggerated care. 'Corehuin wishes to see Jair again before the dream ends, and so do I.' Like Bael and Rhuarc, he had two wives; the other chiefs had only one each, except Timolan, but a widowed chief seldom remained so long. The Wise Ones saw to that if he did not. 'Will any of us ever see the sun rise again in the Three-fold Land?'

'I hope so,' Rand said slowly. *As the plow breaks the earth shall he break the lives of men, and all that was shall be consumed in the fire of his eyes. The trumpets of war shall sound at his footsteps, the ravens feed at his voice, and he shall wear a crown of swords.* The Prophecies of the Dragon gave little hope for anything except victory over the Dark One, and only a chance of that. The Prophecy of Rhuidean, the Aiel Prophecy, said he would destroy them. The bleakness swept through the clans because of him and ancient customs were ripped apart. Even without the Aes Sedai, small wonder if some chiefs pondered whether they were right to follow Rand al'Thor, Dragons on his arms or no. 'I hope so.'

'May you always find water and shade, Rand al'Thor,' Indirian said.

After they left, Rand sat frowning into his cup, finding no answers in the dark tea. Finally he set it beside the tray and pushed his sleeves down. Merana's eyes were intent on him, as if trying to pull out his thoughts. There was a hint of impatience about her, too. He had told her to stay in the corner unless she could hear voices. Doubtless she saw no reason why she should not come out now the clan chiefs were gone. Come out, and dig out what had been said.

'Do you think they believe I dance on Aes Sedai strings?' he said.

Young Narishma gave a start. In truth, he was a little older than Rand, but he had the look of a boy five or six years younger. He glanced at Merana as though she had the answer, and shifted his shoulders uncomfortably. 'I . . . do not know, my Lord Dragon.'

Dashiva blinked and stopped murmuring to himself. Tilting his head, bird-like, he eyed Rand sideways. 'Does it matter, so long as they obey?'

'It matters,' Rand said. Dashiva shrugged, and Narishma frowned thoughtfully; neither seemed to understand, yet maybe Narishma could come to.

Maps littered the stone floor behind the throne on its dais, rolled or folded or spread out where he had left them. He shifted some with the toe of his boot. So much to be juggled at once. Northern Cairhien and the mountains called Kinslayer's Dagger, and the region around the city. Illian and the Plains of Maredo out to Far Madding. The island of Tar Valon and all the surrounding towns and villages. Ghealdan and part of Amadicia. Movement and color in his head. Lews Therin moaned and laughed in the distance, faint mad mutters of killing the Asha'man, killing the Forsaken. Killing himself. Alanna stopped weeping, cutting anguish subdued beneath a thin thread of anger. Rand scrubbed his hands through his hair, pressing hard against his temples. What had it been like to be alone inside his own skull? He could not recall.

One of the tall doors opened to admit one of the Maidens who were standing guard in the corridor. Riallin, with vivid yellow-red hair and a grin for everything, actually managed to appear plump. For a Maiden, anyway. 'Berelain sur Paendrag and Annoura Larisen wish to see the *Car'a'carn*,' she announced. Her voice went from warm and friendly on the first name to cold and flat on the second without disturbing her grin.

Rand sighed and opened his mouth to let them enter, but Berelain did not wait. She stormed in, a somewhat calmer Annoura at her heels. The Aes Sedai shied slightly at the sight of Dashiva and Narishma, and stared curiously when she saw Merana standing in her corner. Not so Berelain.

'What is the meaning of this, my Lord Dragon?' she demanded, brandishing the letter he had had delivered to her this morning. She stalked across the floor to shake it under his nose. 'Why am I to return to Mayene? I have governed well here in your name, and you know it. I could not stop Colavaere having herself crowned, but at least I stopped her changing the laws you made. Why am I to be sent away? And why am I told by letter? Not to my face. By letter, thanked for my services and dismissed like a clerk who's done collecting the taxes.'

Even furious, the First of Mayene was one of the most beautiful women Rand had ever seen. Black hair fell in shining waves to her shoulders, framing a face to make a blind man stare. A man could easily drown in her dark eyes. Today she wore shimmering silver silk, thin and clinging and more suited to entertaining a lover in private. In fact, had the neckline been a hair lower, she would not have been able to wear the dress in public. As it was, he was not sure she should. He had told himself when writing that letter that it was because he had too much to do and no time for arguing with her. The truth was, he enjoyed looking at her too much; for some reason, he had begun feeling that was – not exactly wrong, but almost.

As soon as she appeared, Lews Therin gave over ranting to hum softly, the way he did when admiring a woman. Abruptly Rand realized he was thumbing his earlobe, and felt a shock. Instinctively, he knew that was something else Lews Therin did without thinking, like the humming. He pushed his hand to his side, but for an instant it wanted to rise to his ear again.

Burn you, this is my body! The thought was a snarl. *Mine!* Lews Therin's hum stopped in surprise, and confusion; without a sound, the dead man fled, back into the deepest shadows of Rand's brain.

Rand's silence had an effect. Berelain lowered the letter, and her anger receded. A little. Eyes fixed on his, she drew a deep breath that heated his cheeks. 'My Lord Dragon—'

'You know why,' he cut in. Looking only at her eyes was not easy. Oddly, he found himself wishing Min were there. Very odd. Her viewings would be no help now. 'When you returned from that Sea Folk ship this morning, there was a fellow waiting on the dock with a knife.'

Berelain tossed her head contemptuously. 'He came no closer than three steps. I was accompanied by a dozen of the Winged Guards and Lord Captain Gallenne.' Nurelle had led some of the Winged Guards to Dumai's Wells, but Gallenne commanded the Guards as a whole. She had eight hundred of them in the city aside from those who returned with Nurelle. 'You expect me to turn tail because of a cutpurse?'

'Don't play the fool,' he growled. 'A cutpurse, with a dozen soldiers around you?' Color flared in her cheeks; she knew, all right. He gave her no chance for protests or explanations or any other foolishness. 'Dobraine tells me he's already heard whispers in the Palace that you betrayed Colavaere. Those who supported her might be afraid to say boo to me, but they'll pay to have a knife stuck into you.' And Faile, too, according to Dobraine; that was being taken care of. 'But they won't have a chance, because you are going back to Mayene. Dobraine will take your place here until Elayne claims the Sun Throne.'

She spluttered as if he had dumped cold water down her dress. Her eyes grew dangerously large. He had been glad when she stopped being afraid of him, but now he was not so sure. As she opened her mouth to explode, Annoura touched her arm, and her head whipped around. They exchanged a long look, and Berelain's splutters subsided. She smoothed her skirts and vigorously squared her shoulders. Rand looked away hastily.

Merana hovered at the edge of the ward. He wondered whether she had stepped across and dodged back – how else could she stand right on top of what she could not possibly detect? When his head turned, she moved backward until she almost touched the walls, her eyes never leaving him. By her face, she would have poured his tea every day for ten years to hear what was being said.

'My Lord Dragon,' Berelain said, smiling, 'there is still the matter of the Atha'an Miere.' Her voice was warm honey; the curve of her lips would have sparked thoughts of kisses in a stone. 'The Wavemistress Harine is not pleased to be left sitting on her ship so long. I have visited with her a number of times. I can smooth the difficulties there, which I hardly think Lord Dobraine can. I believe the Sea Folk are vital to you whether or not the Prophecies of the Dragon mention them. You are crucial in their prophecies, though they seem reluctant to say exactly how.'

Rand stared. Why was she struggling so hard to keep a difficult job that had offered few thanks from Cairhienin even before some began wanting to kill her? She was a ruler, used to dealing with rulers and embassies, not street thugs and knives in the dark. Warm honey or no warm honey, it was not for any desire to stay near Rand al'Thor. She had ... well, offered herself to him ... once, but the hard fact was that Mayene was a small country, and Berelain used her beauty as a man would a sword, to keep her land from being swallowed by its more powerful neighbor, Tear. And there, simple as that, he had it. 'Berelain, I don't know what else I can do to guarantee Mayene for you, but I will write out any—' Colors swirled so strongly in his head that his tongue froze. Lews Therin cackled. *A woman who knows the danger and isn't afraid is a treasure only a madman would spurn.*

'Guarantees.' Bleakness engulfed honey, and anger bubbled again, cold this time. Annoura plucked at Berelain's sleeve, but she paid the Aes Sedai no heed. 'While I sit in Mayene with your guarantees, others will serve you. They will ask their rewards, and the service I did here will be faded and old, while theirs is bright and new. If the High Lord Weiramon gives you Illian and asks Mayene in return, what will you say? If he gives you Murandy, and Altara, and everything clear to the Aryth Ocean?'

'Will you serve if it still means leaving?' he asked quietly. 'You will be out of my sight, but not out of my mind.' Lews Therin laughed again, in such a way that Rand nearly blushed. He enjoyed looking, but sometimes the things Lews Therin thought ...

Berelain considered him with stubborn eyes, and he could all but see the questions being toted up behind Annoura's, the careful choosing of which to ask.

The door opened again for Riallin. 'An Aes Sedai has come to see the *Car'a'carn.*' She managed to sound cold and uncertain at the same time. 'Her name is Cadsuane Melaidhrin.' A strikingly handsome woman swept in right behind her, iron-gray hair gathered in a bun atop her head and decorated with dangling gold ornaments, and it seemed everything happened at once.

'I thought you were dead,' Annoura gasped, eyes nearly starting out of her head.

Merana darted through the ward, hands outstretched. 'No, Cadsuane!' she screamed. 'You mustn't harm him! You must not!'

Rand's skin tingled as someone in the room embraced *saidar*, perhaps more than one, and swiftly moving well clear of Berelain, he seized hold of the Source, flooding himself with *saidin*, feeling it fill the Asha'man. Dashiva's face twitched as he glared from one Aes Sedai to another. Despite the Power he held, Narishma grasped his sword hilt with both hands and assumed the stance called Leopard in the Tree, on the brink of drawing. Lews Therin snarled of killing and death, kill them all, kill them now. Riallin raised her veil, shouting something, and suddenly a dozen Maidens were in the room, veiling, spears ready. It was hardly surprising that Berelain stood gaping as if everyone had gone mad.

For someone who had caused all that, this Cadsuane seemed remarkably unaffected. She looked at the Maidens and shook her head, golden stars and moons and birds swaying gently. 'Trying to grow decent roses in northern Ghealdan may be near to death, Annoura,' she said drily, 'but it is not quite the grave. Oh, do calm down, Merana, before you frighten someone. One would think you would have grown a little less excitable since putting off novice white.'

Merana opened and closed her mouth, looking abashed of all things, and the tingling vanished abruptly. Rand did not release *saidin*, though, nor did the Asha'man.

'Who are you?' he demanded. 'What Ajah?' Red, by Merana's reaction, but for a Red sister simply to walk in like this, alone, would require suicidal courage. 'What do you want?'

Cadsuane's gaze lingered on him for no more than a moment, and she did not answer. Merana's lips parted, but the gray-haired woman looked at her, raising one eyebrow, and that was that. Merana actually reddened and lowered her eyes. Annoura was still staring at the newcomer as if at a ghost. Or a giant.

Without a word, Cadsuane swept across the room to the two Asha'man, dark green divided skirts swishing. Rand was beginning to get the feeling that she always moved in that rushing glide, graceful yet wasting no time and allowing nothing to impede her. Dashiva stared her up and down, and sneered. Although looking him straight in the face, she did not seem to notice, any more than she appeared to notice Narishma's hands on his sword when she put a finger under his chin, moving his head from side to side before he could jerk back.

'What lovely eyes,' she murmured. Narishma blinked uncertainly, and Dashiva's sneer turned to a grin, but a nasty one that made his former smirk lighthearted in comparison.

'Do nothing,' Rand snapped. Dashiva had the gall to glower at him before sullenly pressing a fist to his chest in the salute the Asha'man used. 'What do you want here, Cadsuane,' Rand went on. 'Look at me, burn you!'

She did, turning just her head. 'So you are Rand al'Thor, the Dragon Reborn. I'd have thought even a child like Moiraine could have taught you a few manners.'

Riallin put the spear from her right hand with those clutched behind her buckler and flashed Maiden handtalk. For once, none laughed. For once, Rand was sure the talk was not a joke about him. 'Be easy, Riallin,' he said, raising a hand. 'All of you, be easy.'

Cadsuane ignored the byplay too, directing a smile to Berelain. 'So this is your Berelain, Annoura. She is more beautiful than I had heard.' The curtsy she made, bowing her head, was quite deep, yet somehow without any suggestion of obeisance, no hint that she was in any way less. It truly was a courtesy, no more. 'My Lady First of Mayene, I must speak with this young man, and I would retain your advisor. I've heard you have undertaken many duties here. I would not keep you from them.' It was as clear a dismissal as could be, short of holding the door open.

Berelain inclined her head graciously, then smoothly turned to Rand and spread her skirts in a curtsy so deep that he worried whether she would remain even as clothed as she was. 'My Lord Dragon,' she intoned, 'I ask your kind permission to withdraw.'

Rand's return bow was not so practiced. 'Granted, my Lady First, as you wish.' He offered her a hand, to help her rise. 'I hope you will consider my proposal.'

'My Lord Dragon, I will serve you wherever and however you desire.' Her voice was all honey again. For Cadsuane's benefit, he supposed. There was certainly no flirtation on her face, only determination. 'Remember Harine,' she added in a whisper.

When the door closed behind Berelain, Cadsuane said, 'It's always good to see children play, don't you think, Merana?' Merana goggled, head swiveling between Rand and the gray-haired sister. Annoura looked as though only willpower held her upright.

Most of the Maidens followed Berelain, apparently deciding there was to be no killing, but Riallin and two others remained before the door, still veiled. It might have been coincidence that there was one for each Aes Sedai. Dashiva also seemed to think any danger past. He leaned back against the wall with a foot propped, lips moving silently, arms folded, apparently watching the Aes Sedai.

Narishma frowned questioningly at Rand, but Rand only shook his head. The woman was deliberately trying to provoke him. The question was, why provoke a man she must know could still her, or kill her, without exerting himself? Lews Therin muttered the same thing. *Why? Why?* Stepping onto the dais, Rand took up the Dragon Scepter from the throne and sat, waiting to see what would happen. The woman was not going to succeed.

'Rather ornate, wouldn't you say?' Cadsuane said to Annoura, looking around. Aside from all the other gold, broad bands of it ran around the walls above the mirrors, and the cornices were nearly two feet of golden scales. 'I've never known whether Cairhienin or Tairens overdo worse, but either can make an Ebou Dari blush, or even a Tinker. Is that a tea tray? I would like some, if it's fresh, and hot.'

Channeling, Rand scooped up the tray, half expecting to see the metal corrode from the taint, and wafted it to the three women. Merana had brought extra cups, and four still stood unused on the tray. He filled these, replaced the teapot and waited. It floated in midair, supported by *saidin*.

Three very different women in appearance, and three distinctly different reactions. Annoura looked at the tray much as might a coiled viper, gave a tiny shake of her head, and took a small step back. Merana drew a deep breath and slowly picked up a cup with a hand that trembled slightly. Knowing a man could channel and being forced to see it were not at all the same. Cadsuane, though, took her cup and sniffed the vapors with a pleased smile. Nothing could tell her which of the three men had poured the tea, yet she looked across her cup straight at Rand, lounging with one leg over the arm of his chair. 'That's a good boy,' she said. The Maidens passed shocked looks above their veils.

Rand quivered. No. She would not provoke him. For whatever reason, that was what she wanted, and she would not! 'I will ask one more time,' he said. Strange, that his voice could be that cold; inside, he was hotter than the hottest fires of *saidin*. 'What do you want? Answer, or leave. By the door or a window; your choice.'

Again Merana began to speak, and again Cadsuane silenced her, this time by a sharp gesture without looking away from him. 'To see you,' she said calmly. 'I am Green Ajah, not Red, but I have worn the shawl longer than any other sister living, and I have faced more men who could channel than any four Reds, maybe than any ten. Not that I hunted them, you understand, but I seem to have a nose.' Calmly, a woman saying she had been to market once or twice in her life. 'Some fought to the bitter end, kicking and screaming even after they were shielded and bound. Some wept and begged, offering gold, anything, their very souls, not to be taken to Tar Valon. Still others wept from relief, meek as lambs, thankful finally to be done with it. Light's truth, they all weep, at the end. There is nothing left for them but tears at the end.'

The heat inside him erupted in rage. Tray and massive teapot hurtled across the room, smashing a mirror with a thunderous crash and bouncing back in a shower of glass, half-flattened pot spraying tea, tray spinning across the floor bent double. Everyone jumped except Cadsuane. Rand leaped from the dais, clutching the Dragon Scepter so hard his knuckles hurt. 'Is that supposed to frighten me?'

he growled. 'Do you expect me to beg, or to be thankful? To weep? Aes Sedai, I could close my hand and crush you.' The hand he held up shook with fury. 'Merana knows why I should. The Light only knows why I don't.'

The woman looked at the battered tea things as if she had all the time in the world. 'Now you know,' she said at last, calm as ever, 'that I know your future, and your present. The Light's mercy fades to nothing for a man who can channel. Some see that and believe the Light denies those men. I do not. Have you begun to hear voices, yet?'

'What do you mean?' he asked slowly. He could feel Lews Therin listening.

The tingle returned to his skin, and he very nearly channeled, but all that happened was that the teapot rose and floated to Cadsuane, turning slowly in the air for her to examine. 'Some men who can channel begin to hear voices.' She spoke almost absently, frowning at the flattened sphere of silver and gold. 'It is a part of the madness. Voices conversing with them, telling them what to do.' The teapot drifted gently to the floor by her feet. 'Have you heard any?'

Startlingly, Dashiva gave a raucous laugh, shoulders shaking. Narishma wet his lips; he might not have been afraid of the woman before, but now he watched her closely as a scorpion.

'I will ask the questions,' Rand said firmly. 'You seem to forget. I am the Dragon Reborn.' *You are real, aren't you?* he wondered. There was no answer. *Lews Therin?* Sometimes the man did not answer, but Aes Sedai always drew him. *Lews Therin?* He was not mad; the voice was real, not imagination. Not madness. A sudden desire to laugh did not help.

Cadsuane sighed. 'You are a young man who has little idea where he is going or why, or what lies ahead. You seem overwrought. Perhaps we can speak when you are more settled. Have you any objection to my taking Merana and Annoura away for a little while? I've seen neither in quite some time.'

Rand gaped at her. She swooped in, insulted him, threatened him, casually announced she knew about the voice in his head, and with that she wanted to leave and talk with Merana and Annoura?

Is she *mad?* Still no answer from Lews Therin. The man was real. He was!

'Go away,' he said. 'Go away, and . . .' He was not mad. 'All of you, get out! Get out!'

Dashiva blinked at him, tilting his head, then shrugged and started for the door. Cadsuane smiled in such a way that he half expected her to tell him again he was a good boy, then gathered up Merana and Annoura and herded them toward the Maidens, who were lowering their veils and frowning worriedly. Narishma looked at him too, hesitating until Rand gestured sharply. Finally they were all gone, and he was alone. Alone.

Convulsively he hurled the Dragon Scepter. The spearpoint stuck quivering in the back of one of the chairs, the tassels swaying.

'I am not mad,' he said to the empty room. Lews Therin had told him things; he would never have escaped Galina's chest without the dead man's voice. But he had used the Power before he ever heard the voice; he had figured out how to call lightning and hurl fire and form a construct that had killed hundreds of Trollocs. But then, maybe that had been Lews Therin, like those memories of climbing trees in a plum orchard, and entering the Hall of the Servants, and a dozen more that crept up on him unawares. And maybe those memories were all fancies, mad dreams of a mad mind, just like the voice.

He realized he was pacing, and could not stop. He felt as if he had to move or his muscles would tear him apart in spasms. 'I am not mad,' he panted. Not yet. 'I am not—' The sound of the door opening made him whirl, hoping for Min.

It was Riallin again, supporting a short stocky woman in a dark blue dress, with hair more gray than not and a blunt face. A haggard, red-eyed face.

He wanted to tell them to go away, to leave him alone. Alone. Was he alone? Was Lews Therin a dream? If only they would leave him . . . Idrien Tarsin was the head of the school he had founded here in Cairhien, a woman so practical he was not sure she believed in the One Power since she could neither see nor touch it. What could reduce her to this state?

He made himself turn toward her. Mad or not, alone or not,

there was no one else to do what had to be done. Not even this small duty. Heavier than a mountain. 'What is the matter?' he asked, making his voice as gentle as he could.

Suddenly weeping, Idrien stumbled to him and collapsed against his chest. When she was coherent enough to tell her story, he felt like weeping too.

CHAPTER 19

Diamonds and Stars

Merana followed closely as she dared on Cadsuane's heels, a hundred questions bubbling on her tongue, but Cadsuane was not a woman whose sleeve you plucked. She decided who she noticed, and when. Annoura held her silence, too, the pair of them drawn along in the other's wake down the palace corridors, down flights of stairs, polished marble at first, then plain dark stone. Merana exchanged glances with her sister Gray, and felt a moment's pang. She did not know the woman, really, but Annoura wore the steely look of a girl on her way to the Mistress of Novices, determined to be brave. They were not novices. They were not children. She opened her mouth – and closed it; intimidated by the gray bun bobbing ahead of her with its dangling moons and stars and birds and fish. Cadsuane was . . . Cadsuane.

Merana had met her once before, or at least listened to her and been spoken to, when she was a novice. Sisters had come from every Ajah to see the woman, filled with an awe they could not hide.

Once Cadsuane Melaidhrin had been the standard by which every new entry into the novice book was judged. Until Elayne Trakand, none had come to the White Tower in her lifetime who could match that standard, much less surpass it. In more ways than one, her like had not walked among Aes Sedai for a thousand years. A refusal to accept selection as a Sitter was unheard of, yet it was said she had refused, and at least twice. It was said she had spurned being raised head of the Green Ajah, too. It was said she once vanished from the Tower for ten years because the Hall intended to raise her Amyrlin. Not that she had ever spent a day more in Tar Valon than absolutely necessary. Word of Cadsuane came to the Tower, stories to make sisters gape, adventures to make those who dreamed of the shawl shiver. She would end a legend among Aes Sedai. If she was not already.

The shawl had graced Merana's shoulders for over twenty-five years when Cadsuane announced her retirement from the world, her hair already solid gray, and everyone assumed her long dead when the Aiel War erupted another twenty-five years on, but before the fighting was three months old, she reappeared, accompanied by two Warders, men long in the tooth yet still hard as iron. It was said Cadsuane had had more Warders over the years than most sisters had shoes. After the Aiel retreated from Tar Valon, she retired once more, but some said, more than half-seriously, that Cadsuane would never die so long as even a spark of adventure remained in the world.

And that is the sort of nonsense that novices babble, Merana reminded herself firmly. *Even we die eventually.* Yet Cadsuane was still Cadsuane. And if she was not one of those sisters who had appeared in the city after al'Thor was taken, the sun would not set tonight. Merana moved her arms to adjust her shawl and realized it was hanging on a peg in her room. Ridiculous. She needed no reminders of who she was. If only it had been someone other than Cadsuane . . .

A pair of Wise Ones standing in the mouth of a crossing corridor watched them pass, cold pale eyes in stony faces beneath their dark head scarves. Edarra and Leyn. Both could channel, and quite strongly; they might have risen high had they gone to the Tower as girls. Cadsuane went by without seeming to notice the wilders' disapprobation. Annoura did, frowning and muttering, slender braids swaying as she shook her head. Merana kept her own eyes on the floor tiles.

Undoubtedly it would fall to her now, explaining to Cadsuane the ... compromise ... that had been worked out with the Wise Ones last night, before she and the others were brought to the Palace. Annoura did not know – she was no part of it – and Merana had small hope that Rafela or Verin would appear, or anyone else she might somehow foist the duty onto. It *was* a compromise, in a way, and perhaps the best that could be expected under the circumstances, yet she strongly questioned whether Cadsuane would see it so. She wished she did not have to be the one to convince her. Better to pour tea for those cursed men for a month. She wished she had not been so free with her tongue with young al'Thor. Knowing why he had made her serve tea was no balm for being sealed off from every advantage she might have gained from it. She would rather think she had been caught in some *ta'veren* swirling of the Pattern than believe that a young man's eyes, like polished blue-gray gems, had set her babbling from pure fright, but either way, she had handed all the advantage to him on a tray. She wished ...

Wishing was for children. She had negotiated countless treaties, many of which had actually accomplished what was intended; she had ended three wars and stopped two dozen more before they began, faced kings and queens and generals and made them see reason. Even so ... She found herself promising that she would not utter one word of complaint no matter how often that man made her play the maidservant if only Seonid would pop around the next corner, or Masuri, or Faeldrin, or anyone at all. Light! If only she could blink her eyes and find that everything since leaving Salidar had been a bad dream.

Surprisingly, Cadsuane led them straight to the small room that Bera and Kiruna shared, deep in the bowels of the Palace. Where the servants lived. A tight window, set high in the wall yet level with the paving stones of a courtyard outside, let in a little stream of light, but the room seemed murky. Cloaks and saddlebags and a few dresses hung from pegs in the cracked, yellowing plaster walls. Gouges marred the bare wooden floor, though some effort had been made to smooth them. A tiny battered round table stood in one corner, and an equally beaten washstand in another, with a chipped basin and pitcher. Merana eyed the small bed. It did not look that much narrower than the one she was forced to share with Seonid *and* Masuri, two doors farther down. That room was larger by perhaps a pace each way, but not meant for three. Coiren and the others still held in the Aiel tents probably were much more comfortable as prisoners.

Neither Bera nor Kiruna was present, but Daigian was, a plump, pale woman who wore a thin silver chain in her long black hair, with a round moonstone dangling in the middle of her forehead. Her dark Cairhienin dress bore four thin stripes of color across the bodice, and she had added slashes in the skirts, white for her Ajah. A younger daughter of one of the lesser Houses, she had always minded Merana of a pouter pigeon. When Cadsuane entered, Daigian rose on her toes expectantly.

There was only one chair in the room, little more than a stool with an excuse of a back. Cadsuane took that and sighed. 'Tea, please. Two sips of what that boy poured, and I could have used my tongue to sole a shoe.'

The glow of *saidar* immediately surrounded Daigian, though faintly, and a dented tin teapot rose from the table, flows of Fire heating the water as she opened a small brass-bound tea chest.

With no other choice for place to sit, Merana settled onto the bed, adjusting her skirts and shifting on the lumpy mattress while she tried to order her thoughts. This might well be as important a negotiation as she had ever undertaken. After a moment, Annoura joined her, perching on the lip of the mattress.

'I take it by your presence, Merana,' Cadsuane said abruptly, 'that tales of the boy submitting to Elaida are false. Don't look so surprised, child. Did you think I didn't know your ... associations?' She gave that word such a twist, it sounded as filthy as any soldier's expletive. 'And you, Annoura?'

'I am here only to advise Berelain, though the truth of it is, she ignored my advice by coming in the first place.' The Taraboner woman held her head up, voice confident. She was rubbing her thumbs for all she was worth, though. She could not do well at the negotiating table if she was that transparent. 'For the rest,' she said carefully, 'I have reached no decision as yet.'

'A wise decision,' Cadsuane murmured, with a pointed look at Merana. 'It seems that in the last few years far too many sisters have forgotten they possess brains, or discretion. There was a time when Aes Sedai reached their decisions after calm deliberation, with the good of the Tower always in the front of their thoughts. Just remember what the Sanche girl got from meddling with al'Thor, Annoura. Walk too near a forge-fire, and you can be burned badly.'

Merana lifted her chin, working her neck to ease its tightness. Realizing what she was doing, she made herself stop. The woman did not stand that far above her. Not really. Just higher than any other sister. 'If I may ask ...' Too diffident, but worse to stop and start over. '... what are your intentions, Cadsuane?' She struggled to maintain dignity. 'Obviously, you have been ... holding yourself aside ... until now. Why have you decided to ... approach ... al'Thor at this particular time? You were ... rather undiplomatic ... with him.'

'You might as well have slapped his face,' Annoura put in, and Merana colored. Of the two of them, Annoura should have been having the harder time with Cadsuane by far, but she was not the one stumbling over her words.

Cadsuane shook her head in pitying style. 'If you want to see what a man is made of, push him from a direction he doesn't expect. There's good metal in that boy, I think, but he's going to be difficult.' Steepling her fingers, she peered across them at the wall, musing to herself. 'He has a rage in him fit to burn the world, and he holds it by a hair. Push him too far off balance ... Phaw! Al'Thor's not so hard yet as Logain Ablar or Mazrim Taim, but a hundred times as difficult, I fear.' Hearing those three names together clove Merana's tongue to the roof of her mouth.

'You have seen Logain and Taim both?' a staring Annoura said. 'Taim, he is following al'Thor, so I hear.' Merana managed to swallow a relieved sigh. Tales of Dumai's Wells had not had time to spread yet. They would, though.

'I do have ears to catch rumors, too, Annoura,' Cadsuane said acerbically. 'Though I could wish I didn't, for what I hear of that pair. All my work thrown away to be done over. Others' as well, but I did my share. And then there are these blackcoats, these Asha'man.' Taking a cup from Daigian, she smiled warmly and murmured thanks. The round-cheeked White seemed ready to curtsy, though all she did was retreat to a corner and fold her hands. She had been longer a novice, and Accepted, than anyone in living memory, barely allowed to remain in the Tower, gaining the ring by a fingernail and the shawl by an eyelash. Daigian was always self-effacing around other sisters.

Breathing the steam from her teacup, Cadsuane went on, suddenly chatting pleasantly. 'It was Logain, practically on my doorstep, that lured me away from my roses. Phaw! A scuffle at a sheep fair could have lured me from those Light-cursed plants. What's the point if you use the Power, but do it without, and you grow ten thousand thorns for every – Phaw! I actually considered taking the oath as a Hunter, if the Council of Nine would allow it. Well. It was a nice few months, chasing down Logain, but once he was taken, escorting him to Tar Valon appealed as much as the roses. I wandered a bit, to see what I could find, perhaps a new Warder, though it's a bit late for that in any fairness to the man, I suppose. Then I heard of Taim, and I was off to Saldaea as fast as I could ride. There's nothing for a bit of excitement like a man who can channel.' Abruptly her voice hardened, and her gaze. 'Were either of you involved in that ... vileness ... right after the Aiel War?'

Despite herself, Merana gave a confused start. The other woman's eyes spoke of the block and the headsman's axe. 'What vileness? I don't know what you are talking about.'

That accusing glare hit Annoura so hard, she almost fell off the bed. 'The Aiel War?' she gasped, steadying herself. 'The years after, I spent trying to make the so-called Grand Coalition more than a name.'

Merana looked at Annoura with interest. A good many of the Gray Ajah had scurried from capital to capital after the war, in a futile effort to hold together the alliance that had formed against the Aiel, but she had never known Annoura was one of them. She could not be that bad a negotiator if she was. 'So did I,' she said.

Dignity. Since setting out after al'Thor from Caemlyn, she had not retained much of that. The few scraps remaining were too precious to lose. She made her voice calm, and firm. 'What vileness do you mean, Cadsuane?'

The gray-haired woman simply waved the question away, as though she had never spoken the word.

For a moment, Merana wondered whether Cadsuane's wits might be wandering. She had never heard of it happening to a sister, but most Aes Sedai did go into retreat at the close of their lives, far apart from the stratagems and turbulence that none but sisters ever knew. Far from everyone, often as not. Who could say what befell them before the end? One look at the clear, steady gaze regarding her over that teacup quickly disabused her of any such notion. Anyway, twenty-year-old vileness, whatever it had been, certainly could not hold a candle to what the world confronted now. And Cadsuane still had not answered her original questions. What did she intend? And why now?

Before Merana could ask again, the door opened and Bera and Kiruna were herded in by Corele Hovian, a boyishly slim Yellow with thick black eyebrows and a mass of raven hair that gave her something of a wild appearance no matter how neatly she dressed, and she always dressed for a country dance, with masses of embroidery on her sleeves and bodice and up the sides of her skirts. There was barely room to move, with so many people in this confined space. Corele never failed to seem amused, whatever happened, but now she wore a wide smile somewhere between disbelief and outright laughter. Kiruna's eyes flashed in a face of frozen arrogance, while Bera fumed, mouth tight and forehead creased. Until they saw Cadsuane. Merana supposed that for them, it must be as if she had found herself face to face with Alind Dyfelle or Sevlana Meseau or even Mabriam en Shereed. Their eyes bulged. Kiruna's jaw dropped.

'I thought you were dead,' Bera breathed.

Cadsuane sniffed irritably. 'I am growing tired of hearing that. The next imbecile I hear it from is going to yelp for a week.' Annoura began studying the toes of her slippers.

'You'll never guess where I found these two,' Corele said in her lilting Murandian accent. She tapped the side of her upturned nose, the way she did when about to tell a joke, or what she saw as one. Spots of color appeared in Bera's cheeks, and larger in Kiruna's. 'Bera there was sitting meek as a mouse under the eyes of half a dozen of those Aiel wilders, who told me bold as you please that she couldn't come with me until Sorilea – oh, now that woman's a harridan to give you nightmares, she is – I couldn't have Bera until Sorilea was done with her private chat with the *other* apprentice. Our darling Kiruna, there.'

It was no longer a matter of spots. Kiruna and Bera reddened to their hair, refusing to meet anyone's eye. Even Daigian stared at them.

Relief surged through Merana in wonderful waves. She would not have to be the one to explain how the Wise Ones had interpreted that wretched al'Thor's orders that the sisters were to obey them. They were not really apprentices; there were no lessons involved, of course. What could a great lot of wilders, savages at that, teach Aes Sedai? It was just that the Wise Ones liked to know where everyone fit. Just? Bera or Kiruna could tell how al'Thor had laughed – laughed! – and said it made no difference to him and he expected them to be *obedient* pupils. No one was having an easy time bending her neck, least of all Kiruna.

Yet Cadsuane did not demand explanations. 'I expected a dog's dinner,' she said dryly, 'but not a bucket from the midden. Let me see if I have the straight of it. You children who stand in rebellion against a lawfully raised Amyrlin have now somehow associated yourselves with the al'Thor boy, and if you are taking orders from these Aiel women, I assume you take his as well.' Her grunt was disgusted enough for a mouthful of rotten plums. Shaking her head, she peered into her teacup, then fixed the pair again. 'Well, what's one treason more or less? The Hall can put you on your knees from here to Tarmon Gai'don for penance, but they can only take your heads once. What of the rest, out in the Aiel camp? All Elaida's, I suppose. Have they also ... *apprenticed* ... themselves? None of us have been allowed as close as the first row of tents. These Aiel seem to have no love of Aes Sedai.'

'I do not know, Cadsuane,' Kiruna answered, so red-faced she appeared about to catch fire. 'We have been kept apart.' Merana's eyes widened. She had never before heard Kiruna sound deferential.

Bera, on the other hand, drew a deep breath. She already stood straight, yet she seemed to straighten herself for an unpleasant task. 'Elaida is not—' she began heatedly.

'Elaida is overambitious, as near as I can make out,' Cadsuane broke in, leaning forward so abruptly that Merana and Annoura both started back on the bed, though she was not looking at them, 'and she may be catastrophe simmering, but she is still the Amyrlin Seat, raised by the Hall of the Tower in full accordance with the laws of the Tower.'

'If Elaida is a lawful Amyrlin, why have you not obeyed her order to return?' All that betrayed Bera's lack of composure was the stillness of her hands on her skirts. Only a marked effort to keep from clutching or smoothing could hold them so motionless.

'So one of you has a little backbone.' Cadsuane laughed softly, but her eyes did not look mirthful at all. Leaning back, she sipped her tea. 'Now sit down. I have a great many more questions.'

Merana and Annoura rose, offering their places on the bed, but Kiruna simply stood peering at Cadsuane worriedly, and Bera glanced at her friend, then shook her head. Corele rolled her blue eyes, grinning broadly for some reason, but Cadsuane did not seem to care.

'Half the rumors I hear,' she said, 'concern the Forsaken being loose. It would hardly be a surprise, with all else, but do you have any evidence, for or against?'

Before very long, Merana was glad to be sitting; before very long, she knew what laundry felt going through the laundress's mangle. Cadsuane did all the questioning, dodging from topic to topic so you never knew what was coming next. Corele held her peace except for chuckling now and then or shaking her head, and Daigian did not even do that, of course. Merana caught the worst, her and Bera and Kiruna, yet Annoura was certainly not spared. Every time Berelain's advisor relaxed, thinking she was in the clear, Cadsuane skewered her anew.

The woman wanted to know everything, from the al'Thor boy's authority with the Aiel to why a Sea Folk Wavemistress was anchored in the river, from whether Moiraine truly was dead to whether the boy really had rediscovered Traveling and whether Berelain had bedded him or had any intention of it. What Cadsuane thought of the answers was impossible to say, except once, when she learned that Alanna had bonded al'Thor, and how. Her mouth compressed to a thin line and she frowned a hole through the wall, but while everyone else expressed disgust, Merana thought of Cadsuane saying she had considered taking another Warder herself.

The answer was ignorance entirely too often to suit, but saying you did not know failed to quench Cadsuane's appetite; she required every last shred and particle you did know, even if you did not know you knew it. They managed to keep a little back, most of what had to be kept back, yet a few surprising things came out that way, some *very* surprising, even from Annoura, who it turned out had been receiving detailed letters from Berelain almost from the day the girl rode north. Cadsuane demanded answers, but gave none, and that worried Merana. She watched faces grow dogged and defensive and apologetic, and wondered whether her own looked anything similar.

'Cadsuane.' She had to make one more effort. 'Cadsuane, why have you decided to take an interest in him now?' An unblinking gaze met hers for a moment, then Cadsuane turned her attention to Bera and Kiruna.

'So they actually managed to kidnap him right out of the palace,' the gray-haired woman said, holding out her empty cup for Daigian to refill. No one else had been offered tea. Cadsuane's expression and tone were so neutral that Merana wanted to tear her own hair. Al'Thor would not be pleased if he learned Kiruna had revealed the kidnapping, however inadvertently; Cadsuane used any slip of your tongue to pry out more than you meant to say. At least the details of his treatment had not come out. He had made plain how displeased he would be if that happened. Merana thanked the Light that the woman was not staying with any one subject for long.

'You are sure it was Taim? And you are sure these blackcoats didn't arrive on horses?' Bera answered reluctantly, and Kiruna sullenly; they were as certain as they could be; no one had actually seen the Asha'man come or depart, and the ... hole ... that brought them all here could have been made by al'Thor. Which did not satisfy at all, of course.

'Think! You aren't silly girls any longer, or shouldn't be. Phaw! You must have noticed something.'

Merana felt ill. She and the others had spent half the night arguing over what their oath meant before deciding it meant exactly what they had said, with no loopholes to wriggle through. At last even Kiruna conceded that they must defend and support al'Thor as well as obey, that standing aside in the slightest was not permitted. What that might mean when it came to Elaida and the sisters loyal to her really concerned no one. At least, no one admitted any concern. The mere fact of what they had decided was stunner enough. But Merana wondered whether Bera or Kiruna had yet realized what she had. They might just find themselves opposing a legend, not to mention whatever sisters besides Corele and Daigian had chosen to follow her. Worse . . . Cadsuane's eyes rested on her for a moment, giving away nothing, demanding everything. Worse, Merana was sure that Cadsuane knew that very well.

Hurrying along the palace corridors, Min ignored greetings from half a dozen Maidens she knew, just trotted right by without a word in return, never considering that she was being rude. Trotting was not easy in heeled boots. The fool things women did for men! Not that Rand had asked her to wear the boots, but she put them on the first time with him in mind, and she had seen him smile. He liked them. Light, what was she doing, thinking about boots! She should never have gone to Colavaere's apartments. Shivering, blinking back unshed tears, she began to run.

As usual, a number of Maidens were squatting on their heels beside the tall doors worked with gilded rising suns. Their *shoufa* hung about their shoulders and their spears lay across their knees, yet there was nothing casual about them. They were leopards, waiting for something to kill. Usually Maidens made Min uneasy, for all they were friendly enough. Today, she would not have cared if they were veiled.

'He is in a foul temper,' Riallin warned, but made no move to stop her. Min was one of the few allowed to enter Rand's presence without being announced. She straightened her coat and tried to settle herself. She was not sure why she had come. Except that Rand made her feel safe. Burn him! She had never needed anyone to feel safe before.

Just inside the room, she stopped, aghast. Automatically, she pushed the door shut behind her. The place was a shambles. A few glittering shards clung to some of the mirror frames, but most of the glass lay scattered across the floor. The dais was on its side, the throne that had stood atop it just gilded flinders where it had been smashed against a wall. One of the stand-lamps, heavy iron beneath the gilt, had been twisted into a hoop. Rand sat in one of the smaller chairs in his shirtsleeves, arms dangling and head back, staring at the ceiling. Staring at nothing. Images danced about him and colored auras flickered and flared; he was like Aes Sedai in that. She had no need of Illuminators when Rand or an Aes Sedai was in sight. He did not move as she walked farther into the room. He did not seem aware of her at all. Shattered bits of mirror crunched beneath her boots. A foul temper, indeed.

Even so, she felt no fear. Not of him; she could not begin to imagine Rand harming her. For him, she felt enough to nearly purge the memory of Colavaere's apartments from her head. She had long since reconciled herself to being hopelessly in love. Nothing else mattered, not that he was an unsophisticated countryman, younger than she, not who or what he was, not that he was doomed to go mad and die if he was not killed first. *I don't even mind having to share him*, she thought, and knew how tightly she was caught if she could lie to herself. That, she had forced herself to accept; Elayne had a part of him, a claim on him, and so did this Aviendha woman she had yet to meet. What could not be mended must be lived with, so her Aunt Jan always said. Especially when your brains had gone soft. Light, she had always prided herself on keeping her wits.

She stopped beside one of the chairs, where the Dragon Scepter had driven into the thick wooden back so hard that the point stood out nearly a hand behind. In love with a man who did not know, who would send her away should he ever become aware. A man she was sure was in love with her. And with Elayne, and this Aviendha, too; that, she rushed by. What could not be mended ... He was in love with her and refused to admit it. Did he think that just because mad Lews Therin Telamon had killed the woman he loved, he was fated to as well?

'I'm glad you came,' he said suddenly, still staring at the ceiling. 'I've been sitting here alone. Alone.' He gave a bitter bark of a laugh. 'Herid Fel is dead.'

'No,' she whispered, 'not that sweet little old man.' Her eyes stung.

'He was torn apart.' Rand's voice was so tired. So empty. 'Idrien fainted when she found him. She lay in a stupor half the night, and was nearly incoherent when finally roused. One of the other women at the school gave her something to make her sleep. She was embarrassed about that. When she came to me, she started crying again and . . . It had to be Shadowspawn. What else could tear a man limb from limb?' Without raising his head, he smacked a fist down on the chair arm so hard the wood creaked. 'But why? Why was he killed? What could he have told me?'

Min tried to think. She truly did. Master Fel was a philosopher; he and Rand discussed everything from the meaning of parts of the Prophecies of the Dragon to the nature of the hole into the Dark One's prison. He let her borrow books, fascinating books, especially where she had to work to puzzle out what it was they said. He had been a philosopher. He would never lend her a book again. Such a gentle old man, wrapped up in a world of thought and startled when he noticed anything outside it. She treasured a note he had written to Rand. He had said she was pretty, that she distracted him. And now he was dead. Light, she had had too much of death.

'I shouldn't have told you, not like that.'

She gave a start; she had not heard Rand cross the room. His fingers brushed her cheek. Wiping away tears. She was crying.

'I'm sorry, Min,' he said softly. 'I am not a very nice person anymore. A man is dead because of me, and all I can do is worry why he was killed.'

Flinging arms around him, she buried her face against his chest. She could not stop crying. She could not stop trembling. 'I went to Colavaere's apartments.' Images flashed in her head. The empty sitting room, all the servants gone. The bedchamber. She did not want to remember, but now she had begun, she could not stop the words tumbling out. 'I thought, since you'd exiled her, maybe there was some way around the viewing I had of her.' Colavaere had been wearing what must have been her finest gown, dark silk that glistened, with falls of delicate aged-ivory Sovarra lace. 'I thought for once it didn't have to be that way. You're *ta'veren*. You can change the Pattern.' Colavaere had donned a necklace and bracelets of emeralds and firedrops, and rings with pearls and rubies, surely her best pieces, and yellow diamonds had been arranged in her hair, a fair imitation of the crown of Cairhien. Her face . . . 'She was in her bedchamber. Hanging from one of the bedposts.' Bulging eyes and protruding tongue in a blackened, swollen face. Toes a foot above the overturned stool. Sobbing helplessly, Min sagged against him.

His arms went around her slowly, gently. 'Oh, Min, you have more pain than pleasure from your gift. If I could take your pain, I would, Min. I would.'

Slowly it penetrated that he was trembling, too. Light, he tried so hard to be iron, to be what he thought the Dragon Reborn must, but it cut him when somebody died because of him, Colavaere probably no less than Fel. He bled for everyone harmed, and tried to pretend he did not.

'Kiss me,' she mumbled. When he did not move, she looked up. He blinked at her uncertainly, eyes now blue, now gray, a morning sky. 'I'm not teasing.' How often had she teased him, sitting on his lap, kissing him, calling him sheepherder because she dared not say his name for fear he might hear the caress? He put up with it because he thought she *was* teasing and would stop if she believed it did not affect him. Hah! Aunt Jan and Aunt Rana said you should not kiss a man unless you intended to marry him, but Aunt Miren seemed to know a little more of the world. She said you should not kiss a man too casually because men fell in love so easily. 'I'm cold inside, sheepherder. Colavaere, and Master Fel . . . I need to feel warm flesh. I need . . . Please?'

His head lowered so slowly. It was a brother's kiss, at first, mild as milk-water, soothing, comforting. Then it became something else. Not at all soothing. Jerking upright, he tried to pull away. 'Min, I can't. I have no right—'

Seizing two handfuls of his hair, she pulled his mouth back down, and after a little while, he stopped fighting. She was not certain whether her hands began tearing at the laces of his shirt first or his at hers, but of one thing she was absolutely sure. If he even tried to stop now, she was going to fetch one of Riallin's spears, all of them, and stab him.

On her way out of the Sun Palace, Cadsuane studied the Aiel wilders she saw as well as she could without being obvious. Corele and Daigian followed in silence; they knew her well enough by now not to disturb her with chatter, which could not be said of all those who paused a few days at Arilyn's little palace before she sent them on. A great many wilders, every one staring at the Aes Sedai as if at flea-ridden curs covered with running sores, tracking mud over a new rug. Some people looked at Aes Sedai with awe or adoration, others with fear or hate, but Cadsuane had never seen contempt before, not even from Whitecloaks. Even so, any people who produced so many wilders should be sending a river of girls to the Tower.

That would have to be seen to eventually, and to the Pit of Doom with custom if need be, but not now. The al'Thor boy needed to be kept intrigued enough that he allowed her near him, and off-balance enough that she could nudge him where she wanted without him realizing. One way or another, anything that might interfere with that must be controlled or suppressed. Nothing could be allowed to influence him, or upset him, in the wrong way. Nothing.

The shiny black coach was waiting in the courtyard behind a patient team of six matched grays. A serving man rushed to open the door painted with a pair of silver stars atop red and green stripes, bowing to the three of them till his bald head was nearly level with his knees. He was in shirtsleeves and breeches. Since coming to the Sun Palace, she had not noticed anyone in livery yet, except a few wearing Dobraine's colors. No doubt the servants were unsure what to wear and afraid to make a mistake.

'I may skin Elaida when I can lay hands on her,' she said as the coach lurched into motion. 'That fool child has made my task nearly impossible.'

And then she laughed so abruptly that Daigian stared before she could control her eyes. Corele's smile widened in anticipation. Neither understood, and she did not try to explain. All of her life, the fastest way to interest her in anything had been to tell her it was impossible. But then, over two hundred and seventy years had passed since she last encountered a task she could not perform. Any day now might be her last, but young al'Thor would be a fitting end to it all.

Chapter 20

Patterns Within Patterns

Contemptuously Sevanna studied her dusty companions, seated in a circle with her in the small clearing. The nearly leafless branches overhead provided a bit of cool shade, and the place where Rand al'Thor had hurled death lay more than a hundred miles to the west, yet the other women's eyes shifted with an air of looking over shoulders. Without sweat tents, none had been able to clean herself properly, no more than a hasty washing of face and hands at day's end. Eight small silver cups, all different, sat by her side on the dead leaves, and a silver pitcher, filled with water, that had been dented in the retreat.

'Either the *Car'a'carn* is not following,' she said abruptly, 'or he has been unable to find us. Either contents me.'

Some of them actually jumped. Tion's round face paled, and Modarra patted her shoulder. Modarra would have been pretty if she was not so tall, if she did not always try to mother everyone within reach. Alarys became much too intent on straightening skirts already neatly spread around her, attempting to ignore what she did not want to see. Meira's thin mouth drew down, but who could say whether for the others' open fear of the *Car'a'carn* or her own? They had reason to be afraid.

Two full days since the battle, and fewer than twenty thousand spears had regrouped around Sevanna. Therava and most of the Wise Ones who had been to the west were still absent, including all the rest who were tied to her. Some of the missing surely were making their way back to Kinslayer's Dagger, but how many would never again see the sun rise? No one remembered such a slaughter, so many dead in so short a time. Even the *algai'd'siswai* were not truly ready to dance the spears again so soon. Reason to be afraid, yet none for showing it, displaying heart and soul on your face like a wetlander, open and naked for all to see.

Rhiale at least seemed to realize that much. 'If we are to do this thing, let us do it,' she muttered, stiff with embarrassment. She was one who had jumped.

Sevanna took the small gray cube from her pouch and placed it atop the brown leaves in the middle of the circle. Someryn put her hands on her knees, leaning over to examine it until she appeared in danger of falling out of her blouse. Her nose nearly touched the cube. Intricate patterns covered every side, and close up you could see smaller patterns within the larger, and still smaller inside those, and a hint of what seemed smaller yet. How they could have been made, the tiniest, so fine, so precise, Sevanna had no idea. Once she had thought the cube stone, but she was no longer certain. Yesterday she had dropped it accidentally on some rocks without marring one line of the carving. If it *was* carving. The thing must be a *ter'angreal*; that they knew.

'The smallest flow possible of Fire must be touched lightly there, on what looks like a twisted crescent moon,' she told them, 'and another there on the top, on that mark like a lightning bolt.' Someryn straightened very quickly.

'What will happen then?' Alarys asked, combing her hair with her fingers. It seemed an absentminded gesture, but she always found ways to remind everyone that her hair was black instead of common yellow or red.

Sevanna smiled. She enjoyed knowing what they did not. 'I will use it to summon the wetlander who gave it to me.'

'That much you told us already,' Rhiale said in a sour voice, and Tion bluntly asked, 'How will it summon him?' She might fear Rand al'Thor, but not a great deal else. Certainly not Sevanna. Belinde lightly stroked the cube with one bony finger, her sun-bleached eyebrows drawn down.

Maintaining a smooth face, Sevanna irritably prevented her hands from fingering a necklace or adjusting her shawl. 'I have told you all you need know.' Considerably more than they needed, in her opinion, but it had been necessary. Otherwise they would all be back with the spears and the other Wise Ones, eating hard bread and dried meat. Or rather they would all be on the move eastward, watching for any sign of other survivors. Watching for any sign of pursuit. With a late start, they might still cover fifty miles before halting. 'Words will not skin the boar, much less kill it. If you have decided to creep back to the mountains and spend your lives running and hiding, then go. If not, then do what you must, and I will do my part.'

Rhiale's blue eyes stared flat defiance, and Tion's gray. Even Modarra looked doubtful, and she and Someryn lay the most solidly in her grasp.

Sevanna waited, outwardly calm, unwilling to tell them again or ask. Inside, her stomach churned with anger. She would not be beaten because these women had pale hearts.

'If we must,' Rhiale sighed at last. Excepting the absent Therava, she resisted most often, but Sevanna had hopes of her. The spine that refused to bend at all was often the most malleable once it gave way. That was as true for women as men. Rhiale and the others turned their eyes to the cube, some frowning.

Sevanna saw nothing, of course. In fact, she realized that if they did nothing, they could claim the cube failed to work, and she would never know.

Abruptly, though, Someryn gasped, and Meira almost whispered, 'It draws more. Look.' She pointed. 'Fire there and there, and Earth, and Air and Spirit, filling the runnels.'

'Not all of them,' Belinde said. 'They could be filled many ways, I think. And there are places where the flows ... twist ... around something that is not there.' Her forehead furrowed. 'It must be drawing the male part, as well.'

Several drew back a little, shifting shawls, brushing skirts as though to rub away dirt. Sevanna would have given anything to see. Almost anything. How could they be such cowards? How could they let it show?

Finally Modarra said, 'I wonder what would happen if we touched it with Fire elsewhere.'

'Power the callbox too much or in the wrong way, and it may melt,' a man's voice said out of the air. 'It could even ex—'

The voice cut off as the other women surged to their feet, peering in among the trees. Alarys and Modarra went so far as to draw their belt knives, though they had no need of steel when they had the One Power. Nothing moved among the sun-streaked shadows, not so much as a bird.

Sevanna did not stir. She had believed perhaps a third of what the wetlander had told her, not including this, in truth, but she recognized Caddar's voice. Wetlanders always had more names, but that was all he had given. A man of many secrets, she suspected. 'Take your places again,' she ordered. 'And put the flows back where they were. How can I summon him if you fear words?'

Rhiale swung around, mouth gaping and eyes incredulous. Undoubtedly wondering how she knew they had stopped channeling; the woman was not thinking clearly. Slowly, uneasily, they settled in the circle again. Rhiale donned a flatter face than anyone else.

'So you are back,' Caddar's voice said from the air. 'Do you have al'Thor?'

Something in his tone warned her. He could not know. But he did. She abandoned all she had prepared to say. 'No, Caddar. But we still must talk. I will meet you in ten days where we first met.' She could reach that valley in Kinslayer's Dagger sooner, but she needed time to prepare. How did he know?

'Well that you told the truth, girl,' Caddar murmured dryly. 'You will learn I do not like being lied to. Maintain the wayline for location, and I will come to you.'

Sevanna stared at the cube in shock. *Girl?* 'What did you say?' she demanded. *Girl!* She could not believe her ears. Rhiale very pointedly did not look at her, and Meira's mouth twisted in a smile, awkward because so seldom used.

Caddar's sigh filled the clearing. 'Tell your Wise One to continue doing exactly what she is doing – nothing else – and I will come to you.' The forced patience in his tone scraped like a grist-stone. When she had what she wanted from the wetlander, she would dress him in *gai'shain* white. No, in black!

'What do you mean, you will come, Caddar?' Silence answered. 'Caddar, where are you?' Silence. 'Caddar?'

The others exchanged uneasy glances.

'Is he mad?' Tion said. Alarys muttered that he must be, and Belinde angrily demanded to know how long they were to continue this nonsense.

'Until I say to stop,' Sevanna said softly, staring at the cube. A prickle of hope wormed through her chest. If he could do this, then surely he could deliver what he had promised. And maybe . . . She would not hope too much. She looked up through the branches that nearly met above the clearing. The sun still had a way to climb to its peak. 'If he has not come by midday, we will go.' It was too much to expect they would not grumble.

'So we sit here like stones?' Alarys tossed her head in a practiced way, sweeping all of her hair over one shoulder. 'For a wetlander?'

'Whatever he promised you, Sevanna,' Rhiale said with a scowl, 'it cannot be worth this.'

'He is mad,' Tion growled.

Modarra nodded toward the cube. 'What if he can still hear?'

Tion sniffed dismissively, and Someryn said, 'How should we care if a man hears what we say? But I do not relish waiting for him.'

'What if he is like those wetlanders in black coats?' Belinde compressed her lips till they nearly matched Meira's.

'Do not be ridiculous,' Alarys sneered. 'Wetlanders kill such men on sight. Whatever the *algai'd'siswai* claim, that must have been the work of the Aes Sedai. And Rand al'Thor.' That name produced a pained silence, but it did not last.

'Caddar must have a cube like this one,' Belinde said. 'He must have a woman with the gift to make it work.'

'An Aes Sedai?' Rhiale made a noise of disgust in her throat. 'If there are ten Aes Sedai with him, let them come. We will deal with them as they deserve.'

Meira laughed, a dry sound as narrow as her face. 'I think you almost begin to believe they did kill Desaine.'

'Watch your tongue!' Rhiale snarled.

'Yes,' Someryn murmured anxiously. 'Careless words might be heard by the wrong ears.'

Tion's laugh was short and unpleasant. 'The lot of you has less courage than one wetlander.' Which made Someryn snap back, of course, and Modarra too, and Meira spoke words that would have brought a challenge had they not been Wise Ones, and Alarys spoke harsher, and Belinde ...

Their squabbling irritated Sevanna, though it guaranteed they would not conspire against her. But that was not why she raised a hand for silence. Rhiale frowned at her, opening her mouth, and in that moment they heard what she did. Something rustled in the dead leaves among the trees. No Aiel would make so much noise, even if any would approach Wise Ones unbidden, and no animal would come so near people. This time, she rose to her feet with the others.

Two shapes appeared, a man and a woman, breaking enough branches underfoot to wake a stone. Just short of the clearing, they stopped, and the man bent his head slightly to speak to the woman. It was Caddar, in a nearly black coat with lace at his neck and wrists. At least he did not wear a sword. They seemed to be arguing. Sevanna should have been able to hear something of their words, yet the silence was complete. Caddar stood nearly a hand taller than Modarra — tall for a wetlander, or even for an Aiel — and the woman's head reached no higher than his chest. As dark of face and hair as he, and beautiful enough to tighten Sevanna's mouth, she wore bright red silk, cut to expose even more of her bosom than Someryn showed.

As if thinking of the woman called her, Someryn drew close to Sevanna. 'The woman has the gift,' she whispered without taking her eyes from the pair. 'She weaves a barrier.' Pursing her lips, she added, reluctantly, 'She is strong. Very strong.' From her, that meant something indeed. Sevanna had never been able to understand why strength in the Power did not count among Wise Ones — while being thankful that it did not, for her own sake — but Someryn prided herself that she had never encountered a woman near as strong as she. By her tone, Sevanna suspected this woman was stronger.

Right then, she did not care whether the woman could move mountains or barely light a candle. She must be Aes Sedai. She did not have the face, yet some Sevanna had seen did not. That must be how Caddar could put his hand on *ter'angreal*. That was how he could find them and come. So soon; so quickly. Possibilities unfolded, and hope grew. But between him and her, who commanded?

'Stop channeling into that,' she ordered. He might still be able to hear through it.

Rhiale gave her a look that did not stop short of pity. 'Someryn already did, Sevanna.'

Nothing could spoil her mood. She smiled and said, 'Very well. Remember what I said. Let me do all of the talking.' Most of the others nodded; Rhiale sniffed. Sevanna kept her smile. A Wise One could not be made *gai'shain*, but so many worn-out customs had been set aside already that others might follow.

Caddar and the woman started forward, and Someryn whispered again. 'She still holds the Power.'

'Sit next to me,' Sevanna told her hastily. 'Touch my leg if she channels.' How that galled. But she must know.

She sat folding her legs under, and the others joined her, leaving a space for Caddar and the woman. Someryn sat close enough that their knees touched. Sevanna wished she had a chair.

'I see you, Caddar,' she said formally, in spite of his insult. 'Sit, you and your woman.'

She wanted to see how the Aes Sedai reacted, but all she did was arch an eyebrow and smile lazily. Her eyes were as black as his, as black as a raven's. The other Wise Ones let a little coldness show. Had the Aes Sedai at the wells not allowed Rand al'Thor to break free, they surely would have killed or captured every one. This Aes

Sedai must be aware of that, since Caddar plainly knew what had happened, yet she looked anything but afraid.

'This is Maisia,' Caddar said, lowering himself to the ground, a little short of the space left for him. For some reason, he did not like to come within arm's reach. Perhaps he feared knives. 'I told you to use a single Wise One, Sevanna, not seven. Some men might be suspicious.' For some reason, he seemed amused.

The woman, Maisia, paused in the act of smoothing her skirts under when he gave her name, glaring at him with a fury that should have stripped his hide away. Perhaps she had thought to keep her identity hidden. She said nothing, though. After a moment she sat beside him, her smile returning so suddenly it might never have gone. Not for the first time, Sevanna was thankful that wetlanders wore their emotions on their faces.

'You have brought the thing that can control Rand al'Thor?' She did not even glance at the pitcher of water. When he was so rude, why should she continue the forms? She did not remember him being so when they met before. Perhaps the Aes Sedai emboldened him.

Caddar gave her a quizzical look. 'Why, when you do not have him?'

'I will,' she said levelly, and he smiled. So did Maisia.

'When you do, then.' His smile shouted of doubt and disbelief. The woman's mocked. A black robe could be found for her, too. 'What I have will control him once he is taken, but it cannot overcome him. I won't risk him finding out about me until you have him secure.' He did not appear shamed in the slightest by the admission.

Sevanna forced down a stab of disappointment. One hope gone, but others remained. Rhiale and Tion folded their hands and stared straight ahead, beyond the circle, beyond him; he was no longer worth listening to. Of course, they did not know everything.

'What of Aes Sedai? Can this thing control them?' Rhiale and Tion stopped peering beyond the trees. Belinde's eyebrows twitched, and Meira actually looked at her. Sevanna could have cursed their lack of self-control.

Caddar was as blind as all wetlanders, though. He threw back his head and laughed. 'Do you mean to say you missed al'Thor but captured Aes Sedai? You grabbed at the eagle and caught a few larks!'

'Can you provide the same for Aes Sedai?' She wanted to grind her teeth. Surely he had been properly courteous before.

He shrugged. 'Perhaps. If the price is right.' It was dust to him, of no moment. For that matter, Maisia showed no concern either. Strange, if she was Aes Sedai. But she must be.

'Your tongue tosses bright colors on the wind, wetlander,' Tion said in a flat voice. 'What proof of them have you?' For once, Sevanna did not mind that she had spoken out of turn.

Caddar's face tightened for all the world as if he were a clan chief, as if he had heard the insult, but in an instant he was all smiles once more. 'As you wish. Maisia, play with the callbox for them.'

Someryn shifted her skirts, pressing her knuckles against Sevanna's thigh as the gray cube rose a pace into the air. It bounced back and forth as though tossed from hand to hand, then tilted and spun on one corner like a top, faster and faster, until it blurred.

'Would you like to see her balance it on her nose?' Caddar asked with a toothy grin.

Tight-eyed, the dark woman stared straight ahead, her smile clearly forced now. 'I think I have *demonstrated* quite enough, Caddar,' she said coldly. But the cube – the callbox? – continued whirling.

Sevanna waited a slow count of twenty before saying, 'That is sufficient.'

'You may stop now, Maisia,' Caddar said. 'Put it back where it was.' Only then did the cube slowly descend, nestling gently on its original spot. Dark as she was, the woman looked pale. And furious.

Had she been alone, Sevanna would have laughed, and danced. As it was, she had difficulty maintaining a smooth face. Rhiale and the others were too busy staring disdainfully at Maisia to notice. What worked on one woman with the gift would work on another. No need with Someryn and Modarra, perhaps, but Rhiale, and Therava ... She could not appear too eager, not when the others knew there were no Aes Sedai captives.

'Of course,' Caddar went on, 'it will take a little time to provide you with what you wish.' He took on a sly look, trying to hide it;

perhaps another wetlander would not have seen. 'I warn you, the price will not be small.'

In spite of herself, Sevanna leaned forward. 'And the way you traveled here so quickly? How much to make her teach us that?' She managed to keep eagerness from her voice, but she was afraid the contempt she felt came through. Wetlanders would do anything for gold.

Perhaps the man heard it; his eyes certainly widened in surprise before he could regain control. Such as it was. He studied his hands, and his mouth curled faintly. Why should his smile seem pleased? 'That is not something she does,' he said in a voice as smooth as his palms, 'not by herself. It is like the callbox. I can provide you with several, but the price of those is even higher. I doubt what you've gleaned from Cairhien will be enough. Fortunately, you can use the ... traveling boxes to take your people to richer lands.'

Even Meira was hard-pressed to keep her expression from becoming too avid. Richer lands, and no need to make a way through those fools following Rand al'Thor.

'Tell me more,' Sevanna said coolly. 'Richer lands might be of some interest.' Not enough to make her forget the *Car'a'carn*, though. Caddar would give her everything he had promised before she declared him *da'tsang*. As well that he seemed to like wearing black. There would be no need to give him any gold then.

The watcher ghosted through the trees, making no sound. It was wonderful what you could learn with a callbox, especially in a world where there seemed to be only two others. That red dress was easy to follow, and they never looked back even to see whether some of those so-called Aiel were trailing them. Graendal maintained the Mirror of Mists that hid her true form, but Sammael had dropped his, golden-bearded again and just head and shoulders taller than she. He had let the link between them dissolve, too. The watcher wondered whether that was wise, under the circumstances. He had always wondered how much of Sammael's vaunted bravery was really stupidity and blindness. But the man did hold *saidin*; perhaps he was not completely unaware of his danger.

The watcher followed and listened. They had no idea. The True

Power, drawn directly from the Great Lord, could neither be seen nor detected except by who wielded it. Black flecks floated across his vision. There was a price, to be sure, one that grew with each use, but he had always been willing to pay the price when it was necessary. Being filled with the True Power was almost like kneeling beneath Shayol Ghul, basking in the Great Lord's glory. The glory was worth the pain.

'Of course I had to have you with me,' Sammael growled, stumbling over a dead vine. He had never really been at home away from the cities. 'You answered a hundred questions for them just being there. I can hardly believe that silly girl herself actually suggested what I wanted.' He barked a laugh. 'Perhaps I'm *ta'veren* myself.'

A branch that partially blocked Graendal's path flexed away until it snapped with a sharp crack. For a moment it hung in the air as if she intended to strike her companion. 'That silly girl will cut out your heart and eat it, given half a chance.' The branch flew aside. 'I have a few questions of my own. I never thought you would keep your truce with al'Thor any longer than you must, but this . . . ?'

The watcher's eyebrows rose. A truce? A claim as risky as it was false, by all evidence.

'I didn't arrange his kidnapping.' Sammael gave her what he probably thought was a wry look; his scar made it more a snarl. 'Mesaana had a hand in it, though. Maybe Demandred and Semirhage as well, despite how it ended, but Mesaana certainly. Perhaps you ought to reconsider what you think the Great Lord means about leaving al'Thor unharmed.'

Graendal considered that, so much so that she tripped. Sammael caught her by the arm, keeping her on her feet, but as soon as she regained her balance, she jerked free. Interesting, even given what had happened back in that clearing. Graendal's real interest was always the most beautiful plucked from among the most powerful, but she would have flirted, just to pass an hour, with a man she intended to kill or one who wanted to kill her. The only men she never flirted with were those of the Chosen who stood above her for a time. She never accepted being the lesser of any pair.

'Then why continue with them?' Her voice dripped molten lava, although normally she had exquisite control over her emotions.

'Al'Thor in Mesaana's hands is one thing; al'Thor in this savage's is something else. Not that she'll have much chance at him if you really intend sending them off to loot. *Traveling* boxes? What is your game there? Do they hold captives? If you think I will teach them Compulsion, erase it from your mind. One of those women was not negligible. I will not risk strength and skill residing together, in her, or in someone she teaches. Or do you have a binder hidden away with your other toys? For that matter, where were you earlier? I do not like having to wait!'

Sammael stopped, glancing behind them. The watcher stood very still. Swathed in fancloth except for his eyes, he had no worry that he would be seen. Over the years he had learned expertise in many areas Sammael scorned. In some he favored, too.

The gateway opening suddenly, slicing away half of a tree, made Graendal jump. The split trunk leaned drunkenly. Now she also knew Sammael held to the Source.

'Did you think I was telling them the truth?' Sammael said mockingly. 'Small increases in chaos are as important as large. They will go where I send them, do as I wish, and learn to be satisfied with what I give them. As will you, Maisia.'

Graendal let her Illusion fade and stood golden-haired as he, as fair as she had been dark. 'If you call me that again, I will kill you.' Her voice held even less expression than her face. She meant it. The watcher tensed. If she tried, one of the two would die. Should he interfere? Black flecks sped across his eyes, faster, faster.

Sammael met her stare with one just as hard. 'Remember who will be Nae'blis, Graendal,' he said, and stepped through his gateway.

For a moment she stood looking at the opening. A vertical silver slash appeared off to one side, but before her gateway began to align, she let go the weave, slowly, the streak shrinking to a point before winking out. The prickling vanished from the watcher's skin as she released *saidar* as well. With a fixed face, she followed Sammael, and his gateway closed behind her.

The watcher smiled crookedly behind his fancloth skulker's mask. Nae'blis. That explained what had brought Graendal to heel, what had stayed her from killing Sammael. Even she would be blinded by that. An even greater risk for Sammael than claiming truce with Lews Therin, though. Unless, of course, it was true. The Great Lord delighted in setting his servants one against another, to see who was stronger. Only the strongest could stand near his glory. But today's truth need not be tomorrow's. The watcher had seen truth change a hundred times between a single sunrise and sunset. More than once he had changed it himself. He considered going back and killing the eight women in the clearing. They would die easily; he doubted they knew how to form a true circle. The black flecks filled his eyes, a horizontal blizzard. No, he would let that run its course. For now.

To his ears, the world screamed as he used the True Power to rip a small hole and step outside the Pattern. Sammael did not know how truly he spoke. Small increases in chaos could be every bit as important as large.

Chapter 21

Swovan Night

Night came slowly over Ebou Dar, the glow of the white buildings resisting darkness. Small knots and bunches of Swovan Night revelers with little sprigs of evergreen in their hair danced in the streets beneath a bright three-quarter moon, few carrying so much as a lantern as they gamboled to the music of flutes and drums and horns that drifted from inns and palaces, dancing their way from one set of festivities to another, but for the most part the streets lay empty. A distant dog barked, and another, closer, answered furiously until it suddenly yelped and fell silent.

Balanced on his toes, Mat listened, eyes searching the moonshadows. Only a cat moved, slinking along the street. The slap of running bare feet faded. The owner of one pair should be staggering, and the other bleeding. As he bent, his foot kicked a club as long as his arm on the paving stones; heavy brass studs shone in the moonlight. That would have broken his skull for sure. Shaking his head, he wiped his knife on the ragged coat worn by the man at his feet. Open eyes stared at the night sky from a dirty, creased face. A beggar, by the look and smell of him. Mat had not heard of beggars attacking people, but maybe times were harder than he thought. A large jute sack lay near one outstretched hand. The fellows certainly had been optimistic about what they would find in his pockets. The thing could have covered him from head to knees.

To the north, above the city, light suddenly burst in the sky with a hollow boom as glittering streaks of green expanded in a ball, and then another eruption showered red sparkles through the first, then a blue, and a yellow. Illuminators' nightflowers, not as spectacular as they would have been in a moonless, cloudy sky, yet still they took his breath. He could watch fireworks till he fell over from hunger. Nalesean had spoken of an Illuminator – Light, was that only this morning? – but no more nightflowers came. When Illuminators made the sky bloom, as they said, they planted more than four flowers. Plainly someone with coin had made a purchase for Swovan Night. He wished he knew who. An Illuminator who would sell nightflowers would sell more than that.

Slipping the knife back up his sleeve, he gathered his hat from the pavement and walked away hurriedly, his boots echoing, a sound empty as the street. Most shuttered windows here showed not a glimmer of light. A better place for murder probably could not be found in the city. The entire encounter with the three beggars had lasted only a minute or two and had been seen by no one. In this city, you could find three or four fights in a day if you were not careful, but the odds of facing two sets of robbers in one day seemed about as great as the odds of the Civil Guard refusing a bribe. What was happening to his luck? If only those bloody dice would stop rolling in his head. He did not run, but he did not dawdle either, one hand on a hilt beneath his coat and an eye open for anyone moving in the shadows. He saw nothing but a few clumps of people cavorting along the street, though.

In the common room of The Wandering Woman, the tables had been cleared away except for a few near the walls. The flutists and the drummer made shrill music for four laughing lines of people doing what appeared to be half pattern-dance and half jig. Watching, he copied a step. Outland merchants in fine woolens leaped right along with locals in brocaded silk vests or those useless coats slung on their shoulders. He marked out two of the merchants for the way they moved, one slender and one not, yet both with a light grace, and several local women wearing their best, the deep necklines outlined by a little lace or a great deal of embroidery, but none in silk. Not that he would refuse to dance with a woman in silk, of course – he had never turned down a dance with any woman of any age or station – but the rich were in the palaces tonight, or the homes of the wealthier merchants and moneylenders. Those folk near the walls, catching their breath for the next dance, had their faces buried in mugs often as not, or were snatching fresh mugs from trays carried by scurrying serving women. Mistress Anan likely would sell as much wine tonight as in an ordinary week. Ale, too; the local folk must have no taste to their tongues.

Trying another step of the dance, he caught Caira as she tried to hurry by with a tray, pitching his voice loud above the music to ask a few questions and finishing with an order for his dinner, gilded fish, a tangy dish that Mistress Anan's cook prepared to perfection. A man needed his strength to keep up in the dance.

Caira flashed a sultry smile at a fellow in a yellow vest who grabbed a mug from her tray and dropped his coin on it, but for once she had no smile for Mat. In fact, she managed to compress her mouth to a thin line, no small feat. 'Your little rabbit, am I?' With a telling sniff, she went on impatiently. 'The boy is tucked into his bed, where he should be, and I don't know where Lord Nalesean is, or Harnan, or Master Vanin, or anybody else. And Cook said she won't fix anything but soup and bread for those as are drowning their tongues in wine. Though why my Lord wants gilded fish when he has a gilded woman waiting in his room, I'm sure I couldn't say. If my Lord will excuse me, some people need to work for their crust.' She swooped away, proffering her tray and smiling fit to split her face at every man in sight.

Mat frowned after her. A gilded woman? In his room? The chest of gold rested now in a small hollow beneath the kitchen floor, in front of one of the stoves, but the dice in his head drummed like thunder suddenly.

The sounds of merriment faded a little as he slowly climbed the stairs. In front of his door, he paused, listening to the dice. Two attempts to rob him so far today. Twice his skull could have been broken. He was sure that Darkfriend had not seen him, and no one could call her gilded, but ... He fingered a hilt under his coat, then took his hand away as a woman flared in his thoughts, a tall woman falling with the hilt of a knife protruding between her breasts. His knife. Luck would just have to be with him. Sighing, he pushed open the door.

The Hunter that Elayne had made her Warder turned, hefting his unstrung Two Rivers bow, her golden braid drawn over her shoulder. Her blue eyes fastened on him purposefully, and her face fixed itself in determination. She looked ready to drub him with the bow if she did not get what she wanted.

'If this is about Olver,' he began, and suddenly a twist of memory unfolded, a mist thinned over one day, one hour in his life.

There was no hope, with Seanchan to the west and Whitecloaks to the east, no hope and only one chance, so he raised the curled Horn and blew, not really knowing what to expect. The sound came golden as the Horn, so sweet he did not know whether to laugh or cry. It echoed, and the earth and heavens seemed to sing. While that one pure note hung in the air, a fog began to rise, appearing from nowhere, thin wisps, thickening, billowing higher, until all was obscured as if clouds covered the land. And down the clouds they rode, as though down a mountainside, the dead heroes of legend, bound to be called back by the Horn of Valere. Artur Hawkwing himself led, tall and hook-nosed, and behind came the rest, little more than a hundred. So few, but all those the Wheel would spin out again and again to guide the Pattern, to make legend and myth. Mikel of the Pure Heart, and Shivan the Hunter behind his black mask. He was said to herald the end of Ages, the destruction of what had been and the birth of what was to be, he and his sister Calian, called the Chooser, who rode red-masked at his side. Amaresu, with the Sword of the Sun glowing in her hands, and Paedrig, the golden-tongued peacemaker, and there, carrying the silver bow with which she never missed . . .

He pushed the door shut trying to lean against it. He felt dizzy, dazed. 'You are she. Birgitte, for true. Burn my bones to ash, it's impossible. How? How?'

The woman of legend gave a resigned sigh and propped his bow back in the corner next to his spear. 'I was ripped out untimely, Hornsounder, cast out by Moghedien to die and saved by Elayne's bonding.' She spoke slowly, studying him as if to be sure he understood. 'I feared you might remember who I used to be.'

Still feeling hit between the eyes, he flung himself scowling into the armchair beside his table. Who she used to be, indeed. Fists on hips, she confronted him challengingly, no whit different from the Birgitte he had seen ride out of the sky. Even her clothes were the same, though this short coat was red and the wide trousers yellow. 'Elayne and Nynaeve know and kept it from me, true? I weary of secrets, Birgitte, and they harbor secrets as a grain barn harbors rats. They've become Aes Sedai, eyes and hearts. Even Nynaeve is twice a stranger, now.'

'You have your own secrets.' Folding her arms under her breasts, she sat on the foot of his bed. The way she looked at him, you would have thought he was a tavern puzzle. 'For one, you've not told them you blew the Horn of Valere. The smallest of your secrets from them, I think.'

Mat blinked. He had assumed they had told her. After all, she was Birgitte. 'What secrets do I have? Those women know my toe-nails and dreams.' She was Birgitte. Of course. He leaned forward. 'Make them see reason. You're Birgitte Silverbow. You can make them do as you say. This city has a pit-trap at every crossing, and I fear the stakes grow sharper by the day. Make them come away before it's too late.'

She laughed. Put a hand over her mouth and laughed! 'You have the wrong end, Hornsounder. I do not command them. I am

Elayne's Warder. I obey.' Her smile became rueful. 'Birgitte Silverbow. Faith of the Light, I'm not sure I still am that woman. So much of what I was and knew has faded like mist beneath the summer sun since my strange new birth. I'm no hero now, only another woman to make my way. And as for your secrets. What language do we speak, Hornsounder?'

He opened his mouth ... and stopped, really hearing what she had just asked. *Nosane iro gavane domorakoshi, Diynen'd'ma'purvene?* Speak we what language, Sounder of the Horn? The hair on his neck tried to stand. 'The old blood,' he said carefully. Not in the Old Tongue. 'An Aes Sedai once told me the old blood runs strong in— What are you bloody well laughing at now?'

'You, Mat,' she managed while trying not to double over. At least she was not speaking the Old Tongue anymore either. She knuckled a tear from the corner of her eye. 'Some people speak a few words, a phrase or two, because of the old blood. Usually without understanding what they say, or not quite. But you ... One sentence you're an Eharoni High Prince and the next a First Lord of Manetheren, accent and idiom perfect. No, don't worry. Your secret is safe with me.' She hesitated. 'Is mine with you?'

He waved a hand, still too flabbergasted to be offended. 'Do I look like my tongue flaps?' he muttered. Birgitte! In the flesh! 'Burn me, I could use a drink.' Before that was out of his mouth he knew it was the wrong thing to say. Women never—

'That sounds the right notion to me,' she said. 'I could use a pitcher of wine, myself. Blood and ashes, when I saw you'd recognized me, I nearly swallowed my tongue.'

He sat up straight as if he had been jerked, staring.

She met his gaze with a merry twinkle and a grin. 'There's enough noise in the common room, we could talk without being overheard. Besides, I wouldn't mind sitting and looking a bit. Elayne preaches like a Tovan councilor if I ogle a man for longer than a heartbeat.'

He nodded before he thought. Other men's memories told him Tovans were a stark and disapproving people, abstemious to the point of pain; at least they had been, a thousand years gone and more. He was not sure whether to laugh or groan. On the one hand, a chance to talk with Birgitte – Birgitte! He doubted he would ever get over the shock – but on the other, he doubted he would be able to hear the music downstairs for the noise of those dice rattling in his skull. She must be a key to it, somehow. A man with any brains would climb out the window right now. 'A pitcher or two sounds fine to me,' he told her.

A stiff salt breeze up from the bay carried a touch of coolness, for a wonder, but the night felt oppressive to Nynaeve. Music and snatches of laughter drifted into the palace, and faintly from within as well. She had been invited to the ball by Tylin herself, and Elayne and Aviendha too, but all declined, with varying degrees of politeness. Aviendha had said there was only one dance she was willing to do with wetlander men, which made Tylin blink uncertainly. For herself, Nynaeve would have liked to go – only a fool passed up any chance to dance – yet she knew if she had, she would have done exactly what she was doing, sat somewhere worrying and trying not to chew her knuckle to a nub.

So there they all were, closeted in their apartments with Thom and Juilin, anxious as caged cats, while everyone else in Ebou Dar made merry. Well, she was, anyway. What could be keeping Birgitte? How long did it take to tell a man to present himself first thing in the morning? Light, the whole effort was useless, and it was long past time for bed. Long past. If she could only sleep, she could put away memories of the morning's horrible journeys by boat. Worst of all, her weather sense told her a storm was on the way, told her the wind should be howling outside and the rain sheeting down so thick no one could see ten feet. It had taken her some time to understand about the times she Listened to the Wind and seemed to hear lies. At least, she thought she understood. Another kind of storm was coming, not wind or rain. She had no proof, but she would eat her slippers if Mat Cauthon was not part of it somehow. She wanted to sleep for a month, a year, to forget worries until Lan wakened her with a kiss like the Sun King with Talia. Which was ridiculous, of course; that was only a story, and a very improper one at that, and anyway, she was not about to become any man's pet, not even Lan's. She would find him, though, somehow, and bond him hers. She would ... Light! If she had not thought the others would stare at her, she would have paced the soles out of her slippers!

The hours wore on. She read and re-read the short letter Mat had left with Tylin. Aviendha sat quietly beside her high-backed chair, cross-legged on the pale green floor tiles as usual, an ornately gilded leather-bound copy of *The Travels of Jain Farstrider* open on her knees. No anxiety there, not to see, but then the woman would not turn a hair if someone stuffed a viper down her dress. Since returning to the palace she had donned the intricate silver necklace she wore nearly day and night. Except on the boat trip; she had said she did not want to risk it, then. Idly, Nynaeve wondered why she no longer wore her ivory bracelet. There had been an overheard conversation, something about not wearing it until Elayne had its like, which made little sense. And mattered as little as the bracelet, of course. The letter called from her lap.

The sitting-room stand-lamps made reading easy, though Mat's unformed, boyish hand did present difficulties. It was the contents that clenched Nynaeve's middle into knots.

There's nothing here but heat and flies, and we can find plenty of those in Caemlyn.

'Are you sure you didn't tell him anything?' she demanded.

Across the room, Juilin paused with his hand over the stones board, giving her a look of outraged innocence. 'How often must I say so?' Outraged innocence was one of the things men did best, especially when they were guilty as foxes in the henyard. Interesting that the carving around the board's rim was of foxes.

Thom, seated across the lapis-inlaid table from the thief-catcher, looked as little the gleeman in his finely cut coat of bronze wool as he did the man who had once been Queen Morgase's lover. Gnarled and white-haired, with long mustaches and thick eyebrows, he was frustrated patience from his sharp blue eyes to his boot soles. 'I can't see how we could have, Nynaeve,' he said dryly, 'given that you told us next to nothing until tonight. You should have sent Juilin and me.'

Nynaeve sniffed loudly. As if those two had not been running around like chickens with their heads off ever since they arrived, prying into her and Elayne's affairs on Mat's say-so. Those three could not be together two minutes without gossiping, either. Men never could. They ... The truth of it was, she admitted reluctantly, using the men had never occurred to them. 'You'd have gone off carousing and drinking with him,' she muttered. 'Don't tell me you would not.' That must be where Mat was, leaving Birgitte to cool her feet at the inn. That man would find some way to set the whole scheme awry.

'And what if they had?' Leaning beside one of the tall arched windows, peering out at the night through the white-painted iron balcony, Elayne giggled. She was tapping her foot, though how she could make out one tune from all those floating in the darkness was a wonder. 'It is a night for ... carousing.'

Nynaeve frowned at her back. Elayne had been increasingly peculiar all night. If she had not known better, she would have suspected the other woman had been sneaking out to snatch sips of wine. Gulps of it, actually. Even if Elayne had not been under her eye, though, that was impossible. Each of them had had a rather unfortunate experience with too much wine, and neither had again let herself have more than a single cup at a time.

'It is Jaichim Carridin who interests me,' Aviendha said, closing the book and setting it beside her. She refused to consider how odd she looked, sitting on the floor in a blue silk dress. 'Among us, Shadowrunners are killed as soon as found, and not clan, sept, society or first-sister will raise a hand in protest. If Jaichim Carridin is a Shadowrunner, why does Tylin Mitsobar not kill him? Why do we not?'

'Matters are a little more complex here,' Nynaeve told her, though she had wondered the same. Not why Carridin was not killed, of course, but why he was still allowed to come and go as he wished. She had seen him in the palace that very day, after she had been handed Mat's letter, after she had told Tylin what it contained. He had spoken with Tylin above an hour and departed with as much honor as he arrived. She had meant to discuss it with Elayne, but the question of what Mat knew, and how, kept intruding. That man would make trouble. He would, somehow. This business was going to go wrong no matter what anyone said. Bad weather was coming.

Thom cleared his throat. 'Tylin is a weak queen, and Carridin the ambassador of a power.' Placing a stone, he kept his eyes on the board. He sounded as though he was thinking aloud. 'By definition, a Whitecloak Inquisitor cannot be a Darkfriend; at least, that's how it is defined in the Fortress of the Light. If she arrests him, or even charges him, she'll find a Whitecloak legion in Ebou Dar before she can blink. They might leave her the throne, but she'd be a puppet from then on, strings pulled from the Dome of Truth. Aren't you ready to concede yet, Juilin?' The thief-catcher glared at him, then bent to a furious study of the board.

'I did not think her a coward,' Aviendha said disgustedly, and Thom gave her an amused smile.

'You have never faced something you could not fight, child,' he said gently, 'something so strong your only choice is to flee or be consumed alive. Try to hold judgment on Tylin till you have.' For some reason, Aviendha's face reddened. Normally, she hid her emotions so well her face was like stone.

'I know,' Elayne said suddenly. 'We'll find proof even Pedron Niall must accept.' She skipped back into the room. No, she danced. 'We will disguise ourselves and follow him.'

Suddenly, it was no longer Elayne standing there in a green Ebou Dari gown, but a Domani woman in thin clinging blue. Nynaeve leaped up before she could stop, and her mouth tightened with exasperation at herself. Just because she could not see the weaves at the moment was no reason to be startled by Illusion. She darted a glance at Thom and Juilin. Even Thom's mouth hung open. Unconsciously she took a firm grip on her braid. Elayne was going to reveal everything! What was the matter with her?

Illusion worked best the closer you stayed to what was there before, in shape and size at least, so bits of the Ebou Dari dress flashed through the Domani garment as Elayne whirled to examine herself in one of the room's two large mirrors. She laughed and clapped her hands. 'Oh, he will *never* recognize me. Or you, near-sister.' Abruptly a Taraboner woman sat beside Nynaeve's chair, with brown eyes and yellow braids strung with red beads just the shade of her snug-fitting dress of folded silk. She watched Elayne quizzically. Nynaeve's hand tightened on her braid. 'And we can't forget you,' Elayne babbled on. 'I know *just* the thing.'

This time, Nynaeve saw the glow around Elayne. She was furious. Seeing the flows being woven about herself did not tell her what image Elayne gave her, of course. It took looking into one of the mirrors to do that. A Sea Folk woman stared back at her, aghast, with a dozen be-gemmed rings in her ears and twice as many golden medallions dangling from the chain running to her nose ring. Aside from the jewelry, she wore wide trousers of brocaded green silk and not a stitch else, the way women of the Atha'an Miere did out of sight of land. It was just Illusion. She was still decently clothed under the weaving. But ... Beside her reflection she saw those of Thom and Juilin, both fighting grins.

A strangled squawk erupted from her throat. 'Close your eyes!' she shouted at the men and began leaping about, waving her arms, anything to make her dress show through. 'Close them, burn you!' Oh. They had. Bristling with indignation, she stopped capering. They were not fighting those grins anymore, though. For that matter, Aviendha was laughing quite openly, rocking to and fro.

Nynaeve gave her skirts a jerk – in the mirror, the Sea Folk woman seemed to pluck at her trousers – and fixed Elayne with a glare. 'Stop this, Elayne!' The Domani woman stared back, mouth open and eyes wide with incredulity. Only then did Nynaeve realize how angry she was; the True Source beckoned from just beyond the edge of sight. Embracing *saidar*, she slammed a shield between Elayne and the Source. Or rather, she tried to. Shielding someone who already held the Power was not easy even when you were the stronger. Once, as a girl, she had swung Master Luhhan's hammer against his anvil as hard as she could, and the shiver of it ran all the way to her toes. This was about twice that. 'Love of the Light, Elayne, are you drunk?'

The glow around the Domani woman faded away, and so did the Domani woman. Nynaeve knew the weave was gone from around herself, but she still glanced at the mirror and drew a relieved breath to see Nynaeve al'Meara there in yellow-slashed blue.

'No,' Elayne said slowly. Color burned in her face, but it was not embarrassment, or not entirely. Her chin rose, and her voice frosted. '*I* am not.'

The door to the corridor banged open, and Birgitte staggered in with a broad smile. Well, perhaps she did not quite stagger, but she was decidedly unsteady. 'I did not expect you all to remain awake for me,' she said brightly. 'Well, you'll be interested to hear what I have to say. But first ... ' With the too steady steps of someone carrying considerable drink inside, she vanished into her room.

Thom stared at her door with a bemused grin, Juilin with an incredulous one. They knew who she was, the truth of it. Elayne just glared down her nose. From Birgitte's bedchamber came a splashing, as if a pitcher had been upended on the floor. Nynaeve exchanged puzzled looks with Aviendha.

Birgitte reappeared with her face and hair dripping and her coat soaked from shoulders to elbows. 'Now my wits are clearer,' she said, settling into one of the ball-footed chairs with a sigh. 'That young man has a hollow leg and a hole in the bottom of his foot. He even out-drank Beslan, and I was beginning to think wine was water to that lad.'

'Beslan?' Nynaeve said, her voice rising. 'Tylin's son? What was he doing there?'

'Why did you allow it, Birgitte?' Elayne exclaimed. 'Mat Cauthon will corrupt the boy, and his mother will blame us.'

'The *boy* is the same age as you,' Thom told her in stuffy tones.

A baffled look passed between Nynaeve and Elayne. What was his point? Everyone knew that a man did not achieve his proper wits, such as they were, until ten years later than a woman.

The puzzlement faded from Elayne's face, replaced by firmness and no little anger as she focused on Birgitte again. Words were going to be said, words both women might regret tomorrow.

'If you and Juilin will leave us now, Thom,' Nynaeve said quickly. It was extremely unlikely they would see the need on their own. 'You need your sleep to be fresh first thing in the morning.' They sat there, gaping at her like belled fools, so she made her tone firmer. 'Now?'

'This game was done twenty stones ago,' Thom said, glancing at the board. 'What do you say we go down to our own room and start another? I'll spot you ten stones to place as you will any time during the game.'

'Ten stones?' Juilin yelped, scraping back his chair. 'Will you offer me fish broth and milk-bread, as well?'

They argued all the way out, but at the door, each of them glanced back in sullen resentment. She would not put it past them to remain awake all night just because she had sent them to bed.

'Mat won't corrupt Beslan,' Birgitte said dryly as the door closed behind the men. 'I doubt nine feather dancers with a shipload of brandy could corrupt him. They wouldn't know where to begin.'

Nynaeve was relieved to hear it, though something was odd about the woman's tone – likely the drink – but Beslan was not at all the issue. She said so, and Elayne added, 'No, he isn't. You got *drunk*, Birgitte! And *I* felt it. I *still* feel tipsy if I don't concentrate. The bond is *not* supposed to work that way. Aes Sedai don't fall over giggling if their Warders drink too much.' Nynaeve threw up her hands.

'Don't look at me that way,' Birgitte said. 'You know more than I do. Aes Sedai and Warders have always been men and women before. Maybe that's the difference. Maybe we are too alike.' Her grin was skewed slightly. There had not been near enough water in that pitcher. 'That might be embarrassing, I suppose.'

'If we could stay with what is important?' Nynaeve said tightly. 'Such as Mat?' Elayne had her mouth open for a retort to Birgitte, but she closed it quickly, the red spots in her cheeks most definitely chagrin this time. 'Now,' Nynaeve went on. 'Will Mat be here in the morning, or is he in the same revolting state as you?'

'He might come,' Birgitte said, taking a cup of mint tea from Aviendha, who of course sat down on the floor. Elayne frowned at her a moment, then, of all things, folded up her legs and sat beside her!

'What do you mean, he might?' Nynaeve demanded. She channeled, and the chair she had been sitting in floated over to her, and if it banged to the floor, she meant it to. Drinking too much, sitting on the floor. What was next? 'If he expects us to come to him on hands and knees . . . !'

Birgitte took a sip of the tea with a grateful murmur, and oddly, when she looked at Nynaeve again, she did not seem so intoxicated. 'I talked him out of that. I don't think he was really serious. All he wants now is an apology and thanks.'

Nynaeve's eyes popped. She had talked him *out* of that? Apologize? To Matrim Cauthon? 'Never,' she growled.

'For what?' Elayne wanted to know, as if that mattered. She pretended not to see Nynaeve's glare.

'The Stone of Tear,' Birgitte said, and Nynaeve's head whipped around. The woman no longer sounded intoxicated at all. 'He says he went into the Stone, him and Juilin, to free the pair of you from a dungeon you couldn't escape on your own.' She shook her head slowly, in wonder. 'I don't know that I would have done that for anyone short of Gaidal. Not the Stone. He says you gave him a backhanded thanks and made him feel he ought to be grateful you didn't kick him.'

It was true, in a way, but all distorted. There Mat had been with that mocking grin of his, saying he was there to pull their chestnuts off the fire or some such. Even then he had thought he could tell them what to do. 'Only one of the Black sisters was on guard in the dungeon,' Nynaeve muttered, 'and we had taken care of her.' True they hadn't yet been able to figure out how to open the door, shielded. 'Be'lal wasn't really interested in us, anyway – it was just to lure Rand. Moiraine may already have killed him, by then, for all we know.'

'The Black Ajah.' Birgitte's voice was flatter than the floor tiles. 'And one of the Forsaken. Mat never mentioned them. You owe him thanks on your knees, Elayne. Both of you do. The man deserves it. And Juilin, as well.'

Blood rushed to Nynaeve's face. He had never mentioned . . . ? That despicable, despicable man! 'I will not apologize to Matrim Cauthon, not on my deathbed.'

Aviendha leaned toward Elayne, touching her knee. 'Near-sister, I will say this delicately.' She looked and sounded about as delicate as a stone post. 'If this is true, you have *toh* toward Mat Cauthon, you and Nynaeve. And you have made it worse since, just by the actions I have seen.'

'*Toh!*' Nynaeve exclaimed. Those two were always talking about this *toh* foolery. 'We aren't Aiel, Aviendha. And Mat Cauthon is a thorn in the foot to everybody he meets.'

But Elayne was nodding. 'I see. You are right, Aviendha. But what must we *do*? You will have to help me, near-sister. I don't intend to try to become Aiel, but I . . . I want you to be proud of me.'

'We will *not* apologize!' Nynaeve snapped.

'I have pride in knowing you,' Aviendha said, touching Elayne's cheek lightly. 'An apology is a beginning, yet not enough to meet *toh*, now.'

'Are you listening to me?' Nynaeve demanded. 'I said, I will – not – apologize!'

They went right on talking. Only Birgitte looked at her, and the woman wore a smile not far from outright laughter. Nynaeve throttled her braid with both hands. She had known that they should have sent Thom and Juilin.

Chapter 22

Small Sacrifices

Squinting up at the sign above the inn's arched door, a crudely drawn woman with a walking staff peering hopefully into the distance, Elayne wished she were back in her bed instead of up with the sun. Not that she could have slept. Mol Hara Square stood empty behind her except for a few creaking ox- and donkey-carts on their way to the markets, a scattering of women balancing huge baskets on their heads. A one-legged beggar sat with his bowl at a corner of the inn, the first of many who would dot the square later; she had already given him a silver mark, enough to feed him for a week even now, but he tucked it under his ragged coat with a toothless grin and waited on. The sky was still gray, yet the day already promised to scorch. Keeping concentration well enough to ignore the heat was a problem this morning.

The last remnants of Birgitte's morning-after head remained in the back of her own, dwindling but not yet gone. If only her small ability with Healing had not proved too small. She hoped Aviendha and Birgitte would manage to learn something useful about Carridin this morning, in their Ilusion disguises. Not that Carridin would know any of them from a shoemaker, of course, but it was best to be careful. She felt pride that Aviendha had not asked to come along here, had in fact been surprised at the suggestion. Aviendha did not believe she needed anyone to watch her, to make sure she did what was needful.

With a sigh, she straightened her dress, though there was no need. Blue and cream, with a bit of cream-colored Vandalra lace, the garment did make her feel just a touch . . . exposed. The only time she had balked at donning a local fashion was while she and Nynaeve traveled to Tanchico with the Sea Folk, but in its own way, Ebou Dari fashion was almost . . . She sighed again. She was just trying to delay. Aviendha should have come to lead her by the hand.

'I will not apologize,' Nynaeve said suddenly at her shoulder. She clutched her own gray skirts with both hands, staring at The Wandering Woman as though Moghedien herself waited inside. 'I won't!'

'You should have worn white after all,' Elayne murmured, earning a suspicious sideways glance. After a moment, she added, 'You did say it was the color for funerals.' Which produced a satisfied nod, though it was not what she had meant at all. This *would* be disaster if they could not keep peace among themselves. Birgitte had had to settle for an infusion of herbs this morning, and a particularly bitter mix at that, because Nynaeve claimed she was not angry enough to channel. She had gone on in the most dramatic manner about funeral white being the only suitable color, insisted she was not coming, until Elayne dragged her out of their apartments, and announced at least twenty times since that she would not apologize. Peace had to be kept, but ... 'You agreed to this, Nynaeve. No, I don't want to hear any more about the rest of us bullying you. You agreed. So stop sulking.'

Nynaeve spluttered, eyes going wide with outrage. She was not to be diverted, though, despite one fiercely incredulous '*Sulking?*' under her breath. 'We need to discuss this further, Elayne. There is no need to be so hasty. There must be a thousand reasons why this won't work, *ta'veren* or no *ta'veren*, and Mat Cauthon is nine hundred of them.'

Elayne gave her a level look. 'Did you deliberately choose the bitterest herbs that would work this morning?' Wide-eyed outrage turned to wide-eyed innocence, but red stained Nynaeve's cheeks. Elayne pushed open the door. Nynaeve followed, muttering. Elayne would not have been surprised if she stuck out her tongue, too. Sulky was not even in it, this morning.

The smell of breads baking wafted from the kitchens, and all the shutters were open to air out the common room. A plump-cheeked serving woman standing atop a tall stool stretched on tiptoes to take down bedraggled evergreen branches from above the windows, while others replaced tables and benches and chairs that must have been taken away for the dancing. This early, no one else was about, except for a skinny girl in a white apron, sweeping halfheartedly with a brush-broom. She might have been pretty if her mouth had not seemed set in a constant pout. There was surprisingly little mess, considering that inns were supposed to be riotous, even licentious, during festivals. A part of her wished she could have seen it, though.

'Could you direct me to Master Cauthon's rooms?' she asked the skinny girl with a smile, proffering two silver pennies. Nynaeve sniffed. She was tight as the skin on a fresh apple; she had given the beggar one *copper*!

The girl eyed them sullenly – and surprisingly, the coins as well – and mumbled something sour that sounded like, 'A gilded woman last night and ladies this morning.' She gave directions grudgingly. For a moment Elayne thought she intended to scorn the pennies, but on the point of turning away, the girl snatched the silver from her hand without so much as a word of thanks, pausing only to tuck them into the neck of her dress, of all places, before she set to swinging her broom as if to beat the floor to death. Perhaps she had a pocket sewn in there.

'You see,' Nynaeve grumbled under her breath. 'You mark me, he tried to push his attentions on that young woman. That's the sort of man you want me to apologize to.'

Elayne said nothing, only led the way up the railless steps at the back of the room. If Nynaeve did not stop complaining... The first hallway on the right, the girl had said, and the last door on the left, but in front of it, she hesitated, biting her lower lip.

Nynaeve brightened. 'You see it's a bad idea now, don't you? We aren't Aiel, Elayne. I like the girl well enough, for all she's forever fondling that knife of hers, but just think of the absolute drivel she talked. It's impossible. You must know it is.'

'We did not agree to anything impossible, Nynaeve.' Keeping her voice firm took an effort. Some of what Aviendha had suggested, apparently in all seriousness... She actually had suggested letting the man *switch* them! 'What we did agree to is quite possible.' Barely. She rapped loudly on the paneled door with her knuckles. There was a fish carved on the door, a round thing with stripes and a snout. All of the doors had different carvings, most of fish. There was no answer.

Nynaeve puffed out a breath she must have been holding. 'Perhaps he has gone out. We'll just have to come back another time.'

'At this hour?' She rapped once more. 'You say he always lies abed when he can.' Still no sound from inside.

'Elayne, if Birgitte is any indication, Mat got himself juicy as a fiddler last night. He won't thank us for waking him. Why don't we just go away and—'

Elayne lifted the latch and went in. Nynaeve followed with a sigh that could have been heard back in the palace.

Mat Cauthon was sprawled on his bed atop the knitted red coverlet, a folded cloth lying over his eyes and dripping onto the pillow. The room was not very tidy despite the absence of dust. A boot stood on the washstand – the washstand! – next to a white basin full of unused water, the stand-mirror sat askew, as if he had stumbled into it and simply left it tilted back sharply, and his wrinkled coat lay tossed across a ladder-back chair. He wore everything else, including that black scarf he seemed never to take off, and the other boot. The silver foxhead dangled from his unlaced shirt.

The medallion made her fingers itch. If he really was lying there sodden with drink, she might be able to remove it unfelt. One way or another, she intended to find out how the thing absorbed the Power. Finding out how almost anything worked was a fascination to her, but that foxhead was all the puzzles in the world rolled into one.

Nynaeve caught her sleeve and jerked her head toward the door, silently mouthing 'asleep' and something else she could not make out. Probably another plea to go.

'Leave me alone, Nerim,' he mumbled suddenly. 'I told you before; I don't want anything but a new skull. And close the door softly, or I'll pin your ears to it.'

Nynaeve jumped, and tried to pull her toward the door, but she stood her ground. 'It is not Nerim, Master Cauthon.'

Raising his head from the pillow, he used both hands to lift the cloth a trifle and squinted at them with reddened eyes.

Grinning, Nynaeve made no effort at all to hide her pleasure at his wretched state. What Elayne could not understand at first was why she wanted to grin, too. Her one experience with drinking too much had left her with nothing but pity and sympathy for anyone so snared. In the back of her mind she felt Birgitte's head throbbing still, and it came to her. Certainly she could not like Birgitte drowning herself in drink, whatever the reason, but neither could she like the thought that anyone could do anything at all better than her first Warder. A ridiculous thought. Embarrassing. But satisfying, too.

'What are you doing here?' he demanded hoarsely, then winced and lowered his voice. 'It's the middle of the night.'

'It's morning,' Nynaeve said sharply. 'Don't you remember talking with Birgitte?'

'Could you not be so loud?' he whispered, closing his eyes. The next instant, they popped open again. 'Birgitte?' Sitting up abruptly, he swung his legs over the side of the bed. For a time he just sat there, peering at the floorboards, elbows on his knees and the medallion swinging from its thong around his neck. At last he turned his head to look at them balefully. Or perhaps his eyes just made it seem so. 'What did she tell you?'

'She informed us of your demands, Master Cauthon,' Elayne said formally. This must be how it felt to stand before the headsman's block. There was nothing for it but to keep her head high and face whatever came proudly. 'I wish to thank you from my heart for rescuing me from the Stone of Tear.' There, she had begun, and it had not hurt. Not very much.

Nynaeve stood there, glowering, her lips growing tighter and tighter. The woman was *not* going to leave her to do this alone. Elayne embraced the Source almost before she thought, and channeled a thin flow of Air that flicked Nynaeve's earlobe like a snapping finger. The woman clapped a hand to her ear and glowered, but Elayne simply turned coolly back to Master Cauthon and waited.

'I thank you, too,' Nynaeve mumbled sullenly at last. 'From the heart.'

Elayne rolled her eyes in spite of herself. Well, he had asked them to speak more softly. And he did seem to hear. Strangely, he shrugged with embarrassment.

'Oh, that. It was nothing. Likely thing, you'd have gotten yourself free in another tick without me.' His head sank to his hands, and he pressed the damp cloth to his eyes once more. 'On your way out, would you ask Caira to bring me some wine-punch? A slender girl, pretty, with a warm eye.'

Elayne quivered. *Nothing?* The man *demanded* an apology, she *humbled* herself to give it, and now it was *nothing?* He was not deserving of sympathy or pity! She still held *saidar*, and she considered thumping him with a much thicker flow than she had used on Nynaeve. Not that that would do any good so long as he wore the foxhead. Then again, it hung loose, not touching him. Did it offer the same protection when it was not . . . ?

Nynaeve ended her speculation by lunging for him, fingers

clawed. Elayne managed to put herself between them and seize the other woman by the shoulders. For a stretched moment they stood nose-to-nose except for the difference in their heights; with a grimace, Nynaeve finally relaxed, and Elayne felt it was safe to release her.

The man still had his head bowed, all unaware. Whether the medallion protected him or not, she could snatch his bowstave from the corner and beat him till he howled. She felt heat rise in her face: she had stopped Nynaeve from ruining everything, only to think of ruining it herself. Worse, by the smirky, self-satisfied little smile the other woman gave her, she knew very well what had been in her head.

'There is more, Master Cauthon,' she announced, squaring her shoulders. The smile vanished from Nynaeve's face. 'We also wish to apologize for delaying so long in giving you your much deserved thanks. And we apologize ... humbly ... ' She stumbled a little on that. ' ... for the way we have treated you since.' Nynaeve stretched out a beseeching hand that she ignored. 'To show the depth of our regret, we undertake the following promises.' Aviendha had said an apology was only a beginning. 'We will not belittle or demean you in any way, nor shout at you for any reason, nor ... nor attempt to give you orders.' Nynaeve winced. Elayne's mouth tightened too, but she did not stop. 'Recognizing your due concern for our safety, we will not leave the palace without telling you where we are going, and we will listen to your advice.' Light, she had no wish to be Aiel, no wish to do any of this, but she wanted Aviendha's respect. 'If you ... if you decide that we are ... ' Not that she had any intention of becoming a sister-wife – the very *idea* was indecent! – but she did like her. ' ... are putting ourselves in needless danger ... ' It was not Aviendha's fault that Rand had caught both their hearts. And Min's as well. ' ... we will accept bodyguards of your choosing ... ' Fate or *ta'veren* or whatever, what was, was. She loved both women like sisters. ' ... and keep them with us as long as possible.' *Burn* the man for doing this to her! It was not Mat Cauthon she meant. 'This I swear by the Lion Throne of Andor.' She breathed in as if she had run a mile. Nynaeve wore a face like a cornered badger.

His head swiveled toward them ever so slowly, and he lowered the cloth just enough to expose one red-streaked eye. 'You sound like you have an iron rod down your throat, my Lady,' he said mockingly. 'You have my permission to call me Mat.' Odious man! He would not know civility if it bit him on the nose! That sanguine eye slanted toward her. 'What about you, Nynaeve? I heard a lot of "we" from her, but not a word from you.'

'I won't shout at you,' Nynaeve shouted. 'And all the rest, too. I promise, you . . . you . . . !' She gobbled on the edge of swallowing her tongue as she realized she could not call him one of the names he warranted without breaking the promise already. And yet, the effect of her shout was most gratifying.

With a cry, he shuddered and dropped the cloth, clutched his head with both hands. His eyes bulged. 'Flaming dice,' he whimpered, or something very like. It suddenly struck Elayne that he would be a very good source of pithy language. Stablemen and the like always seemed to scrape their tongues clean the moment they saw her. Of course, she had promised herself to civilize him, to make him useful to Rand, but that need not interfere too much with his language. In fact, she realized there was a good deal she had *not* promised not to do. Pointing that out should settle Nynaeve considerably.

After a long moment, he spoke in a hollow voice. 'Thank you, Nynaeve.' He paused to swallow hard. 'I thought you two must be somebody else in disguise, there for a bit. Since I still seem to be alive, we might as well take care of the rest of it. I seem to recall that Birgitte said you wanted me to find something for you. What?'

'You won't find it,' Nynaeve told him in a firm voice. Well, perhaps more hard than firm, but Elayne did not think of calling her down. He merited every wince. 'You will accompany us, and we will find it.'

'Backtracking already, Nynaeve?' Somehow, he managed a derisive sneer, especially hideous with his eyes. 'You just finished promising to do as I say. If you want a tame *ta'veren* on a leash, go ask Rand or Perrin and see what answer you get.'

'We promised no such thing, Matrim Cauthon,' Nynaeve snapped, going up on her toes. 'I promised no such thing!' She looked about to fling herself at him again. Even her braid seemed to bristle.

Elayne kept a better rein on her temper. They would get nowhere bludgeoning him. 'We will *listen* to your advice, and accept it if it is reasonable, Master ... Mat,' she chided gently. Surely he could not really believe they had promised to ... Looking at him, though, she saw that he did. Oh, Light! Nynaeve was right. He *was* going to be trouble.

She held that rein firmly. Channeling again, she lifted his coat from the chair to a proper place on one of the pegs on the wall so she could sit, back straight, arranging her skirts carefully. Keeping her promises to Master Cauthon – Mat – and to herself was going to be difficult, but nothing he said or did could touch her. Nynaeve eyed the only other place to sit, a low carved wooden footstool, and remained standing. One hand moved toward her braid before she folded her arms. Her foot tapped ominously.

'The Atha'an Miere call it the Bowl of the Winds, Master ... Mat. It is a *ter'angreal* ...'

By the end, a light of excitement shone through his sickliness. 'Now, that would be a thing to find,' he murmured. 'In the Rahad.' He shook his head, and flinched. 'I'll tell you this now. Neither of you is setting foot on the other side of the river without four or five of my Redarms each. Not outside the palace, for that matter. Did Birgitte tell you about the note that was stuffed in my coat? I'm sure I told her. And there's Carridin and his Darkfriends; you can't tell me he isn't up to something.'

'Any sister who supports Egwene as Amyrlin is in danger from the Tower.' Bodyguards everywhere? Light! A dangerous light shone in Nynaeve's eyes, and her foot tapped faster. 'We cannot hide, Mast ... Mat, and we will not. Jaichim Carridin will be taken care of in due course.' They had not promised to tell him everything, and they could not let him be diverted. 'There are more important matters afoot.'

'Due course?' he began, voice rising in disbelief, but Nynaeve cut him short.

'Four or five each?' she said sourly. 'That's ridic—' Her eyes shut for a moment, and her tone became milder. Slightly milder. 'I mean to say, it isn't sensible. Elayne and me, Birgitte and Aviendha. You don't have that many soldiers. Anyway, all we really need is you.'

That last came out as though dragged. It was much too much an admission.

'Birgitte and Aviendha don't need minders,' he said absently. 'I suppose this Bowl of the Winds is more important than Carridin, but ... It doesn't seem right, letting Darkfriends walk loose.'

Slowly Nynaeve's face turned purple. Elayne checked her own in the stand-mirror, relieved to see she was maintaining her composure. On the outside, anyway. The man was reprehensible! Minders? She was not sure which would be worse: that he had flung that offhand insult on purpose, or that he had done so without realizing. She eyed herself in the mirror again and lowered her chin a trifle. Minders! She was poise itself.

He studied them with those bloodshot eyes, but saw nothing, apparently. 'Was that all Birgitte told you?' he asked, and Nynaeve snapped back, 'That was quite enough, I'd think, even for you.' Inexplicably, he looked surprised, and quite pleased.

Nynaeve gave a start, then folded her arms around herself tighter. 'Since you're in no condition to go anywhere with us now – don't scowl at me, Mat Cauthon; that isn't demeaning, it's simple truth! – you can spend the morning moving yourself into the palace. And you needn't think we'll help carry your things. I didn't promise to be a packhorse.'

'The Wandering Woman is plenty good enough,' he began angrily, then stopped, a wondering expression spreading over his face. A horrified expression, Elayne would have said. That should teach him to growl when he had a head like a melon. At least, that was what hers had felt like, the time she drank too much. Of course he would not learn from it. Men kept sticking their hands in the fire thinking this time it would not burn, so Lini always said.

'You can hardly expect we'll find the Bowl the first time we try,' Nynaeve went on, '*ta'veren* or no. Going out each day will be much simpler if you don't have to come across the square.' If they did not have to wait for him every morning, was what she meant. According to her, drunkenness was not the only excuse he could find for lying in bed till all hours, far from it.

'Besides,' Elayne added, 'that way, you can keep an eye on us.' Nynaeve made a sound in her throat, very close to a groan. Did she not see that he must be enticed? It was not as if she had promised to actually *allow* him to keep an eye on them.

He seemed not to have heard her or Nynaeve. Haggard eyes stared right through her. 'Why did they bloody well have to stop now?' he moaned, so softly she barely heard. What under the Light did he mean by that?

'The rooms are fit for a king, Master ... Mat. Tylin herself chose them, just down from her own. She has taken a very personal interest. Mat, you wouldn't have us offend the Queen, would you?'

One look at his face, and Elayne hurriedly channeled to push open the window and empty the washbasin through it. If she had ever seen a man about to lose the contents of his stomach, he was staring red-eyed at her right that minute.

'I don't see why you're making such a fuss,' she said. Actually, she supposed she did. Some of the serving women here probably let him paw them, but she doubted many in the palace would, if any. He would not be able to drink and gamble his nights away, either. Tylin surely would not allow a bad example for Beslan. 'We all must make sacrifices.' With an effort she stopped there, not telling him that his was small and only right, theirs monstrous and unjust, no matter what Aviendha said. Nynaeve had certainly railed against *any* sacrifice.

He put his head in his hands again, making strangled noises while his shoulders shook. He was laughing! She hefted the basin on a flow of Air, considering hitting him with it. When he raised his eyes again, though, he looked outraged for some reason. 'Sacrifices?' he snarled. 'If I asked you to make the same, you'd box every ear in sight and pull the roof down on my head!' Could he still be drunk?

She decided to ignore his frightful glare. 'Speaking of your head, if you would like Healing, I'm sure Nynaeve would oblige.' If she had ever been angry enough to channel, she was now.

Nynaeve gave a small jerk and glanced at her from the corner of one eye. 'Of course,' she said hurriedly. 'If you want.' The color in her cheeks confirmed all of Elayne's suspicions about that morning.

Gracious as ever, he sneered. 'You just forget my head. I do very well without Aes Sedai.' And then, just to confuse matters she was sure, he added in a hesitant voice, 'I thank you for asking, though.' Almost as if he meant it!

Elayne managed not to gape. Her knowledge of men was limited to Rand and what Lini and her mother had told her. Was Rand going to be as confusing as Mat Cauthon?

Last thing before going, she remembered to secure a promise that he would start moving to the palace immediately. He kept his word once given, so Nynaeve had made clear, however reluctantly, but leave one crack, and he could find a hundred ways to slip through. *That* she had been all too eager to emphasize. He gave his promise with a bleak, resentful grimace; or maybe that was just his eyes again. When she set the basin down at his feet, he actually looked grateful. She would not feel sympathy. She would not.

Once back in the corridor, with the door to Mat's room closed, Nynaeve shook her fist at the ceiling. 'That man could try the patience of a stone! I'm glad he wants to cuddle with his head! Do you hear me? Glad! He will make trouble. He will.'

'You two will make more trouble for him than he ever could.' The speaker stalked down the hall toward them, a woman with a touch of gray in her hair, a strong face and a commanding voice. She also wore a frown little short of a scowl. Despite the marriage knife hanging into her cleavage, she was too fair for an Ebou Dari. 'I couldn't believe it when Caira told me. I doubt I've ever seen so much foolishness poured into just two dresses.'

Elayne eyed the woman up and down. Not even as a novice had she gotten used to being addressed in that tone. 'And who might you be, my good woman?'

'I might be and am Setalle Anan, the owner of this inn, child,' was the dry reply, and with that, the woman flung open a door across the hallway, seized them each by an arm, and hustled them through so fast Elayne thought her slippers had left the floor.

'You seem under some misapprehension, Mistress Anan,' she said coolly as the woman released them to shut the door.

Nynaeve was in no mood for niceties. Holding her hand so her Great Serpent ring was plain, she said heatedly, 'Now, you look here—'

'Very pretty,' the woman said, and pushed each of them so hard they found themselves sitting side-by-side on the bed. Elayne's eyes popped in disbelief. This Anan woman confronted them, grim-faced, fists on her hips, for all the world like a mother about to castigate her daughters. 'Flaunting that just shows how silly you are. That young man will dandle you on his knee – one on each, I shouldn't wonder, if you allow – he'll take a few kisses and as much else as you're willing to give, but he won't harm you. You can harm him, though, if you keep on with this.'

Harm him? The woman thought they – she thought he had *dandled* – she thought— Elayne did not know whether to laugh or cry, but she stood up, straightening her skirts. 'As I said, Mistress Anan, you are under a misapprehension.' Her voice became smoother as she went on, confusion giving way to calm. 'I am Elayne Trakand, Daughter-Heir of Andor and Aes Sedai of the Green Ajah. I don't know what you think—' Her eyes nearly crossed as Mistress Anan pushed a finger to the tip of her nose.

'Elayne, if that is your name, all that keeps me from dragging you down to the kitchen and washing your mouth out, yours and that other foolish girl's there, is the possibility that you actually can channel somewhat. Or are you silly enough to wear that ring when you can't even do that? I warn you, it will make no difference to the sisters over in the Tarasin Palace. Do you even know about them? If you do, frankly, you are not foolish, you're blind stupid.'

Elayne's temper grew by the word. Foolish girl? Blind stupid? She would not put up with it, especially not right after being forced to crawl to Mat Cauthon. Dandle? Mat Cauthon? She maintained her outward composure, though, but not so Nynaeve.

She glared in a fury, and the glow of *saidar* enveloped her as she bounded to her feet. Flows of Air wrapped Mistress Anan from shoulders to ankles, crushing her skirts and petticoats against her legs, just short of tight enough to topple her. 'I happen to be one of those sisters in the palace. Nynaeve al'Meara of the Yellow Ajah, to be exact. Now would you like me to carry *you* down to the kitchens? I know something of how to wash out a mouth.' Elayne stepped away from the innkeeper's outstretched arm.

The woman had to feel the pressure of the flows, and even a half-wit would have known what those invisible bonds must be, yet she did not blink! Her green-flecked eyes narrowed, no more. 'So one of you can channel, at least,' she said calmly. 'I should let you drag me downstairs, child. Whatever you do to me, you would be in the hands of real Aes Sedai by noon; I'll wager that.'

'Didn't you hear me?' Nynaeve demanded. 'I—!'

The Anan woman did not even pause. 'You'll not only spend the next year blubbering, you will do part of it in front of anyone you told that you are Aes Sedai. Be sure, they'll make you tell. They will turn your liver to water. I should let you go blundering on your way, or else run across to the palace as soon as you loose me. The only reason I don't is that they'll make an example of Lord Mat nearly as much as of you, if they even suspect he's helped you, and as I said, I like the young man.'

'I'm telling you—' Nynaeve tried again, but *still* the innkeeper gave her no chance to tell anything. Tied like a bundle, the woman was a boulder rolling downhill. She was the whole hillside falling, flattening whatever lay in its path.

'Trying to keep up the lie does no good, Nynaeve. You look to be, oh, twenty-one give or take a year, so you might be as much as ten years older if you've already reached the slowing. You might even have worn the shawl four or five years. Except for one thing.' Her head, the only part of her she could move, swiveled toward Elayne. 'You, child, aren't old enough to have slowed yet, and no woman has ever worn the shawl as young as you. Never in the history of the Tower. If you ever were in the Tower, I'll wager you wore white and squeaked every time the Mistress of Novices glanced your way. You had some goldsmith make that ring for you – there are some fool enough, I hear – or maybe Nynaeve stole it for you, if she has any right to hers. Either way, since you can't be a sister, neither can she. No Aes Sedai would travel with a woman who was pretending.'

Elayne frowned, not noticing that she was chewing her lower lip. Slowed. Slowing. How did an innkeeper in Ebou Dar know those words? Maybe Setalle Anan had gone to the Tower as a girl, though she would not have remained long, since she clearly could not channel. Elayne would have known even if her ability had been as small as her own mother's, and Morgase Trakand had had an ability so small she would have been sent away in a matter of weeks probably, had she not then been heir to a strong House.

'Release her, Nynaeve,' she said, smiling. She truly did feel more well-disposed toward the woman, now. It must have been terrible to make that journey to Tar Valon only to be turned away. There was no reason the woman *had* to believe them – something tickled at that, but she could not say what – no reason at all, but if she had made the trip to Tar Valon, maybe she would walk across the Mol Hara. Merilille, or any of the other sisters, could set her straight.

'Release her?' Nynaeve yelped. 'Elayne?'

'Release her. Mistress Anan, I see the only way to convince you is—'

'The Amyrlin Seat and three Sitters couldn't convince me, child.' Light, did she ever let anyone finish a sentence? 'Now, I don't have time for any more games. I can help the pair of you. I know those who can, anyway, some women who take in strays. You can thank Lord Mat that I'm willing to take you to them, but I must know. Were you ever in the Tower, or are you wilders? If you were there, were you put out, or did you run away? The truth. They handle each in a different way.'

Elayne shrugged. They had done what they came for; she was more than ready to stop wasting time and get on with what needed doing next. 'If you won't be convinced, then that's all there is to it. Nynaeve? It is past time we were on our way.'

The flows around the innkeeper vanished, and the glow around Nynaeve too, but Nynaeve stood there watching the woman warily, hopefully. She wet her lips. 'You know a group of women who can help us?'

'Nynaeve?' Elayne said. 'We don't need any help. We *are* Aes Sedai, remember?'

With a wry glance in her direction, Mistress Anan gave her skirts a shake to straighten them and bent to smooth her exposed petticoats. Her real attention was on Nynaeve; Elayne had never felt so completely shunted aside in her life. 'I know a few women who take in the occasional wilder or runaway or woman who failed her test for Accepted or the shawl. There must be at least fifty of them, altogether, though the number changes. They can help you find a life without the risk of a real sister making you wish she'd just skin you and be done. Now, don't lie to me. Were you ever in the Tower? If you've run away, you might as well decide to go back. The Tower managed to find most runaways even during the War of the Hundred Years, so you needn't think this little bother now will stop them. In truth, my suggestion then would be to go across the square and throw yourself on a sister's mercy. It will be a small mercy, I'm afraid, but you can believe me, it's more than you'll find if they have to drag you back. You won't even think of so much as leaving the Tower *grounds* without permission after that.'

Nynaeve drew a deep breath. 'We were told to leave the Tower, Mistress Anan. I will swear to that, however you ask.'

Elayne stared in disbelief. 'Nynaeve, what are you *saying*? Mistress Anan, we *are* Aes Sedai.'

The Anan woman laughed. 'Child, let me talk with Nynaeve, who at least seems old enough to have sense. You tell the Circle that, and they will not take it kindly. They won't care you can channel; they can, too, and they'll smack your bottom or toss you out in the street on your nose if you play the fool.'

'Who is this *Circle*?' Elayne demanded. 'We *are* Aes Sedai. You come across to the Tarasin Palace, and you will see.'

'I'll keep her in hand,' Nynaeve had the gall to say, all the while frowning and grimacing at Elayne as if she were the one who had gone mad.

The Anan woman merely nodded. 'Good. Now take off those rings and put them away. The Circle doesn't allow that sort of pretending. They'll have them melted down to give you a start. Though by the look of your dresses, you have coin. If you stole it, don't let Reanne know. One of the first rules you'll have to learn is, don't steal even if you are starving. They don't want to draw attention.'

Elayne made a fist and thrust it behind her back. And watched Nynaeve meekly slip her ring off and tuck it into her belt pouch. Nynaeve, who howled every time Merilille or Adeleas or any of them forgot she was a full sister!

'Trust me, Elayne,' Nynaeve said.

Which Elayne would have had an easier time of if she had any notion what the woman was up to. Still, she did trust her. Mostly. 'A small sacrifice,' she muttered. Aes Sedai did go without their rings when the need arose, and she had too, while passing for a sister, but it was hers by right, now. Removing that band of gold almost hurt physically.

'Talk to your friend, child,' the Anan woman told Nynaeve impatiently. 'Reanne Corly won't put up with all this sulky pouting, and if you make me waste my morning for nothing . . . Come along, come along. It's lucky for you I like Lord Mat.'

Elayne held on to cool composure by a fingernail. Sulky pouting? Sulky *pouting*? When she had the chance, she was going to kick Nynaeve where it hurt!

CHAPTER 23

Next Door to a Weaver

Nynaeve did want to talk to Elayne, away from the innkeeper's ears, but she did not find the chance right away. The woman marched them out of the room doing a fine imitation of a guard on prisoners, her stony impatience undented by the wary look she cast at Mat's door. At the back of the inn another set of unrailed stone steps led down into a large hot kitchen full of baking smells, where the roundest woman Nynaeve had ever seen was wielding a large wooden spoon like a scepter, directing three others in sliding crusty brown loaves from the ovens and replacing them with rolls of pale dough. A large pot of the coarse white porridge that was eaten for breakfast hereabout bubbled gently on one of the white-tiled stoves.

'Enid,' Mistress Anan addressed the round woman, 'I am going out for a little while. I need to take these two children to someone who has time to mother them properly.'

Wiping broad, floury hands on a piece of white toweling, Enid studied Nynaeve and Elayne disapprovingly. Everything about her was round, her sweaty olive-skinned face, her dark eyes, all of her; she seemed made of very large balls stuffed into a dress. The marriage knife she wore hanging outside her snowy apron sparkled with a full dozen stones. 'Is this the pair of barkers Caira was chattering about, Mistress? Fancy bits for the young Lord's taste, I'd have said. He likes them with a bit of wiggle.' That amused her, by her tone.

The innkeeper shook her head in vexation. 'I told that girl to hold her tongue. I won't let that sort of rumor touch The Wandering Woman. Remind Caira for me, Enid, and use your spoon to get her attention, if need be.' The gaze she turned on Nynaeve and Elayne was so disparaging that Nynaeve nearly gasped. 'Would anyone with half their wits believe these two were Aes Sedai? Spent all their coin on dresses to impress the man, and now they'd starve unless they smile for him. Aes Sedai!' Giving Enid no chance to answer, she seized Nynaeve's ear with her right hand, Elayne's with her left, and in three quick steps had them out into the stableyard.

That was as long as Nynaeve's shock held. Then she pulled free, or tried to, because the woman let go at the same instant and she stumbled half a dozen paces, glaring indignantly. She had not bargained for being dragged about. Elayne's chin rose, her blue eyes so cold Nynaeve would not have been surprised to see frost forming in her curls.

Hands on hips, Mistress Anan seemed not to notice. Or perhaps she simply did not care. 'I can hope no one in there believes Caira after that,' she said calmly. 'If I could have been sure you had the wits to keep your mouths shut, I'd have said and done more, and made certain.' She was calm, but not at all pleasant or soft; they had troubled her morning. 'Now follow me and don't get lost. Or if you do, do not show your faces anywhere near my inn again, or I'll send somebody to the palace to tell Merilille *and* Teslyn. They are two of the real sisters, and they'll probably rip you each down the middle and share you out.'

Elayne shifted her gaze from the innkeeper to Nynaeve. Not a glare, or a frown, yet a very meaning look just the same. Nynaeve wondered whether she was going to be able to go through with this. The thought of Mat convinced her; any chance was better than that.

'We won't lose ourselves, Mistress Anan,' she said, striving for meekness. She thought she did fairly well, considering how foreign meekness was to her. 'Thank you for helping us.' Smiling at the innkeeper, she did her best to ignore Elayne, whose stare became more meaningful, hard as that was to credit. Looks or no looks, she had to make sure the woman continued to think them worth the trouble. 'We are truly grateful, Mistress Anan.'

Mistress Anan eyed her askance, then sniffed and shook her head. When this was done, Nynaeve decided, she was going to drag the innkeeper to the palace, if need be, and *make* the other sisters acknowledge her in Mistress Anan's presence.

This early, the stableyard was empty save for a lone boy of ten or twelve with a bucket and a sieve who sprinkled water to dampen the hard-packed ground against dust. The white plastered stable's doors were wide open, and a barrow sat in front with a dung-fork resting across it. Sounds like a huge frog being stepped on floated out; Nynaeve decided it was a man singing. Would they have to ride to reach their destination? Even a short journey would not be pleasant; walking only across the square and meaning to be back before the sun rose very high, they had brought neither hats nor parasols nor hooded cloaks.

Mistress Anan led them through the stableyard, however, down a narrow alleyway between the stable and a high wall that had drought-bedraggled trees poking above the top. Someone's garden no doubt. A small gate at the end let into a dusty alley so cramped dawn had not completely reached it yet.

'You children keep up now, mind you,' the innkeeper told them, starting away down the dim alley. 'You lose yourselves, and I vow I'll go to the palace myself.'

Nynaeve took a grip on her braid with both hands as she followed, to keep them from the Anan woman's throat. How she yearned for her first gray hairs. First the other Aes Sedai, then the Sea Folk – Light, she did not want to think about them! – and now an innkeeper! No one took you seriously until you had at least a little gray; even an Aes Sedai's ageless face could not possibly do as well in her estimation.

Elayne was lifting her skirts out the dust, though their slippers still kicked up little puffs that settled on the hems of their dresses. 'Let me see,' Elayne said softly, looking straight ahead. Softly, but coolly. Very coolly, in fact. She had a way of slashing someone to tatters without letting her tone heat that Nynaeve admired. Usually. Now, it just made her want to box the other woman's ears. 'We could be back in the palace drinking blueberry tea and enjoying the breezes while we waited for Master Cauthon to move his belongings. Perhaps Aviendha and Birgitte might return with something useful. We could finally be settling exactly what to do with the man. Do we simply follow him along the streets of the Rahad and see what happens, or take him into buildings that look likely, or let him choose? There must be a hundred worthwhile uses for this morning, including deciding whether it's safe to go back to Egwene – ever – after that bargain the Sea Folk wrung out of us. We have to talk about that sooner or later; ignoring it won't help. Instead, we are off on a walk of who knows what length, squinting into the sun the whole way if we keep on as we are, to visit women who feed runaways from the Tower. Myself, I don't have much interest in catching runaways this morning or any morning. But I'm sure you can explain it so I will understand. I do so want to understand, Nynaeve. I would hate to think I'm going to kick you the length of the Mol Hara for nothing.'

Nynaeve's eyebrows drew down. Kick her? Elayne really was becoming violent, spending so much time with Aviendha. Someone ought to slap some sense into that pair. 'The sun isn't high enough to make us squint yet,' she muttered. It would be soon, unfortunately. 'Think, Elayne. *Fifty* women who can channel, helping wilders and women put out of the Tower.' She felt guilty sometimes, using the term wilders; in the mouths of most Aes Sedai, it was an insult, but she intended to make them speak it as a badge of pride one day. 'And she called them "the Circle." That doesn't sound like a few friends to me. It sounds organized.' The alley meandered between high walls and the backs of buildings, many showing bare brick through the plaster, between palace gardens and shops where an open back door revealed silversmiths or tailors or woodcarvers at work. Every so often Mistress Anan looked over her shoulder to make sure they still followed. Nynaeve gave her smiles and nods she hoped would convey eagerness.

'Nynaeve, if *two* women who could channel made a society, the Tower would fall on them like a pack of wolves. How would Mistress Anan know whether they can or not, anyway? Women who can and aren't Aes Sedai do not go about making a show of themselves, you know. Not for very long, anyway. In any case, I can't see it makes a difference. Egwene might want to bring every woman who can channel into the Tower somehow, but that is not what we are about here.' The frosty patience in Elayne's voice tightened Nynaeve's hands on her braid. How could the woman be so dense? She bared her teeth again for Mistress Anan, and managed not to scowl at the innkeeper's back when her head turned forward once more.

'Fifty women isn't two,' Nynaeve whispered fiercely. They could channel; they must be able to; everything hinged on that. 'It's beyond reason that this Circle can be in the same city with a storeroom packed full of *angreal* and such without at least knowing of it. And if they do . . . ' She could not keep satisfaction from honeying her voice. ' . . . we'll have found the Bowl without Master Matrim Cauthon. We can forget those absurd promises.'

'They were not a bribe, Nynaeve,' Elayne said absently. 'I will keep them, and so will you, if you have any honor, and I know you do.' She was spending entirely too much time with Aviendha. Nynaeve wished she knew why Elayne had begun thinking they all had to follow this preposterous Aiel *ji*-whatever-it-was.

Elayne bit her underlip, frowning. All that iciness seemed to have vanished; she was herself again, apparently. Finally she said, 'We would never have gone to the inn without Master Cauthon, so we'd never have met the remarkable Mistress Anan or been taken to this Circle. So if the Circle does lead us to the Bowl, we have to say he was the root cause.'

Mat Cauthon; his name *boiled* in her head. Nynaeve stumbled over her own feet and let go of her braid to lift her skirts. The alley was hardly as smooth as a paved square much less a palace floor. At times, Elayne in a taking was better than Elayne thinking clearly. 'Remarkable,' she muttered. 'I'll "remarkable" her till her eyes cross. No one has ever treated us this way, Elayne, not even people who doubted, not even the Sea Folk. Most people would step wary if a ten-year-old said she was Aes Sedai.'

'Most people don't really know what an Aes Sedai's face looks like, Nynaeve. I think she went to the Tower once; she knows things she couldn't, otherwise.'

Nynaeve snorted, glowering at the back of the woman striding ahead. Setalle Anan might have been to the Tower ten times, a hundred, but she was going to acknowledge Nynaeve al'Meara as Aes Sedai. And apologize. And learn what it was like to be hauled about by her ear, too! Mistress Anan glanced back, and Nynaeve flashed her a rigid smile, nodded as if her neck was a hinge. 'Elayne? If these women do know where the Bowl is ... We don't have to tell Mat how we found it.' That was not quite a question.

'I do not see why,' Elayne replied, then dashed all her hopes by adding, 'But I'll have to ask Aviendha to be sure.'

If she had not thought the Anan woman might abandon them on the spot, Nynaeve would have screamed.

The wandering alley gave way to a street, and there was no talking then to amount to anything. The sun's thin rim glared blindingly above the rooftops ahead; Elayne shaded her eyes with one hand very ostentatiously. Nynaeve refused to. It was not that bad. She barely had to squint at all, really. A clear blue sky mocked her weather sense, that still told her a storm was right on top of the city.

Even this early a few brightly lacquered coaches were about in the winding streets, and a double fistful of brighter sedan chairs, two or sometimes four barefoot bearers in green-and-red striped vests to each, trotting because they carried passengers hidden behind the grilled wooden screens. Carts and wagons rumbled over the paving stones, and people began to fill the streets as shop doors opened and awnings went up, vested apprentices hurrying on errands and men with great rolled carpets balanced on their shoulders, tumblers and jugglers and musicians readying themselves at likely corners and hawkers with their trays of pins or ribbons or shabby fruit. The open-sided fish- and meat-markets had long since been in full cry; all the fishmongers were women, and most of the butchers, too, except those dealing in beef.

Dodging through the crowds, past the coaches and sedan chairs and wagons that seemed to think they had no reason to slow, Mistress Anan set a fast pace to make up for interruptions. There were plenty of those. She seemed to be a well-known woman, hailed by shopkeepers and craftsmen and other innkeepers standing in their doorways. The shopkeepers and craftsmen received a few words, a pleasant nod, but she always stopped to chat a moment with the innkeepers. After the first, Nynaeve wished fervently that she would not again; after the second, she prayed for it. After the third she stared straight ahead and tried in vain not to hear. Elayne's face grew tighter and tighter, colder and colder; her chin rose till it was a wonder she could see to walk.

There was a reason, Nynaeve had to admit grudgingly. In Ebou Dar, someone wearing silk might stroll the length of a square, maybe, but no further. Everybody else in sight wore wool or linen, seldom with much embroidery, except for an occasional beggar who had acquired a cast off silk garment, frayed on every edge and more hole than cloth. She just wished Mistress Anan had chosen some other explanation for why she was leading the pair of them through the streets. She wished she did not have to listen one more time to a tale of two flighty girls who had spent all their money on fine clothes to impress a man. Mat came out of it well, burn him. A fine young fellow, if Mistress Anan had not been married, a beautiful dancer with just a touch of the rogue. All of the women laughed. Not her or Elayne, though. Not the brainless little honeykissers – that was the word she used; Nynaeve could guess what it meant – honeykissers penniless from chasing after a man and their purses full of brass bits and tin to fool fools, witless loobies who would have been reduced to beggary or theft had Mistress Anan not known someone who might give them work in the kitchen.

'She doesn't have to stop at every inn in the city,' Nynaeve growled as she stalked away from The Stranded Goose, three broad stories with an innkeeper who wore large garnets at her ears despite the humble name. Mistress Anan hardly even glanced back to see they followed, now. 'Do you realize we'll never be able to show our own faces in any of those places!'

'I suspect that is exactly the point.' Every word out of Elayne's mouth was chipped from ice. 'Nynaeve, if you've sent us running after a wild pig ...' There was no need to complete the threat. With Birgitte and Aviendha to help, and they would, Elayne could make her life miserable until she was satisfied.

'They will take us right to the Bowl,' she insisted, flapping her hands to shoo a beggar with a horrible purple scar that obliterated one eye; she could recognize flour paste dyed with bluewort when she saw it. 'I know they will.' Elayne sniffed in an offensively expressive manner.

Nynaeve lost count of the number of bridges they crossed, large and small, with barges poling beneath. The sun climbed its own height above the rooftops, then twice. The Anan woman did not follow even so straight a line as she might have – she really did seem to be going out of her way to find inns – but they continued generally east, and Nynaeve thought they must be nearing the river when the hazel-eyed woman suddenly rounded on them.

'You watch your tongues, now. Speak when you're spoken to and not else. You embarrass me, and ...' With a final frown and a mutter half under her breath that she was probably making a mistake, she jerked her head for them to follow again, to a flat-roofed house right opposite.

It was not a large house, two stories without one balcony, cracked plaster and brick showing in several places, and hardly in an agreeable location, with the loud rattling of a weaver's looms to one side and the acrid stinks of a dyer's shop to the other. A maid answered the door, though, a graying woman with a square jaw, shoulders like a blacksmith, and a steely eye unsoftened by the sweat on her face. As Nynaeve followed Mistress Anan in, she smiled. Somewhere in that house, a woman was channeling.

The square-jawed maid obviously knew Setalle Anan on sight, but her reaction was odd. She curtsied with a very real respect, yet she was plainly surprised to see her, and obviously doubtful about her being there. She almost fluttered before letting them in. Nynaeve and Elayne were greeted with no ambivalence, though. They were shown to a sitting room one flight up, and the maid told them firmly, 'Don't stir a toe and don't touch anything, or you'll catch the old what-for,' then vanished.

Nynaeve looked at Elayne.

'Nynaeve, one woman channeling doesn't mean—' The feel changed, swelling for a moment, then subsiding, lower than before. 'Even two women doesn't mean anything,' Elayne protested, but she sounded doubtful. 'That was the most ill-mannered maid I've ever seen.' She took a tall-backed red chair, and after a moment Nynaeve sat too, but she perched on the edge. From eagerness, not nerves. Not nerves at all.

The room was not grand, but the blue-and-white floor tiles glistened, and the pale green walls looked freshly painted. No trace of gilt showed anywhere, of course, yet fine carving covered the red chairs arrayed along the walls and several small tables of a darker blue than the tiles. The lamps hanging from sconces were clearly brass, polished till they shone. Carefully arranged evergreen branches filled the swept hearth, and the lintel above the fireplace was carved, not plain stonework. The carving seemed an odd choice – what people around Ebou Dar called the Thirteen Sins; a man with eyes that nearly filled his whole face for Envy, a fellow with his tongue hanging to his ankles for Gossip, a snarling, sharp-toothed man clutching coins to his chest for Greed, and so on – but all in all, it satisfied her very much. Whoever could afford that room could afford fresh plaster outside, and the only reason not to put it up was to keep low, avoiding notice.

The maid had left the door open, and suddenly voices coming up the hall drifted through.

'I cannot believe you brought them here.' The speaker's tone was tight with incredulity and anger. 'You know how careful we are, Setalle. You know more than you should, and you surely know that.'

'I am very sorry, Reanne,' Mistress Anan answered stiffly. 'I suppose I didn't think. I ... submit myself, both to stand surety for these girls' behavior and to your judgment.'

'Of course not!' Reanne's tone was high with shock, now. 'That is to say . . . I mean, you shouldn't have, but . . . Setalle, I apologize for raising my voice. Say you forgive me.'

'You have no reason to apologize, Reanne.' The innkeeper managed to sound rueful and reluctant at the same time. 'I did wrong to bring them.'

'No, no, Setalle. I shouldn't have spoken to you so. Please, you must forgive me. Please do.'

The Anan woman and Reanne Corly entered the sitting room, and Nynaeve blinked in surprise. From the exchange, she had expected someone younger than Setalle Anan, but Reanne had hair more gray than not and a face full of what might have been smile lines, though they were creased in worry now. Why would the older woman humble herself so to the younger, and why would the younger allow it, however halfheartedly? Customs were different here, the Light knew, some more different than she liked to think about, yet not this much, surely. Of course, she had never gone very far toward being humble with the Women's Circle back home, but this . . .

Of course Reanne could channel – she had expected that; hoped for it, anyway – but she had not expected the strength. Reanne was not as strong as Elayne, or even Nicola – burn that wretched girl! – but she easily equaled Sheriam, say, or Kwamesa or Kiruna. Not many women possessed so much strength, and for all she herself bettered it by a fair margin, she was surprised to find it here. The woman must be one of the wilders; the Tower would have found a way to keep its hands on a woman like this if they had to hold her in a novice dress her whole life.

Nynaeve rose as they came through the doorway, smoothing her skirts. Not from nervousness, certainly; certainly not. Oh, but if only this came out right . . .

Reanne's sharp blue eyes studied the two of them with the air of someone who had just found a pair of pigs in her kitchen, fresh from the sty and dripping mud. She dabbed at her face with a tiny handkerchief, though the interior of the house was cooler than outside. 'I suppose we'll have to do something with them,' she murmured, 'if they are what they claim.' Her voice was quite high even now, musical and almost youthful. As she finished speaking she gave a small start for some reason and eyed the innkeeper sideways, which set off another round of Mistress Anan's reluctant apologies and Mistress Corly's flustered attempts to deflect them. In Ebou Dar, when folk were truly being polite, apologies back and forth could flow for an hour.

Elayne had risen too, wearing a slightly fixed smile. She raised an eyebrow at Nynaeve, cupped her elbow in one hand and laid a finger against her cheek.

Nynaeve cleared her throat. 'Mistress Corly, my name is Nynaeve al'Meara, and this is Elayne Trakand. We are looking for—'

'Setalle has told me all about you,' the blue-eyed woman cut in ominously. However many gray hairs on her head, Nynaeve suspected she was also hard as a stone fence. 'Abide with patience, girl, and I'll deal with you directly.' She turned back to Setalle, blotting her cheeks with the handkerchief. Barely suppressed diffidence once more tinged her voice. 'Setalle, if you will please excuse me, I must question these girls, and—'

'Look who is returned after all these years,' a short, stout woman in her middle years blurted as she barged into the room, nodding at her companion. Despite her red-belted Ebou Dari dress and a tanned face that glistened damply, her accents were pure Cairhienin. Her equally sweaty companion, in the dark, plainly cut woolens of a merchant, was a head taller, no older than Nynaeve, with dark tilted eyes, a strongly hooked nose, and a wide mouth. 'It's Garenia! She—' The flow of words terminated abruptly in confusion as the stout woman realized others were present.

Reanne clasped her hands as if in prayer, or perhaps because she wanted to hit someone. 'Berowin,' she said with an edge, 'one day you will run right off a cliff before you see it under your feet.'

'I am sorry, Eld—' Blushing, the Cairhienin lowered her eyes. The Saldaean became intent on fiddling with a circle of red stones pinned at her breast.

For Nynaeve's part, she gave Elayne a triumphant look. Both newcomers could channel, and *saidar* was still being wielded somewhere in the house. Two more, and while Berowin was not very strong, Garenia stood even above Reanne; she could match Lelaine or Romanda. Not that that mattered, of course, yet this made at least five. Elayne's chin set stubbornly, but then she sighed and gave a small nod. Sometimes it took the most incredible effort to convince her of anything.

'Your name is Garenia?' Mistress Anan said slowly, frowning at the woman in question. 'You look very much like someone I met once. Zarya Alkaese.'

Dark tilted eyes blinked in surprise. Plucking a lace-trimmed handkerchief from her sleeve, the Saldaean merchant touched her cheeks. 'That is my grandmother's sister's name,' she said after a moment. 'I'm told I favor her strongly. Was she well when you saw her? She forgot her family completely after she went off to become Aes Sedai.'

'Your grandmother's sister.' The innkeeper laughed softly. 'Of course. She was well when I saw her, but that was a long time ago. I was younger than you are now.'

Reanne had been hovering at her side, all but grabbing her elbow, and now she leaped in. 'Setalle, I truly am sorry, but I really must ask you to excuse us. You will forgive me not showing you to the door?'

Mistress Anan made her own apologies, as if she was at fault because the other woman could not escort her down, and departed with a last, very dubious look at Nynaeve and Elayne.

'Setalle!' Garenia exclaimed as soon as the innkeeper was gone. 'That was Setalle Anan? How did she—? Light of Heaven! Even after seventy years, the Tower would—'

'Garenia,' Mistress Corly said in an extremely sharp tone. Her stare was sharper still, and the Saldaean's face reddened. 'Since you two are here, we can make up the three for questioning. You girls stay where you are and keep silent.' That last was for Nynaeve and Elayne. The other women withdrew to a corner in a huddle and began conversing in soft murmurs.

Elayne moved nearer Nynaeve. 'I did not like being treated as a novice when I *was* a novice. How long do you intend to continue this farce?'

Nynaeve hissed at her for quiet. 'I'm trying to listen, Elayne,' she whispered.

Using the Power was out of the question, of course. The three would have known on the instant. Fortunately, they wove no barriers, perhaps not knowing how, and sometimes their voices rose just enough.

'... said they may be wilders,' Reanne said, and shock and revulsion bloomed on the other women's faces.

'Then we show them the door,' Berowin said. 'The back door. Wilders!'

'I still want to know who this Setalle Anan is,' Garenia put in.

'If you can't keep your mind on the straight,' Reanne told her, 'perhaps you should spend this turn on the farm. Alise knows how to concentrate a mind wonderfully. Now ...' The words dropped back to a buzz.

Another maid appeared, a slender woman, pretty except for a sullen expression, with a rough gray woolen dress and a long white apron. Setting a green-lacquered tray on one of the small tables, she surreptitiously wiped her cheeks with a corner of her apron and began fussing with blue-glazed cups and a matching teapot. Nynaeve's eyebrows rose. This woman could channel, too, if not to any high degree. What was she doing as a servant?

Garenia glanced over her shoulder, and gave a start. 'What did Derys do to earn penance? I thought fish would sing the day she cracked a rule, much less broke one.'

Berowin sniffed loudly, but her reply was barely audible. 'She wanted to marry. She will advance a turn and go with Keraille the day after the Feast of the Half Moon. That will settle for Master Denal.'

'Perhaps you both wish to hoe the fields for Alise?' Reanne spoke dryly, and the voices fell again.

Nynaeve felt a rush of exultation. She did not care much for rules, at least for other people's rules – other people rarely saw the situation as clearly as she, and thus made stupid rules; why should that woman, Derys, not marry if she wished, for example? – but rules and penances spoke of a society. She *was* right. And another thing. She nudged Elayne until the other woman bent her head.

'Berowin's wearing a red belt,' she whispered. That indicated a Wise Woman, one of Ebou Dar's fabled healers, their care known far and wide as the next best to being Healed by an Aes Sedai, curing just about anything. Supposedly it was all done with herbs and knowledge, but ... 'How many Wise Women have we seen, Elayne? How many could channel? How many were Ebou Dari, or even Altaran?'

'Seven, counting Berowin' was the slow answer, 'and only one I was sure was from here.' Hah! The others plainly had not been. Elayne took a deep breath, though she went on softly. '*None* had anywhere near these women's strength, though.' At least she had not suggested they were mistaken somehow; all of those Wise Women had been able. 'Nynaeve, are you really suggesting that the Wise Women ... *all* the Wise Women ... are ... ? That would be *beyond* incredible.'

'Elayne, this city has a guild for the men who sweep the squares every night! I think we've just found the Ancient Muckety-muck Sisterhood of Wise Women.'

The stubborn woman shook her head. 'The Tower would have had a hundred sisters here years ago, Nynaeve. Two hundred. Anything of the sort would have been squashed flat in short order.'

'Maybe the Tower doesn't know,' Nynaeve said. 'Maybe the guild keeps low enough that the Tower never thought they were worth troubling. There's no law against channeling if you aren't Aes Sedai, only against claiming to be Aes Sedai, or misusing the Power. Or bringing discredit.' That meant doing anything that might possibly cast a bad light on real Aes Sedai, should anyone happen to think you were one, which was going pretty far, to her way of thinking. The real trouble, though, was that she did not believe it. The Tower seemed to know everything, and they probably would break up a quilting circle if the women in it could channel. Yet there had to be some explanation for ...

Only half-aware, she felt the True Source being embraced, but suddenly she became very aware. Her mouth fell open as a flow of Air snared her braid right at the base of her skull and ran her across the room on her toes. Elayne ran right beside her, red-faced with fury. The worst of it was, they were both shielded.

The short run ended when they were allowed to settle their heels in front of Mistress Corly and the other two, all three seated against the wall in red chairs, all surrounded by the glow of *saidar*.

'You were told to be quiet,' Reanne said firmly. 'If we decide to help you, you will have to learn that we expect strict obedience no less than the White Tower itself.' She imbued those last words with a tone of reverence. 'I will tell you that you would have been treated more gently if you had not come to us in this irregular fashion.' The flow gripping Nynaeve's braid vanished. Elayne tossed her head angrily as she was released.

Appalled astonishment became fiery outrage as Nynaeve realized that Berowin held her shield. Most Aes Sedai she had met stood above Berowin; nearly all. Gathering herself, she strained to reach the Source, expecting the weaves to shatter. She would at least show these women she would not be ... The weaves ... stretched. The round Cairhienin woman smiled, and Nynaeve's face darkened. The shield stretched further, further, bulging like a ball. It would not break. That was impossible. Anyone could block her from the Source if they caught her by surprise, of course, and someone weaker could hold the shield once woven, but not *this* much weaker. And a shield did not bend that far without breaking. It was impossible!

'You could burst a blood vessel if you keep at that,' Berowin said, almost companionably. 'We do not try to reach above our station, but skills are honed with time, and this was always nearly a Talent with me. I could hold one of the Forsaken.'

Scowling, Nynaeve gave over. She could wait. Since she had no choice, she could.

Derys came bearing her tray, distributing cups of dark tea. To the three seated women. She never so much as glanced at Nynaeve or Elayne before making a perfect curtsy and returning to her table.

'We could have been drinking blueberry tea, Nynaeve,' Elayne said, shooting such a look at her that she came close to stepping back. Maybe it would be best not to wait too long.

'Be quiet, girl.' Mistress Corly's tone might be calm, but she patted her handkerchief to her face angrily. 'Our report of you says you both are forward and contentious, that you chase after men and lie. To which I add that you cannot follow simple instructions. All of which must change if you seek our help. All of it. This is most irregular. Be grateful we're willing to speak to you.'

'We do seek your help,' Nynaeve said. She wished Elayne would stop glaring so. It was worse than the Corly woman's hard stare. Well, as bad, anyway. 'We desperately need to find a *ter'angreal*—'

Reanne Corly broke in as if she had been standing there silent. 'Usually, we know the girls brought to us beforehand, but we must make certain you are what you say. How many doors to the Tower Library may a novice use, and which?' She took a sip of tea, waiting.

'Two.' The word dripped venom from Elayne's mouth. 'The main doors to the east, when a sister sends her, or the small door at the southwest corner, called the Novice Door, when she goes for herself. How long, Nynaeve?'

Garenia, who held Elayne's shield, channeled another slender flow of Air, not gently. Elayne quivered, then again, and Nynaeve winced, wondering that she did not grab at the back of her skirt. 'A civil tongue is another requirement,' Garenia murmured wryly into her cup.

'That is the right answer,' Mistress Corly said, as if nothing else had happened. Although she did eye the Saldaean woman briefly over her tea. 'Now, how many bridges in the Water Garden?'

'Three,' Nynaeve snapped, mainly because she knew. She had not known about the library, having never been a novice. 'We need to know—' Berowin could not spare anything to channel a flow of Air, but Mistress Corly could, and did. Barely keeping her face smooth, Nynaeve knotted her hands in her skirts to hold them still. Elayne had the gall to give her a small, chilly smile. Chilly, but satisfied.

A dozen more questions hammered at them, from how many floors the novice quarters contained – twelve – to under what circumstances a novice was allowed into the Hall of the Tower – to carry messages or to be expelled from the Tower for a crime; no others – hammered without Nynaeve getting in more than two words, and those two answered silently by the horrible Corly woman. She began to feel like a novice in the Hall; they were not allowed to speak a word either. That was one of the few answers she knew, but luckily Elayne responded promptly when she did not. Nynaeve might have done better had they asked about Accepted, a little better at least, but it was what a novice should know that interested them. She was just glad Elayne was willing to go along, though by her pale cheeks and raised chin, that could not last much longer.

'I suppose Nynaeve was really there,' Reanne said finally, exchanging glances with the other two. 'If Elayne taught her to pass, I think she would have done a better job. Some people live in perpetual fog.' Garenia sniffed, then nodded slowly. Berowin's nod came entirely too promptly for Nynaeve's liking.

'Please,' she said politely. She could be polite when there was reason, whatever anyone said. 'We truly need to find a *ter'angreal* the Sea Folk call the Bowl of the Winds. It's in a dusty old storeroom somewhere in the Rahad, and I think your guild, your Circle, must know where. Please help us.' Three suddenly stony faces stared at her.

'There is no *guild*,' Mistress Corly said coolly, 'only a few friends who found no place in the White Tower ...' Again, that reverential tone. '... and who are foolish enough occasionally to reach out a hand where it's needed. We have no truck with *ter'angreal*, or *angreal*, or *sa'angreal* either. We are not Aes Sedai.' 'Aes Sedai' echoed with veneration, as well. 'In any case, you are not here to ask questions. We have more for you, to see how far you've gone, after which you will be taken to the country and given into the care of a friend. She will keep you until we decide what to do next. Until we can be sure the sisters are not looking for you. You have a new life ahead of you, a new chance, if you can only let yourself see it. Whatever held you back in the Tower does not apply here, whether a lack of dexterity or fear or anything else. No one will push you to learn or do what you cannot. What you are is sufficient. Now.'

'Enough,' Elayne said in a wintery voice. 'Long *enough*, Nynaeve. Or do you intend to wait in the country for however long? They do *not* have it, Nynaeve.' Removing her Great Serpent ring from her belt pouch, she thrust the circle of gold onto her finger. From the way she looked at the seated women, no one would believe her shielded. She was a queen out of patience. She was Aes Sedai to her hair was what she was. 'I am Elayne Trakand, High Seat of House Trakand. I am Daughter-Heir of Andor and Aes Sedai of the Green Ajah, and I *demand* you release me immediately.' Nynaeve groaned.

Garenia grimaced with disgust, and Berowin's eyes widened in horror. Reanne Corly shook her head ruefully, but when she spoke, her voice was iron. 'I had hoped Setalle had changed your mind concerning that particular lie. I know how hard it is, to set out proudly for the White Tower then find yourself faced with returning home to admit failure. But that is never said, even in joke!'

'I made no joke,' Elayne said lightly. Snow was light.

Garenia leaned forward with a scowl, a flow of Air already forming until Mistress Corly raised her hand. 'And you, Nynaeve? Do you persist in this ... madness, too?'

Nynaeve filled her lungs. These women had to know where the Bowl was; they just had to!

'Nynaeve!' Elayne said peevishly. She was not going to let her forget this even if they did have to effect an escape. She had a way of harping on every little misstep in a manner that cut the ground right from under your feet.

'I am an Aes Sedai of the Yellow Ajah,' Nynaeve said wearily. 'The true Amyrlin Seat, Egwene al'Vere, raised us to the shawl in Salidar. She's no older than Elayne; you must have heard.' Not a glimmer of change in those three hard faces. 'She sent us to find the Bowl of the Winds. With it, we can mend the weather.' Not a flicker of change. She tried to hold her anger down; she truly did. It just oozed up despite her. 'You must want that! Look around you! The Dark One is strangling the world! If you have even a hint of where the Bowl might be, tell us!'

Mistress Corly motioned for Derys, who came and took the cups, casting fearful, wide-eyed looks at Nynaeve and Elayne. When she scurried away, out of the room in fact, the three women stood slowly, standing like grim magistrates pronouncing sentence.

'I regret that you will not accept our help,' Mistress Corly said coldly. 'I regret this whole affair.' Reaching into her pouch, she pressed three silver marks into Nynaeve's hand and another three into Elayne's. 'These will take you a little way. You can also get something for those dresses, I should think, if not what you paid. Those are hardly suitable garments for a journey. By tomorrow sunrise, you will be gone from Ebou Dar.'

'We aren't going anywhere,' Nynaeve told her. 'Please, if you know—' She might as well have kept silent. The measured flow of words did not slow.

'At that time we will begin circulating your descriptions, and we will make certain they reach the sisters in the Tarasin Palace. If you are seen after sunrise, we will see that the sisters know where you are, and the Whitecloaks as well. Your choice then will be to run, surrender to the sisters, or die. Go, do not return, and you should live long if you give over this repulsive and dangerous ruse. We are done with you. Berowin, see to them, please.' Brushing between them, she went from the room without looking back.

Sullenly, Nynaeve let herself be herded down to the front door. A struggle would not achieve anything except maybe being thrown out bodily, but she did not like giving up. Light, she did not! Elayne marched, frozen determination to leave and be done shining in every line of her.

In the small entry hall, Nynaeve decided to try once more. 'Please, Garenia, Berowin, if you have any hint, tell us. Any clue at all. You must see how important this is. You must!'

'"The blindest are those who keep their eyes shut,"' Elayne quoted, not quite under her breath.

Berowin hesitated, but not Garenia. She put her face right in Nynaeve's. 'Do you think we're fools, girl? I'll tell you this. If I had my way, we would bundle you out to the farm no matter what you say. A few months of Alise's attentions, and you'd learn to guard your tongue and be grateful for the help you spit on.' Nynaeve considered hitting her on the nose; she did not need *saidar* to use her fist.

'Garenia,' Berowin said sharply. 'Apologize! We do not hold anyone against her will, and you know it well. Apologize immediately!'

And wonder of wonders, the woman who would have stood very close to the top had she been Aes Sedai looked sideways at the woman who would have stood near the bottom, and blushed crimson. 'I ask forgiveness,' Garenia mumbled at Nynaeve. 'My temper gets the better of me sometimes, and I say what I have no right to. I humbly ask forgiveness.' Another sidelong glance at Berowin, who nodded, producing a sigh of open relief.

While Nynaeve was still gaping, the shields were released, and she and Elayne were pushed into the street, the door slamming shut behind them.

Chapter 24

The Kin

Incredible, Reanne thought, watching from a window as the two strange girls vanished down the street among the tradesmen and beggars and occasional sedan chairs. She had returned to the meeting room as soon as the pair was escorted from it. She did not know what to make of them, and their persistent claims in the face of all reason were only part of her confusion.

'They did not perspire,' Berowin whispered at her shoulder.

'Yes?' She would have arranged for the news to reach the Tarasin Palace in the next hour if she had not given her word. And if not for the danger. Fear bubbled in her middle, the same panic that had overtaken her after one passage through the silver arches when she went to test for Accepted. Just as she had every time it had stirred in the years since, she took a fresh grip on herself; in truth, she did not realize that the fear she might run screaming again had long since conquered any possibility that she would. She prayed that those girls would abandon their insanity. She prayed that if they did not, they were caught far from Ebou Dar and either kept silent or were not believed. Precautions would have to be taken, safeguards carried out that had not been used in years. Aes Sedai were as near omnipotent as made no difference, though. That, she knew in her bones.

'Eldest, could it be possible that the older of the two really is . . . ? We channeled, and . . .'

Berowin trailed off miserably, but Reanne did not need to consider, not even setting aside the younger girl. Why would any Aes

Sedai pretend to be less, so much less? Besides, any real Aes Sedai would have put them all on their knees begging mercy, not stood there so submissively.

'We did not channel in front of an Aes Sedai,' she said firmly. 'We broke no rule.' Those rules applied to her as strictly as anyone else; the very first was that they were all one, even those set above for a time. How could it have been otherwise, when those who were above must eventually step down? Only through movement and change could they remain hidden.

'But some of the rumors do mention a girl as Amyrlin, Eldest. And she knew—'

'Rebels.' Reanne put into that all the outraged disbelief she felt. That anyone should *dare* to rebel against the White Tower! It was hardly strange for unbelievable tales to attach to anyone like that.

'What about Logain, and the Red Ajah?' Garenia demanded, and Reanne fixed her with a stare. The woman had gotten herself another cup of tea before coming back up, and she managed to sip defiantly.

'Whatever the truth, Garenia, it is not our place to criticize anything Aes Sedai might do.' Reanne's mouth tightened. That hardly squared with what she felt toward the rebels, but how could any Aes Sedai do such a thing?

The Saldaean bent her neck in acquiescence, though, and perhaps to hide the sullen twist of her mouth. Reanne sighed. She herself had given up dreams of the Green Ajah long long ago, but there were those like Berowin who believed, secretly they thought, that somehow they might one day return to the White Tower, somehow yet become Aes Sedai. And then there were women like Garenia, almost as poor at keeping their wishes secret, though those wishes were ten times as forbidden. They actually would have accepted wilders, and even gone out to find girls who could be taught!

Garenia was not done; she always skirted the edges of discipline, and frequently stepped over. 'What of this Setalle Anan, then? Those girls know about the Circle. The Anan woman must have told them, though how she knows . . . ' She shuddered in a way that would have been entirely too ostentatious for most others, but she had never been able to conceal her emotions. Even when she should.

'Whoever betrayed us to her must be found, and her betrayal punished too. She's an innkeeper, and she must be taught to guard her tongue!' Berowin gasped, wide-eyed with shock, and dropped into a chair so hard she nearly bounced.

'Remember who she is, Garenia,' Reanne said sharply. 'If Setalle had betrayed us, we would be crawling to Tar Valon, begging forgiveness the whole way.' When she first came to Ebou Dar, she had been told the story of a woman made to crawl to the White Tower, and nothing she had seen since of Aes Sedai made her question it in the least. 'She has kept the few secrets she knows from gratitude, and I doubt that has faded. She would have died in her first childbirth if the Kin had not helped her. What she knows comes from careless tongues, when it was thought she could not hear, and the owners of those tongues were punished more than twenty years ago.' Still, she wished there was some way she could bring herself to ask Setalle to be more circumspect. She must have spoken carelessly in front of those girls.

The woman bowed her head again, but her mouth was set stubbornly. At least part of this turn, Reanne decided, Garenia would spend at the retreat, and she would have special instructions to relay with her own stubborn mouth. Alise seldom required more than a week to make a woman decide stubbornness did not pay.

Before she could inform Garenia, though, Derys was curtsying in the doorway, announcing Sarainya Vostovan. As usual, Sarainya swept right in before Reanne could say to admit her. In some ways, the strikingly handsome woman made Garenia appear supple, despite keeping the form of every rule exactly. Reanne was sure she would have worn her hair in braids and bells given the choice, and never mind how that would have looked with her red belt. But then, given the choice she would not have served even one turn with the belt.

Sarainya did curtsy at the door, of course, and kneel before her, head lowered, but fifty years had not made her forget that she would have been a woman of considerable power had she been able to make herself return home to Arafel. Curtsy and the rest all were concessions. When she spoke, in that husky, forceful voice, whether the woman would ever reconcile herself and the problem of Garenia left Reanne's mind.

'Callie is dead, Eldest Sister. Her throat was cut and she apparently had been robbed even of her stockings, but Sumeko says that it was the One Power killed her.'

'That is impossible!' Berowin burst out. 'No Kinswoman would do such a thing!'

'An Aes Sedai?' Garenia said, hesitant for once. 'But how? The Three Oaths. Sumeko must be wrong.'

Reanne raised a hand for silence. Sumeko was never wrong, not in this area. She would have been Yellow Ajah had she not broken down completely while testing for the shawl, and although it was forbidden, despite countless penances, she worked to learn more whenever she thought no one was watching. No Aes Sedai could have done this, obviously, and no Kinswoman would have, but ... Those girls, so insistent, knowing what they should not. The Circle had lasted too long, offered succor to too many women, to be destroyed now.

'This is what must be done,' she told them. That flutter of fear began again, but for once she hardly noticed.

Nynaeve stalked away from the small house in outrage. It was incredible! Those women did have a guild; she knew they did! Whatever they said, she was sure they knew where the Bowl was, too. She would have done whatever was necessary to bring them to tell her. Pretending docility before them for a few hours would have been a deal easier than putting up with Mat Cauthon for the Light knew how many days.

I could have been as acquiescent as they wanted, she thought irritably. *They'd have thought I was a pliable old slipper! I could have...* That was a lie, and it did not take a foul, remembered taste to convince her. Given half a chance, she would have shaken every one of those women till they told her what she wanted to know. She would have given them Aes Sedai till they squeaked!

She scowled sideways at Elayne. The other woman seemed lost in thought. Nynaeve wished she did not know what the woman was thinking about. A wasted morning, and not far short of complete humiliation. She did not like being in the wrong. She was not yet used to admitting she was, really. And now she was going to have to apologize to Elayne. She *truly* hated apologizing. Well, it would be bad enough back in their rooms. With Birgitte and Aviendha still out, it was to be hoped. She was not about to begin in the street, with who knew who streaming by. The throng had thickened, though the sun hardly seemed much higher through the wheeling clouds of seabirds that cried overhead.

Finding their way was not easy, after all those twists and turns. Nynaeve had to ask directions half a dozen times, while Elayne stared in another direction, pretending indifference. She stalked along across bridges, ducked around wagons and carts, jumped out of the way of racing sedan chairs that wove through the crowds, wished Elayne would say something. Nynaeve knew how to nurse a grudge, and the longer she herself kept silent, the worse it was when she spoke, so the longer Elayne walked without speaking, the darker became the image in her mind of how it was going to be back in their rooms. That made her furious. She had admitted she was wrong, if only to herself. Elayne had no right to make her suffer this way. She began wearing such a face that even people who did not notice their rings gave them a clear path. People who did notice usually seemed to find an urgent need to be a street away. Even some sedan-chair bearers skirted around her.

'How old did Reanne look to you?' Elayne asked suddenly. Nynaeve nearly jumped. They were almost back to Mol Hara.

'Fifty years. Maybe sixty. I don't see it matters.' She ran her eyes over the crowd to see if anyone was close enough to hear. A passing hawker, her tray displaying a bitter little yellow fruit called a lemon, tried to swallow her cry in midshout when Nynaeve's gaze rested on her for a moment, with the result that she doubled over her tray coughing and choking. Nynaeve sniffed. The woman probably had been eavesdropping, if not planning to cut a purse. 'They *are* a guild, Elayne, and they *do* know where the Bowl is. I just know they do.' That was not what she had intended to say at all. If she apologized for dragging Elayne into this now, maybe it would not be so bad.

'I suppose they are,' Elayne said absently. 'I suppose they might. How is it that she can have aged so?'

Nynaeve stopped dead in the middle of the street. After all that arguing, after getting them thrown out, she *supposed*? 'Well, *I* suppose she aged the same way as the rest of us, a day at a time. Elayne, if you believed, why did you announce who you were like Rhiannon at the Tower?' She rather liked that; according to the story, what Queen Rhiannon got was far from what she had wanted.

The question did not seem to register with Elayne, for all her education. She pulled Nynaeve to one side as a curtained green carriage rumbled past – the street was not very wide there – over to the front of a seamstress's shop with a wide doorway showing several dressmaker's forms clothed in half-done dresses.

'They were not going to tell us anything, Nynaeve, not if you got down on your knees and begged.' Nynaeve opened her mouth indignantly, then snapped it shut. She had never said anything about begging. Anyway, why should she have been the only one? Better any woman at all than Mat Cauthon. Elayne had a fly up her nose, though, and was not to be distracted. 'Nynaeve, she must have slowed like everyone else. How old is she, to look fifty or sixty?'

'What are you talking about?' Without thinking Nynaeve noted the location in a corner of her mind; the seamstress's work looked quite good, worth closer examination. 'She probably doesn't channel any more than she can help, afraid as she is of being mistaken for a sister. She wouldn't have wanted her face too smooth, after all.'

'You never listened in class, did you?' Elayne murmured. She saw the plump seamstress beaming in the doorway, and drew Nynaeve toward the corner of the building. Considering the amount of lace the seamstress wore on her own dress, the bodice buried in it and pieces of it drooping over her exposed petticoats, she would bear close watching if Nynaeve did order anything. 'Forget clothes for one moment, Nynaeve. Who is the oldest Accepted you remember?'

She gave Elayne a very level look. The woman made it sound as if she never thought of anything else! And she had too listened. Sometimes. 'Elin Warrel, I think. She's about my age, I think.' Of course, the seamstress's own dress would look fine with a more modest neckline and much less lace. In green silk. Lan liked green, though she certainly was not going to choose her dresses for him. He liked blue, as well.

Elayne barked such a laugh that Nynaeve wondered whether she had spoken aloud. Coloring fiercely, she tried to explain – she was sure she could; by Bel Tine – but the other woman gave her no opportunity for a word. 'Elin's sister came to visit her just before you first arrived at the Tower, Nynaeve. Her *younger* sister. The woman had *gray* hair. Well, some of it was. She must have been over *forty*, Nynaeve.'

Elin Warrel was past forty? But ...! 'What are you saying, Elayne?'

No one was close enough to listen, and no one seemed to be giving them a second glance except the still hopeful seamstress, but Elayne lowered her voice to a whisper. 'We *slow*, Nynaeve. Somewhere between twenty and twenty-five, we begin aging more slowly. How much depends on how strong we are, but when doesn't. Any woman who can channel does it. Takima said she thought it was the beginning of achieving the ageless look, though I don't think anyone has ever reached that until they've worn the shawl at *least* a year or two, sometimes five or more. Think. You *know* any sister with gray hair is *old*, even if you aren't supposed to mention it. So if Reanne slowed, and she must have, how old is she?'

Nynaeve did not care how old Reanne was. She wanted to cry. No wonder everyone refused to believe her age. It explained why the Women's Circle back home had looked over her shoulder as if unsure she was old enough to be trusted fully. Achieving a sister's ageless face was all very well, but how long before she had her gray hairs?

Blinking, she turned away angrily. And something struck her a glancing blow on the back of the head. Staggering, she rounded on Elayne in astonishment. Why had the woman hit her? Only, Elayne lay in a heap, eyes closed and a nasty purple lump rising on her temple. Groggily, Nynaeve fell to her knees and gathered her friend into her arms.

'Your friend must be taken ill,' a long-nosed woman said, kneeling beside them, careless of a yellow dress that showed far too much bosom even by Ebou Dari standards. 'Let me help.'

A tall fellow, handsome in his embroidered silk vest except for a rather oily grin, bent to take Nynaeve's shoulders. 'Here, I have a carriage. We'll take you somewhere more comfortable than a paving stone.'

'Go away,' Nynaeve told them politely. 'We don't need your help.'

The man kept trying to raise her to her feet, though, to guide her toward a red carriage, where a startled-appearing woman in blue beckoned vigorously. The long-nosed woman actually tried to lift Elayne, thanking the man for his help and chattering how his carriage sounded a fine idea. A crowd of onlookers seemed to have gathered out of air in a semicircle, women murmuring sympathy about fainting from the heat, men offering to help carry the ladies. A scrawny fellow, bold as you please, reached for Nynaeve's purse almost right under her nose.

Her head still swam enough to make embracing *saidar* difficult, but if all those nattering folk had not fueled her temper, what she saw lying in the street would have. An arrow with a blunt stone head. The one that had grazed her or the one that had struck Elayne. She channeled, and the scrawny cutpurse doubled over, clutching himself and squealing like a pig in briars. Another flow, and the long-nosed woman fell over backward with a shriek twice as high. The man in the silk vest apparently decided they did not need his help after all, because he turned and ran for the carriage, but she gave him a dose anyway. He out-bellowed any outraged bull as the woman in the carriage hauled him in by his vest.

'Thank you, but we don't need any help,' Nynaeve shouted. Politely.

Few remained to hear. Once it became clear that the One Power was being used – and folk suddenly leaping about and yelling for no visible cause made it clear enough to most – they hurried elsewhere. The long-nosed woman gathered herself up and actually jumped onto the back of the red carriage, clinging precariously as the dark-vested driver whipped the horses away through the crowd, people leaping aside. Even the cutpurse hobbled off as fast as he could.

Nynaeve could not have cared less had the earth opened and swallowed the whole lot. Chest aching, she ran fine flows of Wind and Water, Earth, Fire and Spirit mixed and blended, through Elayne. It was a simple weave, no bother despite her faint dizziness, and the result let her breathe again. The bruise was not serious; the bones of Elayne's skull were unbroken. Normally, she would have redirected those same flows into much more complex weaves, the Healing she had discovered herself. At the moment, simpler weaves were all she could manage, though. With just Spirit, Wind and Water, she wove the Healing that Yellows had used since time immemorial.

Elayne's eyes shot open wide, and with a gasp that seemed to take all the air in her, she convulsed like a netted trout, slippered heels drumming on the pavement. That only lasted a moment, of course, but in that moment the bruise shrank and vanished.

Nynaeve helped her to her feet – and a woman's hand appeared, holding a pewter cup full of water. 'Even an Aes Sedai might be thirsty after that,' the seamstress said.

Elayne reached for it, but Nynaeve laid fingers on her wrist. 'No, thank you.' The woman shrugged, and as she turned away, Nynaeve added in a different tone, 'Thank you.' It seemed to come easier the more you said it; she was not sure she liked that.

That ocean of lace heaved as the seamstress shrugged again. 'I make dresses for anyone. I can do better for your coloring than that.' She vanished back into her shop. Nynaeve frowned after her.

'What happened?' Elayne demanded. 'Why wouldn't you let me take a drink? I'm thirsty *and* hungry.'

With a last frown for the seamstress, Nynaeve bent to pick up the arrow.

The other woman needed no explanations. *Saidar* shone around her in a flash. 'Teslyn and Joline?'

Nynaeve shook her head; the slight wooziness seemed to be fading. She did not think those two would stoop to this. She did not think so. 'What about Reanne?' she said quietly. The seamstress was back in the doorway, still hopeful. 'She might want to make sure we leave. Or worse, maybe Garenia.' That was almost as chilling as Teslyn and Joline. And twice as infuriating.

Somehow Elayne managed to look pretty while scowling. 'Whoever it was, we will settle them. You'll see.' The scowl faded. 'Nynaeve, if the Circle does know where the Bowl is, we can find it, but . . .' She bit her lip, hesitating. 'I only know one way to be sure.'

Nynaeve nodded slowly, though she would rather have eaten a handful of dirt. Today had seemed so bright for a time, but then it had spiraled into darkness, from Reanne to . . . Oh, Light, how long before she had her gray hair?

'Don't cry, Nynaeve. Mat can't possibly be that bad. He'll find it for us in a few days, I know.'

Nynaeve only cried harder.

CHAPTER 25

Mindtrap

Moghedien did not want to dream the dream again, but wanting to wake, wanting to scream, did no good. Sleep held her faster than any manacles. The beginning went by quickly, a sketchy blur. No mercy; she would have to relive the rest that much sooner.

She barely recognized the woman who entered the tent where she was held prisoner. Halima, secretary to one of these fools who called themselves Aes Sedai. Fools, yet they held her tightly enough by the band of silver metal around her neck, held her and made her obey. Fast movement, though she prayed for slowness. *The woman channeled to make a light, and Moghedien saw only the light. It had to be* saidin *– among the living, only the Chosen knew how to tap the True Power – the Power that came from the Dark One – and few were fool enough to except in direst need – but that was impossible!* Blurring quickness. *The woman named herself Aran'gar and called Moghedien by name, she gave summons to the Pit of Doom and removed the* a'dam *necklace, flinching at pain no woman should have felt. Again – how many times had she done this? – again Moghedien wove a small gateway in the tent. She Skimmed to give herself time to think in the endless dark, but no sooner did she step onto her platform, like a small enclosed marble balcony complete with a comfortable chair, than she arrived on the black slopes of Shayol Ghul, forever shrouded in twilight, where vents and tunnels emitted steam and smoke and harsh vapors, and a Myrddraal came to her in its dead black garb, like a slug-white, eyeless man, but taller, more massive than any other Halfman. It regarded her arrogantly, and gave its odd name unbidden, and commanded her to come;*

these were not things Myrddraal did with the Chosen. Now she screamed in the depths of her mind for the dream to move faster, to blur beyond seeing, beyond knowing, but *now, as she followed Shaidar Haran's back into the entrance to the Pit of Doom, now all flowed at its normal pace and seemed more real than* Tel'aran'rhiod *or the waking world.*

Tears leaked from Moghedien's eyes, down cheeks that already glistened. She twitched on her hard pallet, arms and legs jerking as she fought desperately, futilely, to wake. She was no longer aware that she dreamed – all seemed real – but deep memories remained, and in those depths, instinct shrieked and clawed for escape.

She was well familiar with the sloping tunnel ceilinged in stone daggers like fangs, the walls glowing with pale light. Many times she had made this downward journey since the day so long ago when she first came to make obeisance to the Great Lord and pledge her soul, but never as now, never with her failure known in all its magnitude. Always before she had managed to hide failures even from the Great Lord. Many times. Things could be done here that could be done nowhere else. Things could happen here that could happen nowhere else.

She gave a start as one of the stone fangs brushed her hair, then gathered herself as best she could. Those spikes and blades still cleared the strange, too-tall Myrddraal easily, but though it overtopped her by head and shoulders and more, she was forced to move her head around their points now. Reality was clay to the Great Lord here, and he often made his displeasure known so. A stone tooth struck her shoulder, and she ducked to go under another. There was no longer enough height in the tunnel for her to straighten as she walked. She bent lower, scurrying crouched in the Myrddraal's wake, trying to get closer. Its stride never changed, but no matter how quickly she scuttled, the interval between them did not lessen. The ceiling descended, the Great Lord's fangs to rend traitors and fools, and Moghedien dropped to hands and knees, crawling, then flattened to elbows and knees. Light flared and flickered in the tunnel, cast from the entrance to the Pit itself, just ahead, and Moghedien slithered on her belly, pulled herself along with her hands, pushed with her feet. Stone points dug at her flesh, caught at her dress. Panting, she wriggled the last distance to the sound of ripping wool.

Staring back over her shoulder, she shivered convulsively. Where the tunnel mouth should have been stood a smooth stone wall. Perhaps the Great Lord had timed it all exactly, and perhaps, had she been slower ...

The ledge on which she lay projected above a black-mottled red lake of molten rock where flames the size of men danced and died and reappeared. Overhead, the cavern rose roofless through the mountain to a sky where wild clouds raced, striated red and yellow and black, as if on the winds of time themselves. It was not the dark-clouded sky seen outside on Shayol Ghul. None of that earned a second glance, and not just because she had seen it many times. The Bore into the Great Lord's place of imprisonment was no closer here than anywhere else in the world, but here she could feel it, here she could bathe in the radiant glory of the Great Lord. The True Power washed around her, so strong here that attempting to channel it would fry her to a cinder. Not that she had any desire to pay the price elsewhere either.

She started to push up to her knees, and something struck her between the shoulder blades, driving her down hard onto the stone ledge, crushing the air from her lungs. Stunned, she struggled for breath, then stared back up over her shoulder. The Myrddraal stood with one massive boot planted firmly on her back. Almost, she embraced saidar, *though channeling here without express permission was a good way to die. The arrogance on the slopes above was one thing, but this!*

'Do you know who I am?' she demanded. 'I am Moghedien!' That eyeless gaze watched her as it might an insect; she had often seen Myrddraal look at ordinary humans that way.

MOGHEDIEN. That voice inside her head flushed away all thought of the Myrddraal; it nearly flushed away all thought. Beside this, any human lover's deepest embrace was a drop of water beside the ocean. HOW DEEP IS YOUR FAILURE, MOGHEDIEN? THE CHOSEN ARE ALWAYS THE STRONGEST, BUT YOU LET YOURSELF BE CAPTURED. YOU TAUGHT THOSE WHO WOULD OPPOSE ME, MOGHEDIEN.

Eyelids fluttering, she fought for coherence. 'Great Lord, I taught them only small things, and I fought them as I could. I taught them a supposed way to detect a man channeling.' She managed to laugh. 'Practicing it gives them such headaches they cannot channel for hours.' Silence. Perhaps as well. They had given up trying to learn that long before her rescue, but the Great Lord did not need to know that. 'Great Lord, you know how I have served you. I serve in the shadows, and your enemies never feel my bite until my venom is working.' She did not quite dare say she had deliberately let herself be captured, to work from within, but she could suggest. 'Great Lord, you know how many of your enemies I brought down in the War of Power. From the shadows, unseen, or if seen, ignored because I could not possibly be a threat.' Silence. And then . . .

MY CHOSEN ARE ALWAYS THE STRONGEST. MY HAND MOVES.

That voice reverberating in her skull turned her bones to boiling honey and her brain to fire. The Myrddraal had her chin in its hand, forcing her head up before her vision cleared enough to see the knife in its other hand. All her dreams were to end here in a slit throat, her body going to feed the Trollocs. Perhaps Shaidar Haran would save a choice cut for itself. Perhaps . . .

No. She knew she was going to die, but this Myrddraal would not eat one shred of her! She reached to embrace saidar, *and her eyes bulged. There was nothing there. Nothing! It was as if she had been severed! She knew she had not – it was said that tearing was the deepest pain anyone could know, beyond any power to deaden – but—!*

In those stunned moments, the Myrddraal forced her mouth open, scraped the blade along her tongue, then nicked her ear. And as it straightened with her blood and saliva, she knew, even before it produced what appeared to be a tiny, fragile cage of gold wire and crystal. Some things could only be done here, some only to those who could channel, and she had brought a number of men and women for this very purpose.

'No,' she breathed. Her eyes could not leave the cour'souvra. *'No, not me! NOT ME!'*

Ignoring her, Shaidar Haran scraped the fluids from the knife onto the cour'souvra. *The crystal turned a milky pink, the first setting. With a flick of its wrist, it tossed the mindtrap out over the lake of molten stone for the second. The gold and crystal cage arched through the air and suddenly stopped, floating at the very spot where it seemed the Bore was, the place where the Pattern lay thinnest of all.*

Moghedien forgot the Myrddraal. She flung out her hands toward the Bore. 'Mercy, Great Lord!' She had never noticed that the Great Lord of the Dark possessed any mercy, but had she been bound in a cell with rabid wolves or with a darath *in moult, she would have begged the same. In the right circumstances, you begged even for the impossible. The* cour'souvra *hung in midair, turning slowly, glittering in the light of leaping fires below. 'I have served you with all my heart, Great Lord. I beg mercy. I beg! MER-CYYYYYYY!'*

YOU MAY SERVE ME STILL.

The voice flung her into ecstasy beyond knowing, but at the same instant the sparkling mindtrap suddenly glowed like the sun, and in the midst of rapture, she knew pain as if she had been immersed in the fiery lake. They blended, and she howled, thrashing like a mad thing, thrashing in endless pain, endless, until after Ages, after nothing remained but agony and the memory of agony, the tiny mercy of darkness overwhelmed her.

Moghedien stirred on the pallet. Not again. Please.

She barely recognized the woman who entered the tent where she was held prisoner.

Please, she shrieked in the depths of her mind.

The woman channeled to make a light, and Moghedien saw only the light.

Deep in sleep, she quivered, vibrating from head to toe. Please!

The woman named herself Aran'gar and called Moghedien by name, she gave summons to the Pit of Doom and—

'Wake, woman,' said a voice like rotted bone crumbling, and Moghedien's eyes popped open. She almost wished for the dream back.

No door or window broke the featureless stone walls of her small prison, and there were no glowbulbs or even lamps, but light came from somewhere. She did not know how many days she had been there, only that tasteless food appeared at irregular intervals, that the single bucket serving for sanitation was emptied at even more irregular times, and soap and a bucket of perfumed water were somehow left for her to clean herself. She was not sure whether that was a mercy or not; the glad thrill at seeing a bucket of water reminded her how far she had fallen. Shaidar Haran was in the cell with her now.

Hurriedly rolling from her pallet, she knelt and put her face to the bare stone floor. She had always done whatever was necessary for survival, and the Myrddraal had been all too glad to teach her what was necessary. 'I greet you eagerly, *Mia'cova.*' The lashed-together title burned on her tongue. 'One Who Owns Me,' it meant, or simply, 'My Owner.' The strange shield Shaidar Haran had used on her – Myrddraal could not, but it did – the shield was not in evidence, yet she did not consider channeling. The True Power was denied her, of course – that could be drawn only with the Great Lord's blessing – but the Source tantalized, though the glow just beyond sight seemed somehow odd. She still did not consider it. Every time the Myrddraal visited, it displayed her mindtrap. Channeling too near your own *cour'souvra* was extremely painful, the nearer, the more the pain; this close, she did not think she would survive a simple touch on the Source. And that was the least of the mindtrap's dangers.

Shaidar Haran chuckled, a rasp of dried, cracked leather. That was another difference about this Myrddraal. Far more cruel than Trollocs, who were merely bloodthirsty, Myrddraal were cold and dispassionate in it. Shaidar Haran often showed amusement, though. So far she felt lucky to have only bruises. Most women would have been on the brink of madness by now, if not beyond.

'And are you eager to obey?' that rustling, grating voice asked.

'Yes, I am eager to obey, *Mia'cova*.' Whatever was necessary to survive. But she still gasped when cold fingers suddenly tangled in her hair. She scrambled to her feet on her own as much as possible, but still was hauled up. At least this time her feet remained on the floor. The Myrddraal studied her, expressionless. Remembering past visits, it required an effort not to flinch, or scream, or simply reach for *saidar* and make an end.

'Close your eyes,' it told her, 'and keep them closed until you are commanded to open them.'

Moghedien's eyes snapped shut. One of Shaidar Haran's lessons had been instant obedience. Besides, with her eyes closed, she could try to pretend that she was somewhere else. Whatever was necessary.

Abruptly the hand in her hair rushed her forward, and she screamed in spite of herself. The Myrddraal meant to run her into the wall. Her hands went up for protection, and Shaidar Haran released her. She staggered at least ten steps – but her cell was not ten paces corner to corner. Wood smoke; she smelled a faint touch of wood smoke. She kept her eyelids firmly closed, though. She meant to continue with no more than bruises, and as few bruises as possible, for as long as she could manage.

'You can look now,' a deep voice said.

She did, cautiously. The speaker was a tall, broad-shouldered young man in black boots and breeches and a flowing white shirt unlaced at the top, who watched her with startlingly blue eyes from a deep, cushioned armchair in front of a marble fireplace where flames danced along long logs. She stood in a wood-paneled room that might have belonged to a wealthy merchant or noble of moderate rank in this time, the furniture lightly carved and touched with gilt, the rugs woven in red-and-gold arabesques. She did not doubt it was somewhere close by Shayol Ghul, though; it did not have the feel of *Tel'aran'rhiod*, the only other possibility. Swiveling her head hastily, she drew a deep breath. The Myrddraal was nowhere to be seen. Tight bands of *cuande* seemed to vanish from around her chest.

'Did you enjoy your time in the vacuole?'

Moghedien felt icy fingers dig into her scalp. She was no researcher or maker, but she knew that word. She did not even think to ask how a young man of this time did, too. Sometimes there were bubbles in the Pattern, though someone like Mesaana would say that was too simple an explanation. Vacuoles could be entered, if you knew how, and manipulated much like the rest of the world – researchers had often done great experiments in vacuoles, so she vaguely remembered hearing – but they were outside the Pattern really, and sometimes they closed up, or perhaps broke off and drifted away. Even Mesaana could not say what happened – except that anything in them at the time was gone forever.

'How long?' She was surprised her voice was so steady. She rounded on the young man, who sat there showing her white teeth. 'I said, how long? Or don't you know?'

'I saw you arrive ...' He paused, lifting a silver goblet from the table beside his chair, eyes smiling at her over the rim as he drank. '...the night before last.'

She could not hide a relieved gasp. The only reason anyone would want to enter a vacuole was that time flowed differently there, sometimes slower, sometimes faster. Sometimes much faster. She would not have been entirely surprised to learn that the Great Lord had really imprisoned her for a hundred years, or a thousand, to emerge into a world already his, to make her way feeding among carrion while the other Chosen stood at the pinnacle. She was still one of the Chosen, in her own mind, at least. Until the Great Lord himself said she was not. She had never heard of anyone being released once a mindtrap was set, but she would find a way. There was always a way for those who were cautious, while those fell who called caution cowardice. She herself had carried a few of that so-called brave sort to Shayol Ghul to be fitted with *cour'souvra*.

Suddenly, it occurred to her that this fellow knew a great deal for a Friend of the Dark, especially one not many years past twenty. He swung one leg over an arm of the chair, lounging insolently under her scrutiny. Graendal might have snatched him, if he had any position or power; only too strong a chin kept him from being pretty enough. She did not think she had ever seen eyes so blue. With his insolence in her very face and what she had had to endure at Shaidar Haran's hands so fresh, with the Source calling her and the Myrddraal gone, she considered teaching this young Friend of the Dark a sharp lesson. The fact that her clothes were grimy added their part; she herself smelled faintly of the perfume in the wash water, but she had had no way to clean the rough woolen dress in which she fled Egwene al'Vere, with its rips from her journey down to the Pit. Prudence prevailed – this room must be close to Shayol Ghul – but barely.

'What is your name?' she demanded. 'Do you have any idea who you are speaking to?'

'Yes, I do, Moghedien. You may call me Moridin.'

Moghedien gasped. Not for the name; any fool could call himself Death. But a tiny black fleck, just large enough to see, floated straight across one of those blue eyes and then across the other in the same line. This Moridin had tapped into the True Power, and more than once. Much more. She knew that some men who could channel survived in this time aside from al'Thor – this fellow was much of a size with al'Thor – but she had not expected the Great Lord to allow one that particular honor. An honor with a bite, as any of the Chosen knew. In the long run, the True Power was far more addictive than the One Power; a strong will could hold down the desire to draw more *saidar* or *saidin*, but she herself did not believe the will existed strong enough to resist the True Power, not once the *saa* appeared in your eyes. The final price was different, but no less terrible.

'You have been given distinction greater than you know,' she told him. As though her filthy dress was the finest streith, she took the armchair opposite him. 'Bring me some of that wine, and I will tell you. Only twenty-nine others have ever been granted—'

To her shock, he laughed. 'You misapprehend, Moghedien. You

still serve the Great Lord, but not quite as you once did. The time for playing your own games has passed. If you had not managed to do some good by accident, you would be dead now.'

'I am one of the Chosen, boy,' she said, fury burning through caution. She sat up straight, facing him with all the knowledge of an Age that made his little different from times of mud huts. As much of that knowledge as she had, anyway, and in some areas, concerning the One Power, no one outstripped her. She almost embraced the Source no matter how close Shayol Ghul lay. 'Your mother probably used my name to frighten you not so many years gone, but know that grown men who could crumple you like a rag sweated when they heard it. You will watch your tongue with me!'

He reached into the open neck of his shirt, and her own tongue clove to the roof of her mouth. Her eyes fixed on the small cage of gold wire and blood-red crystal that he drew out dangling on a cord. She thought vaguely that he tucked another just like it back in, but she had eyes only for her own. It definitely was hers. His thumb stroked, and she felt that caress across her mind, her soul. Breaking a mindtrap did not require much more pressure than he was using. She could be on the other side of the world or farther, and it would not matter a hair. The part of her that was *her* would be separated; she would still see with her eyes and hear with her ears, taste what crossed her tongue and feel what touched her, but helpless within an automaton that was utterly obedient to whoever held the *cour'souvra*. Whether or not there was any way to get free of it, a mindtrap was just what its name implied. She could feel the blood draining from her face.

'You understand now?' he said. 'You still serve the Great Lord, but now it will be by doing as I say.'

'I understand, *Mia'cova*,' she said automatically.

Again he laughed, a deep rich sound that mocked her as he put the mindtrap away beneath his shirt. 'There is no need for that, now you've had your lesson. I will call you Moghedien, and you will call me Moridin. You are still one of the Chosen. Who is there to replace you?'

'Yes, of course, Moridin,' she said tonelessly. Whatever he said, she knew that she was owned.

Chapter 26

The Irrevocable Words

Morgase lay awake, staring at the ceiling through the moonlit darkness, and tried to think of her daughter. A single pale linen sheet covered her, but despite the heat she sweated in a thick woolen sleeping gown, laced tightly to the neck. Sweat hardly mattered; no matter how many times she bathed, no matter how hot the water, she did not feel clean. Elayne must be safe in the White Tower. At times it seemed years since she could make herself trust Aes Sedai, yet whatever the paradox, the Tower was surely the safest place for Elayne. She tried to think of Gawyn – he would be in Tar Valon with his sister, full of his pride for her, so earnest in his desire to be her shield when she needed one – and of Galad – why would they not let her see him? She loved him as much as if he had come out of her own body, and in so many ways he needed it more than the other two. She tried to think of them. It was difficult to think of anything except . . . Wide eyes stared up into the darkness, glistening with unshed tears.

She had always thought she was brave enough to do whatever needed doing, to face whatever came; she had always believed she could pick herself up and continue to fight. In one endless hour, without leaving more than a few bruises that were already fading, Rhadam Asunawa had begun teaching her differently. Eamon Valda had completed her education with one question. The bruise her answer had left on her heart had not faded. She should have gone back to Asunawa herself and told him to do his worst. She should have . . . She prayed that Elayne was safe. Perhaps it was not fair to hope more for Elayne than for Galad or Gawyn, but Elayne would be the next Queen of Andor. The Tower would not miss the chance to put an Aes Sedai on the Lion Throne. If only she could see Elayne, see all her children once more.

Something rustled in the dark bedchamber, and she held her breath, fought against trembling. The faint moonlight barely let her make out the bedposts. Valda had ridden north from Amador yesterday, him and Asunawa, with thousands of Whitecloaks to face the Prophet, but if he had come back, if he . . .

A shape in the darkness resolved into a woman, too short for Lini. 'I thought you might still be awake,' Breane's voice said softly. 'Drink this; it will help.' The Cairhienin woman tried to put a silvery cup into Morgase's hand. It gave off a slightly sour smell.

'Wait until you're summoned to bring me drink,' she snapped, pushing the cup away. Warm liquid spilled onto her hand, onto the linen sheet. 'I was almost asleep when you came stamping in,' she lied. 'Leave me!'

Instead of obeying, the woman stood looking down at her, face shadowed. Morgase did not like Breane Taborwin. Whether Breane truly was nobly born and come down in the world, as she sometimes claimed, or merely a servant who had learned to counterfeit her betters, she obeyed when and as she chose and let her tongue run entirely too free. As she proved now.

'You moan like a sheep, Morgase Trakand.' Even kept low, her voice seethed in anger. She set the cup on the small bedside table with a thump; more of the contents splashed onto the tabletop. 'Bah! Many others have seen far worse. You are alive. None of your bones are broken; your wits are whole. Endure; let the past pass, and go on with your life. You have been so much on edge that the men walk on their toes, even Master Gill. Lamgwin has hardly slept a wink these three nights.'

Morgase flushed with annoyance; even in Andor, servants did not speak so. She caught the woman's arm in a tight grip, but anxiety warred with displeasure. 'They don't know, do they?' If they did, they would try to avenge her, rescue her. They would die. Tallanvor would die.

'Lini and I drape linen over their eyes for you,' Breane sneered, pulling her hand away and flinging it back at her. 'If I could save Lamgwin, I would let them know you for the bleating sheep you are. He sees the Light made flesh in you; I see a woman without courage to accept the day. I will not let you destroy him with your cowardice.'

Cowardice. Outrage welled up in Morgase, yet no words came. Her fingers knotted in the sheet. She did not think she could have decided in cold blood to lie with Valda, but had she, she could have lived with it. She thought she could. Another matter entirely to say yes because she feared facing Asunawa's knotted cords and needles again, feared worse that he would have gotten to eventually. However she had screamed under Asunawa's ministrations, Valda was the one who had showed her the true borders of her courage, so far short of where she had believed. Valda's touch, his bed, could be forgotten, with time, but she would never be able to wash the shame of that 'yes' from her lips. Breane hurled the truth in her face, and she did not know how to reply.

She was spared the need by a rush of boots in the outer room. The bedchamber door flung open, and a running man stopped a pace inside.

'So you're awake; good,' Tallanvor's voice said after a moment. Which allowed her heart to start beating again, allowed her to breathe. She tried to release Breane's hand – she did not remember clasping it – but to her surprise, the woman squeezed once before letting go.

'Something is happening,' Tallanvor went on, striding to the lone window. Standing to one side as if to avoid being seen, he peered into the night. Moonlight outlined his tall form. 'Master Gill, come and tell what you saw.'

A head appeared in the doorway, bald top shining in the darkness. Behind, in the other room, a hulking shadow moved; Lamgwin Dorn. When Basel Gill realized she was still in bed, that faint shining from his scalp jerked as he directed his eyes elsewhere, though he probably had difficulty making out more than the bed itself. Master Gill was even wider than Lamgwin, but not nearly as tall. 'Forgive me, my Queen. I didn't mean to . . .' He cleared his throat violently, and his boots scraped on the floor, shifting. Had he had a cap, he would have been turning it in his hands, or wadding

it nervously. 'I was in the Long Corridor, on my way to ... to ...'
To the jakes, was what he could not bring himself to say to her.
'Anyway, I glanced out one of the windows, and I saw a ... a big
bird, I think ... land on top of the South Barracks.'

'A bird!' Lini's thin voice drove Master Gill to leap into the
room, clearing the doorway. Or maybe it was a sharp poke in his
stout ribs. Lini usually took every advantage her gray hair offered.
She stalked by him still belting her nightrobe. 'Fools! Ox-brained
lummoxes! You woke my ch—!' She stopped with a fierce cough;
Lini never forgot that she had been Morgase's nurse, and her
mother's as well, but she never slipped in front of others. She would
be cross that she had now, and it showed in her voice. 'You woke
your Queen for a *bird*!' Patting her hairnet, she automatically
tucked in a few strands that had escaped in her sleep. 'Have you
been drinking, Basel Gill?' Morgase wondered that herself.

'I don't know it was a bird,' Master Gill protested. 'It didn't look
like any bird, but what else flies, except bats? It was big. Men
climbed off its back, and there was another still on its neck when
it took off again. While I was slapping my face to wake up, another
of the ... things ... landed, and more men climbed down, and then
another came, and I decided it was time to tell Lord Tallanvor.' Lini
did not sniff, but Morgase could almost feel her stare, and it was not
directed at her. The man who had abandoned his inn to follow her
certainly felt it. 'The Light's own truth, my Queen,' he insisted.

'Light!' Tallanvor announced like an echo. 'Something ...
Something just landed atop the North Barracks.' Morgase had never
heard him sound shaken before. All she wanted was to make them
all go away and leave her alone in her misery, but there seemed no
hope. Tallanvor was worse than Breane in many ways. Much worse.

'My robe,' she said, and for once Breane was quick to hand her
one. Master Gill hastily turned his face to the wall while she
climbed from the bed and put on the silk robe.

She strode to the window, tying the sash. The long North
Barracks loomed across the wide courtyard, four hulking floors of
flat-roofed dark stone. Not a light showed, there or anywhere in the
Fortress. All was stillness and silence. 'I see nothing, Tallanvor.'

He drew her back. 'Just watch,' he said.

Another time she would have regretted his hand leaving her shoulder, and been irritated at her own regret as well as his tone. Now, after Valda, she felt relief. And irritation at the relief as well as his tone. He was too disrespectful by miles, far too stubborn, too young. Not much older than Galad.

Shadows moved as the moon did, but nothing else stirred. Off in the city of Amador, a dog bayed, answered by more. Then, as she opened her mouth to dismiss Tallanvor and all of them, darkness atop the massive barracks humped up and hurled itself off the roof.

Something, Tallanvor had called it, and she had no better name. An impression of a long body that seemed thicker than a man was tall; great ribbed wings like a bat's sweeping down as the creature fell toward the courtyard; a figure, a man, sitting just behind a sinuous neck. And then the wings caught air, and the ... something ... soared up, blocking the moonlight as it swept over her head trailing a long, thin tail.

Morgase closed her mouth slowly. The only thought that came to her was Shadowspawn. Trollocs and Myrddraal were not the only Shadow-twisted creatures in the Blight. She had never been taught of anything like this, but her tutors in the Tower said that things lived there no one had ever seen clearly and lived to describe. How could it be so far south, though?

Abruptly a flash of light flared with a great boom in the direction of the main gates, and then again, at two more places along the great outer wall. Those were gates too, she believed.

'What in the Pit of Doom was that?' Tallanvor muttered in a moment of silence before alarm gongs began resounding in the darkness. Shouts rose, and screams, and hoarse cries like some sort of horn. Fire leaped with a crash of thunder, then again elsewhere.

'The One Power,' Morgase breathed. She might not be able to channel, or as well as not, but she could tell that. Notions of Shadowspawn fled. 'It ... it must be Aes Sedai.' She heard someone's breath catch behind her; Lini or Breane. Basel Gill excitedly murmured 'Aes Sedai,' and Lamgwin murmured back too low for her to understand. Off in the darkness, metal clashed on metal; fire bellowed, and lightning streaked from the cloudless sky. Faintly through the din came alarm bells from the city at last, but strangely few.

'Aes Sedai.' Tallanvor sounded doubtful. 'Why now? To rescue you, Morgase? I thought they couldn't use the Power against men, only Shadowspawn. Besides, if that winged creature wasn't Shadowspawn, I will never see one.'

'You don't know what you are talking about!' she said, confronting him heatedly. 'You—!' A crossbow bolt clashed against the windowframe in a spray of stone chips; air stirred against her face as it ricocheted between them and planted itself in one of the bedposts with a solid *tchunk*. A few inches to the right, and all her troubles would have been ended.

She did not move, but Tallanvor pulled her away from the window with an oath. Even by moonlight, she could see his frown as he studied her. For a moment she thought he might touch her face; if he did, she did not know whether she would weep or scream or order him to leave her forever or ...

Instead, he said, 'More likely it's some of those men, those Shamin or whatever they call themselves.' He insisted on accepting the strange, impossible tales that had seeped even into the Fortress. 'I think I can get you out, right now; everything will be confusion. Come with me.'

She did not correct him; few people knew anything about the One Power, much less the differences between *saidar* and *saidin*. His idea had its attractions. They might be able to escape in the bedlam of a battle.

'Take her out into that!' Lini screeched. Flaring lights drowned the moon at the window; crashes and thunders drowned the din of men and swords. 'I thought you had more wits, Martyn Tallanvor. "Only fools kiss hornets or bite fire." You heard her say it's Aes Sedai. Do you think she doesn't know? Do you?'

'My Lord, if it is Aes Sedai ...' Master Gill trailed off.

Tallanvor's hands fell away from her, and he grumbled under his breath, wishing he had a sword. Pedron Niall had allowed him to keep his blade; Eamon Valda was not so trusting.

For an instant, disappointment swelled in her breast. If only he had insisted, had dragged her ... What was the matter with her? Had he tried to drag her anywhere for any reason, she would have had his hide. She needed to take hold of herself. Valda had dented her confidence – no, he had casually ripped it to shreds – but she must cling to those shreds and knit them up again. Somehow. If the tatters were worth knitting up again.

'At least I can find out what is happening,' Tallanvor growled, striding for the door. 'If it isn't your Aes Sedai—'

'No! You will remain here. Please.' She was very glad of the pale darkness, hiding her furiously flushing face. She would have bitten her tongue off before saying that last word, but it had slipped out before she knew. She went on in firmer tones. 'You will remain here, guarding your Queen as you should.'

In the dim light, she could see his face, and his bow seemed quite proper, but she would have wagered her last copper both were angry. 'I will be in your anteroom.' Well, there was no doubt about his voice. For once, though, she cared neither how angry he was nor how little he hid it. Very possibly she might kill the infuriating man with her own hands, but he was not going to die tonight, cut down by soldiers with no way to tell which side he was on.

There was no hope of sleep now even had she been able. Without lighting any lamps, she washed her face and teeth. Breane and Lini helped her dress, in blue silk slashed with green, with spills of snowy lace at her wrists and beneath her chin. It would do very well for receiving Aes Sedai. *Saidar* raged in the night. They had to be Aes Sedai. Who else could it be?

When she joined the men in the anteroom, they were sitting in darkness except for the moonlight through the windows, and the occasional flash of Power-wrought fire. Even a candle might attract unwanted attention. Lamgwin and Master Gill sprang from their chairs respectfully; Tallanvor stood more slowly, and she needed no light to know he regarded her with a sullen frown. Furious that she had to ignore him – she was his Queen! – furious and barely able to keep it from her voice, she ordered Lamgwin to bring more of the tall wooden chairs further from the windows. In silence, they sat and waited. At least, silence on their part. Outside thunderous crashes and roars still echoed, horns cried and men shouted, and through it she felt *saidar* surge and fall and surge again.

Slowly, after at least an hour, the battle dwindled and died. Voices still shouted incomprehensible orders, wounded screamed, and sometimes those strange hoarse horns gave voice, but no more did steel ring on steel. *Saidar* faded; she was sure women still held it inside the Fortress, but she did not think any channeled now. All seemed close to peaceful after the clamor and commotion.

Tallanvor stirred, but she waved him back before he could rise; for a moment she thought he would not obey. Night weakened, and sunlight crept in through the windows, shining on Tallanvor's glower. She held her hands still in her lap. Patience was but one of the virtues that young man needed to learn. Patience stood second only to courage as a noble virtue. The sun rose higher. Lini and Breane began whispering together in increasingly worried tones, shooting glances in her direction. Tallanvor scowled, dark eyes smoldering, sitting rigid in that dark blue coat that fit him so well. Master Gill fidgeted, running first one hand then the other across his gray-fringed head, mopping his pink cheeks with a handkerchief. Lamgwin slouched in his chair, the onetime street tough's heavy-lidded eyes making him seem half asleep, but when he glanced at Breane a smile flickered on his scarred, broken-nosed face. Morgase focused on her breathing, almost like the exercises she had done during her months in the Tower. Patience. If someone did not come soon, she was going to have sharp words to say, Aes Sedai or not!

Despite herself, she jumped at an abrupt pounding on the door to the hallway. Before she could tell Breane to see who was there, the door swung open, banging against the wall. Morgase stared at who entered.

A tall, dark, hook-nosed man stared back at her coldly, the long hilt of a sword rising above his shoulder. Strange armor covered his chest, overlapping plates lacquered glistening gold and black, and he held a helmet on his hip that looked like an insect's head, black and gold and green, with three long, thin green plumes. Two more armored like him came at his heels wearing their helmets, though without plumes; their armor seemed painted rather than lacquered, and they carried crossbows ready. Still more stood in the hall outside, with gold-and-black tasseled spears.

Tallanvor and Lamgwin and even stout Master Gill scrambled to their feet, placing themselves between her and her peculiar visitors. She had to push a way through.

The hook-nosed man's eyes went straight to her before she could demand an explanation. 'You are Morgase, Queen of Andor?' His voice was harsh, and he drawled his words so badly she barely understood. He stepped on her reply. 'You will come with me. Alone,' he added as Tallanvor, and Lamgwin, and Master Gill, all moved forward. The crossbowmen presented their weapons; the heavy quarrels looked made to punch holes in armor; a man would hardly slow one down.

'I have no objection to my people remaining here until I return,' she said a good more calmly than she felt. Who were these people? She was familiar with the accents of every nation, familiar with their armor. 'I am sure you will see to my safety very well, Captain . . . ?'

He did not supply a name, only motioned curtly for her to follow. To her vast relief, Tallanvor made no fuss despite his hot gaze. To her vast irritation, Master Gill and Lamgwin looked to him before stepping back.

In the hallway, the soldiers formed around her, the hook-nosed officer and the two crossbowmen in the lead. A guard of honor, she tried to tell herself. This soon after a battle, wandering around unprotected was worse than foolish; there might be holdouts who would seize a hostage, or kill any who saw them. She wished she believed that.

She tried questioning the officer, but he never spoke a word, never slackened his stride or turned his head, and she stopped trying. None of the soldiers so much as glanced at her; they were hard-eyed men of the kind she knew from her own Queen's Guards, men who had seen fighting before, more than once. But who were they? Their boots struck the floorstones as one in an ominous drumbeat emphasized by the stark Fortress corridors. There was little color, nothing for beauty except scattered tapestries showing Whitecloaks in bloody battle.

She realized they were taking her toward the Lord Captain Commander's quarters, and a queasiness settled in the pit of her stomach. She had grown almost pleasantly accustomed to the way while Pedron Niall lived; she had come to dread it in the few days since he died – but as they rounded a corner, she started at the sight of some two dozen archers marching behind their own officer, men in baggy trousers and boiled leather breastplates painted in horizontal stripes of blue and black. Each man wore a conical steel cap, with a veil of gray steel mail covering his face to the eyes; here and there the ends of mustaches dangled below the veils. The archers' officer bowed to the one leading her guard, who merely raised his hand in reply.

Taraboners. She had not seen a Taraboner soldier in a good many years, but those men were Taraboners in spite of those stripes, or she would eat her slippers. Yet that made no sense. Tarabon was chaos come to life, a hundred-sided civil war between pretenders to the throne and Dragonsworn. Tarabon could never have launched this attack on Amador itself. Unless, incredibly, one claimant had won out over the rest, and over the Dragonsworn, and . . . It was impossible, and it did not explain these strangely armored soldiers, or that winged beast, or . . .

She thought she had seen strangeness. She thought she had known queasiness. Then she and her guard turned another corner and encountered two women.

One was slender, short as any Cairhienin and darker than any Tairen, in a blue dress that stopped well short of her ankles; silver lightning forked across red panels on her breast and the sides of her wide, divided skirts. The other woman, in drab dark gray, stood taller than most men, with golden hair to her shoulders that had been brushed till it glistened and frightened green eyes. A silver leash connected a silver bracelet on the shorter woman's wrist to a necklace worn by the taller.

They stood aside for Morgase's guard, and when the hook-nosed officer murmured '*Der'sul'dam*' – Morgase thought that was it; his slurred accent made understanding difficult – when he murmured in tones nearly but not quite to an equal, the dark woman bowed her head slightly, twitched at the leash, and the golden-haired woman sank to the floor, folding herself with her head on her knees and her palms flat on the floorstones. As Morgase and her guards passed by, the dark woman bent to pat the other fondly on the head, as she might a dog, and worse, the kneeling woman looked up with pleasure and gratitude.

Morgase made the necessary effort to keep walking, to keep her knees from folding, to keep her stomach from emptying itself. The sheer servility was bad enough, but she was certain the woman being patted on the head could channel. Impossible! She walked in a daze, wondering whether this could be a dream, a nightmare. Praying that it was. She had a vague awareness of stopping for more soldiers, these in red-and-black armor, then ...

Pedron Niall's audience chamber – Valda's now, or rather whoever had taken the fortress – was changed. The great golden sunburst remained, set in the floor, but all Niall's captured banners, which Valda had kept as if they were his, were gone, and so were the furnishings, except for the plainly carved high-backed chair Niall and then Valda had used, flanked now by two tall, luridly painted screens. One showed a white-crested black bird of prey with a cruel beak, its white-tipped wings spread wide, the other a black-spotted yellow cat with one paw on a dead, deerlike creature half its size, with long, straight horns and white stripes.

There were a number of people in the room, but that was all she had time to notice before a sharp-faced woman in blue robes stepped forward, one side of her head shaved and the remaining hair in a long brown braid that hung in front of her right shoulder. Her blue eyes, full of contempt, could have done for the eagle's or the cat's. 'You are in the presence of the High Lady Suroth, who leads Those Who Come Before, and succors The Return,' she intoned in that same slurring accent.

Without warning, the hook-nosed officer seized the back of Morgase's neck and bore her down prostrate beside him. Stunned, not least because the breath was knocked out of her, she saw him kiss the floor.

'Release her, Elbar,' another woman drawled angrily. 'The Queen of Andor is not to be treated so.'

The man, Elbar, rose as far as his knees, head bent. 'I abase myself, High Lady. I beg forgiveness.' His voice was as cold and flat as that accent allowed.

'I have small forgiveness for this, Elbar.' Morgase looked up. Suroth took her aback. The sides of her head were shaved, leaving a glossy black crest across the top of her head and a mane that flowed down her back. 'Perhaps when you are punished. Report yourself now. Leave me! Go!' A sweeping gesture flashed fingernails at least an inch long, the first two on each hand a glistening blue.

Elbar bowed on his knees, then rose smoothly, backing away through the door. For the first time Morgase realized none of the other soldiers had followed them in. She realized something else, as well. He gave her one final glance before he vanished, and instead of flickering resentment for the one who had caused his punishment, he ... considered. There would be no punishment; the entire exchange had been arranged beforehand.

Suroth swept toward Morgase, carefully holding her pale blue robe to keep her skirts exposed, snow-white, with hundreds of tiny pleats. Embroidered vines and lush red and yellow flowers spread across the robe. For all her sweeping, Morgase noticed the woman did not reach her until she had regained her feet on her own.

'You are unharmed?' Suroth asked. 'If you are harmed, I will double his punishment.'

Morgase brushed at her dress so she would not have to look at the false smile that never touched the woman's eyes. She took the opportunity to look around the room. Four men and four women knelt against one wall, all young and more than good-looking, all wearing ... She jerked her eyes away. Those long white robes were very nearly transparent! At the far sides of the screens two more pairs of women knelt, one of each in the gray dress, one in the blue embroidered with lightning, bound by the silvery leash from wrist to neck. Morgase was not close enough to say for sure, but she had the sick-making certainty that the two gray-clad women could channel. 'I am quite all right, thank—' A huge reddish brown shape lay sprawled on the floor – a heap of tanned cowskins, perhaps. Then it heaved. 'What is *that*?' She managed not to gape, but the question popped from her tongue before she could stop it.

'You admire my *lopar*?' Suroth swept away a good deal quicker than she had come. The enormous shape raised a great round head for her to stroke it under the chin with a knuckle. The creature put Morgase in mind of a bear, though it was easily half again as big as the largest bear she had ever heard tell of, and hairless to boot, with no muzzle to speak of and heavy ridges surrounding its eyes.

'Almandaragal was given to me as a pup, for my first true-name day; he foiled the first attempt to kill me that same year, when he was only a quarter grown.' There was real affection in the woman's voice. The ... *lopar*'s ... lips peeled back to reveal thick pointed teeth as she stroked; its forepaws flexed, claws sheathing and unsheathing from six long toes on each. And it began to purr, a bass rumble fit for a hundred cats.

'Remarkable,' Morgase said faintly. True-name day? How many attempts had there been to kill this woman that she could speak of 'the first' so casually?

The *lopar* whined briefly when Suroth left it, but quickly settled with its head on its paws. Disconcertingly, its eyes did not follow her, but settled mainly on Morgase, now and then flicking toward the door or the narrow, arrow-slit windows.

'Of course, however loyal a *lopar*, it cannot match *damane*.' No affection touched Suroth's voice now. 'Pura and Jinjin could slay a hundred assassins before Almandaragal blinked his eye.' At the mention of each name, one of the blue-clad women twitched her silvery leash, and the woman at the other end doubled herself as the one in the corridor had. 'We have many more *damane* since returning than before. This is a rich hunting ground for *marath'damane*. Pura,' she added casually, 'was once a ... woman of the White Tower.'

Morgase's knees wobbled. Aes Sedai? She studied the bent back of the woman called Pura, refusing to believe. No Aes Sedai could be made to cringe like that. But any woman who could channel, not just an Aes Sedai, should be able to take that leash and strangle her tormentor. Anyone at all should be able to. No, this Pura could not be. Morgase wondered if she dared ask for a chair. 'That is very ... interesting.' At least her voice was steady. 'But I do not think you asked me here to speak of Aes Sedai.' Of course, she had not been asked. Suroth stared at her, not a muscle moving except that the long-nailed fingers of her left hand twitched.

'Thera!' the sharp-faced woman with half her head shaved barked suddenly. 'Kaf for the High Lady and her guest!'

One of the women in diaphanous robes, the eldest but still young, leaped gracefully to her feet. Her rosebud mouth had a petulant look to it, but she darted behind the tall screen painted with the eagle, and in moments reappeared bearing a silver tray with two small white cups. Kneeling sinuously before Suroth, she bowed her dark head as she raised the tray, so her offering stood higher than she. Morgase shook her head; any servant in Andor asked to do that – or wear that robe! – would have stormed off in a dudgeon.

'Who are you? Where do you come from?'

Suroth raised one of the cups on her fingertips, inhaling the steam rising from it. Her nod was entirely too much permission for Morgase's liking, but she took a cup anyway. One sip, and she stared into her drink in amazement. Blacker than any tea, the liquid was also more bitter. No amount of honey would make it drinkable. Suroth put her own cup to her lips and sighed with enjoyment.

'There are many things we must speak of, Morgase, yet I will be brief at this first talk. We Seanchan return to reclaim what was stolen from the heirs of the High King, Artur Paendrag Tanreall.' Pleasure over the kaf became a different pleasure in her voice, both expectation and certainty, and she watched Morgase's face closely. Morgase could not take her eyes away. 'What was ours, will be ours again. In truth, it always has been; a thief gains no ownership. I have begun the recovery in Tarabon. Many nobles of that land have already sworn to obey, await and serve; it will not be long before all have. Their king – I cannot recall his name – died opposing me. Had he lived, in rebellion against the Crystal Throne and not even of the Blood, he would have been impaled. His family could not be found to be made property, but there is a new King and a new Panarch who have sworn their fealty to the Empress, may she live forever, and the Crystal Throne. The bandits will be eradicated; no longer will there be strife or hunger in Tarabon, but the people will shelter beneath the wings of the Empress. Now I begin in this Amadicia. Soon all will kneel to the Empress, may she live forever, the direct descendant of the great Artur Hawkwing.'

If the serving woman had not gone with the tray, Morgase would have put her cup back. No tremor disturbed the dark surface of the kaf, but much of what the woman spouted was meaningless to her. Empress? Seanchan? There had been wild rumors a year or more ago about Artur Hawkwing's armies come back from across the Aryth

Ocean, but only the most credulous could have believed, and she doubted that the worst gossipmonger in the markets still told the tale. Could it have been truth? In any case, what she did understand was more than enough.

'All honor the name of Artur Hawkwing, Suroth...' The sharp-faced woman opened her mouth angrily, subsiding at the move of a blue-nailed finger by the High Lady '... but his time is long past. Every nation here has an ancient lineage. No land will surrender to you or your Empress. If you have taken some part of Tarabon...' Suroth's indrawn breath hissed, and her eyes glittered. '... remember that it is a troubled land, divided against itself. Amadicia will not fall easily, and many nations will ride to her aid when they learn of you.' *Could* it be true? 'However many you are, you will find no easy game for your spit. We have faced great threats before, and overcome them. I advise you to make peace before you are crushed.' Morgase remembered *saidar* raging in the night, and avoided looking at the – *damane*, had she called them? By strong effort, she managed not to wet her lips.

Suroth smiled that mask's smile again, eyes shining like polished stones. 'All must make choices. Some will choose to obey, await and serve, and will rule their lands in the name of the Empress, may she live forever.'

She took a hand from her cup to gesture, a slight movement of long fingernails, and the sharp-faced woman barked, 'Thera! Poses of the Swan!'

For some reason, Suroth's mouth tightened. 'Not the Swan, Alwhin, you blind fool!' she hissed, half under her breath, though her accent made understanding difficult. The frozen smile returned in an instant.

The serving woman rose from her place at the wall again, running out to the middle of the floor in an odd way, on tiptoe, with her arms swept back. Slowly, atop the flaring golden sun, symbol of the Children of the Light, she began a sort of stylized dance. Her arms unfolded to the sides like wings, then folded back. Twisting, she slid her left foot out, lowering herself over the bending knee, both arms outstretched as if appealing, until arms and body and right leg made a straight, slanted line. Her sheer white robe made the whole thing scandalous. Morgase felt her cheeks growing hot as the dance, if it could be called that, continued.

'Thera is new and not well trained yet,' Suroth murmured. 'The Poses are most often done with ten or twenty *da'covale* together, men and women chosen for the clean beauty of their lines, but sometimes it is pleasant to view only one. It is very pleasant to own beautiful things, is it not?'

Morgase frowned. How could anyone own a person? Suroth had spoken earlier about 'making someone property.' She knew the Old Tongue, and the word *da'covale* was not familiar to her, but thinking it out she came up with 'Person Who Is Owned.' It was disgusting. Horrendous! 'Incredible,' she said dryly. 'Perhaps I should leave you to enjoy the ... dance.'

'In one moment,' Suroth said, smiling at the posturing Thera. Morgase avoided looking. 'All have choices to make, as I said. The old King of Tarabon chose to rebel, and died. The old Panarch was captured, yet refused the Oath. Each of us has a place where we belong, unless raised by the Empress, but those who reject their proper place can also be cast down, even to the depths. Thera has a certain grace. Strangely, Alwhin shows great promise in teaching, so I expect that before many years, Thera will learn the skill in the Poses to go with her grace.' That smile swiveled toward Morgase, that glittering gaze.

A very significant gaze, but why? Something to do with the dancer? Her name, mentioned so often, as if to highlight it. But what ... ? Morgase's head whipped around, and she stared at the woman, up on her toes and slowly pivoting in one spot with her hands flat together and arms stretched up as high as they would go. 'I don't believe it,' she gasped. 'I won't!'

'Thera,' Suroth said, 'what was your name before you became my property? What title did you hold?'

Thera froze in her up-stretched posture, quivering, shooting a look half panic, half terror at sharp-faced Alwhin, a look of pure terror at Suroth. 'Thera was called Amathera, if it pleases the High Lady,' she said breathily. 'Thera was the Panarch of Tarabon, if it pleases the High Lady.'

The cup dropped from Morgase's hand, smashing to bits on the floor, spraying the black kaf. It had to be a lie. She had never met Amathera, but she had heard a description, once. No. Many women of the right age could have large dark eyes and a petulant mouth. Pura had never been Aes Sedai, and this woman . . .

'Pose!' Alwhin snapped, and Thera flowed on without so much as one more glance at Suroth or anyone. Whoever she was, clearly the foremost thought in her head now was an urgent desire not to make a mistake. Morgase concentrated on not vomiting.

Suroth stepped very close, face cold as midwinter. 'All confront choices,' she said quietly. Her voice could have marked steel. 'Some of my prisoners say that you spent time in the White Tower. By law, no *marath'damane* may escape the leash, but I pledge to you that you, who named me to my eyes and called lie on my word, you will not face *that* fate.' The emphasis made quite clear that her pledge covered no other possible fate. The smile that never reached her eyes returned. 'I hope that you will choose to swear the oath, Morgase, and rule Andor in the name of the Empress, may she live forever.' For the first time, Morgase was absolutely certain the woman lied. 'I will speak to you again tomorrow, or perhaps the next day, if I have time.'

Turning away, Suroth glided past the lone dancer to the high-backed chair. As she sat, spreading her robe gracefully, Alwhin barked again. She did not seem to have any other voice. 'All! Poses of the Swan!' The young men and women kneeling against the wall leaped forward to join Thera, joining her movements exactly in a line before Suroth's chair. Only the *lopar*'s gaze still acknowledged Morgase's existence. She did not believe she had ever been dismissed so thoroughly in her life. Gathering her dignity with her skirts, she left.

She did not go far alone of course. Those red-and-black armored soldiers stood in the anteroom like statues with red-and-black tasseled spears, faces impassive in their lacquered helmets, hard eyes seeming to stare from behind the mandibles of monstrous insects. One, not much taller than she, fell in at her shoulder without a word and escorted her back to her rooms, where two Taraboners with swords flanked her door, these in steel breastplates, but still painted in horizontal stripes. They bowed low, hands on their knees, and she thought it was for her until her escort spoke for the first time.

'Honor met,' he said in a harsh, dry voice, and the Taraboners straightened, never glancing at her until he said, 'Watch her well. She has not given the Oath.' Dark eyes flickered toward her above steel veils, but their short bows of assent were for the Seanchan.

She tried not to hurry inside, but once the door was closed behind her, she leaned against it attempting to settle her whirling thoughts. Seanchan and *damane*, Empresses and oaths and people owned. Lini and Breane stood in the middle of the room looking at her.

'What did you learn?' Lini asked patiently, in much the tone in which she had questioned the child Morgase about a book read.

'Nightmares and madness,' Morgase sighed. Suddenly she stood up straight, looking around the room anxiously. 'Where is—? Where are the men?'

Breane answered the unasked question in a dryly mocking tone. 'Tallanvor went to see what he could find out.' Her fists planted themselves on her hips, and her face became deadly serious. 'Lamgwin went with him, and Master Gill. What did *you* find out? Who are these ... *Seanchan*?' She said the name awkwardly, frowning around it. 'We heard that much for ourselves.' She affected not to notice Lini's biting stare. 'What are we to do now, Morgase?'

Morgase brushed between the women, crossing to the nearest window. Not as narrow as those in the audience chamber, it looked down twenty feet or more to the stone paving of the courtyard. A dispirited column of bare-headed, disheveled men, some with blood-stained bandages, shambled across the courtyard under the watchful gaze of Taraboners carrying spears. Several Seanchan stood atop a nearby tower, peering into the distance between the crenellations. One wore a helmet decorated with three slender plumes. A woman appeared in a window across the court, the lightning-embroidered red panel plain on her breast, frowning down at the Whitecloak prisoners. Those stumbling men looked stunned, unable to believe what had happened.

What were they to do? A decision Morgase dreaded. It seemed that she had not made so much as a decision on fruit for breakfast in months without it leading to disaster. A choice, Suroth had said. Aid these Seanchan in taking Andor, or ... One last service she could do for Andor. The tail end of the column appeared, followed by more Taraboners, who were joined by their countrymen they passed. A twenty-foot fall, and Suroth lost her lever. Maybe it was the coward's way out, but she had already proved herself that. Still, the Queen of Andor should not die so.

Under her breath, she spoke the irrevocable words that had been used only twice before in the thousand-year history of Andor. 'Under the Light, I relinquish the High Seat of House Trakand to Elayne Trakand. Under the Light, I renounce the Rose Crown and abdicate the Lion Throne to Elayne, High Seat of House Trakand. Under the Light, I submit myself to the will of Elayne of Andor, her obedient subject.' None of that made Elayne Queen, true, but it cleared the way.

'What are you smiling at?' Lini asked.

Morgase turned slowly. 'I was thinking of Elayne.' She did not think her old nurse had been close enough to hear what no one really needed to.

Lini's eyes widened, though, and her breath caught. 'You come away from there now!' she snapped, and suiting actions to words, seized her arm and physically pulled her from the window.

'Lini, you forget yourself! You stopped being my nurse a long—!' Morgase drew a deep breath and softened her tone. Meeting those frightened eyes was not easy; nothing frightened Lini. 'What I do is for the best, believe me,' she told her gently. 'There's no other way—'

'No other way?' Breane broke in angrily, gripping her skirts till her hands shook. Clearly she would rather have had them wrapped around Morgase's throat. 'What fool nonsense are you spouting now? What if these Seanchan think we killed you?' Morgase compressed her lips; had she become so transparent?

'Shut up, woman!' Lini never got angry, either, or raised her voice, but she did both now, her withered cheeks red. She raised a bony hand. 'You hold your mouth, or I'll slap you sillier than you are!'

'Slap her if you want to slap someone!' Breane shouted back so fiercely that spittle flew. '*Queen* Morgase! She will send you and me and my Lamgwin to the gallows, and her precious Tallanvor too, because she lacks the belly of a *mouse*!'

The door opened to admit Tallanvor and put an abrupt end to it.

No one was about to shout in front of him. Lini pretended to examine Morgase's sleeve as though it might need mending as Master Gill and Lamgwin followed Tallanvor in. Breane put on a bright smile and smoothed her skirts. The men noticed nothing, of course.

Morgase noticed a great deal. For one thing, Tallanvor had a sword belted on, and so did Master Gill, and even Lamgwin, though his was a short-sword. She had always had the feeling he was more comfortable with his fists than any other weapons. Before she could ask how, the skinny little man who brought up the rear closed the door carefully behind him.

'Majesty,' Sebban Balwer said, 'forgive the intrusion.' Even his bow and his smile seemed dry and precise, but as his eyes flicked from her to the other women, Morgase decided that whether the other men noticed the atmosphere in the room or not, Pedron Niall's onetime secretary did.

'I am surprised to see you, Master Balwer,' she said. 'I heard there was some unpleasantness with Eamon Valda.' What she had heard was that Valda had said if he laid eyes on Balwer, he would kick him over one of the Fortress walls. Balwer's smile tightened; he knew what Valda had said.

'He has a plan to take us all out of here,' Tallanvor broke in. 'Today. Now.' He gave her a look not of subject to queen. 'We are accepting his offer.'

'How?' she said slowly, forcing her legs to remain straight. What help could this prissy little stick of a man offer? Escape. She wanted very much to sit down, but she was not going to, not with Tallanvor looking at her in that fashion. Of course, she was not his Queen, now, but he did not know that. Another question occurred. 'Why? Master Balwer, I'll not shun any true offer of help, but why would you risk yourself? These Seanchan will make you regret it, should they find out.'

'I laid my plans before they came,' he said carefully. 'It seemed ... imprudent ... to leave the Queen of Andor in Valda's hands. Consider it my way of repaying him. I know I am not much to look at, Majesty ...' He hid a self-deprecating cough behind his hand. '... but the plan will work. These Seanchan actually make it easier; I would not have been ready for days yet without them. For a newly conquered city, they allow remarkable freedom to anyone willing to say their Oath. Not an hour after sunrise, I obtained a pass allowing myself and up to ten more who have taken the Oath to depart Amador. They believe I intend to buy wine, and wagons to carry it, in the east.'

'It must be a trap.' The words tasted bitter. Better the window than falling into some snare. 'They won't allow you to carry word of them ahead of their army.'

Balwer's head tilted to one side, and he began dry-washing his hands, then stopped abruptly. 'In truth, Majesty, I considered that. The officer who gave me the pass said it did not matter. His exact words: "Tell who you will what you have seen, and let them know they cannot stand against us. Your lands will know soon enough anyway." I have seen several merchants take the Oath this morning and depart with their wagons.'

Tallanvor moved close to her. Too close. She could almost feel his breath. She could feel his eyes. 'We are accepting his offer,' he said for her ears alone. 'If I must bind and gag you, I think he can find a way even so. He seems a very resourceful little fellow.'

She met him stare for stare. The window or ... a chance. If Tallanvor had only held his tongue it would have been much easier to say, 'I accept with gratitude, Master Balwer,' but she said it. She stepped away as if to see Balwer without having to crane past Tallanvor. It was always disturbing being so near to him. He was too young. 'What is to do first? I doubt those guards at the door will accept your pass for us.'

Balwer bowed his head as if acknowledging her foresight. 'I fear they must meet with accidents, Majesty.' Tallanvor eased his dagger in its scabbard, and Lamgwin flexed his hands like the *lopar* flexing its claws.

She did not believe it could be so easy, even after they had packed up what they could carry and the two Taraboners had been stuffed beneath her bed. At the main gates, holding her linen dust-cloak close awkwardly because of the bundle on her back, she bowed, hands on her knees the way Balwer had shown her, while he told the guards that they had all sworn to obey, await and serve. She thought of how to make sure she was not taken alive. It was not until they were actually riding out of Amador, past the last guards, on the horses Balwer had had waiting, that she began to believe. Of course, Balwer probably expected some fine reward for rescuing the Queen of Andor. She had not told anyone that that was done with beyond going back; she knew she had spoken the words, and no one else needed to know. Regretting them was useless. Now she would see what sort of life she could find without a throne. A life far from a man who was much too young and much too disturbing.

'Why is your smile so sad?' Lini asked, reining her slab-sided brown mare closer. The animal looked moth-eaten. Morgase's bay was no better; none of the horses were. The Seanchan might have been willing to let Balwer go with his pass, but not with decent mounts.

'There is a long road ahead, yet,' Morgase told her, and thumped her mare into some semblance of a trot after Tallanvor.

CHAPTER 27

To Be Alone

Slipping the haft of his axe through the loop on his belt opposite his quiver, Perrin took his unstrung longbow from the corner, slung his saddlebags over his shoulder and left the rooms he had shared with Faile without a backward look. They had been happy there – most of the time. He did not think he would ever be back. Sometimes he wondered whether being happy somewhere with Faile meant he would never return there. He hoped not.

The servants he saw in the Palace corridors wore unrelieved black livery; perhaps Rand had ordered it, and perhaps the servants themselves had simply adopted it. They had been uneasy without livery, as though they did not know where they belonged, and black seemed safe as Rand's color because of the Asha'man. Those who saw Perrin scampered away as fast as they could, not waiting for any bows or curtsies. Fear scent drifted behind them.

For once his yellow eyes had nothing to do with anyone being afraid. It might not be safe to loiter near a man at whom the Dragon Reborn had unleashed his rage so publicly this very morning. Perrin eased the shoulder under his saddlebags. A long while had passed since anyone had been able to pick him up and throw him. Of course, no one had ever used the Power to try, before. One moment in particular stuck with him.

He pushed himself up holding his shoulder, sliding his back up the square column that had stopped his flight. He thought a few ribs might have cracked. Around the Grand Hall of the Sun, a scattering of nobles who had come to appeal one thing or another to Rand tried to look anywhere else, tried to pretend they were anywhere else. Only Dobraine watched, shaking his gray head, as Rand stalked across the throne room.

'I will deal with the Aes Sedai as I choose!' Rand shouted. 'Do you hear me, Perrin? As I choose!'

'You've just handed them over to the Wise Ones,' he growled back, shoving away from the column. 'You don't know whether they're sleeping on silk or had their throats cut! You are not the Creator!'

With a snarl of rage, Rand threw his head back. 'I am the Dragon Reborn!' he cried. 'I don't care how they're treated! They deserve a dungeon!' Perrin's hackles stirred as Rand's eyes lowered from the vaulted ceiling. Blue ice would have been warm and soft beside them, the more so because they stared from a face twisted with pain. 'Get out of my sight, Perrin. Do you hear me? Get out of Cairhien! Today! Now! I never want to see you again!' Pivoting on his heel, he strode away with nobles all but throwing themselves to the floor as he passed.

Perrin thumbed a trickle of blood from the corner of his mouth. For one moment there, he had been sure Rand was going to kill him.

Shaking his head to rid himself of the thought, he rounded a corner and nearly ran into Loial. With a large bundle strapped to his back and a scrip big enough to hold a sheep slung on his shoulder, the Ogier was using his long-handled axe as a walking staff. The capacious pockets of his coat bulged with the shapes of books.

Loial's tufted ears perked up at the sight of him, then suddenly drooped. His whole face drooped, eyebrows hanging on his cheeks. 'I heard, Perrin,' he boomed sadly. 'Rand should not have done that. Quick words make long troubles. I know he'll reconsider. Tomorrow, maybe.'

'It's all right,' Perrin told him. 'Cairhien is too ... polished ... for me, anyway. I'm a blacksmith, not a courtier. By tomorrow, I'll be a long way gone.'

'You and Faile could come with me. Karldin and I are going to visit the *stedding*, Perrin. All of them, about the Waygates.' A narrow-faced, pale-haired young fellow standing behind Loial stopped frowning at Perrin to frown at the Ogier. He had a scrip and a bundle, too, and a sword on his hip. Despite the blue coat, Perrin recognized one of the Asha'man. Karldin did not look pleased to recognize Perrin; besides, his smell was cold and angry. Loial peered down the hallway behind Perrin. 'Where is Faile?'

'She's ... meeting me in the stables. We had words.' That was simple truth; Faile seemed to *like* shouting, sometimes. He lowered his voice. 'Loial, I wouldn't talk about that where anyone could hear. The Waygates, I mean.'

Loial snorted hard enough to make a bull jump, but he did drop his tone. 'I don't see anyone but us,' he rumbled. No one more than two or three paces beyond Karldin could have heard clearly. His ears ... lashed was the only word ... and laid back angrily. 'Everyone's afraid to be seen near you. After all you've done for Rand.'

Karldin tugged at Loial's sleeve. 'We have to go,' he said, glaring at Perrin. Anyone the Dragon Reborn shouted at was outside the gates so far as he was concerned. Perrin wondered whether he was holding the Power right then.

'Yes, yes,' Loial murmured, waving a ham-sized hand, but he leaned on his axe, frowning pensively. 'I don't like this, Perrin. Rand chases you away. He sends me off. How I'm to finish my book ... ' His ears twitched, and he coughed. 'Well, that's neither here nor there. But you, me, and the Light only knows where Mat is. He'll send Min away next. He hid from her, this morning. He sent me out to tell her he wasn't there. I think she knew I was lying. He'll be alone, then, Perrin. "It's terrible to be alone." That's what he said to me. He is planning to send all of his friends away.'

'The Wheel weaves as the Wheel wills,' Perrin said. Loial blinked at that echo of Moiraine. Perrin had been thinking of her a lot recently; she had been a restraining influence on Rand. 'Farewell, Loial. Keep safe, and don't trust anyone you don't have to.' He did not quite look at Karldin.

'You don't mean that, Perrin.' Loial sounded shocked; he seemed to trust everyone. 'You cannot. Come with me, you and Faile.'

'We'll meet again, one day,' Perrin told him gently, and hurried past before he had to say more. He did not like lying, especially not to a friend.

In the north stable things were much the same as inside the palace. Grooms saw him walk in, and dropped dung forks and curry combs, crowding out through small doors at the back. Rustles in the loft high above that might have escaped another's ears told of folk hiding there; he could hear anxious, fearful breaths. He brought Stepper out of a green-streaked marble stall, slipped on his bridle and tied the dun stallion to a gilded hitching ring. He went to fetch blanket and saddle from a marble tackroom where half the saddles were mounted with silver or gold. The stable fit very well in a palace, with tall square marble columns and a marble floor, even under the straw in the stalls. He rode out glad to see the back of grandeur.

North of the city he followed the road he had come down so desperately with Rand just a few days before, rode until folds in the land hid Cairhien. Then he turned off to the east, where a fair patch of forest remained, running down one tall hill and over the next, taller one. Just inside the trees, Faile booted Swallow to meet him, Aram heeling her like a hound on his own horse. Aram's face brightened at the sight of him, though that was not saying much; he merely divided his faithful hound looks between him and Faile.

'Husband,' she said. Not too coolly, but razor-sharp anger and spiky jealousy still threaded through the clean scent of her and her herbal soap. She was garbed for travel, with a thin dust-cloak hanging down her back and red gloves that matched the boots peeking out beneath the dark narrow riding skirts she favored. No fewer than four sheathed daggers were tucked behind her belt.

Movement behind her turned into Bain and Chiad. And Sulin, with a dozen more Maidens. Perrin's eyebrows rose. He wondered what Gaul thought of that; the Aielman had said he was looking forward to getting Bain and Chiad alone. Even more surprising were Faile's other companions.

'What are they doing here?' He nodded toward a small cluster who held their horses back. He recognized Selande and Camaille and the tall Tairen woman, all still in men's clothes and wearing swords. The blocky fellow in a fat-sleeved coat who had kept his beard oiled and trimmed to a point despite wearing his hair tied back with a ribbon also looked familiar. The other two men, both Cairhienin, he did not know, but he could guess, by their youth and the ribbon tying their hair if nothing else, that they were part of Selande's 'society'.

'I took Selande and a few of her friends into my service.' Faile spoke lightly, but suddenly she gave off foggy waves of caution. 'They would have gotten themselves into trouble in the city, sooner or later. They need someone to give them direction. Think of them as charity. I won't let them get under your feet.'

Perrin sighed and scratched his beard. A wise man did not tell his wife to her face that she was hiding things. Especially when that wife was Faile; she was going to be as formidable as her mother. If she was not already. Under his feet? How many of these ... puppies ... had she taken on? 'Is everything ready? Pretty soon some idiot back there will decide he can curry favor by bringing Rand my head. I'd like to be gone before that.' Aram growled in his throat.

'No one is going to take your head, husband.' Faile showed white teeth, and went on in a whisper she knew he would catch. 'Except perhaps me.' In a normal voice, she said, 'All is ready.'

In a clear, fairly flat hollow beyond the trees, the Two Rivers men stood beside their horses, a column of twos that wound out of sight around the side of the hill. Perrin sighed again. The red wolfhead banner and the Red Eagle of Manetheren stirred slightly in a hot breeze at the head of the column. Maybe another dozen Maidens squatted on their heels near the banners; on the other side, Gaul wore as close to a sullen expression as Perrin had ever seen on an Aiel.

As he dismounted, two black-coated men came to him, saluting with fist pressed to heart. 'Lord Perrin,' Jur Grady said. 'We've been here since last night. We are ready.'

Grady's weathered farmer's face made Perrin almost comfortable with him, but Fager Neald was another matter. Maybe ten years younger than Grady, he might have been a farmer too for all Perrin knew, but he affected airs and graces, and wore his pitiful mustache waxed to a semblance of points. Where Grady was one of the Dedicated, he was a Soldier, without the silver sword pinned to his collar, but that did not hold him back from speaking. 'Lord Perrin, is it really necessary to take those women with us? They'll be nothing but trouble, they will, the whole lot of them, and you know it well.'

Some of the women he was talking about stood not far from the Two Rivers men, shawls looped over their arms. Edarra appeared the eldest of the six Wise Ones impassively watching the two women Neald had nodded to. In truth, that pair worried Perrin as well. Seonid Traighan, all coolness and reserve in green silk, had been haughtily trying to ignore the Aiel women – most Cairhienin who were not pretending to be Aiel despised them – but when she saw Perrin, she shifted her bay's reins to the other hand and gave Masuri Sokawa a nudge in the ribs. Masuri started – Browns seemed to go off in daydreams fairly often – stared at the Green sister blankly, then directed her stare at Perrin. This one was more the sort she might have given some peculiar and perhaps dangerous animal, one she intended to be sure of before she was done. They had sworn to obey Rand al'Thor, but how would they do obeying Perrin Aybara? Giving orders to Aes Sedai seemed unnatural. But better than the other way around, at least.

'Everybody comes,' Perrin said. 'Let's be gone before we are seen.'
Faile sniffed.

Grady and Neald saluted again and strode out to the middle of the treeless area. Perrin had no idea which of them did what was necessary, but suddenly the now-familiar silvery vertical flash in the air rotated into a gateway not quite tall enough to ride through. Trees showed beyond the opening, not that much different from those on the surrounding hills. Grady strode through immediately, but even so he was nearly knocked down by Sulin and a small horde of veiled Maidens. They seemed to have taken the honor of being first through a gateway for themselves, and were not about to let anyone usurp it.

Foreseeing a hundred problems he had not thought of, Perrin led Stepper through into a land not so hilly. There was no clearing, but it was not so thickly treed as the hollow back in Cairhien, either, the scattered trees were taller, but just as sere, even the pines. He did not recognize much else except for oak and leatherleaf. The air seemed a little hotter.

Faile followed him, but when he turned to the left, she took Swallow right. Aram's head swung worriedly between them until Perrin nodded toward his wife. The onetime Tinker hauled his gelding after her, but quick as he was, he was not before Bain and Chiad, still veiled, and, for all Perrin's orders that the Two Rivers men were to be next, Selande and a good two dozen young Cairhienin and Tairens poured out of the gateway drawing their horses along. Two dozen! Shaking his head, Perrin stopped beside Grady, who turned this way and that, studying the sparse woodland.

Gaul came stalking up as Dannil finally began leading the Two Rivers men out at a run, pulling their horses. Those bloody banners appeared right behind Dannil, going up as soon as they were clear. The man ought to shave those fool mustaches.

'Women are beyond any belief,' Gaul muttered.

Perrin opened his mouth to defend Faile before he realized it must be Bain and Chiad the man was glaring at. To cover, he said, 'Do you have a wife, Grady?'

'Sora,' Grady answered absently, his attention still on the surrounding trees. Perrin would have wagered he held the Power now, for sure. Anyone could see a long way in this, compared to any woods back home, but someone could still sneak up on you. 'She's missing me,' Grady went on, almost to himself. 'You learn to recognize that one right off. I wish I knew why her knee hurts, though.'

'Her knee hurts,' Perrin said flatly. 'Right this minute, it hurts.'

Grady seemed to realize he was staring, and Gaul was too. He blinked, but went right back to his study. 'Forgive me, Lord Perrin. I need to keep a watch.' For a long moment he said nothing, then began slowly, 'It's something a fellow named Canler worked out. The M'Hael doesn't like us trying to figure out things on our own, but once it was done . . .' His slight grimace said perhaps Taim had not been all that easy about it even then. 'We think maybe it's something like the bond between Warders and Aes Sedai. Maybe one in three of us is married; anyway, that's how many wives stayed instead of running off when they learned what their husbands were. This way, when you're apart from her, you know she's all right, and she knows you are. A man likes to know his wife's safe.'

'That he does,' Perrin said. What was Faile up to with those fools? She was mounted on Swallow now, and they were all standing close around, looking up at her. He would not put it past her to leap into this *ji'e'toh* nonsense herself.

Seonid and Masuri glided behind the last of the Two Rivers men with the three Warders they had between them, and the Wise Ones right behind them, which was no surprise. They were along to keep an eye on the Aes Sedai. Seonid gathered her reins as if to mount, but Edarra said something in a low voice, pointing to a fat lopsided oak, and the two Aes Sedai looked at her, heads swiveling as one, then exchanged glances and led their horses to the tree. Matters would go a deal smoother if that pair was always so meek – well, not meek exactly; Seonid's neck was stiff as a rod.

After that came the remounts, a herd of spare horses tied ten to a lead, under the watchful eyes of folk from Dobraine's estates who supposedly knew what they were about. Perrin automatically picked out Stayer, on a lead by himself; the woman taking care of him better know what she was doing. A great many high-wheeled supply carts came through, drivers tugging the horses and shouting as if they feared the gateway might close on them – a great many because carts could not carry as much as wagons, and carts because a wagon and team would not fit through the gateway. It seemed neither Neald nor Grady could make one as big as Rand could, or Dashiva.

When the last cart finally trundled out on a squealing axle, Perrin considered ordering the gateway closed right then, but Neald was the man holding the thing open, and him on the other side of it back in Cairhien. A moment later, it was too late.

Berelain strode through leading a mare as white as Swallow was black, and he offered up small thanks that her gray riding dress had a neck right to her chin. On the other hand, from the waist up, it fit as snugly as any Taraboner dress. Perrin groaned. With her came Nurelle and Bertain Gallenne, the Lord Captain of her Winged Guards, a gray-haired fellow who wore his red eyepatch as another man might a plume in his hat, and then the red-armored Winged Guards themselves, more than nine hundred of them. Nurelle and the rest who had been at Dumai's Wells wore a yellow cord tied high on the left arm.

Climbing onto her mare, Berelain rode off to one side with Gallenne while Nurelle formed the Winged Guards among the trees. There must have been fifty paces between her and Faile, and dozens of trees, but she placed herself where they could stare at each other. Stare with so little expression that Perrin's skin crawled. Putting Berelain at the rear, as far from Faile as he could manage, had seemed a good notion, but he was going to face this every bloody evening. Burn Rand!

Now Neald popped out of the gateway, stroking his ridiculous mustache and preening for anyone who might be watching as the opening vanished. No one was, and he climbed onto his horse with a disgruntled expression.

Mounting Stepper, Perrin rode to a slight rise. Not everyone could see him because of the trees, but it was enough they could hear. A stir ran through the assemblage as he reined in, people shifting for a better look.

'As far as anyone's eyes-and-ears back in Cairhien know,' he said loudly, 'I've been banished, the First of Mayene is on her way back home, and the rest of you have just disappeared like fog in the sun.'

To his surprise, they laughed. A cry of 'Perrin Goldeneyes' went up, and not just from the Two Rivers folk. He waited for it to quiet; that took a while. Faile neither laughed nor shouted, nor did Berelain. Each woman shook her head; neither believed he should tell as much as he intended to. Then they saw each other, and those shaking heads froze as if trapped in amber. They did not like agreeing. It was no surprise when their eyes swung to him with identical expressions. There was an old saying in the Two Rivers, though how you said it and what you meant depended on circumstance and who you were. 'It's always a man's fault.' One thing, he had learned, women were better at than anything else: teaching a man to sigh.

'Some of you may be wondering where we are, and why,' he went on when silence fell at last. A smaller ripple of laughter. 'This is Ghealdan.' Murmurs of awe, and maybe disbelief, at having crossed fifteen hundred miles or more in a step. 'The first thing we have to do is convince Queen Alliandre we aren't here to invade.' Berelain was supposed to talk to Alliandre, and Faile was going to give him fits for it. 'Then we're going to find a fellow who calls himself the Prophet of the Lord Dragon.' That would not be much pleasure, either; Masema had been no joy before he tipped over the edge. 'This Prophet has been causing some problems, but we're going to let him know Rand al'Thor doesn't want anybody frightened into following him, and we'll take him and any of his people who want to come back to the Lord Dragon.' *And we'll frighten the breeches off Masema to do it if need be*, he thought wryly.

They cheered. They whooped and shouted that they would march this Prophet back to Cairhien for the Lord Dragon till Perrin hoped this spot was even farther from any village than it was supposed to be. Even the cart drivers and horse handlers joined in. More than that, he prayed that everything went smoothly, and quickly. The sooner he could put as much distance as possible between Berelain and himself and Faile, the better. No surprises, that was what he wanted once they rode south. It was about time his being *ta'veren* showed itself good for something.

Chapter 28

Bread and Cheese

Mat knew he was in trouble from the day he moved into the Tarasin Palace. He could have refused. Just because the flaming dice started or stopped did not mean he had to *do* anything; usually when they stopped spinning, it was too late not to do something. The problem was, he wanted to know why. Before very many days, he wished he had taken his curiosity by the throat and throttled it.

After Nynaeve and Elayne left his room, once he could manage to reach his feet without his head falling off, he spread the word among his men. Nobody seemed to see the disadvantages. He just wanted to prepare them, but nobody listened.

'Very good, my Lord,' Nerim murmured, tugging Mat's boot onto his foot. 'My Lord will finally have decent rooms. Oh, very good.' For a moment, he seemed to lose his mournful expression. For just a moment. 'I will brush the red silk coat for my Lord; my Lord has stained the blue rather badly with wine.' Mat waited impatiently, put on the coat, and headed for the hall.

'Aes Sedai?' Nalesean muttered as his head popped out at the top of a clean shirt. His round-bellied manservant, Lopin, was hovering behind him. 'Burn my soul, I don't much like Aes Sedai, but . . . The Tarasin Palace, Mat.' Mat winced; bad enough the man could drink a barrel of brandy with no effect the next morning, but did he have to grin so? 'Ah, Mat, now we can forget dice, and play cards with our own kind.' He meant nobles, the only ones who afford to play except for well-to-do merchants who would not remain well-to-do long if they began betting for the stakes nobles did. Nalesean rubbed his hands briskly while Lopin tried to settle his laces; even his beard seemed eager. 'Silk sheets,' he murmured. Whoever heard of silk *sheets*? Those old memories nudged, but Mat refused to listen.

'Full of nobles,' Vanin growled downstairs, pursing his lips to spit. His glance searching for Mistress Anan was automatic now; he decided instead to swallow from the mug of rough wine that was his breakfast. 'Be good to see the Lady Elayne again, though,' he mused. His free hand rose as if to knuckle his forehead; he did not seem aware of the gesture. Mat groaned. That woman had ruined a good man. 'You want me to look in on Carridin again?' Vanin went on as if the rest was unimportant. 'His street's so full of beggars, it's hard to see anything, but he has an awful lot of folk come to call.' Mat told him that would be fine. No wonder Vanin did not care whether the palace was full of nobles and Aes Sedai; he would spend the day sweating in the sun and jostled by the crowds. Much more comfortable.

There was no point trying to warn Harnan and the rest of the Redarms, all shoveling down white porridge and tiny black sausages while they nudged one another in the ribs and laughed about the serving women in the palace, who, they had heard, were all chosen for their beauty and remarkably free with their favors. A true fact, they kept assuring themselves.

Things did not get any better when he went into the kitchens searching for Mistress Anan to settle the bill. Caira was there, but with all her bad temper of the night before doubled; she stuck out her lower lip, glowering at him, and stalked out the door to the stableyard rubbing the back of her skirt. Maybe she had gotten herself into some misery or other, but how she could blame Mat Cauthon was beyond him.

Mistress Anan was out, it seemed – she was always organizing soup kitchens for refugees or leaping into some other good work – but Enid was waving a long wooden spoon at her scurrying helpers and ready to take his coin in her stout hand. 'You squeeze too many melons, my young Lord, and you shouldn't be surprised when a rotten one breaks in your hand,' she said darkly for some reason. 'Or two,' she added after a moment, nodding. She leaned close, tilting up her sweating round face with an intent stare. 'You'll only make trouble for yourself if you say a word. You won't.' That did not sound like a question.

'Not a word,' Mat said. What in the Light was she talking about? It seemed the right response, though, because she nodded and waddled away waving that spoon twice as vigorously as before. For a moment, he had thought she meant to thump him with it. The pure truth was, women all had a violent streak, not just some of them.

One thing and another, it was a relief when Nerim and Lopin got into a shouting match over whose master's baggage would be carried over first. Smoothing their feathers required a good half an hour from him and Nalesean both. A manservant with his dander ruffled could make your life miserable. Then he had to settle which of the Redarms were to have the honor of lugging the chest of gold across and which were to take the horses. Anyway, it was that much longer outside the bloody Tarasin Palace.

Once he was ensconced in his new rooms, though, he almost forgot his troubles at first. He had a large sitting room and a small, what they called a sulking room hereabouts, and an immense bedchamber with the biggest bed he had ever seen, the massive bedposts carved with entwined flowers of all things, and painted red. Most of the furniture was bright red or bright blue, where it was not layered with gilt. A small door near the bed led to a cramped room for Nerim, which the fellow seemed to think was excellent despite a narrow bed and no window. Mat's rooms all had tall arched windows letting onto white wrought-iron balconies that overlooked the Mol Hara. The stand-lamps were gilded, and so were the mirror frames; there were two mirrors in the sulking room, three in the sitting room, and *four* in the bedchamber. The clock – a clock! – on the marble mantel above the fireplace in the sitting room sparkled with gilt, as well. The washbasin and pitcher were red Sea Folk porcelain. He was almost disappointed to discover that the chamber pot under the bed was only plain white pottery. There was even a shelf in the large sitting room with a full dozen books. Not that he read much.

Even given the jarring colors of walls and ceilings and floor tiles, the rooms shouted rich. Any other time, he would have danced a jig. Any time when he was not aware that a woman with chambers right down the hall wanted to stick him in hot water and put a bellows to the fire. If Teslyn or Merilille or one of that lot did not manage it first despite his medallion. Why *had* the dice in his head stopped tumbling as soon as Elayne mentioned these bloody rooms? Curiosity. He had heard a saying on several women's lips back home, usually when he had done something that looked fun at the time. 'Men teach cats curiosity, but cats keep sense for themselves.'

'I'm no bloody cat,' he muttered, stalking out of the bedchamber into the sitting room. He just had to know; that was all.

'Of course you're not a cat,' Tylin said. 'You're a succulent little duckling, is what you are.'

Mat gave a start and stared. Duckling? And a *little* duckling, at that! The woman stood well short of his shoulder. Indignation or no indignation, he managed an elegant bow anyway. She was the Queen; he had to remember that. 'Majesty, thank you for these wonderful apartments. I'd love to talk with you, but I have to go out and—'

Smiling, she advanced across the red-and-green floor tiles, layered blue and white silk petticoats swishing, large dark eyes fixed on him. He had no desire at all to look at the marriage knife nestled in her generous cleavage. Or the larger, gem-studded dagger thrust behind an equally gem-studded belt. He backed away.

'Majesty, I have an important—'

She started humming. He recognized the tune; he had hummed it to a few girls lately. He was wise enough not to try actually singing with his voice, and besides, the words they used in Ebou Dar would have singed his ears. Around here, they called it 'I Will Steal Your Breath With Kisses.'

Laughing nervously, he tried to put a lapis-inlaid table between them, but she somehow got around it first without seeming to increase her speed. 'Majesty, I—'

She laid a hand flat on his chest, back-heeled him into a high-backed chair, and plumped herself down on his lap. Between her and the chair arms, he was trapped. Oh, he could have picked her up and set her on her feet quite easily. Except that she did have that bloody big dagger in her belt, and he doubted his manhandling her would be as acceptable to her as her manhandling him seemed to be. This was Ebou Dar, after all, where a woman killing a man was justified until proven otherwise. He could have picked her up easily, except . . .

He had seen fishmongers in the city selling peculiar creatures called squid and octopus – Ebou Dari actually ate the things! – but they had nothing on Tylin. The woman possessed ten hands. He thrashed about, vainly trying to fend her off, and she laughed softly. Between kisses, he breathlessly protested that someone might walk in, and she just chuckled. He babbled his respect for her crown, and she chortled. He claimed betrothal to a girl back home who held his heart in her hands. She really laughed at that.

'What she does not know cannot harm her,' she murmured, her twenty hands not slowing for an instant.

Someone knocked at the door.

Prying his mouth free, he shouted, 'Who is it?' Well, it was a shout. A high-pitched shout. He was out of breath, after all.

Tylin was off his lap and three paces away so fast it seemed she was just here then there. The woman had the nerve to give him a reproachful look! And then she made a kiss at him.

That barely left her lips before the door opened, and Thom stuck his head in. 'Mat? I wasn't sure that was you. Oh! Majesty.' For a scrawny old gleeman with pretensions, Thom could flourish a bow with the best in spite of his limp. Juilin could not, but he snatched off his ridiculous red hat and did what he could. 'Forgive us. We won't disturb—' Thom began, but Mat broke in hurriedly.

'Come in, Thom!' Snatching his coat back all the way on, he started to stand, then realized that somehow the bloody woman had untied the waist of his *breeches* without him noticing. These two might miss that his shirt was undone to his belly, but they would not miss his breeches falling off. Tylin's blue dress was not mussed at all! 'Juilin, come in!'

'I am glad you find the rooms acceptable, Master Cauthon,' Tylin said, dignity incarnate. Except for her eyes, anyway, when she stood so Thom and Juilin could not see them. Her eyes laced innocuous words with added meaning. 'I look forward to having your company with pleasure; I shall find it interesting, having a *ta'veren* where I can reach out and touch him at will. But I must leave you to your friends, now. No, do not stand; please.' That with just the hint of a mocking smile.

'Well, boy,' Thom said, knuckling his mustaches when she was gone, 'there's luck for you, being welcomed with open arms by the Queen herself.' Juilin became very interested in his cap.

Mat eyed them warily, mentally daring them to say a word more — just one word! — but once he asked after Nynaeve and Elayne, he quit worrying what they suspected. The women were not back. He almost leaped up, breeches or no. They were trying to wiggle out of their agreement already; he had to explain what he meant in between their outbursts of incredulity, in between expressing his opinions of Nynaeve bloody al'Meara and Elayne bloody Daughter-Heir. Not much chance they would have gone off to the Rahad without him, but he would not put it past them to try their hand spying on Carridin. Elayne would demand a confession and expect the man to break down; Nynaeve would try to beat one out of him.

'I doubt they are bothering Carridin,' Juilin said, scratching behind his ear. 'I believe Aviendha and Birgitte are taking a look at him, from what I heard. We didn't see them go. I do not think you need to worry about him knowing what he's seeing even if he walks right by them.' Thom, pouring himself a golden goblet of the wine punch that Mat had found waiting, took up the explanation.

Mat put a hand over his eyes. Disguises made with the Power; no wonder they had slipped away like snakes whenever they wanted. Those women were going to make trouble. That was what women did best. It hardly surprised him to learn that Thom and Juilin knew less about this Bowl of the Winds than he did.

After they left to ready themselves for a trip to the Rahad, he had time to set his clothes to rights before Nynaeve and Elayne came back. He had time to check on Olver, in his room one floor down. The boy's skinny frame had fleshed out somewhat, with Enid and the rest of the cooks at The Wandering Woman stuffing him, but he would always be short even for a Cairhienin, and if his ears shrank to half their size and his mouth to half its width, his nose would still stop him well short of handsome. No fewer than three serving women fussed over him while he sat cross-legged on his bed.

'Mat, doesn't Haesel have the most beautiful eyes?' Olver said, beaming at the big-eyed young woman Mat had met the last time he came to the palace. She beamed back and ruffled the boy's hair. 'Oh, but Alis and Loya are so sweet, I could never choose.' A plump woman just short of her middle years looked up from unpacking Olver's saddlebags to give him a broad grin, and a slender girl with bee-stung lips patted the towel she had just put on his washstand, then flung herself onto the bed to tickle Olver's ribs till he fell over laughing helplessly.

Mat snorted. Harnan and that lot were bad enough, but now these *women* were encouraging the boy! How was he ever going to learn to behave if women did that? Olver ought to be playing in the streets like any other ten-year-old. *He* had had no serving women falling over him in his rooms. Tylin had seen to that, he was sure.

He had time to check on Olver, and to look in on Harnan and the rest of the Redarms, sharing a long room lined with beds not far from the stables, and to saunter down to the kitchens for some bread and beef – he had not been able to face that porridge back at the inn. Still Nynaeve and Elayne had not returned. He finally looked over the books in his sitting room and began reading *The Travels of Jain Farstrider*, though he barely made out a word for worrying. Thom and Juilin came in just as the women finally bustled in exclaiming over finding him there, as if they thought *he* would not keep his word.

He closed the book gently, set it gently on the table beside his chair. 'Where have you been?'

'Why, we went for a walk,' Elayne said brightly, blue eyes wider than he remembered seeing before. Thom frowned and produced a knife from his sleeve, rolling it back and forth through his fingers. He very markedly did not so much as glance at Elayne.

'We had tea with some women your innkeeper knows,' Nynaeve said. 'I won't bore you with talk about needlework.' Juilin started to shake his head, then stopped before she noticed.

'Please, don't bore me,' Mat said dryly. He supposed she knew one end of a needle from the other, but he suspected she would as soon stick one through her tongue as talk about needlework. Neither woman cracked her teeth about civility, confirming his worse suspicions. 'I've told off two fellows to walk out with each of you this afternoon, and there will be two more tomorrow and every day. If you're not inside the palace or under my nose, you'll have bodyguards. They know their turns already. They'll stay with you at all times – *all* times – and you will let me know where you're headed. No more making me worry till my hair falls out.'

He expected indignation and argument. He expected weaseling over what they had or had not promised. He expected that demanding this whole loaf might get him a slice at the end; a butt slice, if his luck was in. Nynaeve looked at Elayne; Elayne looked at Nynaeve.

'Why, bodyguards are a *wonderful* idea, Mat,' Elayne exclaimed, her cheek dimpling in a smile. 'I suppose you were right about that. It's very smart of you to have your men already to a schedule.'

'It *is* a wonderful notion,' Nynaeve said, nodding enthusiastically. 'Very smart of you, Mat.'

Thom dropped the knife with a muffled curse and sat sucking on a nicked finger, staring at the women.

Mat sighed. Trouble; he had known it. And that was before they told him to forget the Rahad for the time being.

Which was how he found himself on a bench in front of a cheap tavern not far from the riverfront called The Rose of the Eldar, drinking from one of the dented tin cups chained to the bench. At least they washed the cups out for each new patron. The stink from a dyer's shop across the way only raised the style of the Rose. Not that it was a shabby neighborhood really, though the street was too narrow for carriages. A fair number of brightly lacquered sedan chairs swayed through the crowd. If far more passersby wore wool and perhaps a guild vest than silk, the wool was as often well cut as frayed. The houses and shops were the usual array of white plaster, and if most were small and even run-down, the tall house of a wealthy merchant stood on a corner to his right and on the left a diminutive palace – smaller than the merchant's house, at least –

with a single green-banded dome and no spire. A pair of taverns and an inn in plain sight looked cool and inviting. Unfortunately, the Rose was the only one where a man could sit outside, the only one in just the right spot. Unfortunately.

'I doubt I've ever seen such splendid flies,' Nalesean grumbled, waving away several choice specimens from his cup. 'What is it we're doing again?'

'You are swilling that foul excuse for wine and sweating like a goat,' Mat muttered, tugging his hat to shade his eyes better. 'I'm being *ta'veren*.' He glared at the dilapidated house, between the dyer's and a noisy weaver's establishment, that he had been told to watch. Not asked – told – that was what it came to, however they phrased it, squirming around their pledges. Oh, they made it sound like asking, made it sound like pleading at the end, which he would believe when dogs danced, but he knew when he had been bullied. 'Just be *ta'veren*, Mat,' he mimicked. 'I know you'll just *know* what to do. Bah!' Maybe Elayne bloody Daughter-Heir and her bloody dimple knew, or Nynaeve with her bloody hands twitching to yank her bloody braid, but he would be burned if he did. 'If the pig-kissing Bowl is in the Rahad, how am I supposed to find it on this flaming side of the river?'

'I do not remember them saying,' Juilin said wryly, and took a long swallow of some drink made from a yellow fruit grown in the countryside. 'You've asked that fifty times, at least.' He claimed the pale drink was refreshing in the heat, but Mat had taken a bite of one of those lemons, and he was not about to swallow anything made from them. With his head still throbbing faintly, he himself drank tea. It tasted as if the tavernkeeper, a scrawny fellow with beady suspicious eyes, had been dumping new leaves and water in yesterday's leavings since the founding of the city. The taste suited his mood.

'What interests me,' Thom murmured over steepled fingers, 'is why they asked so many questions about your innkeeper.' He did not seem very upset at the women still keeping secrets; sometimes, he was decidedly odd. 'What do Setalle Anan and these women have to do with the Bowl?'

Women did pass in and out of the dilapidated house. A steady stream of women, just about, some well dressed if none in silks, and not one man. Three or four wore the red belt of a Wise Woman. Mat had considered following some of them when they left, but it felt too planned. He did not know how *ta'veren* worked – he had never really seen any sign of it in himself – but his luck was always best when everything was random. Like with dice. Most of those little iron tavern puzzles eluded him, however lucky he felt.

He ignored Thom's question; Thom had asked it at least as often as Mat had asked how he was to find the Bowl here. Nynaeve had told him to his face she had not promised to tell him every last thing she knew; she said she would tell him whatever he needed to know; she said . . . Watching her nearly choke from not calling him names was not nearly enough vengeance.

'I suppose I should take a walk down the alley,' Nalesean sighed. 'In case one of those women decides to climb over the garden wall.' The narrow gap between the house and the dyer lay in full view for its whole length, but another alleyway ran along behind the shops and houses. 'Mat, tell me again why we're doing this instead of playing cards.'

'I'll do it,' Mat said. Maybe he would find out how *ta'veren* worked behind the garden wall. He went, and found out nothing.

By the time twilight began creeping over the street and Harnan came with a bald-headed, narrow-eyed Andoran named Wat, the only possible effect of being *ta'veren* he had seen was that the tavernkeeper brewed a fresh pot of tea. It tasted almost as bad as the old.

Back in his rooms in the palace, he found a note, an invitation of sorts, elegantly lettered on thick white paper that smelled like a garden of flowers.

My little rabbit, I expect to have you for dinner tonight in my apartments.

No signature, but he hardly needed one. Light! The woman had no shame at all! There was a red-painted iron lock on the door to the corridor; he found the key and locked it. Then, for good measure, he jammed a chair under the latch on the door to Nerim's room. He could do well enough without dinner. Just as he was about to climb into bed, the lock rattled; out in the hall, a woman laughed at finding the door secured.

He should have been able to sleep soundly then, but for some reason he lay there listening to his belly grumble. Why was she doing this? Well, he knew why, but why him? Surely she had not decided to toss all decency over the barn just to bed a *ta'veren*. He was safe now, anyway. Tylin would not batter down the door, after all. Would she? Not even most birds could get in through the wrought-iron arabesques screening the balconies. Besides, she would need a long ladder to reach that high. And men to carry it. Unless she climbed down from the roof on a rope. Or she could ... The night passed, his stomach rumbled, the sun rose, and he never closed his eyes or had a decent thought. Except that he did make a decision. He thought of a use for the sulking room. He certainly never sulked.

At first light, he sneaked out of his rooms and found another of the palace servants he remembered, a balding fellow named Madic, with a smug, self-satisfied air and a sly twist to his mouth that said he was not satisfied at all. A man who could be bought. Though the startled look that flashed across his square face, and the smirk he barely bothered to hide, said he knew exactly why Mat was slipping gold into his hand. Blood and as his! How many people knew what Tylin was up to?

Nynaeve and Elayne did not seem to, thank the Light. Though that did mean they chided him about missing dinner with the Queen, which they had learned about when Tylin inquired whether he was ill. And worse ...

'Please,' Elayne said, smiling almost as if the word did not pain her, 'you must put your best foot forward with the Queen. Don't be nervous. You'll enjoy an evening with her.'

'Just don't do anything to offend her,' Nynaeve muttered. There was no doubt with her that being civil hurt; her brows drew down in concentration, her jaw tightened, and her hands trembled to pull her braid. 'Be accommodating for once in your— I mean to say, remember she's a decent woman, and don't try any of your— Light, you know what I mean.'

Nervous. Ha! Decent woman. Ha!

Neither seemed the least concerned that he had wasted a whole afternoon. Elayne patted his shoulder sympathetically and asked him please to try another day or two; it certainly was better than tramping through the Rahad in this heat. Nynaeve said the exact same thing, the way women did, but without the shoulder pat. They admitted right out that they intended to spend the day trying to spy on Carridin with Aviendha, though they evaded his question of who it was they thought they might recognize. Nynaeve let that slip, and Elayne gave her such a look he thought he might see Nynaeve's ears boxed for once. They meekly accepted his stricture not to lose sight of their bodyguards, and meekly let him see the disguises they intended to wear. Even after Thom's description, seeing the pair suddenly turn into Ebou Dari women in front of his eyes was almost as big a shock as their meekness. Well, Nynaeve made a sickly stab at meekness, growling when she realized he had meant what he said about the Aiel woman needing no bodyguard, but she came close. Either one of these women folding her hands and answering submissively made him nervous. Both of them together – with Aviendha nodding *approvingly*! – and he was happy to send them on their way. Just to be sure, though, he ignored their suddenly flat mouths and made them demonstrate their disguises for the men he was sending along first. Vanin leaped at the chance to be one of Elayne's guards, knuckling his forehead right and left like a fool.

The fat man had not learned much watching on his own. Just as on the day before, a surprising number of people had come to call on Carridin, including some in silk, but that was not proof they were all Darkfriends. All said and done, the man was the Whitecloak ambassador; more folk who wanted to trade into Amadicia probably went to him than to the Amadician ambassador, whoever he or she was. Vanin did say two women had definitely been watching Carridin's palace, too – the look on his face when Aviendha suddenly turned into a third Ebou Dari woman was a wonder – and also an old man, he thought, though the fellow proved surprisingly spry. Vanin had not managed to get a good look at him despite spotting him three times. Once Vanin and the women left, Mat sent off Thom and Juilin to see what they could uncover concerning Jaichim Carridin and a bent, white-haired old man with an interest in Darkfriends. If the thief-catcher could not discover a way to trip Carridin on his face, it did not exist, and Thom seemed to have a way of putting together all the gossip and rumor in a place and filtering out the truth. All that was the easy part, of course.

For two days he sweated on that bench, with an occasional stroll down the alley beside the dyer's, and the only thing that changed was that the tea got worse again. The wine was so bad, Nalesean began drinking ale. The first day, the tavernkeeper offered fish for a midday meal, but by the smell they had been caught last week. The second day, he offered a stew of oysters; Mat ate five bowls of that despite the bits of shell. Birgitte declined both.

He had been surprised when she caught up to him and Nalesean hurrying across the Mol Hara that first morning. The sun barely made a rim above the rooftops, but already people and carts dotted the square. 'I must have blinked,' she laughed. 'I was waiting the way I thought you'd come out. If you don't mind company.'

'We move fast sometimes,' he said evasively. Nalesean looked at him sideways; of course, he had no idea why they had crept out through a tiny side door near the stables. It was not that Mat thought Tylin would actually leap on him in the halls in broad daylight, but then again, it never hurt to be careful. 'Your company is welcome any time. Uh. Thanks.' She just shrugged and murmured something he did not catch and fell in on the other side of him.

That was the beginning with her. Any other woman he had ever known would have demanded to know thanks for what, and then explained why none were necessary at such length that he wanted to cover his ears, or upbraided him at equal length for thinking they were, or sometimes made it clear she expected something more substantial than words. Birgitte just shrugged, and over the next two days, something startling occurred in his head.

Normally, to him, women were to admire and smile at, to dance with and kiss if they would allow, to snuggle with if he was lucky. Deciding which women to chase was almost as much fun as chasing them, if not nearly so much as catching them. Some women were just friends, of course. A few. Egwene, for one, though he was not sure how that friendship would survive her becoming Amyrlin. Nynaeve was sort of a friend, in a way; if she could forget for one hour that she had switched his bottom more than once and remember he was not a boy anymore. But a woman friend was different from a man; you always knew her mind ran along other paths than yours, that she saw the world with different eyes.

Birgitte leaned toward him on the bench. 'Best be wary,' she murmured. 'That widow is looking for a new husband; the sheath on her marriage knife is blue. Besides, the house is over there.'

He blinked, losing sight of the sweetly plump woman who rolled her hips so extravagantly as she walked, and Birgitte answered his sheepish grin with a laugh. Nynaeve would have flayed him with her tongue for looking, and even Egwene would have been coolly disapproving. By the end of the second day on that bench, he realized he had sat all that time with his hip pressed against Birgitte's and never once thought of trying to kiss her. He was sure she did not want to be kissed by him – frankly, considering the dog-ugly men she seemed to enjoy looking at, he might have been insulted if she had – and she was a hero out of legend whom he still half-expected to leap over a house and grab a couple of the Forsaken by the neck on the way. But that was not it: He would as soon have thought of kissing Nalesean. The same as the Tairen, just exactly the same as, he *liked* Birgitte.

Two days on that bench, up and down to trot down the alley beside the dyer and stare at the tall wall of bare brick at the back of the house's garden. Birgitte could have climbed it, but even she might have broken her neck if she tried wearing a dress. Three times he decided on the spur of the moment to follow a woman coming out of the house, two wearing the red belt of a Wise Woman. Random chance did seem to invoke his luck. One of the Wise Women went around the corner and bought a bunch of shriveled turnips before going back; the other walked two streets over to buy a pair of big, green-striped fish. The third woman, tall and dark in neat gray wool, maybe a Tairen, crossed two bridges before entering a large shop where she was greeted with smiles by a skinny bowing fellow and began supervising the loading of lacquered boxes and trays into sawdust-filled baskets that were then loaded into a wagon. By what he heard, she hoped to fetch a pretty piece of silver with them in Andor. Mat barely managed to escape without buying a box. So much for random luck.

No one else had any either. Nynaeve and Elayne and Aviendha made their pilgrimages to the streets around Carridin's small palace without seeing anyone they recognized, which frustrated them no end. They still refused to say who; it hardly mattered, since the people were not to be seen. That was what they said, showing him enough teeth for six women. The grimaces were supposed to be smiles, he thought. It was a shame Aviendha seemed to have fallen in with the other two so thoroughly, but there was a moment when he was pressing them for an answer, and Elayne snapped at him, staring down her nose, and the Aiel woman whispered something in her ear.

'Forgive me, Mat,' Elayne said earnestly, her face going so red her hair seemed to pale. 'I humbly beg pardon for speaking so. I . . . will beg on my knees, if you wish.' No surprise that her voice faltered at the end.

'No need for that,' he said faintly trying not to goggle. 'You're forgiven; it was nothing.' The oddest thing, though; Elayne looked at Aviendha the whole time she spoke to him and did not twitch an eyelid when he replied, but she heaved a great sigh of relief when Aviendha nodded. Women were just strange.

Thom reported that Carridin gave to beggars frequently, and aside from that, every scrap of word about him in Ebou Dar was the kind to be expected, depending on whether the speaker thought Whitecloaks were murderous monsters or the true saviors of the world. Juilin learned that Carridin had purchased a plan of the Tarasin Palace, which might indicate some Whitecloak intention toward Ebou Dar and might indicate that Pedron Niall wanted a palace for himself and intended to copy the Tarasin. If he still lived; rumors had sprung up in the city that he was dead, but then, half said Aes Sedai had killed him and half said Rand had, which showed their worth. Neither Juilin or Thom had scuffed up a pebble concerning a white-haired old man with a much-worn face.

Frustration with Carridin, frustration with watching the bloody house, and as far as the palace went . . .

Mat found out how things were to go that first night when he finally got back to his rooms. Olver was there, already fed and curled up in a chair with *The Travels of Jain Farstrider* by the light of the stand-lamps, and not at all upset over being moved out of his own room. Madic had been as good as his word; as good as the gold he stuffed in his pouch, anyway. The sulking room now held Olver's bed. Just let Tylin try anything with a child watching her! The Queen had not been idle either, though. He sneaked down to the kitchens like a fox, slipping from corner to corner, flashing down stairs – and found there was no food to be had.

Oh, the smell of cooking permeated the air, roasts turning on spits in the big fireplaces, pots bubbling atop the white-tiled stoves, and cooks kept popping open ovens to prod this or that. There was just no food for Mat Cauthon. Smiling women in pristine white aprons ignored his own smiles and put themselves in his way so he could not get near the sources of those wonderful smells. They smiled and rapped his knuckles when he tried to snatch a loaf of bread or just a bit of honey-glazed turnip. They smiled and told him he must not spoil his appetite if he was to eat with the Queen. They knew. Every last one of them knew! His own blushes as much as anything else drove him back to his rooms, bitterly regretting that odorous fish at midday. He locked the door behind him. A woman who would starve a man might try anything.

He was lying on a green silk carpet playing Snakes and Foxes with Olver when the second note was slipped under his door.

I have been told it is more sporting to take a pigeon on the wing, to watch it flutter, but sooner or later, a hungry bird will fly to the hand.

'What is it, Mat?' Olver asked.

'Nothing.' Mat crumpled the note. 'Another game?'

'Oh, yes.' The boy would play the fool game all day, given a chance. 'Mat, did you try any of that ham they cooked tonight? I never tasted anything—'

'Just throw the dice, Olver. Just throw the bloody dice.'

Coming back for his third night in the palace, he bought bread and olives and ewe's milk cheese on the way, which was just as well. The kitchen still had its orders. The bloody women actually laughed out loud while they wafted steaming platters of meats and fishes just beyond his reach and told him not to spoil his bloody appetite.

He maintained his dignity. He did not grab a platter and run. He made his finest leg, flourishing an imaginary cloak. 'Gracious ladies, your warmth and hospitality overwhelm me.'

His withdrawal would have gone a deal better if one of the cooks had not cackled at his back, 'The Queen will feast on roast duckling soon enough, lad.' Very droll. The other women roared so hard, they must have been rolling on the floor. Very bloody droll.

Bread and olives and salty cheese made a fine meal, with a little water from his washstand to wash it down. There had not been any wine punch in his room since that first day. Olver tried to tell him about some sort of roasted fish with mustard sauce and raisins; Mat told him to practice his reading.

Nobody slipped a note under his door that night. Nobody rattled the lock. He began to think things might turn for the better. Tomorrow was the Festival of Birds. From what he had heard of the costumes some people wore, men and women both, it might be possible Tylin would find herself a new duckling to chase after. Somebody might come out of that bloody house across from The Rose of the Eldar and hand him the bloody Bowl of the Winds. Things just had to turn for the better.

When he woke for his third morning in the Tarasin Palace, the dice were rolling in his head.

CHAPTER 29

The Festival of Birds

Waking to the dice, Mat considered going back to sleep until they went away, but at last he got up feeling grumpy. As if he did not have more than enough on his plate already. He chased Nerim away and dressed himself, eating the last of the bread and cheese from the night before while he did, then went to check on Olver. The boy flashed between bursts of yanking on his clothes in a hurry to be out and stopping entirely with boot or shirt in hand to spout dozens of questions that Mat answered with half a mind. No, they would not go racing today, and never mind the rich races at the Circuit of Heaven, north of the city. Maybe they could go see the menagerie. Yes, Mat would buy him a feathered mask for the festival. If he ever got dressed. That sent him into a flurry.

What really occupied Mat's thoughts were those bloody dice. Why had they started up again? He still did not know why they had before!

When Olver was finally clothed, he followed Mat into the sitting room bubbling with half-heard questions – and bumped him from behind when he stopped dead. Tylin replaced the book Olver had been reading the night before on the table.

'Majesty!' Mat's eyes darted to the door he had locked last night, now standing wide open. 'What a surprise.' He pulled Olver around in front of him, between him and the woman's mocking smile. Well, maybe it was not really mocking, but it surely seemed so right then. She was certainly pleased with herself. 'I was about to take Olver out.

To see the festival. And some traveling menagerie. He wants a feathered mask.' He snapped his mouth shut to stop babbling and started edging toward the door, using the boy as a shield.

'Yes,' Tylin murmured, watching through her eyelashes. She made no move to intervene, but her smile deepened, as if she was just waiting for his foot to land in the snare. 'Much better if he has a companion, instead of running with the urchins, as I hear he does. One hears a good deal about your lad. Riselle?'

A woman appeared in the doorway, and Mat gave a start. A fanciful mask of swirling blue and golden feathers hid most of Riselle's face, but the feathers on the rest of her costume did not hide very much else. She possessed the most spectacular bosom he had ever seen.

'Olver,' she said, sinking to her knees, 'would you like to walk out with me at festival?' She held up a mask like a red-and-green hawk, just the right size for a boy.

Before Mat could open his mouth, Olver broke free and rushed to her. 'Oh, yes, please. Thank you.' The ungrateful little lout laughed as she tied the hawk mask on his face and hugged him to her bosom. Hand in hand, they ran out, leaving Mat gaping.

He recovered himself quickly enough when Tylin said, 'Well for you I am not a jealous woman, my sweet.' She produced the long iron key to his door from behind her gold-and-silver belt, and then another just like it, waggling the pair at him. 'People always keep keys in a box near the door.' That was where he had left his. 'And no one ever thinks there might be a second key.' One key went back behind her belt; the other was turned in the lock with a loud click before joining its fellow. 'Now, lambkin.' She smiled.

It was too much. The woman hounded him, tried to starve him; now she locked them in together like ... like he did not know what. Lambkin! Those bloody dice were bouncing around in his skull. Besides, he had important business to see to. The dice had never had anything to do with finding something, but ... He reached her in two long strides, seized her arm, and began fumbling in her belt for the keys. 'I don't have bloody time for—' His breath froze as the sharp point of her dagger beneath his chin shut his mouth and drove him right up onto his toes.

'Remove your hand,' she said coldly. He managed to look down his nose at her face. She was not smiling now. He let go of her arm carefully. She did not lessen the pressure of her blade, though. She shook her head. *'Tsk, tsk.* I do try to make allowances for you being an outlander, gosling, but since you wish to play roughly ... Hands at your sides. Move.' The knifepoint gave a direction. He shuffled backward on tiptoe rather than have his neck sliced.

'What are you going to do?' he mumbled through his teeth. A stretched neck put a strain in his voice. A stretched neck among other things. 'Well?' He could try grabbing her wrist; he was quick with his hands. 'What are you going to do?' Quick enough, with the knife already at his throat? That was the question. That, and the one he asked her. If she intended to kill him, a shove of her wrist right there would drive the dagger straight up into his brain. 'Will you answer me!' That was not panic in his voice. He was not in a panic. 'Majesty? Tylin?' Well, maybe he was in a bit of a panic, to use her name. You could call any woman in Ebou Dar 'duckling' or 'pudding' all day, and she would smile, but use her name before she said you could, and you found a hotter reception than you would for goosing a strange woman on the street anywhere else. A few kisses exchanged were never enough for permission, either.

Tylin did not answer, only kept him tiptoeing backward, until suddenly his shoulders bumped against something that stopped him. With that flaming dagger never easing a hair, he could not move his head, but eyes that had been focused on her face darted. They were in the bedchamber, a flower-carved red bedpost hard between his shoulder blades. Why would she bring him ...? His face was suddenly as crimson as the bedpost. No. She could not mean to ... It was not decent! It was not possible!

'You can't do this to me,' he mumbled at her, and if his voice was a touch breathy and shrill, he surely had cause.

'Watch and learn, my kitten,' Tylin said, and drew her marriage knife.

Afterward, a considerable time later, he irritably pulled the sheet up to his chest. A silk sheet; Nalesean had been right. The Queen of Altara hummed happily beside the bed, arms twisted behind her to do up the buttons of her dress. All he had on was the foxhead medallion on its cord – much good *that* had done – and the black scarf tied around his neck. A ribbon on her present, the bloody woman called it. He rolled over and snatched his silver-mounted pipe and tabac pouch from the small table on the other side from her. Golden tongs and a hot coal in a golden bowl of sand provided the means for lighting. Folding his arms, he puffed away as fiercely as he frowned.

'You should not flounce, duckling, and you shouldn't pout.' She yanked her dagger from where it was driven into a bedpost beside her marriage knife, examining the point before sheathing it. 'What is the matter? You know you enjoyed yourself as much as I did, and I . . .' She laughed suddenly, and oh so richly, resheathing the marriage knife as well. 'If that is part of what being *ta'veren* means, you must be very popular.' Mat flushed like fire.

'It isn't natural,' he burst out, yanking the pipestem from between his teeth. 'I'm the one who's supposed to do the chasing!' Her astonished eyes surely mirrored his own. Had Tylin been a tavern maid who smiled the right way, he might have tried his luck – well, if the tavern maid lacked a son who liked poking holes in people – but *he* was the one who chased. He had just never thought of it that way before. He had never had the need to, before.

Tylin began laughing, shaking her head and wiping at her eyes with her fingers. 'Oh, pigeon. I do keep forgetting. You are in Ebou Dar, now. I left a little present for you in the sitting room.' She patted his foot through the sheet. 'Eat well today. You are going to need your strength.'

Mat put a hand over his eyes and tried very hard not to weep. When he uncovered them, she was gone.

Climbing out of the bed, he tucked the sheet around him; for some reason, the notion of walking around bare felt uncomfortable. The bloody woman might leap out of the wardrobe. The garments he had been wearing lay on the floor. *Why bother with laces,* he thought sourly, *when you can just* cut *somebody's clothes off!* She had no call to slice up his red coat that way, though. She had just enjoyed peeling him with her knife.

Not quite holding his breath, he pulled open the tall red-and-gilt wardrobe. She was not hiding inside. His choices were limited;

Nerim had most of his coats for cleaning or mending. Dressing quickly, he chose a plain coat of dark bronze silk, then stuffed the sliced rags as far under the bed as he could reach until he could dispose of them without Nerim seeing. Or anyone else, for that matter. Too many people already knew entirely too much of what was going on between him and Tylin; there was no way he could face anybody knowing this.

In the sitting room, he lifted the lid of the lacquerware box by the door, then let it fall with a sigh; he had not really expected Tylin to replace the key. He leaned against the door. The unlocked door. Light, what was he going to do? Move back to the inn? Burn why the dice had stopped before. Only, he would not put it past Tylin to bribe Mistress Anan and Enid, or the innkeeper wherever he went. He would not put it past Nynaeve and Elayne to claim he had broken some agreement and put an end to their promises. Burn all women!

A large parcel elaborately wrapped in green paper sat on one of the tables. It contained an eagle mask in black and gold and a coat covered with feathers to match. There was also a red silk purse holding twenty gold crowns and a note that smelled of flowers.

> *I would have bought you an earring, piglet, but I noticed your ear is not pierced. Have it done, and buy yourself something nice.*

He nearly wept again. *He* gave *women* presents. The world was standing on its head! *Piglet?* Oh, Light! After a minute, he did take the mask; she owed him that much, for his coat alone.

When he finally reached the small, shaded courtyard where they had been meeting each morning beside a tiny round pool of lily pads and brightly spotted white fish, he found Nalesean and Birgitte ready for the Festival of Birds, too. The Tairen had contented himself with a plain green mask, but Birgitte's was a spray of yellow-and-red with a crest of plumes, her golden hair hung loose, with feathers tied all down its length, and she wore a dress with a wide yellow belt, diaphanous beneath more red and yellow feathers. It did not reveal nearly as much as Riselle's, yet it seemed about to every time she moved. He had never thought of her wearing a dress like other women.

'Sometimes it's fun to be looked at,' she said, poking him in the ribs, when he commented. Her grin would have done for Nalesean saying how much fun it was to pinch serving girls. 'There's a lot more to it than feather dancers wore, but not enough to it to slow me down, and anyway, I cannot see we'll have to move quickly on this side of the river.' The dice rattled in his head. 'What kept you?' she went on. 'You didn't make us wait so you could tickle a pretty girl, I hope.' He hoped he was not blushing.

'I—' He was not certain what excuse he would have made, but just then half a dozen men wearing feathered coats strolled into the courtyard, all with those narrow swords on their hips, all but one wearing an elaborate mask with colorful crest and beak that represented no bird ever seen by human eyes. The exception was Beslan, twirling his mask by its ribbon. 'Oh, blood and bloody ashes, what's he doing here?'

'Beslan?' Nalesean folded his hands on the pommel of his sword and shook his head in disbelief. 'Why, burn my soul, he says he intends to spend the festival in your company. Some promise you two made, he says. I told him it would be deadly boring, but he wouldn't believe me.'

'I cannot think it is ever boring around Mat,' Tylin's son said; his bow took them all in, but his dark eyes especially lingered on Birgitte. 'I've never had so much fun as I did drinking with him and the Lady Elayne's Warder on Swovan Night, though truth, I remember little.' He did not seem to recognize that Warder. Strangely, considering the taste she had shown in men – Beslan was fine-looking, maybe a little too fine, not at all her sort – strangely, she smiled slightly, and preened under his scrutiny.

Right then, Mat did not care how out of character she behaved. Obviously Beslan suspected nothing, or that sword of his likely would already be out, but the last thing under the Light Mat wanted was a day in company with the man. It would be excruciating. He had some sense of decency, even if Beslan's mother did not.

The only problem was Beslan, who took that bloody promise to attend all the festivals and feastdays together very seriously. The more Mat agreed with Nalesean that the day they had planned would be dull beyond belief, the more determined Beslan grew. After a bit, his face began to darken, and Mat began to think that sword might be unsheathed yet. Well, a promise was a promise. When he and Nalesean and Birgitte left the palace, half a dozen feathered fools strutted along. Mat was sure it would not have happened had Birgitte been wearing her proper clothes. The whole lot of them kept eyeing her and smiling.

'What was all that twisting around while he was spilling his eyes all over you?' he muttered as they crossed the Mol Hara. He tugged the ribbon holding the eagle mask tighter.

'I did not twist, I moved.' Her primness was so blatantly false, he would have laughed some other time. 'Slightly.' Abruptly her grin was back, and she lowered her voice for his ear alone. 'I told you sometimes it's fun to be looked at; just because they're all too pretty doesn't mean I cannot enjoy them looking. Oh, you'll want to look at her,' she added, pointed to a slender woman who went running by in a blue owl mask and rather fewer feathers than Riselle had worn.

That was one of the things about Birgitte; she would nudge him in the ribs and point out a pretty girl for his eye as readily as any man he had ever known, and expect him to point out in turn what she liked to see, which was generally the ugliest man in sight. Whether or not she chose to go half-naked today – a quarter, anyway – she was . . . well, a friend. A strange world, it was turning out to be. One woman he was beginning to think of as a drinking companion, and another after him as intently as he had ever pursued any pretty woman, in those old memories or his own. More intently; he had never chased any woman who let him know she did not want to be chased. A very strange world.

The sun stood little more than halfway to its peak, but already celebrants filled the streets and squares and bridges. Tumblers and jugglers and musicians with feathers sewn about their clothes performed at every street corner, the music often drowned in laughter and shouting. For the poorer folk a few feathers laced into their hair sufficed, pigeon feathers gathered from the pavement for the street children dodging about and the beggars, but masks and costumes grew more elaborate as purses grew heavier. More elaborate, and frequently more scandalous. Men and women alike were often decked in feathers that revealed more skin than Riselle *or* that woman back in the Mol Hara. No commerce moved in the streets or canals today, though a number of shops seemed to be open – along with every tavern and inn, of course – but here and there a wagon made its way through the throng or a barge was poled along supporting a platform where young men and women posed in bright bird masks that covered their entire heads, with spreading crests sometimes rising a full pace, moving long colorful wings in such a way that the rest of their costumes were exposed only in flashes. Which was just as well, considering.

According to Beslan, these settings, as they were called, were usually presented in guild halls and private palaces and houses. The entire festival normally took place indoors for the most part. It did not snow properly in Ebou Dar even when the weather was as it should be – Beslan said he would like to see this snow, one day – but apparently ordinary winter was cold enough to keep people from running around outdoors all but unclothed. With the heat, everything was spilling into the streets. Wait until night fell, Beslan said; then Mat would really see something. As sunlight faded, so did inhibitions.

Staring at a tall slender woman gliding along through the crowd in mask and feathered cloak and beyond that, six or seven feathers, Mat wondered what inhibitions some of these folk had left to shed. He almost shouted at her to cover herself with that cloak. She was pretty, but out in the *street*, before the Light and everybody?

Those wagons carrying the settings attracted followers, of course, thick knots of men and women who shouted and laughed as they tossed coins, and sometimes folded notes, onto the wagons and squeezed everyone else in the street aside. He became used to fleeing ahead until they could duck down a crossing street, or waiting until the setting went by to cross an intersection or bridge. While waiting, Birgitte and Nalesean tossed coins to filthy urchins and dirtier beggars. Well, Nalesean tossed; Birgitte concentrated on the children, and pressed each coin into a grubby hand like a gift.

In one of those waits, Beslan suddenly put a hand on Nalesean's arm, raising his voice above the crowd and a cacophony of music coming from at least six different places. 'Forgive me, Tairen, but not him.' A ragged man edged back into the throng, warily; gaunt-cheeked and bony, he seemed to have lost whatever pitiful feathers he might have found for his hair.

'Why not?' Nalesean demanded.

'No brass ring on his little finger,' Beslan replied. 'He's not in the guild.'

'Light,' Mat said, 'a man can't even beg in this city without belonging to a guild?' Maybe it was his tone. The beggar leaped for his throat, a knife appearing in his grimy fist.

Without thinking, Mat grabbed the man's arm and spun, slinging him away into the crowd; some people cursed at Mat, some at the sprawling beggar. Some tossed the fellow a coin.

From the corner of his eye, Mat saw a second skinny man in rags try to push Birgitte out of the way to reach him with a long knife. It was a foolish mistake to underestimate the woman because of her costume; from somewhere among those feathers she produced a knife and stabbed him beneath the arm.

'Look out!' Mat shouted at her, but there was no time for warnings; even as he shouted, he drew from his coatsleeve and threw sidearmed. The blade streaked past her face to sink into the throat of yet another beggar flaunting steel before he could plant it in her ribs.

Suddenly there were beggars everywhere with knives, and clubs studded with spikes; screams and shouts rose as people in masks and costumes scrambled to get out of the way. Nalesean slashed a man in rags across the face, sending him reeling; Beslan ran another through the middle, while his costumed cronies fought still others.

Mat had no time to see more; he found himself back-to-back with Birgitte and facing his own adversaries. He could feel her shifting against him, hear her mutter curses, but he was barely conscious of it; Birgitte could take care of herself, and watching the two men in front of him, he was not sure he could do the same. The hulking fellow with the toothless sneer had only one arm and a puckered socket where his left eye had been, but his fist held a club two feet long, encircled by iron bands that sprouted spikes like steel thorns. His rat-faced little companion still had both eyes and several teeth, and despite sunken cheeks and arms that seemed all bone and sinew, he moved like a snake, licking his lips and flicking a rusty dagger from hand to hand. Mat aimed the shorter knife in his own hand first at one, then the other. It was still long enough to reach a man's vitals, and they danced and shuffled, each waiting for the other to leap at him first.

'Old Cully won't like this, Spar,' the bigger man growled, and rat-face darted forward, rusty blade flashing from hand to hand.

He did not count on the knife that suddenly appeared in Mat's left hand and sliced across his wrist. The dagger clattered to the paving stones, but the fellow flung himself at Mat anyway. As Mat's other blade stabbed into his chest, he squealed, eyes going wide, arms wrapping around Mat convulsively. The bald fellow's sneer widened, his club rising as he stepped in.

The grin vanished as two beggars swarmed over him, snarling and stabbing.

Staring incredulously, Mat shoved rat-face's corpse away. The street was clear for fifty paces except for combatants, and everywhere beggars rolled on the pavement, two or three or sometimes four stabbing at one, beating him with clubs or rocks.

Beslan caught Mat's arm. There was blood on his face, but he was grinning. 'Let's get out of here and let the Fellowship of Alms finish its business. There's no honor in fighting beggars, and besides, the guild won't leave any of these interlopers alive. Follow me.' Nalesean was scowling – doubtless he saw no honor in fighting beggars either – and Beslan's friends, several with their costumes awry and one with his mask off so another could dab at a cut across his forehead. The man with the cut was grinning, too. Birgitte bore not a scratch that Mat could see, and her costume looked as neat as it had back in the palace. She made her knife disappear; there was no way she could hide a blade under those feathers, but she did.

Mat made no protest about being drawn away, but he did growl, 'Do beggars always go around attacking people in this . . . this city?' Beslan might not appreciate hearing it called a bloody city.

The man laughed. 'You are *ta'veren*, Mat. There's always excitement around *ta'veren*.'

Mat smiled back with gritted teeth. Bloody fool, bloody city, and bloody *ta'veren*. Well, if a beggar slit his throat, he would not have to go back to the palace and let Tylin peel him like a ripe pear. Come to think of it, she had called him her little pear. Bloody everything!

The street between the dyer's shop and The Rose of the Eldar had its share of revelers, though not many scantily clad. Apparently you had to have coin to go near naked. Though the acrobats in front of the merchant's house on the corner came close, the men barefoot and bare-chested in tight, brightly colored breeches, the women in even tighter breeches and thin blouses. They all had a few feathers in their hair, as did the capering musicians playing in front of the small palace at the far corner, a woman with a flute, another blowing on a tall, twisted black tube covered with levers, and a fellow beating a tambour for all he was worth. The house they had come to watch looked shut up tight.

The tea at The Rose was as bad as ever, which meant it was much better than the wine. Nalesean stuck to the sour local ale. Birgitte said thanks without saying for what, and Mat shrugged it off silently; they grinned at each other and tapped cups. The sun rose, and Beslan sat balancing first one boot on the toe of the other, then the other way around, but his companions began growing restive, no matter how often he pointed out that Mat was *ta'veren*. A scuffle with beggars was hardly proper excitement, the street was too narrow for any settings to pass, the women were not as pretty as elsewhere, and even looking at Birgitte seemed to pall once they realized that she did not intend to kiss even one of them. With protestations of regret that Beslan would not come, they hurried off to find somewhere more exhilarating. Nalesean took a stroll down the alley beside the dyer's, and Birgitte vanished into The Rose's murky interior to find, she said, whether there was anything at all fit to drink hidden in some forgotten corner.

'I never expected to see a Warder garbed like that,' Beslan said, changing his boots around.

Mat blinked. The fellow had sharp eyes. She had not removed her mask once. Well, as long as he did not know about—

'I think you will be good for my Mother, Mat.'

Choking, Mat sprayed tea into the passersby. Several glared at him angrily, and one slender woman with a nice little bosom gave him a coy smile from beneath a blue mask he thought was meant to be a wren. She stamped a foot and stalked off when he did not smile back. Luckily, no one was angry enough to take it beyond glares before they too went on their way. Or maybe unluckily. He would not have minded if six or eight piled on him right then.

'What do you mean?' he said hoarsely.

Beslan's head whipped around in wide-eyed surprise. 'Why, her choosing you for her pretty, of course. Why is your face so red? Are you angry? Why—?' Suddenly he slapped his forehead and laughed. 'You think *I* will be angry. Forgive me, I forget you're an outlander. Mat, she's my mother, not my wife. Father died ten years ago, and she has always claimed to be too busy. I am just glad she chose someone I like. Where are you going?'

He did not realize he was on his feet until Beslan spoke. 'I just . . . need to clear my head.'

'But you're drinking tea, Mat.'

Dodging around a green sedan chair, he half saw the door of the house open and a woman with a blue-feathered cloak over her dress slip out. Unthinkingly – his head was spinning too much to think clearly – he fell in behind her. Beslan *knew*! He *approved*! His own mother, and he . . .

'Mat?' Nalesean shouted behind him. 'Where are you going?'

'If I'm not back by tomorrow,' Mat shouted back absently over his shoulder, 'tell them they'll have to find it for themselves!' He walked on after the woman in a daze, not hearing if Nalesean or Beslan shouted again. The man *knew*! He remembered once thinking that Beslan and his mother were both mad. They were worse! All of Ebou Dar was mad! He was hardly aware of the dice still spinning inside his skull.

From a window of the meeting room, Reanne watched Solain disappear down the street toward the river. Some fellow in a bronze coat followed in her wake, but if he tried to impede her, he would find out soon enough that Solain had no time for men, and no patience with them.

Reanne was not sure why the urge had grown so strong today. For days it had come on almost with the morning and faded with the sun, and for days she had fought – by the strict rules they did not quite dare call laws, that order was given at the half moon, still five nights off – but today . . . She had spoken the order before she thought and been unable to make herself retract until the proper time. It would be well. No one had seen any sign of those two young fools calling themselves Elayne and Nynaeve anywhere in the city; there had been no need to take dangerous chances.

Sighing, she turned to the others who waited until she took her chair before seating themselves. It would be well, as it always had been. Secrets would be kept, as they always had been. But, still . . . She had no touch of Foretelling or anything of that sort, yet perhaps that urge had been telling her something. Twelve women watched her expectantly. 'I think we should consider moving everyone who does not wear the belt to the farm for a little while.' There was little discussion; they were the Elders, but she was the Eldest. In that, at least, there was no harm in behaving as Aes Sedai did.

Chapter 30

The First Cup

'I do not understand this,' Elayne protested. She had not been offered a chair; in fact, when she started to sit, she had been told curtly to remain standing. Five sets of eyes were focused on her, five women with set, grim faces. 'You are behaving as if we've done something *terrible* when what we have *done* is find the Bowl of the Winds!' At least they were on the brink of it, she hoped; the message Nalesean had come running back with was none too clear. Mat had gone off shouting that he had found it. Or something very like, Nalesean allowed; the longer he talked, the more he bounced between absolute certainty and doubt. Birgitte had remained watching Reanne's house; she seemed to be sweaty and bored. In any case, matters were in motion. Elayne wondered how Nynaeve was getting on. Better than herself, she hoped. She had certainly never expected this when she revealed their success.

'You have endangered a secret kept close by every woman to wear the shawl for over two thousand years.' Merilille sat stiff-backed, serenity almost abandoned on the tight-lipped brink of apoplexy. 'You must have been insane! Only madness could excuse this!'

'What secret?' Elayne demanded.

Vandene, flanking Merilille with her sister, adjusted pale green silk skirts irritably and said, 'Time enough for that when you've been properly raised, child. I thought you had some sense.' Adeleas, in a dark gray wool with deep brown trim, nodded, mirroring Vandene's disapproval.

'The child cannot be faulted for revealing a secret she did not know,' Careane Fransi said from Elayne's left, shifting her bulk in her green-and-gilt armchair. She was not stout, but almost, with shoulders as wide and arms as thick as most men.

'Tower law does not allow for excuses,' Sareitha put in quickly, in somewhat self-important tones, her normally inquisitive brown eyes stern. 'Once mere excuses are allowed, inevitably lesser and lesser excuses will become acceptable, until law itself is gone.' Her high-backed chair stood to the right. Only she wore her shawl, but Merilille's sitting room had been arranged as a court, though no one called it that. So far, no one had. Merilille, Adeleas and Vandene confronted Elayne like judges, Sareitha's chair was placed where the Seat of Rebuke would be, and Careane's the Seat of Pardon, but the Domani Green who would have been her defender nodded thoughtfully as the Tairen Brown who would have been her prosecutor continued. 'She has admitted guilt from her own mouth. I recommend that the child be confined to the palace until we leave, with some good hard work to occupy her mind and her hands. I also recommend a firm dose of the slipper at regular intervals to remind her not to go behind sisters' backs. And the same for Nynaeve, as soon as she can be found.'

Elayne swallowed. Confined? Perhaps they did not need to name this a trial for it to be one. Sareitha might not yet have achieved the ageless face, but the weight of the other women's years pressed at Elayne. Adeleas and Vandene with their hair nearly all white, even their ageless faces echoing years. Merilille's hair was glossy black, yet Elayne would not have been surprised to learn she had worn the shawl as long or longer than most women not Aes Sedai lived. For that matter, Careane might have, as well. Not one of them approached her own strength in the Power, but ... All that experience as Aes Sedai, all that knowledge. All that ... authority. A heavy reminder that she was only eighteen and had been in novice white a year ago.

Careane made no move to rebut Sareitha's suggestions. Perhaps she best go on defending herself. 'Plainly this secret you speak of has something to do with the Circle, but—'

'The Kin are no concern of yours, child,' Merilille broke in sharply. Drawing a deep breath, she smoothed gold-slashed skirts of silvery gray. 'I propose to pass sentence,' she said in a cold voice.

'I concur, and defer to your decision,' Adeleas said. She gave Elayne a disappointed frown and shook her head.

Vandene waved her hand dismissively. 'I concur and defer. But I agree with the Seat of Rebuke.' Careane's look might have contained a sliver of sympathy. Maybe a sliver.

Merilille opened her mouth.

The timid knock at the door sounded quite loud in the momentary, thunderous silence.

'What under the Light?' Merilille muttered angrily. 'I told Pol not to let anyone disturb us. Careane?'

Not the youngest, but the lowest in strength, Careane stood and glided to the door. Despite her heft, she always moved like a swan.

It was Pol herself, Merilille's maid, who popped in curtsying left and right. A slender, gray-haired woman usually possessed of a dignity to rival that of her mistress, she wore an anxious frown now, as well she might, barging in after Merilille's instructions. Elayne had not been so glad to see anyone since ... since Mat Cauthon appeared in the Stone of Tear. A horrendous thought. If Aviendha did not say she had met *toh* sufficiently soon, she might just see if asking the man to beat her after all could end the agony.

'The Queen brought this herself,' Pol announced breathily, proffering a letter sealed with a large red lump of wax. 'She said if I didn't give it to Elayne right away, she'd bring it in herself. She said it's about the child's mother.' Elayne almost ground her teeth. The sisters' serving women had all picked up their mistresses' way of talking about Nynaeve and her, if seldom where they could hear.

Furious, she snatched the letter without waiting for Merilille to say she could – if that was what she would have said – and broke the seal with her thumb.

My Lady Elayne,

I greet the Daughter-Heir of Andor with joyous news. I have but just learned that your mother, Queen Morgase, lives and is at present the guest of Pedron Niall in Amador, and wishes above all to be reunited with you so that you may return to Andor together in triumph. I offer escort through the bandits now infesting Altara, so that you may reach your mother's side in safety and all speed. Forgive these few poor words, scribbled in haste, but I know you would wish to learn the wondrous news as soon as possible. Until I can leave you at your mother's side.

Sealed in the Light,
Jaichim Carridin

The paper crumpled in her fist. How *dare* he? The pain of her mother's death, without even a body to be buried, was only beginning to fade, and Carridin *dared* mock her this way? Embracing the True Source, she hurled the foul lies away from her and channeled; fire flared in midair, so hot that only a dust of ash fell to the blue-and-gold floor tiles. *That* for Jaichim Carridin. And as for these... women! The pride of a thousand years of Andoran queens put steel into her backbone.

Merilille surged to her feet. 'You were not given permission to channel! You will release the—!'

'Leave us, Pol,' Elayne said. 'Now.' The serving woman stared, but Elayne's mother had taught her well the voice of command, the voice of a Queen from her throne. Pol bobbed a curtsy and was moving before she realized. Once under way, she hesitated only an instant before hurrying out and closing the door behind her. Whatever was about to happen plainly was for Aes Sedai alone.

'What has gotten into you, child?' Pure fury submerged the remnants of Merilille's regathered calm. 'Release the Source immediately, or I vow, I'll fetch a slipper myself this minute!'

'I am Aes Sedai.' The words came out like winter stone, and Elayne meant them to. Carridin's lies, and these women. Merilille threatened to *slipper* her? They *would* acknowledge her rightful place as a sister. She and Nynaeve had found the Bowl! As good as, anyway, and the arrangements for its use were under way. 'You propose to punish me for endangering a secret apparently known only to sisters, but no one bothered to tell me this secret when I attained the shawl. You suggest punishing me like a novice or Accepted, but I am Aes Sedai. I was raised to the shawl by Egwene al'Vere, the Amyrlin you claim to serve. If you deny that Nynaeve and I are Aes Sedai, then you deny the Amyrlin Seat who sent me to find the Bowl of the Winds, which we have done. I will not have it! I call you to account, Merilille Ceandevin. Submit to the will of the Amyrlin Seat, or *I* will call judgment on *you* as a rebellious traitor!'

Merilille's eyes bulged, and her mouth hung open, but she appeared composed beside Careane or Sareitha, who looked about to choke to death on incredulity. Vandene only seemed mildly taken aback, a thoughtful finger pressed to her lips beneath slightly widened eyes, while Adeleas sat forward, studying Elayne as if seeing her for the first time.

Channeling, Elayne floated one of the tall armchairs to her and sat, composing her skirts. 'You may as well sit, too, Merilille.' She still used the voice of command – apparently it was the only way to make them listen – but she was startled when Merilille actually sank back down slowly, staring at her pop-eyed.

Outside, she maintained a calm, cool façade, but inside, anger bubbled. No, it *boiled*. Secrets. She had always thought Aes Sedai kept too many secrets, even from each other. Especially from each other.

True, she kept some herself, but only at necessity, and not from anyone who needed to know. And these women had thought to punish *her*! 'Your authority comes from the Hall of the Tower, Merilille; Nynaeve's and mine from the Amyrlin Seat. Ours supersedes yours. From now on, you will take your instructions from Nynaeve or me. We will of course listen carefully to any advice you might offer.' She had thought Merilille's eyes bulged before, but now ...

'Impossible,' the Gray spluttered. 'You are—'

'Merilille!' Elayne said sharply, leaning forward. 'Do you still deny the authority of your Amyrlin? Do you still *dare*?' Merilille's mouth worked soundlessly. She wet her lips. She shook her head jerkily. Elayne felt a thrill of exultation; all that about Merilille taking direction was stuff and nonsense, of course, but she *would* be acknowledged. Thom and her mother both said you must begin by asking for ten to get one. Still, that was not enough to damp her anger. She had half a mind to fetch a slipper herself and see how far she could push this. Except, that would shatter everything. They would remember her age fast enough then, and how short a time ago she had put off a novice dress; they might even begin thinking of her as a foolish child again. Which thought stoked her fury anew. But, she contented herself with, 'While you think quietly on what else I should be told as Aes Sedai, Merilille, Adeleas and Vandene will instruct me in this secret I endangered. Do you mean to tell me the Tower has known of the Circle – these Kin, as you call them – all along?' Poor Reanne and her hopes to avoid Aes Sedai notice.

'As near as they could make themselves come to sisters, I suppose,' Vandene replied. Carefully. She studied Elayne as intently as her sister did, now. Though a Green, she had many of the same mannerisms as Adeleas. Careane and Sareitha looked stunned, disbelieving eyes swinging from a silent, red-cheeked Merilille to Elayne and back.

'Even during the Trolloc Wars, women failed their tests, or lacked the strength, or were sent away from the Tower for any of the usual reasons.' Adeleas had adopted a lecturing tone, but not offensively. Browns often did when expounding. 'Under the circumstances, it is hardly surprising that a number feared to go off into the world alone, nor that they might flee to Barashta, as the city that existed here then was called. Though the main part of Barashta was, of course, where the Rahad now stands. Not that a stone of Barashta remains. The Trolloc Wars did not truly envelope Eharon until late, but in the end, Barashta fell as completely as Barsine, or Shaemal, or . . .'

'The Kin . . .' Vandene broke in gently, Adeleas blinked at her, then nodded. '. . . The Kin persisted even after Barashta fell, in the same way they had before, taking in wilders and women put out of the Tower.' Elayne frowned; Mistress Anan had said the Kin took in wilders, too, but Reanne's biggest anxiety had seemed to be making her and Nynaeve prove they were not.

'None ever remained long,' Adeleas added. 'Five years, perhaps ten; then, I suppose, as now. Once they realize that their little group is no replacement for the White Tower, they go off and become village Healers or Wisdoms or the like, or sometimes simply forget the Power, stop channeling, and take up a craft or trade. In any case, they vanish, so to speak.' Elayne wondered how anyone could forget the One Power that way; the urge to channel, the temptation of the Source, was always there, once you learned how. Aes Sedai did seem to believe some women could just put it behind them, though, once they found out they would not be Aes Sedai.

Vandene took up the explanation again; the sisters frequently spoke almost in alternating sentences, each carrying on smoothly where the other left off. 'The Tower has known of the Kin from nearly the beginning, perhaps from the very beginning. At first, no doubt, the Wars took precedence. And despite calling themselves the Kin, they have done just what we want such women to do. They remain hidden, even the fact that they can channel, draw no attention whatsoever to themselves. Over the years, they have even passed along word – secretly of course; carefully – when one of them found a woman falsely claiming the shawl. You said something?'

Elayne shook her head. 'Careane, is there any tea in that pot?' Careane gave a small start. 'I think Adeleas and Vandene might like to wet their throats.' The Domani woman did not quite look at a still-staring Merilille before going to the table where the silver teapot and cups were. 'That doesn't explain why,' Elayne went on.

'Why is knowledge of them such a deep secret? Why haven't they been scattered long ago?'

'Why, the runaways, of course.' Adeleas made it sound the most obvious thing in the world. 'It is a fact that other gatherings have been broken up as soon as found – the last about two hundred years ago – but the Kin do keep themselves small, and quiet. That last group called themselves the Daughters of Silence, yet they were hardly silent. Only twenty-three of them altogether, wilders gathered and trained after a fashion by a pair of former Accepted, but they—'

'Runaways,' Elayne prompted, taking a cup from Careane with a smile of thanks. She had not asked one for herself, but she realized absently that the woman had offered her the first. Vandene and her sister had talked quite a bit about runaways on the way to Ebou Dar.

Adeleas blinked, and pulled herself back to the topic. 'The Kin help runaways. They always have two or three women in Tar Valon keeping watch. For one thing, they approach almost every woman put out, in a very circumspect way, and for another, they manage to find every runaway, whether novice or Accepted. At least, none has made it off the island without their help since the Trolloc Wars.'

'Oh, yes,' Vandene said as Adeleas paused to take a cup from Careane. It had been offered to Merilille first, but Merilille sat slumped and staring bleakly at nothing. 'If anyone does manage to escape, why, we know right where to look, and she almost always ends up back in the Tower wishing her feet had never itched. As long as the Kin don't know we know, anyway. Once that happens, it will be back to the days before the Kin, when a woman running from the Tower might go in any direction. The numbers were larger then – Aes Sedai, Accepted, novices *and* runaways – and some years two out of three escaped clean, others three out of four. Using the Kin, we retake at least nine of ten. You can see why the Tower has preserved the Kin and their secret like precious jewels.'

Elayne could. A woman was not done with the White Tower until it was done with her. Besides, it could not hurt the Tower's reputation for infallibility that it always caught runaways. Almost always. Well, now she knew.

She stood, and to her astonishment, Adeleas did also, and Vandene, waving away Careane's offered tea, and Sareitha. Even Merilille, after a moment. They all looked at her expectantly, even Merilille.

Vandene noticed her surprise, and smiled. 'Another thing you might not know. We are a contentious lot in many ways, we Aes Sedai, each jealous of her place and prerogatives, but when someone is placed above us or stands above us, we tend to follow her fairly meekly for the most part. However we might grumble about her decisions in private.'

'Why, so we do,' Adeleas murmured happily, as if she had just discovered something.

Merilille took a deep breath, absorbing herself for a moment in straightening her skirts. 'Vandene is right,' she said. 'You stand above us in yourself, and I must admit, you apparently have been placed above us. If our behavior calls for penance . . . Well, you will tell us if it does. Where are we to follow you? If I may ask?' There was no sarcasm in any of that; if anything, her tone was more polite than Elayne had heard out of her before.

She thought any Aes Sedai who ever lived would have been proud to control her features as well as she did right then. All she had wanted was for them to admit she really was Aes Sedai. She fought a momentary urge to protest that she was too young, too inexperienced. 'You can never put honey back in the comb,' so Lini used to say when she was a girl. Egwene was no older.

Drawing breath, she smiled warmly. 'The first thing to recall is that we *are* all sisters, in every meaning of the word. We must work together; the Bowl of the Winds is too important for anything less.' She hoped they would all nod so enthusiastically when she told them what Egwene intended. 'Perhaps we should sit again.' They waited for her before folding themselves back into their seats. She hoped Nynaeve was getting on a tenth so well. When she found out about this, Nynaeve was going to faint from shock. 'I have something of my own to tell you about the Kin.'

Fairly soon it was Merilille who looked ready to faint from shock, and even Adeleas and Vandene were not far from it. But they went right on saying, 'Yes, Elayne,' and 'If you say so, Elayne.' Perhaps it would all go smoothly from now on.

*

The sedan chair was rocking through the crowds of revelers along the quay when Moghedien spotted the woman. She was being handed down from a coach at one of the boat landings by a footman in green and white. A wide feathered mask covered her face more completely than Moghedien's did, but she would have known that determined stride, known that woman, from any angle in any light. The carved screens that served as windows in the closed chair were certainly no hindrance. Two fellows with swords on their hips scrambled from the coach roof to follow the masked woman.

Moghedien thumped a fist against the side of the chair, shouting, 'Stop!' The bearers halted so quickly she was almost flung forward.

The crowd jostled past, some shouting curses at her bearers for blocking the way, some shouting more good naturedly. Down here by the river, the throng ran thin enough for her to watch through the gaps. The boat that pulled away from the landing seemed quite distinctive; the roof of the low cabin in the rear was painted red; she did not see that affectation on any of the others waiting at the long stone dock.

She wet her lips, shivering. Moridin's instructions had been explicit, the price of disobedience made excruciatingly clear. But a slight delay would not hurt. Not if he never learned of it, anyway.

Flinging open the door, she climbed out into the street and looked about hastily. There; that inn, right overlooking the docks. And the river. Lifting her skirts, she hurried away without the slightest fear anyone might hire her chair; until she untied the webs of Compulsion on them, the bearers would tell anyone who asked that they were engaged, and stand there until they died of hunger. A path opened ahead of her, men and women in feathered masks leaping aside before she reached them, leaping with squeals and cries as they clutched where they thought they had been stabbed. As they had; there was no time to spin subtle webs on so many minds, but a flurry of needles woven of Air did as well here.

The stout innkeeper at The Oarsman's Pride nearly leaped, too, at the sight of Moghedien striding into her common room in gloriously scarlet silk worked with thread-of-gold and black silk that glistened as richly as the gold. Her mask was a great spray of pitch black feathers with a sharp black beak; a raven. That was Moridin's joke, his command, as was the dress, in fact. His colors were black and red, he said, and she would wear them while she served him. She was in livery, however elegant, and she could have killed everyone who saw her.

Instead, she spun a hasty web on the round-cheeked innkeeper that jerked her up straight and made her eyes pop. No time for subtlety. At Moghedien's command to show her the roof, the woman *ran* up the railless stairs at the side of the room. It was unlikely any of the feather-draped drinkers saw anything unusual in the innkeeper's behavior, Moghedien thought with a small laugh. The Oarsman's Pride probably had never seen a patron of her quality before.

On the flat roof, she quickly weighed the dangers of letting the innkeeper live versus those of killing her. Corpses had a way of pointing a finger, eventually. If you wished to remain quietly hidden in the shadows, you did not kill unless you absolutely had to. Hastily, she adjusted the web of Compulsion, told the woman to go down to her room, to go to sleep and forget ever having seen her. With the haste, it was possible the innkeeper might lose the whole day, or wake somewhat slower of wits than she had been – so much in Moghedien's life would have been so much easier had she possessed a better Talent for Compulsion – but in any case, the woman scurried away, eager to obey, and left her alone.

As the door thumped down flat into the dirty white-tiled roof, Moghedien gasped at the sudden feel of fingers stroking her mind, palping her soul. Moridin did that sometimes; a reminder, he said, as if she needed any more. She almost looked around for him; her skin pebbled as though at a sudden icy breeze. The touch vanished, and she shivered again. Coming or going, it did remind her. Moridin himself could appear anywhere at any time. Haste.

Speeding to the low wall that surrounded the roof, she searched the river spread out below. Scores of boats of every size swept along on their oars between larger vessels, anchored or under sail. Most of the cabins of the sort she sought were plain wood, but there she saw a yellow roof, and there a blue, and there, in midriver and heading southward fast ... Red. It had to be the right one; she could not take any more time here.

She raised her hands, but as balefire launched itself, something flashed around her and she jerked. Moridin *had* come; he *was* there, and he would ... She stared at the pigeons fluttering away. Pigeons! She nearly spewed the contents of her stomach across the roof. A glance at the river made her snarl.

Because she had jerked, the balefire she meant to slice through cabin and passenger instead had sliced diagonally through the middle of the boat, about where the oarsmen had stood, and the bodyguards. Because the rowers had been burned out of the Pattern *before* the balefire struck, the two halves of the craft were now a good hundred paces back up the river. Then again, perhaps it was not a complete disaster. Because that slice from the boat's center had gone at the same time the boatmen really died, the river had had minutes to rush in. The two parts of the boat sank out of sight in a great froth of bubbles even as her eyes shifted to them, carrying their passenger to the depths.

Suddenly, what she had done struck her. She had always moved in the dim places, always kept herself hidden, always ... Any woman in the city who could channel would know someone had drawn a great deal of *saidar*, if not for what, and any eye watching had seen that bar of liquid white fire sear across the afternoon. Fear gave her wings. Not fear. Terror.

Gathering her skirts, she ran back down the stairs, ran through the common room bumping into tables and careening off people trying to get out her way, ran into the street too frightened to think, battering a path through the crowd with her hands.

'Run!' she shrieked, hurling herself into the sedan chair. Her skirts caught in the door; she ripped them free. 'Run!'

The bearers flung themselves into motion, tossing her about, but she did not care. She braced herself with fingers laced through the carved window screens, and shook uncontrollably. He had not forbidden this. He might forgive, or even ignore her independent action here, if she carried out his instructions swiftly, efficiently. That was her only hope. She was going to make Falion and Ispan *crawl*!

Chapter 31

Mashiara

As the boat swept away from the landing, Nynaeve tossed her mask down beside her on the cushioned bench and slumped back with arms folded and braid gripped firmly, scowling at nothing. Scowling at everything. Listening to the Wind still told her a fierce storm was on the way, the kind that tore off roofs and flattened barns, and she almost wished the river would begin to kick up in waves right that minute.

'If it isn't the weather, Nynaeve,' she mimicked, 'then you should be the one to go. The Mistress of the Ships might be insulted if we didn't send the strongest of us. They know Aes Sedai put great store in that. Bah!' That had been Elayne. Except for the 'bah.' Elayne just thought putting up with any amount of nonsense from Merilille would be preferable to facing Nesta again. Once you began badly with someone, it was hard to recover – Mat Cauthon was proof enough of that! – and if they had gotten on any worse with Nesta din Reas Two Moons, she would be sending the lot of them to fetch and carry.

'Horrible woman!' she grumbled, shifting around on the seat cushions. Aviendha had been no better when Nynaeve suggested she go to the Sea Folk; those people had been fascinated by her. She pitched her voice high and finicky, not at all like Aviendha's, but the mood fit. 'We will learn of this trouble when we learn, Nynaeve al'Meara. Perhaps I will learn something watching Jaichim Carridin today.' If not for the fact that nothing whatsoever frightened the

Aiel woman, she would have thought Aviendha fearful from her eagerness to spy on Carridin. A day standing in a hot street jostled by crowds was not amusing, and today would be worse, with the festival. Nynaeve would have thought the woman would enjoy a nice refreshing boat ride.

The boat lurched. A nice refreshing boat ride, she told herself. Nice cool breezes on the bay. Moist breezes, not dry. The boat rolled. 'Oh, blood and ashes!' she moaned. Appalled, she clapped a hand over her mouth and drummed her heels against the front of the bench in righteous outrage. If she had to endure those Sea Folk for long, she would have as much filth coming off of her tongue as Mat did. She did not want to think about him. One more day folding her hands for that ... that *man* ... and she would yank every hair out of her head! Not that he had demanded anything unreasonable so far, but she kept waiting for him to, and his manner ... !

'No!' she said firmly. 'I want to settle my stomach, not rile it.' The boat had begun a slow rocking. She tried to concentrate on her clothes. She was not fixated on clothes the way Elayne sometimes seemed to be, but thinking about silks and laces was soothing.

Everything had been chosen to impress the Mistress of the Ships, to try regaining a little lost ground, for all the good it might do. Green silk slashed with yellow in the skirts, embroidered in gold down the sleeves and across the bodice, with golden lace along the hem, and at her wrists, and just bordering the neckline. Perhaps that should have been higher, to be taken seriously, but she did not own anything higher. Considering Sea Folk customs, it was more than modest. Nesta would have to take her as she was; Nynaeve al'Meara did not go changing herself for anyone.

The yellow opal pins stuck in her braid were her own – a present from the Panarch of Tarabon, no less – but Tylin had provided the gold necklace that fanned emeralds and pearls down to her bosom. A richer piece than she had ever dreamed of owning; a gift for bringing Mat, Tylin had called it, which made no sense at all, but maybe the Queen thought she needed some excuse for such a valuable present. Both gold-and-ivory bracelets came from Aviendha, who had a surprising little stock of jewelry for a woman who so seldom wore more than that one silver necklace. Nynaeve had asked to borrow that pretty roses-and-thorns ivory bracelet that the Aiel woman never wore; surprisingly, Aviendha had snatched it to her bosom as if it was her most precious possession, and of all things, Elayne began comforting her. Nynaeve would not have been surprised to see the pair fall weeping on one another's shoulder.

There was something odd going on there, and if she had not known those two were too sensible for such nonsense, she would have suspected a man at the root of it. Well, Aviendha was too sensible; Elayne did still yearn for Rand, though Nynaeve could hardly fault her for—

Suddenly she felt weaves of *saidar* almost atop her in huge amounts, and . . .

. . . she floundered in salty water over her head, flailing upward to find air, tangled in her skirts, flailing. Her head broke surface, and she gasped for breath amid floating cushions, staring in astonishment. After a moment, she recognized the slanting shape above her as one of the cabin seats, and a bit of the cabin wall. She was inside a trapped pocket of air. Not large; she could have touched both sides without stretching her arms out fully. But how . . . ? An audible thud announced the bottom of the river; the upside-down cabin lurched, tilted. She thought the air pocket shrank a little.

The first order of business, before wondering about anything, was getting out before she used up the air. She knew how to swim – she had splashed in the Waterwood ponds often enough back home – it was just when the water started rocking her about that she minded. Filling her lungs, she doubled over and swam down toward where the door must be, kicking awkwardly because of her skirts. It might help to shed the dress, but she was not about to bob to the surface of the river in nothing but shift and stockings and jewels. She was not about to leave those behind, either. Besides, she could not get out of the dress without loosing her belt pouch, and she would drown before losing what was in there.

The water was black, lightless. Her outstretched fingers struck wood, and she felt across the piercework carving until she found the door, scrabbled down the edge of that – and found a hinge. Muttering imprecations in her head, she cautiously felt her way to the other side. Yes! The latch handle! She lifted it, pushed outward. The door moved maybe two inches – and stopped.

Lungs straining, she swam back up to the pocket, but only long enough to fill them again. This time, finding the door came faster. She stuck her fingers through the crack to find what held the door shut. They sank into mud. Maybe she could dig away a little hillock, or ... She felt higher. More mud. Increasingly frantic, she worked her fingers from the bottom of the crack to the top, and then, refusing to believe, from the top to the bottom. Mud, solid gooey mud, all the way.

This time when she swam back up to the pocket, she grabbed hold of the edge of the seat above her and hung from it, panting, heart beating wildly. The air felt ... thicker.

'I will not die here,' she muttered. 'I will not die here!'

She hammered a fist against the seat until she felt it bruise, fighting for the anger that would allow her to channel. She would not die. Not here. Alone. No one would know where she had died. No grave, just a corpse rotting at the bottom of the river. Her arm fell with a splash. She labored for breath. Flecks of black and silver danced in her eyes; she seemed to be looking down a tube. No anger, she realized dimly. She kept trying to reach for *saidar*, but without any belief that she would touch it, now. She was going to die here after all. No hope. No Lan. And with hope gone, flickering on the edge of consciousness like a guttering candle flame, she did something she had never done before in her life. She surrendered completely.

Saidar flowed into her, filled her.

She was only half-aware of the wood above her suddenly bulging outward, bursting. In rushing bubbles of air she drifted up, out through the hole in the hull into darkness. Vaguely, she knew she should do something. She could almost remember what. Yes. Her feet kicked weakly; she tried to move her arms to swim. They seemed to just float.

Something seized her dress, and panic roused her in thoughts of sharks, and lionfish, and the Light alone knew what else that might inhabit these black depths. A spark of consciousness spoke of the Power, but she flailed desperately with fists and feet, felt her knuckles land solidly. Unfortunately, she also screamed, or tried to. A great quantity of water rushing down her throat washed away scream, *saidar*, and very nearly her final scraps of awareness.

Something tugged on her braid, then again, and she was being towed ... somewhere. She was no longer conscious enough to struggle, or even to be very much afraid of being eaten.

Abruptly her head broke surface. Hands encircled her from behind – hands; not a shark, after all – squeezed hard against her ribs in a most familiar way. She coughed – water spewed from her nose – coughed again, painfully. And drew a shuddering breath. She had never tasted anything so sweet in her life.

A hand cupped her chin, and suddenly she was being towed again. Lassitude washed through her. All she could do was float on her back, and breathe, and stare up at the sky. So blue. So beautiful. The stinging in her eyes was not all from the salty river.

And then she was being pushed upward against the side of a boat, a rude hand beneath her bottom shoving her higher, until two lanky fellows with brass rings in their ears could reach down and haul her aboard. They helped her walk a step or two, but as soon as they let go to help her rescuer, her legs collapsed like towers of soggy mush.

On unsteady hands and knees, she stared blankly at a sword and boots and green coat someone had thrown down on the deck. She opened her mouth – and emptied herself of the River Eldar. The entire river, it seemed, plus her midday meal, and her breakfast; it would not have surprised her at all to see a few fish, or her slippers. She was wiping her lips with the back of her hand when she became aware of voices.

'My Lord is all right? My Lord was down for a very long time.'

'Forget me, man,' said a deep voice. 'Get something to wrap around the lady.' Lan's voice, that she dreamed every night of hearing.

Wide-eyed, Nynaeve barely bit back a wail; the horror she had felt when she thought she was going to die was nothing alongside what flashed through her now. Nothing! This was a nightmare. Not now! Not like this! Not when she was a drowned rat, kneeling with the contents of her stomach spread out before her!

Without thought she embraced *saidar* and channeled. Water fell away from her clothes, her hair, in a rush and washed all evidence of her little mishap out through a scupper hole. Scrambling to her feet, she hurriedly pulled her necklace aright and did her best to straighten her dress and hair, but the soaking in salt water and then the rapid drying had left several stains on the silk and a number of creases that would require a knowledgeable hand with a hot iron to remove. Wisps of hair wanted to fly away from her scalp, and the opals in her braid seemed to dot the bristling tail of an angry cat.

It did not matter. She was calmness itself, cool as an early spring breeze, self-possessed as . . . She spun around before he could come on her from behind and startle her into disgracing herself completely.

She only realized how quickly she had moved when she saw that Lan was just then taking his second step from the railing. He was the most beautiful man she had ever seen. Soaking wet in shirt and breeches and stockings, he was gorgeous, with his dripping hair clinging to the angles of his face, and . . . A split purple bruise was rising on his face, as from a blow. She clapped a hand to her mouth, remembering her fist connecting.

'Oh, no! Oh, Lan, I'm so sorry! I didn't mean to!' She was not really aware of crossing the space between them; she was just there, stretching up on toetips to lay fingers gently on his injury. A deft weave of all Five Powers, and his tanned cheek was unblemished. But he might have been hurt elsewhere. She spun the weaves to Delve him; new scars made her wince inside, and there was something odd, but he seemed healthy as a prime bull. He was also very wet, from saving her. She dried him as she had herself; water splashed around his feet. She could not stop touching him. Both hands traced his hard cheeks, his wonderful blue eyes, his strong nose, his firm lips, his ears. She combed that silky black hair into place with her fingers, adjusted the braided leather band that held it. Her tongue seemed to have a life of its own, too. 'Oh, Lan,' she murmured. 'You really are here.' Somebody giggled. Not her – Nynaeve al'Meara did not giggle – but somebody did. 'It isn't a dream. Oh, Light, you're here. How?'

'A servant at the Tarasin Palace told me you'd gone to the river, and a fellow at the landing said what boat you had taken. If Mandarb hadn't lost a shoe, I would have been here yesterday.'

'I don't care. You're here now. You're here.' She did *not* giggle.

'Maybe she is Aes Sedai,' one of the boatmen murmured, not quite low enough, 'but I still say she's one duckling who means to stuff herself in that wolf's jaws.'

Nynaeve's face flashed pure scarlet, and she snatched her hands to her sides, her heels thumping to the deck. Another time, she would have given the fellow what for, and no mistake. Another time, when she could think. Lan crowded everything else out of her head. She seized his arm. 'We can talk more privately in the cabin.' Had one of the oarsmen snickered?

'My sword and—'

'I'll bring it,' she said, snatching up his things from the deck on flows of Air. One of those louts *had* snickered. Another flow of Air pulled open the cabin door, and she hustled Lan and his sword and the rest inside and slammed it behind them.

Light, she doubted if even Calle Coplin back home had ever been as bold as this, and as many merchants' guards knew Calle's birthmark as knew her face. But it was not the same at all. Not at all! Still, no harm in being just a tad less ... eager. Her hands went back to his face – only to straighten his hair some more; just that – and he caught her wrists gently in his big hands.

'Myrelle holds my bond, now,' he said quietly. 'She is lending me to you until you find a Warder of your own.'

Calmly pulling her right hand free, she slapped his face as hard as she could swing. His head hardly moved, so she freed the other hand and slapped him harder with that. 'How could you?' For good measure, she punctuated the question with another slap. 'You knew I was waiting!' One more seemed called for, just to drive the point home. 'How could you do such a thing? How could you let her?' Another slap. 'Burn you, Lan Mandragoran! Burn you! Burn you to the Pit of Doom! Burn you!'

The man – the *bloody* man! – did not say one word. Not that he could, of course; what defense could he offer? He just stood there while she rained blows at him, making no move, unblinking eyes looking peculiar, as well they might with the way she reddened his cheeks for him. If her slaps made little impression on him, though, the palms of her hands began to sting like fury.

Grimly, she clenched a fist and punched him in the belly with all her might. He grunted. Slightly.

'We will talk this over calmly and rationally,' she said, stepping back from him. 'As adults.' Lan just nodded and sat down and pulled his boots over to him! Pushing bits of hair out of her face with her left hand, she stuck the right behind her so she could flex her sore fingers without him seeing. He had no right being that hard, not when she wanted to hit him. Too much to hope she had cracked a rib in him.

'You should thank her, Nynaeve.' How could the man sound so calm! Stamping his foot firmly into one boot, he bent to pick up the other, not looking at her. 'You wouldn't want me bonded to you.'

The flow of Air seized a handful of his hair and bent his head up painfully. 'If you dare – if you even dare – to spout that drivel about not wanting to give me a widow's weeds, Lan Mandragoran, I'll . . . I'll . . . ' She could not think of anything strong enough. Kicking him was not near enough. Myrelle. Myrelle and her Warders. Burn him! Removing his hide in strips would not be enough!

He might as well not have been bent over with his neck craned. He just rested his forearms across his knees, and watched her with that odd look in his eyes, and said, 'I thought about not telling you, but you have a right to know.' Even so, his tone became hesitant; Lan was never hesitant. 'When Moiraine died – when a Warder's bond to his Aes Sedai is snapped – there are changes . . . '

As he continued, her arms snaked around herself, hugging tightly to keep her from shivering. Her jaw ached, for she kept it clamped shut. She released the flow holding him as if a hand springing away, released *saidar*, but he only straightened and went on relating this horror without so much as a flinch, went on watching her. Suddenly she understood his eyes, colder than winter's heart. The eyes of a man who knew he was dead and could not make himself care, a man waiting, almost eager, for that long sleep. Her own eyes stung with not weeping.

'So you see,' he concluded with a smile that touched only his mouth; an accepting smile, 'when it's done, she will have a year or more of pain, and I will still be dead. You are spared that. My last gift to you, *Mashiara*.' *Mashiara*. His lost love.

'You are to be my Warder until I find one?' Her voice startled her with its levelness. She could not break down in tears now. She would not. Now, more than ever before, she had to gather all her strength.

'Yes,' he said cautiously, tugging on his other boot. He had always seemed something of a half-tame wolf, and his eyes made him seem much less than half tame now.

'Good.' Adjusting her skirts, she resisted the urge to cross the cabin to him. She could not let him see her fear. 'Because I have found him. You. I waited and wished with Moiraine; I won't with Myrelle. She is going to give me your bond.' Myrelle would, if she had to drag the woman to Tar Valon and back by her hair. For that matter, she might drag her just for the principle of it. 'Don't say anything,' she said sharply when he opened his mouth. Her fingers brushed her belt pouch, where his heavy gold signet ring lay wrapped in a silk handkerchief. With an effort, she moderated her tone; he was ill, and harsh words never helped sickness. It was an effort, though; she wanted to berate him up one side and down the other, wanted to pull her braid out by the roots every time she thought of him and that woman. Fighting to keep her voice calm, she went on.

'In the Two Rivers, Lan, when somebody gives another a ring, they are betrothed.' That was a lie, and she half-expected him to jump to his feet in outrage, but he only blinked warily. Besides, she had read about the notion in a story. 'We have been betrothed long enough. We are going to be married today.'

'I used to pray for that,' he said softly, then shook his head. 'You know why it can't be, Nynaeve. And even if it could, Myrelle—'

Despite all her promises to keep her temper, to be gentle, she embraced *saidar* and stuffed a gag of Air into his mouth before he could confess what she did not want to hear. So long as he did not confess, she could pretend nothing had happened. When she got hold of Myrelle, though! Opals pressed hard into her palm, and her hand leaped from her braid as if burned. She occupied her fingers with brushing his hair again while he glared at her indignantly above his gaping mouth. 'A small lesson for you in the difference between wives and other women,' she said lightly. Such a struggle. 'I would appreciate it very much if you did not mention Myrelle's name again in my presence. Do you understand?'

He nodded, and she released the flow, but as soon as he had worked his jaw a moment, he said, 'Naming no names, Nynaeve, you know she's aware of everything I feel, through the bond. If we were man and wife . . .'

She thought her face might burst into flame. She had never thought of that! Bloody Myrelle! 'Is there any way to make sure she knows it is me?' she said finally, and her cheeks nearly did flash to fire. Especially when he fell back against the cabin wall laughing in astonishment.

'Light, Nynaeve, you are a hawk! Light! I haven't laughed since . . .' His mirth faded, the coldness that had dimmed in his eyes for an instant returning. 'I do wish it could be, Nynaeve, but—'

'It can and will,' she broke in. Men always seemed to get the upper hand if you let them talk too long. She plumped herself down on his knees. They were not married yet, true, but he was softer than the unpadded benches on this boat. She shifted a bit to make herself more comfortable. Well, no harder than the benches, anyway. 'You might as well reconcile yourself, Lan Mandragoran. My heart belongs to you, and you've admitted yours belongs to me. *You* belong to me, and I will not let you go. You will be my Warder, and my husband, and for a very long time. I will not let you die. Do you understand *that*? I can be as stubborn as I have to be.'

'I hadn't noticed,' he said, and her eyes narrowed. His tone sounded awfully . . . dry.

'As long as you do now,' she said firmly. Twisting her neck, she peered through the piercework in the hull behind him, then craned around to peer through the carving at the front of the cabin. Long stone docks thrusting out from the stone quay passed by; all she could see ahead were more docks, and the city gleaming white in the afternoon sun. 'Where are we going?' she muttered.

'I told them to put us ashore as soon as I had you aboard,' Lan said. 'It seemed best to get off the river as fast as possible.'

'You . . . ?' She clamped her teeth shut. He had not known where she was headed or why; he had done the best he could with what he did know. And he *had* saved her life. 'I can't go back to the city yet,

Lan.' Clearing her throat, she changed her tone. However gentle she had to be with him, that much syrup would make her sick up all over again. 'I have to go to the Sea Folk ships, to *Windrunner*.' Much better; light, but not too light, and firm.

'Nynaeve, I was right behind your boat. I saw what happened. You were fifty paces ahead of me, and then fifty paces behind, sinking. It had to be balefire.' He did not need to say more; she said it for him, and with more knowledge than he could.

'Moghedien,' she breathed. Oh, it could have been another of the Forsaken, or one of the Black Ajah perhaps, but she knew. Well, she had beaten Moghedien not once, but twice. She could do so a third time, if necessary. Her face must not have shared her confidence.

'Don't be afraid,' Lan said, touching her cheek. 'Don't ever be afraid while I'm near. If you have to face Moghedien, I'll make sure you are angry enough to channel. I seem to have some talent in that direction.'

'You'll never make me angry again,' she began, and stopped, staring at him wide-eyed. 'I'm not angry,' she said slowly.

'Not now, but when you need to be—'

'I'm not angry,' she laughed. She kicked her feet in delight, and pounded her fists on his chest, laughing. *Saidar* filled her, not just with life and joy, but this time, with awe. With feathery flows of Air, she stroked his cheeks. 'I am not angry, Lan,' she whispered.

'Your block is gone.' He grinned, sharing her delight, but the grin put no warmth into his eyes.

I will take care of you, Lan Mandragoran, she promised silently. *I will not let you die.* Leaning on his chest, she thought of kissing him, and even ... *You are not Calle Coplin*, she told herself firmly.

A sudden, horrible thought struck her. All the more horrible because it had not come earlier. 'The boatmen?' she said quietly. 'My bodyguards?' Wordlessly, he shook his head, and she sighed. Bodyguards. Light, they had needed her protection, not the other way around. Four more deaths to lay at Moghedien's feet. Four on top of thousands, but these were personal, as far as she was concerned. Well, she was not about to settle Moghedien this moment.

Getting to her feet, she began seeing what she could do about her clothes. 'Lan, will you turn the boatmen around? Tell them to row for all they have.' As it was, she would not see the palace again before nightfall. 'And find out if one of them has such a thing as a comb.' She could not face Nesta like this.

He picked up his coat and sword and gave her a bow. 'As you command, Aes Sedai.'

Pursing her lips, she watched the door close behind him. Laughing at her, was he? She would wager someone on *Windrunner* could perform a marriage. And from what she had seen of the Sea Folk, she would wager Lan Mandragoran would find himself promising to do as he was told. They would see who laughed then.

Lurching and rolling, the boat began to swing around, and her stomach lurched with it.

'Oh, Light!' she groaned, sinking onto the bench. Why could she not have lost that along with her block? Holding *saidar*, aware of every touch of the air on her skin, only made it worse. Letting go did not help. She was *not* going to sick up again. She *was* going to make Lan hers once and for all. This was going to be a wonderful day yet. If only she could stop feeling that storm on the way.

The sun sat luridly just above the rooftops by the time Elayne rapped on the door with her knuckles. Revelers danced and cavorted in the street behind her, filling the air with laughter and song and the scent of perfume. Idly, she wished she had had a chance really to enjoy the festival. A costume like Birgitte's might have been fun. Or even one like that she had seen on the Lady Riselle, one of Tylin's attendants, first thing this morning. As long as she could have kept her mask on. She rapped again, harder.

The gray-haired, square-jawed maid opened the door, fury suddenly painting her face when Elayne lowered her green mask. 'You! What are you doing back—?' Fury turned to ghastly paleness as Merilille removed her mask, and Adeleas and the others did the same. The woman jerked with each ageless face revealed, and even for Sareitha's. By that time, maybe she saw what she expected to see.

With a sudden cry, the maid tried to push the door shut, but Birgitte darted past Elayne, her feathered shoulder knocking it back open. The servant staggered a few steps, then gathered herself, but whether to run or shout, Birgitte was there beforetime, gripping her arm just below the shoulder.

'Easy,' Birgitte said firmly. 'We don't want any fuss or shouting, now do we?' It did seem she was only holding the woman's arm, almost supporting her, but the maid stood very straight indeed and very still. Staring wide-eyed at her captor's plume-crested mask, she shook her head slowly.

'What is your name?' Elayne asked, as everyone crowded into the entry hall behind her. The closing door muted the noise from outside. The maid's eyes darted from one face to the next as if she could not bear to gaze at any one for long.

'C-c-cedora.'

'You will take us to Reanne, Cedora.' This time, Cedora nodded; she looked about to cry.

Cedora stiffly led the way upstairs with Birgitte still holding her arm. Elayne considered telling her to release the woman, but the last thing she wanted was a shouted alarm and everyone in the house fleeing in all directions. That was why Birgitte used muscle instead of Elayne herself channeling. She thought Cedora was more frightened than hurt, and everybody was to be at least a little frightened this evening.

'In th-there,' Cedora said, nodding to a red door. The door to the room where Nynaeve and she had had that unfortunate interview. She opened it and went in.

Reanne was there, seated with the fireplace carved with the Thirteen Sins at her back, and so were another dozen women Elayne had never seen before, occupying all of the chairs against the pale green walls, sweating with the windows tight and curtains drawn. Most wore Ebou Dari dresses, though only one possessed the olive skin; most had lines on their faces and at least a touch of gray; and every last woman of them could channel to one degree or another. Seven wore the red belt. She sighed in spite of herself. When Nynaeve was right, she let you know it until you wanted to scream.

Reanne bounded to her feet in the same red-faced fury Cedora had shown, and her first words were almost identical as well. 'You! How dare you show your face . . . ?' Words and fury drained away together for the same reason, too, as Merilille and the others entered on Elayne's heels. A yellow-haired woman in red belt and plunging neckline made a faint sound as her eyes rolled up in her head and she slid bonelessly from her red chair. No one moved to help her. No one even glanced at Birgitte as she escorted Cedora to a corner and planted her there. No one seemed to breathe. Elayne felt a great desire to shout 'boo' just to see what would happen.

Reanne swayed, white-faced, and visibly tried to gather herself with slight success. It took her only a moment to scan the five cool-faced Aes Sedai lined up before the door and decide who must be in charge. She wobbled across the floortiles to Merilille and sank to her knees, head bowed. 'Forgive us, Aes Sedai.' Her voice was worshipful, and only a little steadier than her knees had been. She babbled, in fact. 'We are only a few friends. We have done nothing, certainly nothing to bring discredit to Aes Sedai. I swear that, whatever this girl has told you. We would have told you of her, but we were afraid. We only meet to talk. She has a friend, Aes Sedai. Did you catch her, too? I can describe her for you, Aes Sedai. Whatever you wish, we will do. I swear, we—'

Merilille cleared her throat loudly. 'Your name is Reanne Corly, I believe?' Reanne flinched and whispered that it was, still peering at the floor at the Gray sister's feet. 'I fear you must address yourself to Elayne Sedai, Reanne.'

Reanne's head jerked up in a *most* satisfactory way. She stared at Merilille, then by slow increments turned eyes as big as her face to Elayne. She licked her lips. She drew a deep, long breath. Twisting around on her knees to face Elayne, she bowed her head once more. 'I beg your forgiveness, Aes Sedai,' she said leadenly. 'I did not know. I could not—' Another long, hopeless breath. 'Whatever punishment you decree, we accept humbly, of course, but please, I beg you to believe that—'

'Oh, stand up,' Elayne broke in impatiently. She had wanted to make this woman acknowledge her as much as she had Merilille or any of the others, but the groveling sickened her. 'That's right. Stand on your feet.' She waited until Reanne complied, then walked over and sat in the woman's chair. There was no need for cringing, but she wanted no doubts who was in charge. 'Do you still deny knowing about the Bowl of the Winds, Reanne?'

Reanne spread her hands. 'Aes Sedai,' she said guilelessly, 'none of us would ever use a *ter'angreal*, much less an *angreal* or *sa'angreal*.' Guileless, and wary as a fox in a city. 'I assure you, we make no pretense of being anything even near to Aes Sedai. We are just these few friends you see, tied together by once having been allowed to enter the White Tower. That is all.'

'Just these few friends,' Elayne said dryly over steepled fingers. 'And Garenia, of course. And Berowin, and Derys, and Alise.'

'Yes,' Reanne said reluctantly. 'And them.'

Elayne shook her head very slowly. 'Reanne, the White Tower knows about your Kin. The Tower has *always* known.' A dark woman with a Tairen look to her, though wearing a blue-and-white silk vest with the sigil of the goldsmiths' guild, gave a strangled scream and pressed both plump hands to her mouth. A lean, graying Saldaean wearing the red belt crumpled with a sigh to join the yellow-haired woman on the floor, and two more swayed as if they might.

For her part, Reanne looked to the sisters in front of the door for confirmation, and saw it, as she thought. Merilille's face was more icy than serene, and Sareitha grimaced before she could stop herself. Vandene and Careane were both tight-lipped, and even Adeleas seemed included, turning her head this way and that to study the women along the walls as she might have insects previously unknown to her. Of course, what Reanne saw and what was were not the same. They had all accepted Elayne's decision, but no amount of 'Yes, Elayne . . .' could make them like it. They would have been here two hours ago if not for a great deal of 'But, Elayne . . .' tossed in. Sometimes leading meant herding.

Reanne did not faint, but fear filled her face, and she raised pleading hands. 'Do you mean to destroy the Kin? Why now, after so long? What have we done that you should come down on us now?'

'No one will destroy you,' Elayne told her. 'Careane, since nobody else is going to help those two, would you, please?' Jumps and blushes ran around the room, and before Careane could move, two women were crouching over each one who had fainted, lifting her up and waving smelling salts under her nose. 'The Amyrlin Seat desires every woman who can channel to be connected to the Tower,' Elayne went on. 'The offer is open to any of the Kin who wish to accept.'

Had she woven flows of Air around every one of those women, she could not have frozen them more still. Had she squeezed those flows tight, she could not have produced more bulging eyes. One of the women who had fainted suddenly gasped and coughed, pushing away the tiny vial of smelling salts that had been held still too long. That broke everyone free in a deluge of voices.

'We can become Aes Sedai after all?' the Tairen in the goldsmith's vest asked excitedly, at the same time that a round-faced woman with a red belt at least twice as long as anyone else's burst out with, 'They will let us learn? They will teach us again?' A deluge of painfully eager voices. 'We can really ... ?' and 'They will actually let us ... ?' from every side.

Reanne rounded on them fiercely. 'Ivara, Sumeko, all of you, you forget yourselves! You speak in front of Aes Sedai! You speak in – front of – Aes Sedai.' She passed a hand over her face, trembling. An embarrassed silence descended. Eyes fell and blushes rose. With all those lined faces, all that gray and white hair, Elayne still was minded of nothing so much as a group of novices having a pillow-fight after Last had tolled when the Mistress of Novices walked in.

Hesitantly, Reanne looked at her across her fingertips. 'We truly will be allowed to return to the Tower?' she mumbled into her hand.

Elayne nodded. 'Those who can learn to become Aes Sedai will have the chance, but there will be a place for all. For any woman who can channel.'

Unshed tears shone in Reanne's eyes. Elayne was not sure, but she thought the woman whispered, 'I can be Green.' It was very hard not to rush over and throw her arms around her.

None of the other Aes Sedai showed any signs of giving way to emotion, and Merilille certainly was of sterner stuff. 'If I may ask a question, Elayne? Reanne, how many ... of you will we be taking in?' Doubtless that pause covered a change from 'how many wilders and women who could not make it the first time.'

If Reanne noticed or suspected, she ignored it or did not care. 'I cannot believe there are any who would refuse the offer,' she said breathlessly. 'It may take some time to send word to everyone. We remain spread out, you see, so . . .' She laughed, a touch nervously and still not far from tears '. . . so Aes Sedai would not notice us. At present there are one thousand seven hundred and eighty-three names on the roll.'

Most Aes Sedai learned to cover shock with an outward show of calm, and only Sareitha allowed her eyes to widen. She also mouthed silent words, but Elayne knew her well enough to read her lips. *Two thousand wilders! Light help us!* Elayne made a great show of adjusting her skirts until she was sure her own face was under control. Light help them, indeed.

Reanne misunderstood the silence. 'You expected more? Accidents do take some every year, or natural deaths, as with everyone else, and I fear the Kin have grown fewer in the last thousand years. Perhaps we have been too cautious in approaching women when they leave the White Tower, but there has always been the fear that one of them might report being questioned, and . . . and . . .'

'We are not disappointed in the least,' Elayne assured her, making soothing gestures. Disappointed? She very nearly giggled hysterically. There were nearly twice as many Kinswomen as there were Aes Sedai! Egwene could never say she had not done her part to bring women who could channel to the Tower. But if the Kin refused wilders . . . She must stick to the point; conscripting the Kin had only been incidental. 'Reanne,' she said gently, 'do you think perhaps you might happen to recall where the Bowl of the Winds is, now?'

Reanne blushed a sunset. 'We've never touched them, Elayne Sedai. I don't know why they were gathered. I've never heard of this Bowl of the Winds, but there is a storeroom such as you describe over—'

Belowstairs, a woman channeled briefly. Someone screamed in purest terror.

Elayne was on her feet in a flash, as were they all. From somewhere in that feathered dress, Birgitte produced a dagger.

'That must have been Derys,' Reanne said. 'She's the only other one here.'

Elayne darted forward and caught her arm as she started for the door. 'You aren't Green yet,' she murmured, and was rewarded with a lovely dimpled smile, surprised and pleased and diffident all at once. 'We will handle this, Reanne.'

Merilille and the others arrayed themselves to either side, ready to follow Elayne out, but Birgitte was at the door before any of them, grinning as she put hand to latch. Elayne swallowed and said nothing. That was the Warder's honor, so the gaidin said; first to go in, last to come out. But she still filled herself with *saidar*, ready to crush anything that threatened her Warder.

The door opened before Birgitte could lift the latch.

Mat sauntered in, pushing the slender maid Elayne remembered ahead of him. 'I thought you might be here.' He grinned insolently, ignoring Derys' glares, and went on, 'when I found a bloody great lot of Warders drinking at my least favorite tavern. I've just come back from following a woman to the Rahad. To the top floor of a house with nobody living on it, to be precise. After she left, the floor was so dusty, I could see right away which room she'd gone to. There's a flaming big rusted lock on the door, but I'll bet a thousand crowns to a kick in the bottom, your Bowl is behind it.' Derys aimed a kick at him, and he pushed her away, pulling a small knife from his belt to bounce on his palm. 'Will one of you tell this wildcat whose side I'm on? Women with knives make me uneasy, these days.'

'We already know all about that, Mat,' Elayne said. Well, they had been just about to learn all about it, and the stunned look on his face was *priceless*. She felt something from Birgitte. The other woman gazed at her without any particular expression, but that little knot of emotion in the back of Elayne's head radiated disapproval. Aviendha probably would not think much of it, either. Opening her mouth was one of the most difficult things Elayne had ever done. 'I must thank you, though, Mat. It is entirely due to you that we have found what we were looking for.' His gaping astonishment was almost worth the agony.

He closed his mouth quickly, though opening it again to say, 'Then let's hire a boat and fetch this bloody Bowl. With any luck, we can leave Ebou Dar tonight.'

'That is ridiculous, Mat. And don't tell me I'm demeaning you. We are not crawling about the Rahad in the dark, and we are not leaving Ebou Dar until we have used the Bowl.'

He tried to argue, of course, but Derys took the opportunity of his attention being elsewhere to try kicking him again. He dodged around Birgitte, yelping for somebody to help him, while the slender woman darted after him.

'He is your Warder, Elayne Sedai?' Reanne asked doubtfully.

'Light, no! Birgitte is.' Reanne's mouth fell open. Having answered a question, Elayne asked one, a question she could not have brought herself to ask another sister. 'Reanne, if you don't mind telling me, how old are you?'

The woman hesitated, glancing at Mat, but he was still dodging to keep a grinning Birgitte between him and Derys. 'My next naming day,' Reanne said as if it was the most ordinary thing in the world, 'will be my four hundred and twelfth.'

Merilille fainted dead away.

CHAPTER 32

Sealed to the Flame

Elaida do Avriny a'Roihan sat regally in the Amyrlin Seat, the tall vine-carved chair painted now in only six colors instead of seven, a six-striped stole on her shoulders, and ran her gaze around the circular Hall of the Tower. The Sitters' painted chairs had been rearranged along the stair-fronted dais that encircled the chamber beneath the great dome, spaced out to account for only six Ajahs instead of seven now, and eighteen Sitters stood obediently. Young al'Thor knelt quietly beside the Amyrlin Seat; he would not speak unless given leave, which he would not be today. Today, he was merely another symbol of her power, and the twelve most favored Sitters glowed with the link that she herself controlled to keep him safe.

'The greater consensus is achieved, Mother,' Alviarin said meekly at her shoulder, bowing humbly against the Flame-topped staff.

Down on the floor, below the dais, Sheriam screamed wildly and had to be restrained by the Tower Guard at her side. The Red sister shielding her sneered in contempt. Romanda and Lelaine clung to a cold outward dignity, but most of the others shielded and guarded on the floor wept quietly, perhaps in relief that only four women had been ordered the ultimate penalty, perhaps in fear of what else was to come. The most ashen faces belonged to the three who had dared sit in a rebel Hall for the now-dissolved Blue. Every rebel had been cast out from her Ajah until Elaida granted permission to request reacceptance, but the onetime Blues knew they confronted difficult years working their way into her good graces, years before they would be allowed to enter any Ajah at all. Until then, they lay in the palm of her hand.

She stood, and it seemed the One Power flowing through her from the circle was a manifestation of her power. 'The Hall concurs with the will of the Amyrlin Seat. Let Romanda be the first to be birched.' Romanda's head jerked; let her see how much dignity she could retain until her stilling. Elaida gestured curtly. 'Take the prisoners away, and bring in the first of the poor deluded sisters who followed them. I will accept their submission.'

There was a cry among the prisoners, and one tore free from the Guard gripping her arm. Egwene al'Vere threw herself onto the steps at Elaida's feet, hands outstretched, tears streaming down her cheeks.

'Forgive me, Mother!' the girl wept. 'I repent! I will submit; I do submit. Please, do not still me!' Brokenly, she sagged facedown, shoulders shaking with sobs. 'Please, Mother! I repent! I do!'

'The Amyrlin Seat can show mercy,' Elaida said exultantly. The White Tower had to lose Lelaine and Romanda and Sheriam as examples, but she could keep this girl's strength. She *was* the White Tower. 'Egwene al'Vere, you have rebelled against your Amyrlin, but I will show mercy. You will be dressed in novice white again, until I myself judge you ready to be raised further, but this very day you shall be the first to take a Fourth Oath on the Oath Rod, of fealty and obedience to the Amyrlin Seat.'

The prisoners began falling on their knees, crying out to be allowed to take that oath, to prove their true submission. Lelaine was one of the first, and neither Romanda nor Sheriam the last. Egwene crawled up the steps to kiss the hem of Elaida's dress.

'I yield myself to your will, Mother,' she murmured through her tears. 'Thank you. Oh, thank you!'

Alviarin seized Elaida's shoulder, shook her. 'Wake up, you fool woman!' she growled.

Elaida's eyes popped open to the dim light of a single lamp held by Alviarin, bending over her bed with a hand on her shoulder. Still only half awake, she mumbled, 'What did you say?'

'I said, "Please wake up, Mother,"' Alviarin replied coolly. 'Covarla Baldene has returned from Cairhien.'

Elaida shook her head, trying to clear away the tag end of the dream. 'So soon? I did not expect them for another week at least. Covarla, you say? Where is Galina?' Foolish questions; Alviarin would not know what she meant.

But in that cool crystalline tone, the woman said, 'She believes Galina dead or a prisoner. I fear the news is . . . not good.'

What Alviarin should or should not know rushed out of Elaida's head. 'Tell me,' she demanded, throwing off the silk sheet, but as she rose and belted a silk robe over her nightdress, she heard only snatches. A battle. Hordes of Aiel women channeling. Al'Thor gone. Disaster. Distractedly, she noticed that Alviarin was neatly garbed in a silver-embroidered white dress, with the Keeper's stole around her neck. The woman had waited till she clothed herself to bring her this!

The case clock in her study softly chimed Second Low as she entered the sitting room. The small hours of the morning; the worst time to receive dire news. Covarla rose hastily from one of the red-cushioned armchairs, her implacable face sagging with weariness and worry, and knelt to kiss Elaida's ring. Her dark riding dress still bore the dust of travel, and her pale hair needed the use of a brush, but she had donned the shawl she had worn as long as Elaida had been alive.

Elaida barely waited for the woman's lips to touch the Great Serpent before pulling her hand away. 'Why were you sent?' she said curtly. Snatching up her knitting from where she had left it in a chair, she sat and began to work the long ivory needles. Knitting served many of the same purposes as fondling her carved ivory miniatures, and she surely needed soothing now. Knitting helped her think, too. She had to think. 'Where is Katerine?' If Galina was dead, Katerine should have taken charge ahead of Coiren; Elaida had made it clear that once al'Thor was taken, the Red Ajah was in charge.

Covarla stood slowly, as if uncertain she should. Her hands tightened on the red-fringed shawl looped over her arms. 'Katerine is among the missing, Mother. I stand highest among those who ...' Her words trailed off as Elaida stared at her, fingers frozen in the act of passing wool over one of the needles. Covarla swallowed and shifted her feet.

'How many, daughter?' Elaida asked finally. She could not believe her voice was so calm.

'I cannot say how many escaped, Mother,' Covarla said hesitantly. 'We dared not wait to make a thorough search, and—'

'How many?' Elaida shouted. With a shudder, she made herself concentrate on her knitting; she should not have shouted; giving way to anger was weakness. Loop the yarn, pull through and push down. Soothing motions.

'I – I brought eleven other sisters with me, Mother.' The woman paused, breathing hard, and then, when Elaida said nothing, rushed on. 'Others may be making their way back, Mother. Gawyn refused to wait longer, and we dared not remain without him and his Younglings, not with so many Aiel about, and the ...'

Elaida did not hear. Twelve returned. Had any more escaped, they would have sped back to Tar Valon, would have been here as soon as Covarla, surely. Even if one or two were injured, traveling slowly ... Twelve. The Tower had not suffered a disaster of this magnitude even during the Trolloc Wars.

'These Aiel wilders must be taught a lesson,' she said, trampling over whatever Covarla was babbling. Galina had thought she could use Aiel to divert Aiel; what a fool the woman had been! 'We will rescue the sisters they hold prisoner, and teach them what it means to defy Aes Sedai! And we will take al'Thor again.' She would not let him get away, not if she had to personally lead the entire White Tower to take him! The Foretelling had been certain. She *would* triumph!

Casting an uneasy glance at Alviarin, Covarla shifted her feet again. 'Mother, those men – I think—'

'Do not think!' Elaida snapped. Her hands clasped the knitting needles convulsively, and she leaned forward so fiercely that Covarla actually raised a hand as though to fend off an attack. Alviarin's presence had slipped from Elaida's mind. Well, the woman knew what she knew, now; that could be dealt with later. 'You have maintained secrecy, Covarla? Aside from informing the Keeper?'

'Oh, yes, Mother,' Covarla said hastily. Her head bobbed with eagerness, glad that she had done something right. 'I entered the city alone, and hid my face until I reached Alviarin. Gawyn meant to accompany me, but the bridge guards refused to let any member of the Younglings pass.'

'Forget Gawyn Trakand,' Elaida ordered sourly. That young man remained alive to trouble her plans, it seemed. If Galina did turn out to be alive still, she would pay for failing in that, on top of letting al'Thor escape. 'You will leave the city as circumspectly as you entered, daughter, and keep yourself and the others well hidden in one of the villages beyond the bridge towns until I send for you. Dorlan will do nicely.' They would have to sleep in barns in that tiny hamlet, which had no inn; the least their bungling deserved. 'Go, now. And pray that someone above you does arrive soon. The Hall will demand amends for this unparalleled catastrophe, and at the moment, it seems you stand highest among those at fault. Go!'

Covarla's face went white. She tottered so making her curtsy to leave, Elaida thought she might fall. Bunglers! She was surrounded by fools, traitors and bunglers!

As soon as Elaida heard the outer door close, she hurled down her knitting and sprang to her feet, rounding on Alviarin. 'Why have I not heard of this before? If al'Thor escaped – what was it you said? Seven days ago? – if he escaped seven days ago, someone's eyes-and-ears must have seen him. Why was I not informed?'

'I can only pass on to you what the Ajahs pass to me, Mother.'

Alviarin adjusted her stole calmly, not a whit ruffled. 'Do you really mean to court a third debacle by attempting to rescue the captives?'

Elaida sniffed dismissively. 'Do you really believe wilders can stand before Aes Sedai? Galina let herself be surprised; she must have.' She frowned. 'What do you mean, a *third* debacle?'

'You didn't listen, Mother.' Shockingly, Alviarin sat without being given permission, crossing her knees and serenely arranging her skirts. 'Covarla thought they might have held out against the wilders – though I believe she is nowhere near as certain as she tried to pretend – but the men were another matter. Several hundred of them in black coats, all channeling. She was very certain of that, and so are the others, apparently. Living weapons, she called them. I think she nearly soiled herself just remembering.'

Elaida stood as if poleaxed. Several hundred? 'Impossible. There can't be more than—' She walked to a table that seemed all ivory and gilt, and poured herself a goblet of wine punch. The lip of the crystal pitcher rattled against the crystal goblet, and almost as much punch went onto the golden tray.

'Since al'Thor can Travel,' Alviarin said suddenly, 'it seems logical at least some of these men can, too. Covarla is quite sure that was how they arrived. I suppose he is rather upset at his treatment. Covarla seemed somewhat uneasy about it; she implied that a number of the sisters were. He might feel he owes you something. It would not be pleasant to have those men suddenly stepping out of thin air right here in the Tower, would it?'

Elaida practically tossed the punch down her throat. Galina had been instructed to begin making al'Thor supple. If he came for revenge . . . If there really were hundreds of men who could channel, or even one hundred . . . She had to think!

'Of course, if they were coming, I believe they would have by now. They would not have wasted surprise. Perhaps even al'Thor doesn't wish to confront the full Tower. I suppose they have all returned to Caemlyn, to their Black Tower. Which means, I fear, that Toveine has a most unpleasant shock awaiting her.'

'Pen an order for her to return immediately,' Elaida said hoarsely. The punch did not seem to help. She turned, and gave a start to find

Alviarin right in front of her. Maybe there were not even one hundred – not *even* one hundred? At sunset, *ten* would have seemed madness – but she could not take the chance. 'Write it out yourself, Alviarin. Now; right now.'

'And how is it to be gotten to her?' Alviarin tilted her head, icily curious. For some reason, she wore a faint smile. 'None of *us* can Travel. The ships will put Toveine and her party ashore in Andor any day now, if they have not already. You told her to divide into small groups and avoid villages, so as to give no warning. No, Elaida, I am afraid Toveine will regather her forces near Caemlyn and attack the Black Tower without any word from us reaching her.'

Elaida gasped. The woman had just called her by name! And before she could begin to splutter with outrage, worse came.

'I think you are in great trouble, Elaida.' Cold eyes stared into Elaida's and cold words slid smoothly from Alviarin's smiling lips. 'Sooner or later, the Hall will learn of the disaster with al'Thor. Galina might have satisfied the Hall, possibly, but I doubt Covarla will; they will want someone ... higher ... to pay. And sooner or later, we will all learn Toveine's fate. It will be difficult to keep this on your shoulders then.' Casually, she adjusted the Amyrlin's stole around Elaida's neck. 'In fact, it will be impossible if they learn any time soon. You will be stilled, made an example, the way you wanted to make Siuan Sanche. But there might be time to recover, if you listen to your Keeper. You must take good advice.'

Elaida's tongue felt frozen. The threat could not have been clearer. 'What you have heard tonight is Sealed to the Flame,' she said thickly, but she knew that the words were useless before they were out of her mouth.

'If you mean to reject my advice ...' Alviarin paused, then began to turn away.

'Wait!' Elaida pulled down the hand she had stretched out unaware. Stripped of the stole. Stilled. Even after that, they would make her howl. 'What—?' She had to stop and swallow. 'What advice does my Keeper offer?' There had to be some way to stop this.

Sighing, Alviarin came close again. Closer, in fact; much too near for anyone to stand to the Amyrlin, their skirts almost touching. 'First, I fear you must abandon Toveine to whatever comes, for the moment at least. And also Galina and whoever else was taken prisoner, whether by the Aiel or the Asha'man. Any attempted rescue now must mean discovery.'

Elaida nodded slowly. 'Yes. I can see that.' She could not take her horrified eyes away from the other woman's demanding gaze. There had to be a way! This could not be happening!

'And I think it is time to reconsider your decision about the Tower Guard. Don't you really think the Guard should be increased after all?'

'I – can see my way clear to do that.' Light, she had to think!

'So good,' Alviarin murmured, and Elaida flushed with helpless rage. 'Tomorrow, you will personally search Josaine's rooms, and Adelorna's.'

'Why under the Light would I—?'

The woman tugged her striped stole again, roughly this time almost as if to yank it off or saw through her neck with it. 'It seems that Josaine found an *angreal* some years ago and never turned it in. Adelorna did worse, I fear. She removed an *angreal* from one of the storerooms without permission. When you have found them, you will announce their punishment immediately. Something quite stiff. And at the same time you will hold up Doraise, Kiyoshi and Farellien as models of preserving the law. You will give each a present; a fine new horse will do.'

Elaida wondered whether her eyes were going to pop right out of her face. 'Why?' From time to time a sister kept an *angreal* to herself in defiance of the law, but the penance was seldom more than a stern slap on the knuckles. Every sister knew the temptation. And the rest! The effect was obvious. Everyone would believe Doraise and Kiyoshi and Farellien had exposed the other two. Josaine and Adelorna were Green, the others Brown, Gray and Yellow respectively. The Green Ajah would be furious. They might even try to get back at the others, which would incite those Ajahs, and ... 'Why do you want to do this, Alviarin?'

'Elaida, it should be enough for you that it is my advice.'

Mocking, honeyed ice suddenly turned to cold iron. 'I want to hear you say that you will do as you are told. There's no point in me working to keep the stole on your neck, otherwise. Say it!'

'I—' Elaida tried to look away. Oh, Light, she had to think! Her belly was clenched in a knot. 'I will – do – as I – am told.'

Alviarin smiled that chilly smile. 'You see, that did not hurt very much.' Suddenly she stepped back, spreading her skirts in a moderate curtsy. 'With your permission, I will withdraw and let you find some sleep in what remains of the night. You have an early morning ahead, with orders to issue for High Captain Chubain and apartments to search. We have to decide when to let the Tower know about the Asha'man, too.' Her tone made it clear that she would decide. 'And perhaps we should begin planning our next move against al'Thor. It is about time the Tower stood openly and called him to heel, don't you think? Think well. I give you good night, Elaida.'

Dazed, wanting to sick up, Elaida watched her go. Stand openly? That would *invite* attack by these – what had the woman called them? – these Asha'man. This could not be happening to her. Not to her! Before she realized what she was doing, she hurled the goblet across the room to shatter against a tapestry of flowers. Seizing the pitcher with both hands, she raised it overhead with a shriek of fury and flung that too, in a spray of punch. The Foretelling had been so certain! She would . . . !

Abruptly she stopped, frowning at the tiny shards of crystals clinging to the tapestry, the larger pieces scattered across the floor. The Foretelling. Surely that had spoken of her triumph. *Her* triumph! Alviarin might have her minor victory, but the future belonged to Elaida. As long as Alviarin could be gotten rid of. But it had to be done quietly, in some way so that even the Hall would want silence. A way that would not point to Elaida until it was too late, should Alviarin gain wind. And suddenly it came to her. Alviarin would not believe if she was told. No one would.

Could Alviarin have seen her smile then, the woman's knees would have turned to jelly. Before she was done, Alviarin would envy Galina, alive or dead.

*

Pausing in the hallway outside Elaida's apartments, Alviarin studied her hands by the light of the stand-lamps. They did not shake, which surprised her. She had expected the woman to fight harder, to resist longer. But it was begun, and she had nothing to fear. Unless Elaida learned that no fewer than five Ajahs had passed mention of al'Thor to her in the last few days; the deposing of Colavaere had sent every Ajah's agent in Cairhien flying for a pen. No, if Elaida did learn, she was safe enough, with the hold she had on the woman now. And with Mesaana as patron. Elaida, though, was finished whether she realized or not. Even if the Asha'man failed to trumpet crushing Toveine's expedition – and she was sure they would crush it, after what Mesaana had told her of events of Dumai's Wells – all the eyes-and-ears in Caemlyn truly would gain wings once they learned. Lacking a miracle, such as the rebels appearing at the gates, Elaida would suffer Siuan Sanche's fate in a matter of weeks. In any case, it had begun, and if she wished she knew what 'it' was, all she really had to do was obey. And watch. And learn. Perhaps she would wear the seven-striped stole herself when all was done.

In the early morning sunlight streaming through her windows, Seaine dipped the pen, but before she could write the next word, the door to the hall opened and the Amyrlin swept in. Seaine's thick black eyebrows rose; she would have expected anyone else at all before Elaida, perhaps not excluding Rand al'Thor himself. Still, she set the pen down and rose smoothly, pulling down the silver-white sleeves she had pushed up to keep clear of the ink. She made the degree of curtsy proper to the Amyrlin Seat from a Sitter in her own apartments.

'I do hope you haven't found any White sisters hiding away *angreal*, Mother.' After all these years, a touch of Lugard still clung to her voice. She did hope it quite fervently. Elaida's descent on the Greens a few hours ago, while most of them slept, was probably still producing wails and gnashing of teeth. In living memory no one had been ordered birched for keeping back an *angreal*, and now there were to be two. The Amyrlin must have been in one of her infamous cold furies.

But if she had been then, no sign of it remained now. For a moment she regarded Seaine silently, cool as a winter pond in her red-slashed silks, then glided to the carved sideboard where painted ivory miniatures of Seaine's family stood. All years dead, but she still loved every one.

'You did not stand to raise me Amyrlin,' Elaida said, picking up the picture of Seaine's father. She set it down hastily and took up her mother instead.

Seaine's eyebrows almost rose again, but she tried to make it a rule not to let herself be surprised more than once in a day. 'I was not informed that the Hall was sitting until afterward, Mother.'

'Yes, yes.' Abandoning the paintings, Elaida glided to the fireplace. Seaine had always had a fondness for cats, and carved wooden cats of every sort crowded the mantlepiece, some in amusing poses. The Amyrlin frowned at the display, then squeezed her eyes shut and gave her head a tiny shake. 'But you remained,' she said, turning quickly. 'Every Sitter who was not informed fled the Tower and joined the rebels. Except you. Why?'

Seaine spread her hands. 'What else could I do but stay, Mother? The Tower must be whole.' *Whoever the Amyrlin*, she added to herself. *And what's wrong with my cats, if I may ask?* Not that she ever would aloud, of course. Sereille Bagand had been a fierce Mistress of Novices before being raised Amyrlin Seat, the very year she herself earned the shawl, and a fiercer Amyrlin than Elaida could be with a sore tooth. Seaine had had the proprieties driven into her too hard and deep for mere years to shift. Or any dislike for the woman who wore the stole. One did not have to like an Amyrlin.

'The Tower must be whole,' Elaida agreed, rubbing her hands together. 'It must be whole.' Now, why was she nervous? She had ninety-nine kinds of temper, all hard as a knife and twice as sharp, but nervous the woman was not. 'What I say to you now is Sealed to the Flame, Seaine.' Her mouth twisted wryly, and she shrugged, giving her stole an irritable twitch. 'If I knew how to make it stronger, I would,' she said, dry as yesterday's dust.

'I will hold your words in my heart, Mother.'

'I want you – I command you – to undertake an inquiry. And

you must indeed hold it in your heart. The wrong ear hearing of it might mean death, and disaster for the whole Tower.'

Seaine's eyebrows twitched. Death and disaster for the whole Tower? 'In my heart,' she said again. 'Will you sit yourself, Mother?' That was proper, in her own apartments. 'May I pour you some mint tea? Or plum punch?'

Waving away the offer of refreshment, Elaida took the most comfortable chair, carved by Seaine's father as a gift when she received the shawl, though of course the cushions had been replaced many times since. The Amyrlin made the country chair seem a throne, all stiff back and iron countenance. Most ungraciously, she did not give permission for Seaine to sit, too, so Seaine folded her hands and remained standing.

'I have thought long and hard on treason, Seaine, since my predecessor and her Keeper were allowed to escape. Helped to escape. Treason must have been at the core of that, and I fear only a sister, or sisters, could have effected it.'

'That would certainly be a possibility, Mother.' Elaida frowned at the interruption.

'We can never be sure who has the shadow of treason in her heart, Seaine. Why, I suspect that someone arranged for an order of mine to be countermanded. And I have reason to believe that someone has communicated privately with Rand al'Thor; to what end, I cannot say, but that surely is treason against me, and against the Tower.'

Seaine waited for more, but the Amyrlin only looked back at her, slowly smoothing her red-slashed skirts as if unaware. 'Exactly what inquiry do you wish me to make, Mother?' she asked cautiously.

Elaida bounded to her feet. 'I charge you to follow the stench of treason, no matter where it leads or how high, even to the Keeper herself. What you find, whoever it leads to, you will bring before the Amyrlin Seat alone, Seaine. No one else must know. Do you understand me?'

'I understand your commands, Mother.'

Which, she thought, once Elaida departed even more swiftly than she had come, was about all she did understand. She took the chair the Amyrlin had vacated in order to think, fists pressed beneath her chin in just the way her father had always sat thinking. Everything fell to logic, eventually.

She would not have stood against Siuan Sanche – she had proposed the girl as Amyrlin in the first place! – but once it was done and all the forms followed, however sparely, aiding her escape certainly had been treason, and deliberately countermanding an Amyrlin's order just as much. Possibly communicating with al'Thor was, too; that depended on what was communicated, with what intent. Finding who had changed the Amyrlin's command would be difficult without knowing what command. At this late date, learning who might have helped Siuan escape stood about as much chance of success as learning who might be writing to al'Thor. So many pigeons flew into and out of the Tower cots every day that at times the sky seemed to be raining feathers. If Elaida knew more than she said, she had certainly gone around the barn. This all made very little sense. Treason would make Elaida boil with rage, but she had not been angry. She had been nervous. And anxious to be gone. And secretive, as if she did not want to tell everything she knew or suspected. Almost as though she was afraid to. What kind of treason would make Elaida nervous or afraid? Death and disaster for the whole Tower.

Like the pieces of a blacksmith's puzzle, all fell into place, and Seaine's eyebrows tried to climb onto her scalp. It fit; it all fit. She felt the blood draining from her face; her hands and feet suddenly icy. Sealed to the Flame. She had said she would keep this in her heart, but everything had changed since she spoke those words. She only let herself be afraid when it was logical to be, and right then, she was terrified. She could not face this alone. But who? Under the circumstances, who? This answer came much more easily. Gathering herself took a little time, but she hurried from her rooms and out of the White quarters walking a good deal faster than she usually did.

Servants scurried through the corridors as always, though she walked so quickly that she was past most before they could begin bow or curtsy, but there seemed fewer sisters about than the early hour could account for. Many fewer. Yet if most were staying close to their quarters for some reason, those few made up for it in one way. Sisters swanned along the tapestry-hung hallways, faces all serenity, and their eyes seemed to have steam behind them. Here and there two or three women spoke together, with sharp eyes darting to see who might be listening. Always two or three of the same Ajah. Even yesterday, she was sure she had still seen women sharing friendship between Ajahs. Whites were supposed to put emotion away entirely, but she had never seen the reason for blinding herself, as some did. Suspicion made the air in the Tower like hot jelly. Not a new thing, unfortunately – the Amyrlin had begun it with her harsh measures, and the rumors abut Logain had only exacerbated the situation – but this morning seemed worse than ever.

Talene Minly came around a corner ahead of her, for some reason with her shawl not just across her shoulders, but spread down her arms as though to display the green fringe. For that matter, she realized that every Green she had seen this morning wore her shawl. Talene, golden-haired and statuesque and lovely, had stood to depose Siuan, but she had come to the Tower while Seaine was Accepted, and that decision had not dented their long friendship. Talene had had reasons Seaine accepted if not agreed with. Today, her friend stopped, watching her warily. So many sisters seemed to watch one another that way of late. Another time, she would have stopped, but not with what made her head want to burst open like a spoiled melon. Talene was a friend, and she thought she would be sure of her, but thinking was not enough for this. Later, if possible, she would approach Talene. Hoping it possible, she hurried past with only a nod.

In the Red quarters, the mood was even worse, the air thicker. As with other Ajah, there were many more rooms than there were sisters to fill them now – that had been so long before the first rebel fled – but the Red was the largest of the Ajahs, and sisters filled the levels still in use. Reds frequently wore their shawls when there was no need, but even here, every last woman sported her red fringe like a banner. Conversations stopped as Seaine approached, and cold eyes followed her in a bubble of icy silence. She felt an invader deep in enemy country as she crossed those peculiar floor tiles, white with the teardrop Flame of Tar Valon in red. But then, any part of the

Tower might be enemy country. Looking another way, those scarlet flames might be taken for red Dragon's Fangs. She had never believed those irrational tales about the Reds and false Dragons, but ... Why would none of them deny it?

She had to ask directions. 'I will not disturb her if she is busy,' she said. 'We were close friends, once, and I would like us to be again. Now more than ever, the Ajahs cannot afford to drift apart.' All true, though the Ajahs seemed to splitting apart rather than drifting, but the Domani woman listened with a face that could have been cast in copper. There were not many Domani Reds, and those few usually meaner than snakes caught in a fence.

'I will show you, Sitter,' the woman said at last, and not very respectfully. She led the way, then watched while Seaine knocked on the door, as though she could not be trusted here alone. The door panels were carved with the Flame, too, lacquered the color of fresh blood.

'Come!' a brisk voice called from within. Seaine opened the door hoping she was right.

'Seaine!' Pevara exclaimed cheerfully. 'What brings you here this morning? Come! Shut the door and sit!' It was as if all the years since they were novice and Accepted together had melted away. Quite plump and not tall – in truth, for a Kandori, she was short – Pevara was also quite pretty, with a merry twinkle in her dark eyes and a ready smile. It was sad that she had chosen Red, no matter how good her reasons, because she still liked men. The Red did attract women who were naturally suspicious of men, of course, but others chose it because the task of finding men who could channel was important. Whether they liked men, or disliked them, or did not care one way or the other in the beginning, however, not many women could belong to the Red for long without taking a jaundiced view of all men. Seaine had reason to believe Pevara had served a penance shortly after attaining the shawl for saying that she wished she had a Warder; since reaching the safer heights of the Hall, she had openly said Warders would make the Red Ajah's work easier.

'I cannot tell you how happy I am to see you,' Pevara said once they were ensconced in armchairs carved in the spirals popular in

Kandor a hundred years ago, with delicate, butterfly-painted cups of blueberry tea in hand. 'I've often thought how I should go to you, but I admit to fearing what you would say after I gave you the cut direct so many years ago. Sworn on the blade, Seaine, I'd not have done it, except Tesien Jorhald practically had me by the scruff of my neck, and I was too new to the shawl to have much backbone yet. Can you forgive me?'

'Of course, I can,' Seaine replied. 'I understood.' The Red firmly discouraged friendships outside the Ajah. Quite firmly, and quite efficiently. 'We cannot go against our Ajahs when we are young, and later, it seems impossible to retrace our steps. A thousand times I've remembered us whispering together after Last – Oh, and the pranks! Do you recall when we dusted Serancha's shift with powdered itchoak? – but I'm shamed to say it took being terrified out of my wits to stir my feet. I do want us to be friends again, but I need your help, too. You are the only one I'm sure I can trust.'

'Serancha was a prig then, and still is,' Pevara laughed. 'The Gray is a good place for her. But I can't believe you terrified at anything. Why, you never decided it was logical to be afraid until we were back in our beds. Short of a promise to stand in the Hall without knowing what for, whatever help I can give is yours, Seaine. What do you need?'

Brought to the point, Seaine hesitated, sipping her tea. Not that she had any doubts about Pevara, but pushing the words out of her mouth was ... difficult. 'The Amyrlin came to see me this morning,' she said finally. 'She instructed me to make an inquiry, Sealed to the Flame.' Pevara frowned slightly, but she did not say that in that case Seaine should not be speaking of it. Seaine might have planned how to carry out most of their pranks as girls, but Pevara had been the one with the audacity to think of most, and she had provided most of the nerve to go through with them. 'She was very circumspect, but after a little thought, it was clear to me what she wanted. I am to hunt out ... ' at the last, courage failed her tongue ' ... Darkfriends in the Tower.'

Pevara's eyes, as dark as her own were blue, became stone, and swept to the mantle above her fireplace, where miniatures of her own family made a precise line. They had all died while she was a novice, parents, brothers and sisters, aunts, uncles and all, murdered in a quickly suppressed uprising of Darkfriends who had become convinced the Dark One was about to break free. That was why Seaine had been sure she could trust her. That was why Pevara had chosen Red – though Seaine still thought she could have done as well and been happier as a Green – because she believed a Red hunting men who could channel had the best chance of finding Darkfriends. She had been very good at it; that plump exterior covered a core of steel. And she possessed the courage to say calmly what Seaine had been unable to bring herself to utter.

'The Black Ajah. Well. No wonder Elaida would be circumspect.'

'Pevara, I know she's always denied its existence harder than any three other sisters combined, but I'm certain sure that's what she meant, and if she is convinced . . .'

Her friend waved her off. 'You have no need to convince me, Seaine. I have been sure the Black Ajah exists for . . .' Strangely, Pevara became hesitant, peering into her teacup like a fortune-teller at a fair. 'What do you know of events right after the Aiel War?'

'Two Amyrlins dying suddenly in the space of five years,' Seaine said carefully. She assumed the other woman meant events in the Tower. Truth to tell, until being raised a Sitter nearly fifteen years ago, just a year after Pevara, she had not given much attention to anything outside the Tower. And not that much inside, really. 'A great many sisters died in those years, as I recall. Do you mean to say you think the . . . the Black Ajah had a hand in that?' There; she had said it, and the name had not burned her tongue.

'I don't know,' Pevara said softly, shaking her head. 'You've done well to wrap yourself deep in philosophy. There were . . . things . . . done then, and Sealed to the Flame.' She drew a troubled breath.

Seaine did not press her; she herself had committed something akin to treason breaking that same seal, and Pevara would have to decide on her own. 'Looking at reports will be safer than asking questions with no idea who we're really asking. Logically, a Black sister must be able to lie despite the Oaths.' Otherwise, the Black Ajah would have been revealed long since. That name seemed to be coming more easily with use. 'If any sister wrote that she did one thing when we can prove she did another, then we have found a Darkfriend.'

Pevara nodded. 'Yes, but we mustn't confine ourselves. Perhaps the Black Ajah has no hand in the rebellion, but I cannot think they would let this turmoil pass without taking advantage. We must look closely at the last year, I think.'

To that, Seaine agreed reluctantly. There would be fewer pieces of paper to read and more questions to ask concerning recent months. Deciding who else to make part of the inquiry was even harder. Especially after Pevara said, 'You were very brave coming to me, Seaine. I've known Darkfriends to kill brothers, sisters, parents, to try hiding who they are and what they've done. I love you for it, but you were very brave indeed.'

Seaine shivered as if a goose had walked on her grave. Had she wanted to be brave, she would have chosen Green. She almost wished Elaida had gone to someone else. There was no turning back now, though.

CHAPTER 33

A Bath

The days after sending Perrin away seemed endless to Rand, and the nights longer. He retreated to his rooms and stayed there, telling the Maidens to allow no one to enter. Only Nandera was allowed past the doors with the gilded suns, bringing his meals. The sinewy Maiden would set down a covered tray and list those who had asked to see him, then give him a look of rebuke when he repeated that he would see no one. Often he heard disapproving comments from the Maidens outside before she pulled the door shut behind her; he was intended to hear, else they would have used handtalk. But if they thought to chivy him out by claiming that he was sulking ... The Maidens did not understand, and might not if he explained. If he could have brought himself to.

He picked at the meals without appetite, and tried to read, but his favorite books could divert him for only a few pages even in the beginning. At least once every day, though he had promised himself he would not, he lifted the massive wardrobe of polished blackwood and ivory in his bedchamber, floated it aside on flows of Air and carefully unraveled the traps he had set and the Mirror of Mists that made the wall seem smooth, all inverted so no other eyes but his could see. There, in a niche hollowed out with the Power, stood two small statues of white stone about a foot tall, a woman and a man, each in flowing robes and holding a clear crystal sphere overhead in one hand. The night he set the army in motion toward Illian he had gone to Rhuidean alone to fetch these *ter'angreal*: if he needed them, he might not have much time. That was what he had told himself. His hand would stretch toward the bearded man, the only one of the pair a man could use, stretch out and stop, shaking. One finger touching, and more of the One Power than he could imagine could be his. With that, no one could defeat him, no one stand against him. With that, Lanfear had said once, he could challenge the Creator.

'It is mine by right,' he muttered each time, with his hand trembling just short of the figure. 'Mine! I am the Dragon Reborn!'

And each time, he made himself draw back, reweaving the Mask of Mirrors, reweaving the invisible traps that would burn anyone to a cinder who tried to pass them without the key. The huge wardrobe wafted back into place like a feather. He was the Dragon Reborn. But was that enough? It would have to be.

'I am the Dragon Reborn,' he whispered at the walls sometimes, and sometimes shouted at them, 'I am the Dragon Reborn!' Silently and aloud he raged at those who opposed him, the blind fools who could not see and those who refused to see, for ambition or avarice or fear. He was the Dragon Reborn, the only hope of the world against the Dark One. And the Light help the world for it.

But his rages and thoughts of using the *ter'angreal* were only attempts to escape other things, and he knew it. Alone, he picked at his meals, though less every day, and tried to read, though seldom, and attempted to find sleep. That he tried more often as the days passed, not caring whether the sun was down or high. Sleep came in fitful snatches, and what harrowed his waking thoughts, also stalked his dreams and chased him awake too soon for any rest. No amount of shielding could keep out what was already inside. He had the Forsaken to face, and sooner or later the Dark One himself. He had fools who fought him or ran away when their only hope was to stand behind him. Why would his dreams not let him be? From one dream he always sprang awake before it more than began, to lie there filled with self-loathing and muddled with lack of sleep, but the others ... He deserved them all, he knew.

Colavaere confronted him sleeping, her face black and the scarf she had used to hang herself still buried in the swollen flesh of her neck. Colavaere, silent and accusing, with all the Maidens who had died for him arrayed behind her in silent staring ranks, all the women who died because of him. He knew every face as well as his own, and every name but one. From those dreams, he woke weeping.

A hundred times he hurled Perrin across the Grand Hall of the Sun, and a hundred times he was overwhelmed by blazing fear and rage. A hundred times, he killed Perrin in his dreams and woke to his own screams. Why had the man chosen the Aes Sedai prisoners to use for their argument? Rand tried not to think about them; he had done his best to ignore their existence from the beginning. They were too dangerous to keep long as captives, and he had no idea what to do with them. They frightened him. Sometimes he dreamed of being bound inside the box again, of Galina and Erian and Katerine and the rest taking him out to beat him, dreamed and woke whimpering even after he convinced himself his eyes were open and he was outside. They frightened him because he feared he might give way to the fear and the anger, and then ... He tried not to think of what he might do then, but sometimes he dreamed it, and woke shaking in a cold sweat. He would not do that. Whatever he had done, he would not do that.

In dreams he gathered the Asha'man to attack the White Tower and punish Elaida; he leaped from a gateway filled with righteous anger and *saidin* – and learned that Alviarin's letter had been a lie, saw her stand alongside Elaida, saw Egwene beside her, too, and Nynaeve, and even Elayne, all with Aes Sedai faces, because he was too dangerous to let run free. He watched the Asha'man destroyed by women who had years of studying the One Power behind them, not just a few months of harsh tutoring, and from those dreams, he could never wake until every man in a black coat was dead, and he stood alone to face the might of the Aes Sedai. Alone.

Again and again Cadsuane spoke those words about madmen hearing voices, till he flinched at them as at blows of a whip, flinched in his sleep when she appeared. In dreams and waking, he called to Lews Therin, shouted at him, screamed for him, and only silence answered. Alone. That small bundle of sensations and emotions in the back of his head, the sense of Alanna's almost touch, slowly became a comfort. In many ways, that frightened him most of all.

On the fourth morning, he woke groggily from a dream of the White Tower, flinging up a hand to shield grainy eyes from what he thought was a flare of *saidar*-wrought fire. Dust motes sparkled in the sunlight streaming through the window to reach his bed, with its great square blackwood bedposts inlaid with ivory wedges. Every piece of furnishing in the room was polished blackwood and ivory, square and stark and heavy enough to suit his mood. For a moment he lay there, but if sleep returned, it would only bring another dream.

Are you there, Lews Therin? he thought without any hope of answer, and wearily pushed himself to his feet, tugging his wrinkled coat straight. He had not changed his clothes since first shutting himself away.

When he staggered into the anteroom, at first he thought he was dreaming again, the dream that always woke him straight off in shame and guilt and loathing, but Min looked up at him from one of the tall gilded chairs, a leather-bound book on her knees, and he did not wake. Dark ringlets framed her face, big dark eyes so intent he almost felt her touch. Her breeches of brocaded green silk fit her like a second skin, and her coat of matching silk hung open, a cream-colored blouse rising and falling with her breath. He prayed to wake. It had not been fear, or anger, or guilt over Colavaere, or Lews Therin's disappearance that drove him to shut himself away.

'There's a feast of sorts in four days,' she said brightly, 'at the half moon. The Day of Repentance, they call it for some reason, but there will be dancing that night. Sedate dancing, I hear, but any dancing is better than none.' Carefully tucking a thin strip of leather into the book, she placed it on the floor beside her. 'That's just time to have a dress made, if I set the seamstress to work today. That is, if you mean to dance with me.'

He pulled his eyes away from her, and they fell on a cloth-covered tray beside the tall doors. Just the thought of food made him queasy. Nandera was not supposed to let anyone in, burn her! Least of all, Min. He had not mentioned her by name, but he had said no one! 'Min, I – I don't know what to say. I—'

'Sheepherder, you look like what the dogs fought over. Now I understand why Alanna was so frantic, even if I don't see how she knew. She practically begged me to speak to you, after the Maidens turned her away for about the fifth time. Nandera wouldn't have let *me* in if she wasn't in a lather about you not eating, and even so, I had to do a little begging myself. You owe me, country boy.'

Rand flinched. Images of himself flashed in his head; him tearing at her clothes, forcing himself on her like a mindless beast. He owed her more than he could ever pay. Raking a hand through his hair, he made himself turn to face her. She had tucked her feet up so she sat cross-legged in the chair, leaning her fists on her knees. How could she look at him so calmly? 'Min, there's no excuse for what I did. If there was any justice, I'd go to the gallows. If I could, I'd put the rope around my neck myself. On oath, I would.' The words tasted bitter. He was the Dragon Reborn, and she would have to wait on justice until the Last Battle. What a fool he had been to want to live past Tarmon Gai'don. He did not deserve to.

'What are you talking about, sheepherder?' she said slowly.

'I'm talking about what I did to you,' he groaned. How could he have done that, to anyone, but most of all to her? 'Min, I know how hard it is for you to be in the same room with me.' How could he recall the soft feel of her so, the silkiness of her skin? After he had torn her clothes off. 'I never thought I was an animal, a monster.' But he was. He loathed himself for what he had done. And loathed himself worse because he wanted to do it again. 'The only excuse I have is madness. Cadsuane was right. I did hear voices. Lews Therin's voice, I thought. Can you—? No. No, I have no right to ask you to forgive me. But you have to know how sorry I am, Min.' He was sorry. And his hands ached to run down her bare back, over her hips. He *was* a monster. 'Bitterly sorry. At least know that.'

She sat there motionless, staring at him as if she never before had seen his like. Now, she could stop pretending. Now, she could say what she really thought of him, and however vile it was, it would not be half vile enough.

'So that's why you've been keeping me away,' she said finally. 'You listen to me, you wooden-headed numbskull. I was ready to cry myself to dust because I'd seen one death too many, and you, you were about to do the same for the same reason. What we did, my innocent lamb, was comfort one another. Friends comfort one another at times like that. Close your mouth, you Two Rivers hayhair.'

He did, but only to swallow. He thought his eyes were going to fall onto the floorstones. He nearly spluttered getting words out. '*Comforted?* Min, if the Women's Circle back home heard what we did called comforting, they'd be lining up to peel our hides if we were *fifty!*'

'At least it's "we," now, instead of "I,"' she said grimly. Rising smoothly, she advanced toward him shaking a furious finger. 'Do you think I'm a doll, farmboy? Do you think I am too dimwitted to let you know if I didn't want your touch? Do you think I couldn't let you know in no uncertain terms?' Her free hand produced a knife from under her coat, gave it a flourish and tucked it back without slowing the torrent. 'I remember ripping your shirt off your back because you couldn't pull it over your head fast enough to suit me. That's how little I wanted your arms around me! I did with you what I've never done with any man – and don't you think I was never tempted! – and you say it was all you! As if I wasn't even there!'

The back of his legs hit a chair, and he realized he had been backing away from her. Frowning up at him, she muttered, 'I don't think I *like* you looking down at me right now.' Abruptly she kicked him hard on the shin, planted both hands on his chest, and shoved. He toppled into the chair so hard it nearly went over backward. Ringlets swayed as she gave her head a toss and adjusted her brocaded coat.

'That's as may be, Min, but—'

'That's as *is*, sheepherder,' she cut in firmly, 'and if you say different again, you had best shout for the Maidens and channel for all you're worth, because I'll thump you around this room till you squeal for mercy. You need a shave. And a bath.'

Rand took a deep breath. Perrin had such a serene marriage, with a smiling, gentle wife. Why was it that he always seemed drawn to women who spun his head like a top? If only he knew the tenth part of what Mat did about women, he would have known what to say to all that, but as it was, all he could do was blunder on. 'In any case,' he said cautiously, 'there's only one thing I can do.'

'And what might that be?' She folded her arms tight beneath her breasts, and her foot began tapping ominously, but he knew this was the right thing to do.

'Send you away.' Just as he had Elayne, and Aviendha. 'If I had any self-control, I wouldn't have—' That foot started tapping faster. Maybe better to leave that alone. Comforted? Light! 'Min, anyone close to me is in danger. The Forsaken aren't the only ones who would harm somebody near me just on the chance it might harm me, too. And now there's me, as well. I can't control my temper any more. Min, I nearly killed Perrin! Cadsuane was right. I'm going mad, or there already. I have to send you away so you'll be safe.'

'Who is this Cadsuane?' she said, so calmly that he gave a start at noticing that her foot was still tapping. 'Alanna mentioned that name as if she was the Creator's sister. No, don't tell me; I don't care.' Not that she gave him one hair of a gap to tell anything. 'I don't care about Perrin, either. You would hurt me as soon as him. I think that great public fight of yours was a fake, is what I think. I don't care about your temper, and I don't care whether you're mad.

You can't be very mad, or you'd not be worrying about it so. What I do care about . . .'

She bent until those very big, very dark eyes were level with his, not a great distance away, and suddenly there was such a light glaring in them that he seized *saidin*, ready to defend himself. 'Send me away to be safe?' she growled. 'How dare you? What right do you think you have to send me anywhere? You need me, Rand al'Thor! If I told you half the viewings I've had about you, half your hair would curl and the rest fall out! You dare! You let the Maidens face any risk they want, and you want to send me away like a child?'

'I don't love the Maidens.' Floating deep in the emotionless Void, he heard those words spring from his tongue, and shock shattered the emptiness and sent *saidin* flying.

'Well,' Min said, straightening. A small smile added more curve to her lips. 'That's out of the way.' And she sat down on his lap.

She had said he would not hurt Perrin any more than he would her, but he had to hurt her now. He had to, for her own good. 'I love Elayne, too,' he said brutally. 'And Aviendha. You see what I am?' For some reason, that did not seem to faze her at all.

'Rhuarc loves more than one woman,' she said. Her smile seemed almost of Aes Sedai serenity. 'So does Bael, and I never noticed any Trolloc's horns on either. No, Rand, you love me, and you can't back out of that. I ought to string you up on tenterhooks for what you've put me through, but . . . Just so you'll know, I love you, too.' The smile faded in a frown of internal struggle, and finally she sighed. 'Life would be a deal easier sometimes if my aunts hadn't brought me up to be fair,' she muttered. 'And to be fair, Rand, I have to tell you that Elayne loves you, too. So does Aviendha. If both of Mandelain's wives can love him, I suppose three women can manage to love you. But I'm here, and if you try to send me away, I'll tie myself to your leg.' Her nose wrinkled. 'Once you start bathing again, anyway. But I won't go, no matter what.'

Just exactly like a top, his head spun. 'You – *love* me?' he said incredulously. 'How do you know what Elayne feels? How do you know anything about Aviendha? Light! Mandelain can do what he likes, Min; I'm not Aiel.' He frowned. 'What was that you said about telling me half of what you see? I thought you told me everything. And I am too sending you somewhere safe. And stop doing your nose like that! I don't smell!' He jerked the hand he had been scratching with from under his coat.

Her arched eyebrow spoke volumes, but of course her tongue had to have its bit, too. 'You dare take that tone? Like you don't believe it?' Suddenly her voice began to rise by the word, and she augured a finger against his chest as though she meant to drive it through him. 'Do you think I'd go to *bed* with a man I did not love? Do you? Or maybe you think you aren't worth loving? Is that it?' She made a sound like a stepped-on cat. 'So I'm some little bit of fluff without a brain in her head, falling in love with a worthless lout, am I? You sit there gaping like a sick ox and slander my wits, my taste, my—'

'If you don't quiet down and talk sense,' he growled, 'I swear, I'll smack your bottom!' That leaped out of nowhere, out of sleepless nights and confusion, but before he could begin to form an apology, she smiled. The woman smiled!

'At least you're not sulking anymore,' she said. 'Don't ever whine, Rand; you are no good at it. Now, then. You want sense? I love you, and I will not go. If you try to send me away, I'll tell the Maidens you ruined me and cast me aside. I'll tell everybody who will listen. I will—'

He raised his right hand and studied the flat of his palm, where the branded heron stood clear, then looked at her. She eyed his hand warily and shifted herself on his knees, then conspicuously ignored everything except his face.

'I won't go, Rand,' she said quietly. 'You need me.'

'How do you do it?' he sighed, slumping back in the chair. 'Even when you stand me on my head, you make all my troubles shrink.'

Min sniffed. 'You need to be stood on your head more often. Tell me. This Aviendha. I don't suppose there is any chance she's bony and scarred, like Nandera.'

He laughed in spite of himself. Light, how long since he had laughed with pleasure? 'Min, I'd say she is as pretty as you, but how can you compare two sunrises?'

For a moment she stared at him with a small smile, as if she could not decide whether to be surprised or delighted. 'You are a very dangerous man, Rand al'Thor,' she murmured, leaning toward him slowly. He thought he might fall into her eyes and be lost. All those times before when she sat on his lap and kissed him, all those times he had thought she was only teasing a country boy, he had nearly crawled out of his skin wanting to kiss her forever. Now, if she kissed him again now ...

Taking her firmly by the arms, he stood and set her on her feet. He loved her, and she loved him, but he had to remember that he wanted to kiss Elayne forever when he thought about her, and Aviendha. Whatever Min said about Rhuarc or any Aielman, she had made a poor bargain the day she fell in love with him. 'You said half, Min,' he said quietly. 'What viewings haven't you told me?'

She looked up at him with what almost might have been frustration, except of course that it could not have been. 'You're in love with the Dragon Reborn, Min Farshaw,' she grumbled, 'and best you remember it. Best you did, too, Rand,' she added, pulling away. He let her go reluctantly, eagerly; he did not know which. 'You've been back in Cairhien half a week, and you still have done nothing about the Sea Folk. Berelain thought you might drag your feet again. She left me a letter, asking me to keep reminding you, only you wouldn't let me— Well, never mind that. Berelain thinks they're important to you somehow; she says you're the fulfillment of some prophecy of theirs.'

'I know all about that, Min. I—' He had thought to leave the Sea Folk out of being tangled with him; they were not mentioned in the Prophecies of the Dragon that he could find. But if he was going to let Min stay near him, let her risk the dangers ... She had won, he realized. He had watched Elayne walk away with his heart sinking, watched Aviendha go with his stomach in knots. He could not do it again. Min stood there waiting. 'I'll go to their ship. I'll go today. The Sea Folk can kneel to the Dragon Reborn in all his splendor. I don't suppose there was ever any hope for anything else. Either they're mine, or they're my enemies. That is how it always seems to be. Will you tell me about those viewings, now?'

'Rand, you should study what they're like before you—'

'The viewings?'

She folded her arms and frowned up at him through her lashes. She chewed her lip and frowned at the door. She shook her head and muttered under her breath. At last she said, 'There is only one, really. I was exaggerating. I saw you and another man. I couldn't make out either face, but I knew one was you. You touched, and seemed to merge into one another, and ...' Her mouth tightened worriedly, and she went on in a very small voice. 'I don't know what it means, Rand, except that one of you dies, and one doesn't. I— Why are you grinning? This isn't a joke, Rand. I do not know which of you dies.'

'I'm grinning because you've given me very good news,' he said, touching her cheek. The other man had to be Lews Therin. *I'm not just insane and hearing voices*, he thought, jubilant. One lived and one died, but he had known for a long time that he was going to die. At least he was not mad. Or not as far mad as he had feared. There was still the temper he could barely control. 'You see, I—'

Suddenly he realized that he had gone from touching her cheek to cupping her face in both hands. He pulled them away as if burned. Min pursed her lips and gave him a reproving look, but he was not going to take advantage of her. It would not be fair to her. Luckily, his stomach rumbled loudly.

'I need something to eat, if I'm going to see the Sea Folk. I saw a tray ...'

Min made a sound more snort than sniff as he turned away, but the next moment she was sailing toward the tall doors. 'You need a bath, if *we're* going to the Sea Folk.'

Nandera was delighted, nodding enthusiastically and sending Maidens running. Though she did lean close to Min and say, 'I should have let you in the first day. I wanted to kick him, but it is not done, kicking the *Car'a'carn*.' By her tone, it should have been done. She spoke softly, yet not so softly he could not hear. He was sure that was deliberate; she directed too sharp a glare at him for it not to be.

Maidens lugged in the big copper tub themselves, flashing handtalk once they set it down, laughing and too excited to let the

Sun Palace servants do the work, or bring in the stream of buckets filled with hot water, either. Rand had a hard time taking his own clothes off. For that matter, he had a hard time washing himself, and he could not escape Nandera lathering his hair. Flaxen-haired Somara and fiery-haired Enaila insisted on shaving him as he sat chest-deep in the tub, concentrating so intently they seemed afraid they might cut his throat. He was used to that from other times they had refused to let him handle brush and razor himself. He was used to the Maidens who stood around watching, offering to scrub his back or his feet, hands flickering in silent chatter and still more than half-scandalized at the sight of someone *sitting* in water. Besides, he managed to get rid of some, at least, by sending them off carrying orders.

What he was not used to was Min, sitting cross-legged on the bed with her chin on her hands, watching the whole thing in very evident fascination. In all the crowd of Maidens, he had not realized she was there until he was naked, and all there was to do then was sit down as fast as he could, splashing water over the sides of the tub. The woman would have done very well as a Maiden herself. She discussed him with the Maidens quite openly, with never a blush! He was the one who blushed.

'Yes, he is very modest,' she said, agreeing with Malindare, a woman more rounded than most Maidens, with the darkest hair Rand had seen on any Aiel. 'Modesty is a man's crowning glory.' Malindare nodded soberly, but Min wore a grin that nearly split her cheeks.

And, 'Oh, no, Domeille; it would be a shame to spoil such a pretty face with a scar.' Domeille, grayer than Nandera, leaner, and with a thrusting chin, insisted that he was not pretty enough to do without a scar to set off what beauty he had. Her words. The rest was worse. The Maidens had always seemed to enjoy making his face red. Min certainly did.

'You have to dry off sooner or later, Rand,' she said, holding up a long piece of white toweling with both hands. She stood a good three paces from the tub, and the Maidens had all backed into a watching ring. Min's smile was so innocent any magistrate would have found her guilty on that alone. 'Come and get dry, Rand.'

He had never been so relieved to pull on clothes in his life.

By that time, all his orders had been carried out, and everything was in readiness. Rand al'Thor might have been routed in a bathtub, but the Dragon Reborn was going to the Sea Folk in a style that would send them plummeting to their knees with awe.

CHAPTER 34

Ta'veren

All was ready as Rand had ordered in the courtyard at the front of the Sun Palace. Or almost all. The morning sun slanted shadows from the stepped towers, so only ten paces in front of the tall bronze gates stood in full light. Dashiva and Flinn and Narishma, the three Asha'man he had retained, waited beside their horses, even Dashiva resplendent with the silver sword and red-and-gold Dragon on his black collar, though he still managed to handle the sword at his hip as if constantly surprised to find it there. A hundred of Dobraine's armsmen sat their mounts behind Dobraine himself with two long banners that hung down in the still air, their dark armor newly lacquered so it glistened in the sun, and silk streamers of red and white and black tied below the heads of their lances. They raised a cheer when Rand appeared, his swordbelt with its gilded Dragon buckle strapped over a red coat heavy with gold.

'Al'Thor! Al'Thor! Al'Thor!' filled the courtyard. People crowding the archers' balconies joined in, Tairen and Cairhienin in their silks and laces who just a week before had no doubt cheered Colavaere as loudly. Men and women who would as soon he had never returned to Cairhien, some of them, waving their arms and giving voice. He raised the Dragon Scepter to acknowledge them, and they roared louder.

A thunderous roll of drums and a blare of trumpets rose through the cheers, produced by a dozen more of Dobraine's men who wore crimson tabards with the black-and-white disc on the chest, half carrying long trumpets draped in identical cloths, the other half with kettle drums also decorated slung on either side of the horses. Five Aes Sedai in their shawls came to meet him as he descended the broad stairs. At least, they glided toward him. Alanna gave him one searching look with those big dark penetrating eyes – the tiny knot of emotions in his skull said she was calmer, more relaxed, than he ever remembered – one searching look, then she made a small motion, and Min touched his arm and went aside with her. Bera and the others made small curtsies, inclining their heads slightly, as Aiel streamed out of the palace behind him. Nandera led two hundred Maidens – they were not about to be outshone by the 'oathbreakers' – and Camar, a rangy Bent Peak Daryne grayer than Nandera and half a head taller than Rand, led two hundred *Seia Doon* who would not be outshone by *Far Dareis Mai*, let alone Cairhienin. They swung past on either side of him and the Aes Sedai to ring the courtyard. Bera like a proud farmwife and Alanna like some darkly beautiful queen, in their green-fringed shawls, and plump Rafela, even darker wrapped in her blue, watching him anxiously, and cool-eyed Faeldrin, yet another Green, her thin braids worked with colored beads, and slim Merana in her gray, whose frown made Rafela seem a picture of Aes Sedai serenity. Five.

'Where are Kiruna and Verin?' he demanded. 'I called for all of you.'

'So you did, my Lord Dragon,' Bera answered smoothly. She made another curtsy, too; only the slightest dip, but it took him aback. 'We could not find Verin; she is somewhere in the Aiel tents. Questioning the ...' her smooth tone faltered for one instant '... the prisoners, I believe, in an attempt to learn what was planned once they reached Tar Valon.' Once he reached Tar Valon; she knew enough not to blurt that where anyone could hear. 'And Kiruna is ... consulting with Sorilea on a matter of protocol. But I'm quite certain she will be more than happy to join us if you send a personal summons to Sorilea. I could go myself, if you—'

He waved that away. Five should be enough. Perhaps Verin could learn something. Did he want to know? And Kiruna. A matter of *protocol*? 'I'm glad you are getting on with the Wise Ones.' Bera started to speak, then closed her mouth firmly. Whatever Alanna was saying to Min, scarlet spots had flared in Min's cheeks and had raised her chin, though oddly, she seemed to be replying calmly enough. He wondered whether she would tell him. One thing he was sure of about women was that every last one had secret places in her heart, sometimes shared with another woman but never with a man. The only thing he was sure of about women.

'I didn't come out here to stand all day,' he said irritably. The Aes Sedai had arranged themselves with Bera in the lead, the others half a step back. If it had not been her, it would have been Kiruna. Their own arrangements, not his. He did not really care so long as they held to their oaths, and he might have left it alone if not for Min and Alanna. 'Merana will speak for you from now on; you will take your orders from her.'

By the suddenly widened eyes, you would have thought he had slapped every one of them. Including Merana. Even Alanna's head whipped around. Why should they be startled? True, Bera or Kiruna had done almost all the talking since Dumai's Wells, but Merana had been the ambassador sent to Caemlyn.

'If you are ready, Min?' he said, and without waiting for a reply strode out into the courtyard. The big, fiery-eyed black gelding he had ridden back from Dumai's Wells had been brought out for him, with a high-cantled saddle all worked in gold and a crimson saddlecloth embroidered with the disc of black-and-white at each corner. The trappings suited the animal, and his name. Tai'daishar; in the Old Tongue, Lord of Glory. Horse and trappings both suited the Dragon Reborn.

As he mounted, Min led up the mouse-colored mare she had ridden back, snugging on her riding gloves before swinging into the saddle. 'Seiera's a fine animal,' she said, patting the mare's arched neck. 'I wish she was mine. I like her name, too. We call the flower a blue-eye around Baerlon, and they grow everywhere in the spring.'

'She's yours,' Rand said. Whichever Aes Sedai the mare belonged to would not refuse to sell to him. He would give Kiruna a thousand crowns for Tai'daishar; she could not complain then; the finest stallion of Tairen blood stock never cost a tenth of that. 'Did you have an interesting conversation with Alanna?'

'Nothing that would interest you,' she said off-handedly. But a faint touch of red stained her cheeks.

He snorted softly, then raised his voice. 'Lord Dobraine, I've kept the Sea Folk waiting long enough, I think.'

The procession drew crowds along the broad avenues and filled the windows and rooftops as word raced ahead. Twenty of Dobraine's lancers led, to clear the way, along with thirty Maidens and as many Black Eyes, then drummers, booming away – *Droom, droom, droom, DROOM-DROOM* – and the trumpeters punctuating that with flourishes. Shouts from the onlookers nearly drowned drums and trumpets alike, a wordless roar that could have been rage as easily as approbation. The banners streamed out, just ahead of Dobraine and behind Rand, the white Dragon Banner and the scarlet Banner of the Light, and veiled Aiel trotted alongside the lancers, whose streamers also floated in the air. Now and then a few flowers were hurled at him. Maybe they did not hate him. Maybe they only feared. It had to do.

'A train worthy of any king,' Merana said loudly, to be heard.

'Then it's enough for the Dragon Reborn,' he replied sharply. 'Will you stay back? And you, too, Min.' Other rooftops had held assassins. The arrow or crossbow bolt meant for him would not find its target in a woman today.

They did fall behind his big black, for all of three paces, and then they were right beside him again, Min telling him what Berelain had written about the Sea Folk on the ships, about the Jendai Prophecy and the Coramoor, and Merana adding what she knew of the prophecy, though she admitted that was not very much, little more than Min had.

Watching the rooftops, he listened with half an ear. He did not hold *saidin*, but he could feel it in Dashiva and the other two, right behind him. He did not feel the tingle that would announce the Aes Sedai embracing the Source, but he had told them not to, without permission. Perhaps he should change that. They did seem to be keeping their oath. How could they not? They were Aes Sedai. A fine thing if he took an assassin's blade while one of the sisters tried to decide whether serving meant saving him or obeying meant not channeling.

'Why are you laughing?' Min wanted to know. Seiera pranced closer, and she smiled up at him.

'This is no laughing matter, my Lord Dragon,' Merana said acidly on the other side. 'The Atha'an Miere can be very particular. Any people grow fastidious when it comes to their prophecies.'

'The world is a laughing matter,' he told her. Min laughed along with him, but Merana sniffed and went right back to the Sea Folk as soon as he stopped.

At the river, the high city walls ran out into the water, flanking long gray stone docks that stretched out from the quay. Riverships and boats and barges of every kind and size were tied everywhere, the crews on deck to see the commotion, but the vessel Rand sought stood ready and waiting, lashed end-on to the end of a dock where all the laborers had already been cleared off. A longboat, it was called, a low narrow splinter without any masts, just one staff in the bow, four paces tall, topped by a lantern and another at the stern. Nearly thirty paces in length and lined with as many long oars, it could not carry the cargo a sailing vessel the same size would, but it had no need to depend on the wind, either, and with a shallow draft, it could travel day and night, using rowers in shifts. Longboats were employed on the rivers for cargoes of importance and urgency. It had seemed appropriate.

The captain bowed repeatedly as Rand came down the boarding ramp with Min on his arm and the Aes Sedai and Asha'man at his heels. Elver Shaene was even skinnier than his craft in a yellow coat of Murandian cut that hung to his knees. 'It's an honor to be carrying you, my Lord Dragon,' he murmured, mopping his bald head with a large handkerchief. 'An honor, it is. An honor, indeed. An honor.'

Plainly the man would rather have had his ship brim full of live vipers. He blinked at the Aes Sedai's shawls and stared at their ageless faces and licked his lips, eyes flickering from them to Rand uneasily. The Asha'man dropped his mouth open once he put their black coats together with rumor, and thereafter he avoided so much as a glance in their direction. Shaene watched Dobraine lead the men with the banners aboard, and the trumpeters, and the drummers lugging their drums, then eyed the horsemen lining the dock as if he suspected they might want to board, too. Nandera, with twenty Maidens, and Camar with twenty Black Eyes, all with *shoufa* wrapped around their heads though unveiled, made the captain step hastily to put the Aes Sedai between him and them. The Aiel wore scowls, for the heartbeat that needing to veil might slow them, but the Sea Folk might well know what a veil meant, and it would hardly do for them to think they were under attack. Rand thought Shaene's handkerchief might yet rub away what thin gray fringe of hair he had left.

The longboat swept away from the dock on its long oars, the two banners rippling in the bows, and the drums pounding, and the trumpets blaring. Out in the river, people appeared on the decks of ships to watch, even climbed into the rigging. On the Sea Folk ship they came out, too, many in bright colors unlike the drab clothing on the other vessels. The *White Spray* was a larger craft than most of the rest, yet somehow sleeker as well, with two tall masts raked back sharply and spars laid across them squarely where nearly all the other ships had slanting spars longer than the masts to hold most of their sails. Everything about it spoke of difference, but in one thing, Rand knew, the Atha'an Miere had to be like everyone else. They could either agree to follow him on their own or be forced to it; the Prophecies said he would bind together the people of every land – 'The north shall he tie to the east, and the west shall be bound to the south,' it said – and no one could be allowed to stand aside. He knew that now.

Sending out orders from his bath, he had not had an opportunity to give details of what he intended on reaching *White Spray*, so he announced them now. The details produced grins among the Asha'man, as expected – well, Flinn and Narishma grinned;

Dashiva blinked absently — and frowns among the Aiel, also as expected. They did not like being left behind. Dobraine merely nodded; he knew he was only here for show today. What Rand did not expect was the Aes Sedai reaction.

'It shall be as you command, my Lord Dragon,' Merana said, making one of those small curtsies. The other four exchanged glances, but they were curtsying and murmuring 'as you command' right behind her. Not one protest, not one frown, not a single haughty stare or recital of why it should be done any way but what he wanted. Could he begin to trust them? Or would they find some Aes Sedai way to wriggle around their oath as soon as his back was turned?

'They will keep their word,' Min murmured abruptly, just as if she had read his thoughts. With an arm wrapped around his and both hands holding his sleeve, she kept her voice for his ears alone. 'I just saw these five in your hand,' she added in case he did not understand. He was not sure he could fix his mind around that, even if she had seen it in a viewing.

He did not have long to try. The longboat flew through the water, and in no time at all was backing oars some twenty paces from the much taller *White Spray*. Drums and trumpets fell silent, and Rand channeled, making a bridge of Air laced with Fire that connected the longboat's railing to that of the Sea Folk ship. With Min on his arm, he started across, to every eye but that of an Asha'man, walking upward on nothing.

He half expected Min to falter, at least at first, but she simply walked at his side as though there were stone beneath her green-heeled boots.

'I trust you,' she said quietly. She smiled, too, partly a comforting smile, and partly, he thought, because she was amused at reading his mind once more.

He wondered how much she would trust if she knew that this was as far as he could weave a bridge like this. One pace further, one foot, and the whole thing would have given way at the first step. At that point it became like trying to lift yourself with the Power, an impossibility; even the Forsaken did not know why, any more than they knew why a woman could make a longer bridge than a man even if she was not as strong. It was not a matter of weight; any amount of weight could cross any bridge.

Just short of *White Spray*'s railing, he stopped, standing in midair. For all Merana's descriptions, the people staring back at him were a shock. Dark women and bare-chested men with colorful sashes that dangled to the knee, and gold or silver chains around their necks and rings in their ears, in their noses of all places on some of the women, who wore a rainbow of blouses above their dark, baggy breeches. None had any more expression than an Aes Sedai who was trying hard. Four of the women, despite being barefoot like the rest, wore bright silks, two of them brocades, and they had more necklaces and earrings than anyone else as well, with a chain strung with gold medallions running from an earring to a ring in the side of the nose. They said nothing, only stood together watching him, sniffing at small, lacy golden boxes that hung from chains around their necks. He addressed himself to them.

'I am the Dragon Reborn. I am the Coramoor.'

A collective sigh ran through the crew. Not among the four women, though.

'I am Harine din Togara Two Winds, Wavemistress to Clan Shodein,' announced the one with the most earrings, a handsome, full-mouthed woman in red brocade wearing five fat little gold rings in each ear. There were white streaks through her straight black hair, and fine lines at the corners of her eyes. She had an impressive dignity. 'I speak here for the Mistress of the Ships. If it pleases the Light, the Coramoor may come aboard.' For some reason she gave a start, and so did the three with her, but that sounded entirely too much like permission. Rand stepped onto the deck with Min wishing he had not waited.

He let the bridge go, and *saidin*, but immediately felt another bridge replace it. In short order the Asha'man and the Aes Sedai were with him, the sisters no more flustered than Min had been, though perhaps one or two did straighten her skirts a bit more than necessary. They were still not so easy around the Asha'man as they pretended.

The four Sea Folk women took one look at the Aes Sedai and

immediately gathered in a close huddle, whispering. Harine did a lot of the talking, and so did a young, pretty woman in green brocade with eight earrings altogether, but the pair in plain silk put in occasional comments.

Merana coughed delicately, and spoke softly into the hand she used to cover it. 'I heard her name you the Coramoor. The Atha'an Miere are great bargainers, I've heard, but I think she gave away something, then.' Nodding, Rand glanced down at Min. She was squinting at the Sea Folk women, but as soon as she noticed his look, she shook her head ruefully; she saw nothing yet that might help him.

Harine turned so calmly there might never have been any hasty conference. 'This is Shalon din Togara Morning Tide, Windfinder to Clan Shodein,' she said with a small bow toward the woman in green brocade, 'and this is Derah din Selaan Rising Wave, Sailmistress of *White Spray*.' Each woman bowed slightly as she was named, and touched fingers to her lips.

Derah, a handsome woman a little short of her middle years, wore plain blue and also eight earrings, though earrings, nose ring, and the chain that ran between was finer than Harine's or Shalon's. 'The welcome of my ship to you,' Derah said, 'and the grace of the Light be upon you until you leave his decks.' She made a small bow toward the fourth woman, in yellow. 'This is Taval din Chanai Nine Gulls, Windfinder of *White Spray*.' Only three rings hung from each of Taval's ears, fine like those of the Sailmistress. She looked younger than Shalon, no older than himself.

Harine took it up again, gesturing toward the raised stern of the ship. 'We will speak in my cabin, if it pleases you. A soarer is not a large vessel, Rand al'Thor, and the cabin is small. If it pleases you to come alone, all here stand surety for your safety.' So. From the Coramoor to plain Rand al'Thor. She would take back what she had given, if she could.

He was about to open his mouth and agree – anything to get this done; Harine was already moving that way, still gesturing for him to follow, the other women with her – when Merana gave another tiny cough.

'The Windfinders can channel,' she murmured hastily into her hand. 'You should take two sisters with you, or they'll feel they've gained the upper hand.'

Rand frowned. The upper hand? He *was* the Dragon Reborn, after all. Still . . . 'I will be pleased to come, Wavemistress, but Min here goes everywhere with me.' He patted Min's hand on his arm — she had not let go an instant — and Harine nodded. Taval was already holding the door open; Derah made one of those small bows, gesturing him toward it.

'And Dashiva, of course.' The man gave a start at his name, as if he had been asleep. At least he was not staring wide-eyed around the deck like Flinn and Narishma. Staring at the women. Stories spoke of the alluring beauty and grace of Sea Folk women, and Rand could certainly see that — they walked as if they would begin dancing on the next step, swaying sinuously — but he had not brought the men here to ogle. 'Keep your eyes open!' he told them harshly. Narishma colored, jerking himself stiffly erect, and pressed fist to chest. Flinn simply saluted, but both seemed more alert. For some reason, Min looked up at him with the tiniest wry smile.

Harine nodded a little more impatiently. A man stepped out from the crew, in baggy green silk breeches and with an ivory-hilted sword and dagger thrust behind his sash. More white-haired than she, he also wore five fat little rings in each ear. She waved him away even more impatiently. 'As it pleases you, Rand al'Thor,' she said.

'And of course,' Rand added, as though an afterthought, 'I must have Merana, and Rafela.' He was not certain why he chose the second name — perhaps because the plump Tairen sister was the only one not Green except Merana — but to his surprise, Merana smiled in approval. For that matter, Bera nodded, and so did Faeldrin, and Alanna.

Harine did not approve. Her mouth tightened before she could control it. 'As it pleases you,' she said, not quite so pleasantly as before.

Once he was inside the stern cabin, where everything except a few brass-bound chests seemed built into the walls, Rand was not so sure the woman had not gained whatever she wanted just bringing him there. For one thing, he was forced to stand hunched over, even between the roof beams, or whatever they were called on a ship. He had read several books about ships, but none mentioned that. The chair he was offered at the foot of the narrow table would not pull out, being fastened to the deck, and once Min showed him how to unlatch the chair arm and swing it out so he could sit, his knees hit the bottom of the table. There were only eight chairs. Harine sat at the far end, her back to the stern's red-shuttered windows, with her Windfinder to her left and the Sailmistress to her right and Taval below her. Merana and Rafela took the chairs below Shalon, while Min sat to Rand's left. Dashiva, with no chair, took a place beside the door, standing upright quite easily, though the roof beams almost brushed his head, too. A young woman in a bright blue blouse, with one thin earring in each ear, brought thick cups of tea, brewed black and bitter.

'Let's be done with this,' Rand said testily as soon as the woman left with her tray. He left his cup on the table after one sip. He could not stretch out his legs. He hated being confined. Thoughts of being doubled inside the chest flashed in his head, and it was all he could do to rein his temper. 'The Stone of Tear has fallen, the Aiel have come over the Dragonwall, all the parts of your Jendai Prophecy have come to pass. I am the Coramoor.'

Harine smiled across her cup, a cool smile with no amusement in it. 'That may be so, as it pleases the Light, but—'

'It *is* so,' Rand snapped despite a warning glance from Merana. She went so far as to nudge his leg with her foot. He ignored that, too. The cabin walls seemed closer, somehow. 'What is it that you don't believe, Wavemistress? That Aes Sedai serve me? Rafela, Merana.' He gestured sharply.

All he wanted was for them to come to him and be seen to come, but they set down their cups and rose gracefully, glided to either side of him – and knelt. Each took one of his hands in both of hers and pressed her lips to the back of it, right on the shining goldenmaned head of the Dragon that wound around his forearm. He just managed to conceal his shock, not taking his eyes from Harine. Her face went a little gray.

'Aes Sedai serve me, and so will the Sea Folk.' He motioned the sisters back to their seats. Oddly, they looked a touch surprised.

'That is what the Jendai Prophecy says. The Sea Folk will serve the Coramoor. I *am* the Coramoor.'

'Yes, but there is the matter of the Bargain.' That word was plainly capitalized in Harine's tone. 'The Jendai Prophecy says you will bring us to glory, and all the seas of the world will be ours. As we give to you, you must give to us. If I do not make the Bargain well, Nesta will hang me naked in the rigging by my ankles and call the First Twelve of Clan Shodein to name a new Wavemistress.' A look of utter horror stole across her face as those words came out of her mouth, and her black eyes went wider and wider by the word with disbelief. Her Windfinder goggled at her, and Derah and Taval tried so hard not to, their eyes fastened to the table, that it seemed their face might break.

And suddenly, Rand understood. *Ta'veren*. He had seen the effects, the sudden moments when the least likely thing happened because he was near, but he had never known what was going on before until it was finished. Easing his legs as best he could, he leaned his arms on the table. 'The Atha'an Miere will serve me, Harine. That is given.'

'Yes, we will serve you, but—' Harine half-reared out her chair, spilling her tea. 'What are you doing to me, Aes Sedai?' she cried, trembling. 'This is not fair bargaining!'

'We do nothing,' Merana said calmly. She actually managed to drink a swallow of that tea without wincing.

'You are in the presence of the Dragon Reborn,' Rafela added. 'The Coramoor your prophecy calls you to serve, as I believe.' She laid a finger to one round cheek. 'You said you speak for the Mistress of the Ships. Does that mean your word is binding on the Atha'an Miere?'

'Yes,' Harine whispered hoarsely, falling back in her seat. 'What I say binds every ship, and all to the Mistress of the Ships herself.' It was impossible for one of the Sea Folk to go white in the face, yet staring at Rand, she came as near as she could.

He smiled at Min, to share the moment. At last a people would come to him without fighting every step of the way, or splitting apart like the Aiel. Maybe Min thought he wanted her help to clinch matters, or maybe it was *ta'veren*. She leaned toward the

Wavemistress. 'You will be punished for what happens here today, Harine, but not so much as you fear, I think. At least, one day you will be the Mistress of the Ships.'

Harine frowned at her, then glanced to her Windfinder.

'She is not Aes Sedai,' Shalon said, and Harine seemed caught between relief and disappointment. Until Rafela spoke.

'Several years ago, I heard reports of a girl with a remarkable ability to see things. Are you she, Min?'

Min grimaced into her cup, then nodded reluctantly; she always said that the more people knew what she could do, the less good came of it. Glancing across the table at the Aes Sedai, she sighed. Rafela only nodded, but Merana was staring at her, hazel eyes avid in a mask of serenity. No doubt she expected to corner Min as soon as possible and find out what this talent was and how it worked, and no doubt Min expected it too. Rand felt a prickle of irritation; she should have known he would protect her from being bothered. A prickle of irritation, and a warmth that he could protect her from that, at least.

'You may trust what Min says, Harine,' Rafela said. 'The reports I heard say that what she sees always seems to come true. And even if she does not realize it, she has seen something else.' Her round face tilted to one side, and a smile curved her mouth. 'If you will be punished for what happens here, then it must mean you will agree to whatever your Coramoor wants.'

'Unless I agree to nothing,' Harine blustered. 'If I make no Bargain . . .' Her fists clenched on the tabletop. She had already admitted she had to make the Bargain. She had admitted the Sea Folk would serve.

'What I require of you is not onerous,' Rand said. He had thought about this since deciding to come. 'When I want ships to carry men or supplies, the Sea Folk will give them. I want to know what is happening in Tarabon and Arad Doman, and in the lands between. Your ships can learn – will learn – what I want to know; they call in Tanchico and Bandar Eban and a hundred fishing villages and towns between. Your ships can travel farther out to sea than anyone else's. The Sea Folk will keep watch as far west in the Aryth Ocean as they can sail. There is a people, the Seanchan, who live beyond the Aryth Ocean, and one day, they will come to try to conquer us. The Sea Folk will let me know when they come.'

'You require much,' Harine muttered bitterly. 'We know of these Seanchan, who come from the Islands of the Dead, it seems, from which no ship returns. Some of our ships have encountered theirs; they use the One Power as a weapon. You require more than you know, Coramoor.' For once, she did not pause at the title. 'Some dark evil has descended upon the Aryth Ocean. No ship of ours has come from there in many months. Ships that sail west, vanish.'

Rand felt a chill. He turned the Dragon Scepter, made from part of a Seanchan spear, in his hands. Could they have returned already? They had been driven back once, at Falme. He carried the spearhead to remind him that there were more enemies in the world than those he could see, but he had been sure it would take the Seanchan years to recover from their defeat, driven into the sea by the Dragon Reborn and the dead heroes called back by the Horn of Valere. Was the Horn still in the White Tower? He knew it had been taken there.

Suddenly he could not bear the confines of the cabin any longer. He fumbled with the latch on the chair arm. It would not open. Gripping the smooth wood, he tore the arm off in splinters with one convulsive heave. 'We've agreed the Sea Folk will serve me,' he said, pushing himself up. The low ceiling made him hunch over the table threateningly. The cabin did feel smaller. 'If there is any more to your Bargain, Merana and Rafela here will see to it with you.' Without waiting for an answer, he spun for the door, where Dashiva appeared to be muttering to himself again.

Merana caught him there, caught his sleeve and spoke swiftly and low. 'My Lord Dragon, it would be for the best if you remained. You have seen what your being *ta'veren* has done already. With you here, I believe she will continue to reveal what she wants to hide and give agreement before we give anything.'

'You are Gray Ajah,' he told her harshly. 'Negotiate! Dashiva, come with me.'

On deck, he drew deep breaths. The cloudless sky was open overhead. Open.

It took him a moment to notice Bera and the other two sisters, watching him expectantly. Flinn and Narishma kept to what they were supposed to do, a quarter of an eye on the ship and the rest on the riverbanks, the city on one side and the half-rebuilt granaries on the other. A ship in midriver was a vulnerable place to be if one of the Forsaken decided to strike. For that matter, anywhere was a dangerous place then. Rand could not understand why one of them had not at least tried to destroy the Sun Palace around his ears.

Min took his arm, and he gave a start.

'I'm sorry,' he said. 'I shouldn't have left you.'

'That's all right,' she laughed. 'Merana is already setting to work. I think she means to get you Harine's best blouse, and maybe her second best as well. The Wavemistress looked like a rabbit caught between two ferrets.'

Rand nodded. The Sea Folk were his, or as good as. What matter whether the Horn of Valere was in the White Tower? He was *ta'veren*. He was the Dragon Reborn, and the Coramoor. The golden sun still burned well short of its noon peak. 'The day is young yet, Min.' He could do anything. 'Would you like to see me settle the rebels? A thousand crowns to a kiss, they're mine before sunset.'

CHAPTER 35

Into the Woods

Sitting cross-legged on Rand's bed, Min watched him, in his shirtsleeves, rooting through the coats in the huge ivory-inlaid wardrobe. How could he sleep in this room, with all its black, heavy furniture? A part of her thought absently about moving everything out, replacing it with some carved pieces she had seen in Caemlyn lightly touched with gilding, and pale draperies and linens that he would find less oppressive. Odd; she had never cared one way or another about furniture, or linens. But that one tapestry of a battle, of a lone swordsman surrounded by enemies and about to be overwhelmed – that definitely had to go. Mostly, though, she just watched him.

There was such an intent look in his morning-blue eyes, and the snowy shirt tightened across the broad of his back when he turned to reach deep into the wardrobe's interior. He had very good legs, and marvelous calves, shown off well in dark close-fitting breeches, with his boots turned down. Sometimes he frowned, combing fingers through dark reddish hair; no amount of brushing could make it ruly; it always curled slightly around his ears and on the nape of his neck. She was not one of those fool women who tossed their brains at a man's feet along with their hearts. It was just that sometimes, near him, thinking clearly became a trifle difficult. That was all.

Coat after embroidered silk coat came out and was tossed to the floor atop the one he had worn to the Sea Folk ship. Could the negotiations still be going half so well without his *ta'veren* presence? If only she had a really useful viewing of the Sea Folk. As always to her eyes, images and colorful auras flickered around him, most gone too quickly to make out, all but one meaningless to her at the moment. That one viewing came and went a hundred times a day, and whenever Mat or Perrin were present, it encompassed them, too, and sometimes others. A vast shadow lurked over him, swallowing up thousands upon thousands of tiny lights like fireflies that hurled themselves into it in an attempt to fill up the darkness. Today, there seemed to be countless tens of thousands of fireflies, but the shadow seemed larger, too. Somehow that viewing represented his battle with the Shadow, but he almost never wanted to know how it stood. Not that she could really say, except that the shadow always seemed to be winning, to one degree or another. She sighed with relief to see the image go.

A tiny stab of guilt made her shift her seat on the coverlet. She had not really lied when he asked what viewings she had kept back. Not really. What good to tell him he would almost certainly fail without a woman who was dead and gone? He became bleak too easily as it was. She had to keep his spirits up, make him remember to laugh. Except . . .

'I don't think this is a good idea, Rand.' Saying that might be a mistake. Men were strange creatures in so many ways; one minute they took reasonable advice, and the next did just the opposite. Deliberately did the opposite, it seemed. For some reason, though, she felt . . . protective . . . toward this towering man who could probably lift her with either hand. And that without his channeling.

'It is a wonderful idea,' he said, tossing down a blue coat with silver embroidery. 'I'm *ta'veren*, and today it seems to be working in my favor for a change.' A green coat with gold embroidery went to the floor.

'Wouldn't you rather comfort me again?'

He stopped dead, staring at her with a silver-worked red coat hanging forgotten in his hands. She hoped she was not blushing. Comforting. *Where did that idea ever come from?* she wondered silently. The aunts who had raised her were gentle, kind women, but they had strong notions of proper behavior. They had disapproved of her wearing breeches, disapproved of her working in stables, the job she loved best, since it brought her into contact with horses. There was no question what they would think of *comforting*, with a man she was not married to. If they ever found out, they would ride all the way from Baerlon just to skin her. And him, too, of course.

'I . . . need to keep moving while I'm sure it is still working,' he said slowly, then turned quite quickly back to the wardrobe. 'This will do,' he exclaimed, pulling out a plain coat of green wool. 'I didn't know this was in there.'

It was the coat he had worn coming back from Dumai's Wells, and she could see his hands tremble as he remembered. Trying to be casual, she got up and went to put her arms around him, crushing the coat between them as she laid her head against his chest.

'I love you' was all she said. Through his shirt she could feel the round, half-healed scar on his left side. She could recall when he got it as if it were yesterday. That had been the first time she ever held him in her arms, while he lay unconscious and near death.

His hands pressed against her back, squeezing her tight, squeezing the breath out of her, but then, disappointingly, they fell away. She thought he muttered something about 'not fair' under his breath. Was he thinking about the Sea Folk while she hugged him? He should be, really. Merana was a Gray, yet it was said the Sea Folk could make a Domani sweat. He should be, but ... She thought about kicking his ankle. Gently he moved her away and began pulling on the coat.

'Rand,' she said firmly, 'you can't be sure it will have any effect, just because it did on Harine. If you being *ta'veren* always affected everything, you'd have every ruler kneeling at your feet by now, and the Whitecloaks, too.'

'I'm the Dragon Reborn,' he replied haughtily, 'and today I can do anything.' Scooping up his sword belt, he fastened it around his waist. It bore a plain brass buckle, now. The gilded Dragon lay atop the coverlet on the bed. Gloves of thin black leather went on to cover the golden-maned heads on the backs of his hands and the herons branded on his palms. 'But I don't look like him, do I?' He spread his arms, smiling. 'They won't know until it's too late.'

She almost threw up her hands. 'You don't look much like a fool, either.' And let him take that how he would. The idiot eyed her askance, as if he was not sure. 'Rand, as soon as they see the Aiel, they will either run or start fighting. If you won't take any of the Aes Sedai, at least take those Asha'man. One arrow, and you're dead, whether you're the Dragon Reborn or a goatherd!'

'But I *am* the Dragon Reborn, Min,' he said seriously. 'And *ta'veren*. We are going alone, just you and me. That is, if you still want to come.'

'You're not going anywhere without me, Rand al'Thor.' She stopped herself from saying he would trip over his own feet if he did. This euphoria was almost as bad as the dark bleakness. 'Nandera won't like this.' She did not know exactly what went on between him and the Maidens – something very peculiar indeed, by the things she had seen – but any hope that that might stop him guttered out when he grinned like a small boy evading his mother.

'She won't know, Min.' He even had a twinkle in his eye! 'I do this all the time, and they never know.' He held out a gloved hand, expecting her to jump when he called.

There really was nothing to do but straighten her green coat, glance into the stand-mirror to make sure of her hair – and take his hand. The trouble was, she *was* all too ready to leap if he crooked a finger; she just wanted to make sure he never found out.

In the anteroom, he made a gateway atop the golden Rising Sun set in the floor, and she let him lead her through onto a hilly forest floor carpeted with dead leaves. A bird flashed away, flaring red wings. A squirrel appeared on a branch and chittered at them, lashing a furry white-tipped tail.

It was hardly the sort of woods she remembered from near Baerlon; there were not many real forests anywhere close to the city of Cairhien. Most of the trees stood four or five or even ten paces apart, tall leatherleafs and pines, taller oaks and trees she did not know, running across the flat she and Rand stood on and up a slope that began only a few spans off. Even the undergrowth seemed thinner than back home, the bushes and vines and briars spread out in patches, though some of those were not small. Everything was brown and dry. She plucked a lace-edged handkerchief from her sleeve and dabbed at the sweat that suddenly seemed to pop out on her face.

'Which way do we go?' she asked. By the sun, north lay over the slope, the direction she would choose. The city should lie about seven or eight miles in that direction. With luck, they could walk all the way back without encountering anyone. Or better, given her heeled boots and the terrain, not to mention the heat, Rand could decide to give up and make another gateway back to the Sun Palace. The palace rooms were cool compared to this.

Before he could answer, crackling brush and leaves announced someone coming. The rider who appeared on a long-legged gray gelding with bright-fringed bridle and reins was a Cairhienin woman, short and slender in a dark blue, nearly black, silk riding dress, horizontal slashes of red and green and white running from her neck to below her knees. The sweat on her face could not diminish her pale beauty, or make her eyes less than large dark pools. A small clear green stone hung on her forehead from a fine golden chain fastened in black hair that fell in waves to her shoulders.

Min gasped, and not for the hunting crossbow the woman carried casually raised in one green-gloved hand. For a moment, she was sure it was Moiraine. But . . .

'I do not recall seeing either of you in the camp,' the woman said in a throaty, almost sultry, voice. Moiraine's voice had been crystal. The crossbow lowered, still quite casually, until it pointed rock-steady at Rand's chest.

He ignored it. 'I thought I might like to take a look at your camp,' he said with a slight bow. 'I believe you are the Lady Caraline Damodred?' The slender woman inclined her head, acknowledging the name.

Min sighed regretfully, but it was not as if she had really expected Moiraine to turn up alive. Moiraine was the only viewing of hers that had ever failed. But Caraline Damodred herself, one of the leaders of the rebellion against Rand here in Cairhien, and a claimant to the Sun Throne . . . He really was pulling all the threads of the Pattern around him, to have her appear.

Lady Caraline slowly raised the crossbow to one side; the cord made a loud snap, launching the broadhead bolt into the air.

'I doubt one would do any good against you,' she said, walking her gelding slowly toward them, 'and I would not like you to think I was threatening you.' She looked once at Min – just a glance that ran head to toe, though Min was sure everything about her was filed away – but aside from that, Lady Caraline kept her eyes on Rand. She drew rein three paces away, just far enough he could not reach her afoot before she could dig in her heels. 'I can only think of one gray-eyed man with your height who might suddenly appear out of nowhere, unless perhaps you are an Aiel in disguise, but perhaps you will be so kind as to supply a name?'

'I am the Dragon Reborn,' Rand said, every bit as arrogant as he had been with the Sea Folk, yet if any *ta'veren* swirling of the Pattern was at work, the woman on the horse gave no evidence.

Rather than leaping down to fall to her knees, she merely

nodded, pursing her lips. 'I have heard so very much about you. I have heard you went to the Tower to submit to the Amyrlin Seat. I have heard you mean to give the Sun Throne to Elayne Trakand. I have also heard that you killed Elayne, and her mother.'

'I submit to no one,' Rand replied sharply. He stared up at her with eyes fierce enough to snatch her out of the saddle by themselves. 'Elayne is on her way to Caemlyn as we speak, to take the throne of Andor. After which, she will have the throne of Cairhien as well.' Min winced. Did he have to sound like a pillow stuffed full of haughty? She had hoped he had calmed down a bit after the Sea Folk.

Lady Caraline laid her crossbow across the saddle in front of her, running a gloved hand along it. Perhaps regretting that loosed bolt? 'I could accept my young cousin on the throne – better she than some, at least – but . . . ' Those big dark eyes that had seemed so liquid suddenly became stone. 'But I am not sure I can accept you in Cairhien, and I do not mean only your changes to laws and customs. You . . . change fate by your very presence. Every day since you came, people die in accidents so bizarre no one can believe them. So many husbands abandon their wives, and wives their husbands, that no one even comments upon it now. You will tear Cairhien apart just by remaining here.'

'Balance,' Min broke in hastily. Rand's face was so dark, he looked ready to burst. Maybe he had been right to come after all. Certainly there was no point letting him throw this meeting away in a tantrum. She gave no one a chance to speak. 'There is always a balance of good against bad. That's how the Pattern works. Even he doesn't change that. As night balances day, good balances harm. Since he came, there hasn't been a single stillbirth in the city, not one child born deformed. There are more marriages some days than used to be in a week, and for every man who chokes to death on a feather, a woman tumbles head over heels down three flights of stairs and, instead of breaking her neck, stands up without a bruise. Name the evil, and you can point to the good. The turning of the Wheel requires balance, and he only increases the chances of what might have happened anyway in nature.' Suddenly she colored, realizing they were both looking at her. Staring, more like.

'Balance?' Rand murmured, eyebrows lifting.

'I've been reading some of Master Fel's books,' she said faintly. She did not want anyone to think she was pretending to be a philosopher. Lady Caraline smiled at her tall saddlebow and toyed with her reins. The woman was *laughing* at her. She would show this woman what she could laugh at!

Abruptly a tall black gelding with the look of a warhorse came crashing through the undergrowth, ridden by a man well into his middle years, with close-cropped hair and a pointed beard. Despite his yellow Tairen coat, the fat sleeves striped with green satin, eyes of a startling pretty blue looked out of his damp, dark face, like pale polished sapphires. Not a particularly pretty man, but those eyes made up for a too-long nose. He carried a crossbow in one leather-gauntleted hand, and brandished a broadhead bolt in the other.

'This came down inches from my face, Caraline, and it has your markings! Just because there's no game is no reason—' He became aware of Rand and Min just then, and his drawn crossbow lowered toward them. 'Are these strays, Caraline, or did you find spies from the city? I've never believed al'Thor would continue to let us sit here unhindered.'

Half a dozen more riders appeared behind him, sweating men in fat-sleeved coats with satin stripes and perspiring women in riding dresses with wide, thick lace collars. All carrying crossbows. The last of those riders had not halted, horses stamping and tossing heads, before twice as many came struggling through the brush from another direction and pulled up near Caraline, slight, pale men and women in dark clothes with stripes of color sometimes to below the waist. All with crossbows. Servants afoot came after, laboring and panting with the heat, the men who would dress and carry any downed game. It hardly seemed to matter that none had more than a skinning knife at his belt. Min swallowed, and unconsciously began patting her cheeks with her handkerchief a little more vigorously. If even one person recognized Rand before he knew it . . .

Lady Caraline did not hesitate. 'Not spies, Darlin,' she said, turning her horse to face the Tairen newcomers. The High Lord Darlin

Sisnera! All that was needed now was Lord Toram Riatin. Min wished Rand's *ta'veren* tugging at the Pattern could be just a little less complete. 'A cousin and his wife,' Caraline went on, 'come from Andor to see me. May I present Tomas Trakand – from a minor branch of the House – and his wife Jaisi.' Min almost glared at her; the only Jaisi she had ever known had been a dusty prune before she was twenty, and sour and bad-tempered to boot.

Darlin's gaze swept over Rand again, lingered a moment on Min. He lowered his crossbow and bowed his head just a hair, a High Lord of Tear to a minor noble. 'You are welcome, Lord Tomas. It takes a brave man to join us in our present circumstances. Al'Thor may loose the savages on us any day.' The Lady Caraline gave him an exasperated look that he made a show of not seeing.

He noted that Rand's return bow was no more than his, however; noted, and frowned. A darkly handsome woman in his retinue muttered angrily under her breath – she had a long hard face, well-practiced in anger – and a stout fellow, scowling and sweating in a red-striped coat of pale green, heeled his horse forward a few steps as if thinking to ride Rand down.

'The Wheel weaves as the Wheel wills,' Rand said coolly, as though he noticed nothing. The Dragon Reborn to ... The Dragon Reborn to just about anybody, was what it was. Arrogance on a mountaintop. 'Not much happens as we expect. For instance, I heard you were in Tear, in Haddon Mirk.'

Min wished she dared speak up, dared say something to soothe him. She settled for stroking his arm. Casually. A wife – now there was a word that suddenly sounded fine – a wife idly patting her husband. Another fine word. Light, it was hard being fair! It was hardly *fair*, having to be fair.

'The High Lord Darlin is but lately come by longboat with a few of his close friends, Tomas.' Caraline's throaty tone never changed, but her gelding suddenly pranced, no doubt at a sharp heel, and under cover of regaining control she turned her back to Darlin and shot Rand a brief warning frown. 'Do not trouble the High Lord, Tomas.'

'I do not mind, Caraline,' Darlin said, slinging his crossbow from his saddle by a loop. He rode a little closer and rested an arm on his tall saddlebow. 'A man should know what he is stepping into. You may have heard the tales about al'Thor going to the Tower, Tomas. I came because Aes Sedai approached me months ago with suggestions that might happen, and your cousin informed me she had received the same. We thought we might put her on the Sun Throne before Colavaere could take it. Well, al'Thor is no fool; never believe he is. Myself, I think he played the Tower like a harp. Colavaere is hanged, he sits secure behind Cairhien's walls – without an Aes Sedai halter, I'll wager, no matter what rumor says – and until we find some way to extricate ourselves, we sit in his hand, waiting for him to make a fist.'

'A ship brought you,' Rand said simply. 'A ship could take you away.' Abruptly Min realized he was gently patting her hand on his arm. Trying to soothe her!

Startlingly, Darlin threw back his head and laughed. A great many women would forget his nose for those eyes and that laugh. 'So it would, Tomas, but I've asked your cousin to marry me. She will not say yes or no, but a man cannot abandon even a possible wife to the mercies of the Aiel, and she will not leave.'

Caraline Damodred drew herself up on her saddle, face cold enough to shame an Aes Sedai, but suddenly auras of red and white flashed around her and Darlin, and Min knew. The colors never seemed to matter, but she knew that they would marry – after Caraline had led him a merry chase. More, to her eyes a crown suddenly appeared on Darlin's head, a simple golden circlet with a slightly curved sword lying on its side above his brows. The king's crown he would wear one day, though of what country, she could not say. Tear had High Lords instead of a king.

Image and auras vanished as Darlin pulled his horse around to face Caraline. 'There's no game to be found today. Toram has already returned to camp. I suggest we do the same.' Those blue eyes scanned the surrounding trees quickly. 'It seems your cousin and his wife have lost their horses. They will wander, in a careless moment,' he added to Rand, in a kindly tone. He knew very well they had no horses. 'But I'm sure Rovair and Ines will give up their mounts. A walk in the air will do them good.'

The stout man in the red-striped coat swung down from his tall bay immediately, with a toadying smile for Darlin and one markedly less warm if just as greasy for Rand. The angry-faced woman was a moment later in climbing stiffly from her silver-gray mare. She did not look pleased.

Neither was Min. 'You mean to go into their camp?' she whispered as Rand led her to the horses. 'Are you mad?' she added before thinking.

'Not yet,' he said softly, touching her nose with the tip of one finger. 'Thanks to you, I know that.' And he boosted her onto the mare, then climbed into the bay's saddle and heeled the animal up beside Darlin.

Heading north and a little toward the west, across the slope, they left Rovair and Ines standing beneath the trees frowning at one another sourly. As they fell in behind with the Cairhienin, the other Tairens shouted laughing wishes that the pair would enjoy the walk.

Min would have ridden alongside Rand, but Caraline put a hand on her arm, drawing her in back of the two men. 'I want to see what he does,' Caraline said quietly. Which one, Min wondered. 'You are his lover?' Caraline asked.

'Yes,' Min told her defiantly, once she could catch a breath. Her cheeks felt like fire. But the woman only nodded, as if it were the most natural thing in the world. Maybe it was, in Cairhien. Sometimes she realized that all the sophistication she had picked up talking to worldly people was about as thick as her blouse.

Rand and Darlin rode knee to knee just ahead, the younger man half a head taller than the older, each wrapped in pride like a cloak. But talking, just the same. Listening was not easy. They spoke quietly, and the dead leaves rustling under the horses' hooves, fallen branches cracking, often was enough to muffle their words. The cry of a hawk overhead or the chattering of a squirrel in a tree drowned them. Still, it was possible to overhear snatches.

'If I may say so, Tomas,' Darlin said at one point, as they headed down after the first rise, 'and under the Light I offer no disrespect, you are fortunate in having a beautiful wife. The Light willing, I will have one as beautiful myself.'

'Why do they not speak of something important?' Caraline muttered.

Min turned her head to hide a small smile. The Lady Caraline did not look half as displeased as she sounded. She herself had never cared whether anyone thought her pretty or not. Well, until she met Rand, anyway. Maybe Darlin's nose was not all that long.

'I would have let him take Callandor from the Stone,' Darlin said some time later, as they climbed a sparsely treed slope, 'but I could not stand aside when he brought Aiel invaders into Tear.'

'I've read the Prophecies of the Dragon,' Rand said, leaning forward on the bay's neck and urging the animal on. A fine glossy appearance the horse had, but no more bottom than his owner, Min suspected. 'The Stone had to fall before he could take Callandor,' Rand continued. 'Other Tairen lords follow him, so I hear.'

Darlin snorted. 'They cringe and lick his boots! I could have followed, if that was what he wanted, if . . . ' With a sigh, he shook his head. 'Too many ifs, Tomas. There is a saying in Tear. "Any quarrel can be forgiven, but kings never forget." Tear has not been under a king since Artur Hawkwing, but I think the Dragon Reborn is very like a king. No, he has attainted me with treason, as he calls it, and I must go on as I began. The Light willing, I may see Tear sovereign on its own land once more before I die.'

It had to be *ta'veren* work, Min knew. The man would never have spoken this way to someone casually met, Caraline Damodred's supposed cousin or not. But what did Rand think? She could hardly wait to tell him about the crown.

Topping that hill, they suddenly came on a knot of spearmen, some with a dented breastplate or helmet, most without either, who bowed as soon they saw the party. To left and right through the trees, Min could see other groups of sentries. Below, the camp lay spread out in what seemed a permanent haze of dust, down a nearly treeless slope and across the hill-valley and up the next hill. Each of the few tents was large, with some noble's banner hanging limply on a staff above the peak. Almost as many horses stood tied to picket lines as there were people, and thousands of men and a handful of women wandered among the cookfires and wagons. None raised a cheer as their leaders rode in.

Min studied them over the handkerchief she pressed to her

nose against the dust, not caring whether Caraline saw what she was doing. Dispirited faces watched them pass, and grim faces, people who knew they were in a trap. Here and there a House's *con* stood stiffly above some man's head, yet most seemed to be wearing whatever they could find, bits and pieces of armor that often neither matched nor fitted very well. A good many, though, men too tall for Cairhien, wore red coats under their battered breastplates. Min eyed a nearly obscured white lion worked on a filthy red sleeve. Darlin could only have brought a few people with him on a longboat, perhaps no more than his hunting party. Caraline looked to neither side as they rode through the camp, but whenever they came near those men in red coats, her mouth tightened.

Darlin dismounted before a tremendous tent, the largest Min had ever seen, larger than any she had ever imagined, a great red-striped oval, shining in the sunlight like silk, with no fewer than four high conical peaks, each with the Rising Sun of Cairhien stirring above in a lazy breeze, gold on blue. The strumming of harps drifted out amid the murmur of voices, like the sounds of geese. As servants took away the horses, Darlin offered his arm to Caraline. After a very long pause, she laid her fingers lightly on his wrist with no expression whatsoever, letting him escort her inside.

'My Lady wife?' Rand murmured with a smile, extending his arm.

Min sniffed and put her hand atop his. She would rather have hit him. He had no right to make a joke of that. He had no right to bring her here, *ta'veren* or no *ta'veren*. He could be killed here, burn him! But did he care if she spent the rest of her life weeping? She touched one of the striped doorflaps as they went in, and shook her head in wonder. It *was* silk. A *silk* tent!

No sooner were they inside than she felt Rand stiffen. Darlin's shrunken retinue, and Caraline's, jostled around them with insincere murmurs of apology. Between the four main tentpoles, long trestle tables groaning with food and drink stood about the colorful carpets that had been laid for a floor, and there were people everywhere, Cairhienin nobles in their finery, a few soldiers with the fronts of the heads shaved and powdered, plainly men of high rank by the fine cut of their coats. A handful of bards strolled playing through the crowd, picked out as much by a loftier air than any noble as by the carved and gilded harps they carried. Yet Min's eyes flew as if pulled to the sure source of Rand's worry, three Aes Sedai talking together in shawls fringed green and yellow and gray. Images and colors flashed around them, but not a thing she could make sense of. A swirl in the crowd revealed another, a comfortably round-faced woman. More images, more flaring colors, but all Min needed was the red-fringed shawl looped over her plump arms.

Rand tucked her hand under his arm and patted it. 'Don't worry,' he said softly. 'Everything is going well.' She would have asked him what they were doing there, but she was afraid he would tell her.

Darlin and Caraline had vanished into the crowd along with their followers, yet as a bowing serving man with stripes of red, green and white on his dark cuffs offered a tray of silver goblets to Rand and Min, she reappeared, shaking off the importunings of a hatchet-faced fellow in one of those red coats. He glared at her back as she took a goblet of punch and waved the servant away, and Min's breath caught at the aura that suddenly flashed around him, bruised hues so dark they seemed nearly black.

'Don't trust that man, Lady Caraline.' She could not stop herself. 'He will murder anyone he thinks is in his way; he'll kill for a whim, kill anybody.' She clamped her teeth shut before saying more.

Caraline glanced over her shoulder as the hatchet-faced man turned away abruptly. 'I could believe it easily of Daved Hanlon,' she said wryly. 'His White Lions fight for gold, not Cairhien, and loot worse than the Aiel. Andor became too hot for them, it seems.' That with an arch glance at Rand. 'Toram has promised him a great deal of gold, I think, and estates I know.' She tilted her eyes up to Min. 'Do you know the man, Jaisi?'

Min could only shake her head. How to explain what she did know about Hanlon now, that his hands would be red with more rapes and murders before he died? If she had known when or who . . . But all she knew was that he would. Anyway, telling about a viewing never changed it; what she saw happened, no matter who she warned. Sometimes, before she had learned better, it had happened because she warned.

'I've heard of the White Lions,' Rand said coldly. 'Look among them for Darkfriends, and you won't be disappointed.' They had been some of Gaebril's soldiers; Min knew that much, and little more, except that Lord Gaebril had really been Rahvin. It stood to reason that soldiers serving one of the Forsaken would include Darkfriends.

'What of him?' Rand nodded toward a man across the tent whose long dark coat had as many stripes as Caraline's dress. Very tall for a Cairhienin, perhaps less than a full head shorter than Rand, he was slender except for broad shoulders, and strikingly good-looking, with a strong chin and just a touch of gray at his dark temples. For some reason, Min's eyes were drawn to his companion, a skinny little fellow with a large nose and wide ears, in a red silk coat that did not fit him very well. He kept fingering a curved dagger at his belt, a fancy piece with a golden sheath and a large red stone capping the hilt that seemed to catch the light darkly. She saw no auras around him. He seemed vaguely familiar. They were both looking at her and Rand.

'That,' Caraline breathed in a tight voice, 'is Lord Toram Riatin himself. And his constant companion these past days, Master Jeraal Mordeth. Odious little man. His eyes make me want to take a bath. They both make me feel unclean.' She blinked, surprised at what she had said, but recovered quickly. Min had the feeling little put Caraline Damodred off her stride for long. In that, she was very like Moiraine. 'I would be careful were I you, Cousin Tomas,' she went on. 'You may have wrought some miracle or *ta'veren*-work on me – and perhaps even on Darlin – though I cannot say what it might come to – I make no promises – but Toram hates you with a passion. It was not so bad before Mordeth joined him, yet since . . . Toram would have us attack the city immediately, in the night. With you dead, he says, the Aiel would go, but I think it is you dead he seeks now even more than he does the throne.'

'Mordeth,' Rand said. His eyes were locked to Toram Riatin and the skinny fellow. 'His name is Padan Fain, and there are one hundred thousand golden crowns on his head.'

Caraline nearly dropped her goblet. 'Queens have been ransomed for less. What did he do?'

'He ravaged my home because it was my home.' Rand's face was frozen, his voice ice. 'He brought Trollocs to kill my friends because they were my friends. He is a Darkfriend, and a dead man.' Those last words came through clenched teeth. Punch splashed to the carpet as the silver goblet bent in his gloved fist.

Min felt sick for him, for his pain – she had heard what Fain had done in the Two Rivers – but she put a hand on Rand's chest in near panic. If he gave way now, channeled with who knew how many Aes Sedai around ... 'For the Light's sake, take hold of yourself,' she began, and a woman's voice spoke pleasantly behind her.

'Will you present me to your tall young friend, Caraline?'

Min looked over her shoulder, right into an ageless face, cool-eyed beneath iron-gray hair pulled up into a bun from which dangled small golden ornaments. Swallowing a squeak, Min coughed. She had thought Caraline had taken her in in one glance, but these cool eyes seemed to know things about her she herself had forgotten. The Aes Sedai's smile, as she adjusted her green-fringed shawl, was not nearly so pleasant as her voice.

'Of course, Cadsuane Sedai.' Caraline sounded shaken, but she smoothed her tone well before she finished introducing her visiting 'cousin' and his 'wife'. 'But I fear Cairhien is no place for them at present,' she said, all self-possession once more, smiling regret that she could not keep Rand and Min longer. 'They have agreed to take my advice and return to Andor.'

'Have they?' Cadsuane said dryly. Min's heart sank. Even if Rand had not spoken of her, it was clear from the way she looked at him that she knew him. Tiny golden birds and moons and stars swayed as she shook her head. 'Most boys learn not to stick their fingers into the pretty fire the first time they are burned, Tomas. Others need to be spanked, to learn. Better a tender bottom than a seared hand.'

'You know I'm no child,' Rand told her sharply.

'Do I?' She eyed him from head to toe, and made it seem no very great distance. 'Well, it seems I shall soon see whether or not you need spanking.' Those cool eyes drifted to Min, to Caraline, and with a final hitch to her shawl, Cadsuane herself drifted away into the crowd.

Min swallowed the lump in her throat, and was pleased to see Caraline do the same, self-possession or no. Rand – the blind fool! – stared after the Aes Sedai as though intending to go after her. This time it was Caraline who laid a hand on Rand's chest.

'I take it you know Cadsuane,' she said breathily. 'Be careful of her; even the other sisters stand in awe of her.' Her throaty tones took on a note of gravity. 'I have no idea what will come of today, but whatever it is, I think it is time you were gone, "Cousin Tomas." Past time. I will have horses—'

'This is your cousin, Caraline?' said a deep rich man's voice, and Min jumped in spite of herself.

Toram Riatin was even better-looking close up than at a distance, with the sort of strong male beauty and air of worldly knowledge that would have attracted Min before she met Rand. Well, she still found them attractive, just not as much as she did Rand. His firm-lipped smile was quite appealing.

Toram's gaze fell to Caraline's hand, still on Rand's chest. 'The Lady Caraline is to be my wife,' he said lazily. 'Did you know that?'

Caraline's cheeks reddened angrily. 'Do not say that, Toram! I have told you I will not, and I will not!'

Toram smiled at Rand. 'I think women never know their minds until you show them. What do you think, Jeraal? Jeraal?' He looked around, scowling. Min stared at him in amazement. And he was so pretty, with just the right air of . . . She wished she could call up viewings at will. She very much wanted to know what the future held for this man.

'I saw your friend scurry off that way, Toram.' Mouth twisted with distaste, Caraline gave a vague wave of her hand. 'You will find him near the drink, I think, or else bothering the serving girls.'

'Later, my precious.' He tried to touch her cheek, and looked amused when she stepped back. Without a pause he transferred his amusement to Rand. And the sword at his side. 'Would you care for a little sport, cousin? I call you that because we will be cousins, once Caraline is my wife. With practice swords, of course.'

'Certainly not,' Caraline laughed. 'He is a boy, Toram, and scarce knows one end of that thing from the other. His mother would never forgive me, if I allowed—'

'Sport,' Rand said abruptly. 'I might as well see where this leads. I agree.'

Chapter 36

Blades

Min did not know whether to groan or shout or sit down and cry. Caraline, staring wide-eyed at Rand, seemed in the same quandary.

With a laugh, Toram began rubbing his hands together. 'Listen, everyone,' he shouted. 'You are going to see some sport. Clear a space. Clear a space.' He strode off, waving people away from the center of the tent.

'Sheepherder,' Min growled, 'you're not wool-brained. You don't have *any* brains!'

'I would not put it quite so,' Caraline said in a *very* dry voice, 'but I suggest you leave, now. Whatever ... tricks ... you think you might use, there are seven Aes Sedai in this tent, four of them Red Ajah lately arrived from the south on their way to Tar Valon. Should one of them so much as suspect, I very much fear that whatever might have come of today, never will. Leave.'

'I won't use any . . . tricks.' Rand unbuckled his sword belt and handed it to Min. 'If I've touched you and Darlin in one way, maybe I can touch Toram in another.' The crowd was pushing back, opening up an area twenty paces across between two of the great centerpoles. Some looked to Rand, and there was a great deal of rib nudging and sly laughter. The Aes Sedai were offered pride of place, of course, Cadsuane and her two friends on one side, four ageless women in Red Ajah shawls on the other. Cadsuane and her companions were eyeing Rand with open disapproval and as close to irritation as any Aes Sedai ever let show, but the Red sisters looked more concerned with those three. At least, although they stood directly opposite, they managed to seem oblivious of the presence of any other sisters. No one could be that blind without trying.

'Listen to me, *cousin.*' Caraline's low voice almost crackled with urgency. She stood very close, her neck craned to look up at him. Barely reaching his chest, she seemed ready to box his ears. 'If you use none of your *special* tricks,' Caraline went on, 'he can hurt you badly, even with practice swords, and he will. He has never liked another touching what he thinks is his, and he suspects every pretty young man who speaks to me of being my lover. When we were children, he pushed a friend – a friend! – down the stairs and broke his back because Derowin rode his pony without asking. Go, cousin. No one will think less; no one expects a boy to face a blademaster. Jaisi . . . whatever your real name is . . . help me convince him!'

Min opened her mouth – and Rand laid a finger across her lips. 'I am who I am,' he smiled. 'And I don't think I could run from him if I wasn't. So, he's a blademaster.' Unbuttoning his coat, he strode out into the cleared area.

'Why must they be so stubborn when you least wish it?' Caraline whispered in tones of frustration. Min could only nod in agreement.

Toram had stripped to shirt and breeches, and carried two practice swords, their 'blades' bundles of thin lathes tied together. He raised an eyebrow at the sight of Rand with his coat simply hanging open. 'You will be confined in that, cousin.' Rand shrugged.

Without warning, Toram tossed one of the swords; Rand caught it out of the air by the long hilt.

'Those gloves will slip, cousin. You want a firm grip.'

Rand took the hilt in both hands and turned slightly sideways, blade down and left foot forward.

Toram spread his hands as if to say he had done all he could. 'Well, at least he knows how to stand,' he laughed, and on the last word darted forward, practice sword streaking for Rand's head with all his might behind it.

With a loud clack, bundled lathes met bundled lathes. Rand had moved nothing except his sword. For a moment, Toram stared at him, and Rand looked back calmly. Then they began to dance.

That was all Min could call it, that gliding, flowing movement, wooden blades flickering and spinning. She had watched Rand practice the sword against the best he could find, often against two or three or four at once, but that had been nothing to this. So beautiful, and so easy to forget that had those lathes been steel, blood could have flowed. Except that no blade, steel or lathes, touched flesh. Back and forth they danced, circling one another, swords now probing, now slashing, Rand attacking, now defending, and every movement punctuated by those loud clacks.

Caraline gripped Min's arm hard without taking her eyes from the contest. 'He is also a blademaster,' she breathed. 'He must be. Look at him!'

Min was looking, and hugging Rand's sword belt and scabbarded blade as if they were him. Back and forth in beauty, and whatever Rand thought, Toram already wished his blade was steel. Cold rage burned on his face, and he pressed harder, harder. Still no blade touched anything but another, yet now Rand backed away constantly, sword darting to defend, and Toram moved forward, attacking, eyes glittering with icy fury.

Outside, someone screamed, a wail of utter horror, and suddenly the huge tent snapped up into the air, vanishing into a thick grayness that hid the sky. Fog billowed on every side, filled with distant shrieks and bellows. Thin tendrils wafted into the clear inverted bowl left by the tent. Everyone stared in amazement. Almost everyone.

Toram's lathe blade smashed into Rand's side with a bone-crack sound, doubling him over. 'You are dead, cousin,' Toram sneered, lifting his sword high to strike again – and froze, staring, as part of the heavy gray mist overhead ... solidified. A tentacle of fog, it might have been, a thick three-toed arm, reaching down, closed around the stout Red sister, snatching her into the air before anyone had a chance to move.

Cadsuane was the first to overcome shock. Her arms rose, shaking back her shawl, her hands made a twist, and a ball of fire seemed to shoot upward from each palm, streaking into the mist. Above, something suddenly burst into flame, one violent gout that vanished immediately, and the Red sister fell back into sight, dropping with a thud facedown on the carpets near where Rand knelt on one knee clutching his side. At least, she would have been facedown had her head not been twisted around so her dead eyes stared up into the fog.

Whatever scraps of composure remained in the tent fled with that. The Shadow had been given flesh. Screaming people fled in every direction, knocking over tables, nobles clawing past servants and servants past nobles. Buffeted, Min fought her way to Rand with fists and elbows and his sword as a club.

'Are you all right?' she asked, pulling him to his feet. She was surprised to see Caraline on the other side, helping him, too. For that matter, Caraline looked surprised.

He took his hand from beneath his coat, fingers thankfully free of blood. That half-healed scar, so tender, had not broken open. 'I think we best move,' he said, taking his sword belt. 'We have to get out of this.' The inverted bowl of clear air was noticeably smaller. Almost everyone else had fled. Out in the fog, screams rose, most cutting off abruptly but always replaced by new.

'I agree, Tomas,' Darlin said. Sword in hand, he planted himself with his back to Caraline, between her and the fog. 'The question is, in which direction? And also, how far do we have to go?'

'This is his work,' Toram spat. 'Al'Thor's.' Hurling down his practice sword, he stalked to his discarded coat and calmly donned it. Whatever else he was, he was no coward. 'Jeraal?' he shouted at the fog as he fastened his sword belt. 'Jeraal, the Light burn you, man, where are you? Jeraal!' Mordeth – Fain – did not answer, and he went on shouting.

The only others still there were Cadsuane and her two

companions, faces calm but hands running nervously over their shawls. Cadsuane herself might have been setting out for a stroll. 'I should think north,' she said. 'The slope lies closer that way, and climbing may take us above this. Stop that caterwauling, Toram! Either your man's dead, or he can't hear.' Toram glared at her, but he did stop shouting. Cadsuane did not appear to notice or care, so long as he was silent. 'North, then. We three will take care of anything your steel can't handle.' She looked straight at Rand when she said that, and he gave a whisker of a nod before buckling his sword belt and drawing his blade. Trying not to goggle, Min exchanged glances with Caraline; the other woman's eyes looked as large as teacups. The Aes Sedai knew who he was, and she was going to keep anyone else from knowing.

'I wish we had not left our Warders back in the city,' the slim Yellow sister said. Tiny silver bells in her dark hair chimed as she tossed her head. She had almost as commanding an air as Cadsuane, enough that you did not realize how pretty she was at first, except that that toss of her head seemed . . . well . . . a touch petulant. 'I wish I had Roshan here.'

'A circle, Cadsuane?' the Gray asked. Head turning this way and that to peer at the fog, she looked like a plump, pale-haired sparrow with her sharp nose and inquisitive eyes. Not a frightened sparrow, but one definitely ready to take wing. 'Should we link?'

'No, Niande,' Cadsuane sighed. 'If you see something, you must be able to strike at it without waiting to point it out for me. Samitsu, stop worrying about Roshan. We have three fine swords here, two of them heron-mark, I see. They will do.'

Toram showed his teeth on seeing the heron engraved on the blade Rand had unsheathed. If it was a smile, it held no mirth. His own bared blade bore a heron, too. Darlin's did not, but he gave Rand and his sword a weighing look, then a respectful nod that was considerably deeper than he had offered plain Tomas Trakand, of a minor branch of the House.

The gray-haired Green had taken charge, clearly, and she kept it despite attempted protests from Darlin, who like many Tairens seemed not to relish Aes Sedai a great deal, and Toram, who just seemed to dislike anyone giving orders but himself. For that matter, so did Caraline, but Cadsuane ignored her frowns as completely as she did the men's voiced complaints. Unlike them, Caraline appeared to realize complaints would do no good. Wonder of wonders, Rand meekly let himself be placed to Cadsuane's right as she quickly arranged everyone. Well, not exactly meekly – he stared down his nose at her in a way that would have made Min slap him if he did it to her; Cadsuane just shook her head and muttered something that reddened his face – but at least he kept his mouth shut. Right then, Min almost thought he would announce who he was. And maybe expect the fog to vanish in fear of the Dragon Reborn. He smiled at her as though fog in this weather was nothing, even a fog that snatched tents and people.

They moved into the thick mist in a formation like a six-pointed star, Cadsuane herself in the lead, an Aes Sedai at each of two other points, a man with a sword at three. Toram, of course, protested loudly at bringing up the rear until Cadsuane mentioned the honor of the rear guard or some such. That quieted him down. Min had no objection whatsoever to her own position with Caraline in the center of the star. She carried a knife in either hand, and wondered whether they would be any use. It was something of a relief to see the dagger in Caraline's fist tremble. At least her own hands were steady. Then again, she thought she might be too frightened to shake.

The fog was cold as winter. Grayness closed around them in swirls, so heavy it was difficult to see the others clearly. Hearing was all too easy, though. Shrieks drifted through the murk, men and women crying out, horses screaming. The fog seemed to deaden sound, make it hollow, so that thankfully, those awful sounds seemed distant. The mist ahead began to thicken, but fireballs immediately shot from Cadsuane's hands, sizzling through the icy gray, and the thickening erupted in one roaring flare of flame. Roars behind, light flashing against the fog like lightning against clouds, spoke of the other two sisters at work. Min had no desire to look back. What she could see was more than enough.

Past trampled tents half obscured by gray haze they moved, past bodies and sometimes parts of bodies not nearly obscured enough. A leg. An arm. A man who was not there from the waist down.

Once a woman's head that seemed to grin from where it sat on the corner of an overturned wagon. The land began to slope upward, steeper. Min saw her first living soul besides them, and wished she had not. A man wearing one of the red coats staggered toward them, waving his left arm feebly. The other was gone, and wet white bone showed where half his face had been. Something that might have been words bubbled though his teeth; and he collapsed. Samitsu knelt briefly beside him, putting her fingers against the bloody ruin of his forehead. Rising, she shook her head, and they moved on. Upslope, and up, until Min began wondering whether they were climbing a mountain instead of a hill.

Right in front of Darlin, the fog suddenly began to take on form, a man-high shape, but all tentacles and gaping mouths full of sharp teeth. The High Lord might have been no blademaster, but he was not slow either. His blade sliced through the middle of the still-coalescing shape, looped and slashed it top to bottom. Four clouds of fog, thicker than the surrounding mist, settled to the ground. 'Well,' he said, 'at least we know steel can cut these ... creatures.'

The thicker chunks of fog oozed together, began to rise once more.

Cadsuane stretched out a hand, droplets of fire falling from her fingertips; one bright flash of flame seared the solidifying fog from existence. 'But no more than cut, so it seems,' she murmured.

Ahead to their right, a woman suddenly appeared in the swirling gray, silk skirts held high as she half ran, half fell down the slope toward them. 'Thank the Light!' she screamed. 'Thank the Light! I thought I was alone!' Right behind her the fog drew together, a nightmare all teeth and claws, looming above her. Had it been a man, Min was sure Rand would have waited.

His hand rose before Cadsuane could move, and a bar of ... something ... liquid white fire brighter than the sun ... shot out over the running woman's head. The creature simply vanished. For a moment there was clear air where it had been, and along the line that bar had burned, until the fog began closing in. A moment while the woman froze where she stood. Then, shrieking at the top of her lungs, she turned and ran from them, still downslope, fleeing what she feared more than nightmares in these mists.

'You!' Toram roared, so loudly that Min spun to face him with her knives raised. He stood pointing his sword at Rand. 'You are him! I was right! This is your work! You will not trap me, al'Thor!' Suddenly he broke away at an angle, scrambling wildly up the slope. 'You will not trap me!'

'Come back!' Darlin shouted after him. 'We must stick together! We must . . . ' He trailed off, staring at Rand. 'You *are* him. The Light burn me, you are!' He half-moved as if to place himself between Rand and Caraline, but at least he did not run.

Calmly, Cadsuane picked her way across the slope to Rand. And slapped his face so hard his head jerked. Min's breath caught in shock. 'You will not do that again,' Cadsuane said. There was no heat in her voice, just iron. 'Do you hear me? Not balefire. Not ever.'

Surprisingly, Rand only rubbed his cheek. 'You were wrong, Cadsuane. He's real. I'm certain of it. I know he is.' Even more surprisingly, he sounded as if he very much wanted her to believe.

Min's heart went out to him. He had mentioned hearing voices; he must mean that. She raised her right hand toward him, forgetting for the moment that it held a knife, and opened her mouth to say something comforting. Though she was not entirely sure she would ever be able to use that particular word innocuously again. She opened her mouth – and Padan Fain seemed to leap out of the mists behind Rand, steel gleaming in his fist.

'Behind you!' Min screamed, pointing with the knife in her outstretched right hand as she threw the one in her left. Everything seemed to happen at once, half-seen in wintery fog.

Rand began to turn, twisting aside, and Fain also twisted, to lunge for him. For that twist, her knife missed, but Fain's dagger scored along Rand's left side. It hardly seemed to more than slice his coat, yet he screamed. He screamed, a sound to make Min's heart clench, and clutching his side, he fell against Cadsuane, catching at her to hold himself up, pulling both of them down.

'Move out of my way!' one of the other sisters shouted – Samitsu, Min thought – and suddenly, Min's feet jerked out from under her. She landed heavily, grunting as she hit the slope together with Caraline, who snapped a breathless, 'Blood and fire!'

Everything at once.

'Move!' Samitsu shouted again, as Darlin lunged for Fain with his sword. The bony man moved with shocking speed, throwing himself down and rolling beyond Darlin's reach. Strangely, he cackled with laughter as he scampered to his feet and ran off, swallowed in the murk almost immediately.

Min pushed herself up shaking.

Caraline was much more vigorous. 'I will tell you now, Aes Sedai,' she said in a cold voice, brushing at her skirts violently, 'I will not be treated so. I am Caraline Damodred, High Seat of House ...'

Min stopped listening. Cadsuane was sitting on the slope above, holding Rand's head in her lap. It had only been a cut. Fain's dagger could not have more than touched ... With a cry, Min threw herself forward. Aes Sedai or no, she pushed the woman away from Rand and cradled his head in her arms. His eyes were closed, his breathing ragged. His face felt hot.

'Help him!' she screamed at Cadsuane, like an echo of the distant screams in the mist. 'Help him!' A part of her said that did not make much sense after pushing her away, but his face seemed to burn her hands, to burn sense.

'Samitsu, quickly,' Cadsuane said, standing and rearranging her shawl. 'He's beyond my Talent for Healing.' She laid a hand on the top of Min's head. 'Girl, I will hardly let the boy die when I haven't taught him manners, yet. Stop crying, now.'

It was very strange. Min was fairly sure the woman had done nothing to her with the Power, yet she believed. Teach him manners. A fine tussle that would be. Unfolding her arms from around his head, not without reluctance, Min backed away on her knees. Very strange. She had not even realized that she *was* crying, yet Cadsuane's reassurance was enough to stop the flow of tears. Sniffing, she scrubbed at her cheeks with the heel of her hand as Samitsu knelt beside him, placing fingertips on his forehead. Min wondered why she did not take his head in both hands, the way Moiraine did.

Abruptly Rand convulsed, gasping and thrashing so hard that a flailing arm knocked the Yellow over on her back. As soon as her fingers left him, he subsided. Min crawled nearer. He breathed more easily, but his eyes were still closed. She touched his cheek. Cooler than it had been, but still too warm. And pale.

'Something is amiss,' Samitsu said peevishly as she sat up. Pulling Rand's coat aside, she gripped the slice in his bloodstained shirt and ripped a wide gap in the linen.

The cut from Fain's dagger, no longer than her hand and not deep, ran right across the old round scar. Even in the dim light, Min could see that the edges of the gash looked swollen and angry, as if the wound had gone untended for days. It was no longer bleeding, but it should have been gone. That was what Healing did: wounds knitted themselves up right before your eyes.

'This,' Samitsu said in a lecturing tone, lightly touching the scar, 'seems like a cyst, but full of evil instead of pus. And this ...' She drew the finger down the gash. '... seems full of a different evil.' Suddenly she frowned at the Green standing over her, and her voice became sullen and defensive. 'If I had the words, Cadsuane, I would use them. I have never seen the like. Never. But I will tell you this. I think if I had been one moment slower, perhaps if you had not tried first, he would be dead now. As it is ...' With a sigh, the Yellow sister seemed to deflate, her face sagging. 'As it is, I believe he will die.'

Min shook her head, trying to say no, but she could not seem to make her tongue move. She heard Caraline murmuring a prayer. The woman stood gripping one of Darlin's coatsleeves with both hands. Darlin himself frowned down at Rand as though trying to make sense of what he saw.

Cadsuane bent to pat Samitsu's shoulder. 'You are the best living, perhaps the best ever,' she said quietly. 'No one has the Healing to compare with you.' With a nod, Samitsu stood, and before she was on her feet, she was all Aes Sedai serenity once more. Cadsuane, scowling down at Rand with her hands on her hips, was not. 'Phaw! I will not allow you to die on me, boy,' she growled, sounding as though it were his fault. This time, instead of touching the top of Min's head, she rapped it with a knuckle. 'Get to your feet, girl. You're no milksop – any fool can see that – so stop pretending. Darlin, you will carry him. Bandages must wait. This fog is not leaving us, so we had better leave it.'

Darlin hesitated. Maybe it was Cadsuane's peremptory frown, and maybe the hand Caraline half-raised to his face, but abruptly, he sheathed his sword, muttering under his breath, and hoisted Rand across his shoulders with arms and legs dangling.

Min took up the heron-mark blade and carefully slid it into the scabbard hanging from Rand's waist. 'He will need it,' she told Darlin, and after a moment, he nodded. A lucky thing for him he did; she had bundled all her confidence into the Green sister, and she was not about to let anyone think differently.

'Now be careful, Darlin,' Caraline said in that throaty voice once Cadsuane made their marching order clear. 'Be sure to stay behind me, and I will protect you.'

Darlin laughed till he wheezed, and was still chuckling when they began climbing through the cold fog and the distant shrieks once more, with him carrying Rand in the center and the women in a circle around him.

Min knew she was only another pair of eyes, just like Caraline on the other side of Cadsuane, and she knew the knife she carried unsheathed was no use against the mist-shapes, but Padan Fain might still be alive out there. She would not miss again. Caraline carried her dagger too, and by the looks she cast over her shoulder at Darlin staggering uphill under Rand's weight, maybe she also intended to protect the Dragon Reborn. And then again, maybe it was not him. A woman could forgive any amount of nose for that laugh.

Shapes still formed in the mist and died by fire, and once a huge something tore a shrieking horse in two off to their right before any Aes Sedai could slay it. Min was quite noisily sick after that, and not a bit ashamed; people were dying, but at least the people had come here by their own choice. The meanest soldier could have run away yesterday had he chosen, but not that horse. Shapes formed and died, and people died, screaming always in the distance, it seemed, though they still stumbled past torn carrion that had been human an hour gone. Min began to wonder whether they would ever see daylight again.

With shocking suddenness and no warning, she stumbled into it, one moment surrounded by gray, the next with the sun burning golden high overhead in a blue sky, all so bright she had to shade her eyes. And there, perhaps five miles across all but treeless hills, Cairhien rose solid and square on its own prominences. Somehow, it did not look quite real anymore.

Staring back at the edge of the fog, she shivered. It was an edge, a billowing wall, stretching though the trees on this hilltop, and far too straight, with no eddies or thinning. Just clear air here, and there, thick gray. A little more of a tree right in front of her became visible, and she realized the mist was creeping back, perhaps being burned off by the sun. But far too slowly to make the retreat natural. The others stared at it just as hard as she, even the Aes Sedai.

Twenty paces off to their left, a man suddenly scrambled into the clear air on all fours. The front of his head was shaved, and by the battered black breastplate he wore, he was a common soldier. Staring about wildly, he did not appear to see them, and went scrambling on down the hillside, still on hands and knees. Farther to the right, two men and a woman appeared, all running. She had stripes of color across the front of her dress, but how many was hard to say since she had gathered her skirts as high as she could to run faster, and she matched the men stride for stride. None of them looked to either side, only launched themselves down the hill, falling, tumbling and coming back to their feet running again.

Caraline studied the slim blade of her dagger for a moment, then thrust it hard into its sheath. 'So vanishes my army,' she sighed.

Darlin, with Rand still unconscious across his shoulders, looked at her. 'There is an army in Tear, if you call.'

She glanced at Rand, hanging like a sack. 'Perhaps,' she said. Darlin turned his head toward Rand's face with a troubled frown.

Cadsuane was all practicality. 'The road lies that way,' she said pointing west. 'It will be faster than walking cross-country. An easy stroll.'

Easy was not what Min would have called it. The air seemed twice as hot after the fog's cold; sweat rolled out of her, and seemed to drain her strength. Her legs wobbled. She tripped over exposed roots and fell flat on her face. She tripped over rocks and fell. She tripped over her own heeled boots and fell. Once her feet just went out from under, and she slid a good forty paces down the hillside on the seat of her breeches, arms flailing until she managed to snag a sapling. Caraline went sprawling as many times, and maybe more; dresses were not made for this sort of travel, and before long – after a tumble head over heels ended with her skirts around her ears – she was asking Min the name of the seamstress who made her coat and breeches. Darlin did not fall. Oh, he stumbled and tripped and skidded every bit as much as they, but whenever he started to fall, something seemed to catch him, to steady him on his feet. In the beginning he glared at the Aes Sedai, all proud Tairen High Lord who would carry Rand out without any help. Cadsuane and the others affected not to see. They never fell; they simply walked along, chatting quietly among themselves, and caught Darlin before he could. By the time they reached the road, he looked both grateful and hunted.

Standing in the middle of the broad road of hard-packed earth, in sight of the river, Cadsuane flung up a hand to stop the first conveyance that appeared, a rickety wagon drawn by two moth-eaten mules and driven by a skinny farmer in a patched coat who hauled on his reins with alacrity. What did the toothless fellow think he had run into? Three ageless Aes Sedai, complete with shawls, who might have stepped down from a coach a moment before. A sweat-soaked Cairhienin woman, of high rank by the stripes on her dress; or maybe a beggar who had clothed herself from a noblewoman's rag closet, by the state of that dress. An obvious Tairen nobleman, with sweat dripping from his nose and pointed beard and carrying another man across his shoulders like a sack of grain. And herself. Both knees out of her breeches, and another tear in the seat that her coat covered, thank the Light, though one sleeve hung by a few threads. More stains and dust than she wanted to think about.

Not waiting for anyone else, she drew a knife from her sleeve – popping most of those few threads – and gave it a flourish the way Thom Merrilin had taught her, hilt snaking through her fingers so the blade flashed in the sun. 'We require a ride to the Sun Palace,' she announced, and Rand himself could not have done better. There were times when being peremptory saved argument.

'Child,' Cadsuane said chidingly, 'I'm sure Kiruna and her friends would do everything they could, but there isn't a Yellow among them. Samitsu and Corele really are two of the best ever. Lady Arilyn has very kindly lent us her palace in the city, so we will take him—'

'No.' Min had no idea where she found the courage to say that word to this woman. Except . . . It was Rand they were talking about. 'If he wakes . . .' She stopped to swallow; he *would* wake. 'If he wakes in a strange place surrounded by strange Aes Sedai again, I can't imagine what he might do. You don't want to imagine it.' For a long moment she met that cool gaze, and then the Aes Sedai nodded.

'The Sun Palace,' Cadsuane told the farmer. 'And as fast as you can make these fleabags move.'

Of course, it was not quite so simple, even for Aes Sedai. Ander Tol had a wagonload of scraggly turnips he intended to sell in the city, and no intention of going anywhere near the Sun Palace, where, he told them, the Dragon Reborn ate people, who were cooked on spits by Aiel women ten feet tall. Not for any number of Aes Sedai would he venture within a mile of the palace. On the other hand, Cadsuane tossed him a purse that made his eyes pop when he looked inside, then told him she had just bought his turnips and hired him and his wagon. If he did not like the notion, he could give the purse back. That with her fists on her hips and a look on her face that said he might just eat his wagon on the spot if he tried giving the purse back. Ander Tol was a reasonable man, it turned out. Samitsu and Niande unloaded the wagon, turnips simply flying into the air to land in a tidy pile by the roadside. By their icy expressions, this was in no way a use to which they had ever expected to put the One Power. By Darlin's expression, standing there with Rand still on his shoulders, he was relieved they had not called on him to do it. Ander Tol sat the wagon seat with his jaw trying to reach his knees, fingering the purse as though wondering whether it was enough after all.

Once they were settled in the wagon bed, with the straw that had been beneath the turnips all gathered to make a bed for Rand, Cadsuane faced Min across him. Master Tol was flapping his reins and finding a surprising turn of speed in those mules. The wagon lurched and jounced horribly, the wheels not only shaking but apparently out of round. Wishing she had kept just a little of the straw for herself, Min was amused to see Samitsu and Niande growing tighter in the face as they were bounced up and down. Caraline smiled at them quite openly, the High Seat of House Damodred not bothering to hide her pleasure that the Aes Sedai were for once riding rough. Though in truth, slight as she was, she bounced higher and came down with harder thumps than they. Darlin, holding on to the side of the wagon, appeared unaffected however hard he was shaken; he kept frowning and looking from Caraline to Rand.

Cadsuane was another who apparently did not care whether her teeth rattled. 'I expect to be there before nightfall, Master Tol,' she called, producing more flapping if no more speed. 'Now tell me,' she said, turning to Min. 'Exactly what happened the *last* time this boy woke surrounded by strange Aes Sedai?' Her eyes caught Min's and held them.

He wanted it kept secret, if it could be, for as long as it could be. But he was dying, and the only chance he had that Min saw rested in these three women. Maybe knowing could not help. Maybe knowing could at least make them understand something of him. 'They put him in a box,' she began.

She was not sure how she went on – except that she had to – or how she kept from bursting into tears – except that she was not going to break down again when Rand needed her – but somehow she continued through the confinement and the beatings without a tremor in her voice, right to Kiruna and the rest kneeling to swear fealty. Darlin and Caraline looked stunned. Samitsu and Niande looked horrified. Though not for the reason she would have supposed, it turned out.

'He ... *stilled* three sisters?' Samitsu said shrilly. Suddenly she slapped a hand over her mouth and twisted around to lean over the side of the swaying wagon and retch loudly. Niande joined her almost before she began, the pair of them hanging there, emptying their bellies.

And Cadsuane ... Cadsuane touched Rand's pale face, brushed strands of hair from his forehead. 'Do not be afraid, boy,' she said softly. 'They made my task harder, and yours, but I will not hurt you more than I must.' Min turned to ice inside.

Guards at the city gates shouted at the racing wagon, but Cadsuane told Master Tol not to stop, and he flailed at his mules all the harder. People in the streets leaped out of the way to avoid being run down, and the wagon's progress left behind shouts and curses, overturned sedan chairs, and coaches run into street vendors' stalls. Through the streets and up the broad ramp to the Sun Palace, where guards in Lord Dobraine's colors spilled out as though preparing to fight off hordes. While Master Tol was squealing at the top of his lungs that Aes Sedai made him do it, the soldiers saw Min. Then they saw Rand. Min had thought she was in a whirlwind before, but she had been wrong.

Two dozen men tried to reach into the wagon at once to lift Rand out, and those who managed to lay hands on him, handled him as gently as a babe, four to either side with their arms beneath. Cadsuane must have repeated a thousand times that he was not dead as they hurried into the Palace and along corridors that seemed longer than Min remembered, with more Cairhienin soldiers crowding along behind. Nobles began appearing from every doorway and crossing hall, it seemed, faces bloodless, staring as Rand passed. She lost track of Caraline and Darlin, realized she could not remember seeing them since the wagon, and, wishing them well, forgot them. Rand was the only thing she cared about. The only thing in the world.

Nandera was with the *Far Dareis Mai* guarding the doors to Rand's rooms, with their gilded Rising Suns. When the graying Maiden saw Rand, stone-faced Aiel composure shattered. 'What has happened to him?' she wailed, eyes going wide. 'What has happened?' Some of the other Maidens began to moan, a low, hair-raising sound like a dirge.

'Be quiet!' Cadsuane roared, slapping her hands together in a thundercrack. 'You, girl. He needs his bed. Hop!' Nandera hopped. Rand was stripped and in his bed in a twinkling, with Samitsu and Niande both hovering over him, the Cairhienin chased out and Nandera at the door repeating Cadsuane's instructions that he was not to be disturbed by anyone, all so fast Min felt dizzy. She hoped one day to see the confrontation between Cadsuane and the Wise One Sorilea; it had to come, and it would be memorable.

Yet if Cadsuane thought her instructions were really going to keep everyone out, she was mistaken. Before she had more than moved a chair, floating it on the Power, to sit beside Rand's bed, Kiruna and Bera strode in like the two faces of pride, ruler of a court and ruler of her farmhouse.

'What is this I hear about—?' Kiruna began furiously. She saw Cadsuane. Bera saw Cadsuane. To Min's amazement, they stopped with their mouths hanging open.

'He is in good hands,' Cadsuane said. 'Unless one of you has suddenly found more Talent for Healing than I recall?'

'Yes, Cadsuane,' they said meekly. 'No, Cadsuane.' Min closed her own mouth.

Samitsu took an ivory-inlaid chair against the wall, spreading her dark yellow skirts, and sat with her hands folded, watching Rand's chest rise and fall beneath the sheet. Niande went to Rand's bookshelf and selected a book before she sat near the windows. *Reading!* Kiruna and Bera started to sit, then actually looked to Cadsuane and waited for her impatient nod before they sat down.

'Why aren't you doing something?' Min shouted.

'That is what I might ask,' Amys said, walking into the room. The youthful, white-haired Wise One stared at Rand for a moment, then shifted her deep brown shawl and turned to Kiruna and Bera. 'You may go,' she said. 'And Kiruna, Sorilea wishes to see you again.'

Kiruna's dark face paled, but the pair of them rose and curtsied, murmuring, 'Yes, Amys,' even more meekly than for Cadsuane before leaving with embarrassed glances at the Green sister.

'Interesting,' Cadsuane said when they were gone. Her dark eyes locked with Amys' blue, and Cadsuane, at least, seemed to like what she saw. At any rate, she smiled. 'I should like to meet this Sorilea. She is a strong woman?' She seemed to emphasize the word 'strong.'

'The strongest I have ever known,' Amys said simply. Calmly. You would never have thought Rand lay senseless in front of her. 'I do not know your Healing, Aes Sedai. I trust that you have done what can be done?' Her tone was flat; Min doubted how much Amys did trust.

'What can be done, has been,' Cadsuane sighed. 'All we can do now is wait.'

'While he dies?' a man's harsh voice said, and Min jumped.

Dashiva strode into the room, his plain face contorted in a scowl. 'Flinn!' he snapped.

Niande's book thudded to the floor from apparently nerveless fingers; she stared at the three men in black coats as she would have at the Dark One himself. Pale-faced, Samitsu muttered something that sounded like a prayer.

At Dashiva's command, the grizzled Asha'man limped to the bed on the opposite side from Cadsuane and began running his hands along the length of Rand's still body a foot above the sheet. Young Narishma stood frowning by the door, fingering the hilt of his sword, those big dark eyes trying to watch all three Aes Sedai at once. The Aes Sedai, and Amys. He did not look afraid; just a man confidently waiting for those women to show themselves his enemies. Unlike the Aes Sedai, Amys ignored the Asha'man except for Flinn. Her eyes followed him, smooth face utterly expressionless. But her thumb ran along the haft of her belt knife in a very expressive manner.

'What are you doing?' Samitsu demanded, leaping up from her chair. Whatever her unease about Asha'man, concern for her unconscious patient had overcome it. 'You, Flinn or whoever you are.' She started toward the bed, and Narishma flowed to block her. Frowning, she tried to go around, and he put a hand on her arm.

'Another boy with no manners,' Cadsuane murmured. Of the three sisters, only she displayed no alarm whatsoever at the Asha'man. Instead, she studied them over steepled fingers.

Narishma flushed at her comment and removed his hand, but when Samitsu tried to go around him again, he once more stepped in front of her.

She settled for glaring past his shoulder. 'You, Flinn, what are you doing? I won't have you killing him with your ignorance! Do you hear me?' Min practically danced from foot to foot. She did not think an Asha'man would kill Rand, not on purpose, but ... He trusted them, but ... Light, even Amys did not seem sure, frowning from Flinn to Rand.

Flinn stripped the sheet down to Rand's waist, exposing the wound. The gash looked neither better nor worse than she remembered, a gaping, angry, bloodless wound slicing across the round scar. He appeared to be sleeping.

'He can't do any worse than Rand already is,' Min said. Nobody paid her any mind.

Dashiva made a guttural sound, and Flinn looked at him. 'You see something, Asha'man?'

'I have no Talent for Healing,' Dashiva said, twisting his mouth wryly. 'You're the one who took my suggestion and learned.'

'What suggestion?' Samitsu demanded. 'I insist that you—'

'Be quiet, Samitsu,' Cadsuane said. She seemed to be the only one in the room who was calm aside from Amys, and from the way the Wise One kept stroking her knife hilt, Min was not certain about her. 'I think the last thing he wants to do is harm the boy.'

'But, Cadsuane,' Niande began urgently, 'that man is—'

'I said, be quiet,' the gray-haired Aes Sedai told her firmly.

'I assure you,' Dashiva said, managing to sound oily and harsh at the same time, 'Flinn knows what he is about. Already he can do things you *Aes Sedai* never dreamed of.' Samitsu sniffed; loudly. Cadsuane merely nodded and sat back in her chair.

Flinn traced his finger along the puffy gash in Rand's side and across the old scar. That did seem more tender. 'These are alike, but different, as if there's two kinds of infection at work. Only it isn't infection; it's ... darkness. I can't think of a better word.' He shrugged, eyeing Samitsu's Yellow-fringed shawl as she frowned at him, but it was a considering look she gave him now.

'Get on with it, Flinn,' Dashiva muttered. 'If he dies ...' Nose wrinkled as though at a bad smell, he seemed unable to look away from Rand. His lips moved as he talked to himself, and once he made a sound, half sob, half bitter laugh, without his face changing one line.

Drawing a deep breath, Flinn looked around the room, at the Aes Sedai, at Amys. When he caught sight of Min, he gave a start, and his leathery face reddened. Hastily he rearranged the sheet to cover Rand to his neck, leaving only the old wound and the new exposed.

'I hope nobody minds if I talk,' he said, beginning to move callused hands above Rand's side. 'Talking seems to help a mite.' He squinted, focusing on the injuries, and his fingers writhed slowly. Very much as though he was weaving threads, Min realized. His tone was almost absent, only part of his mind on the words. 'It was Healing made me go to the Black Tower, you might say. I was a soldier, till I took a lance in my thigh; couldn't grip a saddle proper after that, or even walk far. That was the fifteenth wound I took in near forty years in the Queen's Guards. Fifteen that counted, anyway; it don't if you can walk or ride, after. I seen a lot of friends die in them forty years. So I went, and the M'Hael taught me Healing. And other things. A rough sort of Healing; I was Healed by an Aes Sedai once – oh, nigh on thirty years back now – and this hurts, compared to that. Works as well, though. Then one day, Dashiva here – pardon; Asha'man Dashiva – says he wonders why it's all the same, no matter if a man's got a broke leg or a cold, and we got to talking, and ... Well, he's got no feel for it, himself, but me, seems I got the knack you might say. The Talent. So I started thinking, what if I ... ? There. Best I can do.'

Dashiva grunted as Flinn abruptly sat back on his heels and wiped the back of his hand across his forehead. Sweat beaded on his face, the first time Min had seen an Asha'man perspire. The slash in Rand's side was not gone, yet it seemed a little smaller, less red and angry. He still slept, but his face seemed less pale.

Samitsu darted past Narishma so quickly he had no chance to intervene. 'What did you do?' she demanded, laying fingers on Rand's forehead. Whatever she found with the Power, her eyebrows climbed halfway to her hair, and her tone leaped from imperious to incredulous. 'What did you do?'

Flinn shrugged his shoulders regretfully. 'Not much. I couldn't really touch what's wrong. I sort of sealed them away from him, for a time, anyhow. It won't last. They're fighting each other, now. Maybe they'll kill off each other, while he heals himself the rest of the way.' Sighing, he shook his head. 'On the other hand, I can't say that they won't kill him. But I think he has a better chance than he did.'

Dashiva nodded self-importantly. 'Yes; he has a chance, now.' You would have thought he had done the Healing himself.

To Flinn's evident surprise, Samitsu rounded the bed to help him rise. 'You will tell me what you did,' she said, regal tone at strong odds with the way her quick fingers straightened the old man's collar and smoothed his lapels. 'If only there was some way you could *show* me! But you will describe it. You must! I will give you all the gold I possess, bear your child, whatever you wish, but you *will* tell me all that you can.' Apparently not sure herself whether she was commanding or begging, she led a very bemused Flinn over by the windows. He opened his mouth more than once, but she was too busy trying to make him talk to see it.

Not caring what anyone thought, Min climbed onto the bed and lay so she could tuck Rand's head under her chin and wrap her arms around him. A chance. Furtively she studied the three people gathered around the bed. Cadsuane in her chair, Amys standing opposite, Dashiva leaning against one of the square bedposts at the foot, all with unreadable auras and images dancing around them. All with their eyes intent on Rand. No doubt Amys saw some disaster for the Aiel if Rand died, and Dashiva, the only one with any expression, a dark yet worried scowl, disaster for the Asha'man. And Cadsuane . . . Cadsuane, who was not only known to Bera and Kiruna, but made them jump like girls for all their oaths to Rand. Cadsuane would not hurt Rand 'any more than she had to.'

Cadsuane's gaze met Min's for a moment, and Min shivered. Somehow, she would protect him while he could not protect himself, from Amys, and Dashiva, and Cadsuane. Somehow. Unconsciously, she began to hum a lullaby, rocking Rand gently. Somehow.

Chapter 37

A Note from the Palace

The day after the Festival of Birds dawned to strong winds off the Sea of Storms that actually cut the heat in Ebou Dar. A sky without a cloud and the red-gold dome of the sun on the horizon gave promises for once the wind died, though. Mat hurried down through the Tarasin Palace with his green coat undone and his shirt only half-laced in anticipation. He did not quite jump at every sound, but he did give a start, considerably more wide-eyed than he liked, whenever one of the serving women passed, swishing her petticoats and smiling at him. Every last one of them smiled, in a particularly ... knowing ... way. It was all he could do not to run.

At the last, he slowed, easing onto the shaded walk bordering the stableyard almost on tiptoe. Between the fluted columns of the walk, yellowish reedy plants in big red pottery bowls and vines with wide, red-striped leaves dangling from metal baskets on chains formed a thin screen. Unconsciously, he tugged his hat lower to obscure his face. His hands ran along his spear – an *ashandarei*, Birgitte called it – unthinkingly fingering the haft as if he might need to defend himself. The dice tumbled inside his head fiercely, yet that had nothing to do with his uneasiness. The source of that was Tylin.

Six closed coaches with the green Anchor and Sword of House Mitsobar lacquered on the doors already waited in line before the tall arched outer gates with teams hitched and liveried drivers mounted. He could see Nalesean yawning in a yellow-striped coat on the far side of them, and Vanin sat slumped atop an upended barrel not far from the stable doors, apparently asleep. Most of the other Redarms were squatting patiently on the stableyard flagstones; a few tossed dice in the shadow of the huge white stables. Elayne stood between Mat and the coaches, just the other side of the screen of plants. Reanne Corly was with her, and close by, seven more of the women who were at that peculiar meeting he had burst into the evening before; Reanne was the only one not wearing the red belt of a Wise Woman. He had half-expected them not to appear this morning. They had the features of women used to ordering their own lives and others', and most had at least a bit of gray in their hair, yet they watched fresh-faced Elayne with an air of expectation, seemingly on their toes, as though ready to jump at her command. The whole lot caught less than half his attention, though; none of them was the woman who had him ready to jump out of his skin. Tylin made him feel ... well ... 'helpless' was the only word that seemed to fit, however ridiculous it seemed.

'We do not need them, Mistress Corly,' Elayne said. The Daughter-Heir sounded like a woman patting a child on the head. 'I've told them to remain here until we return. We will attract less attention, especially across the river, without anyone recognizably Aes Sedai.' Her notion of what to wear visiting the roughest part of the city without attracting attention was a wide green hat with green-dyed plumes, a light dust-cloak of green linen worked in golden scrolls hanging down her back, and a high-necked green silk riding dress with gold embroidery climbing the divided skirts and thickly emphasizing the oval that exposed half her bosom. She even wore one of those necklaces for a marriage knife. That broad band of woven gold would make every thief's hand in the Rahad itch. She carried no weapon beyond a small belt knife. But as to that, what weapon did a woman who could channel need? Of course, every one of those red belts had a curved dagger tucked behind it. So did Reanne's belt of plain worked leather.

Reanne removed a large blue straw hat, frowned at it, then put it back on and retied the ribbons. Elayne's tone did not seem to be what was bothering her. She put on a diffident smile with the hat, and a timid tone. 'But why does Merilille Sedai think we are lying, Elayne Sedai?'

'They all do,' one of the red-belts said breathlessly. All of them wore Ebou Dari dresses in sober colors, with narrow plunging necklines and skirts sewn up on one side to expose layered petticoats, but only this one, bone-lean and with more white than black in her long hair, had the olive skin and dark eyes of an Ebou Dari. 'Sareitha Sedai called me liar to my face, about our numbers, about—' She cut off short at a frown and a 'Be quiet, Tamarla' from Reanne; Mistress Corly might be ready to curtsy and simper for a child if the child was Aes Sedai, but she kept a tight rein on her companions.

Mat frowned up at the windows overlooking the stableyard, those he could see from where he stood. Elaborate white wrought-iron screens covered some, white wooden screens of intricately carved piercework others. Not likely Tylin was up there; not likely she would appear in the stableyard. He had been very careful not to wake her getting dressed. Besides, she would not try anything here. At least, he did not think she would. Then again, was anything past the woman who had had half a dozen serving women seize him in the halls last night and drag him into her apartments? The bloody woman treated him like a toy! He was not going to put up with it anymore. He was not. Light, who was he trying to fool? If they did not grab this Bowl of the Winds and get out of Ebou Dar, Tylin would be pinching his bottom and calling him her little pigeon again tonight.

'It's your ages, Reanne.' Elayne did not exactly sound hesitant – she never did that – but her tone became very careful. 'It is considered rude among Aes Sedai to speak of age, but ... Reanne, apparently no Aes Sedai since the Breaking has lived as long as any of you in the Knitting Circle claim.' That was the odd name these Kin gave their ruling council. 'In your own case, not by over a hundred years.' The red-belts gasped, going wide-eyed. A slender brown-eyed woman with pale honey hair gave a nervous giggle and instantly covered her mouth at Reanne's whip-quick 'Famelle!'

'That can't be possible,' Reanne said faintly to Elayne. 'Surely, Aes Sedai must—'

'Good morning,' Mat said, stepping past the screen of plants. The whole discussion was idiotic; everyone knew Aes Sedai lived longer than anybody else. Instead of wasting time, they should be on their way to the Rahad. 'Where are Thom and Juilin? And Nynaeve.' She had to have come back last night, or Elayne would have been in a swivet. 'Blood and ashes, I don't see Birgitte either. We need to be on our way, Elayne, not standing around. Is Aviendha coming?'

She frowned at him slightly, with just a flicker of her eyes toward Reanne, and he knew she was deciding what performance to give him. Wide-eyed innocence might damage her standing with these women as much as flashing her dimple at him would; Elayne always expected that dimple to work where all else failed. Her chin rose slightly. 'Thom and Juilin are helping Aviendha and Birgitte watch Carridin's palace, Mat.' It was to be the Daughter-Heir in near full-bloom. Not the whole flowering, since she surely knew how he would react to that, but a voice full of certainty, cool blue eyes demanding, and that pretty face chill if not exactly frozen with arrogance. Was there any woman in the world who was just one person? 'Nynaeve will be down shortly, I'm sure. There is no reason for you to come, you know, Mat. Nalesean and your soldiers are a more than adequate bodyguard. You could enjoy yourself right here in the palace until we return.'

'Carridin!' he cried. 'Elayne, we aren't staying in Ebou Dar to settle Jaichim Carridin. We are getting the Bowl, then you or Nynaeve is going to make a gateway, and we are leaving. Is that clear? And I'm going with you to the Rahad.' Enjoy himself! The Light only knew what Tylin would get up to if he remained in the palace all day. The very thought made him want to laugh hysterically.

Icy stares stabbed at him from the Wise Women; stout Sumeko pursed her lips angrily, and Melore, a plump Domani in her middle years whose bosom he had enjoyed eyeing yesterday, planted fists on hips with a face like a thunderhead. They should have known from yesterday that he was not intimidated by Aes Sedai, yet even Reanne gave him such a scowl he half thought she might try to box his ears. Apparently, if they were going to fall all over themselves around Aes Sedai, then everybody else had to as well.

Elayne struggled with herself visibly. Her lips compressed, but one thing he had to give her; she was too smart to go on with what obviously would not work. On the other hand, she was snooty to the bone, however she tried. And the other women were watching. 'Mat, you know we cannot leave until we have used the Bowl.' That haughty chin remained high, and her tone was at best halfway between explaining and telling. 'It might require days for us to be sure of how to use it, perhaps even half a week or more, and we might as well finish Carridin if we can in that time.' Such a crackle entered her voice on the Whitecloak's name that you might have thought she bore the man a personal grudge, but something else leaped out and clamped a fist on his thoughts.

'Half a week!' Feeling strangled, he put a finger behind the scarf knotted around his neck and tugged to ease it. Tylin had used that length of black silk to tie his hands last night before he knew what she was doing. Half a week. Or more! Despite his best efforts, his voice became a touch frantic. 'Elayne, surely you can use the Bowl anywhere. It doesn't have to be here. Egwene must want you back as soon as possible; she can use a friend or two, I'll wager.' By the last he had seen, she could use a few hundred. Maybe once he got these women back, Egwene would be ready to give up that nonsense about being Amyrlin and let him take her to Rand along with Elayne and Nynaeve and Aviendha. 'And what about Rand, Elayne? Caemlyn. The Lion Throne. Blood and ashes, you know you want to reach Caemlyn quick as you can so Rand can give you the Lion Throne.' For some reason, her face grew darker almost by the word, and her eyes flashed. He would have said she was indignant, except of course that she had no cause.

She opened her mouth angrily to argue as soon as he finished, and he set himself, ready to list her promises and to the Pit of Doom with what that did to her in the eyes of Reanne and the rest. By their faces, they would have snubbed him short already in her place.

Before anyone could say anything, though, a round graying woman in House Mitsobar livery was curtsying, first to Elayne, then to the women wearing red belts, and finally to him. 'Queen Tylin sends this, Master Cauthon,' Laren said, holding out a basket with a striped cloth over the contents and small red flowers woven around the handle. 'You did not breakfast, and you must maintain your strength.'

Mat's cheeks warmed. The woman merely looked at him, but she had seen considerably more of him than when she first showed him into Tylin's presence. Considerably more. She had brought supper on a tray last night, while he tried to hide under the silk bedsheet. He did not understand it. These women had him jumping about and blushing like a girl. He just could not understand.

'Are you sure you wouldn't rather remain here?' Elayne asked. 'I'm sure Tylin would enjoy your company for breakfast. The Queen said she finds you wonderfully entertaining and courteously compliant,' she added in a doubtful tone.

Mat fled for the coaches with the basket in one hand and his *ashandarei* in the other.

'Are all northern men so shy?' Laren said.

He risked a glance over his shoulder without stopping, and heaved a sigh of relief. The serving woman was already gathering her skirts, turning to walk though the screen of plants, and Elayne was motioning Reanne and the Wise Women into a circle close around her. Even so, he shivered. Women were going to be the death of him yet.

Rounding the nearest coach, he nearly dropped the basket at the sight of Beslan seated on the coach step, sunlight gleaming along the narrow blade of his sword as he examined the edge. 'What are you doing here?' Mat exclaimed.

Beslan slid the sword into its sheath, a grin splitting his face. 'Coming with you to the Rahad. I suspect you'll find more fun for us.'

'There had better be some fun,' Nalesean yawned into his hand. 'I didn't get very much sleep last night, and now you drag me off when there are Sea Folk women about.' Vanin sat up on his barrel, looked around, found nothing moving, and settled himself back again with his eyes shut.

'There'll be no *fun* if I can help it,' Mat muttered. *Nalesean* had not gotten much sleep? Hah! The whole lot of them had been out enjoying themselves at the festival. Not that he had not enjoyed himself in patches, but only when he could forget he was with a woman who thought he was some sort of bloody doll. 'What Sea Folk women?'

'When Nynaeve Sedai returned last night, she brought a dozen or more, Mat.' Beslan blew out his breath, and his hands made swaying motions. 'The way they move, Mat ...'

Mat shook his head. He was not thinking clearly; Tylin was scrambling his brains. Nynaeve and Elayne had told him about the Windfinders, reluctantly and in sworn secrecy, after trying to hold back even where Nynaeve wanted to go, much less why. And not a single blush at the effort, either. 'Women keep promises in their own way,' so the saying went. Come to think of it, Lawtin and Belvyn were not with the rest of the Redarms. Maybe Nynaeve thought to make up for the other by keeping them with her now. '... In their own way.' But if she had the Windfinders already in the palace, surely it would not take half a week to use the Bowl. Light, please not!

As if thinking of her had been a summons, Nynaeve came strolling through the screen of plants into the stableyard. Mat's jaw dropped. The tall man in a dark green coat on her arm was Lan! Or rather, she was on his, clinging to it with both hands, smiling up at him. With any other woman, Mat would have said she was moon-eyed and dreaming, but this was Nynaeve.

She gave a start once she realized where she was, and took a hasty step to one side, though she still held on to Lan's hand for a moment. Her choice of dress was no better than Elayne's, all blue silk and green embroidery, cut low enough to show a heavy gold ring that would have rattled on her two thumbs together, dangling into her cleavage on a thin gold chain. The wide hat she carried by its ribbons was trimmed with blue plumes, her dust-cloak green linen embroidered in blue. She and Elayne made the other women drab by comparison in their woolens.

In any case, whether or not she had been calf-eyes a moment before, she was all herself now, shifting her braid around. 'Join the other men now, Lan,' she said peremptorily, 'and we can go. The last four coaches are for the men.'

'As you say,' Lan replied, bowing with a hand on his sword hilt. She watched him stride toward Mat with an expression of wonder, probably unable to believe he was obeying so meekly, then gave herself a shake and recovered her bristly self again. Gathering up Elayne and the other women, she herded them toward the first two coaches like a woman shooing geese. By the way she shouted for someone to open the stableyard gates, no one would have known she had been the one delaying their departure. She shouted at the drivers, too, setting them to snatching up their reins and flourishing their long whips; it was a marvel they waited for anyone to climb aboard.

Scrambling awkwardly after Lan and Nalesean and Beslan into the third coach, Mat propped his spear across the door and sat down hard with the basket on his lap as the coach lurched forward. 'Where did you come from, Lan?' he burst out as soon as introductions were out of the way. 'You're the last man I expected to see. Where have you been? Light, I thought you were dead. I know Rand's afraid you are. And letting Nynaeve order you around. Why in the Light would you do that?'

The stone-faced Warder seemed to consider which question to answer. 'Nynaeve and I were married last night by the Mistress of the Ships,' he said finally. 'The Atha'an Miere have several ... unusual ... marriage customs. There were surprises for both of us.' A small smile touched his mouth, if nothing else. He shrugged slightly; seemingly that was all the answer he intended to give.

'The blessing of the Light be upon you and your bride,' Beslan murmured politely with as much of a bow as the confines of the coach would allow, and Nalesean mumbled something, though it was plain from his expression that he thought Lan must be mad. Nalesean had had a good bit of Nynaeve's company.

Mat just sat there swaying with the coach's motion and staring. Nynaeve *married*? *Lan* married to *Nynaeve*? The man *was* mad. No wonder his eyes looked so bleak. Mat would as soon have stuffed a rabid fox down his own shirt. Only a fool married, and only a madman would marry Nynaeve.

If Lan noticed that not everyone was overjoyed, he gave no sign. Except for his eyes, he looked no different than Mat remembered. Maybe a little harder, if that was possible. 'There is something more important,' Lan said. 'Nynaeve doesn't want you to know, Mat, but you need to hear it. Your two men are dead, killed by Moghedien. I am sorry, but if it is any consolation, they truly were dead before they knew. Nynaeve thinks Moghedien must be gone, or she'd have tried again, but I am not so certain. It seems she has a personal enmity toward Nynaeve, although Nynaeve managed to avoid telling me why.' Again the smile; Lan seemed unaware of it. 'Not all of it, at least, and it does not matter. Best you know what might be facing us beyond the river, though.'

'Moghedien,' Beslan breathed, eyes shining. The man was probably seeing *fun*.

'Moghedien,' Nalesean breathed, but in his case, it was more of a groan, and he gave his pointed beard a fitful jerk.

'Those bloody flaming women,' Mat muttered.

'I hope you don't include my wife,' Lan said coldly, one hand gripping the hilt of his sword, and Mat quickly raised his own hands.

'Of course not. Just Elayne and . . . and the Kin.'

After a moment, Lan nodded, and Mat breathed a small sigh of relief. It would be just like Nynaeve to get him killed by her husband – her husband! – when sure as bread was brown, she would have hidden the fact that one of the Forsaken might be in the city. Even Moghedien did not really frighten him, not so long as he had the foxhead around his neck, but the medallion could not protect Nalesean or any of the rest. No doubt Nynaeve thought she and Elayne would do that. They let him bring along the Redarms, all the while laughing up their sleeves at him while they—

'Aren't you going to read my mother's note, Mat?'

Until Beslan mentioned it, he had not realized there was a sheet of paper, folded small, tucked in between the basket and the striped cloth. Just enough showed to reveal the green seal impressed with the Anchor and Sword.

He broke the wax with his thumb and unfolded the page, holding it so Beslan could not see what was written. As well he did; or then again, considering how the other man saw things, maybe it did not matter. Either way, Mat was just as glad no eyes but his saw those words. His heart sank deeper by the line.

Mat, my sweet,

I am having your things moved to my apartments. So much more convenient. By the time you return, Riselle will be in your old rooms to look after young Olver. He seems to enjoy her company.

I have seamstresses coming to measure you. I will enjoy watching that. You must wear shorter coats. And new breeches, of course. You have a delightful bottom. Duckling, who is this Daughter of the Nine Moons I made you think of? I have thought of several delicious ways to make you tell me.

Tylin

The others were all looking at him expectantly. Well, Lan was simply looking, but his gaze was more unnerving than the rest; that stare seemed almost . . . dead.

'The Queen thinks I need new clothes,' Mat said, stuffing the note into his coat pocket. 'I think I'll take a nap.' He pulled the brim of his hat down over his eyes, but he did not close them, staring out the window, where the tied-back curtain let in occasional eddies of dust. It also let in the wind, though, which was considerably better than the heat of a closed coach.

Moghedien and Tylin. Of the two, he would rather confront Moghedien. He touched the foxhead hanging in the open neck of his shirt. At least he had some protection against Moghedien. Against Tylin, he had no more than he did against the Daughter of the bloody Nine Moons, whoever she was. Unless he could find some way to make Nynaeve and Elayne leave Ebou Dar before tonight, everybody was going to know. Sullenly, he tugged his hat lower. These flaming women really were making him act like a girl. In another minute, he was afraid, he might just start crying.

CHAPTER 38

Six Stories

Mat would have gotten out and pulled the coach himself, if he could. He thought they might have moved faster. The streets were already full with the sun not all the way up, wagons and carts wending their way noisily through the crowds and windblown dust to shouts and curses both from drivers and those forced to get out of the way. So many barges slid along the canals on the bargemen's poles that a man almost could have walked the canals like streets, stepping from one barge to the next. A noisy hum hung over the gleaming white city. Ebou Dar seemed to be trying to make up for time lost yesterday, not to mention at High Chasaline and the Feast of Lights, and well it might, considering that tomorrow night was the Feast of Embers, with Maddin's Day, celebrating the founder of Altara, two days after that, and the Feast of the Half Moon the following night. Southerners had a reputation for industry, but he thought it was because they had to work so hard to make up for all the festivals and feastdays. The wonder was that they had the strength for it.

Eventually the coaches did reach the river, drawing up at one of the long stone landings that jutted out into the water, all lined with steps for boarding the boats tied alongside. Sticking a wedge of dark yellow cheese and a butt end of bread into his pocket, he stuffed the basket well under the seat. He was hungry, but someone in the kitchens had been in too much of a hurry; most of the basket was filled by a clay pot full of oysters, but the kitchens had forgotten to cook them.

Scrambling down behind Lan, he left Nalesean and Beslan to help Vanin and the others down from the last coaches. Nearly a dozen men and not even the Cairhienin really small, they had been jammed in like apples in a barrel and clambered out stiffly. Mat strode ahead of the Warder toward the lead coach, the *ashandarei* slanted across his shoulder. Nynaeve and Elayne were both going to get a piece of his mind no matter who was listening. Trying to keep Moghedien hidden! Not to mention two of his men dead! He was going to—! Suddenly very conscious of Lan towering behind him like a stone statue with that sword on his hip, he amended his thoughts. The Daughter-Heir at least was going to hear about keeping that sort of secret.

Nynaeve was standing on the landing, tying on her blue-plumed hat and talking back up into the coach when he reached it. '. . . will work out, of course, but who would think the Sea Folk, of all people, would demand such a thing, even just in private?'

'But, Nynaeve,' Elayne said as she stepped down with her green-plumed hat in her hand, 'if last night was as glorious as you say, how can you complain about—?'

That was when they became aware of him and Lan. Of Lan, really. Nynaeve's eyes opened wider and wider, filling her face as it reddened to shame two sunsets. Maybe three. Elayne froze with one foot still on the coach step, giving the Warder such a frown you would have thought he had sneaked up on them. Lan gazed down at Nynaeve, though, with no more expression than a fence post, and for all Nynaeve appeared ready to crawl under the coach and hide, she stared up at Lan as if no one else existed in the world. Realizing her frown was wasted there, Elayne took her foot off the step and moved out of the way of Reanne and the two Wise Women who had shared the coach, Tamarla and a graying Saldaean woman named Janira, but the Daughter-Heir did not give up; oh, no. She transferred that scowl to Mat Cauthon, and if it altered a whit, it was to deepen. He snorted and shook his head. Usually when a woman was in the wrong, she could find so many things to blame on the nearest man that he wound up thinking maybe he really was at fault. In his experience, old memories or new, there were only two times a woman admitted she was wrong: when she wanted something, and when it snowed at midsummer.

Nynaeve seized at her braid, but not as if her heart was in it. Her fingers fumbled and fell away, and she started wringing her hands instead. 'Lan,' she began unsteadily, 'you mustn't think I would talk about—'

The Warder cut in smoothly, bowing and offering her his arm. 'We are in public, Nynaeve. Whatever you want to say in public, you may. May I escort you to the boat?'

'Yes,' she said, nodding so vigorously that her hat nearly fell off. She straightened it hurriedly with both hands. 'Yes. In public. You will escort me.' Taking his arm, she regained some measure of composure, at least insofar as her face went. Gathering her dust-cloak in her free hand, she practically dragged him across the quay toward the landing.

Mat wondered whether she might be ill. He rather enjoyed seeing Nynaeve dropped a peg or six, but she hardly ever let it last two breaths. Aes Sedai could not Heal themselves. Maybe he should suggest to Elayne that she deal with whatever was wrong with Nynaeve. He avoided Healing like death or marriage himself, but it was different for other people as he saw it. First, though, he had a few choice words to say about secrets.

Opening his mouth, he raised an admonitory finger . . .

. . . and Elayne poked him in the chest with hers, her scowl beneath that plumed hat so cold it made his toes hurt. 'Mistress Corly,' she said in the icy voice of a queen pronouncing judgment, 'explained to Nynaeve and me the significance of those red flowers on the basket, which I see you at least have shame enough to have hidden.'

His face went redder than Nynaeve's had thought of. A few paces away, Reanne Corly and the other two were tying on hats and adjusting dresses the way women did every time they stood up, sat down or moved three steps. Yet despite giving their attention to their clothes, they had enough left over for glances in his direction, and for once they were neither disapproving nor startled. He had not known the bloody flowers meant anything! *Ten* sunsets would not have done for his face.

'So!' Elayne's voice was low, for his ears alone, but it dripped disgust and contempt. She gave her cloak a twitch, to keep it from touching him. 'It's true! I could not *believe* it of you, not even you! I'm *sure* Nynaeve couldn't. Any promise I made to you is *abolished*! I will not keep any promise to a man who could *force* his attentions on a woman, on *any* woman, but *especially* on a Queen who has offered him—'

'*Me* force *my* attentions on *her*!' he shouted. Or rather, he tried to shout; choking made it come out in a wheeze.

Seizing Elayne's shoulders, he pulled her away from the carriages a little distance. Shirtless dockmen in stained green leather vests hurried by, carrying sacks on their shoulders or rolling barrels along the quay, some pushing low barrows loaded with crates, all giving the coaches a wide berth. The Queen of Altara might not have much power, but her sigil on a coach door ensured that commoners would give it room. Nalesean and Beslan were chatting as they led the Redarms onto the landing, Vanin bringing up the rear and staring gloomily at the choppy river; he claimed to have a tender belly when it came to boats. The Wise Women from both coaches had gathered around Reanne, watching, but they were not close enough to overhear. He whispered hoarsely just the same.

'You listen to me! That woman won't take no for an answer; I say no, and she *laughs* at me. She's starved me, bullied me, chased me down like a stag! She has more hands than any six women I ever met. She threatened to have the serving women undress me if I didn't let her—' Abruptly, what he was saying hit him. And who he was saying it to. He managed to close his mouth before he swallowed a fly. He became very interested in one of the dark metal ravens inlaid in the haft of the *ashandarei*, so he would not have to meet her eyes. 'What I mean to say is, you don't understand,' he muttered. 'You have it all backwards.' He risked a glance at her under the edge of his hatbrim.

A faint blush crept into her cheeks, but her face became solemn as a marble bust. 'It . . . appears that I may have misunderstood,' she said soberly. 'That is . . . very *bad* of Tylin.' He thought her lips twitched. 'Have you considered practicing different smiles in a mirror, Mat?'

Startled, he blinked. 'What?'

'I have heard reliably that that is what young women do who attract the eyes of kings.' Something cracked the sobriety of her voice, and this time her lips definitely twitched. 'You might try batting your eyelashes, too.' Catching her lower lip with her teeth, she turned away, shoulders shaking, dust-cloak streaming behind as she hurried toward the landing. Before she darted beyond hearing, he heard her chortle something about 'a taste of his own medicine.' Reanne and the Wise Women scurried in her wake, a flock of hens following a chick instead of the other way around. The few bare-chested boatmen up out of their boats stopped coiling lines or whatever they were doing and bowed their heads respectfully as the procession went by.

Snatching off his hat, Mat considered throwing it down and jumping on it. Women! He should have known better than to expect sympathy. He would like to throttle the bloody Daughter-Heir. And Nynaeve, too, on general principle. Except, of course, that he could not. He had made promises. And those dice were still using his skull for a dice cup. And one of the Forsaken might be around somewhere. Settling the hat squarely back on his head, he marched down the landing, brushed past the Wise Women and caught up to Elayne. She was still trying to fight down giggles, but every time she cut her eyes his way, the color in her cheeks renewed itself and so did the giggles.

He stared straight ahead. Bloody women! Bloody promises. Removing his hat long enough to pull the leather cord from around his neck, he reluctantly shoved it in her direction. The silver foxhead dangled beneath his fist. 'You and Nynaeve will have to decide which of you wears this. But I want it back when we leave Ebou Dar. You understand? The moment we leave—'

Suddenly he realized he was walking alone. Turning, he found Elayne standing stock still two paces back, staring at him with Reanne and the rest clustered behind her.

'What's the matter now?' he demanded. 'Oh. Yes, I know all about Moghedien.' A skinny fellow with red stones on his brass-hoop earrings, bending over a mooring line, jerked around so fast at that name that he pitched over the side with a loud yell and a louder splash. Mat did not care who heard. 'Trying to keep her secret – and two of my men dead! – after you promised. Well, we'll talk about that later. I made a promise, too; I promised to keep the pair of you alive. If Moghedien shows up, she'll go after you two. Now, here.' He pushed the medallion at her again.

She shook her head slowly in puzzlement, then turned to murmur to Reanne. Only after the older women were on their way toward where Nynaeve stood beckoning them at the head of a flight of boat stairs did Elayne take the foxhead, turning it over in her fingers.

'Do you have any notion what I would have done to have this for study?' she said quietly. 'Any notion at all?' She was tall for a woman, but she still had to look up at him. She might never have seen him before. 'You are a troublesome man, Mat Cauthon. Lini would say I was repeating myself, but *you* ...!' Expelling her breath, Elayne reached up to pull his hat off and slip the cord over his head. She actually tucked the foxhead into his shirt and patted it before handing him his hat. 'I won't wear that while Nynaeve doesn't have one, or Aviendha, and I think they feel the same. You wear it. After all, you can hardly keep your promise if Moghedien kills *you*. Not that I think she's still here. I think she believes she killed Nynaeve, and I would not be surprised if that was all she came for. You must be careful, though. Nynaeve says there's a storm coming, and she doesn't mean this wind. I ...' That faint blush returned to her cheeks. 'I am sorry I laughed at you.' She cleared her throat, looking away. 'Sometimes I forget my duty to my subjects. You are a worthy subject, Matrim Cauthon. I will see that Nynaeve understands the right of ... of you and Tylin. Perhaps we can help.'

'No,' he spluttered. 'I mean, yes. I mean ... That is ... Oh, kiss a flaming goat if I know what I mean. I almost wish you didn't know the truth.' Nynaeve and Elayne sitting down to discuss him with Tylin over tea. Could he ever live that down? Could he ever again look any of them in the eye afterward? But if they did not ... He was between the wolf and the bear with nowhere to run. 'Oh, sheep swallop! Sheep swallop and bloody buttered onions!' He nearly wished she would call him down for his language the way Nynaeve would, just to change the subject.

Her lips moved silently, and for an instant he had the strange impression that she was repeating what he had just said. Of course not. He was seeing things; that was all. Aloud, she said, 'I understand.' Sounding just as if she did. 'Come along, now, Mat. We can't waste time standing in one spot.'

Gaping, he watched her lift skirts and cloak to make her way along the landing. She understood? She understood, and not one acid little comment, not one cutting remark? And he was her subject. Her *worthy* subject. Fingering the medallion, he followed. He had been sure the fight would be to ever get it back. If he lived as long as *two* Aes Sedai, he still would never understand women, and noblewomen were purely the worst.

When he reached the steps Elayne had gone down, the boat's two brass-earringed oarsmen were already using their long sweeps to push the vessel away. Elayne was herding Reanne and the last of the Wise Women into the cabin, and Lan stood up in the bows with Nynaeve. A shout from Beslan called him on to the next boat, which held all of the men except the Warder.

'Nynaeve said there wasn't room for any of us,' Nalesean said as the boat rocked its way out into the Eldar. 'She said we'd crowd them.' Beslan laughed, looking around their own boat. Vanin sat beside the cabin door with his eyes closed, trying to pretend he was somewhere else. Harnan and Tad Kandel, an Andoran despite being as dark as either of the boatmen, had climbed atop the cabin; the rest of the Redarms hunkered about the deck, trying to keep out of the way of the rowers. Nobody went into the cabin, all apparently waiting to see whether Mat and Nalesean and Beslan wanted it.

Mat put himself beside the tall bowpost, peering after the other boat, crawling on its sweeps just ahead. The wind whipped the dark choppy waters, and his scarf as well, and he had to hold on to his hat. What was Nynaeve up to? The other nine women on the second boat were all in the cabin, leaving the deck to her and Lan. They stood up in the bows, Lan with his arms folded, Nynaeve gesturing as though explaining. Except that Nynaeve seldom explained anything. Better say never than seldom.

Whatever she was doing, it did not last long. There were whitecaps out in the bay, where Sea Folk rakers and skimmers and soarers heaved at their anchors. The river was not so bad, but the boat still wallowed more than Mat remembered from any previous trip. Before long, Nynaeve was draped over the railing, losing her breakfast while Lan held her. That reminded Mat of his own belly; tucking his hat under his arm so it could not blow away, he pulled out the wedge of cheese.

'Beslan, is this storm likely to break before we can come back from the Rahad?' He took a bite of the sharp-tasting cheese; they had fifty different sorts in Ebou Dar, all good. Nynaeve was still hanging over the side. How much had the woman eaten this morning? 'I don't know where we'll shelter if we're caught.' He could not think of a single inn he had seen in the Rahad that he would take the women into.

'No storm,' Beslan said, seating himself on the railing. 'These are the winter trade winds. The trades come twice a year, in late winter and late summer, but they have to blow much harder before it comes to storm.' He directed a sour look out toward the bay. 'Every year those winds bring – brought – ships from Tarabon, and Arad Doman. I wonder whether they ever will again.'

'The Wheel weaves,' Mat began, and choked on a crumb of cheese. Blood and ashes, he was starting to sound like some grayhair resting his aching joints in front of the fireplace. Worrying about taking the women into a rough inn. A year ago, half a year, he would have taken them, and laughed when their eyes popped, laughed at every prim sniff. 'Well, maybe we'll find you some fun in the Rahad, anyway. At the least, somebody will try to cut a purse, or pull Elayne's necklace off.' Maybe that was what he needed to clean the taste of sobriety from his tongue. Sobriety. Light, what a word to apply to Mat Cauthon! Tylin must be scaring him more than he thought, if he was shriveling up this way. Maybe he needed some of Beslan's sort of fun. That was crazy – he had never seen the fight he would not rather walk around – but maybe . . .

Beslan shook his head. 'If anyone can find it, you can, but . . . We'll be with seven Wise Women, Mat. Seven. With just one at your side, you could slap a man, even in the Rahad, and he would swallow his tongue and walk away. And the women. What's the fun of kissing a woman without the risk she'll decide to stick a knife in you?'

'Burn my soul,' Nalesean muttered into his beard. 'It sounds as though I've dragged myself from bed for a dull morning.'

Beslan nodded in commiseration. 'If we're lucky, though ... The Civil Guard does send patrols to the Rahad occasionally, and if they're after smugglers, they always dress like anyone else. They seem to think nobody will notice a dozen or so men together carrying swords, whatever they wear, and they're always surprised when the smugglers ambush them, which is what nearly always happens. If Mat's *ta'veren* luck works for us, we might be taken for the Civil Guard, and some smugglers might attack us before they see the red belts.' Nalesean brightened and began rubbing his hands together.

Mat glared at them. Maybe Beslan's sort of fun was not what he needed. For one thing, he had more than enough of women with knives. Nynaeve still hung over the side of the boat ahead; that would teach her to gorge herself. Wolfing down the last of the cheese, he began on the bread and tried to ignore the dice in his head. An easy trip with no trouble did not sound bad at all. A quick trip, with a quick departure from Ebou Dar.

The Rahad was everything he remembered, and everything Beslan feared. The wind made climbing the cracked gray stone steps at the boat landing into a perilous feat, and after that, it grew worse. Canals ran everywhere, just as across the river, but here the bridges were plain, the grimy stone parapets broken and crumbling; half the canals were so silted that boys waded waist-deep in them, and hardly a barge was to be seen. Tall buildings stood crowded together, blocky structures with scabrous once-white plaster gone in huge patches to reveal rotting red brick, bordering narrow streets with broken paving stones. In those streets where even the fragments had not been ripped up. Morning did not really reach into the shadows of the buildings. Dingy laundry hung drying from every third window, except where a structure stood empty. Some did, and those windows gaped liked eye sockets in a skull. A sour sweet smell of decay permeated the air, last month's chamber pots and ancient refuse moldering wherever it had been flung, and for every fly on the other side of the Eldar, a hundred buzzed here in clouds of green and blue. He spotted the peeling blue door of The Golden Crown of Heaven and shuddered at the thought of taking the women in there if the storm broke, despite what Beslan said. Then he shuddered again for having shuddered. Something was happening to him, and he did not like it.

Nynaeve and Elayne insisted on taking the lead, with Reanne between them and the Wise Women close behind. Lan stayed at Nynaeve's shoulder like a wolfhound, hand on sword hilt, eyes constantly searching, radiating menace. In truth, he was probably enough protection for two dozen pretty sixteen-year-old girls carrying sacks of gold, even here, but Mat insisted that Vanin and the rest keep their eyes open. In fact, the former horsethief and poacher kept so close to Elayne that anyone could have been forgiven for thinking he was her Warder, if a rather fat and rumpled one. Beslan rolled his eyes expressively at Mat's instructions, and Nalesean irritably stroked his beard and muttered that he could still be in bed.

Men strutted arrogantly along the streets with often ragged vests and no shirts, wearing great brass hoops in their ears and brass finger rings set with colored glass, one knife or sometimes two stuck behind their belts. Hands hovering near those knives, they stared as though daring someone to give the wrong twist to a look. Others skulked from corner to corner, doorway to doorway with hooded eyes, imitating the slat-ribbed dogs that sometimes snarled from a dark alleyway barely wide enough for a man to squeeze into. Those men hunched over their knives, and there was no way to tell which would run and which stab. By and large, the women made any of the men appear humble, parading in worn dresses and twice as much brass jewelry as the men. They carried knives too, of course, and their bold dark eyes sent ten sorts of challenge in every glance. In short, the Rahad was the sort of place where anyone wearing silk could hardly hope to walk ten steps without being cracked over the head. After which they had best hope to wake stripped to the skin and tossed onto a pile of rubbish in an alley, since the alternative was not to wake at all. But . . .

Children darted from every second door with chipped pottery cups of water, sent by their mothers in case the Wise Women wished a drink. Men with scarred faces and murder etched into their eyes stared openmouthed at seven Wise Women together, then bobbed jerky bows and inquired politely if they could be of assistance, was there anything that required carrying? Women, sometimes with as many scars and always eyes to make Tylin flinch, curtsied awkwardly and breathlessly asked whether they might supply directions, had anyone made a bother of themselves to bring so many Wise Women? If so, the strong implication was, Tamarla and the rest had no need of troubling themselves if they would just supply the name.

Oh, they glared at the soldiers as hotly as ever, though even the hardest flinched away from Lan after a single look. And, oddly enough, from Vanin. A few of the men growled at Beslan and Nalesean whenever they gazed too long at a woman's deep neckline. Some growled at Mat, though he could not understand why; unlike those two, he was never in danger of his eyeballs falling down the front of a woman's dress. He knew how to look discreetly. Nynaeve and Elayne were ignored, for all their finery, and so was Reanne in her red wool dress; they did not have the red belt. But they did have the protection of those belts. Mat realized that Beslan had been right. He could empty his purse on the ground, and no one would pick up a copper, at least so long as the Wise Women remained. He could pinch the bottom of every woman in sight, and even if she had apoplexy, she would walk away.

'What a pleasant walk,' Nalesean said dryly, 'with such interesting sights and smells. Did I tell you I didn't get much sleep last night, Mat?'

'Do you want to die in bed?' Mat grumbled. They might as well all have stayed in bed; they were bloody useless here, that was for sure. The Tairen snorted indignantly. Beslan laughed, but he probably thought Mat meant something else.

Across the Rahad they marched, until Reanne finally stopped in front of a building exactly like every other, all flaking plaster and crumbling brick, the same Mat had followed another woman to yesterday. No laundry hung from these windows; only rats lived in there. 'In here,' she said.

Elayne's eyes climbed slowly to the flat roof. 'Six,' she murmured in tones of great satisfaction.

'Six,' Nynaeve sighed, and Elayne patted her arm as though sympathizing with her.

'I wasn't really sure,' she said. So Nynaeve smiled and patted *her*.

Mat did not understand a word of it. So the building had six floors. Women behaved very strangely sometimes. Well, most of the time.

Inside, a long hallway carpeted with dust ran dimly to the back, the far end lost in shadows. Few of the doorways held doors, and those were rough planks. One opening, almost a third of the way down the hall, led to a narrow flight of steep stone-faced steps climbing upward. That was the way he had gone the day before, following footprints in the dust, but he thought some of those other openings must be crossing corridors. He had not taken time to look around then, but the building was too deep and too wide for this floor to be served by only the one they saw. It was too big for only one way in.

'Really, Mat,' Nynaeve said when he told off Harnan and half the Redarms to find any back way in and guard it. Lan kept so close to her side, he might have been glued there. 'Don't you see by now there's no need?'

Her tone was so mild that Elayne must have passed on the truth about Tylin, but if anything, that only soured his mood further. He did not want *anyone* to know. Bloody useless! But those dice were still rattling around in his head. 'Maybe Moghedien likes back doors,' he said dryly. Something chittered in the dark end of the hall, and one of the men with Harnan cursed loudly about rats.

'You told him,' Nynaeve breathed furiously at Lan, one hand snapping shut on her braid.

Elayne made an exasperated sound. 'This is no time to stop for an argument, Nynaeve. The Bowl is upstairs! The Bowl of the Winds!' A small ball of light suddenly appeared, floating in front of her, and without waiting to see whether or not Nynaeve was coming, she gathered her skirts and darted up the stairs. Vanin dashed after her with a startling turn of speed for his bulk, followed by Reanne and most of the Wise Women. Round-faced Sumeko and Ieine, tall and dark and pretty despite the lines at the corners of her eyes, hesitated, then remained with Nynaeve.

Mat would have gone, too, if Nynaeve and Lan had not been in his way. 'Would you let me by, Nynaeve?' he asked. He deserved to be there, at least, when this fabulous bloody Bowl was uncovered. 'Nynaeve?' She was so focused on Lan she seemed to have forgotten anyone else. Mat exchanged glances with Beslan, who grinned and squatted easily with Corevin and the remaining Redarms. Nalesean leaned against the wall and yawned ostentatiously. Which was a mistake with all that dust about; the yawn turned into a coughing fit that darkened his face and doubled him over.

Even that did not distract Nynaeve. Carefully, she took her hand away from her braid. 'I am not angry, Lan,' she said.

'Yes, you are,' he replied calmly. 'But he had to be told.'

'Nynaeve?' Mat said. 'Lan?' Neither one so much as flickered an eye his way.

'I would have told him when I was ready, Lan Mandragoran!' Her mouth clamped shut, but her lips writhed as though she were talking to herself. 'I will not be angry with you,' she went on in a much milder tone, and that sounded addressed to herself as well. Very deliberately she tossed her braid back over her shoulder, jerked that blue-plumed hat straight, and clasped her hands at her waist.

'If you say so,' Lan said mildly.

Nynaeve quivered. 'Don't you take that tone with me!' she shouted. 'I tell you, I'm not angry! Do you hear me?'

'Blood and ashes, Nynaeve,' Mat growled. 'He doesn't think you're angry. I don't think you're angry.' A good thing women had taught him to lie with a straight face. 'Now could we go upstairs and fetch this bloody Bowl of the Winds?'

'A marvelous idea,' said a woman's voice from the door to the street. 'Shall we go up together and surprise Elayne?' Mat had never seen the two women who walked into the hall before, but their faces were Aes Sedai faces. The speaker's was long and cold as her voice, her companion's framed by scores of thin dark braids worked with colored beads. Nearly two dozen men crowded in behind them, bulky fellows with heavy shoulders, clubs and knives in hand. Mat shifted his grip on the *ashandarei*; he knew trouble when he saw it, and the foxhead on his chest was cool, almost cold against his skin. Somebody was holding the One Power.

The two Wise Women nearly fell over dropping curtsies as soon as they saw those ageless features, but Nynaeve certainly knew trouble, too. Her mouth worked soundlessly as the pair came down the hallway, her face all consternation and self-recrimination. Behind him, Mat heard a sword leaving its scabbard, but he was not about to look back to see whose. Lan just stood there, which meant of course that he looked like a leopard ready to pounce.

'They're Black Ajah,' Nynaeve said at last. Her voice started faint and gained strength as she went on. 'Falion Bhoda and Ispan Shefar. They committed murder in the Tower, and worse since. They're Darkfriends, and ...' Her voice faltered for an instant. '... they have me shielded.'

The newcomers continued to advance serenely. 'Have you ever heard such nonsense, Ispan?' the long-faced Aes Sedai asked her companion, who stopped grimacing at the dust long enough to smirk at Nynaeve. 'Ispan and I come from the White Tower, while Nynaeve and her friends are rebels against the Amyrlin Seat. They'll be punished severely for that, and so will anyone who helps them.' With a shock, Mat realized the woman did not know; she thought that he and Lan and the others were just hired strongarms. Falion directed a smile at Nynaeve; it made a blizzard warm by comparison. 'There's someone who will be overjoyed to see you when we take you back, Nynaeve. She thinks you are dead. Better the rest of you go now. You don't want to meddle in Aes Sedai affairs. My men will see you to the river.' Without taking her eyes from Nynaeve, Falion motioned for the men behind her to come forward.

Lan moved. He did not draw his sword, and against Aes Sedai he should have had no chance if he had, no chance in any case, but one moment he was standing still and the next he had thrown himself at the pair. Just before he struck, he grunted as though hit hard, but he crashed into them, carrying both Black sisters to the dusty floor. That opened the sluicegates wide.

Lan pushed himself to hands and knees, shaking his head groggily, and one of the bulky fellows raised an iron-strapped club to smash his skull. Mat stabbed the fellow in the belly with his spear as Beslan and Nalesean and the five Redarms rushed to meet the Darkfriends' shouting charge. Lan staggered to his feet, sword sweeping out to open a Darkfriend from crotch to neck. There was not much room to work sword or *ashandarei* in the corridor, but the tight quarters were what allowed them to face odds of two to one or worse without being overcome in the first moment. Grunting men struggled with them face-to-face, elbowing each other for room to stab or swing a club at them.

Small spaces remained clear around the Black sisters, and around Nynaeve; they saw to that themselves. A wiry Andoran Redarm almost bumped into Falion, but at the last instant he jerked into the air and flew across the hallway, knocking down two of the heavy-shouldered Darkfriends in his flight before smacking into the wall and sliding down, the back of his head leaving a bloody smear on the cracked, dusty plaster. A bald-headed Darkfriend squeezed through the line of defenders and rushed at Nynaeve with outstretched knife; he yelled as his feet were suddenly jerked back from him, a yell that cut off when his face hit the floor so hard that his head bounced.

Obviously Nynaeve was no longer shielded, and if the chilly silver foxhead sliding around Mat's chest as he fought was not enough indication that she and the Black sisters were in some sort of struggle, the way they glared at her and she at them, ignoring the battle around them, shouted the fact. The two Wise Women looked on in horror; they had their curved knives in their fists, but they huddled against the wall, staring from Nynaeve to the other two with eyes wide and mouths hanging open.

'Fight,' Nynaeve snapped at them. She turned her head just a fraction, so she could see them as well as Falion and Ispan. 'I cannot do it alone; they're linked. If you don't fight them, they will kill you. You know about them, now!' The Wise Women gaped at her as though she had suggested spitting in the Queen's face. In the midst of shouts and grunts, Ispan laughed melodiously. In the midst of shouts and grunts, a shrill scream echoed down the stairs.

Nynaeve's head swung that way. Suddenly she staggered, and her head swung back like a wounded badger's, with a scowl that should have made Falion and Ispan leave right then if they had any sense. Nynaeve spared an agonized glance for Mat, though. 'There was channeling upstairs,' she said through her teeth. 'There's trouble.'

Mat hesitated. More likely, Elayne had seen a rat. More likely... He managed to knock aside a dagger thrust at his ribs, but there was no room to stab back with the *ashandarei* or use the haft like a quarterstaff. Beslan stabbed past him and took his attacker through the heart.

'Please, Mat,' Nynaeve said tightly. She never begged. She would cut her own throat first. 'Please.'

With a curse, Mat pulled himself out of the fight and dashed up the steep, narrow stairs, taking all six flights in the dark stairwell at a dead run. There was not a single window to give light. If it was just a rat, he was going to shake Elayne till her teeth ... He burst out onto the top floor, not much brighter than the stairwell with only one window at the street end, burst into a scene from nightmare.

Women lay sprawled everywhere. Elayne was one, half on her back against the wall, eyes closed. Vanin crouched on his knees, blood streaming from nose and ears, feebly trying to pull himself up against the wall. The last woman on her feet, Janira, fled toward Mat as soon as she saw him. He had thought of her as a hawk, with her hooked beak of a nose and sharp cheekbones, but her face was pure terror now, those dark eyes wide and stark.

'Help me!' she screamed at him, and a man caught her from behind. He was an ordinary looking fellow, maybe a little older than Mat, of the same height and slender in a plain gray coat. Smiling, he took Janira's head between his hands and twisted sharply. The sound of her neck breaking was like a dry branch snapping. He let her drop in a boneless heap and gazed down at her. For a moment, his smile looked ... rapturous.

By the light of a pair of lanterns, a small knot of men just beyond Vanin were prying open a door to the squeal of rusted hinges, but Mat hardly noticed. His eyes went from Janira's crumpled corpse to Elayne. He had promised to keep her safe for Rand. He had promised. With a cry, he launched himself at the killer, *ashandarei* extended.

Mat had seen Myrddraal move, but this fellow was quicker, hard as that was to believe. He just seemed to flow from in front of the spear, and seizing the haft, he pivoted, flinging Mat past him five paces down the hall.

Breath left when he hit the floor in a small cloud of dust. So did the *ashandarei*. Struggling for air, he pushed himself up, foxhead dangling from his open shirt. Dragging a knife from under his coat, he flung himself at the man again just as Nalesean appeared at the head of the stairs, sword in hand. Now they had him, however quick he . . .

The man made a Myrddraal seem stiff. He slid around Nalesean's thrust as though there was not a bone in his body, right hand shooting out to seize Nalesean's throat. His hand came away with a liquid, ripping sound. Blood fountained past Nalesean's beard. His sword dropped, ringing on the dusty stone floor, and he clutched both hands to his ruined neck, red running through his fingers as he fell.

Mat crashed into the killer's back, and they all three hit the floor together. He had no compunctions against stabbing a man in the back when it was necessary, especially a man who could tear somebody's throat out. He should have let Nalesean stay in bed. The thought came sadly as he drove the blade home hard, then a second time, a third.

The man twisted in his grip. It should not have been possible, but somehow the fellow rolled over beneath him, pulling the knife hilt out of his hand. Nalesean's staring eyes and bloody throat were a reminder right before his eyes. Desperately he grabbed the man's wrists, one hand slipping a little in the blood that ran down the fellow's hand.

The man smiled at him. With a knife sticking out of his side, he smiled! 'He wants you dead as much as he wants her,' he said softly. And as if Mat was not holding him at all, his hands moved toward Mat's head, driving Mat's arms back.

Mat pushed frantically, threw all of his weight against the fellow's arms to no avail. Light, he might as well have been a child fighting a grown man. The fellow was making a game of it, taking his bloody time. Hands touched his head. Where was his flaming luck? He gave a heave with what seemed his last strength – and the medallion fell against the man's cheek. The man screamed. Smoke rose around the edges of the foxhead, and a sizzle like bacon frying. Convulsively, he hurled Mat away with hands and feet both. This time, Mat flew ten paces and slid.

When he scrambled to his feet, half-dazed, the man was already up, hands trembling at his face. A raw red brand marked where the foxhead had fallen. Gingerly, Mat fingered the medallion. It was cool. Not the cool of someone channeling nearby – maybe they were still at it below, but that was too far off – just the cool of silver. He had no notion what this fellow was, except that he certainly was not human, but between that burn and three stab wounds, with the knife hilt still jutting out beneath his arm, he had to be slowed enough for Mat to get past him to the stairs. Avenging Elayne was all very well, and Nalesean too, but it was not going to happen today, apparently, and there was no call to supply a reason for avenging Mat Cauthon.

Jerking the knife out of his side, the man hurled it at him. Mat snagged it out of the air without thinking. Thom had taught him to juggle, and Thom said he had the quickest hands he had ever seen. Flipping the knife around so he held it properly, pointed slanted up, he noticed the gleaming blade, and his heart sank. No blood. There should have been at least a smear of red, but the steel shone, bright and clean. Maybe even three stab wounds were not going to slow this – whatever he was.

He risked a glance over his shoulder. The other men were streaming out of that door they had pried open, the door those footprints had led him to yesterday, but their arms seemed full of rubbish, small half-rotted chests, a cask with cloth-wrapped objects bulging through missing staves, even a broken chair and a cracked mirror. They must have had orders to take everything. Paying no attention whatever to Mat, they hurried toward the far end of the hall and vanished around a corner. There had to be another set of stairs back there. Maybe he could follow them down at a distance. Maybe . . . Just before the doorway they had come out of, Vanin made another effort to stand, and fell back. Mat bit back a curse. Lugging Vanin was going to slow him, but if his luck was in . . . It had not saved Elayne, but maybe . . . From the corner of his eye, he saw her move, lifting a hand to her head.

The man in the gray coat saw it, too. With a smile, he turned toward her.

Sighing, Mat tucked the useless knife into its scabbard. 'You can't have her,' he said loudly. Promises. One jerk broke the leather cord around his neck; the silver foxhead dangled a foot below his fist. It made a low hum as he whirled it in a double loop. 'You can't bloody have her.' He started forward, keeping the medallion spinning. The first step was the hardest, but he had a promise to keep.

The fellow's smile faded. Watching the flashing foxhead warily, he backed away on his toes. The same light that glittered on the whirling silver, from the single window, made a halo around him. If Mat could drive him that far, maybe he could see whether a six-story drop would do what a knife could not.

Brand livid on his face, the fellow backed away, sometimes half-reaching as if to try grabbing past the medallion. And suddenly, he darted to one side, into one of the rooms. This one had a door that he pulled shut behind him. Mat heard the bar drop.

Maybe he should have left it there, but without thinking, he raised a foot and slammed the heel of his boot against the center of the door. Dust leaped off the rough wood. A second kick, and rotten bar-catches gave way, along with a rusted hinge. The door fell in, hanging at a slanted angle.

The room was not entirely dark. A little light reached it from the window at the end of the hall, just one door away, and a broken triangle of mirror leaning against the far wall spread a faint illumination. That mirror let him see everything without going in. Aside from that and a piece of a chair, there was nothing else to see. The only openings were the doorway and a rathole beside the mirror, but the man in the gray coat was gone.

'Mat,' Elayne called faintly. He hurried away from the room as much as toward her. There was shouting somewhere below, but Nynaeve and the rest would have to take care of themselves for the moment.

Elayne was sitting up, working her jaw and wincing, when he knelt beside her. Dust covered her dress, her hat hung askew, some of the plumes broken, and her red-gold hair looked as if she had been dragged by it. 'He hit me so hard,' she said painfully. 'I don't think anything is broken, but ...' Her eyes latched on to his, and if he had ever thought she looked at him as if he were a stranger, he saw it for true now. 'I saw what you did, Mat. With him. We might as well have been chickens in a box with a weasel. Channeling wouldn't touch him; the flows melted the way they do with your ...' Glancing at the medallion still hanging from his fist, she drew a breath that did interesting things to that oval cut-out. 'Thank you, Mat. I apologize for everything I ever did or thought.' She sounded as though she really meant it. 'I keep building up *toh* toward you,' she smiled ruefully, 'but I am *not* going to let you beat me. You are going to have to let me save you at least once to balance matters.'

'I'll see what I can arrange,' he said dryly, stuffing the medallion into a coat pocket. *Toh?* Beat her? Light! The woman was definitely spending too much time with Aviendha.

Once he helped her to her feet, she looked at the hallway, at Vanin with his blood-smeared face, and the women lying where they had fallen, and she grimaced. 'Oh, Light!' she breathed. 'Oh, blood and bloody flaming ashes!' Despite the situation, he gave a start. It was not just that he had never expected to hear those words out of her mouth; they seemed peculiar, as if she knew the sounds but not the meanings. Somehow, they made her sound younger than she looked.

Shaking off his arm, she discarded her hat, just tossing it aside, and hurried to kneel beside the nearest Wise Woman, Reanne, and take her head in both hands. The woman lay limp, face down and arms stretched out as though she had been tripped up running. Toward the room everyone had been after, toward her attacker, not away.

'This is beyond me,' Elayne muttered. 'Where is Nynaeve? Why didn't she come up with you, Mat? Nynaeve!' she shouted toward the stairs.

'No need to shriek like a cat,' Nynaeve growled, appearing in the stairwell. She was looking back over her shoulder down the stairs, though. 'You hold her tight, you hear me?' she shrieked like a cat. She carried her hat, and shook it at whoever she was shouting at. 'You let her get away, too, and I'll box your ears till you hear bells next year!'

She turned, then, and her eyes nearly bulged out of her head. 'The Light shine on us,' she breathed, hurrying to bend over Janira. One touch, and she straightened, wincing painfully. He could have told her the woman was dead. Nynaeve seemed to take death personally. Giving herself a shake, she went on to the next, Tamarla, and this time it appeared there was something she could Heal. It also appeared Tamarla's injuries were not simple, because she knelt over her, frowning. 'What happened here, Mat?' she demanded without looking around at him. Her tone made him sigh; he might have known she would decide it was his fault. 'Well, Mat? What happened? Will you speak up, man, or do I have to—' He never learned what threat she intended to offer.

Lan had followed Nynaeve out of the stairwell, of course, with Sumeko right at his heels. The stout Wise Woman took one look at the hall and immediately lifted her skirts and ran to Reanne. She did give Elayne one worried glance before lowering herself to her knees and beginning to move her hands over Reanne in an odd way. That was what pulled Nynaeve up short.

'What are you doing?' she said sharply. Not halting what she was doing to Tamarla, she spared the round-faced woman only short glances, but they were as piercing as her voice. 'Where did you learn that?'

Sumeko gave a start, but her hands did not stop. 'Forgive me, Aes Sedai,' she said in a breathless, disjointed rush. 'I know I'm not supposed to ... She'll die if I don't ... I know I wasn't supposed to keep trying to ... I just wanted to learn, Aes Sedai. Please.'

'No, no, go on,' Nynaeve said absently. Most of her attention was fixed on the woman under her hands, but not all. 'You seem to know a few things even I— That is to say, you have a very interesting way with the flows. I suspect you'll find that a great many sisters want to learn from you.' Half under her breath, she added, 'Maybe now they'll leave me alone.' Sumeko could not have heard that last, but what she did hear dropped her chin to her considerable chest. Her hands barely paused, though.

'Elayne,' Nynaeve went on, 'would you look for the Bowl, please? I suspect that door is the one.' She nodded to the correct door, standing open like half a dozen others. That made Mat blink until he saw two tiny cloth-wrapped bundles lying in front of it where the looters must have dropped them.

'Yes,' Elayne muttered. 'Yes, I can do that much, at least.' Half-raising a hand toward Vanin, still on his knees, she let it fall with a sigh and strode through the doorway, which almost immediately emitted a cloud of dust and the sound of coughing.

The more-than-plump Wise Woman had not been the only one

following Nynaeve and Lan. Ieine stalked out of the stairwell, forcing the Taraboner Darkfriend in front of her by means of an arm twisted up into her back and a fist clutching the back of her neck. Ieine's jaw was set, her mouth tight; her face was half frightened certainty that she would be skinned alive for manhandling an Aes Sedai, and half determination to hold on no matter what. Nynaeve had that effect on people, sometimes. The Black sister was wide-eyed with terror, sagging so she surely would have fallen except for Ieine's grip. She must have been shielded, certainly, and with equal surety she probably would have chosen being skinned to whatever was going to happen to her. Tears began leaking from her eyes, and her mouth sagged in silent sobs.

Behind them came Beslan, who gave a sad sigh at the sight of Nalesean and a sadder for the women, and then Harnan and three of the Redarms, Fergin and Gorderan and Metwyn. Three who had been at the front of the building. Harnan and two of the others had bloody gashes in their coats, but Nynaeve must have Healed them below. They did not move as if they still had injuries. They looked very subdued, though.

'What happened at the back?' Mat asked quietly.

'Burn me if I know,' Harnan replied. 'We walked right into a knot of shoulderthumpers with knives in the dark. There was one, moved like a snake . . . ' He shrugged, touching the bloodstained hole in his coat absentmindedly. 'One of them got a knife into me, and the next I remember is opening my eyes with Nynaeve Sedai bending over me and Mendair and the others dead as yesterday's mutton.'

Mat nodded. One who moved like a snake. And got out of rooms like one, too. He looked around the hallway. Reanne and Tamarla were on their feet — straightening their dresses, of course — and Vanin, peering into the room where Elayne was apparently trying out some more curses, seemingly with no more success than earlier. It was hard to tell because of the coughing. Nynaeve stood, helping up Sibella, a scrawny yellow-haired woman, and Sumeko was still working on Famelle, with her pale-honey hair and big brown eyes. But he was never going to admire Melore's bosom again; Reanne knelt to straighten her limbs and close her eyes, while Tamarla performed the same service for Janira. Two Wise Women dead, and six of his Redarms. Killed by a ... man ... the Power would not touch.

'I've found it!' Elayne shouted excitedly. She strode back out into the hall holding a wide round bundle of rotted cloth she would not let Vanin take from her. Coated in gray from head to toe, she looked as if she had lain down and rolled in the dust. 'We have the Bowl of the Winds, Nynaeve!'

'In that case,' Mat announced, 'we are bloody well getting out of here now.' Nobody argued. Oh, Nynaeve and Elayne insisted on all the men making sacks out of their jackets for things they rooted out of the room – they even loaded the Wise Woman down, and themselves – and Reanne had to go down and recruit men to carry their dead down the boat landing, but nobody argued. He doubted if the Rahad had ever seen as odd a procession as made its way to the river, or one that moved more quickly.

CHAPTER 39

Promises to Keep

'We are bloody well getting out of here now,' Mat said again later, and this time there was argument. There had been argument for the past half-hour, near enough. Outside, the sun was past its noon peak. The trade winds cut the heat a little; stiff yellow curtains fastened over the tall windows bulged and snapped at gusts. Three hours back in the Tarasin Palace, the dice still bouncing in his head, and he wanted to kick something. Or somebody.

He tugged at the scarf tied around his neck; it felt as though the rope that had given him the scar under that scarf was back and tightening slowly. 'Love of the Light, are you all blind? Or just deaf?'

The room Tylin had provided was large, with green walls and high blue ceiling, and no furnishings but gilded chairs and small tables set with pearlshell, yet it was crowded even so. It seemed so, anyway. Tylin herself sat before one of the three marble fireplaces with her knees crossed, watching him with those dark eagle's eyes and a small smile, idly kicking her layered blue and yellow petticoats, idly toying with the jeweled hilt of her curved knife. He suspected Elayne or Nynaeve had spoken to her. They were there, too, seated to either side of the Queen, somehow in clean dresses and apparently even bathed, though they had only been out of his sight for minutes at a stretch since returning to the palace. They almost matched Tylin for regal dignity in their bright silks; he was not sure who they wanted to impress, with all that lace and elaborate embroidery. They looked ready for a royal ball, not a journey. He himself was still in his muck, with his dusty green coat hanging open and the silver foxhead caught in the neck of his half-undone shirt. Knotting the leather cord had shortened it, but he wanted the medallion touching his skin. He was around women who could channel, after all.

Truth, those three women could probably have crowded the room by themselves. Tylin could have done it by herself, so far as he was concerned; if Nynaeve or Elayne *had* spoken to her, it was a very good thing that he was going. They three could have done it alone, but . . .

'This is preposterous,' Merilille announced. 'I've never heard of any Shadowspawn called a *gholam*. Have any of you?' That was directed to Adeleas and Vandene, Sareitha and Careane. Facing Tylin, the cool-eyed Aes Sedai serenity of all five made a fair job of turning their high-backed armchairs into thrones. He could not understand why Nynaeve and Elayne just sat like lumps, coolly serene too, but absolutely silent. They knew, they understood, and for some reason, Merilille and that lot slathered their tongues with meekness for them, now. Mat Cauthon, on the other hand, was a hairy-eared lout who needed to be kicked, and from Merilille on down, they were all ready to do the kicking.

'I saw the thing,' he snapped, 'Elayne saw the thing, Reanne and the Wise Women saw it. Ask any of them!'

Gathered at one end of the room, Reanne and the five surviving Wise Women shrank back like huddling hens, afraid of actual questions. All but Sumeko, anyway; thumbs tucked behind her long red belt, the round woman kept frowning at the Aes Sedai, then shaking her head, frowning, then shaking her head. Nynaeve had had a considerable talk with her in the privacy of the cabin on the boat coming back, and Mat thought that had something to do with her newfound attitude. He had caught mention of Aes Sedai more than once; not that he had been trying to eavesdrop. The rest seemed to be wondering whether they should offer to fetch tea. Only Sumeko had even appeared to consider the offer of a chair. Sibella, flapping bony arms in shock, had nearly fainted.

'No one denies the word of Elayne Aes Sedai, Master Cauthon,' said Renaile din Calon Blue Star in a cool deep voice. Even had the dignified woman in silks to match the red-and-yellow floor tiles not been named to him earlier, the old memories meshed into his own would have identified her as Windfinder to the Mistress of the Ships by the ten fat gold rings in her earlobes, those in each ear connected by a golden chain and half-hidden by the narrow wings of white in her straight black hair. The medallions clustered along the finer chain that ran to her nose ring would tell him what clan she came from among other things. So would the tattoos on her slim dark hands. 'What we question is the danger,' she continued. 'We do not like leaving the water without good cause.'

Nearly twenty Sea Folk women stood gathered behind her chair, a riot of colorful silks and earrings and medallions on chains for the most part. The first odd thing he had noticed about them was their attitude toward the Aes Sedai. They were perfectly respectful, on the surface at any rate, but he had never before seen anyone look at Aes Sedai *smugly*. The second odd thing came from those other men's memories; he did not know a great deal about the Sea Folk from them, but enough. Every Atha'an Miere, man or woman, began as the lowest deckhand whether they were destined one day to become the Master of the Blades or the Mistress of the Ships herself, and every step of the way between, the Sea Folk were sticklers for rank to make any king or Aes Sedai look a sloven. The women behind Renaile were a peculiar lot by any measure – Windfinders to Wavemistresses rubbing shoulders with Windfinders from soarers, by their medallions – but two wore bright blouses of plain wool above the dark oily breeches of deckhands, each with a single thin ring in her left ear. A second and third ring in the right indicated they were being trained as Windfinders, but with two more to earn, not to mention the nose ring, it would be a long while yet that either would find herself called to haul sail whenever the deckmaster needed her, and find the deckmaster's flail across her rump if she did not move quickly enough. Those two did not belong in this gathering by any memory he had; normally, the Windfinder to the Mistress of the Ships would not even have spoken to one of them.

'Very much as I said, Renaile,' Merilille said, icily condescending. She had certainly noticed those smug glances. That tone did not change as she shifted her attention to him. 'Do not grow petulant, Master Cauthon. We are willing to listen to reason. If you have any.'

Mat gathered patience; he hoped he could find enough. Maybe if he used both hands and both feet. '*Gholam* were created in the middle of the War of the Power, during the Age of Legends,' he began from the beginning. Almost from the beginning of what Birgitte had told him. He turned, facing each group of women as he spoke. Burn him if he was going to let one bunch think they were more important. Or that he was bloody pleading with them. Especially since he was. 'They were made to assassinate Aes Sedai. No other reason. To kill people who could channel. The One Power won't help you; the Power won't touch a *gholam*. In fact, they can sense the ability to channel, if they're within, say, fifty paces of you. They can feel the power in you, too. You won't know the *gholam* until it's too late. They look just like anybody else. On the outside. Inside ... *Gholam* have no bones; they can squeeze themselves under a door. And they're strong enough to rip a door off steel hinges with one hand.' Or rip out a throat. Light, he should have let Nalesean stay in bed.

Suppressing a shiver, he pressed on. The women, all of them, watched him, almost not appearing to blink. He would not let them see him shiver. 'There were only six *gholam* made – three male and three female; at least, that's what they look like. Apparently even the Forsaken were a little uneasy about them. Or maybe they just decided six was enough. Either way, we know one is in Ebou Dar, probably kept alive since the Breaking in a stasis-box. We don't know if any others were put into that box, but one is more than enough. Whoever sent him – and it had to be one of the Forsaken – knew to follow us across the river. He had to have been sent after the Bowl of the Winds, and by what he said to me, to kill Nynaeve or Elayne, maybe both.' He spared them a quick look, soothing and sympathetic; nobody could feel easy knowing that thing was after them. In return he received a puzzled frown from Elayne, just the smallest wrinkling of her forehead, and from Nynaeve a slight wave of the hand, an impatient wave, to get on with it.

'To continue,' he said, shooting the pair of them a glare. It was very hard not to sigh, dealing with women. 'Whoever sent the *gholam* has to know the Bowl is here in the Tarasin Palace, now. If he, or she, sends the *gholam* here, some of you are going to die. Maybe a lot of you. I can't protect all of you at once. Maybe he'll get the Bowl, too. And that's on top of Falion Bhoda; small chance she's alone, even with Ispan a prisoner, so that means we have the Black Ajah to worry about, as well. Just in case the Forsaken and *gholam* aren't enough for you.' Reanne and the Wise Women drew themselves up even more indignantly than Merilille and her friends at mention of the Black Ajah, and the Aes Sedai, stiffening and gathering skirts, looked ready to stalk out in a huff. Press on; that was all he could do. 'Now. Now do you see why you all have to leave the palace and take the Bowl somewhere the *gholam* doesn't know about? Somewhere the Black Ajah doesn't know? Do you see why it has to be done now?'

Renaile's sniff would have startled geese in the next room. 'You merely repeat yourself, Master Cauthon. Merilille Sedai says she has never heard of this *gholam*. Elayne Sedai says there was a strange man, a creature, but little else. What is this . . . *stasis*-box? You have not explained that. How do you know what you claim to know?

Why should we go any further from the water than we are on the word of a man who creates fables from air?'

Mat looked to Nynaeve and Elayne, though with little hope. If they would only open their mouths, this could have been finished long since, but they gazed back at him, practicing expressionless Aes Sedai masks till their jaws must be creaking. He could not understand their silence. A barebones account of events in the Rahad had been all they gave, and he was willing to bet they would not have mentioned the Black Ajah at all had there been any other way to explain showing up in the palace with an Aes Sedai bound and shielded. Ispan was being held in another part of the palace, her presence known only to a handful. Nynaeve had forced some concoction down her throat, a foul-smelling mix of herbs that bulged the woman's eyes going down and had her giggling and stumbling in short order, and the rest of the Knitting Circle occupied the room with her for guards. Unwilling guards, but very assiduous; Nynaeve had made it extremely clear that should they let Ispan get away, they had best start running before she laid hands on them again.

He very carefully did not look toward Birgitte, standing beside the door with Aviendha. The Aiel woman wore an Ebou Dari dress; not the plain wool she had returned in, but a silver-gray silk riding dress that jarred with her plain-sheathed horn-handled belt knife. Birgitte had been quick to shed her own dress for her usual short coat and wide trousers, these dark blue and dark green. A quiver already hung at her hip. She was the source of everything he knew about *gholam* – and stasis-boxes – except what his eyes had seen in the Rahad. And he would not have revealed that on a hot grill.

'I read a book once that talked about—' he began, and Renaile cut him off.

'A book,' she sneered. 'I will not abandon the salt for a book Aes Sedai do not know.'

Suddenly it struck Mat that he was the only man present. Lan had gone off at Nynaeve's command, gone as tame as Beslan had at his mother's. Thom and Juilin were packing to leave. Had probably finished packing by now. If there was any use to it; if they ever did leave. The only man, surrounded by a wall of women who apparently intended to let him beat his head against that wall till his brains were scrambled. It made no sense. None. They looked at him, waiting.

Nynaeve, in yellow-slashed lace-trimmed blue, had pulled her braid over her shoulder so it hung down between her breasts, but that heavy gold ring – Lan's ring, he had learned – was carefully positioned to show anyway. Her face was smooth, and her hands rested in her lap, yet sometimes her fingers twitched. Elayne, in green Ebou Dari silk that made Nynaeve seem covered up despite the smoky lace collar under her chin, gazed back at him with eyes like cool pools of deep blue water. Her hands lay in her lap too, but now and again she would begin to trace the thread-of-gold embroidery that covered her skirts, then immediately stop. Why did they not say something? Were they trying to get back at him? Was it just a case of 'Mat wants to be in charge so much, let him see how well he can do without us'? He might have believed it of Nynaeve, any time but this anyway, but not of Elayne, not anymore. So why?

Reanne and the Wise Women did not huddle away from him as they did from the Aes Sedai, but their manner toward him had changed. Tamarla gave him a decently respectful nod. Honey-haired Famelle went so far as a friendly smile. Strangely, Reanne blushed, a pale stain. But they did not count as opposition, really. The six women had not said a dozen unprompted words between them since entering this room. Every one would jump if Nynaeve or Elayne snapped her fingers, and keep jumping until told to stop.

He turned to the rest of the Aes Sedai. Faces infinitely calm, infinitely patient. Except... Merilille's eyes flickered past him toward Nynaeve and Elayne for one instant. Sareitha began slowly smoothing her skirts under his gaze, seemingly unaware of doing so. A dark suspicion bloomed in his mind. Hands moving on skirts. Reanne's blush. Birgitte's ready quiver. A murky suspicion. He did not really know of what. Just that he had been going about this the wrong way. He gave Nynaeve a stern look, and Elayne a sterner. Butter would not have melted on their bloody tongues.

Slowly he walked toward the Sea Folk. He just walked, but he heard someone with Merilille sniff, and Sareitha muttered, 'Such insolence!' Well, he was about to show them insolence. If Nynaeve and Elayne did not like it, they should have taken him into their confidence. Light, but he hated being used. Especially when he did not know how, or why.

Stopping in front of Renaile's chair, he studied the dark faces of the Atha'an Miere women behind it before looking down to her. She frowned, stroking a knife set with moonstones thrust behind her sash. She was a handsome woman rather than pretty, somewhere in her middle years, and under different circumstances he might have enjoyed looking at her eyes. They were large black pools a man could spend an evening just gazing into. Under different circumstances. Somehow, the Sea Folk were the fly in the cream pitcher, and he had not a clue how to pluck it out. He managed to keep his irritation under control. Barely. What to bloody do?

'You can all channel, I understand,' he said quietly, 'but that doesn't mean much to me.' As well be straight from the start. 'You can ask Adeleas or Vandene how much I care whether a woman can channel.'

Renaile looked past him toward Tylin, but it was not to the Queen she spoke. 'Nynaeve Sedai,' she said dryly, 'I believe there was no mention in your bargain of my having to listen to this young oakum picker. I—'

'I don't bloody care about your bargains with anybody else, you daughter of the sands,' Mat snapped. So his irritation was not that well under control. A man could only take so much.

Gasps rose among the women behind her. Something over a thousand years ago a Sea Folk woman had called a Shiotan soldier a son of the sands just before trying to plant a blade in his ribs; the memory lay tucked inside Mat Cauthon's head, now. It was not the worst insult among the Atha'an Miere, but it came close. Renaile's face gorged with blood; hissing, eyes bulging in fury, she leaped to her feet, that moonstone-studded dagger flashing in her fist.

Mat snatched it out of her hand before the blade could reach his chest and shoved her back into her chair. He did have quick hands. He could still hold on to his temper, too. No matter how many women thought they could dance him for a puppet, he could—

'You listen to me, you bilge stone.' All right; maybe he could not hold it. 'Nynaeve and Elayne need you, or I'd leave you for the *gholam* to crack your bones and the Black Ajah to pick over what's left. Well, as far as you're concerned, I'm the Master of the Blades, and my blades are bare.' What that meant exactly, he had no idea, except for having once heard, 'When the blades are bare, even the Mistress of the Ships bows to the Master of the Blades.' 'This is the bargain between you and me. You go where Nynaeve and Elayne want, and in return, I won't tie the lot of you across horses like packsaddles and haul you there!'

That was no way to go on, not with the Windfinder to the Mistress of the Ships. Not with a bilgeboy off a broken-backed darter, for that matter. Renaile quivered with the effort of not going for him with her bare hands, and never mind her dagger in his hand. 'It is agreed, under the Light!' she growled. Her eyes nearly started out of her head. Her mouth worked, confusion and disbelief chasing one another across her face. This time, the gasps sounded as if the wind had ripped the curtains down.

'It is agreed,' Mat said quickly, and touching fingers to his lips, he pressed them to hers.

After a moment, she did the same, fingers trembling against his mouth. He held out the dagger, and she stared dully at it before taking it from him. The blade went back into its jeweled sheath. It was not polite to kill someone you had sealed a bargain with. At least, not until the terms were fulfilled. Murmurs began among the women behind her chair, rising, and Renaile stirred herself to clap her hands once. That silenced Windfinders to Wavemistresses as quickly as the two deckhands in training.

'I think I have just made a bargain with a *ta'veren*,' she said in that cool, deep voice. The woman could teach Aes Sedai how to pull themselves together quickly. 'But one day, Master Cauthon, if it pleases the Light, I think you will walk a rope for me.'

He did not know what that meant, except that she made it sound unpleasant. He made his best leg. 'All things are possible, if it pleases the Light,' he murmured. Courtesy paid, after all. But her smile was disturbingly hopeful.

When he turned back to the rest of the room, you would have

thought he had horns and wings, for the stares. 'Is there any further argument?' he asked in a wry tone, and did not wait for answers. 'I thought not. In that case, I suggest you pick out some spot well away from here, and we can be on our way as soon as you bundle up your belongings.'

They made a show of discussion. Elayne mentioned Caemlyn, sounding at least half-serious, and Careane suggested several remote villages in the Black Hills, all easily reached by gateway. Light, anywhere was easily reached by gateway. Vandene spoke of Arafel, and Aviendha suggested Rhuidean, in the Aiel Waste, with the Sea Folk women growing glummer the farther from the sea were the places named. All a show. To Mat, at least, that was clear by Nynaeve's impatient fiddling with her braid despite the suggestions coming hot and fast.

'If I may speak, Aes Sedai?' Reanne said timidly at last. She even raised her hand. 'The Kin maintain a farm on the other side of the river, a few miles north. Everyone knows it is a retreat for women who need contemplation and quiet, but no one connects it to us. The buildings are large and quite comfortable, if there's any need to stay long, and—'

'Yes,' Nynaeve broke in. 'Yes, I think that sounds just the thing. What do you say, Elayne?'

'I think it sounds wonderful, Nynaeve. I know Renaile will appreciate staying close to the sea.' The other five sisters practically piled on top of her saying how agreeable it sounded, how superior to any other suggestion.

Mat rolled his eyes to the heavens. Tylin was a study in not seeing what lay under her nose, but Renaile snapped at it like a trout taking a lacewing. Which was the point, of course. For some reason she was not to know that Nynaeve and Elayne had had everything arranged beforehand. She led the rest of the Sea Folk women out to gather whatever belongings they had brought before Nynaeve and Elayne could change their minds.

Those two would have followed Merilille and the other Aes Sedai, but he crooked a finger at them. They exchanged glances – he would have had to talk an hour to say as much as passed in those looks – then, somewhat to his surprise, came to him. Aviendha and

Birgitte watched from the door, Tylin from her chair.

'I am very sorry to have used you,' Elayne said before he could get a word out. Her smile flashed that dimple at him. 'We did have reasons, Mat; you must believe that.'

'Which you do not need to know,' Nynaeve put in firmly, flipping her braid back over her shoulder with a practiced toss of her head that made the gold ring bounce on her bosom. Lan *must* be insane. 'I must say, I never expected you to do what you did. Whatever in the world made you think of trying to *bully* them? You could have ruined everything.'

'What's life if you don't take a chance now and then?' he said blithely. As well by him if they thought it was planned instead of temper. But they had used him again without telling him, and he wanted a bit back for that. 'Next time you have to make a bargain with the Sea Folk, let me make it for you. Maybe that way, it won't turn out as badly as the last one.' Spots of color blooming in Nynaeve's cheeks told him he had hit the mark squarely. Not bad shooting blindfolded.

Elayne, though, just murmured 'A most *observant* subject' in tones of rueful amusement. Being in her good books might turn out less comfortable than being in her bad.

They swept toward the door without letting him say more. Well, he had not really thought they would explain anything. Both were Aes Sedai to the bone. A man learned to live with what he had to.

Tylin had all but slipped from his mind, but he had not from hers. She caught him up before he took two steps. Nynaeve and Elayne paused at the door with Aviendha and Birgitte, watching. So they saw when Tylin pinched his bottom. Some things, nobody could learn to live with. Elayne put on a face of commiseration, Nynaeve of glowering disapproval. Aviendha fought laughter none too successfully, while Birgitte wore her grin openly. They *all* bloody knew.

'Nynaeve thinks you are a little boy needing protection,' Tylin breathed up at him. 'I know you are a grown man.' Her smoky chuckle made that the dirtiest comment he had ever heard. The four women by the door got to watch his face turn beet red. 'I will miss you, pigeon. What you did with Renaile was magnificent. I do so admire masterful men.'

'I'll miss you, too,' he muttered. To his shock, that was simple truth. He was leaving Ebou Dar just in time. 'But if we meet again, I'll do the chasing.'

She chortled at him, and those dark eagle's eyes almost glowed. 'I admire masterful men, duckling. But not when they try being masterful with me.' Seizing his ears, she pulled his head down where she could kiss him.

He never saw Nynaeve and the others go, and he walked out on unsteady legs, tucking his shirt back in. He had to return to fetch his spear from the corner, and his hat. The woman had no shame. Not a scrap of it.

He found Thom and Juilin, coming out of Tylin's apartments, followed by Nerim and Lopin, Nalesean's stout man, who each lugged a large wicker pannier made for a packsaddle. Loaded with his belongings, he realized. Juilin carried Mat's unstrung bow and had his quiver slung on one shoulder. Well, she had said she was moving him.

'I found this on your pillow,' Thom said, tossing him the ring he had bought what seemed a year ago. 'A parting gift, it seems; there were loversknots and some other flowers strewn over *both* pillows.'

Mat jammed the ring onto his finger. 'It's mine, burn you. I paid for it myself.'

The old gleeman knuckled his mustaches and coughed in a failed effort to stifle a sudden wide grin. Juilin snatched off that ridiculous Taraboner hat and became engrossed in studying the inside of it.

'Blood and flaming—!' Mat drew a deep breath. 'I hope you two spared a moment for your own belongings,' he said levelly, 'because as soon as I grab Olver, we're on our way, even if we happen to leave a moldy harp or a rusty sword-breaker behind.' Juilin tugged at the corner of his eye with one finger, whatever that was supposed to mean, but Thom actually frowned. Insults to Thom's flute or his harp were insults to himself.

'My Lord,' Lopin said mournfully. He was a dark, balding man, rounder than Sumeko, and his black Tairen commoner's coat, tight to the waist then flaring, like Juilin's, fit very tightly indeed.

Normally almost as solemn as Nerim, now he had reddened eyes, as though he had been weeping. 'My Lord, is there any chance I might remain to see Lord Nalesean buried? He was a good master.'

Mat hated saying no. 'Anybody left behind might be left for a long time, Lopin,' he said gently. 'Listen, I'll need someone to help look after Olver. Nerim has his hands full with me. For that matter, Nerim will go back to Talmanes, you know. If you'd like, I will take you on myself.' He had grown used to having a manservant, and these were hard times for a man hunting work.

'I would like that very much, my Lord,' the fellow said lugubriously. 'Young Olver reminds me much of my youngest sister's son.'

Only, when they entered Mat's former rooms, the Lady Riselle was there, much more decently clothed than when he had last seen her, and quite alone.

'Why should I have kept him tied to me?' she said, that truly marvelous bosom heaving with emotion as she planted her fists on her hips. The Queen's duckling, it seemed, was not supposed to take a snappish tone with the Queen's attendants. 'Clip a boy's wings too far, and he will never grow to a proper man. He read his pages aloud sitting on my knee – he might have read all day, had I allowed it – and did his numbers, so I let him go. Why are you in such a bother? He promised to return by sunset, and he seems to set a great store by his promises.'

Propping the *ashandarei* in its old corner, Mat told the other men to drop their burdens and go find Vanin and the remaining Redarms. Then he left Riselle's spectacular bosom and ran all the way to the rooms Nynaeve and the other women shared. They were all there, in the sitting room, and so was Lan, with his Warder's cloak already draped down his back and saddlebags on his shoulders. His saddlebags, and Nynaeve's, it seemed. A good many bundles of dresses and not-so-small chests stood about the floor. Mat wondered if they would make Lan carry those, too.

'Of course you have to go find him, Mat Cauthon,' Nynaeve said. 'Do you think we would just abandon the child?' To hear her, you would have thought that was exactly what *he* had intended.

Suddenly he was deluged with offers of help, not just Nynaeve and Elayne proposing to put off going to the farm, but Lan and Birgitte and Aviendha offering to join the search. Lan was stone cold about it, grim as ever, but Birgitte and Aviendha ...

'My heart would break if anything happened to that boy,' Birgitte said, and Aviendha added, just as warmly, 'I have always said you do not care for him properly.'

Mat ground his teeth. In the streets of the city, Olver might well elude eight men until he appeared back at the palace at sunset. He did keep his promises, but small chance he would give up one moment of freedom he did not have to. More eyes would mean a quicker search, especially if all of the Wise Women were brought into it. For the space of three heartbeats he hesitated. He had his own promises to keep, though he was wise enough not to put it that way.

'The Bowl is too important,' he told them. 'That *gholam* is still out there, and maybe Moghedien, and the Black Ajah for sure.' The dice thundered in his head. Aviendha would not appreciate being lumped in with Nynaeve and Elayne, but he did not care right then. He addressed Lan and Birgitte. 'Keep them safe until I can reach you. Keep all of them safe.'

Startlingly, Aviendha said, 'We will. I promise.' She fingered the hilt of her knife. Apparently she did not understand she was one of those to be kept safe.

Nynaeve and Elayne did. Nynaeve's sudden glare tried to bore a hole through his skull; he expected her to yank on her braid, but strangely, her hand only fluttered toward it before being put firmly to her side. Elayne contented herself with raising her chin, those big blue eyes frosty. No dimple here.

Lan and Birgitte understood, too.

'Nynaeve is my life,' Lan said simply, putting a hand on her shoulder. The odd thing was, she suddenly looked very sad, and then just as suddenly, her jaw set as though she was preparing to walk through a stone wall and make a large hole.

Birgitte gave Elayne a fond look, but it was to Mat she spoke. 'I will,' she said. 'Honor's truth.'

Mat tugged at his coat uncomfortably. He still was not sure how much he had told her while drunk. Light, but the woman could soak it up like dry sand. Even so, he gave the proper response for a Barashandan lord, accepting her pledge. 'The honor of blood; the truth of blood.' Birgitte nodded, and from the startled looks he received from Nynaeve and Elayne, she still kept his secrets close. Light, if any Aes Sedai ever found out about those memories, they might as well know he had blown the Horn as well; foxhead or no foxhead, they would stretch him out till they dug out every last why and how.

As he was turning to go, Nynaeve caught his sleeve. 'Remember the storm, Mat. It's going to break soon; I know it. You take care of yourself, Mat Cauthon. Do you hear me? Tylin has directions for the farm, when you get back with Olver.'

Nodding, he made his escape, the dice in his head like echoes of his running boots. Was it during the search that he was supposed to take care of himself, or while getting the directions from Tylin? Nynaeve and her Listening to the Wind. Did she think a little rain was going to melt him? Come to think, once they used the Bowl of the Winds, it would rain again. It seemed years since rain last fell. Something tugged at his thoughts, something about the weather, and Elayne, which made no sense, but he shrugged it off. One thing at a time, and the one thing right now was Olver.

The men were all waiting in the Redarms' long room near the stables, everyone on their feet except Vanin, who lay sprawled on one of the beds with his fingers laced over his belly. Vanin said a man had to take rest when he could. He swung his boots over and sat up when Mat entered, though. He cared about Olver as much as any of the others; Mat was just afraid the man was going to start teaching him how to steal horses and poach pheasants. Seven sets of eyes focused on Mat intently.

'Riselle said Olver's wearing his red coat,' he told them. 'He gives them away, sometimes, but any urchin you see in a good red coat probably knows where Olver last was. Everybody goes in a different direction. Make loops out from the Mol Hara, and try to be back after about an hour. Wait till everybody is back before you go out again. That way, if somebody finds him, the rest of us won't still be looking tomorrow. Does everybody understand?' They nodded.

Sometimes it amazed him. Lanky Thom with his white hair and

mustaches, who had been a Queen's lover once, and more willingly than himself, not to mention more than a lover, if you believed half he said. Square-jawed Harnan with that tattoo on his cheek and more elsewhere, who had been a soldier all his life. Juilin with his bamboo staff and his sword-breaker on his hip, who thought himself as good as any lord even if the idea of carrying a sword himself still made him uneasy, and fat Vanin, who made Juilin look a bootlicker by comparison. Skinny Fergin, and Gorderan, nearly as wide in the shoulders as Perrin, and Metwyn, whose pale Cairhienin face still looked like a boy's despite being years older than Mat. Some of them followed Mat Cauthon because they thought he was lucky, because his luck might keep them alive when the swords were out, and some for reasons he was not really sure of, but they followed. Not even Thom had ever more than protested an order of his. Maybe Renaile had been more than luck. Maybe his being *ta'veren* did more than dump him in the middle of trouble. Suddenly he felt ... responsible ... for these men. It was an uncomfortable feeling. Mat Cauthon and responsibility did not go together. It was unnatural.

'Take care of yourselves, and look sharp,' he said. 'You know what's out there. There's a storm coming.' Now why had he said that? 'Move. We're wasting light.'

The wind still blew strongly, sweeping dust across the Mol Hara Square with its statue of a long-dead queen posing above the fountain, but there was no other sign of a storm. Nariene had been noted for her honesty, but not enough to have been depicted completely bare-chested. The afternoon sun burned high in a sky without a cloud, but people rushed through the square as quickly as they had in the morning cool. That was gone, wind or no, down here on the ground. The paving stones seemed a griddle under his boots.

Glaring across the square at The Wandering Woman, Mat headed toward the river. Olver had not gone off with the street urchins half as often while they were staying at the inn; he had been too content ogling the serving girls and Setalle Anan's daughters. So much for the dice telling him he had to move into the palace. Anything he had done since leaving – anything he wanted to do, he amended, thinking of Tylin and her eyes; and her hands – any of it could have been done just as well from there. Those dice spun now, and he wished they would just go away.

He tried to move quickly, dodging impatiently around trundling carts and wagons, cursing at lacquered sedan chairs and coaches that nearly ran him down, eyes darting in search of a red coat close to the ground, but the bustle in the streets slowed him to a meander. Which was just as well, in truth. No point dashing by the boy without seeing him. Wishing he had brought Pips out of the palace stables, he frowned at the people streaming past; a man on horseback could have moved no faster in the throng, but up in the saddle, he could have seen farther. Then again, asking questions from a saddle would have been awkward; not many folk actually rode inside the city, and some people had a tendency to shy away from anyone on a horse.

Always the same question. The first time he asked was at a bridge just below the Mol Hara, of a fellow selling honey-baked apples from a tray hanging from a strap around his neck. 'Have you seen a boy, about so high, in a red coat?' Olver liked sweets.

'Boy, my Lord?' the fellow said, sucking his few remaining teeth. 'Seen a thousand boys. Don't remember no coat, though. Would my Lord like one apple, or two?' He scooped up two with bony fingers and pushed them at Mat; the way they gave under his fingers, they were softer than any baking could account for. 'Did my Lord hear about the riot?'

'No,' Mat said sourly, and pushed on. At the other end of the bridge, he stopped a plump woman with a tray of ribbons. Ribbons held no fascination for Olver, but her red petticoats flashed beneath a skirt sewn up nearly to her left hip, and the cut of her bodice revealed rounded cleavage to equal Riselle's. 'Have you seen a boy ... ?'

He heard about the riot from her, too, and from half the people he asked. That rumor, he suspected had begun with events at a certain house in the Rahad that very morning. A wagon driver with her long whip coiled around her neck even told him the riot had been across the river, once she allowed as how she never noticed boys unless they ran under her mules. A square-faced man who sold honeycomb – incredibly dry-looking honeycomb – said the riot had been down near the light tower at the end of the Bay Road, on the eastern side of the mouth of the bay, which was about as likely a place for rioting as the middle of the bay itself. There were always a thousand rumors in any city, if you listened, and he was forced to listen to snatches of all of them, it seemed. One of the most remarkably pretty women he had ever seen, standing outside a tavern – Maylin was a serving girl at The Old Sheep, but her only task seemed to be standing outside to attract customers, which she certainly did – told him there had been a battle that morning, in the Cordese Hills west of the city, she thought. Or maybe in the Rhannon Hills, across the bay. Or maybe ... Remarkably pretty, Maylin, but not very bright; Olver might have watched her for hours, so long as she never opened her mouth. But she could not remember seeing any boy in a ... What color coat had he said, again? He heard about riots and battles, he heard about enough strange things seen in the sky or the hills to populate the Blight. He heard that the Dragon Reborn was about to descend on the city with thousands of men who could channel, that the Aiel were coming, an army of Aes Sedai – no, it was an army of Whitecloaks; Pedron Niall was dead, and the Children intended to avenge him, though why in Ebou Dar was not exactly clear. You might have thought the city would be hip-deep in panic with all the tales floating around, but the fact was, even those who told a tale usually only half-believed it. So, he heard all sorts of nonsense, but not a word about any boy in a red coat.

A few streets from the river, he began hearing thunder, great hollow booms that seemed to roll in from the sea. People looked up curiously at the cloudless sky, scratched their heads, and went on about their business. So did he, questioning every seller of sweets or fruit he saw, and every pretty woman afoot. All to no avail. Reaching the long stone quay that ran the whole length of the river side of the city, he paused, studying the gray docks stretching out into the river and the ships tied to them. The wind blew strong, heaving vessels at their mooring lines, grinding them against the stone docks despite the bags stuffed with wool hung down between for fenders. Unlike horses, ships did not interest Olver except as a way to go from here to there, and ships were men's business in Ebou

Dar even if the lading they carried often was not. Women on these docks would either be merchants keeping an eye on their goods or hard-armed members of the cargo-loaders' guild, and there would be no sweet-sellers here.

About to turn away, he realized almost no one was moving. The docks usually bustled, yet on every ship he could see, crewmen lined the rails and had climbed into the rigging to stare toward the bay. Barrels and crates stood abandoned while shirtless men and wiry women in green leather vests crowded together at the ends of the docks to peer between the ships, south, toward the thunder. Down that way, black smoke rose in thick towering columns, slanting sharply north on the wind.

Hesitating only a moment, he trotted out along the nearest dock. At first, ships tied to the long fingers of stone to the south blocked his view of anything except the smoke. Because of the way the shoreline lay, though, each dock stuck out farther than the next down; once he pushed into the murmuring crowd at the end, the broad river made an open path of choppy green water to the wave-tossed bay.

At least two dozen ships were burning out on the wide expanse of the bay, maybe more, engulfed in flame from end to end. A number of others had already settled, only a bow or stern still above water and that sliding under. Even as he looked, the bow of a broad two-masted ship flying a large banner of red and blue and gold, the banner of Altara, suddenly flew apart with a roar, a boom like thunder, and fast-thickening tendrils of smoke wafted away on the wind as the vessel began settling by the head. Hundreds of vessels were in motion, every craft in the bay, three-masted Sea Folk rakers and skimmers and two-masted soarers, coastal ships with their triangular sails, riverships under sail or sweep, some fleeing upriver, most trying to beat out to sea. Scores of other ships swarmed into the bay before the wind, great bluff-bowed vessels as tall as any of the rakers, crashing through the rolling waves, throwing aside spray. His breath caught as he suddenly made out square, ribbed sails.

'Blood and bloody ashes,' he muttered in shock. 'It's the flaming Seanchan!'

'Who?' demanded a stern-faced woman crowded next to him. A dark blue woolen dress of fine cut marked her a merchant as much as did the leather folder she carried for her bills of lading or the guild pin over one breast, a silver quill pen. 'It's the Aes Sedai,' she announced in tones of conviction. 'I know channeling when I see it. The Children of the Light will do for them, just as soon as they arrive. You'll see.'

A lanky, gray-haired woman in a grimy green vest twisted around to confront her, fingering the wooden hilt of her dagger. 'Hold your tongue about Aes Sedai, you flaming penny-grubber, or I'll peel you and stuff a Whitecloak down your bleeding gullet!'

Mat left them waving their arms and shouting at one another, and pushed clear of the crowd, running for the quay. Already he could see three – no, four – huge creatures circling over the city to the south on great pinions like those of a bat. Figures clung to the creatures' backs, apparently in some sort of saddles. Another flying creature appeared, and more. Below them, flame suddenly fountained above the rooftops with a roar.

People ran now, buffeting Mat as he struggled through the streets. 'Olver!' he shouted, hoping to be heard above other shouts from every side, and the screams. 'Olver!'

Abruptly, everybody seemed to be heading the other way, battering past him. Stubbornly he forced on against the tide. And came to a street where what all those folk fled from was made plain.

A Seanchan column rushed by, a hundred or more men in helmets like insects' heads and armor of overlapping plates, all riding animals like cats the size of horses, but covered in bronze scales rather than fur. Leaning forward in their saddles, blue-streamered lances slanted, they galloped toward the Mol Hara without looking to either side. Though 'gallop' was not quite the word for the way those creatures moved; the speed was right, but they ... flowed. It was time to be gone; past time. As soon as he found—

As the end of the column went by a flash of red, waist high, caught his eye among the crowd in the street beyond the intersection. 'Olver!' He darted across almost on the heels of the last scaled creature, pushing into the crowd in time to see a wide-eyed woman snatch up a little girl in a red dress and run with the child clutched to her bosom. Wildly, Mat pressed ahead, shouldering people aside when they bumped into him, bumping into more than a few himself. 'Olver! Olver!'

Twice more he saw a column of fire rise briefly above the rooftops, and smoke drifted to the sky in a dozen places. Several times he heard those booming roars, much closer than the bay, now. Inside the city, he was sure; more than once the ground quivered beneath his boots.

And then the street was clearing again, people fleeing in every direction, down alleys and into houses and shops, for Seanchan on horses were coming. Not all were armored men; near the head of that small thicket of lances rode a dark woman in a blue dress. Mat knew the large red panels on her skirts and bosom were worked with silver lightning. A silver leash, gleaming in the sun, ran from her left wrist to the neck of a woman in gray, a *damane*, who trotted beside the *sul'dam*'s horse like a pet dog. He had seen more of Seanchan at Falme than he wanted to, but unconsciously he paused at the mouth of an alleyway, watching. The roars and fires had showed that somebody in the city was trying to fight back, at least, and now he was going to see such an attempt.

The Seanchan were not the only reason everyone else had gotten out of sight. At the other end of the street, a good hundred mounted men swung long-pointed lances down. They wore baggy white breeches and green coats, and the gold cords on the officer's helmet glittered. With a collective shout, a hundred or more of Tylin's soldiers hurled themselves toward the city's attackers. They outnumbered the Seanchan in front of them by at least two to one.

'Bloody fools,' Mat muttered. 'Not like that. That *sul'dam* will—'

The only movement among the Seanchan was the woman in the lightning-marked dress raising her hand to point, as one might launch a hawk, or send off a hound. The golden-haired woman at the other end of the silvery leash took a small step forward. The foxhead medallion cooled against his chest.

Underneath the head of the Ebou Dari charge, the street suddenly erupted, paving stones and men and horses flying into the air with a deafening roar. The concussion knocked Mat flat on his back, or maybe it was the way the ground seemed to leap from under his feet. He pulled himself up in time to see the front of an inn across the way suddenly collapse into the street in a cloud of dust, exposing the rooms within.

Men and horses lay everywhere, pieces of men and horses, those still alive thrashing, around a hole in the ground half as wide as the street. Screams from the wounded filled the air. Fewer than half the Ebou Dari staggered to their feet, dazed and stumbling. Some seized up the reins of horses as wobbly-legged as they, heaving themselves into saddles, kicking the animals into some semblance of a run. Others just ran afoot. All away from the Seanchan. Steel they could face, but not this.

Running, Mat realized, seemed a particularly fine idea right then. A glance back down the alley showed dust and rubble piled at least a story high. He darted down the street ahead of the fleeing Ebou Dari, keeping as close to the walls as possible, hoping none of the Seanchan would think he was one of Tylin's soldiers. He should never have worn a green coat.

The *sul'dam* apparently was not satisfied. The foxhead went cool again, and from behind another roar hammered him to the pavement, pavement that jumped up to meet him. Through the ringing in his ears, he heard masonry groan. Above him, the white-plastered brick wall began leaning outward.

'What happened to my bloody luck?' he shouted. He had time for that. And just time to realize, as brick and timbers crashed down on him, that the dice in his head had just stopped dead.

CHAPTER 40

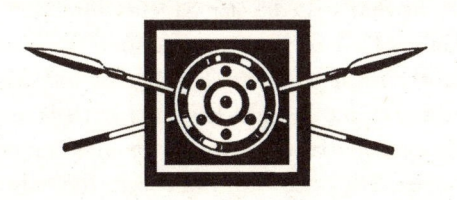

Spears

Mountains rose all around Galina Casban, little more than large hills behind but snowcapped peaks ahead and higher peaks beyond those, yet she really saw none of them. The stones of the slope bruised her bare feet. She panted, lungs laboring already. The sun baked overhead as it had for seemingly endless days, burning the sweat out of her in rivers. Anything other than putting one foot in front of the other seemed beyond her. Strange that with all the sweat coming out of her, she could not find any moisture in her mouth.

She had been Aes Sedai fewer than ninety years, her long black hair untouched as yet by gray, but for nearly twenty of those she had been head of the Red Ajah – called the Highest by other Red sisters, in private; considered by other Reds equal to the Amyrlin Seat – and for all but five of the years she had worn the shawl, she had been of the Black Ajah, in truth. Not to the exclusion of her duties as a Red, but superior to them. Her place on the Supreme Council of the Black Ajah was next to that of Alviarin herself, and she was one of only three who knew the name of the woman who led their hooded meetings. She could speak any name in those meetings – a king's – and know that name belonged to the dead. It had happened, with a king and with a queen. She had helped to break two Amyrlins, twice helped turn the most powerful woman in the world into a squealing wretch eager to tell all she knew, had helped make it seem that one of those had died in her sleep and had seen the other deposed and stilled. Such things were a duty, like the need to exterminate men with the ability to channel, not actions she took pleasure in beyond that of tasks well done, but she had enjoyed leading the circle that stilled Siuan Sanche. Surely all those things meant that Galina Casban was herself among the mightiest of the world, among the most powerful. Surely they did. They must.

Her legs wavered like springs that had lost their tempering, and she fell heavily, unable to catch herself with arms and elbows tightly bound behind her. The once-white silk shift, the only garment left to her, tore again as she slid on the loose rocks, scraping her welts. A tree stopped her. Face pressed against the ground, she began to sob. 'How?' she moaned in a thick voice. 'How can this happen to me?'

After a time she realized that she had not been pulled to her feet; no matter how often she fell, she had never before been allowed a moment's respite. Blinking away tears, she raised her head.

Aiel women covered the mountainside, several hundred of them scattered among the barren trees with their spears, the veils they could raise in an instant hanging down their chests. Galina wanted to laugh. Maidens; they called these monstrous women Maidens. She wished she could laugh. At least there were no men present, a small mercy. Men made her skin crawl, and if one could see her now, less than half-clothed . . .

Anxiously, her eyes sought for Therava, but most of the seventy or so Wise Ones stood together looking at something farther up the slope, blocking her view. There seemed to be a murmur of voices from the front of them. Maybe the Wise Ones were conferring about something. Wise Ones. They had been brutally efficient in teaching her the correct names; never just Aiel woman, and never wilder. They could smell contempt, however she hid it. Of course, you did not have to try hiding what had been seared out of you.

Most of the Wise Ones were looking away, but not all. The glow of *saidar* surrounded a young, pretty, red-haired woman with a delicate mouth who watched Galina with large, intent blue eyes. Perhaps as a sign of their own disdain, they had chosen the weakest of their number to shield her this morning. Micara was not truly weak in the Power – none of them were that – but even smarting from shoulders to knees as she was, Galina could have broken

Micara's shield with little effort. A muscle in her cheek spasmed uncontrollably; it always did when she thought of another escape attempt. The first had been bad enough. The second ... Shuddering, she fought not to sob again. She would not make the attempt again until she was sure of complete success. Very sure. Absolutely sure.

The mass of Wise Ones parted, turning to follow Therava with their eyes as the hawk-faced woman strode toward Galina. Suddenly panting once more, with apprehension, Galina tried to struggle to her feet. Hands bound and muscles watery, she had only reached her knees when Therava bent over her, necklaces of ivory and gold clattering softly. Seizing a handful of Galina's hair, Therava forced her head back sharply. Taller than most men, the woman did that even when they were standing, craning Galina's neck painfully to make her look up into the Wise One's face. Therava was somewhat stronger in the Power than she, which relatively few women were, but that was not what made Galina tremble. Cold deep blue eyes stabbed into her own, held her more tightly than Therava's rough hand; they seemed to strip her soul naked as easily as the Wise One handled her. She had not begged yet, not when they made her walk all day with hardly a drop of water, not when they forced her to keep up as they ran for hours, not even when their switches made her howl. Therava's cruel hard face, staring down at her impassively, made her want to beg. Sometimes she woke at night, stretched out tight between the four stakes where they bound her, woke whimpering from dreams that her whole life would be lived under Therava's hands.

'She is collapsing already,' the Wise One said in a voice like stone. 'Water her, and bring her.' Turning away, she adjusted her shawl, Galina Casban forgotten until there was need to recall her; to Therava, Galina Casban was less important than a stray dog.

Galina did not try to rise; she had been 'watered' often enough by now. It was the only way they let her drink. Aching for moisture, she did not resist when a blocky Maiden took her by the hair as Therava had and pulled her head back. She just opened her mouth as far as she could. Another Maiden, with a puckered scar slanting across nose and cheek, tilted a waterskin and slowly poured a trickle into Galina's waiting mouth. The water was flat and warm; it was delicious. She swallowed convulsively, awkwardly, holding her jaws wide. Almost as much as water to drink, she wanted to move her face under that thin stream, to let it run over her cheeks and forehead. Instead she kept her head very steady, so that every drop went down her throat. Spilling water was cause for another beating; they had thrashed her in sight of a creek six paces wide for spilling a mouthful over her chin.

When the waterskin was finally taken away, the blocky Maiden hauled her to her feet by her bound elbows. Galina groaned. The Wise Ones were gathering their skirts over their arms, exposing their legs well above soft knee-high boots. They could not be going to run. Not again. Not in these mountains.

The Wise Ones loped forward as easily as if on level ground. An unseen Maiden cut Galina across the back of her thighs with a switch, and she stumbled to a semblance of a run, half-dragged by the blocky Maiden. The switch slashed her legs whenever they faltered. If this run continued the rest of the day, they would take turns, one Maiden wielding the stick and another dragging. Laboring up slopes and nearly sliding down, Galina ran. A tawny mountain cat, striped in shades of brown and heavier than a man, snarled at them from a rocky ledge above; a female, lacking the tufts on her ears and the wide cheeks. Galina wanted to shout at her to flee, to run before Therava caught her. The Aiel ran on by the snarling animal, unconcerned, and Galina wept with jealousy for the cat's freedom.

She would be rescued eventually, of course; she knew that. The Tower would not allow a sister to remain in captivity. Elaida would not allow a Red to be held. Surely Alviarin would send rescue. Someone would, anyone, to save her from these monsters, especially from Therava. She would promise anything for that deliverance. She would even keep those promises. She had been broken free of the Three Oaths on joining the Black Ajah, replacing them with a new trinity, but at that moment she truly believed she would keep her word, if it brought rescue. Any promise, to anyone who would free her. Even a man.

By the time low tents appeared, their dark colors fading into the forested mountainsides as well as the cat had, Galina had two

Maidens supporting her, pulling her along. Shouts rose from every side, glad cries of greeting, but Galina was dragged on behind the Wise Ones, deeper into the camp, still running, stumbling.

Without warning the hands left her arms. She pitched forward on her face and lay there with her nose in the dirt and dead leaves, sucking air through her gaping mouth. She coughed on a piece of leaf, but she was too weak to turn her head. The blood pounded her ears, but voices came to her and slowly began to make sense.

'... Took your time, Therava,' a familiar-sounding woman's voice said. 'Nine days. We have been back long since.'

Nine days? Galina shook her head, scrubbing her face on the ground. Since the Aiel had shot her horse from under her, memory blended all the days into a melange of thirst and running and being beaten, but surely it had been longer ago than nine days. Weeks, certainly. A month or more.

'Bring her in,' the familiar voice said impatiently.

Hands pulled her up, shoved her forward, bending her to go under the edge of a large tent with the sides raised all around. She was thrown down on layered carpets, the edge of a red-and-blue Tairen maze overlapping gaudy flowers beneath her nose. With difficulty, she raised her head.

At first, she saw nothing but Sevanna, seated on a large yellow-tasseled cushion in front of her. Sevanna with her hair like fine spun gold, her clear emerald eyes. Treacherous Sevanna, who had given her word to distract attention by raiding into Cairhien, then broken her pledge by trying to free al'Thor. Sevanna, who at the least might take her from Therava's clutches.

She struggled up onto her knees, and for the first time realized there were others in the tent. Therava sat on a cushion to Sevanna's right, at the head of a curving line of Wise Ones, fourteen women who could channel in all, though Micara, who still held the shield on her, stood at the foot of the line rather than sitting. Half of them had been among the Wise Ones who captured her with such scornful ease. She would never again be so careless about Wise Ones; never again. Short, pale-faced men and women in white robes moved behind the Wise Ones, wordlessly offering trays of gold or silver with small cups, and more did the same on the other side of the tent, where a gray-haired woman in an Aiel coat and breeches of brown and gray sat to Sevanna's left, at the head of a line of twelve stone-faced Aielmen. Men. And she wore nothing but her shift, ripped and gaping in a number of places. Galina clamped her teeth shut to stifle a scream. She forced her back stiff to keep from trying to burrow into the rugs and hide from those cold male eyes.

'It seems that Aes Sedai can lie,' Sevanna said, and the blood drained from Galina's face. The woman could not know; she could not. 'You made pledges, Galina Casban, and broke them. Did you think you could murder a Wise One and then run beyond the reach of our spears?'

For a moment, relief froze Galina's tongue. Sevanna did *not* know about the Black Ajah. Had she not abandoned the Light long ago, she would have thanked the Light. Relief stilled her tongue, and a tiny spark of indignation. They *attacked* Aes Sedai and were angry when some of them died? A tiny spark was all she could manage. After all, what was Sevanna's twisting facts alongside days of beatings and Therava's eyes? A pained, croaking laugh bubbled up at the absurdity of it. Her throat was so dry.

'Be thankful some of you still live,' she managed past her laughter. 'Even now it is not too late to rectify your mistakes, Sevanna.' With an effort, she swallowed rueful mirth before it turned to tears. Just before. 'When I return to the White Tower, I will remember those who assist me, even now.' She would have added, 'and those who do otherwise,' but Therava's unwavering stare set fear fluttering in her middle. For all she knew, Therava still might be allowed to do whatever she wished. There had to be some way to induce Sevanna to . . . take charge of her. That tasted bitter, yet anything was better than Therava. Sevanna was ambitious, and greedy. In the midst of frowning at Galina, she had caught sight of her own hand and directed a brief, admiring smile at rings set with large emeralds and firedrops. She wore rings on half her fingers, and necklaces of pearls and rubies and diamonds fit for any queen draped across the swell of her bosom. Sevanna could not be trusted, but perhaps she could be bought. Therava was a force of nature; as well try to buy a flood or an avalanche. 'I trust that you will do what is right, Sevanna,' she finished. 'The rewards of friendship with the White Tower are great.'

For a long moment, there was silence except for the whisper of the white robes as the servants moved with their trays. Then . . .

'You are *da'tsang*,' Sevanna said. Galina blinked. She was a *despised* one? Certainly they had displayed their contempt plainly, but why—?

'You are *da'tsang*,' a round-faced Wise One she did not know intoned, and a woman a hand taller than Therava repeated, 'You are *da'tsang*.'

Therava's hawklike face might have been carved from wood, yet her eyes, fixed on Galina, glittered accusingly. Galina felt nailed to the spot where she knelt, unable to move a muscle. A hypnotized bird watching a serpent slither nearer. No one had ever made her feel that way. No one.

'Three Wise Ones have spoken.' Sevanna's satisfied smile was almost welcoming. Therava's face was stark. The woman did not like whatever had just happened. Something *had* happened, even if Galina did not know what. Except that it appeared to have delivered her from Therava. That was more than enough for the moment. More than enough.

When Maidens cut her bonds and stuffed her into a black wool robe, she was so grateful she almost did not care that they tore off the remnants of her shift first, in front of those ice-eyed men. The thick wool was hot and itchy and scratchy on her welts, and she welcomed it as though it were silk. Despite Micara still shielding her, she could have laughed as the Maidens led her out of the tent. It did not take long for that desire to vanish entirely. It did not take her long to begin wondering whether begging on her knees before Sevanna would do any good. She would have done it, could she have gotten to the woman, except that Micara made it plain she was not going anywhere she was not told to go, or speak a word unless spoken to.

Arms folded, Sevanna watched the Aes Sedai, the *da'tsang*, stagger down the mountainside and stop, beside a Maiden squatting on her heels with a switch, to drop the head-shaped stone she had been carrying in her hands. The black hood turned in Sevanna's direction for a moment, but the *da'tsang* quickly bent to pick up another large stone and turned to labor back up the fifty paces to where Micara waited with another Maiden. There she dropped that stone, picked up another, and started back down. *Da'tsang* were always shamed with useless labor; unless there was great need, the woman would not be allowed to carry even a cup of water, yet toil without purpose would fill her hours till she burst of shame. The sun had a long way to climb yet, and many more days lay ahead.

'I did not think she would condemn herself out of her own mouth,' Rhiale said at Sevanna's shoulder. 'Efalin and the others are all but sure she openly admitted killing Desaine.'

'She is mine, Sevanna.' Therava's jaw tightened. She might have taken the woman, but *da'tsang* belonged to no one. 'I intended to dress her in *gai'shain* robes of silk,' she muttered. 'What is the purpose of this, Sevanna? I expected to have to argue against cutting her throat, not this.'

Rhiale tossed her head, casting a sidelong glance at Sevanna. 'Sevanna intends to break her. We have had long talks of what to do should we capture any Aes Sedai. Sevanna wants a tame Aes Sedai to wear white and serve her. An Aes Sedai in black will do well enough, though.'

Sevanna shifted her shawl, irritated by the woman's tone. Not quite mocking, but all too aware that she wanted somehow to use the Aes Sedai's channeling as though it were Sevanna's own. It would be possible. Two *gai'shain* passed the three Wise Ones, carrying a large brass-strapped chest between them. Short and pale-faced, husband and wife, they had been Lord and Lady in the treekillers' lands. The pair bowed their heads more meekly than any Aiel in white ever could have managed; their dark eyes were tight with fear of a harsh word, much less a switch. Wetlanders could be tamed like horses.

'The woman is tamed already,' Therava grumbled. 'I have looked into her eyes. She is a bird fluttering in the hand and afraid to fly.'

'In nine days?' Rhiale said incredulously, and Sevanna shook her head vigorously.

'She is Aes Sedai, Therava. You saw her face go pale with fury when I accused her. You heard her laugh as she spoke of killing Wise Ones.' She made a vexed, angry sound. 'And you heard her threaten us.' The woman had been as slippery as the treekillers, speaking of rewards and letting the threat if no rewards came shout silently. But what else could be expected of Aes Sedai? 'It will take long to break her, but this Aes Sedai will beg to obey if it takes a year.' Once she did that ... Aes Sedai could not lie, of course; she had expected Galina to deny her accusation. Once she swore to obey ...

'If you want to make an Aes Sedai obey you,' a man's voice said behind her, 'this might help.'

Incredulous, Sevanna spun about to find Caddar standing there, and beside him the woman – the Aes Sedai – Maisia, both dressed in dark silk and fine lace as they had been six days ago, each with a bulging sack hanging incongruously from one shoulder by a strap. Caddar held out a smooth white rod about a foot long in one dark hand.

'How did you come here?' she demanded, then compressed her lips in anger. Plainly he had come as he had before; she was just surprised at him appearing, in the middle of the camp. She snatched the white rod he offered, and as always he stepped back beyond arm's reach. 'Why have you come?' she amended. 'What is this?' A little slimmer than her wrist, the rod was smooth except for a few odd, flowing symbols incised on one flat end. It felt not quite like ivory, not quite like glass. Very cool to the touch.

'You might call it an Oath Rod,' Caddar said, showing teeth in what was doubtless meant for a smile. 'It only came into my hands yesterday, and I immediately thought of you.'

Sevanna clamped her hands tight around the rod to keep from hurling it away. Everyone knew what the Aes Sedai's Oath Rod did. Trying not even to think, much less speak, she thrust it behind her belt and took her hands away.

Rhiale frowned at the rod at Sevanna's waist, and her eyes rose slowly, coldly, to Sevanna's face. Therava adjusted her shawl in a clatter of bracelets, and gave a hard, thin smile. There would never be any chance of one of them touching the rod, and maybe no chance of any other Wise One doing so either. But there was still Galina Casban. One day she would break.

Raven-eyed Maisia, a little behind Caddar, smiled almost as

faintly as Therava. She had seen, and understood. She was observant, for a wetlander.

'Come,' Sevanna told Caddar. 'We will drink tea in my tent.' She certainly would not share water with him. Lifting her skirts, she started up the slope.

To her surprise, Caddar was also observant. 'All you need do is have your Aes Sedai' – walking easily beside her on his long legs, he grinned suddenly, toothily, at Rhiale and Therava – 'or any woman who can channel hold the rod and speak whatever promises you wish while someone channels a little Spirit into the number. The marks on the end of the rod?' he added, raising his eyebrows insultingly. 'You can use it to release her, too, but that is more painful. Or so I understand.'

Sevanna's fingers touched the rod lightly. More glass than ivory, and very cool. 'It only works on women?' She ducked into the tent ahead of him. The Wise Ones and the leaders of the warrior societies were gone, but the dozen treekiller *gai'shain* remained, kneeling patiently to one side. No one person had ever kept a dozen *gai'shain* before, and she possessed more. There would have to be a new name for them, though, since they would never put off the white.

'Women who can channel, Sevanna,' Caddar said, following her in. The man's tone was incredibly insolent. His dark eyes shone with open amusement. 'You will have to wait until you have al'Thor before I give you what will control him.'

Removing the sack from his shoulder, he sat. Not on a cushion near hers, of course. Maisia was not afraid of a blade in her ribs; she lounged on an elbow almost at Sevanna's side. Sevanna eyed her sideways, then casually undid another lace of her own blouse. She did not recall the woman's bosom being as round as that. For that matter, her face seemed even more beautiful, as well. Sevanna tried not to grind her teeth.

'Of course,' Caddar went on, 'if you mean some other man – there is a thing called a binding chair. Binding people who cannot channel is more difficult than binding those who can. Perhaps a binding chair survived the Breaking, but you will have to wait while I find it.'

Sevanna touched the rod again, then impatiently ordered one of the *gai'shain* to bring tea. She could wait. Caddar was a fool. Sooner or later he would give her everything she wanted of him. And now the rod could break Maisia free of him. Surely then the woman would not protect him. For his insults, he would wear black. Sevanna took a small green porcelain cup from the tray the *gai'shain* held and gave it to the Aes Sedai with her own hands. 'It is flavored with mint, Maisia. You will find it refreshing.'

The woman smiled, but those black eyes ... Well, what could be done to one Aes Sedai could be done to two. Or more.

'What of the traveling boxes?' Sevanna demanded curtly.

Caddar waved the *gai'shain* away and patted the sack beside him. 'I brought as many *nar'baha* – that is what they were called – as many as I could find. Enough to transport all of you by nightfall, if you hurry. And I would, if I were you. Al'Thor means to finish you, it seems. Two clans are coming up from the south, and two more are moving to come down from the north. With their Wise Ones, all ready to channel. Their orders are to stay until every last one of you is dead or a prisoner.'

Therava sniffed. 'A reason to move, certainly, wetlander, but not to run. Even four clans cannot sweep Kinslayer's Dagger in a day.'

'Didn't I say?' Caddar's smile was not at all pleasant. 'It seems al'Thor has bound some Aes Sedai to him, too, and they have taught the Wise Ones how to Travel without a *nar'baha*, over short distances, at least. Twenty or thirty miles. A recent rediscovery, it seems. They could be here – well, today. All four clans.'

Maybe he lied, yet the risk ... Sevanna could imagine all too well being in Sorilea's grip. Not allowing herself to shiver, she sent Rhiale to inform the other Wise Ones. Her voice betrayed nothing.

Reaching into his bag, Caddar drew out a gray stone cube, smaller than the callbox she had used to summon him, and much plainer, with no marking but a bright red disc set in one face. 'This is a *nar'baha*,' he said. 'It uses *saidin*, so none of you will see anything, and it has limits. If a woman touches it, it won't work for days afterward, so I will have to hand them out myself, and it has other limits. Once opened, the gateway will remain for a fixed time, sufficient for a few thousand to go through if they don't waste time, and the *nar'baha* needs three days to recover afterward. I have enough extra to carry us where we need to go today, but . . .'

Therava leaned forward so intently she looked about to fall over, but Sevanna hardly listened. She did not doubt Caddar, exactly; he would not dare betray them, not while he hungered for the gold the Shaido would give him. There were small things, though. Maisia seemed to study him over her tea. Why? And if there was such need for speed, why was there no urgency in his voice? He would not betray, but she would take precautions anyway.

Maeric frowned at the stone cube the wetlander had given him, then at the . . . hole . . . that had appeared when he pressed the red spot. A hole, five paces wide and three high, in midair. Beyond lay rolling hills, not low, covered with brown grass. He did not like things to do with the One Power, especially with the male part of it. Sevanna stepped through another, smaller, hole with the wetlander and a dark woman, following the Wise Ones Sevanna and Rhiale had chosen out. Only a handful of Wise Ones remained with the Moshaine Shaido. Through that second hole, he could see Sevanna talking with Bendhuin. The Green Salts sept would find themselves with few Wise Ones, too; Maeric was sure of it.

Dyrele touched his arm. 'Husband,' she murmured, 'Sevanna said it would only remain open a short while.'

Maeric nodded. Dyrele always saw straight to the point. Veiling himself, he ran forward and leaped through the hole he had made. Whatever Sevanna and the wetlander said, he would send none of his Moshaine through before he knew it was safe.

He landed heavily on a slope covered with dead grass and nearly pitched head-over-heels down the hill before he caught himself. For a moment he stared back up at the hole. On this side, it hung more than a foot above the ground.

'Wife!' he shouted. 'There is a drop!'

Black Eyes leaped through, veiled and spears ready, and Maidens, also. As well try to drink sand as try to keep Maidens from being among the first. The rest of the Moshaine followed at a run, *algai'd'siswai* and wives and children, jumping down on the fly, craftsfolk and traders and *gai'shain*, most pulling heavily loaded packhorses and mules, near to six thousand altogether. His sept, his people. They still would be once he went to Rhuidean; Sevanna could not keep him from becoming clan chief for much longer.

Scouts began spreading out immediately, while the sept still rushed out of the hole. Lowering his veil, Maeric shouted orders that sent a screen of *algai'd'siswai* toward the crests of the surrounding hills while everyone else remained concealed below. There was no telling who or what lay beyond those hills. Rich lands, the wetlander claimed, but this part did not look rich to him.

The rush of his sept became a flood of *algai'd'siswai* he did not really trust, men who had fled their own clans because they did not believe Rand al'Thor was truly the *Car'a'carn*. Maeric was not sure what he himself believed, but a man did not abandon sept and clan. These men called themselves *Mera'din*, the Brotherless, a fitting name, and he had two hundr—

The hole suddenly snapped into a vertical slash of silver that sliced through ten of the Brotherless. Pieces of them fell onto the slope, arms, legs. The front half of a man slid almost to Maeric's feet.

Staring at the place where the hole had been, he stabbed at the red spot with his thumb. Useless, he knew, but ... Darin, his eldest son, was one of the Stone Dogs waiting as a rear guard. They would have been the last through. Suraile, his eldest daughter, had remained with the Stone Dog for whom she was thinking of giving up the spear.

His eyes met Dyrele's, as green and beautiful as the day she had laid the wreath at his feet. And threatened to cut his throat if he did not pick it up. 'We can wait,' he said softly. The wetlander had said three days, but maybe he was wrong. His thumb stabbed the red spot again. Dyrele nodded calmly; he hoped there would be no need to cry in one another's arms once they could be alone.

A Maiden came skittering down the slope from above, hurriedly lowering her veil, and actually breathing hard. 'Maeric,' Naeise said, not even waiting for him to see her, 'there are spears to the east, only a few miles and running straight at us. I think they are Reyn. At least seven or eight thousand of them.'

He could see other *algai'd'siswai* running toward him. A young

Brother to the Eagle, Cairdin, slid to a stop, speaking as soon as Maeric saw him. 'I see you, Maeric. There are spears no more than five miles to the north, and wetlanders on horses. Perhaps ten thousand of each. I do not think any of us broke the crest, but some of the spears have turned toward us.'

Maeric knew before the grizzled Water Seeker named Laerad opened his mouth. 'Spears coming over a hill three or four miles to the south. Eight thousand or more. Some of them saw one of the boys.' Laerad never wasted words, and he would never say which boy, who in truth could be anyone without gray hair, to Laerad.

There was no time for wasting words, Maeric knew. 'Hamal!' he shouted. No time for proper courtesy to a blacksmith, either.

The big man knew something was wrong; he scrambled up the slope, likely moving faster than he had since first picking up a hammer.

Maeric handed him the stone cube. 'You must press the red spot and keep pressing it, no matter what happens, no matter how long it takes for that hole to open. That is the only way out for any of you.' Hamal nodded, but Maeric did not even wait for him to say that he would. Hamal would understand. Maeric touched Dyrele's cheek, careless of how many eyes were on them. 'Shade of my heart, you must prepare to put on white.' Her hand strayed toward the hilt of her belt knife – she had been a Maiden when she made his wreath – but he shook his head firmly. 'You must live, wife, roofmistress, to hold together what remains.' Nodding, she pressed fingers to his cheek. He was astonished; she had always been very reserved in public.

Raising his veil, Maeric shoved one spear high above his head. 'Moshaine!' he roared. 'We dance!'

Up the slope they followed him, men and Maidens, nearly a thousand strong counting the Brotherless. Perhaps they could be counted among the sept. Up the slope and west; that way lay the nearest and the fewest. Perhaps they might buy enough time, though he did not really believe that. He wondered whether Sevanna had known of this. Ah, the world had grown very strange since Rand al'Thor came. Some things could not change, though. Laughing, he began to sing.

*'Wash the spears, while the sun climbs high.
Wash the spears, while the sun falls low.
Wash the spears; who fears to die?
Wash the spears; no one I know!'*

Singing, the Moshaine Shaido ran to dance their deaths.

Frowning, Graendal watched the gateway close behind the last of the Jumai Shaido. The Jumai and a great many Wise Ones. Unlike with the others, Sammael had not simply knotted this web so it would fall apart eventually. At least, she assumed he held it to the last; the closing, right on the heels of the last brown-and-gray-clad men, was too fortuitous otherwise. Laughing, Sammael tossed away the bag, still holding a few of those useless bits of stone. Her own empty sack was long since discarded. The sun sat low behind the mountains to the west, half of a glowing red ball.

'One of these days,' she said dryly, 'you will be too smart for your own good. A *fool* box, Sammael? Suppose one of them had understood?'

'None did,' he said simply, but he kept rubbing his hands together and staring at where the gateway had been. Or maybe at something beyond. He still held the Mirror of Mists, giving him the illusion of added height. She had dropped hers as soon as the gateway closed.

'Well, you certainly managed to put a panic into them.' Around them lay the evidence: a few low tents still standing, blankets, a cookpot, a rag doll, all sorts of rubbish lying where it had fallen. 'Where did you send them? Somewhere ahead of al'Thor's army, I suppose?'

'Some,' he said absently. 'Enough.' His staring introspection vanished abruptly, and his disguise as well. The scar across his face seemed especially livid. 'Enough to cause trouble, particularly with their Wise Ones channeling, but not so many that anyone will suspect me. The rest are scattered from Illian to Ghealdan. As to how or why? Maybe al'Thor did it, for his own reasons, but I certainly wouldn't have wasted most of them if it was my work, now would I?' He laughed again; caught up in his own brilliance.

She adjusted the bodice of her dress to cover a start. Competing that way was remarkably silly – she had told herself that ten thousand times, and never listened once – remarkably silly, and now the dress felt as if it might fall off. Which had nothing to do with her start. He did not know Sevanna had taken every Shaido woman who could channel with her. Was it finally time to abandon him? If she threw herself on Demandred's mercy . . .

As if reading her thoughts, he said, 'You're tied to me as tightly as my belt, Graendal.' A gateway opened, revealing his private rooms in Illian. 'The truth doesn't matter anymore, if it ever has. You rise with me, or fall with me. The Great Lord rewards success, and he's never cared how it was achieved.'

'As you say,' she told him. Demandred had no mercy. And Semirhage . . . 'I rise or fall with you.' Still, something would have to be worked out. The Great Lord rewarded success, but she would not be pulled down if Sammael failed. She opened a gateway to her palace in Arad Doman, to the long columned room where she could see her pets frolicking in the pool. 'But what if al'Thor comes after you himself? What then?'

'Al'Thor isn't going after anyone,' Sammael laughed. 'All I have to do is wait.' Still laughing, he stepped his gateway and let it close.

The Myrddraal moved from the deeper shadows, becoming visible. In its eyes, the gateways had left a residue – three patches of glowing mist. It could not tell one flow from another, but it could distinguish *saidin* from *saidar* by the smell. *Saidin* smelled like the sharp edge of a knife, the point of a thorn. *Saidar* smelled soft, but like something that would grow harder the harder it was pressed. No other Myrddraal could smell that difference. Shaidar Haran was like no other Myrddraal.

Picking up a discarded spear, Shaidar Haran used it to upend the bag Sammael had discarded, and then to stir the bits of stone that fell out. Much was happening outside the plan. Would these events churn chaos, or . . .

Angry black flames raced down the spear haft from Shaidar

Haran's hand, the hand of the Hand of the Shadow. In an instant the wooden haft was charred and twisted; the spearhead dropped off. The Myrddraal let the blackened stick fall and dusted soot from its palm. If Sammael served chaos, then all was well. If not . . .

A sudden ache climbed the back of its neck; a faint weakness washed along its limbs. Too long away from Shayol Ghul. That tie had to be severed somehow. With a snarl, it turned to find the edge of shadow that it needed. The day was coming. It would come.

Chapter 41

A Crown of Swords

Tossing, Rand dreamed, wild dreams where he argued with Perrin and begged Mat to find Elayne, where colors flashed just beyond sight and Padan Fain leaped at him with a flashing blade, and sometimes he thought he heard a voice moaning for a dead woman in the heart of a fog, dreams where he tried to explain himself to Elayne, to Aviendha, to Min, to all three at once, and even Min looked at him with scorn.

'. . . not to be disturbed!' Cadsuane's voice. Part of his dreams?

The voice frightened him; in his dream he shouted for Lews Therin, and the sound echoed through a thick mist where shapes moved and people and horses died screaming, a fog where Cadsuane followed him implacably while he ran, panting. Alanna tried to soothe him, but she was afraid of Cadsuane, too; he could feel her fear as strongly as his own. His head hurt. And his side; the old scar was fire. He felt *saidin*. Someone held *saidin*. Was it him? He did not know. He struggled to wake.

'You'll kill him!' Min shouted. 'I won't let you kill him!'

His eyes opened, staring up at her face. Not looking at him, she had his head wrapped in her arms and was glaring at someone away from the bed. Her eyes were red. She had been crying, but no longer. Yes, he was in his own bed, in his rooms in the Sun Palace. He could see a heavy square blackwood bedpost set with wedges of ivory. Coatless in a cream silk blouse, Min lay curled around him protectively, atop the linen sheet that covered him to the neck. Alanna was afraid; that lay shivering in the back of his head. Afraid for him. For some reason, he was sure of that.

'I think he is awake, Min,' Amys said gently.

Min looked down, and her face, framed in dark ringlets, beamed with a sudden smile.

Carefully – because he felt weak – he removed her arms and sat up. His head whirled dizzily, but he forced himself not to lie back again. His bed was ringed.

To one side stood Amys, flanked by Bera and Kiruna. Amys' too-youthful features bore no expression at all, but she brushed back her long white hair and shifted her dark shawl as though tidying herself after a struggle. Outwardly the two Aes Sedai were serene, yet with determined serenity, a queen ready to fight for her throne, a country woman ready to fight for her farm. Oddly, if he had ever seen three people stand together – and not just physically – it was those three, shoulder-to-shoulder as one.

On the opposite side of the bed, Samitsu, with those silver bells in her hair, and a slender sister with thick black eyebrows and a wild look to her raven hair stood with Cadsuane, who had her fists planted on her hips. Samitsu and the raven-haired Aes Sedai wore yellow-fringed shawls and had jaws set every bit as firmly as Bera or Kiruna, yet Cadsuane's stern stare made all four appear hesitant. The two groups of women were not staring at one another, but at the men.

At the foot of the bed were Dashiva with the silver sword and red-and-gold Dragon glittering his collar, and Flinn and Narishma, all grim-faced, trying to watch the women on both sides of the bed at once. Jonan Adley stood beside them, his black coat looking singed on one sleeve. *Saidin* filled all four men, to overflowing it seemed. Dashiva held almost as much as Rand could have. Rand looked to Adley, who nodded slightly.

Abruptly, Rand realized that he was not wearing anything beneath the sheet that had fallen to his waist, and nothing above except a bandage wound around his middle. 'How long have I been asleep?' he asked. 'How is it I'm alive?' He touched the pale bandage gingerly. 'Fain's dagger came from Shadar Logoth. Once I saw it kill a man in moments with a scratch. He died fast, and he died hard.' Dashiva muttered a curse with Padan Fain's name in it.

Samitsu and the other Yellow exchanged startled looks, but Cadsuane merely nodded, the golden ornaments around her iron-gray bun swaying. 'Yes; Shadar Logoth; that would explain several matters. You can thank Samitsu that you're alive, and Master Flinn.' She did not glance toward the grizzled man with his fringe of white hair, but he grinned as though she had given him a bow; in truth, surprisingly, the Yellows did nod to him. 'And Corele, here, of course,' Cadsuane went on. 'Each has done a part, including some things I think have not been done since the Breaking.' Her voice turned grim. 'Without all three, you would be dead by now. You still may die unless you let yourself be guided. You must rest, without exertion.' His stomach rumbled suddenly, loudly, and she added, 'We've only been able to get a little water and broth down you since you were hurt. Two days is a long time without food for a sick man.'

Two days. Only two. He avoided looking at Adley. 'I'm getting up,' he said.

'I won't let them kill you, sheepherder,' Min said with an obstinate glint in her eyes, 'and I won't let you kill you, either.' She put her arms around his shoulders as if to hold him where he was.

'If the *Car'a'carn* wishes to rise,' Amys said flatly, 'I will have Nandera bring in the Maidens from the corridor. Somara and Enaila will be especially happy to give him just the assistance he needs.' The corners of her mouth twitched toward a smile. Once a Maiden herself, she knew close enough to everything of that situation.

Neither Kiruna nor Bera smiled; they frowned at him as at an absolute fool.

'Boy,' Cadsuane said dryly, 'I've already seen more of your hairless bottomcheeks than I wish to, but if you want to flaunt them in front of all six of us, perhaps someone will enjoy the show. If you fall on your face, though, I may just spank you before I put you back to bed.' By Samitsu's face, and Corele's, they would be happy to assist her.

Narishma and Adley stared at Cadsuane in shock, while Flinn tugged at his coat as though arguing with himself. Dashiva, though, barked a rough laugh. 'If you want us to clear the women out . . .' The plain-faced man began preparing flows; not shields, but complex weaves of Spirit and Fire that Rand suspected would put anyone they were laid on in too much pain to think of channeling.

'No,' he said quickly. Bera and Kiruna would obey a simple order to go, and if Corele and Samitsu had helped keep him alive, he owed them more than pain. But if Cadsuane thought nakedness would hold him where he was, she was in for a surprise. He was not sure the Maidens had left him any modesty at all. With a smile for Min, he unwound her arms, tossed back the sheet, and climbed out of the bed on Amys' side.

The Wise One's mouth tightened; he could almost see her considering whether to call for the Maidens. Bera gave Amys an agonized, uncertain look, while Kiruna hurriedly turned her back, her cheeks darkening. Slowly he walked to the wardrobe. Slowly because he expected he might give Cadsuane her chance if he tried to move quickly.

'Phaw!' she muttered behind him. 'I vow, I *should* smack the stubborn boy's bottom.' Someone grunted what might have been agreement, or just disapproval of what he was doing.

'Ah, but it's such a pretty bottom, now isn't it that?' someone else said in a lilting Murandian accent. That must have been Corele.

A good thing he had his head inside the wardrobe. Maybe the Maidens had not peeled away as much modesty as he thought. Light! His face felt hot as a furnace. Hoping the motions of dressing would cover any wobbles, he climbed into his clothes hurriedly.

His sword stood propped in the back of the wardrobe, sword belt wound around the dark boarhide scabbard. He touched the long hilt, then took his hand away.

Barefoot, he turned back to the others while still tying the laces of his shirt. Min still sat cross-legged on the bed in her snug green silk breeches, by her expression unable to decide between approval and frustration. 'I need to talk with Dashiva and the other Asha'man,' he said. 'Alone.'

Min scrambled off the bed and ran to hug him. Not tightly; she was very careful of his bandaged side. 'I've waited too long to see you awake again,' she said, sliding an arm around his waist. 'I need to be with you.' She emphasized that just a tad; she must have had a viewing. Or maybe she just wanted to help steady his legs; that arm seemed to offer support. Either way, he nodded; he was not all that steady. Laying a hand on her shoulder, he suddenly realized that he did not want the Asha'man to know how weak he was any more than Cadsuane or Amys.

Bera and Kiruna made reluctant curtsies and started for the door, then hesitated when Amys did not move right away. 'So long as you do not intend to leave these rooms,' the Wise One said, not in the slightest as though speaking to her *Car'a'carn*.

Rand raised a naked foot. 'Do I look as though I'm going anywhere?' Amys sniffed, but with a glance at Adley, she gathered up Bera and Kiruna and departed.

Cadsuane and the other two were only a moment more in going. The gray-haired Green glanced at Adley, too. It could not be much of a secret that he had been gone from Cairhien for days. At the door, she paused. 'Don't do anything foolish, boy.' She sounded like a stern aunt cautioning a shiftless nephew, without much expectation he would listen. Samitsu and Corele followed her out, dividing their frowns between him and the Asha'man. As they vanished, Dashiva laughed, a sharp wheeze, shaking his head; he actually sounded amused.

Rand stepped away from Min to fetch his boots from beside the wardrobe and take a rolled pair of stockings from inside. 'I'll join you in the anteroom as soon as I'm booted, Dashiva.'

The plain-faced Asha'man gave a start. He had been frowning at

Adley. 'As you command, my Lord Dragon,' he said, pressing fist to heart.

Waiting until the four men were gone, Rand sat down in a chair with a feeling of relief and began pulling on his stockings. He was sure his legs felt stronger just for being up and moving. Stronger, but they still did not want to support him very well.

'Are you sure this is wise?' Min said, kneeling beside his chair, and he gave her a startled look. If he had talked in his sleep during those two days, the Aes Sedai would have known. Amys would have had Enaila and Somara and fifty more Maidens waiting when he woke.

He tugged the stocking the rest of the way up. 'Do you have a viewing?'

Min sat back on her heels, folded her arms beneath her breasts and gave him a firm look. After a moment, she decided it was not working and sighed. 'It's Cadsuane. She is going to teach you something, you and the Asha'man. All the Asha'man, I mean. It's something you have to learn, but I don't know what it is, except that none of you will like learning it from her. You aren't going to like it at all.'

Rand paused with a boot in hand, then stuffed his foot in. What could Cadsuane, or any Aes Sedai, teach the Asha'man? Women could not teach men, or men women; that was as hard a fact as the One Power itself. 'We will see' was all he said.

Plainly that did not satisfy Min. She knew it would happen, and so did he; she was never wrong. But what *could* Cadsuane possibly teach him? What would he let her teach him? The woman made him unsure of himself, uneasy in a way he had not felt since before the Stone of Tear fell.

Stamping his foot to settle it in the second boot, he fetched his sword belt from the wardrobe, and a red coat worked in gold, the same he had worn to the Sea Folk. 'What bargain did Merana make for me?' he asked, and she made an exasperated sound in her throat.

'None, as of this morning,' she said impatiently. 'She and Rafela haven't left the ship since we did, but they've sent half a dozen messages asking if you're well enough to return. I don't think the bargaining has gone well for them without you. I suppose it's too much to hope that's where you're going.'

'Not yet,' he told her. Min said nothing, but she said it very loudly, fists on her hips and one eyebrow raised high. Well, she would know most of it soon enough.

In the anteroom, all the Asha'man except Dashiva sprang out of their chairs when Rand appeared with Min. Staring at nothing and talking to himself, Dashiva did not notice until Rand reached the Rising Sun set in the floor, and then he blinked several times before rising.

Rand addressed himself to Adley while fastening the Dragon-shaped buckle of his sword belt. 'The army's reached the hillforts in Illian already?' He wanted to take one of the gilded armchairs, but would not let himself. 'How? It should have been several more days at the best. At best.' Flinn and Narishma looked as startled as Dashiva; none of them had known where Adley and Hopwil had gone – or Morr. Deciding who to trust was always the difficulty, and trust a razor's edge.

Adley drew himself up. There was something about his eyes, beneath those thick eyebrows. He had seen the wolf, as they said in Cairhien. 'The High Lord Weiramon left the foot behind and pressed forward with the horse,' he said, reporting stiffly. 'The Aiel kept up, of course.' He frowned. 'We encountered Aiel yesterday. Shaido; I don't how they got there. There were maybe nine or ten thousand, altogether, but they didn't seem to have any Wise Ones who could channel with them, and they didn't really slow us down. We reached the hillforts at noon today.'

Rand wanted to snarl. Leaving the foot behind! Did Weiramon think he was going to take palisaded forts on hilltops with horsemen? Probably. The man probably would have left the Aiel behind too, if he could have outrun them. Fool nobles and their fool honor! Still, it did not matter. Except to the men who died because the High Lord Weiramon was contemptuous of anyone who did not fight from horseback.

'Eben and I began destroying the first palisades soon as we arrived,' Adley went on. 'Weiramon didn't much like that; I think he would have stopped us, but he was afraid to. Anyway, we began setting fire to the logs and blowing holes in the walls, but before we more than started, Sammael came. A man channeling *saidin*, at least, and a lot stronger than Eben or me. As strong as you, my Lord Dragon, I'd say.'

'He was there right away?' Rand said incredulously, but then he understood. He had been sure Sammael would stay safe in Illian behind defenses woven of the Power if he thought he had to face Rand; too many of the Forsaken had tried, and most were dead now. In spite of himself, Rand laughed – and had to hug his side; laughing hurt. All that elaborate deception to convince Sammael he would be anywhere but with the invading army, to bring the man out of Illian, and all made unnecessary by a knife in Padan Fain's hand. Two days. By this time, everybody who had eyes-and-ears in Cairhien – which certainly included the Forsaken – knew that the Dragon Reborn lay on the edge of death. As well toss wet wood on the fire as think otherwise. 'Men scheme and women plot, but the Wheel weaves as it will'; that was how they said it in Tear. 'Go on,' he said. 'Morr was with you last night?'

'Yes, my Lord Dragon; Fedwin comes every night, just like he's supposed to. Last night, it was plain as Eben's nose we'd reach the forts today.'

'I don't understand any of this.' Dashiva sounded upset; a muscle in his cheek was twitching. 'You've lured him out, but to what purpose? As soon as he feels a man channel with anything near your strength, he'll flee back to Illian and whatever traps and alarms he has woven. You won't get at him there; he will know as soon as a gateway opens within a mile of the city.'

'We can save the army,' Adley burst out, 'that's what we can do. Weiramon was still sending charges against that fort when I left, and Sammael cuts every one to rags despite anything Eben or I can do.' He shifted the arm with the singed sleeve. 'We have to strike back and run immediately, and even so, he nearly burned us where we stood, more than once. The Aiel are taking casualties too. They're only fighting the Illianers who come out – the other hill-forts must be emptying, so many were coming when I left – but any time Sammael sees fifty of us together, Aiel or anybody, he rips them apart. If there were three of him, or even two, I'm not sure I'd find anybody alive when I go back.' Dashiva stared at him as if at a madman, and Adley shrugged suddenly, as though feeling the lightness of his bare black collar compared with the sword and Dragon on the older man's. 'Forgive me, Asha'man,' he muttered, abashed, then added in a still lower voice, 'But we can at least save them.'

'We will,' Rand assured him. Just not the way Adley expected. 'You're all going to help me kill Sammael today.' Only Dashiva looked startled; the other men just nodded. Not even the Forsaken frightened them anymore.

Rand expected argument out of Min, maybe a demand to come along, but she surprised him. 'I expect you would as soon no one found out you're gone before they have to, sheepherder.' He nodded and she sighed. Perhaps the Forsaken had to depend on pigeons and eyes-and-ears just like anyone else, but being too sure could be fatal.

'The Maidens will want to come if they know, Min.' They would want to, and he would be hard-pressed to refuse. If he could refuse. Yet the disappearance even of Nandera and whoever she had on guard might be too much.

Min sighed again. 'I suppose I could go talk to Nandera. I might be able to keep them out in the hallway for an hour, but they won't be pleased with me when they find out.' He almost laughed again before he remembered his side; they definitely would not be pleased with her, or with him. 'More to the point, farmboy, Amys won't be pleased. Or Sorilea. The things I let you get me into.'

He opened his mouth to tell her he had not asked her to do anything, yet before he could utter a word, she moved very close. Looking up at him through long lashes, she put a hand on his chest, tapping her fingers. She smiled warmly and kept her voice soft, but the fingers were a giveaway. 'If you let anything happen to you, Rand al'Thor, I'll give Cadsuane a hand whether she needs one or not.' Her smile brightened for a moment, almost cheerily, before she turned for the doors. He watched her go; she might make his head spin sometimes – nearly every woman he had ever met had done that at least a time or two – but she did have a way of walking that made him want to watch.

Abruptly he realized Dashiva was watching as well. And licking his lips. Rand cleared his throat loudly enough to be heard over the sound of the door closing behind her. For some reason, the plain-faced man raised his hands defensively. It was not as though Rand glared at him; he could not go around glaring at men just because Min wore tight breeches. Surrounding himself with the emptiness of the Void, he seized *saidin* and forced frozen fire and molten filth into the weaves for a gateway. Dashiva leaped back as it opened. Maybe having a hand sliced off would teach the man not to lick his lips like a goat. Something crooked and red spiderwebbed across the outside of the Void.

He stepped through onto bare dirt, with Dashiva and the others right behind, releasing the Source as soon as the last stepped clear. A sense of loss rushed in as *saidin* left, as awareness of Alanna dwindled. The loss had not seemed so great while Lews Therin was there; not so huge.

Overhead, the golden sun was more than halfway down to the horizon. A gust of wind swept dust from under his boots without leaving any coolness behind. The gateway had opened in a cleared area, marked off by a rope strung between four wooden posts. At each corner stood a pair of guards in short coats and baggy trousers stuffed into their boots, swords that appeared slightly serpentine hanging at their sides. Some had heavy mustaches that hung to their chins or thick beards, and all had bold noses and dark eyes that seemed tilted. As soon as Rand appeared, one of them went running.

'What are we doing here?' Dashiva said, looking about incredulously.

Around them stretched hundreds of sharp-peaked tents, gray and dusty white, tents and picket-lines of already saddled horses. Caemlyn lay not many miles away, hidden behind the trees, and the Black Tower not much farther, but Taim would not know of this unless he had a spy watching. One of Fedwin Moor's tasks had been to listen – to feel – for anyone trying to spy. In a ripple of murmurs spreading outward from the ropes, men with bold noses and serpentine swords rose from their heels and turned to stare expectantly toward Rand. Here and there women stood as well; Saldaean women often rode to the wars with their husbands, at least among the nobles and officers. There would be none of that today, though.

Ducking under the rope, Rand strode directly to a tent no different from any other except for the banner on the staff in front, three simple red blossoms on a field of blue. The kingspenny did not die back even in Saldaean winters, and when fires blackened the forests, those red flowers were always the first to reappear. A blossom nothing could kill: the sign of House Bashere.

Inside the tent, Bashere himself was already booted and spurred, and his sword on his hip. Ominously, Deira was with him, in a riding dress the same shade as her husband's gray coat, and if she wore no sword, the long dagger at her belt of heavy silver rondels would do to go on with. The leather gauntlets tucked behind that belt spoke of someone meaning to ride hard.

'I hadn't expected this for days yet,' Bashere said, rising from a folding camp chair. 'Weeks, I hoped, in truth. I had hoped to have most of Taim's leavings armed the way young Mat and I planned – I've gathered every maker of crossbows I could find into a manufactory, and they're starting to produce them like a sow dropping piglets – but as it is, no more than fifteen thousand have crossbows and know what to do with them.' With a questioning look, he lifted a silver pitcher from atop the maps spread out on his folding table. 'Do we have time for punch?'

'No punch,' Rand said impatiently. Bashere had spoken before about the men Taim found who could not learn to channel, but he had scarcely listened. If Bashere thought he had trained them well enough, that was all that mattered. 'Dashiva and three more Asha'man are waiting outside; as soon as Morr joins them, we'll be ready.' He eyed Deira ni Ghaline t'Bashere, towering over her diminutive husband with her hawk's beak of a nose and her eyes that made a hawk's look mild. 'No punch, Lord Bashere. And no wives. Not today.'

Deira opened her mouth, her dark eyes all but glowing suddenly.

'No wives,' Bashere said, knuckling his heavy gray-streaked mustaches. 'I will pass the order.' Turning to Deira, he held out his hand. 'Wife,' he said mildly. Rand winced, mild tone or no, and waited for the eruption.

Deira's mouth thinned. She scowled down at her husband, a hawk ready to stoop on a mouse. Not that Bashere looked anything like a mouse, of course; just a much smaller hawk. She drew a deep breath; Deira could make drawing a deep breath seem a thing that should cause the earth to tremble. And unhooking her sheathed dagger from her belt, she laid it in her husband's hand. 'We will talk of this later, Davram,' she said. 'At length.'

One day when he had time, Rand decided, he was going to make Bashere explain how he did that. If there ever was time.

'At length,' Bashere agreed, grinning through his mustaches as he stuffed the dagger behind his own belt. Maybe the man was simply suicidal.

The rope had been taken down outside, and Rand stood waiting with Dashiva and the other Asha'man while nine thousand Saldaean light horse arrayed themselves behind Bashere in a column of threes. Somewhere behind them, fifteen thousand men who called themselves the Legion of the Dragon would be gathering afoot. Rand had glimpsed them, every one in a blue coat made to button up the side so the red-and-gold Dragon across the chest would not be broken. Most carried steel-armed crossbows; some bore heavy unwieldy shields instead, but not one carried a pike. Whatever odd notion Mat and Bashere had cooked up, Rand hoped it would not lead a lot of this legion to death.

Morr grinned eagerly while he waited, all but bouncing on his toes. Perhaps he was simply glad to be back in his black coat with the silver sword on his collar, yet Adley and Narishma wore almost identical grins, and for that matter, Flinn's was not far off. They knew where they were going now, and what to do there. Dashiva scowled at nothing as usual, his lips moving silently. As usual. Also silent, scowling, were the Saldaean women gathered behind Deira, watching from one side. Eagles and falcons, feathers ruffled and furious. Rand did not care how they grimaced and frowned; if he could face Nandera and the rest of the Maidens after keeping them back from this, then the Saldaean men could put up with any number of lengthy discussions. Today, the Light willing, no women would die because of him.

So many men could not be lined up in a minute, even when they had been awaiting the order, but in a remarkably short time, Bashere raised his sword and called, 'My Lord Dragon!'

A shout rippled down the great column behind him. 'The Lord Dragon!'

Seizing the Source, Rand made a gateway between the posts, four paces by four, and ran through as he tied off the weave, filled with *saidin* and the Asha'man on his heels, into a great open square surrounded by huge white columns, each topped with a marble wreath of olive branches. At the two ends of the square stood nearly identical purple-roofed palaces of columned walks and high balconies and slender spires. Those were the King's Palace and the slightly smaller Great Hall of the Council, and this was the Square of Tammaz, in the heart of Illian.

A skinny man in a blue coat, with a beard that left his upper lip bare, stood gaping at the sight of Rand and the black-coated Asha'man leaping out of a hole in midair, and a stout woman, in a green dress cut high enough to show green slippers and her ankles in green stockings, pressed both hands to her face and stood rooted right in front of them, her dark eyes popping. All the people were stopping to stare, hawkers with their trays, carters halting their oxen, men and women and children with their mouths hanging open.

Rand thrust his hands high and channeled. 'I am the Dragon Reborn!' The words boomed across the square, amplified by Air and Fire, and flames shot up from his hands a hundred feet. Behind him, the Asha'man filled the sky with balls of fire streaking in every direction. All save Dashiva, who made blue lightnings crackle in a jagged web above the square.

No more was needed. A shrieking flood of humanity fled in all directions, away from the Square of Tammaz. They fled just in time. Rand and the Asha'man darted aside from the gateway, and Davram Bashere led his wildly screaming Saldaeans into Illian, a flood of horsemen waving their swords as they poured out. Straight ahead Bashere led the center line of the column, just as they had planned what seemed so long ago, while the other two lines peeled off to either side. They streamed away from the gateway, breaking apart into smaller groups, galloping into the streets leading out of the square.

Rand did not wait to see the last of the horsemen exit. With well under a third out of the gateway, he immediately wove another, smaller opening. You did not need to know a place at all to Travel if you only intended to go a very short distance. Around him he felt Dashiva and the rest weaving their gateways, but he was already stepping through his own, letting it close behind him atop one of the slender towers of the King's Palace. Absently he wondered whether Mattin Stepaneos den Balgar, the King of Illian, was somewhere below him at that moment.

The top of the spire stretched no more than five paces across, surrounded by a wall of red stone not quite chest-high on him. At fifty paces, it was the highest point in all of the city. From there he could see across rooftops glittering beneath the afternoon sun, red and green and every color, to the long earthen causeways that cut through the vast tall-grass marsh surrounding city and harbor. A sharp tang of salt hung in the air. Illian had no need of walls, with that all-enveloping marsh to stop an attacker. Any attacker who could not make holes in the air. But then, walls would have done no good either.

It was a pretty city, the buildings mainly of pale dressed stone, a city crisscrossed by as many canals as streets, like traceries of blue-green from this height, but he did not stop to admire it. Low across the roofs of taverns and shops and spired palaces he directed flows of Air and Water, Fire and Earth and Spirit, turning as he did so. He did not try to weave the flows, simply swept them out over the city and a good mile out over the marsh. From five other towers came flows sweeping low, and where they touched one another uncontrolled, light flashed and sparks flared and clouds of colored steam burst, a display any Illuminator might have envied. A better way to frighten people under their beds and out of the way of Bashere's soldiers, he could not imagine, though that was not the reason for it.

Long ago he had decided that Sammael must have wards woven throughout the city, set to give an alarm should anyone channel *saidin*. Wards inverted so no one except Sammael himself could find them, wards that would tell Sammael exactly where that man was channeling so he could be destroyed on the instant. With luck, every one of those wards was being triggered now. Lews Therin had been sure Sammael would sense them wherever he was, even at a distance. That was why the wardings should be useless now; that sort had to be remade once triggered. Sammael would come. Never in his life had he relinquished anything he considered his, however shaky his claim, not without a fight. All that from Lews Therin. If he was real. He had to be. Those memories had too much detail. But could not a madman dream his fancies in detail, too?

Lews Therin! he called silently. The wind blowing across Illian answered.

Below, the Square of Tammaz stood deserted and silent, empty except for a few abandoned carts. Edge-on, the gateway was invisible except for the weaves.

Reaching down to those weaves, Rand untied the knot and, as the gateway winked from existence, reluctantly released *saidin*. All the flows vanished from the sky. Maybe some of the Asha'man still held on to the Source, but he had told them not to. He had told them that any man he felt channeling in Illian once he himself stopped, he intended to kill without warning. He did not want to find out afterward that the channeler had been one of them. He leaned on the wall, waiting, wishing he could sit. His legs ached and his side burned however he stood, yet he might need to see as well as feel a weave.

The city was not entirely quiet. From several directions he could hear distant shouts, the faint clash of metal. Even moving so many men to the border, Sammael had not left Illian entirely unprotected. Rand turned, trying to watch in every direction. He thought Sammael would come to the King's Palace or that other at the far end of the square, but he could not be certain. Down one street he saw a band of Saldaeans clashing with an equal number of mounted men in shining breastplates; more Saldaeans suddenly galloped in from one side, and the fight vanished from his sight behind buildings. In another direction he spotted some of the Legion of the Dragon, marching across a canal's low bridge. An officer marked by a tall red plume on his helmet strode ahead of some twenty men carrying wide shields as tall as their shoulders, followed by perhaps two hundred more with heavy crossbows. How would they fight?

Shouts and steel ringing on steel in the distance, the faint screams of dying men.

The sun slid downward, and shadows lengthened across the city. Twilight, and the sun a low crimson dome in the west. A few stars appeared. Had he been wrong? Would Sammael simply go elsewhere, find another land to master? Had he been listening to anything other than his own mad ramblings?

A man channeled. For a moment, Rand froze, staring at the Great Hall of the Council. That had been enough of *saidin* for a gateway; he might not have felt a much smaller channeling, the length of the square. It had to be Sammael.

In an instant he had seized the Source, woven a gateway and leaped through with lightning ready to fly from his hands. It was a large room, lit by huge mirrored golden stand-lamps and others hanging on chains from the ceiling, with snowy marble walls carved in friezes showing battles, and ships crowding the marsh-bordered harbor of Illian itself. At the far end of the room, nine heavily carved and gilded armchairs stood like thrones atop a high stair-fronted white dais, the center chair with a back higher than any other. Before he could release the gateway behind him, the tower-top where he had stood exploded. He felt the wash of Fire and Earth even as a storm of stone fragments and dust struck through the gateway, knocking him down on his face. Pain stabbed his side as he landed, a sharp red lance digging into the Void where he floated, and that as much as anything else made him release the gateway. Someone else's pain; someone else's weakness. He could ignore them, in the Void.

He moved, forcing another man's muscles to work, pushed himself up and scrambled away in a lurching run toward the dais just as hundreds of red filaments burned down through the ceiling, burned through the sea-blue marble floor in a wide circle all around where the residue of his gateway was still fading. One stabbed through the heel of his boot, through his heel, and he heard himself cry out as he fell. Not his pain, in side or foot. Not his.

Rolling onto his back, he could see the remnants of those burning red wires still, fresh enough to make out Fire and Air woven in a way he had not known. Enough to make out exactly the direction they had come from. Black holes in the floor and ornately worked white plaster ceiling high overhead hissed and crackled loudly at the touch of the air.

His hands rose, and he wove balefire. Began to weave it. Someone else's cheek stung from a remembered slap, and Cadsuane's voice hissed and crackled in his head like the holes the red filaments had made. *Never again, boy; you will never do that again.* It seemed that he heard Lews Therin whimpering in distant fear of what he was about to lose, what had almost destroyed the world once. Every flow but Fire and Air fell away, and he wove as he had seen. A thousand fine hairs of red blossomed between his hands, fanning out slightly as they shot upward. A circle of the ceiling two feet across fell in stone chips and plaster dust.

Only after he had done it did he think that there might be someone between him and Sammael. He intended to see Sammael dead this day, but if he could do it without killing anyone else ... The weaves vanished as he pulled himself to his feet once more and limped hurriedly to the doors in the side of the hall, tall things with every panel set with nine golden bees the size of his fist.

A small flow of Air pushed one door open before he reached it, too small to be detected at any distance. Hobbling into the corridor, he sank to one knee. That other man's side was fire, his heel agony. Rand pulled his sword up and leaned on it, waiting. A cleanshaven fellow with plump pink cheeks peered around a corner down the way; enough of his coat showed to name him a servant. At least, a coat green on one side and yellow on the other looked like livery. The fellow saw Rand and, very slowly, as though he might not be noticed if he moved slowly enough, slid back out of sight. Sooner or later, Sammael would have to ...

'Illian belongs to me!' The voice boomed in the air, from every direction, and Rand cursed. That had to be the same weave he himself had used in the square, or something very like; it required so little of the Power he might not have felt the actual flows had he been within ten paces of the man. 'Illian is mine! I won't destroy what belongs to me killing you, and I won't let you destroy it, either. You had the nerve to come after me here? Do you have the courage to follow me again?' A sly mocking tone entering that thundering voice. 'Do you have the courage?' Somewhere above, a gateway opened and closed; Rand had no doubt that was what it was.

The courage? Did he have the *courage*? 'I'm the Dragon Reborn,' he muttered, 'and I'm going to kill you.' Weaving a gateway, he stepped through, to a place floors above.

It was another hallway, lined with wall hangings showing ships at sea. At the far end, the last crimson sliver of the sun shone through a colonnaded walk. The residue of Sammael's gateway hung in the air, the dissipating flows like faintly glowing ghosts. Not so faint Rand could not make them out, though. He began to weave, then stopped. He had leaped up here without a thought of a trap. If he copied what he saw exactly, he would step out wherever Sammael had, or so close as made no difference. But with just a slight alteration; no way to be sure whether the change was fifty feet or five hundred, yet either was close enough.

The vertical silver slash began to rotate open, revealing the shadow-cloaked ruins of greatness, not quite as dark as the hallway. Seen through the gateway, the sun was a slightly thicker slice of red, half-hidden by a shattered dome. He knew that place. The last time he had gone there, he had added a name to that list of Maidens in his head; the first time, Padan Fain had followed and become more than a Darkfriend, worse than a Darkfriend. That Sammael had fled to Shadar Logoth seemed like coming full circle in more ways than one. There was no time to waste now that he was opening the way. Before the gateway stopped widening, he ran through into the ravaged city that once had been called Aridhol, ran limping, letting the weave go as he ran, boots crunching on broken paving stones and dead weeds.

The first corner he came to, he ducked around. The ground shook under his feet as roars sounded back the way he had come, light flashing atop flash in the twilight darkness; he felt the wash of Earth and Fire and Air. Shrieks and bellows rose through the thunderous crashes. *Saidin* pulsing inside him, he hobbled away without looking back. He ran, and with the Power filling him, even in the dark shadows he could see clearly.

All around the great city lay, huge marble palaces each with four and five domes of different shapes painted crimson by the setting sun, bronze fountains and statues at every intersection, great stretches of columns running to towers that soared across the sun. They soared when intact, at least; more ended in abrupt jaggedness than not. For every dome that stood whole, ten were broken eggshells with the top hacked off or one side gone. Statues lay toppled in fragments, or stood with missing arms, or heads. Swiftly deepening darkness raced across sprawling hills of rubble, the few stunted trees clinging to their slopes twisted shapes like broken fingers against the sky.

A fan of bricks and stone spread across the way from what might have been a small palace; half its front missing, the rest of the columned façade leaned drunkenly toward the street. He stopped in the middle of the street, just short of the fan, waiting, feeling for another to use *saidin*. Clinging to the sides of the street was not a good idea, and not simply because any building might fall at any time. A thousand unseen eyes seemed to watch from windows like gouged eye sockets, to watch with a nearly palpable sense of anticipation. Distantly he felt the new wound in his side throbbing, a slash of flame, echoing the evil that clung to the very dust of Shadar Logoth. The old scar clenched like a fist. The pain of his foot seemed very distant indeed. Closer, the Void itself pulsated around him, the Dark One's taint on *saidin* beating in time with the knife slash across his ribs. A dangerous place by daylight, Shadar Logoth. By night . . .

Down the street, beyond a spired monument miraculously standing straight, something moved, a shadowed shape darting across the way in the darkness. Rand almost channeled, but he could not believe Sammael would go scuddling that way. When he first stepped into the city, when Sammael tried to destroy everything around his gateway, he had heard horrible screams. They had barely registered, then. Nothing lived in Shadar Logoth, not even rats. Sammael must have brought henchmen, fellows he did not mind killing in an attempt to reach Rand. Maybe one of them could lead Rand to Sammael. He hurried forward as fast as he could, as soundlessly as he could. Shattered pavement crunched under his boots with a sound like bones snapping. He hoped it was loud only to his *saidin*-enhanced ears.

Stopping at the base of the spire, a thick stone needle covered with flowing script, he peered ahead. Whoever had moved was gone; only fools or the madly brave went inside in Shadar Logoth at night. The evil that stained Shadar Logoth, the evil that had murdered Aridhol, had not died with Aridhol. Farther along the street, a tendril of silver-gray fog wavered out of a window, creeping toward another that came to meet it from a wide gap in a high stone wall. The depths of that gap shone as though a full moon lay inside. With the night, Mashadar roamed its city prison, a vast presence that could appear in a dozen places at once, a hundred. Mashadar's touch was not a pleasant way to die. Inside Rand, the taint on *saidin* beat harder; the distant fire in his side flickered like ten thousand lightnings, one on top of the last. Even the ground seemed to pound beneath his boots.

He turned, half-thinking to leave now. Very likely, Sammael had gone, now that Mashadar was out. Very likely the man had lured him here in the hope he would search the ruins until Mashadar killed him. He turned, and stopped, crouching against the spire. Two Trollocs were creeping down that street, bulky shapes in black mail, half again as tall as him, or more. Spikes stood out on the shoulders and elbows of their armor, and they carried spears with long black points and wicked hooks. To his *saidin*-filled eyes, their faces stood out clearly, one distorted by an eagle's beak where mouth and nose should have been, the other by a boar's tusked snout. Every line of their creeping shouted fear; Trollocs loved killing, loved blood, but Shadar Logoth terrified them. There would be Myrddraal about; no Trolloc would have entered this city without Myrddraal to drive it. No Myrddraal would have entered without Sammael driving. All of which meant Sammael must still be here, or these Trollocs would be running for the gates, not hunting. And they were hunting. That boar's snout was snuffling the air for a scent.

Abruptly a figure in rags leaped from a window above the Trollocs, falling on them with spear already stabbing. An Aiel, a woman, *shoufa* wrapped around her head but veil hanging. The eagle-beaked Trolloc shrieked as her spearpoint stabbed deep into its side, stabbed again. As its companion fell, kicking, boar-snout spun with snarl, thrusting viciously, but she ducked low under the black hooked point and stabbed up into the creature's stomach, and it went down in a thrashing heap with the other.

Rand was on his feet and running before thought. 'Liah!' he shouted. He had thought her dead, abandoned here by him, dead for him. Liah, of the Cosaida Chareen; that name blazed on the list in his head.

She whirled to confront him, spear ready in one hand, round bull-hide buckler in the other. The face he remembered as pretty despite scars on both cheeks was contorted with rage. 'Mine!' she hissed threateningly through her teeth. 'Mine! No one may come here! No one!'

He stopped in his tracks. That spear waited, eager to seek his ribs too. 'Liah, you know me,' he said softly. 'You know me. I'll take you back to the Maidens, back to your spear-sisters.' He held out his hand.

Her rage melted into a twisted frown. She tilted her head to one side. 'Rand al'Thor?' she said slowly. Her eyes widened, falling to the dead Trollocs, and a look of horror spread across her face. 'Rand al'Thor,' she whispered, fumbling the black veil into place across her face with the hand that held her spear. 'The *Car'a'carn*!' she wailed. And fled.

He hobbled after her, scrambling over piles of rubble spread across the street, falling, ripping his coat, falling again and nearly ripping it off, rolling and picking himself up on the run. The weakness of his body was distant, and the pain of it, but even floating deep in the Void, he could only push that body so hard. Liah vanished into the night. Around the next black-shadowed corner, he thought.

He limped around that as fast as he could. And nearly ran into four black-mailed Trollocs and a Myrddraal, inky cloak hanging unnaturally still down its back as the Fade moved. The Trollocs snarled in surprise, yet shock lasted less than a heartbeat. Hooked spears and scythe-curved swords rose; the Myrddraal's dead-black blade was in its fist, a blade that gave wounds almost as deadly as Fain's dagger.

Rand did not even try to draw the heron-mark sword at his side. Death in a tattered red coat, he channeled, and a sword of fire was in his hands, pulsing darkly with the throb of *saidin*, sweeping an eyeless head from its shoulders. Simpler to have destroyed them all the way he had seen the Asha'man kill at Dumai's Wells, but changing the weaves now, trying to change, might take a fatal moment. Those swords could kill even him. He danced the forms in a darkness lit by the flame in his hands, shadows flying across faces above him, faces with wolves' muzzles and goats' faces contorted in screams as his fiery blade sliced through black mail and the flesh beneath as if they were water. Trollocs depended on numbers and overwhelming ferocity; facing him, and that sword of the Power, they might as well have stood stock-still, unarmed.

The sword vanished from his hands. Still poised at the end of the form called Twisting the Wind, he stood among death. The last Trolloc to fall still thrashed, goat horns scraping on the fragmented pavement. The headless Myrddraal yet flung its arms about, of course, booted feet scrabbling wildly; Halfmen did not die quickly, even headless.

No sooner did the sword disappear than silver lightning lanced down from the cloudless, starry sky.

The first bolt struck with a deafening roar not four paces away. The world turned white, and the Void collapsed. The ground bounced under him as another bolt struck, and another. He had not realized he was on his face until then. The air crackled. Dazed, he pushed himself up, half falling as he ran from a hail of lightning that ripped the street apart to a thunder of collapsing buildings. Straight ahead he staggered, not caring where, so long as it was away.

Suddenly his head cleared enough for him to see where he was, reeling across a vast stone floor covered with tumbled chunks of stone, some as big as he. Here and there, dark uneven holes gaped in the floorstones. All around rose high walls, and tier upon tier of deep balconies that ran all the way around. Only a small portion of what had once been a vast roof remained, at one corner. Stars shone bright overhead.

He lurched another step, and the floor gave way beneath him. Desperately he flung out his hands; with a jolt, the right hand caught hold of a rough edge. He dangled into pitch blackness. The fall beneath his boots might be a few spans into a basement, or a mile for all he could tell. He could latch bands of Air to the jagged rim of the hole above his head to help pull himself out, except ... Somehow, Sammael had sensed the relatively small amount of *saidin* used in the sword. There had been a delay before the lightnings struck, but he could not say how long he had taken killing the Trollocs. A minute? Seconds?

With a heave, he swung his left arm up, trying to catch the edge of the hole. Pain no longer buffered by the Void stabbed through his side like a dagger going in. Spots danced in his vision. Worse, his right hand slipped on crumbling stone, and he could feel his fingers weakening. He was going to have to ...

A hand grabbed his right wrist. 'You are a fool,' a man's deep voice said. 'Count yourself lucky I don't care to see you die today.' The hand began drawing him up. 'Are you going to help?' the voice demanded. 'I don't intend to carry you on my shoulders, or kill Sammael for you.'

Shaking off his shock, Rand reached up and grabbed the rim of the hole, pulling despite the agony of his side. Despite the agony, he managed to acquire the Void again, too, and seize *saidin*. He did not channel, but he wanted to be ready.

His head and shoulders came above the floor, and he could see the other man, a big fellow little older than he, with hair black as the night and a coat black as an Asha'man's. Rand had never seen him before. At least he was not one of the Forsaken; those faces he knew. He thought he did, anyway. 'Who are you?' he demanded.

Still heaving, the man barked a laugh. 'Just say I'm a wanderer passing through. Do you really want to talk now?'

Saving his breath, Rand struggled upward, getting his chest over the lip, his waist. Abruptly he realized that a glow bathed the floor around them like the glow of a full moon.

Twisting to look over his shoulder, he saw Mashadar. Not a tendril, but a shining silver-gray wave rolling out of one of the balconies, arching over their heads. Descending.

Without a thought, his free hand rose, and balefire shot upward, a bar of liquid white fire slicing across the wave sinking toward them. Dimly he was aware of another bar of pale solid fire rising from the other man's hand that was not clasping his, a bar slashing the opposite way from his. The two touched.

Head ringing like a struck gong, Rand convulsed, *saidin* and the Void shattering. Everything was doubled in his eyes, the balconies, the chunks of stone lying about the floor. There seemed to be a pair of the other man overlapping one another, each clutching his head between two hands. Blinking, Rand searched for Mashadar. The wave of shining mist was gone; a glow remained in the balconies above, but dimming, receding, as Rand's eyes began to clear. Even mindless Mashadar fled balefire, it seemed.

Unsteadily, he got to his feet and offered a hand. 'I think we best move quickly. What happened there?'

The other man pushed himself up with a grimace at Rand's proffered hand. He was easily as tall as Rand, rare except among the Aiel. 'I don't know what happened,' he snarled. 'Run, if you want to live.' He suited his own words immediately, dashing toward a row of open arches. Not in the nearest wall. Mashadar had come from that one.

Fumbling for the Void, Rand limped after him as fast as he could, but before they were completely across the floor, the lightnings fell again, a storm of silver arrows. The two of them darted through the archways pursued by the thunder of walls and floor collapsing behind them, by clouds of dust and a hail of stones. Shoulders hunched and an arm across his face, Rand ran coughing through a broad room where trembling arches supported the ceiling and bits of stone rained down.

He burst out into a street before he knew it, stumbling three steps before stopping. The pain in his side made him want to bend over, but he thought his legs might give way if he did. His wounded foot throbbed; it seemed a year ago that that red wire of Fire and Air had stabbed his heel. His rescuer stood watching him; covered with dust head to toe, the fellow managed to look a king.

'Who are you?' Rand asked again. 'One of Taim's men? Or did you teach yourself? You can go to Caemlyn, you know, to the Black Tower. You don't have to live afraid of Aes Sedai.' For some reason, saying that made him frown; he could not understand why.

'I have never been afraid of Aes Sedai,' the man snapped, then drew a deep breath. 'You probably should leave here now, but if you intend to stay and kill Sammael, you had better try thinking like him. You have shown you can. He always liked destroying a man in sight of one of that man's triumphs, if he could. Lacking that, somewhere the man had marked as his would do.'

'The Waygate,' Rand said slowly. If he could be said to have marked anything in Shadar Logoth, it had to be the Waygate. 'He's waiting near the Waygate. And he has traps set.' Wards as well, it seemed, like those in Illian, to detect a man channeling. Sammael had planned this well.

The man laughed wryly. 'You can find the way, it seems. If you're led by the hand. Try not to stumble. A great many plans will have to be relaid if you let yourself be killed now.' Turning, he started across the street for an alleyway just ahead of them.

'Wait,' Rand called. The fellow kept on, not looking back. 'Who are you? What plans?' The man vanished into the alley.

Rand teetered after him, but when he reached the mouth of the narrow alley, it was empty. Unbroken walls ran a good hundred paces to another street, where a glow told of yet another part of Mashadar abroad, but the man was gone. Which was purely impossible. The fellow had had time to make a gateway, of course, if he knew how, but the residue would have been visible, and besides, that much of *saidin* being woven so near would have shouted at him.

Suddenly he realized that he had not felt *saidin* when the man made balefire, either. Just thinking of that, of the two streams touching, made his vision double again. Just for an instant, he could see the man's face again, sharp where everything else blurred. He shook his head until it cleared. 'Who in the Light are you?' he whispered. And after a moment, 'What in the Light are you?'

Whoever or whatever, the man was gone, though. Sammael was still in Shadar Logoth. With an effort he managed to regain the Void once more. The taint on *saidin* vibrated now, humming its way deep into him; the Void itself vibrated. But the weakness of watery muscles and the pain of injuries faded. He *was* going to kill one of the Forsaken before this night was done.

Limping, he ghosted through the dark streets, placing his feet with great care. He still made noise, but the night was full of noise now. Shrieks and guttural cries sounded in the distance. Mindless Mashadar killed whatever it found, and Trollocs were dying in Shadar Logoth tonight as they had once long, long ago. Sometimes down a crossing street he saw Trollocs, two or five or a dozen, occasionally with a Halfman but most often not. None saw him, and he did not bother them. Not simply because Sammael would detect any channeling. Those Trollocs and Myrddraal that Mashadar did not kill were still dead. Sammael had almost certainly brought them by the Ways, but apparently he did not realize just how Rand had marked the Waygate here.

Well short of the square where the Waygate lay, Rand stopped and looked around. Nearby, a tower stood seemingly whole. Not nearly as tall as some, its top still rose more than fifty paces above the ground. The dark doorway at its base was empty, the wood long rotted away and the hinges gone to dust. Through blackness relieved only by faint starlight through the windows, he climbed the winding stairs slowly, small clouds puffing up beneath his boots, every second step a stab of pain up his leg. Distant pain. On the towertop, he leaned against the smooth parapet to catch his breath. The idle thought came that he would never hear the end if Min learned of this. Min, or Amys, or Cadsuane for that matter.

Across missing rooftops, he could see the great square that had been one of the most important in Aridhol. Once an Ogier grove had covered this part of the land, but within thirty years after the Ogier who had built the oldest parts of the city departed, the residents had cut down the trees to make room for expanding Aridhol. Palaces and the remains of palaces surrounded the huge square, the glow of Mashadar shining deep inside a few windows, and a huge mound of rubble covered one end, but in the center stood the Waygate, apparently a tall broad piece of stone. He was not close enough to see the delicately carved leaves and vines that covered it, but he could make out the toppled pieces of high fence that had once surrounded it. Power-wrought metal, lying in a heap, they gleamed untarnished in the night. He could also see the trap he had woven around the Waygate, inverted so no eye but his could see it. No way to tell by looking whether the Trollocs and Halfmen really had passed through it, yet if they had, they would die before long. A nasty thing. Whatever traps Sammael had made down there were invisible to him, but that was expected. Likely they were not very pleasant either.

At first, he could not see Sammael, but then someone moved among the fluted, flaring columns of a palace. Rand waited. He wanted to be sure; he had only one chance. The figure stepped forward, out of the columns and a pace into the square, head swinging this way and that. Sammael, with snowy lace shining at his throat, waiting to see Rand walk into the square, into the traps. Behind him, the glow in the windows of the palace brightened. Sammael peered into the darkness lying across the square, and Mashadar oozed out of the windows, thick billows of silver-gray fog sliding together, merging as they loomed above his head. Sammael walked a little to one side, and the wave began to descend, slowly picking up speed as it fell.

Rand shook his head. Sammael was his. The flows needed for balefire seemed to gather themselves, despite the far echo of Cadsuane's voice. He raised his hand.

A scream tore the darkness, a woman shrieking in agony beyond knowing. Rand saw Sammael turn to stare toward the great mound of rubble even as his own eyes flashed that way. Atop the mound a shape stood outlined against the night sky in coat and breeches, a single thin tendril of Mashadar touching her leg. Arms outstretched, she thrashed about, unable to move from the spot, and her wordless wail seemed to call Rand's name.

'Liah,' he whispered. Unconsciously he reached out, as though he could stretch his arm across the intervening distance and pull her away. Nothing could save what Mashadar touched, though, no more than anything could have saved him had Fain's dagger plunged into his heart. 'Liah,' he whispered. And balefire leaped from his hand.

For less than a heartbeat, the shape of her still seemed to be there, all in stark blacks and snowy whites, and then she was gone, dead before her agony began.

Screaming, Rand swept the balefire down toward the square, the rubble collapsing on itself, swept down death out of time – and let *saidin* go before the bar of white touched the lake of Mashadar that now rolled across the square, billowing past the Waygate toward rivers of glowing gray that flowed out from another palace on the other side. Sammael had to be dead. He had to be. There had not been time for him to run, no time to weave a gateway, and if he had, Rand would have felt *saidin* being worked. Sammael was dead, killed by an evil almost as great as himself. Emotion raced across the outside of the Void; Rand wanted to laugh, or perhaps cry. He had come here to kill one of the Forsaken, but instead he had killed a woman he had abandoned here to her fate.

For a long time he stood on the towertop while the waning moon crossed the sky, almost at its half, stood watching Mashadar fill the square completely, till only the very top of the Waygate rose above the surface of the fog. Slowly it began to ebb away, hunting elsewhere. If Sammael had been alive, he could have killed the Dragon Reborn easily then. Rand was not sure that he would have cared. Finally he opened a gateway for Skimming and made a platform, a railless disc, half white and half black. Skimming was slower than Traveling; it took him at least half an hour to reach Illian, and the whole way, he burned Liah's name into his mind again and again, flailing himself with it. He wished he could cry. He thought he had forgotten how.

They were waiting for him in the King's Palace, in the throne room. Bashere, and Dashiva and the Asha'man. It was exactly like the room he had seen at the other end of the square, down to the standlamps and the scenes carved into the marble walls and the long white dais. Exactly the same except for being slightly larger in every dimension, and instead of nine chairs on the dais, there was only a great gilded throne with leopards for its arms and nine fist-sized golden bees that would stand above the head of whoever sat in it. Wearily Rand sat himself down on the steps at the front of the dais.

'I take it Sammael is dead,' Bashere said, looking him up and down in his ragged coat and dust.

'He's dead,' Rand said. Dashiva sighed loudly with relief.

'The city is ours,' Bashere went on. 'Or I should say, yours.' He laughed suddenly. 'The fighting stopped quick enough once the right people found out it was you. Not much to it, in the end.' Dried blood made a black stain down one torn sleeve of his coat.

'The Council has been waiting eagerly for you to come back. Anxiously, you might say,' he added with a wry grin.

Eight sweating men had been standing at the far end of the throne room since Rand came in. They wore dark silk coats with gold or silver embroidery on the lapels and sleeves, and falls of lace at their throats and wrists. Some wore a beard that left the upper lip shaved clean, but every one had a broad sash of green silk slanted across his chest, with nine golden bees marching up it.

At Bashere's gesture they came forward, bowing to Rand at about every third step, for all the world as though he wore the finest garments sewn. A tall man seemed to be the leader, a round-faced fellow with one of those beards, with a natural dignity that appeared strained by worry. 'My Lord Dragon,' he said, bowing again and pressing both hands to his heart. 'Forgive me, but Lord Brend do be nowhere to be found, and—'

'He won't be,' Rand said flatly.

A muscle in the man's face jumped at Rand's tone, and he swallowed. 'As you do say, my Lord Dragon,' he murmured. 'I do be Lord Gregorin den Lushenos, my Lord Dragon. In Lord Brend's absence, I do speak for the Council of Nine. We do offer you . . .' A hand at his side waved vigorously at a shorter, beardless man, who stepped forward bearing a cushion draped with a length of green silk. '. . . we do offer you Illian.' The shorter man whipped the cloth away, revealing a heavy gold circlet, two inches wide, of laurel leaves. 'The city do be yours, of course,' Gregorin went on anxiously. 'We did put an end to all resistance. We do offer you the crown, and the throne, and all of Illian.'

Rand stared at the crown on its cushion, not moving a muscle. People had thought he meant to make himself a king in Tear, feared he would in Cairhien and Andor, but no one had *offered* him a crown before. 'Why? Is Mattin Stepaneos so willing to give up his throne?'

'King Mattin did disappear two days ago,' Gregorin said. 'Some of us do fear . . . We do fear Lord Brend may have something to do with it. Brend does have . . .' He stopped to swallow. 'Brend did have a great deal of influence with the king, some might say too much, but he did be distracted in recent months, and Mattin had begun to reassert himself.'

Strips of grimy coatsleeve and pieces of shirtsleeve dangled as Rand reached to pick up the Laurel Crown. The Dragon wound around his forearm glittered in the lamplight as brightly as the golden crown. He turned it in his hands. 'You still haven't said why. Because I conquered you?' He had conquered Tear, and Cairhien too, but some turned on him in both lands still. Yet it seemed to be the only way.

'That do be part,' Gregorin said dryly. 'Even so, we might have chosen one of our own; kings have come from the Council before. But the grain you did order sent from Tear has your name on every lip with the Light. Without that, many would be dead of starvation. Brend did see every stick of bread go to the army.'

Rand blinked, and snatched one hand from the crown to suck on a pricked finger. Almost buried among the laurel leaves of the crown were the sharp points of swords. How long ago had he commanded the Tairens to sell grain to their ancient enemy, sell it or die for refusing? He had not realized they kept on after he began preparations to invade Illian. Maybe they feared to bring it up, but they had feared to stop, too. Maybe he had earned some right to this crown.

Gingerly he set the circle of laurel leaves on his head. Half those swords pointed up, half down. No head would wear this crown casually or easily.

Gregorin bowed smoothly. 'The Light illumine Rand al'Thor, King of Illian,' he intoned, and the seven other lords bowed with him, murmuring, 'The Light illumine Rand al'Thor, King of Illian.'

Bashere contented himself with a bow of his head – he was uncle to a queen, after all – but Dashiva cried out, 'All hail Rand al'Thor, King of the World!' Flinn and the other Asha'man took it up.

'All hail Rand al'Thor, King of the World!'

'All hail the King of the World!'

That had a good sound to it.

The story spread as stories will, and changed as stories change with time and distance, spreading out from Illian by coasting ship, and merchant trains of wagons, and pigeons sent in secret, spreading in ripples that danced with other ripples and made new. An army had come to Illian, the stories said, an army of Aiel, of Aes Sedai appearing from thin air, of men who could channel riding winged beasts, even an army of Saldaeans, though not many believed that one. Some tales said the Dragon Reborn had been presented the Laurel Crown of Illian by the Council of Nine, and others by Mattin Stepaneos himself on bended knee. Some said the Dragon Reborn had wrenched the crown from Mattin's head, then stuck that head on a spike. No, the Dragon Reborn had razed Illian to the ground and buried the old king in the rubble. No, he and his army of Asha'man had burned Illian out of the earth. No, it was Ebou Dar he had destroyed, after Illian.

One fact, though, turned up again and again in those tales. The Laurel Crown of Illian had been given a new name. The Crown of Swords.

And for some reason, men and women who told the tales often found a need to add almost identical words. The storm is coming, they said, staring southward in worry. The storm is coming.

Master of the lightnings, rider on the storm,
wearer of a crown of swords, spinner-out of fate.
Who thinks he turns the Wheel of Time,
may learn the truth too late.

> From a fragmentary translation
> of *The Prophecies of the Dragon*,
> attributed to Lord Mangore Kiramin,
> Sword-bard of Aramelle and Warder to
> Caraighan Maconar, into what was
> then called the vulgar tongue,
> circa 300 AB

The end of
the seventh book of
The Wheel of Time®

Look out for
THE PATH OF DAGGERS
Book Eight of The Wheel of Time®

Rand al'Thor, the Dragon Reborn, has conquered the city of Illian, struck down Sammael the Forsaken and shattered the armies of the invading Seanchan. Nynaeve, Aviendha and Elayne have broken the Dark One's hold on the world's weather and are poised to retake the throne of Andor. And Egwene al'Vere, leader of the exiled Aes Sedai, marches her army towards the White Tower.

But Rand and the Asha'man that follow him are slowly being corrupted by the madness that comes to the male wielders of the One Power. If they cannot remove the Dark One's taint from the True Source then none will survive to fight the Last Battle against the Shadow.

And as Rand struggles to maintain his sanity the Seanchan launch their counter-strike.

Glossary

A note on dates in this glossary. The Toman Calendar (devised by Toma dur Ahmid) was adopted approximately two centuries after the death of the last male Aes Sedai, recording years After the Breaking of the World (AB). So many records were destroyed in the Trolloc Wars that at their end there was argument about the exact year under the old system. A new calendar, proposed by Tiam of Gazar, celebrated freedom from the Trolloc threat and recorded each year as a Free Year (FY). The Gazaran Calendar gained wide acceptance within twenty years after the Wars' end. Artur Hawkwing attempted to establish a new calendar based on the founding of his empire (FF, From the Founding), but only historians now refer to it. After the death and destruction of the War of the Hundred Years, a third calendar was devised by Uren din Jubai Soaring Gull, a scholar of the Sea Folk, and promulgated by the Panarch Farede of Tarabon. The Farede Calendar, dating from the arbitrarily decided end of the War of the Hundred Years and recording years of the New Era (NE), is currently in use.

a'dam (AYE-dam): A device for controlling a woman who can channel, usable only by either a woman who can channel or a woman who can be taught to channel, and having no effect on any woman who cannot channel. It creates a link between the two women. The Seanchan version consists of a collar and bracelet connected by a leash, all of silvery metal, but one example of a version without the leash has been made, and another, unique, variant is believed to exist which allows a woman to control a man who can channel. If such a man is linked by an ordinary *a'dam* to a woman who can channel, the likely result is death for both. When an *a'dam* is worn by a woman who can channel, simply touching the *a'dam* results in pain for a man who also can. *See also* linking, Seanchan.

Age of Legends: Age ended by the War of the Shadow and the Breaking of the World. A time when Aes Sedai performed wonders now only dreamed of.

Aiel War (976–78 NE): When King Laman (LAY-mahn) of Cairhien cut down *Avendoraldera*, four clans of the Aiel crossed the Spine of the World. They looted and burned the capital city of Cairhien as well as many other cities and towns, and the conflict extended into Andor and Tear. By the conventional view, the Aiel were finally defeated at the Battle of the Shining Walls, before Tar Valon; in fact, Laman was killed in that battle, and having done what they came for, the Aiel recrossed the Spine. *See also* Cairhien; Spine of the World.

Ajah (AH-jah): Societies among the Aes Sedai, seven in number and designated by colors: Blue, Red, White, Green, Brown, Yellow and Gray. All Aes Sedai except the Amyrlin Seat belong to one. Each follows a specific philosophy of the use of the One Power and the purposes of the Aes Sedai. The Red Ajah bends its energies to finding men who can channel, and to gentling them. The Brown forsakes the mundane world and dedicates itself to seeking knowledge, while the White, largely eschewing both the world and the value of worldly knowledge, devotes itself to questions of philosophy and truth. The Green Ajah (called the Battle Ajah during the Trolloc Wars) holds itself ready for Tarmon Gai'don, the Yellow concentrates on the study of Healing, and Blue sisters involve themselves with causes and justice. The Gray are mediators, seeking harmony and consensus.

A Black Ajah, dedicated to serving the Dark One, is officially and vehemently denied.

algai'd'siswai: In the Old Tongue, 'fighters of the spear,' or 'spear fighters.' The name given to those Aiel who carry the spear and regularly take part in battle as opposed to those who follow crafts.

Altara (al-TAH-rah): A nation on the Sea of Storms, though in truth little unifies it except a name. The people of Altara think of themselves as inhabitants of a town or village, or as this lord's or that lady's people, first, and only second if at all as Altaran. Few nobles pay taxes to the crown or offer more than lip service, and that often slight. The ruler of Altara (currently Queen Tylin Quintara of House Mitsobar; TIE-lihn quin-TAHR-ah; MIHT-soh-bahr) is seldom more than the most powerful noble in the land, and at times has not even really been that. The Throne of the Winds holds so little power that many powerful nobles have scorned to take it when they could have. The banner of Altara is two golden leopards on a field checked four-by-four in red and blue. The sigil of House Mitsobar is a green anchor and sword, crossed. *See also* Wise Woman.

Amys (ah-MEESE): Wise One of Cold Rocks Hold, and a dreamwalker. An Aiel of the Nine Valleys sept of the Taardad Aiel. Wife of Rhuarc (ROARK), sister-wife to Lian (lee-AHN), who is roofmistress of Cold Rocks Hold. Amys is sister-mother to Aviendha.

angreal (ahn-gree-AHL): Remnants of the Age of Legends that allow anyone capable of channeling to handle a greater amount of the Power than is safe or even possible unaided. Some were made for use by women, others by men. Rumors of *angreal* usable by both men and women have never been confirmed. Their making is no longer known, and few are known to remain in existence. *See also sa'angreal; ter'angreal.*

Asha'man (AH-shah-mahn): (1) In the Old Tongue, 'Guardian' or 'Defender,' with a strong implication that this is a defender of truth and justice. (2) The name taken by followers of the Dragon Reborn, men who have come to what is now being called the Black Tower in order to learn how to channel. Some have dreamed of channeling despite all the dire risks, while others remain only because passing the test for the ability to learn has itself started them on the road to channeling, and they now must learn to control it before it kills them. They train not only in using the One Power, but in the use of the sword and in fighting with hands and feet. The Asha'man, who wear distinctive black coats, are divided according to the level of knowledge they have achieved, the lowest being a Soldier. The next level is a Dedicated, marked by a pin in the shape of a silver sword worn on the coat collar. The highest level is called simply an Asha'man, marked by a red-and-gold enameled pin in the shape of a Dragon worn on the coat collar opposite the silver sword. Unlike Aes Sedai, who go to great lengths to make sure that those they train are not allowed to move dangerously fast, the Asha'man are pushed hard from the beginning, most especially in learning to use the Power as a weapon. As a result, where the death or stilling of a novice of the White Tower during her training would be something spoken of with horror for years, at the Black Tower it is expected that a certain number of Asha'man Soldiers will die or be burned out attempting to learn. The existence of the Asha'man, and their connection to the Dragon Reborn, has caused a reevaluation among some Aes Sedai of the immediate necessity for gentling, but many have not changed their view at all. *See also* gentling, stilling.

Asunawa, Rhadam (ah-soo-NAH-wah, RAH-dam): High Inquisitor of the Hand of the Light. In his eyes, meddling with the One Power is usurping the Creator's power and is the cause of all the world's ills. He wants more than anything else to destroy anyone and everyone who can channel or even wishes to; they must confess their sin under the ministrations of the Hand of the Light, and then die. *See also* Questioners.

Atha'an Miere (AH-thah-AHN MEE-air): *See* Sea Folk.

Band of the Red Hand: (1) A legendary band of heroes (*Shen an Calhar*) from the Trolloc Wars who died at the Battle of Aemon's Field, when Manetheren fell. (2) A military formation which gathered to follow Mat Cauthon, and which is currently shadowing the rebel Aes Sedai and their army with orders to carry Egwene al'Vere to Rand al'Thor and safety, should she express a wish to flee from her current situation, and also any other sisters who might wish to join her.

Berelain sur Paendrag (BEH-reh-lain suhr PAY-ehn-DRAG): First of Mayene, Blessed of the Light, Defender of the Waves, High Seat of House Paeron (pay-eh-ROHN). A beautiful and willful young woman, and a skillful ruler. *See also* Mayene.

Birgitte (ber-GEET-teh): Warder to Elayne Trakand, believed to be possibly the first female Warder ever, a fact that causes a number of difficulties, few of them expected. Birgitte is in truth the legendary hero of that name, who was one of those bound to be called back by the Horn of Valere, but she was ripped out of *Tel'aran'rhiod* into the world of the flesh during a struggle with Moghedien and was only saved from death by being bonded by Elayne. Except for her beauty and skill with a bow, she is little like the stories of her. *See also* Forsaken; Horn of Valere; Warder.

Bryne, Gareth (BRIHN, GAH-rehth): Once Captain-General of the Queen's Guards in Andor, now commanding an army for those Aes Sedai in rebellion against the authority of Elaida do Avriny a'Roihan. Considered one of the greatest generals living. His relationship with Siuan Sanche troubles him nearly as much as it does her. The sigil of House Bryne is a wild bull, the rose crown of Andor around its neck. Gareth Bryne's personal sigil is three golden stars, each of five rays.

cadin'sor (KAH-dihn-sohr): Garb of Aiel *algai'd'siswai*: coat and breeches in browns and grays that fade into rock or shadow, along with soft, laced knee-high boots. In the Old Tongue, 'working clothes,' though this is of course an imprecise translation. *See also algai'd'siswai.*

Cadsuane Melaidhrin (CAD-soo-ain meh-LIE-drihn): An Aes Sedai of the Green Ajah who has approached legendary status among Aes Sedai while still alive, though in truth most sisters believe she must be years dead by now. Thought to have been born around 705 NE in Ghealdan, which would make her the oldest living Aes Sedai, she was also the strongest in the Power found for a thousand years or more until the advent of Nynaeve, Elayne and Egwene and even they do not far out-step her. Although a Green, over the years she has confronted and captured more men who could channel by far than any other living sister; a little-known oddity is that the men she brought to the White Tower tended to live markedly longer after being gentled than those brought by other sisters.

Cairhien (KEYE-ree-EHN): Both a nation along the Spine of the World and the capital city of that nation. Savaged during the Aiel War, the nation of Cairhien was in no way fully recovered when the assassination of King Galldrian (998 NE) plunged the country into a war for the succession which was itself interrupted by the invasion of the Shaido Aiel in what many call the Second Aiel War, although the city itself was saved by Aiel intervention under Rand al'Thor. Subsequently most nobles of Cairhien, along with many from Tear, swore fealty to the Dragon Reborn, but in a land where the Game of Houses has been raised to an art, it is hardly surprising that even many who swore are ready to maneuver for whatever advantage they can find. The banner of Cairhien is a many-rayed golden sun rising on a field of sky blue.

calendar: There are 10 days to the week, 28 days to the month and 13 months to the year. Several feastdays are not part of any month; these include Sunday (the longest day of the year), the Feast of Thanksgiving (once every four years at the spring equinox), and the Feast of All Souls Salvation, also called All

Souls Day (once every ten years at the autumn equinox). While many feasts and festivals are celebrated everywhere (such as the Feast of the Lights, which ends the old year and begins the new), every land has its own as well, and in many instances so do individual towns and villages. In general, the Borderlands have the fewest festivals and feastdays, while the cities of Illian and Ebou Dar have the most.

Caraighan Maconar (kah-RYE-gihn mah-CON-ahr): Legendary Green sister (212–373 AB), the heroine of a hundred adventures, credited with exploits that even some Aes Sedai consider improbable despite their inclusion in the records of the White Tower, such as single-handedly putting down a rebellion in Mosadorin and quelling the Comaidin Riots at a time when she had no Warders. Considered by the Green Ajah to be the archetype of a Green sister. *See also* Ajah.

Children of the Light: Society of strict ascetic beliefs, owing allegiance to no nation and dedicated to the defeat of the Dark One and the destruction of all Darkfriends. Founded during the War of the Hundred Years to proselytize against an increase in Darkfriends, they evolved during the war into a completely military society. Extremely rigid in beliefs, and certain that only they know the truth and the right. Consider Aes Sedai and any who support them to be Darkfriends. Known disparagingly as Whitecloaks. Their sign is a golden sunburst on a field of white. *See also* Questioners.

Darkfriends: Adherents of the Dark One. They believe they will gain great power and rewards, even immortality, when he is freed. Secretive of necessity, they organize into groups called 'circles,' with members of one circle rarely if ever known to members of another. Rank in the outside world has no bearing on rank with the circles; a king or queen who was a Darkfriend would be expected to obey a beggar who gave the proper signs. Among themselves, they sometimes use the ancient name Friends of the Dark.

Dragonsworn: General term used for supporters of the Dragon Reborn, usually by those who either oppose him or at least think to remain neutral. In fact, many given that name have never sworn any sort of oath, and it is frequently applied to brigands as well, some of whom claim the name in the hope that it will quell resistance. A great many atrocities have been committed by people claiming to be Dragonsworn.

Ebou Dar: The capital city of Altara. One of the great ports, and a city with many odd customs for an outsider to assimilate. *See also* Altara.

Elaida do Avriny a'Roihan (eh-LY-da doh AHV-rih-nee ah-ROY-han): An Aes Sedai, formerly of the Red Ajah, now raised to the Amyrlin Seat, though opposed by another claiming that title. Once advisor to Queen Morgase of Andor. She sometimes has the Foretelling.

Flame of Tar Valon: Symbol of Tar Valon, the Amyrlin Seat, and the Aes Sedai. A stylized representation of a flame: a white teardrop, point upward.

Forsaken, the: Name given to thirteen of the most powerful Aes Sedai of the Age of Legends, thus among the most powerful ever known, who went over to the Dark One during the War of the Shadow in return for the promise of immortality and were imprisoned along with the Dark One when his prison was resealed. Their own name for themselves was 'the Chosen.' The names given to them are still used to frighten children. They were: Aginor (AGH-ih-nohr), Asmodean (ahs-MOH-dee-an), Balthamel (BAAL-thah-mell), Be'lal (BEH-lahl), Demandred (DEE-man-drehd), Graendal (GREHN-dahl), Ishamael (ih-SHAH-may-EHL), Lanfear (LAN-feer), Mesaana (meh-SAH-nah), Moghedien (moh-GHEH-dee-ehn), Rahvin (RAAV-ihn), Sammael (SAHM-may-EHL), and Semirhage (SEH-mih-RHAHG). It is believed by those with some current knowledge that only Demandred and Sammael survive among the men, and only Graendal, Mesaana, Moghedien and Semirhage among the women. A number of strange encounters, however, suggest the possibility either that several new Chosen have been selected by the Dark One or that the Lord of the Grave has in some cases reached beyond death.

Gaidin (GYE-deen): In the Old Tongue, 'Brother to Battles.' A title used by Aes Sedai for the Warders. *See also* Warder.

gai'shain (GYE-shain): In the Old Tongue, 'Pledged to Peace in Battle' is as close a translation as is possible. An Aiel taken prisoner by other Aiel during raid or battle is required by *ji'e'toh* to serve his or her captor humbly and obediently for one year and a day, touching no weapon and doing no violence. A Wise One, a blacksmith, a child, or a woman with a child under the age of ten may not be made *gai'shain*. Since the revelation that the ancestors of the Aiel were in fact pacifist followers of the Way of the Leaf, a good many *gai'shain* refuse to put off white when their time ends. Additionally, although by tradition as strong as law no one who does not follow *ji'e'toh* can be made *gai'shain*, the Shaido Aiel have begun putting Cairhienin and other prisoners into *gai'shain* robes, and many have come to believe that since these people do not follow *ji'e'toh*, there is no need to release them at the end of the year and a day.

Gawyn (GAH-wihn) of House Trakand (trah-KAND): Queen Morgase's son, and Elayne's brother, who will be First Prince of the Sword when Elayne ascends to the throne. Half-brother to Galad Damodred. A man caught in more than one cleft stick; he depises Aes Sedai yet has sworn to serve them, and he hates Rand al'Thor yet has sworn not to raise a hand against him, all because he loves Egwene al'Vere beyond reason. He does not know that Egwene herself has not only become Aes Sedai, but the Amyrlin Seat opposing the Amyrlin he recognizes. His sign is a white boar.

gentling: The removal of a man's ability to channel. Considered necessary by most people because any man who channels will go insane from the taint on *saidin* and almost certainly commit atrocities with the Power in his madness before the taint kills him. One who has been gentled can still sense the True Source, but cannot touch it. Whatever madness has come before gentling is arrested but not cured, and if it is done soon enough, the rotting death brought by the taint can be averted. A man who is gentled, however, inevitably stops wanting to live; those who do not succeed in committing suicide usually die anyway within a year or two. Once believed permanent, gentling is now known by some to be susceptible to a highly specialized form of Healing. *See also* stilling.

Great Lord of the Dark: Name by which Darkfriends refer to the Dark One, claiming that to speak his true name would be blasphemous.

Hall of the Tower, the: The legislative body of the Aes Sedai, traditionally consisting of three Sitters in the Hall from each of the seven Ajahs. At present, there is a Hall sitting in the White Tower, which contains no Sitters for the Blue, and a Hall among those Aes Sedai who oppose Elaida do Avriny a'Roihan. This rebel Hall contains no Red Sitters. While the Amyrlin Seat is by law the absolute power in the White Tower, in fact her power has always depended on how well she could lead, manage or intimidate the Hall, as there are many ways that the Hall can balk any Amyrlin's plans. There are two levels of agreement that may be required for items to pass the Hall, the lesser consensus and the greater consensus. The greater consensus requires that every sister who is present must stand, and that a minimum of eleven Sitters be present; the presence of at least one Sitter from each Ajah is also required, except when the matter before the Hall is the removal of an Amyrlin or Keeper, in which case the Ajah from which she was raised will not be informed of the vote until after it has been taken. The lesser consensus also requires a quorum of eleven Sitters, but only two-thirds of those present need stand for an item to pass. Another difference is that there is no requirement for all Ajahs to be represented in the lesser consensus except in the case of a declaration of war by the White Tower, one of several matters left to the lesser consensus which many might think would require the greater. The Amyrlin Seat may call for any Sitter to resign her chair, or indeed for all to, and that call must be heeded. This is seldom done, however, as nothing stops an Ajah from returning the same Sitter or Sitters except a custom that sisters not serve again in the Hall after leaving it. As an indication of how serious such a call for a mass resignation would be, it is reliably believed that it has happened exactly four times in the more than three-thousand-year history of the White Tower, and that while two of those resulted in the selection of an entirely, or nearly, new Hall, the other two resulted in the resignation and exile of the Amyrlin involved.

Horn of Valere (vah-LEER): The legendary object of the Great Hunt of the Horn, it can call back dead heroes from the grave to fight against the Shadow. A new Hunt of the Horn has been called, and sworn Hunters for the Horn can now be found in many nations. Few even among the Aes Sedai know that the Horn has actually been found and used, or that it is now hidden in the White Tower.

Illian (IHL-lee-an): A great port on the Sea of Storms, capital city of the nation of the same name. An ancient enemy of Tear. The banner of Illian is nine golden bees on a field of green.

Juilin Sandar (JUY-lihn sahn-DAHR): A thief-catcher from Tear. A man in love with perhaps the very last woman he would ever have thought he could be.

length, units of: 10 inches = 1 foot; 3 feet = 1 pace; 2 paces = 1 span; 1000 spans = 1 mile; 4 miles = 1 league.

Lini (LIHN-nee): Childhood nurse to the Lady Elayne, and before her to Elayne's mother, Morgase, as well as to Morgase's mother. A woman of vast inner strength, considerable perception, and a great many sayings, who has never quite admitted that any of her charges has grown up completely.

linking: The ability of women who can channel to combine their flows of the One Power. While the combined flow is not as great as the sum total of the individual flows, it is directed by the person who leads the link and can be used much more precisely and to far greater effect than the individual flows could be. Men cannot link their abilities without the presence of a woman or women in the circle. Entering a link is normally a voluntary act, requiring at least acquiescence, but under certain circumstances, a sufficient circle already formed can bring another woman forcibly into the circle as long as no man is part of it. Insofar as is known, a man cannot be forced into a circle, no matter how large. Up to thirteen women can link without the presence of a man. With the addition of one man, the circle can increase to twenty-six women. Two men can take the circle to include forty-three women, and so on until the limit of six men and sixty-six women is reached. There are links that include more men and fewer women, but except in the linking of one man and one woman, two men and one woman or two men and two women, there must always be at least one more woman in the circle than there are men. In most circles, either a man or a woman can control the link, but a man must control in the circle of seventy-two as well as in mixed circles of fewer than thirteen but more than four. Although men are in general stronger in the Power than women, the strongest circles are those which contain as near as possible to equal numbers of men and women.

Logain Ablar (loh-GAIN): Born 972 NE in Ghealdan, once claimed to be the Dragon Reborn. Captured after carrying war across Ghealdan, Altara and Murandy, he was taken to the White Tower and gentled, later escaping in the confusion after Siuan Sanche was deposed. The accidental restoration of his ability to channel was the first indication that such a loss was not permanent. Confined after his Healing, he escaped again, and his present whereabouts are unknown. *See also* gentling; stilling.

Mayene (may-EHN): City-state on the Sea of Storms, hemmed in and historically oppressed by Tear. The ruler of Mayene is styled the First, which title was once the First Lord or Lady; Firsts claim to be descendants of Artur Hawkwing. The banner of Mayene is a golden hawk in flight on a field of blue.

Mazrim Taim (MAHZ-rihm tah-EEM): A man who raised havoc in Saldaea until he was defeated and captured, although he later escaped, apparently with the aid of some of his followers. Not only able to channel, but of great strength, he is now the M'Hael (MA'kHAIL; 'leader,' in the Old Tongue) of the Asha'man. *See also* Asha'man.

Melaine (meh-LAYN): A Wise One of the Jhirad sept of Goshien Aiel. A dreamwalker. Moderately strong in the One Power. Married to Bael (BAYL), clan chief of the Goshien. Sister-wife to Dorindha (dohr-IHN-dah), roofmistress of Smoke Springs Hold.

Moiraine Damodred (mwah-RAIN DAHM-oh-drehd): An Aes Sedai of the Blue Ajah, born into the then-reigning House of Cairhien, who vanished into a *ter'angreal* in Cairhien while battling Lanfear, apparently killing both herself and the Forsaken. Since she had already located the Dragon Reborn and killed the Forsaken Be'lal, she is already looked upon as one of those near-mythical sisters who are held as legendary heroes. *See also* Forsaken.

Morgase (moor-GAYZ): By the Grace of the Light, Queen of Andor, Defender of the Realm, Protector of the People, High Seat of House Trakand. Now in exile and believed dead, murdered by the Dragon Reborn, or so many think. Her sign is three golden keys. The sign of House Trakand is a silver keystone.

near-sister; near-brother: Aiel kinship terms meaning friends as close as first-sisters or first-brothers. Near-sisters often adopt one another formally as first-sisters in an elaborate ceremony carried out before Wise Ones, after which they are recognized by other

Aiel as truly born twins, though a pair of twins with two mothers. Near-brothers almost never do this.

Oaths, Three: The oaths taken by an Accepted on being raised to Aes Sedai. Spoken while holding the Oath Rod, a *ter'angreal* that makes oaths binding. They are: (1) To speak no word that is not true. (2) To make no weapon with which one man may kill another. (3) Never to use the One Power as a weapon except against Shadowspawn, or in the last extreme of defense of her own life, or that of her Warder or another Aes Sedai. The second oath was the first adopted after the War of the Shadow. The first oath, while held to the letter, is often circumvented by careful speaking. It is believed that the last two are inviolable.

Old Tongue: The language spoken during the Age of Legends. It is generally expected that nobles and the educated can speak it, but most actually know only a few words. Translation is often difficult, as it is a language capable of many subtly different meanings. *See also* Age of Legends.

Padan Fain (PAD-an FAIN): Once a peddler trading into the Two Rivers, and a Darkfriend, he was transformed at Shayol Ghul, not only to enable him to find the young man who would become the Dragon Reborn as a hound finds prey for the hunter, but to ingrain the need to find him. The pain of this transformation induced in Fain a hatred both of the Dark One and of Rand al'Thor. While following al'Thor, he encountered the trapped soul of Mordeth in Shadar Logoth, and this soul tried to take Fain's body. Because of what had been made of Fain, though, the result was an amalgamation that was mostly Fain and that has abilities beyond what either man had originally, though Fain does not understand them fully yet. Most men feel fear at a Myrddraal's eyeless gaze; Myrddraal feel fear at Fain's gaze.

Prophet, the: More elaborately, the Prophet of the Lord Dragon. Title claimed by Masema Dagar, a onetime Shienaran soldier, who preaches the rebirth of the Dragon Reborn. He has achieved a great following in Ghealdan and northern Amadicia, in part because of spreading knowledge that the Dragon has indeed been Reborn and in part because of the extreme brutality his followers visit not only on anyone who refuses to acknowledge the Dragon Reborn, but on those who refuse to acknowledge the authority of the Prophet as the hand and voice of the Dragon Reborn.

Questioners, the: An order within the Children of the Light. Avowed purposes are to discover the truth in disputations and uncover Darkfriends. In the search for truth and the Light, their normal method of inquiry is torture; their normal manner that they know the truth already and must only make their victim confess to it. They refer to themselves as the Hand of the Light, the Hand that digs out truth, and at times act as if they were entirely separate from the Children and the Council of the Anointed, which commands the Children. The head of the Questioners is the High Inquisitor, who sits on the Council of the Anointed. Their sign is a blood-red shepherd's crook. *See also* Children of the Light.

Rhuidean (RHUY-dee-ahn): A great city, the only one in the Aiel Waste and totally unknown to the outside world. Abandoned for nearly three thousand years. Once men among the Aiel were allowed to enter Rhuidean only once, in order to be tested inside a great *ter'angreal* for fitness to become clan chief (only one in three survived), and women only twice, for testing to become Wise Ones, the second time in the same *ter'angreal*, though with a considerably higher survival rate than the men. Now the city is inhabited again, by Aiel, and a great lake occupies one end of the valley of Rhuidean, fed by an underground ocean of fresh water and in turn feeding the only river in the Waste.

sa'angreal (SAH-ahn-GREE-ahl): Remnants of the Age of Legends that allow channeling much more of the One Power than is otherwise possible or safe. A *sa'angreal* is similar to, but more powerful than, an *angreal*. The amount of the Power that can be wielded with a *sa'angreal* compares to the amount that can be handled with an *angreal* as the Power wielded with the aid of an *angreal* does to the amount that can be handled unaided. The making of them is no longer known. As with *angreal*, there are male and female *sa'angreal*. Only a handful remain, far fewer even than *angreal*.

Sea Folk, the: More properly, the Atha'an Miere (AH-thah-AHN MEE-air), the People of the Sea. They live most of their lives on their ships and strongly dislike going any distance from the ocean. Relatively little is known of their customs, giving rise to an air of exotic mystery and often to fanciful tales. Most seaborne trade is carried by Sea Folk ships, which include the fastest by far and most of the largest, and they are considered by the inhabitants of port cities to be bargainers who outstrip the more widely known Domani. As survival at sea often depends on instant obedience, it should be no surprise that the Atha'an Miere stick strictly to their hierarchy, though there are surprising fluidities at some points. The Atha'an Miere are divided into numerous clans, both large and small, each headed by a Wavemistress. Below her are the Sailmistresses, the ships' captains of the clan. A Wavemistress has vast authority, yet she is elected to that position by the twelve senior clan Sailmistresses, who are referred to as the First Twelve of that clan, and she can be removed by the order of the Mistress of the Ships to the Atha'an Miere. The Mistress of the Ships has a level of authority any shorebound king or queen would envy, yet she also is elected, for life, by unanimous vote of the twelve senior Wavemistresses, who are called the First Twelve of the Atha'an Miere. (The term 'the First Twelve' is also used for the twelve senior Wavemistresses or Sailmistresses present in any gathering.) The position of Master of the Blades is held by a man who may or may not be the husband of the Mistress of the Ships. His responsibilities are the defense and the trade of the Sea Folk, and below him are the Swordmasters of Wavemistresses and the Cargomasters of Sailmistresses, who hold like positions and duties; for each of them, any authority outside these areas is held only as delegated by the woman he serves. Where any vessel sails and when is always up to the Sailmistress, but since trade and finances are totally in the hands of the Cargomaster (or, at higher levels, of the Swordmaster or the Master of the Blades), a close degree of cooperation is required. Every Sea Folk vessel, however small, and also every Wavemistress, has a Windfinder, a woman who is almost always able to channel and skilled in Weaving the Winds, as the Atha'an Miere call the manipulation of weather. The Windfinder to the Mistress of the Ships has authority over the Windfinders to the Wavemistresses, who in turn have authority over Windfinders to the Sailmistresses of their clans. One peculiarity of the Sea Folk is that all must begin at the very lowest rank and work their way up, and that anyone other than the Mistress of the Ships can be demoted by those above, even to the very bottom again in extreme instances.

Seanchan (SHAWN-CHAN): (1) Descendants of the armies Artur Hawkwing sent across the Aryth Ocean, who conquered the lands there. They believe that any woman who can channel must be controlled for the safety of everyone else, and any man who can channel must be killed for the same reason. (2) The land from which the Seanchan come.

Shayol Ghul (SHAY-ol GHOOL): A mountain in the Blasted Lands, beyond the Great Blight. Site of the Dark One's prison.

sister-wife: Aiel kinship term. Aiel women who are near-sisters or first-sisters, and who discover they love the same man or simply do not want a man to come between them, will both marry him, thus becoming sister-wives. Women who love the same man will sometimes try to find out whether they can become near-sisters and adopted first-sisters, a first step to becoming sister-wives. An Aielman faced with this situation has the choice of marrying both women or neither; if he has a wife who decides to take a sister-wife, he finds himself with a second wife.

siswai'aman: In the Old Tongue: 'spears of the dragon,' with a strong implication of ownership. The name taken by a good many men among the Aiel, but no women. These men do not actually acknowledge the name – nor do any others, in fact – but they wear a strip of red cloth wound around the forehead with a disc, half black and half white, above the brows. Although *gai'shain* normally are prohibited from wearing anything that would be worn by an *algai'd'siswai*, a large number of *gai'shain* have taken to wearing the headband. *See also gai'shain.*

Sorilea (soh-rih-LEE-ah): The Wise One of Shende Hold, a Jarra Chareen. Barely able to channel, she is also the oldest living Wise One, though not by as much as many think.

Spine of the World: A towering mountain range, with few passes, which separates the Aiel Waste from the lands to the west. Also called the Dragonwall.

stilling: The removal of a woman's ability to channel. A woman who has been stilled can sense but not touch the True Source. Officially, stilling is the result of trial and sentence for a crime, and was last carried out in 859 NE. Novices have always been required to learn the name and crimes of all women who have suffered judicial stilling. When the ability to channel is lost accidentally, it is called being burned out, though 'stilling' is often used for that also. Women who are stilled, however it occurs, seldom survive long; they seem to simply give up and die unless they find something to replace the emptiness left by the One Power. While it has always been believed that stilling was permanent, lately a method of Healing it has been discovered, though there appear to be limits to this which are yet to be explored.

Stone of Tear: A great fortress in the city of Tear, said to have been made with the One Power soon after the Breaking of the World. Attacked and besieged unsuccessfully countless times, it fell in a single night to the Dragon Reborn and a few hundred Aiel, thus fulfilling two parts of the Prophecies of the Dragon.

Talents: Abilities in the use of the One Power in specific areas. Aptitude in various Talents varies widely from individual to individual and is seldom related to the strength of the individual's ability to channel. There are major Talents, the best-known and most widespread of which is Healing. Other examples are Cloud Dancing, the control of weather, and Earth Singing, which involves controlling movements of the earth, for example preventing, or causing, earthquakes or avalanches. There are also minor Talents, seldom given a name, such as the ability to see *ta'veren* or to duplicate the chance-twisting effect of *ta'veren*, though in a very small and localized area rarely covering more than a few square feet. Many Talents are now known only by their names and sometimes vague descriptions. Some, such as Traveling (the ability to shift from one place to another without crossing the intervening space) are only now being rediscovered. Others, such as Foretelling (the ability to foretell future events, but in a general way), and Delving (the location of ores and possibly their removal from the ground, although the term is now also used for the variant of Healing which is used to examine someone's health and physical condition) are found rarely. Another Talent long thought lost is Dreaming, interpreting the Dreamer's dreams to foretell future events in more specific fashion than Foretelling. Some Dreamers had the ability to enter *Tel'aran'rhiod*, the World of Dreams, and (it is said) even other people's dreams. The last acknowledged Dreamer previously was Corianin Nedeal (coh-ree-AHN-ihn neh-dee-AHL), who died in 526 NE, but there is now another.

Tallanvor, Martyn (TAL-lahn-vohr, mahr-TEEN): Former Guardsman-Lieutenant of the Queen's Guards, who loves Morgase more than life or honor. *See also* Morgase.

ta'veren (tah-VEER-ehn): A person around whom the Wheel of Time weaves all surrounding life-threads, perhaps ALL life-threads. This weaving is little understood except that it seems in many ways an alteration of chance; what might happen, but only rarely, does. The effect can at times be quite localized. Someone influenced by a *ta'veren* may say or do what they would only have said or done one time in a million under those circumstances. Events occur of seeming impossibility, such as a child falling a hundred feet from a tower unharmed. At other times the effect seems to extend to influencing history itself, though often by means of the localized effects. This, it is believed, is the real reason that *ta'veren* are born, in order to shift history and restore a balance to the turning of the Wheel.

Tear (TEER): A nation on the Sea of Storms. Also the capital city of that nation, a great seaport. The banner of Tear is three white crescent moons slanting across a field half red, half gold. *See also* Stone of Tear.

ter'angreal (TEER-ahn-GREE-ahl): Remnants of the Age of Legends that use the One Power. Unlike *angreal* and *sa'angreal*, each *ter'angreal* was made to do a particular thing. Some *ter'angreal* are used by Aes Sedai, but the original purposes of many are unknown. Some require channeling, while others may be used by anyone. Some will kill, or destroy the ability to channel of any woman who uses them. Like *angreal* and *sa'angreal*, the making of them has been lost since the Breaking of the World. *See also angreal*; *sa'angreal*.

Thom Merrilin (TOM MER-rih-lihn): A not-so-simple gleeman and traveler.

Tinkers: Properly, the Tuatha'an (too-AH-thah-AHN), also called the Traveling People. A wandering folk who follow a totally pacifist philosophy called the Way of the Leaf, which allows no violence for any reason. Tuatha'an who fall away from this belief are called 'the Lost,' and are no longer acknowledged by any others.

treekillers: Disparaging term used by the Aiel for Cairhienin, along with 'oathbreakers.' Both refer to King Laman's cutting down of *Avendoraldera*, a gift from the Aiel, an act which violated the oaths given at the time the gift was given. To the Aiel, both terms rank with the worst that anyone can be called. *See also* Aiel War.

Valda, Eamon (VAHL-dah, AY-mon): An impatient Lord Captain of the Children of the Light, a man who believes you can't make dinner without breaking eggs and sometimes it is necessary to burn down the barn to get rid of the rats. He sees himself as a pragmatist, and will take whatever advantage offers itself. He is sure that Rand al'Thor is only a puppet of the White Tower and very likely cannot even channel. Hatred of Darkfriends (which of course include Aes Sedai) is the central pillar of his life. *See also* Children of the Light.

Warder: A warrior bonded to an Aes Sedai. The bonding is a thing of the One Power: by it he gains such gifts as quick healing, the ability to go long periods without food, water, or rest, and the ability to sense the taint of the Dark One at a distance. Warder and Aes Sedai share certain physical and emotional knowledge of one another through the bond. So long as a Warder lives, the Aes Sedai to whom he is bonded knows he is alive however far away he is, and when he dies she will know the moment and manner of his death. While most Ajahs believe an Aes Sedai may have one Warder bonded to her at a time, the Red Ajah refuses to bond any Warders at all, and the Green Ajah believes an Aes Sedai may bond as many as she wishes. Ethically the Warder must accede to the bonding voluntarily, but it has been known to happen against the Warder's will. What the Aes Sedai gain from the bonding is a closely held secret. By all known historical records, Warders have always been men, but recently a woman has been bonded, revealing certain differences in the effects. *See also* Birgitte.

weight, units of: 10 ounces = 1 pound; 10 pounds = 1 stone; 10 stone = 1 hundredweight; 10 hundredweight = 1 ton.

wilder: A woman who has learned to channel the One Power on her own; only one in four survive this. Such women usually build barriers against knowing what it is they are doing, but if these can be broken down, wilders are frequently among the most powerful of channelers. The term is often used in derogatory fashion.

Wise One: Among the Aiel, Wise Ones are women chosen by other Wise Ones and trained in healing, herbs and other things. They have great authority and responsibility, as well as great influence with sept and clan chiefs, though these men often accuse them of meddling. A good many Wise Ones can channel to one degree or another; they find every Aiel woman born with the spark in her and most of those who can learn. The fact that Wise Ones can channel is not spoken of among Aiel, by custom; as a result many Aiel do not know for sure which Wise Ones can and which cannot. Also by custom, Wise Ones avoid all contact with Aes Sedai, even more so than other Aiel. Traditionally, Wise Ones have stood outside all feuds and battle, but this custom has recently been shattered, perhaps beyond mending. What this may do to the protections accorded Wise Ones under the Aiel belief of *ji'e'toh* has yet to be seen.

Wise Woman: One of the fabled healers of Ebou Dar, distinguished by the wearing of a red belt. Their abilities with herbs and medical knowledge are spoken of as far away as the Borderlands as being the next best to actual Healing by an Aes Sedai. Although Ebou Dar is a cosmopolitan city where outlanders frequently join the city's many guilds, the oddity has been noted that Wise Women who actually are Ebou Dari are in truth quite rare.

Robert Jordan was born in 1948 in Charleston, South Carolina, and died in 2007. He taught himself to read when he was four with the incidental aid of a twelve-years-older brother, and was tackling Mark Twain and Jules Verne by five. He is a graduate of the Citadel, the Military College of South Carolina, with a degree in physics, and served two tours in Vietnam with the US Army. Among his decorations are the Distinguished Flying Cross with bronze oak leaf cluster, the Bronze Star with 'V' and bronze oak leaf cluster, and two Vietnamese Gallantry Crosses with Palm. He has written historical novels, and dance and theatre criticism, but it is the many volumes of his epic Wheel of Time® series that have made him one of the bestselling and best-loved fantasy writers of modern times.

Find out more about Robert Jordan and other Orbit authors by registering for the free monthly newsletter at www.orbitbooks.net.

Enter the monthly Orbit sweepstakes at

www.orbitloot.com

With a different prize every month,
from advance copies of books by your favourite authors to exclusive merchandise packs,
we think you'll find something you love.

orbit

facebook.com/OrbitBooksUK
@orbitbooks_uk
@OrbitBooks
www.orbitbooks.net